Comedies

Poetry

A Word Carved on A Sill
Weep Before God
Wildtrack
Letters to Five Artists
Feng
Open Country
Poems 1949–1979

Fiction

Hurry on Down
Living in the Present
The Contenders
A Travelling Woman
Nuncle and Other Stories
Strike the Father Dead
The Young Visitors
Death of the Hind Legs and Other Stories
The Smaller Sky
A Winter in the Hills
The Life Guard
The Pardoner's Tale
Where the Rivers Meet

Autobiography

Sprightly Running
Dear Shadows

Criticism

Preliminary Essays
Essays on Literature and Ideas
The Living World of Shakespeare
A House for the Truth
Professing Poetry

Biography

Samuel Johnson

John Wain has also edited

Johnson as Critic
Johnson on Johnson
Interpretations
Contemporary Reviews of Romantic Poetry
Selected Poems of Thomas Hardy
Personal Choice: A Poetry Anthology
Anthology of Contemporary Poetry
An Edmund Wilson Celebration
Everyman's Book of English Verse
The Oxford Library of English Poetry
The Oxford Library of Short Novels

Comedies

John Wain

HUTCHINSON
LONDON SYDNEY AUCKLAND JOHANNESBURG

This edition first published in 1990 by
Hutchinson

Random Century Group Ltd
20 Vauxhall Bridge Road, London SW1V 2SA

Random Century Australia (Pty) Ltd
20 Alfred Street, Milsons Point, Sydney NSW 2061,
Australia

Random Century (NZ) Ltd
PO Box 40–086, Glenfield, Auckland 10, New Zealand

Random Century South Africa (Pty) Ltd
PO Box 337, Bergvlei 2012, South Africa

British Library Cataloguing in Publication Data
Wain, John, 1925–
Comedies
I. Title
823.914

ISBN 0 09 174404 0

Phototypeset by Input Typesetting Ltd, London

Printed and bound in Great Britain by
Clays Ltd, St Ives plc

COMEDIES

Being

VOLUME TWO of WHERE THE RIVERS MEET

1990

It is hard for men to fight when they know only what they are fighting against and not what they are fighting for.

Arthur Koestler

'Comedy is When You Die but They Don't Bury You Because You Can Still Walk.'

Title of a story by William Saroyan

Note

The characters in this book are imaginary, but the historical events that form its background did of course happen, and I have taken care to get them right, the idea being to combine a convincing, imaginative story and a reliable history. The imaginative side of it is my own responsibility, but many people were helpful in filling gaps in my knowledge of matters of fact: notably Raymond Hodgkins, Professor P. A. Brunt, Vernon Bogdanor, John Peach, Laszlo Solymar, Professor Nicholas Kurti, F.R.S., and my wife Pat. Jean Kimber, nowadays Mrs Jean Cook, provided me with invaluable insight into the life of her father Cecil Kimber, originator and presiding genius of M.G. cars.

The book continues the story of *Where the Rivers Meet* (1988), but it is meant to read straightforwardly on its own.

J.W.
Oxford, 1990

Comedies

1

The October of 1933 had come in with a salvo of fine weather, bathing Oxford in that particularly bright early-autumn light which always brings out the beauty of stone and leaf, etching more sharply the shadows that slant from chimney-stack and gable and archway, adding a richness to every colour.

At about a quarter to two on an early day in that month, my wife Heather and I sat in the backyard of one of the pubs in St Giles' Street, finishing a modest lunch of bread and cheese and a glass of beer apiece.

On a bench in the sunshine, we ate and drank in reflective silence, as if we were both preoccupied with thoughts we were not quite ready to disclose. Finally, Heather asked, 'When will they meet, d'you know?'

'I suppose about half-past two.'

'What is it now?'

'About a quarter to.'

'My God,' she said quietly. 'Another three-quarters of an hour before they even start.'

'And no one knows how long till they finish,' I said.

'Well, they'll have to stop by dinner-time, presumably.'

'Oh, yes. In fact Bax says he's never known one go on beyond five o'clock.'

'So if they run to form you'll know in another three and a quarter hours.'

'Well, that's when the meeting should break up. How long it will take them to get round to informing me I don't know. All I can do is hang around and see to it that Frank knows where I am.'

By 'Frank' I meant the head porter of Episcopus College, Frank Penney, who was on duty in the College lodge just across the road from where we were sitting. The meeting we were speaking of was a Fellows' Meeting, the first one of the academic year 1933–34. One of the items to be discussed, probably a long way down the agenda, was whether I, Peter Leonard, was to be elected to a Junior Research Fellowship.

For me, the decision was crucial. It would affect the next stage in my life, and that next stage would affect all the other stages. I knew that the only kind of work in which I could be happy and fulfilled was as an historian. To work as an historian, unless you had private means, it was necessary to have a University post. The only University I wanted to work at was Oxford, whose methods I was used to and whose standards I aimed at. The best avenue to a post at Oxford began with a research appointment at my own College, Episcopus, and to fail at this point would set me back years.

This was one reason why we had had such a light lunch. I couldn't answer for Heather, but I didn't believe I could have eaten anything more substantial. Another reason was lack of funds. I was unemployed: we were living largely on borrowed money and having to watch every penny. The salary for the Episcopus Fellowship was small, but it would be something, and it would be supplemented by a number of benefits in kind: free lunches and dinners, for example. And a free place to live, if I had been single, and in a position to take it up. So enduring the suspense of the next couple of hours, perhaps more, was going to be tough.

Heather, who had also finished her lunch, now said, 'I'm going to do a bit of shopping and get back to the flat.' She never called it 'home'. 'What will you do? Are you coming?'

'No, I think I'll hang about.'

'Suit yourself,' she said, preparing to go.

'You're so calm,' I said. 'I envy you.'

She was standing up now. From her erect height, a fair-haired young Valkyrie, she looked down at me; not unsympathetically, but coolly.

'Well,' she said, 'as I'm sure I don't need to tell you, apart from the money, of course, the whole thing matters much less to me than it does to you.'

I opened my mouth to say something in protest at this, but closed it again. Why get into a barney just at this point? Let Heather have any attitude that seemed natural to her; it would all come out in the wash.

'I'll come on back to the flat,' I said, 'when I've got something to tell you.'

'O.K., fine,' she said cheerfully. I stood up and we kissed. That kiss reassured me. The physical link between us, at any rate, had not slackened yet. The warm, responsive pressure of her firm lips under mine sent a crackle through my blood vessels.

With a smile and a wave, she was gone; into the pub, through the bar, out through the door into St Giles' Street. I watched her for as long as I could keep her in sight. Then I slumped down again on the sun-warmed bench. The afternoon seemed very quiet and very empty. There was nothing, absolutely nothing, I actually *wanted* to do.

What would I normally feel like doing on a beautiful autumn afternoon like this? Go across and sit in Episcopus garden, probably. Well, why not? I felt an obscure reluctance to enter the place; I tried to track down a cause for this and came to the conclusion that it arose from mere timidity, a cowardly feeling that I ought to keep away until my fate was settled one way or the other. But *why* ought I? My hesitation was followed by a surge of bravado. Episcopus was my College whether I became a Fellow or not. I had matriculated there, I had belonged to it for three years and lived within its walls for two; what more natural than that I should go and enjoy the garden, today or any day.

I went out into the street and strode in through the College lodge like Mighty Mouse in a temper.

Then, of course, I lost myself in the beauty of the leaves and the flower-beds and the green shadows on the lawn and the gracious east wall of the quadrangle that looked out benignly on the garden. I sat there on a comfortable bench of seasoned wood, and it all said to me, 'Relax, little man. We will go on as we have for centuries, whatever you think or don't think, whatever you do or don't do. And whether you are technically One of Us or not, you can still come and sit here and look about you, and we will smile as we are smiling now, and isn't that something to be glad of?' At least, I like to think that was what it said, but one can never *quite* interpret these messages.

One thing is certain: I did actually forget, for half an hour or even longer, that my fate was being decided somewhere in the College. It would only be one item on a long agenda, of course, and probably ranked lower in importance than parking space for the Fellows' cars or whether to install window-boxes and if so, how much more would the odd-job men need in wages. But it was an item nevertheless, and when it was decided my life would change.

2

When I did remember the meeting, I looked at my watch – but foolishly, since I had no means of knowing when my particular business would be discussed. Was I already at that moment a Fellow of the College, or had I just joined the grey, anonymous ranks of those who at one time and another had tried for a Fellowship and been refused?

Visitors were coming into the garden now; incredibly enough, to them and to the rest of the world, it was an ordinary weekday afternoon. A grey-haired woman with 'Middle West' written all over her sat down on the other half of my bench and showed signs of wanting to start a conversation. Not now, lady, not now. I got up and went through into the quad. The Junior Common Room would be empty now, in the middle of the afternoon, and peaceful, sleeping at the top of its staircase, its newspapers and magazines littered about. I had a sudden clear mental vision of it, the room I knew so well that would soon be out of bounds to me. If I became a Fellow, I would of course be expected to use the Senior Common Room, and if I didn't, well, I would still have the right to come in and out of the College as a visitor, but I wouldn't exactly be welcomed in the J.C.R., which was for the benefit of the undergraduates. Either way, this afternoon was the last when I would have a right to be in that easy, casual, battered room.

I went through into the front quad. The J.C.R was really two rooms. There was a small antechamber where the day's newspapers were laid out on a table, and a larger room beyond it where people usually sat. I went through into the larger room. Unexpectedly, it was not empty. There was a man standing at the table on which the J.C.R. Suggestions Book was kept. He was looking down at this book and methodically turning its pages. I recognized him at once as Carshalton. He was, like me, a graduate of Episcopus College, and of my own generation, and I would have greeted him with more pleasure if he had not happened to be the man I most disliked of all the men in my year. I disliked his cold self-seeking, his unwavering eye on the main chance, and the obsessive pains he took over what a later generation would have called 'his image'. It was this concern which had led him to tell people that his parents lived in Shanghai, whereas in fact I knew on the testimony of a pre-College acquaintance of his that they came from Hounslow.

Why was Carshalton in the J.C.R. in the middle of the afternoon, leafing through the J.C.R. book? I was going to sit down without speaking to him, but he nodded to me: 'Hello, Leonard.' 'Hello,' I said. I left the conversation there, sat down, picked up a newspaper and pretended to read it, while I kept an eye on him to see what he was up to. The J.C.R. book, the thick bound volume in which people wrote their suggestions and comments and various officers of the J.C.R. answered when necessary, was among other things a scrapbook of undergraduate life at Episcopus. Studying Carshalton over the top of the newspaper, all at once I knew with absolute certainty what he was after. He wanted to find the page on which someone had copied the satiric verses that Lamont, the College poet, had come up with in response to the suggestion that someone ought to commemorate Carshalton's heroic misadventure: the occasion when, after determined string-pulling, he had managed to get himself invited on a shooting-weekend at a country house and had actually succeeded in winging his host.

And then what? Obvious. Then he would tear it out. He would put that page in his pocket, knowing that a new generation of undergraduates, with their own busy little lives to lead, would be unlikely to miss it. And if they did, they would have no way of recovering it. Well, I had stopped that little game. As an historian

I don't approve of the mutilation of records. I was going to sit here, until either he cleared off or the place filled up so much that he couldn't tear the page out without being seen and questioned.

So we were stuck there, I sitting on a sofa with my newspaper, and Carshalton with the J.C.R. book on the table in front of him.

Finally he got to a page that he paused over for longer than usual. I was pretty sure he must have found the poem. I had a bet with myself that the next thing he'd do would be to look over at me. I sat and waited. He looked over at me.

'Re-living your carefree student days?' I asked him.

He didn't reply for a moment, then he put down the book as if realizing he was beaten. 'Congratulations on your First,' he said in a formal, uncongratulatory monotone.

'Thanks,' I said, equally flatly.

To my surprise, because he had never shown the slightest interest in me, he pursued the topic.

'You thinking of using it academically?'

'I might,' I said. 'If there happens to be a vacancy.'

'There'll be one,' he said, looking at me with those deep-set little eyes, 'for a man with a First.'

'Well, we'll see,' I said, wanting to keep the topic away, and with it my anxiety. 'And you? Have you found a job yet?'

'Yes,' he said, 'I'm going to teach at Sarah Lawrence.'

'What's Sarah Lawrence?'

'It's a women's college, near New York.'

This startled me.

'What are you going to teach?' I asked.

'History, of course. That's what I read here.'

'Well, I know that. It's just that I didn't know you were intending to go into academic work.'

He nodded, just one decisive nod, and said, 'Initially.'

Initially. What a strange answer, I thought. Did he mean he was going to start out as a university teacher and after five years or so become a circus performer or a shoe salesman instead? 'And America's what you want, is it?' I asked.

'It's what I want,' he said, nodding again, 'and even if it wasn't, it's what I can get. There aren't enough Firsts to go round. American universities take a good Second.'

I really didn't care what he was going for. America was a long way off and that on its own, as far as I was concerned, made it a good place for Carshalton to go to.

I was in any case saved having to make any reply, because at that moment a couple of undergraduates came in, and by good luck one of them wanted to write something in the J.C.R. book, so he carried it away to a different part of the room and started scrawling in it, the other one looking over his shoulder and giggling.

'I say, that'll annoy Tim.'

'Well, he ought to be annoyed, it'll do him good.'

'Are you going to put in anything about that squash rackets business?'

'No, I'm not on very good ground there. A bit shaky. You know what happened to that one I left at L.M.H.'

They both giggled extravagantly then, making me wonder briefly what on earth could have happened to a squash racket at Lady Margaret Hall that would seem

4

so funny to even a pair of idiots like these. I remembered them as first-year dunderheads, but they were second year now, and ought to be beginning to grow up.

Carshalton sat down and waited for a while, but the two lads moved over to the dartboard at one end of the room and started a game. The dartboard had been an innovation, the more serious students feeling that it gave the J.C.R. a flavour of the tap-room and made it undignified, the darts faction pointing out that since Episcopus didn't have a beer cellar there was nowhere else to put it. I relaxed. Carshalton would have to give up.

'When are you off to America?' I asked him.

'Tomorrow,' he said.

That meant he would have no chance to sneak in here on another quiet afternoon. The record was intact, and Lamont's poem saved for posterity.

'You won't be here to take your degree, then,' I said.

'I'll take it *in absentia*. I'll be at work by that time.'

I nodded and went out, pausing to say goodbye to him and wish him luck. Not that Carshalton needed good luck. He wasn't the type to leave anything to luck.

I went down the stairs, and as I went through the lodge Frank Penney called to me from his window, 'There's a note here for you, sir.'

I went in and opened it. It was on the President's notepaper. The decision? No, he wanted to give me that himself: a message in his spidery but still firm old handwriting: 'Please come and see me as soon as you get this. T.R.S.'

I went along. The butler let me into the President's lodging. I waited a few minutes in the large room upstairs, looking at the paintings on the walls. My mind was a complete blank. Then the President appeared and congratulated me on having been elected to a Research Fellowship. Salterton went into the routine explanation of what my duties and rights would be, and how I could not be dismissed before the end of my tenure – 'Except,' he added, 'for behaviour of a scandalous nature'; by which we both understood that he meant entering into physical intimacy with a young person of the female sex and allowing the fact to become known. He then shook hands with me. I was an Oxford don. A baby don, a donling, it was true, but still a don. I had been elected a Fellow of Episcopus College.

'You'll be undertaking some particular course of study, Leonard?' he asked me. I noticed that he didn't call me 'Mr Leonard'. That was because dons in those days called each other by their surnames whether they were of equal seniority or not. It was *de rigueur* and to address anybody as 'Mr' (worse still, 'Dr', or 'Professor') was, in Common-Room society, a blunder. A few months ago, when I was still an undergraduate, Salterton would probably have called me 'Mr Leonard'. Thus the lopping-off of the title was a sign of welcome, of acceptance.

'I'm going to do a D.Phil.,' I said in answer to his question.

He looked slightly disapproving at that, and I remembered that his generation, already middle-aged when the Doctorate of Philosophy ceased to be purely honorary and became one that any Tom, Dick or Harry could get just by writing a thesis, still looked down on it as a tinsel affair, designed mainly to swell the coffers of the University by attracting American graduate students. But it was too late to apologize for the D.Phil.; I was a man of the twentieth century, he of the nineteenth.

He murmured something polite and I took my leave. The Peter Leonard who went down those stairs was a different one from the Peter Leonard who had

5

gone up them ten minutes earlier. Some things stayed the same, of course; my relationship with Heather, for one. But before going back to North Parade to see how *that* was getting on, I couldn't resist taking a fresh look at the rooms I was supposed to occupy as a Fellow – had I not secretly abandoned the required bachelor status. I went and got the key from the lodge – they promised to let me have one of my own in the next twenty-four hours – and went back and up the stairs to where I was to live. Or pretend to be living.

It was all wonderfully neat and clean and airy. The paint smelt so fresh. Those of the scouts who had been kept on for the 'staircase work' had obviously given it a complete going-over during the vac.; while I was getting married and worrying myself sick, they had been cheerfully creaming paint on to wood. As I stood there, looking round the swept, empty room, my new scout came in. The dons on the whole had a better level of scout than the undergraduates; there was some overlap, but a spavined old whinger like my former scout Arthur would never have been put on a staircase that included a don's quarters. This man was much younger, brisker and more efficient. I knew him by sight. His name was Robert. We talked briefly of furniture, carpets and curtains. He asked if there was anything of my own I wanted to import, in addition to what the College provided. Behind the question I sensed generations of young Oxford Fellows who came from homes with antique furniture, beautiful carpets and curtains, things they had been accustomed to during their growing-up years and now wanted to bring to Oxford so as to go on living among them, together with a cherished painting or two. I came from the Bargeman's Arms in Oseney Town and the furniture in my old bedroom was needed where it was. I told him I would let the College provide everything. He nodded, giving no sign whether this decision made him admire or despise me, and we arranged to meet at eleven the next morning so that I could pick out a sofa and some chairs from a College store-room. He would get them moved in at once, and the room would be ready for me to occupy from the day after tomorrow; or, if there were a few small joinery jobs to be done, in a week at the outside.

'You got somewhere to stay until then, sir, I suppose?' he asked.

For a wild instant I felt like answering, 'Yes, I shall stay with my wife in our flat in North Parade,' and after he had gone I wondered what his reaction would have been if I had. Perhaps I should have done. I don't suppose he would have made trouble for me – he was a good-natured chap – and it would have been good to have an ally close to the centre of things.

As I left my room, letting the door lock itself behind me, there, just arrived at the top of the stairs, was the man with whom I was to share the landing and bathroom. We had already met. His name was McLennan. He had sandy hair, freckles and steel-rimmed glasses. He was a Junior Research Fellow like myself, but already of twelve month's standing. He congratulated me on being elected and we chatted of this and that; clearly he wanted to be friendly.

'Look here,' he said, 'we're standing out here in the passage, your rooms aren't furnished yet – do come into mine and have a glass of sherry while we get to know each other.'

McLennan was perfectly amiable, the suggestion he made was obviously sensible and yet I didn't want to go into his sitting room and sit there holding a glass of sherry and making conversation with him. I wanted to see Heather, to talk to her, to tell her the news. But how could I get rid of McLennan? It would be dangerous to begin our relationship by appearing to him as an oddball. And it would be impossible to say, 'I must hurry away – my wife's expecting me.'

So I had to go and sit down while he prattled on. He was completely wrapped up in his work: every detail of it, from the largest to the smallest, seemed to fascinate him. He was an economist and he said, disarmingly, that he would be glad to have an historian living beside him; he was sure that he would enjoy discussing points of economic history with someone who would see the same facts from a different angle. I groaned inwardly. How was I going to manage any kind of life with Heather if, in addition to all the other calls on my time at College, I had McLennan hanging about waiting for the next leisurely discussion of economic history as seen from his and my angles?

When I stood up to go he said, 'Shall I see you at dinner?'

'No,' I said. 'I didn't put down.'

'Well, that's natural enough.' He grinned. 'I suppose you wanted to see how the election would go before you . . .'

'It's not only that.' I was beginning to get a bit fed up with his college-bound attitude. 'I'm technically still an undergraduate. Degree-giving isn't until next week, so I shan't be a B.A. until then. Time enough to join the festivities when I am.'

'Well, I don't know about festivities,' McLennan said seriously, 'but now you're a Fellow you'll obviously be dining in most nights, if only because it's hard to make ends meet without. I mean, one's stipend isn't all that much.' He looked at me soberly through his steel-rimmed glasses. How typical of him, I thought, to call it by its correct name, 'stipend'. As if we were all a gang of vicars.

'I must be off. I'll start dining after next week, when I become a B.A., I said. 'I'd feel a fool sitting there in an undergraduate gown, and anyway there's probably a statute against it.'

'Well, it might be awkward,' he agreed, still without a spark of humour. 'I was forgetting, of course. You took Schools last term. Congratulations on your First, by the way. I hear it was a good one.'

You hear that, do you, Mr McLennan? Who's been talking about me behind my back?

'Well, I'll be off,' I said. 'Thanks for the sherry.'

As I went down the stairs, I thought how little I was looking forward to dining at High Table and all that Senior Common Room mullarkey. In particular, I did not relish the looking-over I knew I would get. Still, I reflected, in these slightly more liberal times the looking-over, at any rate for an Episcopus man, came *after* the election. I had heard all those stories about candidates for Fellowships in Victorian times who were invited to dinner and watched to see if they had tolerable table manners, things like cherry pies being served, to see what the wretched man did with the stones.

Well, if it had to be cherry pie it wouldn't matter if I flipped the stones in Salterton's eyes. I was a Fellow. . . . All of a sudden I needed to share my elation. Of course, there were plenty of people who wished me well and who would be glad of the news. My parents, down in their little riverside pub, the Bargeman's Arms in Oseney Town (though to them it would be, like all the rest of my strange life, something a little remote and off stage). Geraldine too, and Harry Goodenough. My brother Brian. But obviously there was someone who came before any of them.

I pedalled out to North Parade on my bike, got there slightly out of breath, hurried up the drab staircase to our flat, and in. Now for the good news.

Heather was in the tiny kitchen, at the sink, and she neither turned to face me nor gave any sign that she knew I had come in.

7

I had been eager to embrace her, but now I just let my arms fall to my sides. 'Well?'

'Well, what?' She still did not turn round.

Christ! I said to myself. This looks like trouble.

'I thought,' I said carefully, 'you might be, well, just a bit interested to know if you're married to an unemployed man or to a Fellow of Episcopus.'

At that she whirled to face me. It was as if I had laid a whip across her back. 'Oh, you Oxford people make me sick. The way you stand there and say *a Fellow of Episcopus* . . . so impressed with yourself, aren't you, as if being a Fellow of Episcopus gave you an extra pair of balls or something.'

'All right, sweetheart,' I said. My initial dismay was draining off, and being replaced by a cold anger. I controlled it. I could feel the depth of her icy resentment. But what at? Where did my offence lie?

'Heather, can't we sit down and talk sensibly?'

'I can talk standing up. This isn't a bloody tutorial or whatever you call it.'

'I'm trying to talk about a career and a lifetime's work and a secure home for you and our children — '

'Child. I don't suppose I shall go through all this again.'

'All right, child, then. I'm trying to talk about doing responsible work and having a decent position in society and having something to offer — '

'Position in society! That's rich! How about me? Being a bloody don's wife, spending all my time with a lot of gossiping snobby North Oxford biddies while you sit around drinking port.'

'Oh port, port, I wish it had never been invented. I'll sit around drinking water if you like, just as long as I get a chance to spend my life as a professional historian, which is the only way I'll ever be (a) fulfilled and happy, and (b) any use to the human race.'

'I don't know what use to the human race it is to have you sitting around arguing over things that happened a million years ago and a-ing and b-ing and c-ing. It's not as if you could go back and change anything.'

'That's the sort of thing Phil would say, if he was articulate enough to string a sentence together. You know better than that. You know we can learn a lot from looking back at the way we've travelled.'

'If you mean me personally, no there isn't one damn' thing I can learn, given when I was born and where. I've been in a hopeless position from the start and that's how it'll go on. All the a-ing and b-ing and c-ing in the world won't do me any good.'

'Well, that may be so, but at least the immediate news is good. At least I've got the Episcopus job. That means our future is reasonably assured. Materially, we'll never have to go short.'

Heather bent forward slightly from the hips and looked at me incredulously.

'Never go short? Is that what I heard you say? Did you really say that?'

'Well, yes, damn it, you did. I grew up in a pub in Oseney Town, a working-class pub. By the standards that I grew up with, an Oxford don gets a damn' good salary, good working conditions, plenty of free time — '

'And what does his wife get?'

'Well, don't be silly, she gets what he gets.'

'Oh yes. It bloody looks like it, when I have to skulk out here in this hole while you swan around in Episcopus. Face it and be honest for once. Do those stuffed shirts who elected you even know I exist?'

Oh, God, I thought. Are we going to have all *that* again?

8

'Well, naturally they don't know you exist as my wife. But they'd have no quarrel with you personally.'

'No, not as long as I'm very much somewhere else and they don't have to see me or hear me or smell me. I'm a woman, and that's a crime in their eyes, isn't it?'

I was reminded suddenly of the original statutes of New College: *Male laundresses will be preferred.* The thought silenced me, and Heather drove home her point in a low intense voice that seemed able to blister the paint off the woodwork. 'If they'd known you were married to me you wouldn't have got the job.'

'To you or anyone. There's no personal grudge against — '

'No, we're all the same, one's as bad as another, the crime is to set up and live with any dirty leper of a woman, it doesn't matter which.'

'Oh, Heather, we've been over this so many times. Most of these chaps are married. If you looked into it you'd find that the average Oxford don has a wife and children and a family home. It's just that for career reasons it's as well not to get married very early on. I don't suppose it's the only job like that. Very likely it's the same in the Army or Navy.'

'Oh, to hell with the Army and Navy. I'm me and I'm carrying your child and we had to get married in secret and we're scared to death of anyone finding out. And now I've got to lurk and skulk about while you pretend to your God-Almighty friends that I don't exist. It was probably a mistake bringing me here. Probably I ought to have stayed out with my parents at Cogges and let you visit me just when you felt like it.'

'You wouldn't have stood for that.'

She opened her eyes very wide. 'And that's why we didn't? Because I wouldn't have stood for it? Well, I can see now you'd have been all for it. Out of sight's out of mind, isn't it?'

All this time, I had been standing up. Suddenly, now, I sank down on to one of the shiny, lumpy armchairs, prey to a weariness so intense that I felt my knees would give way at any moment and send me sprawling. Heather, her feet firmly planted on the floor, stared down at me with hostility making the blue of her eyes ice-cold.

'For God's sake, Heather,' I said, 'I'm going to be a good husband to you and a good father to our baby, and I'm going to work hard and have a successful career — '

'Especially that.'

'No, not especially that, just a career that'll keep me in steady work and in funds so that we don't go short of anything. Surely that's worth a bit of — '

'A bit – you mean a lot, don't you? Years and years of pretending I'm your girl-friend instead of your wife and that the baby's a bastard. Well, I'll tell you one thing, he'll have the mentality of a bastard because those are the thoughts that are going into him now, all the time, whenever I breathe.'

'He? Why not she?'

Heather shook her head. 'It'll be a boy, I just know it will. Another male to push me down into a box and shut the lid on me. It's happened all along, years and years of my brother Tom, and now you.'

Fatigued and discouraged as I was, I could hardly help seeing the monstrous unfairness of this, but I was at a loss to know where to get hold of so unwieldy a mass of slanders. So I just said, mildly, 'Heather, I'm tired and hungry. Are we going to have anything to eat?'

9

'Well, I haven't cooked anything, if that's what you're asking me. I thought you'd be down at College getting the feed-bag on.'

'For your information, Heather, now and in the future, I have to sign on by ten a.m. if I want to have dinner in College. So there's no question of my suddenly taking it into my head to — '

'All right, don't bother to tell me. I'm not interested in all the rules and regulations.'

I stood up, went over to the door and paused with my hand on the doorknob. 'I'm going out to get some fish and chips from that place in Walton Street. I think I've got enough money. I'm going to get two fish and as many chips as I can afford. In other words I'll assume you'll join me. If you don't, I'll just eat the lot myself.'

She said nothing. But when I got back she had warmed two plates in the oven and put out knives and forks and salt and vinegar. We shared the fish and chips, and then we went to bed, made love and fell asleep.

I had known Geraldine all through my undergraduate career, and the only time she ever wore a skirt was when she had to don academic dress, that ceremonial black-and-white 'subfusc' that Oxford (unlike Cambridge) insists on at all high moments in a student's life. Thus one of the rare occasions when I got a good look at the skirt-wearing Geraldine was when all our generation turned up for the Conferment of Degrees in the Sheldonian. We were only a few days into the Michaelmas Term, but I was already impatient to get the business done; my lack of graduate status was beginning to hamper the conduct of my daily life.

With relief, therefore, I went through the interminable droning and bowing and being marshalled in through this door and out through that door, under the gaze of a gallery full of onlookers, mostly proud parents in their best clothes. My own parents I had not bothered to alert. Their low-key approach to my University career seemed to me entirely sensible, and beyond remarking that my degree would soon be 'made official' I hadn't even mentioned the ceremony.

After the men had all been mystically transformed into Bachelors of Arts we waited on the side benches while the women took their turn; it was then, sitting back and relaxing, that I took my first leisurely look at Geraldine in a skirt. My other old friend Harry Goodenough, who always saw anything clearly as long as he could see it in terms of Shakespeare, had certainly got her right in his production of *Twelfth Night* when he cast her as the Shakespearean heroine who has to dress as a boy and really look like one, yet still come over as feminine. Conversely, in female dress she kept some of that boyish quality, and I knew that if she caught my eye and gave her sudden grin, it would have had all her usual cheeky flavour. I wondered, for the thousandth time, why I had not gone after her seriously – but it was too late now.

I was fond of her all the same, and waited about outside to grab her and take her off for a drink at the King's Arms. She was with her parents, one look at whom told me a lot about what she was reacting against. They had the absolutely standard plushy middle-class appearance, obviously from some well-trimmed suburb in Surrey, with expensive clothes (the mother was wearing a fur coat, even though the autumn day was quite mild) and no doubt there was a glossy car parked somewhere. I saw now why Geraldine had been so determined not to conform. The struggle must have started long before she got to Oxford. This couple would never give up trying to process her, and if she had successfully

10

resisted them for years she must have been able to eat her St Hilda's dons for breakfast.

She seemed to be on reasonable terms with them, too, and of course on this occasion they were basking in pride. The father had a camera slung around his neck, and as we stood in the forecourt of the Sheldonian he couldn't resist snapping picture after picture. Geraldine in a skirt! And with a cap and gown on! He must have known he would never have another chance like this to prove that his daughter knew how to behave, complete with a Certificate of Life-Worthiness to enlarge and put on the sideboard. Snap, snap, snap he went.

'Here,' she said laughing. 'Come and stand here, Peter. Daddy, this is a friend of mine, Peter Leonard. It's his degree day too, and he's going to be a major historian. Take a picture of me standing beside him and then in future years you can use it to prove I knew the right people at Oxford.'

'Splendid, splendid,' he beamed and caught the pair of us in characteristic stance, I looking straight ahead with a rather solemn expression, and Geraldine with one elbow crooked, leaning on my shoulder as you might lean against a mantelpiece.

That done, she shook off her parents, at the price of promising to join them at their hotel for dinner in one hour precisely, and NOT BE LATE, and she and I went to the King's Arms, which had now been open for about fifteen minutes.

A good many people had had the same idea, and the place was a sea of black and white. We crushed in somehow; I saw a lot of people I recognized, and in particular Harry Goodenough so we got into a corner with him and caught up on our news.

Mine first: I didn't tell them anything about Heather. She wasn't present, since it had been agreed between us that this was to be treated as an ordinary day, and I didn't know how she would get on with Harry and Geraldine anyway. So I briefly told them instead about my Fellowship and let it go at that. Next, Geraldine. She would be working in Oxford too, as a part-time probationary lecturer at Ruskin College. Her students would mostly be older men (no women, in those days) on study leave from industrial jobs, their fees paid by the trade unions.

'You have to be Left, of course,' she said. 'Ruskin is a Socialist foundation.'

'You're not exactly rule-of-thumb Left,' I said.

'No,' she agreed, 'but I'm certainly not Right, and I wear trousers. It was the trousers that did it. They saw at once that I was a class dissident.'

I wasn't sure how serious she was – one spends a lot of time at Oxford not being sure how serious people are – but there was no time to thrash the matter out; it was Harry's turn. And he had good news too. His exams had been a typical H. G. performance – he had not bothered much with those parts that didn't interest him, but he had blazed into the Shakespeare paper, and anything else that seemed to him to have a bearing on Shakespeare, with such gusto and passion that, after one of the longest vivas anyone could remember, they had given him a Second (one of the examiners remarking that it ought really to have been a Fourth or a First), and his College had come up with a grant that would keep him while he did a year's work, sorting out his ideas on the general topic of 'Shakespearean Stage Production: the Way Forward'. This surprised me: academic prejudice against the theatre was very strong at that time. Only later – some years later, in fact – did I learn through some snippet of English Faculty gossip that Goodenough, at his viva, had tangled up one of the country's leading Shakespearean scholars in a stubborn wrangle about proof corrections in the

1623 Folio and to what extent it was possible to locate the points at which a new compositor had taken over. The pundit in question had lost his temper with Harry, and afterwards had felt very contrite and written him a long letter of recommendation which got him the grant.

Our exchange of news over, we gave our attention to another round of drinks, and eventually a lot of people left and we stayed on. And somehow there always seemed to be a full glass in my hand, and we sat in our corner, and there we were, the three of us, Geraldine and Harry and I, and after all they were the best friends I had made during those three growing-up years, and my glass emptied and filled, emptied and filled.

We were three young people in academic dress, all in work, all on the threshold of professional life, all a little drunk, and fond of each other; and suddenly it seemed ridiculous that I had never told them about Heather.

So I told them about Heather. And the coming baby.

Harry was on the ball straight away. 'Is that the girl who dropped in on you when I was visiting you in those awful digs you had in the Iffley Road?'

'Oh yes. I'd forgotten you'd seen her.'

'Well, you didn't give me much chance to get acquainted with her, and I remember thinking that I didn't blame you. If I had something like that up my sleeve I'd certainly keep it to myself.'

'Yes, but she was a she, not an it,' Geraldine said rather severely. 'And so far from being a pet ferret he was carrying up his sleeve, or a card he was going to play at the right moment, or whatever the image is in your squalid male mind, Harry, she was a real woman with real needs and wishes — '

'All right, Geraldine, I'm not one of your miners at Ruskin. She was a real woman and now she's Mrs Leonard, which I take it is what she wanted.'

'God help her,' said Geraldine quietly.

I was taken slightly aback by this remark, which she made with no hint of irony, her face serious.

'Do you really feel sorry for her, Geraldine?' I asked.

'Of course.'

'Well, why? I'm not all that obnoxious, am I? And besides, getting married is what most girls still seem to want, even today.'

'Oh . . .' She made a gesture of impatience, flipping one hand sideways. 'Men are always saying *most girls want this, most girls want that*, because they assume the female sex is an entirely conventional block, and they can apply silly generalizations to every individual girl they come across.' I had the feeling that she was really speaking to her parents; addressing them over my shoulder, so to speak.

'Yes, but you can't brush it off just like that. Heather is an individual, and you said you were sorry for her.'

'I'm not brushing it off. I hope your Heather *is* happy, but I can't say I'd be very happy myself in her situation. What about the College authorities? In their eyes she's committed a crime simply by being a female animal. Her relationship with you has resulted in *her* having a baby, not you, and she's the one who's the pariah. Good God, I thought the whole point of marriage was that it was a *public* relationship. Any couple can decide to go to bed together, any couple can decide to live together, but the whole idea of marriage is that you stand up and say to the world, "I've chosen this person," and bring the families and friends on both sides into the picture.'

'Well, that's one kind of marriage,' I said defensively, 'but it doesn't happen to be our kind. Ours started with a personal relationship and when we found

12

we'd made a baby we thought we ought to go official for the baby's sake. But we didn't do it for the families' sakes. They were slightly appalled, if anything.'

'I'm not surprised. Fancy having to watch your daughter skulking like a kept woman.'

Harry was more indulgent. 'Frankly, old man, I think you're on to a good thing. She looked gorgeous to me. I'd like to cast her as Paulina, assuming of course that Paulina was a good deal younger than Leontes. You know, queenly. Straight-backed. Does she ever act?'

I felt like saying, 'She acts all the time. She's a woman.' But I stopped myself, fortunately, before any such cheap remark could, as Homer puts it, 'escape from me through the fence of my teeth'. And then I realized I had been going to say something so spiteful simply because I was angry at Geraldine's reaction.

And why was I angry? Because it got me on a nerve. What nerve? Guilt. Deep down, and not in fact all that deep, I was ashamed of going along with the Oxford shibboleth, this inherited monastic notion that one's sexual needs were undignified; if one satisfied them outside marriage, that was disreputable; if within marriage, then one had committed a career-wrecking blunder and became a non-person, no longer either accepted in Common-Room society, or even eligible for employment. God Almighty, what foolishness! How right Geraldine was to pity any woman stuck with me!

Still, it is never pleasant to be criticized. But what, after all – given that I longed so intensely for a life spent in historical study – what else could I do?

The mill ground on. At about five past seven the next evening, I went into the Senior Common Room at Episcopus. I had calculated it nicely: I didn't want to rush in unceremoniously a couple of seconds before we moved into Hall for the meal; nor, on the other hand, did I want to be standing about in tongue-tied self-consciousness for any longer than I had to. I had my gown on, of course, and my dinner jacket, black tie, stiff shirt, all the costume and grease-paint. The drill was that we met in the Common Room, where sherry and glasses were laid out on the sideboard, went into Hall for dinner, then into a kind of drawing room for dessert, and finally into a third room, known as the smoking room, for coffee. So that everyone who dined at Episcopus visited four locations in turn, and very gracefully and beautifully furnished they all were. Presumably the conversation was supposed to live up to the surroundings, and I didn't think that, even if I were there fifty years, I would ever be able to rise to it, especially while trying to eat meat and two veg and drink a succession of wines in the appropriate order. At least, that was how I felt at first, but as the meal-time wore on I began to recover. Bax, my old tutor and now my head of department, had something to do with it. Straight away, when I first came in, he greeted me, gave me a glass of sherry and introduced me to several Fellows who had previously only been names to me. Trust him to do his social duty! That started me off on the right foot, and from then on I gradually climbed back to something like confidence. The wine warmed me, the food was good, or at any rate better than I was used to (and free!), and I was seated between two men who passed the occasional remark in an amicable way. After dinner we went into the room where dessert was waiting.

At dessert we had to avoid sitting next to whomever we had sat next to at dinner, a sensible practice because it broke up long obsessive conversations and allowed fresh topics to be started. I was lucky enough – or was it luck? Did the benign old man not move towards me from a fatherly wish to put me at my ease?

– to find myself beside venerable Weatherby, the physicist of so much repute. After a day spent in unguessable labyrinths of speculation about the nature of matter, he seemed glad to make ordinary conversation; he was interested to learn that my origins were local and asked me questions about my boyhood in the Thames Valley, attending carefully as if I were a traveller from fabled Cathay. He himself, it appeared, came from the Lake District, and soon he was telling me about that region as it had been in the 1880s, when he was growing up there. I relaxed in the gentle rays of his benignity; the port circulated, I took a glass, and its deeply releasing glow worked on me as it had on that far-off evening – was it really only last summer? – in poor Gadsby's rooms. Listening to Weatherby, but with not quite all my attention, I had leisure to look round the table and begin to get used to the faces I saw and the personalities which seemed to go with them. But of course there was too much to be hoisted in all at once: procedures, etiquettes, faces, names, facts, impressions. Some of the men, like Weatherby and the aged President Salterton, were wrinkled sages with their roots in another age; then there was a stratum of younger men like Bax, mature and seasoned but advanced no further into life than early middle age; and finally there were men of about my own generation – none, indeed, quite as young as myself, but recognizably a crop produced by the same weather and climate. McLennan, with his innocuous, flavourless voice and manner, was already perfectly adapted to the routines, already a 'good Common Room man', blandly and earnestly discussing some cleverish point with exactly the right blend of tact and persistence; one or two others, whose names I did not yet know, were talking mainly to one another, while energetically cracking nuts, peeling oranges and pushing along the decanters in their silver holders, filling their glasses each time round with port or madeira or claret.

On the whole it was the seniors I found most memorable. The young were more or less standardized and more or less similar to myself, but the older men had had time to be moulded, by what they had studied and what they had lived through, into gnarled lumps of character; their minds had grain and texture. Even so, I was a long way from getting all the names of these older Fellows, even though the College, like all colleges, was much smaller in those days, with only fifteen regular Fellows and half-a-dozen odds and sods like myself. One man I do remember among the seniors was a man named Tonson, whom I noticed because he had been sitting near me at dinner and quite near me over dessert afterwards, and also because he seemed even shyer than I was. He had a round face, a fringe of silver hair round the sides of an otherwise bald head, and large thoughtful eyes behind round lenses. His voice was very quiet and it seemed an effort to him to speak to anyone. I eventually gathered from what I could pick up of the talk around me that he knew about Arabic and the Islamic world – the man sitting across from him, raising his voice so it carried across the broad expanse of the table, was questioning him about the Muslim attitude to Christianity and in particular towards the person of Jesus. This seemed an odd subject to take up over dinner, but – as I was in the process of learning – an Oxford don will discuss anything, anywhere.

'Well, of course, the Qu'ran accepts his status as above ordinary humanity,' Tonson said. I noticed that he pronounced 'Qu'oran' in what was presumably the correct Arabic way. 'The prophet Mahomet accepted the tradition of the virgin birth, which meant that Jesus was of a higher order of beings than he was himself.'

'What about the Crucifixion?' the other man asked in a rather barking way.

14

He seemed intent on questioning Tonson rather like a police-court magistrate trying to pin down a slippery witness. 'What is their attitude to the doctrine of the Atonement?'

'They don't believe in the Crucifixion,' I heard Tonson say.

'Don't believe in it? What about the eye-witness accounts?'

'They accept the eye-witness accounts,' Tonson said, 'but they believe a phantom was crucified on that occasion.'

I didn't hear any more because at that moment I was asked to pass a napkin by the man who sat almost opposite me, only a little way to my right. I knew him by sight and name; he was, I guessed, in his late twenties, his name was Watson and I knew he was some sort of scientist. I had seen him about for a couple of years, since he had come from another college to take up a junior teaching fellowship at Episcopus. There was something about him I had never quite liked, and now, covertly looking at him in the intervals of following Weatherby's Lake District reminiscences, I felt that same impression again. What was it about Watson? His voice (drawling and slightly supercilious), or his face (round and chubby, with small eyes and a large mouth, below which was an aggressive little chin)? Taking in his face, hearing his voice, I was reminded of the old jingle:

> I do not like thee, Doctor Fell;
> The reason why I cannot tell;
> But this I know, I know full well;
> I do not like thee, Doctor Fell.

Ah, well, no need to bother about Watson now, or perhaps ever. Weatherby beside me, warming to his theme, was telling me about the customs in the neighbourhood of Grasmere in his boyhood, at a time when the sturdy dalesmen had influenced the young Wordsworth and made him eager to found his new poetry on 'the real language of men', not of the heterogeneous nomads of the city streets but of these strong, deliberate people who lived their lives close to earth, air, water, stone and wood, sheep and dogs. I began to pay more attention; this could hardly fail to interest an historian. Could it be that the legend was true, and the after-dinner conversation of dons was indeed an education in itself? The port came round again; almost mechanically I filled my glass, passed it to my left, and asked some question of Weatherby, really interested in his answer.

He talked on, warming to his subject, bringing the whole vanished world before my eyes, and I was oblivious of what went on around me until I was pulled back to the present by an outbreak of mild facetiousness among the men sitting across the table from me. 'You're in luck, Parsons.' 'Parsons has got a buzz.' 'Would you mind ringing the bell, President?'

I had to have it explained to me, of course. As a decanter goes round, unless only a very few men are dining, it becomes empty and a fresh one is called for. If the remaining amount in the old decanter is exactly a glassful, so be it, and the next man starts with a new one. But if the decanter runs out when his glass is only half-filled, or two-thirds – if, in short, there is a decent amount of empty space still available – then, in order not to mix decanters or bins or vintages or whatever it is, he is given a fresh glass, fills it from the new decanter and, without paying any more than his flat-rate contribution to the evening's wine, enjoys a little extra.

The man Parsons – about whom I remember nothing across the years except his name, his long, bony face and the fact that he soon afterwards disappeared from Oxford, I think to America – Parsons, then, had a buzz, and acknowledged the small nugget of luck with a good-humoured grin. His right-hand neighbour, Watson, also grinned but not good-humouredly.

'You were lucky at my expense, Parsons,' he remarked in a voice that was clearly not intended to be *sotto voce*. 'If we all had our rights that buzz would have been mine.'

'How so?' Parsons asked idly.

'The decanter would have lasted until it reached me,' said Watson silkily, 'if everybody had taken an equal share.'

'Well, surely everybody did take an equal share.'

'Not quite.' Watson's eyes rested on my glass. 'Our most recently elected Fellow seems to have the engaging habit of drinking port from his claret glass.'

Several pairs of eyes turned to my glass. I would get over the embarrassment, of course; it was not the end of the world, merely a harmless *gaffe*; but at that moment I felt that it was the end of the world. Everyone had, as part of his standard equipment – fruit-knife, finger-bowl, etc. – two glasses. The slightly smaller one was for fortified wines, port or madeira. The larger one was for claret. The first time the port came round, I filled my port glass. The second time, intent on Weatherby's conversation, I had filled my claret glass by mistake, thus taking more port than I was entitled to.

If anyone had noticed, they had given no sign. But then, if anyone had happened to notice so trivial a mistake made by a youthful newcomer, so lately come from the rough-and-ready world of the undergraduate, he would not have thought it worth a moment's attention. Except, apparently, for Watson. As a boy, he had doubtless pulled the wings off flies. Now, for this moment, I was a fly and I had alighted where he could grab me. Looking at him for a second across the table, before turning back to my conversation with Weatherby, I made a silent vow that never, never again would I get into Watson's cobweb.

And in this way, with several lessons well and truly learnt, ended my first dinner as a Fellow of Episcopus College. Not daring to go up to my room because I was certain that McLennan would come knocking on the door, I took my raincoat and went straight out of College and turned my hurrying footsteps towards North Parade.

Heather was already in her dressing-gown.

'I had a long bath,' she said, 'for something to do.'

'I'm sorry,' I said. 'It must have been pretty deadly.'

'Listen, you can't keep on for three years saying you're sorry.' Her voice was quite gentle. 'We're stuck with it, so let's do it sensibly. I've got enough providing and planning for the baby to keep me pretty busy, and to be fair, you were here most of the day. It will be no good if you're going to be a crushed mass of guilt all the time.'

'Well, yes, but. . . .'

'I'm sorry I gave you a bad time last night. It sounds silly, I know, but it was the first time it really . . . well . . . dawned on me, that you really will be away so much. I've thought about it now and I'm over it.'

'Darling,' I said, 'that's wonderful and you're a wonderful girl.'

I held her close and we kissed. I could feel the baby now, but she had so much vitality in her body that that extra quickening of life round her midriff didn't make her seem any less desirable. We went to bed and she said she could smell port on my breath and she liked it. So I set about proving that a couple of glasses of fortified wine, even if one was enough to fill a claret glass, didn't affect my potency.

With the arrival of autumn, and the settling of immediate domestic problems, it was high time to get down to some serious work. The events of the spring of 1742 had been milling about uneasily in my mind for months, and now at last I had a chance to give them some uninterrupted – or very little interrupted – attention. I quickly formed the habit of spending most of each day in the Upper Reading Room of the Bodleian Library, a building that, with its view of a jumble of towers and spires, its beautiful painted frieze, its gold-lettered books ranged in spacious open shelves and its general atmosphere of studious calm, has always seemed to me everything that a library should be. For me, and for others like me, it was more; it was a special club and gathering point, for, though conversation was impossible except for a murmured greeting, one could count on finding one's friends there, each at an accustomed desk and half-hidden behind a wall of appropriate volumes. The two I usually saw were Geraldine and Harry Goodenough; like me, both were doing research and both tended to spend the morning in the library, so it was a rare week-day that did not find the three of us taking a half-hour break to go across the road for a cup of coffee in the King's Arms. They were happy times and at first I tried to include Heather in them, thinking it might heal the breach I could see opening wider and wider between her and 'Oxford'. She came a few times, but then she gave up.

'It's your territory, not mine. Bloody intellectuals. Never talk about anything real.'

I was genuinely puzzled by this. Harry, it was true, never discussed anything that he could not find treated in Shakespeare, but then Shakespeare's range is wide enough for most people, taking in life, death, hell, heaven, immortality, love, hate, youth, age, tenderness, lust, political power, avarice, treachery, loyalty, assassination and disguised identity, not to speak of madness and hallucination. As for Geraldine, the things she talked about were real enough by the most mundane standards – working conditions, factory legislation, movements of population. 'Being at Ruskin has made me much more Left,' she announced quite early on. 'I thought of myself as a Socialist when I went there, but I didn't know what Socialism was about – I'd been brought up where I never even met any working-class people.'

'Except me,' I said.

'You! You're a toff. You never did a manual job in your life.'

'I've rolled beer barrels about. And poured out bottled beer over my finger in the correct way. And washed glasses. And I have a brother who was an apprentice at Morris Motors.'

'Yes, you've told me about that brother of yours. He did his engineering apprenticeship, but he isn't on a factory floor now, is he? He's a glamorous figure, a racing driver.'

'Well, not exactly a racing driver. Brian's a mechanic with M.G. But he's in the thick of it, one way or another. He's in the *équipe*.'

'There you are – *équipe*! Fancy French words already.'

'Yes, Geraldine, the language of motor-racing is full of French terms like the language of cookery. Any big race anywhere is a Grand Prix. But that's not my brother's fault.'

'You're just trying to side-track me. All I'm saying is that your family isn't working class and as for yourself, you're just a *bourgeois* like me.'

17

'*Bourgeoise*, you mean. Who's using fancy French words now?'

'Some of the chaps I teach,' she ignored my red herring, 'are miners. They tell me what it's like down the pit. I can't believe what I'm hearing sometimes. It's absolutely inhumanly awful.'

'And that's made a Socialist of you?'

'Of course it has. We send these men down into that hell because we need the coal, we have to use economic coercion to get them down there because no one in their right mind would go anywhere near the place, and these men aren't only in their right minds, they're often highly intelligent – and then on top of that we keep them in poverty and subjection, and if it happens to suit the market we throw them out of work altogether and let them rot on the dole. And finally, to cap it all, we look down on them.'

'Not guilty to that charge, at least,' I said. 'I've never looked down on a miner.'

'You've probably never met one.'

'You saw me talking to one the other day, as it happens.' As I spoke I forgave myself for bringing in that honest man, Fred Armitage's father, as argument fodder; it seemed to diminish him as a human being, which was far from my intention, but I had to keep my end up somehow. I was *not* a snob. I did *not* think a coal-miner was beneath me as a human being.

'Oh well, when I said "We" do this and that I meant society, not you personally. Nor me, for that matter. They're going to take me down the pit next vac.'

'My God,' I said involuntarily, 'a bit rough, that, for . . .'

I was going to say 'for a woman', but thank goodness something happened to shut me up. Our conversation was interrupted.

We happened to be by ourselves over our coffee that morning, so I was giving my whole attention to Geraldine, and quite unprepared for the interruption. But in any case, when this one came it was clear that the interrupter was a real professional, someone who had been interrupting conversations for years, a young woman, slightly above medium height, with frizzy dark-blonde hair and rimless glasses and wearing a grey dress, who marched up from somewhere behind my back, swiftly circled me, plumped herself down beside Geraldine and began talking to her as if I didn't exist.

There was obviously no doing anything about it, so I sat back, drank my coffee, and took a quiet look at the newcomer. She was of our own generation, but already there was something middle-aged about her bearing. One had the distinct impression that on arriving at Oxford at the age of about eighteen, having already been head girl at school, she had decided that one day she was going to be Principal of Somerville at the very least, and had begun straight away to groom herself for it. Rather large-boned, very determinedly *there*, she leaned over dark, slender Geraldine like an Alsatian towering over a Scotch terrier. Geraldine clearly did not like her, and I can't say I took to her much either. She had a way of staring at you intently through her rimless spectacles that was unnerving; it was like walking down a quiet country lane in the evening, enjoying the last streaks of the sunset, and suddenly finding oneself caught in the beam of a powerful searchlight.

She seemed to be talking business with Geraldine. The words 'class' and 'written work' cropped up. I gathered, listening idly, that they were both taking part in some University Extension Programme, perhaps run from Ruskin. After a while, during a brief lull while our invader drew breath, Geraldine tried to deflect some of her attention towards me.

'Molly, this is Peter Leonard, of Episcopus. Molly Whitworth.'

18

'Episcopus?' The searchlight spectacles were turned on me. 'An undergraduate then, are you?'

'A Research Fellow, actually.'

Molly Whitworth's expression changed almost perceptibly. To say that she looked at me with more respect or more interest would be quite wrong. She showed no trace of either. It was more as if an object she had at first taken to be an umbrella stand had turned out to be a human being. I was at any rate *homo sapiens*, though she evidently entertained no hope that I would show any sign of *sapientia*.

'What are you researching on?' she asked briskly, as if to get the information filed before spinning me into the litter-basket.

'An episode in the War of the Austrian Succession. Lord Stair's hopes of using the Pragmatic Army for a direct invasion of France.'

She looked at me with what I supposed was amused contempt. 'You expect people to be interested in that?'

'Well, historians are.'

She sniffed, dismissively. 'I suppose it's the sort of thing that makes careers.'

I felt my neck growing hot, a sure sign of anger. This must be how Brian felt when people sneered about M.G.

'I happen to be interested in eighteenth-century foreign policy,' I said. 'What's your subject, or haven't you got one?'

'Now then, you two,' said Geraldine, 'don't start building up hostility. It's too early in the day.'

Her tone was cheerful and slightly conciliatory; obviously, she wanted to damp down any rising conflict, and up to a point she succeeded. Molly Whitworth stared at me briefly, said in a colourless tone, 'My subject is philosophy,' and then dismissed me from her attention, picking up the threads of her discussion with Geraldine. When the details of this scheme, whatever it was, were firmly in place, she rose, said goodbye to Geraldine and dropped in my direction a distant nod. Then she walked rapidly to the door and out.

'Sorry about that,' Geraldine said.

'She doesn't seem like a typical friend of yours.'

'She isn't. But we were contemporaries at College. So of course, I know her. I know her more than I really want to, in fact.'

'Is she as clever as she thinks she is?'

'Well, conventionally, she's clever, all right. She got a First, and she's off to Cambridge because she's engaged to a don there and they're getting married in the New Year. That's why she's so keen to give these classes before she goes. Saving every cent for her trousseau, I suppose. But she's interested in money, anyway. Reads the *Financial Times* over breakfast, then goes into the telephone box and rings up her stockbroker. Honestly, I've seen her do it. She plays the gilt-edged or whatever they call it. Makes quite a profit, I believe.'

'Good God,' I said.

'And the other thing she's interested in, apart from money, is men.'

'Well, a lot of girls are, I suppose.'

'Yes, they are, but she's interested in them in a very direct way. She likes them in bed. She's one of the very few women I know in College who really are out for sex and no questions asked. Most of them have high-souled ideas about finding a compatible partner for life, and getting, of all things, *married*.'

I was about to say that I was surprised to hear that Molly Whitworth had made a hobby of sex when her face came back into my mind. Yes, I could see it. A kind of avidity. That sudden intense scrutiny could, I reflected, go along with a voracious sexual nature. All the same . . .

'I don't want to sound malicious,' I said as we got up to go back to the library, 'but if she's so keen on sex it's a pity nature didn't make her a bit better looking.'

'Oh, she gets on all right. It's easy pickings for a girl at Oxford. There are so many men about and they're so short of female company, or female anything for that matter.'

I was silent, reflecting on how true this was. Did I go on to wish that, during my pre-Heather days of greatest privation, I had been acquainted with Molly Whitworth? I did not. With the best will in the world, and there certainly had been times when I *had* the best will in the world, I would simply have found her so off-putting that the show would never have got on the road.

2

As the autumn went on, Heather became majestically pregnant. Straight-backed as ever, she sailed behind her belly like a sixteenth-century galleon in a trade wind. She started attending the ante-natal clinic at the Radcliffe Hospital and they said the baby was due in February, which of course I could have told them. It was that excursion to Fish Hill to see, or rather to disregard, the gliding display which had done the trick. As we lay on that lovely hillside, with her awful brother swooping around us in his silent flying machine, I had so filled her with my eager life fluid that she could have had no response but to conceive.

Her splendidly fruitful appearance caused me pride at a deep level, though at a shallow level it was somewhat embarrassing and sometimes appeared to me as one more of our problems. We used to go shopping together in Oxford market every Saturday morning. Why Oxford market? Because the food there was excellent, fresh and abundant? Yes, but also because in those days one didn't meet dons there. Oxford market had not become smart in those days. Housewives shopped there, and people who kept boarding houses, and occasionally a college chef would come in rather grandly, confer with butcher or poulterer, and place a bulk order. But dons never went there. Other people did their catering for them, and if they wanted anything personal in the way of fruits or sweets or exotic dishes, they went to Grimbly Hughes. It was not until the arrival of the formidable Mrs Palm, in the late thirties, that the market acquired any *chic* – hers being the only shop in Oxford to stock the Central European delicacies so missed by the bewildered refugees.

So to the market Heather and I went. And the stallholders, naturally, treated us as a young married couple. 'Your wife left these for you to pick up,' they would say, handing me a bag of apples or potatoes. 'When's the baby due? Coming along nicely, I expect?' It never occurred to them, naturally, that my perfectly respectable – well, perfectly legal, anyway – marriage to Heather was something to be guiltily concealed. If it had, it would have confirmed them in their ingrained belief that those clever people in 'the colleges' were no doubt all very well so long as they were actually bent over their books, but were totally adrift when it came to dealing with ordinary common-sense life – a point of view that, as the months went by, I often came to sharing.

As Heather rounded, I began gently insisting that we took these Saturday market trips by bus. At first she protested, saying that she liked to walk and she was sure that it did her good, but I said it was important not to tire herself, so we used to go and stand at the bus-stop in the Banbury Road and ride the two or three stages into Cornmarket Street, getting out within a few paces of the market entrance. Very convenient. And also very discreet. It meant that I didn't have to walk right past the front entrance of my College with a woman who was visibly breeding. Furtive? Contemptible? Of course. But that is what I did.

Meanwhile the Burrell family remained at arm's length. Heather's brother Tom, sadly, had nothing to do with us. Since she had got married to me, his attitude to her was the same as if she had gone on the streets. Mrs Burrell was evidently so deeply hurt and sorrowful that she couldn't yet bring herself to open communication, and her husband had no will of his own in any case; one might just as well have asked Phil, that strange, lumpish, almost half-witted creature who seemed to be all they could afford by way of a hand on the farm, why he didn't come to visit us. We managed to avoid going there at Christmas (we told each set of parents we were going to the other and then spent the day quietly in the flat, as far as possible ignoring the whole shooting-match) but finally as January wended its weary way through the calendar, Mrs Burrell's curiosity – plus her natural solicitude towards Heather and her first grand-child – drove her up the shiny stairs to our horrible little flat. She chose a time when she had a pretty good idea I would not be at home, but as things turned out I was, a fact that enveloped her in icy distaste and embarrassment as a fish arrives from the shop wrapped in wet newspaper.

'Oh,' she said when I opened the door to her knock. There was a flat, dismissive sound to that 'Oh'. It meant, 'Oh, *you're* here, are you?' She cast a glance past me. 'Where's Heather?'

'I'm in the kitchen, Mother,' Heather called. She billowed in, just about getting through the narrow doorway, and bestowed a daughterly kiss.

'Won't be long now, evidently,' Mrs Burrell said.

'Well, you know the date they gave us. I don't see why they should be far wrong.'

Her mother turned and looked around the shabby, skimpily-furnished flat.

'Not much of a place to bring a baby up in,' she said. She spoke as if addressing the room in general, but obviously the remark was aimed at me – the seducer, the betrayer, the failer to provide.

'I don't know about *bringing up*,' I said. 'The baby won't remember this place. And we'll be into something much better before he or she is three.'

'Oh, never mind all that,' said Heather. 'Sit down, Mother, and have a cup of tea.'

'I didn't come here to be waited on. I came to see if there was anything I could do.'

'Well, that's kind of you, but we're perfectly well organized, thanks.'

I doubt it, her mother's expression said.

'I suppose they're taking you into hospital to have the baby?'

'I've told you they are.'

'Is it far?'

'I've told you that too. It's the maternity ward of the Radcliffe Infirmary, which is about eight minutes' walk from here.'

'*Walk*? You're not going to *walk*, I suppose?'

'I expect we can cross that bridge when we come to it.'

Mrs Burrell turned to me, her face now flaming with accusation. 'What arrangements have you made for Heather to get to the hospital?'

Realizing that I hadn't actually considered the matter yet, I said uncomfortably, 'When the baby starts coming on I'll get a taxi.'

'A taxi?' Witheringly. 'You don't know much about childbirth, do you?'

'I expect to learn.a lot in the next few weeks.'

'That's all very well, but I'll thank you not to learn on my daughter.' A point to her there. 'If you knew anything about childbirth you'd know there's something called the breaking of the waters. It lets loose a lot of fluid . . . amniotic fluid,' she added condescendingly, as if I were likely to think it was lighter fluid. 'It's going to be pretty embarrassing if that happens in a taxi, don't you think?'

Frankly, it seemed to me that embarrassment would be just about the least of my problems.

'Mother, don't fuss,' said Heather. 'When I get the first contractions, I'll take steps to get to the hospital one way or the other. Obviously they're not going to send an ambulance for a perfectly healthy woman who only lives a few yards away.'

'It's bad enough,' said Mrs Burrell with a stagey little sigh, 'to have our first grandchild born in a *hospital*.' She made it sound as if the hospital were the workhouse. 'All the Burrells have been born at home for generations. You and Tom were born at Jasmine Farm, of course.'

'Speaking of Jasmine Farm,' I said, maliciously, 'how's everybody? All well, I hope?'

'Tom and my husband are very well, thank you.' (Only *I* am cut to the quick by this *mésalliance*.)

'And Phil? Still making himself useful around the place, I hope?'

Mrs Burrell gave me a look that . . . but on second thoughts I can't call it a look. It was a signed, sealed promise, witnessed by an unseen posse of lawyers, that if ever she had the power to do so, she would boil me in oil. I had a sudden glimpse of how much she must hate having Phil around. Why, I wondered, if she hated Phil's presence so much, did she put up with it? Money, I supposed. That was the explanation of most things. It was, after all, the explanation of why Heather and I were living unofficially in this rat-hole while I had official lodgings in those tall, elegant rooms in Episcopus. Economic motivation; in other words, money. I supposed a degenerate like Phil would come cheap.

'I think,' Mrs Burrell turned back to Heather, 'that when the day approaches I'd better stay near the telephone. The moment you get the first contractions, ring up and I'll drive in and take you to the hospital.'

'Heavens, there's no need for that.'

'Further discussion,' said Mrs Burrell, rising, 'is the thing there's no need for. It makes far more sense to have me around with the car. Peter won't mind stepping out to the telephone.' Lazy, irresponsible, inefficient bastard that he is, her tone supplied. I suppose he can afford a few coins for a brief call, it added.

She kissed Heather, ignored me of course, and went over to the door, but with her hand on the knob she stopped and turned to Heather once more.

'Your father and I were discussing some suitable names for the baby. We thought of — '

'It's settled,' Heather said abruptly. 'Michael.'

Mrs Burrell swallowed and said, 'And if it's a girl?'

'Amanda.'

When Mrs Burrell, confounded, had closed the door behind herself and we could hear her going down the comfortless linoleum-covered stairs, I said, 'Michael? Amanda? Any special reason?'

'No, they just came into my head. I had to shut her up. She might have come out with some name I actually wanted, and then I couldn't have used it.'

I think that was the moment when I first realized just how deeply Heather hated her mother. And anyway, Michael was all right with me, if she still liked the name when she had had time to consider.

The reason I was at home that day, at the unlikely time of three o'clock in the afternoon, was an increasingly familiar one: atonement. The previous night had been the first I spent in College, in my newly resplendent rooms. Robert had come up to me after lunch with the unwelcome news that everything had been completed to the carpenters' satisfaction; various window-fittings and shelves had taken longer than expected, but I was now free to move in, which he assumed I would do immediately. There was nothing for it but to comply; it was already over a week since my election, and I had not yet spent a night in College. Exactly how Heather would adjust to being left by herself, I had no idea; there were still, as there had always been, whole areas of her mind that were opaque to me. But I knew it was not going to be easy for her.

I didn't have dinner in College that night. I ate at home, picking up some sausages in the market when I finished my day's reading, to have with mashed potatoes and fried onions. We prepared the food together and chatted and were companionable, but all the time I knew I was going to have to tell her, and soon, that I had to gather up pyjamas and toothbrush and get down to College. I waited until we had eaten and were enjoying a cup of tea, which we both preferred to coffee in the evening. The teapot and cups and milk-jug on the table in the circle of electric light seemed a perfect symbol of desirable domesticity, and I was in a mood, yet again, to curse the single-sex collegiate structure of Oxford University. But the admission had to be made sooner or later, so as I filled Heather's cup for a second time, I blurted it out: my College room was ready and I had to get down there and sleep, *tonight*.

She took it quietly, which didn't particularly reassure me because quite often she took things quietly and the really seismic upheavals came later. But at least it was something, not to have a screaming fit there and then.

About ten o'clock she said, 'When do you have to go?'

'Oh, not for ages. I've got a key, I can let myself in any time.'

Soon afterwards she went to the bathroom and instead of coming back into the sitting room, she went into the bedroom. I heard the springs creak as she got into bed. I went and sat by her. She was in her night-dress, looking composed and beautiful in the way that pregnant women do.

'Let me get in beside you,' I said, beginning to undo my shirt.

She smiled. 'Is there really any point? You'll hardly go off to sleep if you've got to get up again, and you won't have any other motive, I imagine.'

'You imagine wrong,' I said, getting in. All at once I knew it was important to make love to Heather. I didn't feel much in the way of actual physical desire for her just then, but the act of love as a means of showing affection and tenderness was another matter. And even with a Himalayan bulge like Heather's it was still possible, we had discovered, if we lay on our sides. I won't pretend it was the best I ever had, but it was good because it was saying something, and I know Heather was glad of it.

Afterwards we lay awake, talking like good friends, for a long time. Perhaps, I thought, perhaps it's all going to be all right – perhaps we shall get over this awkward beginning to our married life without too much damage. I had great faith in something I vaguely labelled 'the passage of the years'. I thought 'the years' were on my side. Perhaps sometimes, in some lives, they are.

At about two o'clock I got up and dressed, kissed Heather on the cheek, went downstairs and cycled through lonely windy streets to Episcopus, and the small side door to which I had been given a key. And the following day I made sure I got away from College as soon as possible. Heather was glad to see me, and accepting, and not even her mother's visit spoiled our afternoon together.

So life fell into its new pattern. I ought to have been happy, and indeed mostly

I was happy. I had got rid of the constraints and disciplines of undergraduate life. I no longer had to live in greasy lodgings with the landlady patrolling the stairs to make sure I slept by myself. (I could visit my wife whenever I chose, as long as I kept up appearances by sleeping in College about three nights out of four.) And finally, I was accepted as a scholar and treated as one. I no longer had to scramble through an essay a week, whether I was interested in the subject or not, and take it to a tutor whose job it was to riddle it with bullet holes. I could read and gather facts, and meditate, and perceive relationships, and speculate as to chains of cause and effect, at my own pace. In the Bodleian, I was unquestioningly allowed access to rare documents and manuscripts, and so, presumably, I would be in any library anywhere. Mr Peter Leonard, Fellow of Episcopus College, Oxford. The super-civilized and super-learned people who looked after these special collections greeted me with words and gestures that said, 'You are one of us.' It was all very heady. I could think, of course, of a great many people who would not have found it heady at all, who would have found it tedious and irrelevant to their concerns, but I can say, quite genuinely and not caring for the moment whether or not it sounds priggish, that study was my wealth and that knowledge and illumination were my adventures. I was a natural scholar. Ultimately, I and my kind were the reason why Oxford University had come into existence over 700 years previously and why it was still in existence. We had been there all along and we would still be there when the tiny posturing smart set of snobs and hard-faced social climbers whose exploits got into the newspapers had vanished like a puff of scented smoke.

This conviction, which had been strengthening within me during the four brief years of my academic life, received a fillip about this time from my chance acquaintance with two totally genuine, totally committed scholars of an altogether un-Oxonian kind.

Heather and I often used to have a beer and sandwich lunch at the Rose and Crown, a public house a few yards from our dwelling. It was a habit we got into immediately on moving into the flat, and in order to see something of her during the day I would cycle up from the Bodleian for lunch, rather than have it free of charge at College. I looked forward to these lunch-time conversations, took care not to be late for them, and often arrived so super-punctually that I was in the Rose and Crown some minutes before she arrived, and so began to discern a pattern in the daily life of the place, recognizing the regulars and knowing what time they usually came in. Soon I realized that it was impossible to go into the place between 12.30 and 1.30 – except sometimes at weekends – without seeing a pair of middle-aged men, different in appearance but alike in dozens of scarcely definable details that marked them as Continental Europeans. They always sat together and were perpetually deep in conversation. Passing their table one day I heard their voices clearly for the first time; both men had thick German accents.

Since Oxford had been an international centre of learning from before 1200 A.D., there was nothing intrinsically surprising in two men of Continental origin meeting in one of its taverns. In the mid-thirties it was even less surprising: Hitler had tightened his grip on Germany and the Nazi persecution of Jews had grown in cruelty and intensity until, by the later months of 1934, German Jewish scholars of world reputation were having to flee, bringing with them nothing but the clothes they stood up in. To Oxford, as to every University in England and America, they presented at once a glorious opportunity and a sad puzzle. The arrival of so many gifted individuals, nurtured in a different tradition but sharing the same goals of knowledge and understanding, was a stimulus to the native intelligence so great that to find anything comparable one would have to go back to the arrival in England of the Huguenots in the seventeenth century. On the other hand, to fit them into the system, in terms of jobs and salaries, was extremely difficult. The slow, decentralized methods of Oxford, the recruitment of the academic body by means of individual election to Fellowships at individual colleges – none of this equipped Oxford to handle a sudden influx of new minds.

And the newcomers, for their part, found Oxford equally difficult. Most of them had been professors at home; and the professor, in a Continental University, was the supreme authority-figure, never contradicted, always deferred to. How strange these men must have found the relaxed, democratic Oxford system, the long, disputatious faculty meetings at the conclusion of which the professor has only his single vote, no more power than the humblest Research Fellow! What a way to run a University – what a way for that matter to run a country! Could such a ramshackle, open-textured society really hope to take on a disciplined nation like Germany in total warfare and come out alive? (For they were all, each and every one, certain that war was coming.) And if not, where would that leave them, the refugees? Would they not, in a year or two, be back with brown-shirted Nazi stormtroopers stamping around the streets?

Nussbaum and Katz, the two men I saw in the pub, were both classical scholars, both highly eminent within that overarching similarity, and the bond created by their common heritage as German Jews. The similarity notwithstanding, they were startlingly different. Nussbaum was tall and heron-like; he had the habit, common among wading birds that live on fish in streams, of holding himself perfectly motionless, looking down – at a book, a newspaper, a litter of miscellaneous papers, or just the top of the table. Short, broad-built Katz, by contrast, was filled with an energy and a geniality that made it difficult for him to keep still. He smiled readily and even, again unlike Nussbaum, now and then laughed. With all this Nussbaum was never depressing, never just a wet blanket: he had a strong, mordant intelligence, and his opinions, expressed in his own idiosyncratic idiom, were always bracing, however gloomy. It was not depression that radiated from Nussbaum, but tragedy. He seemed to speak, in his thick German accent, from the centre of great events: one felt that the heavy cloak of history was about his shoulders.

I heard, by eavesdropping, snatches of conversation between these two for months before I ventured to insert myself into their conversation. This didn't, in fact, turn out to be very difficult; it was my own reserve, not theirs, that I had to work at breaking down, since they had been brought up in a culture spared the English assumption that it is bad form to speak to a stranger. Before long I felt able to ask them a personal question: why they conducted their private conversations each day in laborious English rather than in their native German.

Was it my imagination, or did the two of them exchange glances for an instant, when I said that, as if it confirmed some shared expectation? 'So at last someone has asked that question,' the glances said.

'Will you explain ower decission?' asked stocky Katz of lanky Nussbaum.

'No, Hans, you explain it.'

'But yoor English iss the better.'

'The more reason vy you should explain. Somm sinks are better explained imperfectly.'

Katz nodded and turned his large face patiently to me. 'I haff forty-five years. Mine friend Otto has forty-seven years. Ve both knew ze English from ze written page, but not in ze speaking. Zer pronounciation of English iss highly idiosyncratic. Sometimes viz clessical colleaks ve are speakink in Lettin, but always ve are pronouncink ze Lettin in zer Cherman menner. Ze langvage ve are hearink inside ower heads iss always Cherman. Never vill it be renversed. Ve haff too much old.'

I nodded sympathetically.

'Ve are hearink inside ower heads,' Katz continued, 'always ze langvage of Goethe, of Beethoven, of Kant and Hegel, of Schliemann. Zat iss gut. But it is also zer langvage of men who are tryink to kill us. Zat iss bed.' He paused, struggling for words that would make it real to me. 'Zey are sayink to the vorld in the langvage of Schiller and Hölderlin and Schubert that they are filled viss hate. Ven ve in ower heads hear zer langvage, ve are hearink the voice of men who haff hate for us.'

'Jawohl,' Nussbaum breathed, assenting out of some depths of his own memories. 'Hate, hate, and more hate.'

'Ve are conversink in English,' Katz said to me, 'in first line, for reason of tect. Ve are in country off English langvage, ve employ langvage off ower hosts and protectors. But iss more. Ven ve hear English, ve are hearink langvage of decent. Of justice. In dese country, people not kilt for belongink to zer race.'

'Iss more,' Nussbaum put in. 'In England man is not put in chail for his political convictions.'

They both stared at me for a moment after making this declaration, as if they expected me to say something, but I felt totally unequal to the situation. All I could do was offer a sympathetic expression and say, 'I understand.' This was inadequate, but at least it had the merit of being true. I did understand.

In the absence of any suitable vacant positions in the colleges, Katz and Nussbaum were both employed by the Oxford University Press. They worked for tiny salaries, proof-reading and generally overseeing the printing of Greek and Latin texts, and each had a cramped little lodging in Jericho, which fortunately in those days was a low-rent area. The O.U.P. would doubtless have paid them a better wage if its funds had not been stretched so far, but it had in fact more or less invented their jobs out of thin air to accommodate these learned fugitives – of whom there were a good many others, mathematicians and philosophers as well as classical and Biblical scholars. The individuals concerned felt deep gratitude; the world in general, as far as I could tell, showed no interest in the matter at all. If Oxford University Press had expected any gratitude from the educated classes as a whole for their generous policy, they must have been disappointed.

A couple of days before the date the doctor had given us for the arrival of the baby, I stopped going to the Bodleian and spent the time at the flat with Heather. I also stopped sleeping the night in College. To Hell with them! This was more important. At it turned out, my spell of purdah didn't last long. The baby arrived punctually. At three o'clock in the afternoon on the exact date we had been given, Heather got the first unmistakable contractions. I got out of the flat like a scalded cat in the direction of the cab rank in St Giles' Street, which I reached in about four minutes' determined pedalling. As I approached the rank I saw that there was only one taxi there, and I prayed that some bastard wouldn't come and take it from under my nose in those last few moments. Mercifully, a couple more cabs arrived just as I did, so the situation was easy. I commandeered the leading taxi, got him to wait a few seconds while I ditched the bike in College, and then we were on our way. Glancing at my watch as we hummed up the Banbury Road, I calculated that the taxi would draw up at our flat not more than eight minutes after the first announcement of the imminent arrival. Pretty good going.

When we got there, though, I was surprised and angered to find that for all my promptness the going had not been good enough. The Burrell family Ford was parked at the kerb in the spot where the taxi ought to have been decanting me. What in God's earth was going on?

Asking the taxi-driver to wait a moment, I hurried upstairs. Mrs Burrell was there, of course, and in command of the show.

Heather, sitting in an armchair with her feet up on a stool, looked pale but composed and cheerful. She knew her mother had no real power to mess up this grand occasion, however much she fussed and domineered.

'Good timing,' I said to Mrs Burrell.

'I intended to call today,' she said, 'this being the day it was expected. Well, Heather seems to have everything ready.'

'She's had everything ready for weeks,' I said. 'And I've got a taxi outside.' I wondered if we were making any impression on her conviction that we were a couple of juvenile delinquents who couldn't manage anything without her.

'Oh,' she waved a hand dismissively. 'A taxi won't be necessary. I'll drive her in.'

'Mind if I come along?' I asked. The hostility between us had almost reached the point of open screaming by now.

She gave me a look that said, 'If you must,' and I went down the stairs to turn the driver away and pay him off. As I turned back from the cab I ran smack into Harry Goodenough.

'Just off out?' he said. 'I was hoping to drop in.'

Even at such a whirling moment, I was glad to see him. His broad, amiable face, his unkempt straggling hair, the burly body that made him move as clumsily yet as purposefully as a bear, were all in their way reassuring. There was a generosity about Harry that I needed at a time like this. A fanatical Shakespeare scholar, he was the opposite of everything that was petty, niggling, competitive.

'It's really good you've come, Harry,' I said. 'I feel it'll bring us luck. But the fact is, this isn't exactly the moment for a social — '

At that moment Mrs Burrell and Heather appeared in the doorway behind me. As I turned, thinking to introduce Harry, a spasm of pain crossed Heather's face and she steadied herself against the lintel.

'Into the car, dear,' Mrs Burrell commanded. 'I wish we had an ambulance and you could lie down. At least it's better than a taxi.'

Anger rallied Heather and she replied, in a stronger voice, 'Oh, I don't need to lie *down*, for Christ's sake.'

'No need to blaspheme, dear, especially at such a time.'

'Oh, just get me there, will you, or I'll start walking.'

Mrs Burrell opened the car door and Heather got into the passenger seat. All of a sudden I couldn't bear to get in with them.

'I'll follow on foot,' I said to Mrs Burrell. 'I'll be there almost as soon as you will.'

She looked outraged, but then I think everything I did outraged her.

They drove off and Harry said, 'Christ, I've put my foot in it a few times, but never like this. What a moment to choose.'

'Nonsense, Harry, you haven't put your foot in it at all. Something drew you here on this particular day at this particular hour because you're a very intuitive person and you wish us well.'

'Well, it's nice of you to put it that way, and I certainly do wish you well, but to turn up in the middle ... I suppose the Mistress Overdone person is her mother.'

'The reference goes over my head, though I've been reading a bit of Shakespeare lately, hoping it might key me in to the thought processes of the early seventeenth century.'

'It'll do that all right. But I thought you were an eighteenth-century man?'

'Don't insult me, Harry. Shakespeare's your man, but I've heard you talk for hours about the Middle Ages. Antecedents are half the battle, as you know.'

'Well, of course, Shakespeare was born into an England that was largely medieval. But the pace of social change was exceptionally ...'

I could see that I had made a mistake. He was all ready for a discussion on Shakespeare's medieval inheritance and its modification there on the pavement.

'Harry, my wife is having a — '

'Oh, God, I'm sorry. Look, get your bike and — '

'My bike's at Episcopus. I'll have to walk.'

'Well, come on then!'

Despite his awkwardness Harry kept up a terrific pace between North Parade and Walton Street. We had breath to speak only once and that was when he asked me, 'D'you want a boy or a girl?'

'I just want a baby, that's all.'

'What names have you got ready?'

'Michael,' I wheezed.

'And if it's a girl?'

'It'll be a boy,' I said. I have no idea why, but I knew the baby's gender already. Michael was still a couple of streets away, and still warm and protected inside Heather's body, but he was beginning to fight his way out, and the first signal had been sent to me. 'It's a boy,' I said to Harry as we pounded along, 'and we're calling him Michael.'

And so it was.

When I got to the hospital a couple of minutes later, and Harry took his leave, I went in and waited. Not for very long, as it turned out. Heather had Michael after about three hours' labour, which I gathered was regarded as unusually fast. But of course her case was uncomplicated, and Michael was absolutely perfect. I wasn't actually present at the moment of birth – that custom hadn't come in yet: fathers were banished from the scene – but I saw him very soon afterwards, and heard his yells. As I told Harry Goodenough, I had been reading Shakespeare lately, trying to fill at least the major gaps, and now my mind recalled the words of King Lear:

> When we are born, we cry that we are come
> To this great stage of fools.

You can say that again, I thought, as I looked down at the little scarlet-faced creature who was going to know me as Dad. I was as big a fool as any of them, but I had to live with it, and for the moment I was content to do so. Even the presence of Mrs Burrell hardly affected me at all.

My first duty, of course, was to tell my parents the news and, as I came out of the hospital at the Walton Street entrance, I fully intended to get straight down to Oseney and do so. But my feet, of their own accord, turned briskly right instead of left, and I soon realized why. They were insisting that before I talked to anyone, anyone at all, I should walk about for a while under a clear, empty sky in a clear, empty space; and of course the nearest such space was Port Meadow. So I hastened along to Walton Well Road and over the railway bridge, and my pace slackened only after I felt the grass under my feet and saw the great green clearness opening out in front of me to the north, all the way to Wolvercote.

'Port Meadow' is, of course, a misnomer. A meadow is a field where the grass is allowed to grow tall and then cut for hay. Port Meadow is a pasture, where the grass is cropped directly by the animals, and has been so ever since the Anglo-Saxons first cleared it for agricultural use. It is also nowhere near a 'Port' or entrance to the city, but I was not concerned with such matters as I walked there on this wide, starlit winter night with the frozen grass crisping beneath my feet. It was eerie to be out there in the winter darkness – it had always been a summer place for me – but I was glad I had come. A few poor shivering horses, some with blankets thrown over them, were out in the open even at that time of year: one or two came towards me in the pathetic hope that I was bringing food. Sorry, poor creatures, I have not come to provide for you. But I am nevertheless a provider, from this time on; there is a new young life that depends on me and that is a trust I shall keep.

I walked out into the middle of Port Meadow, avoiding the long streaks of flooded ground which were perfectly visible in the pale starlight. As I stood there I saw myself as a link in a huge living chain – a humble enough link, but important to the whole. Here it was, this great stretch of grassland, with the river flowing down its western side and the canal standing along its eastern. Behind me was the town, encircled by a wide area of fertile countryside; it must have always been a magnet for the country people, bringing them in to sell their produce. Century after century, the first light of dawn had seen carts lumbering along rutted roads from all the villages into the wide streets and squares where stalls could be set up. And the flow had not only been of goods and money, but of human beings. How many country fellows, attracted by the opportunities of town life, had settled in Oxford and married town girls, how many town dwellers, like myself, had been drawn for one reason or another into marriage with a daughter of the country; each one no doubt thinking of his or her own case as somehow special and individual?

All at once the cold of the February night struck through to my bones. I hurried along the river bank to the towpath that led down to the Botley Road bridge, wanting suddenly to be away from the wide lonely space, to relax and talk and laugh in my parents' friendly place where the river flowed peacefully beside the lighted windows of the Bargeman's Arms.

As I spent more time at Episcopus, more of the fellows began to take on recognizable identities. One of these was the chaplain, Fanshawe. He had been there during my time as a student, but since I was not a chapel-goer he had never impinged on my life. That statement on its own would convey the kind of chaplain he was: the kind who sat still and minded his own business and waited for people to come to him, rather than going out like a salesman. I sat next to him once or twice at meals and found him perfectly easy to get on with; a lean, rather dried-up man in his middle forties, with thinning fair hair and gold-rimmed spectacles. He was reserved but not stand-offish; if you said something to him he said something meaningful in reply, otherwise he left you alone.

He was good at leaving people alone. I reflected that he had, fairly obviously, taken the second of the two available choices open in our time to a man of the cloth. As the Church progressively lost its political power under the blows of modern scepticism, the individual clergyman could either end up as a blend of P.R. man and social worker, or he could lose himself thankfully in the cool shadows of theological speculation, the problems of church history, or even the vaguer expanses of ecumenicity. Fanshawe was, I understood, quite a good scholar, and as for the rest he saw it as his duty to conduct the statutory services in chapel – neither more nor less than were laid down – and to 'be available' at certain times in the week to undergraduates who wanted to discuss matters relating to the religious life.

Oddly enough, Fanshawe is connected in my mind with an early episode in the life of our son, Michael. We had bought him a pram: Heather saw it advertised on a card in a shop window, going cheap, and she went round to the address mentioned and inspected it. It was almost an antique, but that was nothing against it. One of the things that modern people forget, or have never known, about the 1930s is that they were a deflationary period – everything became slightly cheaper all the time; whenever a new model of anything, from a typewriter to a motor-lorry, came on to the market, it was always slightly cheaper than the model before. The result was that instead of rushing out to buy new things, to get ahead of inevitable price rises, one hung on to them to take advantage of future price cuts. People ran their cars and their washing machines for what would now seem incredible lifetimes. This pram was no exception. It had probably begun life being wheeled out by some nursemaid in a long snow-white apron. It had large wheels at the rear and smaller ones at the front, solid rubber tyres that were probably the last word in technology when they were fitted, and a hood in black fabric that could be raised and lowered with shiny electro-plated handles. Across the top had originally stretched a canopy, doubtless with a fringed silk cover, but this had been a casualty of the years; you could just see the sockets where the four stalks of the thing had fitted into the *carrosserie*.

In this regal conveyance, it was often my lot to wheel Michael along North Parade. I was chary of longer excursions, still hoping to keep up my absurd double life as a bachelor don living in College, and to be fair to Heather she never press-ganged me into wider outings. Shopping in the immediate vicinity was another matter, though. There was a grocery barely fifty yards from the door of our flat, and she would often get me to wheel Michael along there and back, for bread or milk or potatoes, because the motion of the pram, even on a short journey, usually sent him to sleep.

So it happened that one afternoon at about four o'clock I was in the little North Parade provision shop, loading a basket with all the things Heather had told me to get while at the same time keeping an eye on Michael through the window, in his stately Edwardian pram on the pavement outside. A familiar enough, calm enough situation. But then the bell in the shop gave its *ting*! to announce another customer, and of all people it was Fanshawe. What the hell did he want? He lived in College; what could he need in the way of groceries?

He recognized me immediately (he had that much of the clergyman about him), and gave me his shy smile. I had finished my business at the counter, but it was impossible to hurry out without exchanging at least a word or two. So we stood there, rather stiffly, trying to think of things to say, and in the intervals of our disjointed conversation, Fanshawe bought a packet of ginger-nuts – a present, perhaps, for some old lady he was going to have tea with. We left the shop together. This was serious; at any moment I might find myself strolling along with him. Quickly, as I came out over the threshold of the shop I formed a plan

31

of action. A little further down the street, to our left, was a florist's. I would go there. I would have business in the flower shop and I would just have to pray that Fanshawe did not. Ignoring the pram with Mike in it (he wasn't asleep, I heard him burbling to himself as I went past, but mercifully he wasn't crying), I turned to the left. Fanshawe also turned to the left. I approached the door of the flower shop. Fanshawe also approached the door of the flower shop. I made a silent vow that if he came into the florist's with me I would hit him with a twelve-pound bag of fertilizer and make my escape. But when I pushed open the shop door he said pleasantly, 'Well, I'll see you tonight, if you're dining.'

'Yes. No, that is,' I said. 'I forgot. Flowers. I must get some flowers.' And I barged through the door of the flower shop like a drunken elephant.

Then, of course, a cool young woman in a smock came up to me and I was forced to buy something. But at least Fanshawe had taken himself off.

The cheapest spray of flowers in the place still cost far more than I wanted to spend. Salaries at Episcopus were paid quarterly, and we were so catastrophically poor that I used to wonder nervously if my frayed jackets and trousers, my shirts with obviously turned collars, were conspicuously noticeable to my colleagues. Their sartorial standard was not all that high, but at least their clothes were of good quality and fairly new, even if they did often look as if they had been slept in; it was another matter to walk around all day in clothes that were past praying for, and I longed for the day when I could get one decent jacket and one new pair of trousers. The miserable bunch of freesias that I bought 'for Heather' pushed that day back a little further; this in itself was lowering enough, but not so lowering as the shabby feeling I had as I walked back to where I had left Mike in his pram. He had started a little fretful series of whimperings now, not exactly crying but signalling that he would start crying at any moment unless something good happened, and I felt terribly contrite.

I wasn't going to take him back to the flat till he fell asleep, so I wheeled him the length of North Parade two or three times, not bothering about shops, scorning concealment, not caring who saw me. Fuck Fanshawe! Let him show up again if he liked. He didn't, though. And Heather was pleased with the flowers. She said I shouldn't have spent the money, but I told her I was overwhelmed by a sudden feeling that I needed to give her a present. I told her the sight of the flowers in the shop window had made me think how beautiful they were, and then I thought how beautiful *she* was, and I knew I had to do something, however small, to match up the one beauty with the other. In fact, the way I plastered her over with bullshit, anyone would have thought we weren't married at all.

In my second year as a Research Fellow, Bax asked me casually if I could fit in a little teaching. 'Just a couple of tutorials a week,' he said. 'We've got rather a lot of men doing a Special Subject in the Eighteenth Century this term, and if you could set them a weekly essay and generally look after them, it would save the fag of having to send them out.'

He knew damn' well, of course, that I'd be delighted to fit it in. Tutorial work was paid at the rate of a pound an hour, so my income went up from £6 to £8 a week; more important still, it made me feel like a real don; most important of all, it let me know that Episcopus had their eye on me for a teaching fellowship one day, if I shaped up reasonably well. I knew Bax would be hovering in the background to make sure that I didn't let these undergraduates down. He would, in his usual unobtrusive way, be supervising my supervision of them.

I felt very important as I sat in my grand sitting room; I had put my most

32

impressive books on the shelves near the fireplace, where they would be conspicu-
ous, and generally set the scene. I was about four years older than the two lads
I was tutoring, but of course I tried to make myself seem at least forty years
older. I took them one at a time, not only to give each of them my anxious
attention but because I got a pound a time for single tutorials but for a pair I
would only have got thirty shillings.

We were now in the summer term of that second year of my apprenticeship
and things seemed reasonably bright with me. Heather had settled down well
enough to our marriage, Michael was over a year old and very bouncing, my
professional prospects looked pretty hopeful, I was young and interested in my
work and the sun shone down on the green leaves and the golden stones and the
sweetly flowing river. One beautiful day, about mid-afternoon, I went in to
Episcopus College lodge to find that someone had left a note in my pigeonhole.
The someone was my dear friend Geraldine. The only reason why I didn't
recognize her handwriting was that it was such a hasty scrawl; the paper was a
leaf torn from a notebook; obviously she had been on the wing. It read: 'Mass
demonstration Cutteslowe tomorrow. Starts mid-morning. Can you come? Shall
telephone for answer 6–7. G.'

Cutteslowe: that pinpointed it straight away. Ever since the previous December
there had been rumblings and mutterings about the extraordinary structure that
has since gone down in history as 'the Cutteslowe Wall'. This, an actual brick
wall, became one of the most overt expressions of that class prejudice that is
always latent in English life.

As the Banbury Road moves out northward from Oxford, a little beyond the
confines of classic North Oxford and close to the traffic roundabout which signals
the exit from the city, there are a couple of residential streets, Carlton Road and
Wentworth Road, which slope gently down towards the River Cherwell. At their
ends, in the lower-lying ground near the river, the City Council had some years
earlier built the large Cutteslowe Housing Estate for the benefit of some of its
poorer citizens. A little later, a private company built somewhat grander (though
still not conspicuously grand) dwellings on either side of these two roads up
closer to where they joined the Banbury Road. So things stood still until, probably
in response to a rumour that Cutteslowe Estate was to be expanded to take in
'slum clearance' tenants, the company – concerned to keep up the exclusive
nature of the district and therefore the property value of the houses – actually
blocked off those two roads just below their houses with bricks and mortar.
(Though always referred to as 'the Cutteslowe Wall', it was in fact two walls.)
Indignation ran high, especially as the Council tenants had to go a long way
round to get to the main road with its bus service and shops.

All this I knew. I had taken an unexcited interest in the affair. I thought the
wall was offensive and deserved to be removed, but it didn't keep me awake at
night because I assumed that it would be removed, and soon. After all, it was
blocking two public thoroughfares. What I had not allowed for was the fact that
lawyers, trained in such devious matters, could point out that the roads on the
farther side of the wall had been built by the Council, whereas those on the City
side had been laid down by the housing company, who had also put in the
services. They could therefore claim that one road stopped and a couple of feet
further on another and different road began, and in this couple of feet they could,
if they wished, build a wall. It was nonsense, of course, but it might be seen as
nonsense that could stand up in court.

For once, popular resentment had found a target that was not the University.

33

It was no Town and Gown matter, but a straight clash of social groupings; on the one hand the Council tenants, who represented the lowest incomes and the least privileged positions in the community; on the other, people who saw themselves as belonging to another class, and wanted to keep themselves apart. I was sure that the second group would be overruled, and I was mildly interested to see how it would be done.

But why mass demonstrations? Had it gone as far as that? And why did Geraldine want *me* to turn out and watch, or perhaps take part? Could I really make any difference?

At about half-past six the porter in the lodge put Geraldine through. Since I had an undergraduate with me who had just finished reading his essay and was waiting for my comments, I had to ask her to ring back in half an hour or so. No, she said, she couldn't, she wouldn't be near a telephone; I must say *now*.

'I'm truly sorry, but I can't get to Cutteslowe during the day tomorrow,' I said. Then, stretching the truth, 'I've got a big teaching load this term and there are a lot of chaps coming to see me. I couldn't put them off without much more notice than you've given me.'

Her voice sounded hard and impatient. 'Oh, nonsense. If you attached any importance to helping out with this, you'd cancel without a second thought. You'd just pin a notice on your door or something.'

'I *wouldn't*, Geraldine. I do the job I'm paid to do. It may not be very important in world terms but I believe in it and I do it.'

'But you're *needed* here. Every person of good will is needed.'

'Look, I'll be a camp follower. I won't make any arrangements for tomorrow night. I won't sign on for dinner and I won't tell Heather I'm going home to eat. Then if you come round I can pour you a drink or take you out for a meal and hear a full account of how it's all gone. Moral support. Don't underestimate it.'

'Oh, all right, if that's all you're good for,' she said and rang off. I turned my attention back to my student, who I noticed was looking at me interestedly. I had forgotten for the moment that I wasn't alone. Fortunately I hadn't said 'home to my wife', because I was supposed to be a bachelor living in College. But I had talked about going home to Heather. He would know, then, that I had a set-up somewhere with a woman called Heather. Gossip, gossip. Of course the belief that I had a mistress in the town somewhere would probably send up my prestige among the undergraduates, making me seem a slightly more dashing figure. What a lot of nonsense! I thought for the millionth time.

Would Heather mind that, having decided not to eat in College, I was spending the time with Geraldine rather than being at home? Well, I was and that was that. Geraldine's friendship was absolutely necessary to my existence. Heather knew that.

So, the next evening, when at seven o'clock I finished my day's tutoring, I didn't go into Hall. McLennan knocked on my door and asked if I were 'dining', as he always put it, and I said No, and after I heard his feet pattering decorously down the staircase I opened a bottle of wine and poured myself a drink and sat down in front of the fire to wait for Geraldine.

While I waited I thought about her. It was easy to see, I decided, why I needed her in my life. She was the diagram of all the things I wasn't. I was dreamy, frequently listless, generally indecisive. Geraldine was always alert, always highly charged with energy, completely certain about the next step in front of her.

On this occasion I could see it must be a pretty big step. As soon as she hurried into the room I could tell by the brightness of her eyes and the general set of her face, tense and expectant, that she had just done, or was about to do, something very important.

'Sit down and tell me,' I said. 'Something's happened.'

'In one sense,' she said crisply, 'nothing at all's happened. The demonstration came to nothing.'

'How can a demonstration come to nothing? You mean nobody came?'

'Two thousand people came. Thanks,' she said, taking a glass of wine from me. 'Two thousand people came and yet nothing happened.'

'Well, fill me in,' I said.

'Everybody assembled. At the very beginning they were just standing about aimlessly in knots, but very soon Abe got there and after that it was organized.'

'Abe?'

'Abe Lazarus. Don't tell me you haven't heard of him.'

'Well, I have now,' I said.

'If you knew anything about ordinary life in this city,' Geraldine said severely, 'you'd know that Abe Lazarus is one of the most important figures in trade unionism in this area.'

'I'm not at Ruskin College.'

'He's got wonderful achievements to his credit. He got a deal for the work-people at Firestone that everybody said was impossible. I tell you, they'd follow him anywhere. He's proved his worth to them. And he's not just a trade union man, he's a Communist. He runs the Oxford Party.'

'Oh, well, no wonder. They're always very good at demonstrations and strikes. They're trained for it, aren't they?'

'They're trained to fight for the working class,' Geraldine said, fixing me with her piercing eye. 'If that means working through strikes and mass protests, they'll do that. Today's demonstration would have been nothing without them.'

'I thought you said it was nothing anyway.'

'Well, the walls across Carlton Road and Wentworth Road are still standing. To that extent it was nothing. But it proved one thing to me and to everybody else there. The Communists are the only progressive force in the country that's likely to get anything done. The only ones with the organization and the *will*.'

When Geraldine said the last word a light of such intensity flashed out from her eyes that for a moment I felt frightened. That kind of will can do a lot of good. But it can also do a lot of harm.

'What happened was quite simple, and quite expected,' she said, setting down her glass and leaning back to tell me the story. 'After Abe and the Committee got there they started handing out picks and shovels and crowbars. They were going to demolish the wall; that was the whole object of the exercise. Abe made a speech – short and very much to the point. He just pointed out the obvious things: that these Council tenants were Oxford citizens like any others, ratepayers and all the rest of it, and citizens of what called itself a free society, with votes and equal status in law, and the wall was a class insult, and they weren't going to put up with it another hour. Everybody gave a great cheer and they were just surging forward when in that magic, soundless way they have, the police were there. All at once, a line of them, with their hands joined, just standing there facing us with their backs to the blasted wall. And then the sergeant or inspector or whoever he was spoke to us through a megaphone and told us that anyone who damaged the wall would be charged with assault. I should have thought you'd have to damage a *person* to be charged with that.'

'Oh,' I said. 'So you just stood there looking at each other? You and the police?'

'Yes, it swayed back and forth a bit and of course there was some cat-calling and what-not. I won't deny there was something in me that would have liked to see the chaps rush forward and go for the coppers. I don't usually want to use violent means – but I did feel a wave of frustration and anger and something very close to hate. I thought of all those smug little people in the more superior houses ensconced behind the wall and saying to one another, "We shall be all right, dear, the law is here to protect us." Why is it always people like that that the law seems to protect? Why doesn't the law do something about the unemployed and the slum-dwellers and the country people living in cottages that let rain through the roof?'

'The law does, ultimately, tackle that kind of problem,' I said, 'but it does take a long time. Hamlet mentions "the law's delay" as one of the inescapable evils of human life. Shaftesbury's Factory Acts took a long time.'

'They took too damned long. Anyway, we can't hang about any more in the way the nineteenth century did. The world's in too much of a mess, it's on the brink of such a godawful total collapse. We have to act, and that means getting decisive leadership.'

'So you're going to get it from Abe Lazarus,' I said, filling her glass.

'Precisely,' she said, nodding composedly. 'In the first instance from him, and then spreading out in concentric rings across the world.'

'Geraldine, you're trying to tell me something.'

'I'm not trying to, I'm telling you. Here.' And she took from her trouser pocket – those skimpy, adolescent trousers that were so much a part of her personality! – a piece of cardboard about three inches by two. I looked at it. Her Party card. Signed by Abe Lazarus as Secretary of the local branch and by Geraldine as the loyal member.

'You joined there and then?'

'A lot of people did. Hundreds, I should think.'

'So,' I said thoughtfully, 'the Cutteslowe Wall has benefited the Communist Party if it hasn't benefited anybody else.'

'Every bit of injustice and stupid arrogance will benefit the Communist Party,' she said, 'until the day when the Communist Party comes to power.'

'And after that,' I said, 'the acts of injustice and stupid arrogance, which human beings commit just because they *are* human beings, will be blamed on the Communist Party because it'll be the ruling party. But with this difference. If there are any demonstrations they won't be dispersed peacefully with a warning against committing assault. There'll be the kind of instant clamp-down that has people being machine-gunned in the street, and beaten to death in sound-proof cells.'

'My word,' she said, 'you have been listening to the propaganda, haven't you?'

'I'm an historian. I look at evidence, not at slogans. There hasn't been much evidence coming out of the Soviet system in recent years, but what has come out has been pretty chilling. And the mere fact that there's been so little information, that the lid's screwed down so tightly, is a piece of evidence in itself.'

For a moment I thought we were going to quarrel. She was silent, and her face was very set. Then, as she slid the Party card back into her pocket, she turned and gave me a forgiving smile.

'Peter,' she said, 'you always were a slow mover.'

'True enough,' I said.

'You're jelly-bellied.'

'You could put it like that.'

36

'I can't believe that things I can see so utterly clearly, you can't see at all. But I realize you'll need time. Your inlet valve for new thoughts and ideas is *tiny*.'

'Um.'

'I shall need six months to convert you. May I have six months, Peter?'

'Of course,' I said. 'But why are you bothering?'

'A little bit for your sake,' she said, serious now, 'but quite a lot for the Party's. We need intellectuals.'

We! I thought. She's been in the Party a couple of hours and already it's We! That was how she was: so open, so welcoming to anything that seemed to her a solution of real human problems. And it was her openness, her welcoming, that made her so terribly vulnerable.

One of the things that happened over the next month or two was that I began to know Katz and Nussbaum somewhat better, through seeing them so often in the Rose and Crown, and to appreciate them as distinct individuals. Nussbaum was stately and melancholy; when he made a pronouncement in his deep, sorrowful voice, it was as if you were listening to the inexorable bells of History tolling to mark apocalyptic events. Katz, though he had just as much in his past and in his future prospects to make him sombre, was ineradicably cheerful. His broad dish-like face, his great moon spectacles, went very easily with smiling, and when he smiled it seemed to flood his body with enjoyment so that he could not keep still, but bounced up and down at the knees.

The extent of Katz's cheerfulness was not really apparent to me until the day I first happened into him on his own, without Nussbaum. It was not that Nussbaum made Katz unhappy, or lowered his vitality; but the stately melancholy that Nussbaum injected into the air around him seemed to make Katz's mercurial upward leaps into blitheness hard to take seriously. Without Nussbaum, on the other hand, his cheerfulness radiated out into the air like heat from an electric fire.

It was in Walton Street that I met him, bouncing along towards the University Press. He greeted me with eager friendliness. 'Ah, Leonard. You haff a moment to spare?' (I hadn't said I had any time to spare. He just assumed I must have.) 'Komm and let me show you my kingdom. It vill be of interest to you.'

He led me, unprotesting, across the wide, college-like quadrangle of the University Press, through a doorway, up an interminable stairway to a landing, along the landing, then up another stairway. We were now at the very top of the building. Skylights admitted a pale light at intervals along the corridor. Katz led the way to a door at the far end, produced a key and opened it. 'Enter!' he said grandly. 'My kingdom. Here I am absolute ruler. Monarch of all I surwey.' His English had made excellent progress lately; only *v* and *w* still sometimes bedevilled him.

Amid the many objects that met my view I made out a deal table and a wooden chair, books and papers, obviously, but also cardboard boxes, files, photographic negatives, insecure piles of manuscript and typescript. The tiny space had obviously been a store-room, and a very small one at that; a broom-cupboard, even, or at any rate a cleaners' depository for mops and pails and tins of polish and buckets. Now it was Katz's kingdom.

'You are familiar with my field of work?' he asked me proudly. 'I haff mentioned it to you?'

'Well, I know that you and Nussbaum are both classical scholars.'

Katz smiled as if I had said something funny. 'Iss blanket term, my friend. Classical scholars have many areas of interest.'

Silently I accepted the rebuke.

'Otto Nussbaum is orthodox classical scholar. Follower of main stream of preoccupation, since *renascentia*. He studies manuscripts and printed texts, main sources of the classical tradition all across Europe. Copied from one scribe to another all across the Dark Ages, the Middle Ages, right up to printing days, then edited and printed, edited and printed. He is in a tradition. Could be at ease in the company of Scaliger or Grotius, Bentley or Lachmann. No reason against that. Such scholars are necessary. Guardians of knowledge that has been gathered very slowly and painfully. But I am different breed. I am papyrologist.'

He spoke with such pride, up there in his little broom-cupboard, with the piles of clutter all around him, that I suddenly felt I loved him. Learning mattered so much to him; the sifting and salvaging of whatever remained of a supreme age of human achievement seemed to him so abundantly worth living for, so much more worth serving than money and power and the vulgar forms of success, that I saw him, in that moment, clearly for what he was: a good and true man, an example. But he was speaking. He was asking me, 'You know of course, vat are the *papyri?*'

'Well,' I hedged. 'It's stuff written on that material made from the papyrus plant, isn't it? A kind of reed that grows in swamps . . .'

'Chief writing material during classical times,' Katz said reverently. 'Mostly survived in Egypt in dry climate. But not stored in libraries like European manuscripts. Thrown away or used casually. Some wrapped round mummies. Nearly all fragments. Haff to be fitted together. It is asking a man's lifetime to become even fairly competent at this.'

'What kind of stuff is mostly on them?'

'Two kinds. Documentary and literary. I am in literary field. This is vy I can talk with Otto. Ve share perspectives. Much of the material on papyrus is Homeric. Vorks of Homer were chief means of education during all classical times. But ve haff other finds. Menander. Poem by Sappho. Callimachus.'

He became lost in thought for a moment and then said abruptly, 'Exile iss vorse for me than for Otto.'

'Exile from Germany, you mean?'

'Yes. Personally, from family and friends and habits and langvage, is eqval I suppose. But professionally, is more inconwenient. His field iss not so much different. German classical scholarship iss best in the vorld. But the kind Otto follows is qvite well done in England. Some respectable vork at English universities. Some good editions issued here.' His hand circled, indicating the University Press all around him. 'But for me, is severe handicap. Study of papyrology iss more methodical in Germany. You are familiar with this standard vork?'

He shovelled about among the mass of books and papers on the table and came up with a stout volume, which he laid open before me. I looked at it. *Einführung in due Papyruskünde*, by a man named Schubart. 'I'm afraid not,' I said.

'No? In that case it iss even less likely that you vill be acquainted with Mitteis and Wilcken.'

'Mitteis and . . . ?'

'*Grundzüge und Chrestomathie der Papyruskünde*,' Katz said with a slow, beautiful relish. 'Four volumes, nineteen-twelve.'

'Very much out of my field, I'm afraid.'

'Not to be helped,' said Katz, cheering up again. 'The vorld's vork must be subdiwided. Specialization is necessary evil.' He got the *v* right that time. 'You must go, my friend? Goodbye. Ve shall meet in the public house. I am glad you haff seen my kingdom.'

'You work here all the time? What is it you're engaged on?'

'An edition, my friend. That is what every papyrologist will be engaged on, for many decades to come. There is enormous editing work to be done.'

I went down the long passage and the steep stairs, thinking: many decades to come? How many decades will come? How much time is left? For the planet, perhaps, a great deal – but for such people as Katz and me, how much?

Public functions, ceremonial occasions . . . looking back, my life at that time seems to have consisted almost entirely of them. When I wasn't being presented for my degree, or being sworn in as a reader at the Bodleian, or being initiated into Common Room society, then there were the Dinners. Oxford life, at Senior Common Room level, is strung out on formal dinners in the same way that power cables are strung on pylons. There is a dinner to mark the end of term, a dinner to mark Somebody-or-other's benefaction, to commemorate this or that. In itself this is harmless enough, and the dinner is invariably a good one, well enough calculated to fulfill its primary function, which is of course to knit the college into a social unity. But these dinners, to a youthful taste, go on far too long; naturally, since going on for a long time is one of the very things they are designed to do, so that Fellows who are very much occupied in distant laboratories and libraries during the working week can relax and have time to get to know each other. But young men don't particularly enjoy sitting over their food for a long time, and I have memories of paralysing boredom, sitting there in my uncomfortable boiled shirt, having long since had enough port, enough nuts, enough grapes and oranges, longing to get up and move about.

There were the Dinners, then, and there had been my (more or less disastrous) wedding day, and, by the unstoppable process of time, another formal occasion had landed on me in the Long Vac. after my first year: Michael had to be christened. It never occurred to Heather or me to do without this observance. He *had* to be baptized, just as his presence *in utero* meant that we *had* to get married. In those days that was how people thought.

On the other hand, I was still determined to keep the whole shady business of my matrimony under the carpet. Having got this far, and been through so much tension and difficulty, I wasn't going to spoil it now. I even took a detached interest – like a psychoanalyst observing an interesting case of some rare neurosis that fortunately it wasn't his responsibility to treat – in the battle against Mrs Burrell that had to be fought all over again. She must have known in the silence of her own mind that the same reasons which had kept me from announcing to the world my wedding to her daughter must equally keep me from announcing the baptism of our child. But the silence of her own mind was an empty space she took care never to enter. She preferred clamour, and clatter, and shrill indignation, and isn't it a shame that we should come to this, and I'm only thankful my mother didn't live to see what we've come to.

We bulldozed it through, however, and fixed the christening, discreetly, again in the local church of South Leigh, for late July. The aged parson tut-tutted a bit.

'It's usual, you know,' he said to me, the silvery rims of his glasses glinting

39

coldly in the summer-morning sunshine that came through the vicarage window, 'to present a child for baptism as soon as practicable after the birth.'

'This is as soon as is practicable,' I said curtly. I wasn't in a mood for any of his arm-twisting.

'The child is in normal health, I understand?'

'Yes. It's not because he's ill that we haven't brought him before.'

Exactly why, in that case, it was, I thought none of his business.

'Mrs Burrell tells me,' he persisted, 'that the birth took place in February. I should have been perfectly happy to christen him in March, which would have been more usual.'

'Usual? In some communities he would have had to walk through the Cherwell till it closed over his head. In others . . .'

'More in keeping with Anglican practice as we understand it in these parts.'

I let it go, silently accepting his rebuke. After all, unless he actually went so far as to *refuse* to baptize Michael, it was no skin off my nose.

Did I think that if Michael died before we got round to having the holy water sprinkled on him, and the holy words said, he would go to hell? I did not. I thought the notion a typically sick idea of the early Christian Fathers. Most of those venerable maniacs were Middle Easterners or North Africans, and neither region has made much of a contribution to the world fund of compassion or common sense. To this crew I was to entrust the indoctrination of my infant son? Never.

Social convention within an Anglo-Saxon community, however, was another matter, and to the christening party at Jasmine Farm we all duly repaired one Saturday in July. In some ways it was a re-run of the damp little gathering of the previous August; in others, it was much better. Certainly I felt better. I was buoyed up by the deep instinctive pride of procreation: this child was my son, the issue of my body through the body of the woman I had chosen, who had chosen me. Rationally, of course, it was nothing to be proud of. All I had done was to knock Heather up, which any man could have done and most would have been glad to get a chance. Carshalton could have done it. Kent could have done it. Even that poor bastard Phil could have done it. Obviously he wasn't impotent, if he had wagged his big wang at the adolescent Heather round the corner of the barn. But as things turned out, I had done it and I was proud of myself. I was also very proud of Mike. With what may have been a foolish partiality, I considered him an exceptionally beautiful baby. It was too early to say whether he more resembled Heather or me; sometimes it seemed to me that I caught a look of her, and sometimes she said that she caught a look of me. We spent hours watching him, and very happy hours they were. That, at least, had gone right.

My brother Brian had come along to the Burrells' farm at High Cogges, and he brought Primrose Ravenscroft with him. He never went anywhere without her nowadays. If the term had been in use in our social circle, one would have said they were engaged. They were in fact looking for somewhere to live, and once that was settled they would be getting married. I was quite certain Brian had got on to a winning streak there. Primrose, though I found her opaque, was very beautiful, and seemed to have become even more so in recent months, perhaps in consequence of being so much adored by Brian, who never took his eyes off her unless there was a racing car to look at. I got my eyes on her once or twice during the christening party, and on one of these occasions I noticed her looking at Heather with an expression I couldn't quite read. It certainly wasn't sisterly love, and yet it wasn't hostile either. As Primrose's eyes rested for a moment on my wife's face, I saw in them a certain detachment, even a touch of wonder: what does it feel like, she seemed to be asking, to be that kind of woman? The kind who lies down with a man and gets up pregnant, and then has to turn the heat on him and make him marry her; the kind, in other words, who responds to experience rather than initiating it. And suddenly I knew, with absolute certainty, that this would never have happened to Primrose. That wild freedom inside her, that gipsy strain in her blood that showed in her wild high cheekbones, the totally untamed quality (if Heather was like a well-cared-for race-horse, Primrose was like a chamois of the mountains), would have stopped her from running down the grooves marked by society. She was untamed, as a wild animal is untamed, and wild animals pay a terrible price in terms of starvation and untended injuries and epidemics that sweep them away, but one price they do not pay, and that price Heather and I had paid. I moved my eyes away from Primrose. I felt uncomfortable, diminished, in her presence.

Another person was there in whose presence I did not feel in the least diminished, but I felt something almost as bad – irritation, aggressiveness, impatience, all the emotions that stop one from taking calm and wise decisions. Yes, Tom was among those who had come to launch Michael into life, and I personally could have well done without him. To be fair, he was at least free of any hypocritical pretence of having changed his mind about me; with that square, fighter's face above those powerful shoulders, he still glared across the room at me as if he would have liked to punch me on the jaw if he could have got away with it in front of so many witnesses.

'Can't think what your brother's doing here,' I muttered to Heather during a brief moment when we found ourselves alone at Jasmine Farm. 'Pressure from your mother, I suppose.'

'No, I don't think so. Tom's stubborn enough that if he really made up his mind not to come, even Mother wouldn't budge him. I think it's more likely to be just his idea of the Correct Thing.'

'Why should he care about that, when he disapproves of me so much?'

'Tom's a funny mixture. He's very conventional. Approval and disapproval don't come into it. His nephew's getting christened, that's how he sees it. Put on your best suit and be there.'

'I suppose so. I'm not really familiar with that Empire-building type.'

'I wish I could say I wasn't. Watch out.'

This last caution, delivered in an undertone, referred to the fact that Heather could see, over my shoulder, the approaching figure of Mrs Burrell, who seemed to be everywhere at once, giving instructions, monitoring the distribution of food and drink, and breaking up individual conversations whenever they threatened to become enjoyable and interesting.

One pair who found themselves thrust into juxtaposition by her constant stirring motion were, on the face of it, very ill-suited. Recalling Tom's blank refusal to get to know Brian at the wedding, when they had first come face to face, I watched with a certain amount of trepidation as, wedged into a corner, they had no option but to begin talking. I need not have worried. Tom had overheard Brian, in some previous conversation, mention the name 'Brooklands' – which was not surprising, since the majority of his sentences contained the name. M.G., with whom he worked, had a more or less perpetual involvement there, whether in racing or attempting various records, and the road between Oxford and Brooklands must have seemed to Brian like his own backyard. I was standing a little way off, but I moved nearer to hear how the conversation developed.

'I heard you mention Brooklands. I know a lot of chaps who fly from there.' Tom's tone was challenging, as if only he had the right to an acquaintance with the great Mecca of speed and skill.

'Yes, there is a lot of flying from Brooklands. A. V. Roe — '

'You don't have to tell me about Roe. Mind you, that flying speed record was never official. Only two people ever saw it and they were just employees.'

'Yes,' Brian said evenly, 'the carpenter and a chap who was a gamekeeper in the woods. But it doesn't matter much, does it? Flying isn't what Brooklands is about.'

'Not what it's about? It's pretty well the most important aerodrome in the country.'

'That may be, but flying isn't what it's about. Racing cars is what it's about.'

'Oh, come on. You don't expect me to swallow that, do you? Flying is the most important development of the age. It's going to change everything – transport, military strategy, everything. Rushing about in racing cars is just a hobby for a few overgrown schoolboys.'

Brian's jaw tightened. I knew the sign. I prayed he wouldn't start throwing punches. 'Look,' he said, 'do you want to talk about this seriously, or d'you just want to — '

'Of course I want to talk about it seriously. What else is there?'

'Well, to start with, you're in too much of a hurry to separate the two. Aeroplanes here, racing cars there, as if they were in different worlds. You talk as if the engine of a racing car wasn't very similar to an aero engine. They both have the same high-compression — '

'Well, there may be similarities, but the aircraft industry's perfectly capable of developing its own engines. It doesn't have to wait for a lot of chaps to blast off in racing cars. Alcock and Brown — '

'Nothing tests an engine like racing,' said Brian patiently. 'Racing tests every component of an engine hundreds of times over on every lap. You can't test something like that a thousand feet up in the air. There'd be too many fatal accidents.'

A knot of people pushed between me and the pair of them, someone claimed my attention, then I had to go and pose for my photograph with Heather and Michael. It all took time and when I got back to plug into the Tom-and-Brian dialogue again I could see they had made progress. By standing up to Tom and not being over-awed, Brian had established his own solidity as an opponent, and in any case by now they had gone beyond mere opposition. Since both their talk was of engines and high-octane fuels, and speeds and records, and of Brooklands, they were rapidly turning into allies.

'Look,' Brian was saying, 'I can see I shall have to fill you in on some background. You flying types always think anything that runs along the ground can't be technically advanced. You think of cars the way I do of trains, silly overgrown steam-kettles. But when you're up in the air, what's keeping you moving forward? The engine. And it's the racing designer who's giving you that engine.'

'Oh, come. There's lots of — '

'Not the racing designer on his own, I grant that, but him more than any other single person. Look, I work on racing cars.'

'I think I might have guessed that by now.'

'I work at M.G.'

'Well, I've heard that outfit's doing pretty well,' Tom conceded.

'*Pretty well?* Playing it down a bit, aren't you? Look, already this season – and it's not over – we've won the Ulster T.T. Outright. We went to Italy and won the Junior Coppa Acerbo. Outright. We went to America and won the Auto Club Grand Prix. Outright. And on top of that, how many class H international records do you think we hold.'

'Oh, a lot, I expect. My point is simply — '

'No. Not a lot. Every single one of them.'

'All right, you've made your — '

'And to top it up,' Brian said relentlessly, 'we hold every single one of the Class G records too. Every last one of them.'

'Just freeze it there for a moment, will you?' said Tom, holding up his hand like a traffic policeman. He was grinning now. 'I've listened while you talked about your racing cars. Now will you listen while I tell you a bit about flying?'

'No, I haven't finished yet.'

'Well, look here, I'll make you an offer. If we go down to the Green Man and I stand you a drink, will you let *me* talk for a change?'

Brian considered. He spotted Primrose, approaching through the crush. 'Primrose, Tom and I are going down to the Green Man.'

'No.'

'What do you mean, no?'

'Tom and you and I are going to the Green Man,' she said. 'You're not leaving me alone with this lot.'

I wasn't meant to hear the last sentence, but I did and I concurred with its sentiments. The party at Jasmine Farm was damp and lumpy. The three of them down there at the Green Man would be animated and happy. The two men would be talking about things that filled them with passion. Racing cars and aeroplanes. At what altar? Brooklands. Why should young men not love speed, and noise, and danger, and competition? My own life, at that moment, seemed dreary. But then Brian had always had a gift for making me feel like that.

I would have loved to go down to the pub and have a few drinks with the three of them, but of course it was out of the question. I had to stay and swell the throng at the lunch *à la fourchette* which Mrs Burrell had painstakingly provided at the farmhouse. We were dispiritingly few in number as it was; the christening had been at eleven in the morning, precisely so that the moment it was over my parents could hare back to Oxford and open the Bargeman's on time; it was Saturday, always a busy day. Work, work, work – everybody I knew seemed to be forever working, and always with an eye on the clock and the calendar. Certainly I was like that myself. I supposed there were people who had leisure; not the poor devils who couldn't get a job because of the Depression, but people who had bank balances, and investments, and didn't work because they didn't need to. But I never seemed to meet these people. Or had I met them without knowing it? Were some of my fellow undergraduates at Episcopus like that?

So I stayed and rather gloomily munched my way through some of the egg sandwiches and drank coffee from a little painted cup. If I hadn't been there my side of the family would not have been represented at all, except insofar as Heather could be said to belong to it now. And Michael, of course; but Michael was here *hors concours*. He would have to cope with his own problems when he grew up. No need to saddle him with mine.

Heather and I had agreed that we would get back to North Parade as soon as we decently could, but it was a matter of waiting for a lift. Not quite knowing what was happening, we dawdled about. Michael went heavily to sleep in his Moses basket, and it seemed unwise to wake him; he might howl. Then Brian and Primrose came back, without Tom, who had gone off somewhere, evidently feeling he had done enough by being present at the ceremony. I went up to Brian to see if he could fix us a lift. But it seemed he had something more important to talk about, and he took me outside to be sure of not being overheard.

'Look,' he said when we were well away from the house. 'I ought to warn you. There's a big upheaval coming in this family.'

All I could think of to say was, 'Another one?'

'They won't get over this one,' he said. 'At least the old man won't. But there's no help for it.'

'Well, come on,' I said.

'Tom's just let me into his plans. He's leaving the nest.'

Absurdly enough, the first thing I felt was a little twinge of envy. I didn't like Tom, had no reason to like him, but it seemed unfair that he obviously liked Brian so much that he had confided his plans to him during their first conversation.

'I suppose,' I said pettishly, 'that he's old enough to know his own mind. He must be about twenty-five.'

'He's twenty-six. That's partly why he doesn't want to wait any longer. He's going into the Raff.'

'The Raff?' I was not, at that time, familiar with this way of referring to the Royal Air Force. But of course as soon as the syllable was out I realized what it must mean. What else would Tom do but join the Raff?

'You see what it will do to the old man,' Brian was going on. Heather had silently joined us and was listening. 'It'll finish him. His daughter was a help about the place, and she's gone. With Tom going as well, he'll never be able to manage.'

'He'll have to take on another hand.'

'It's all very well to say that; I don't suppose he can afford it.' Brian shrugged. 'Still, neither you nor I can stop it. And looking at Tom, he's not the kind of bloke who'd stay on a small farm for ever. Specially one he didn't even own. Anyway, he's off.'

'When?'

'Oh, pretty soon. Next week, I think he said. It's all fixed and he hasn't said a word to his parents. He knows they'd hit the ceiling and he just doesn't want all the fuss.'

'Why are you telling me?'

'Because, sonny, when the tidal wave hits his family some of it's bound to wash over you, and you might as well be ready. The parents are more or less bound to come round and try to involve Heather. You'll have to stand firm and not let them bother her too much.'

'All right. Thanks for the warning.'

'You're welcome. Look, are you ready for off yet?'

'We could be in about five minutes.'

'O.K. The atmosphere's bad here, isn't it?'

I had to agree. We left as soon as we could. I hoped it would be a long time before I had to see Jasmine Farm again. As we drove out of the yard I saw Phil peering round the corner of a shed, his eyes invisible under the brim of his awful old mackintosh hat.

3

Now that I was a donling, there were all sorts of comforts and conveniences available to me that were quite unknown in undergraduate life. It was very much as if a citizen of Ancient Rome had somehow been able to transform himself suddenly from a plebeian to a patrician. One of these comforts was a good pot of coffee that was put in the Common Room every morning towards eleven, and one could drop in and help oneself. Having occasion one morning to be in College to change a book at the library, I went over to get a cup and found Bax reading a newspaper. When he had finished looking at it he handed it to me on his way out.

'Looks as if at least one of your generation is well launched on a career,' he said drily.

I looked at the page he had left open. It was an article headed 'Will Oxford Still Not Fight?' The letterpress referred to the famous Oxford Union debate earlier that same year which had carried the motion that 'This house will never again fight for King and Country'. It was decorated with familiar photographs of Tom Tower, Eights on the river, and people in gowns, so that the readers of the paper should not mistake it for an article about Dar-es-Salaam or Wolver-hampton.

In those days the newspapers were rather different from what we have now. The term 'gutter press' had been in use for some time, but although the mass market popular sheets were commonplace and vulgar, they were still comparatively respectable. The heavies, for their part, had changed very little since Victorian times and still aimed at stately, Macaulayesque prose. The middle-range papers, the ones that landed on the breakfast tables of 'ordinary decent' God-fearing, art-hating English people, were pompous and self-righteous ('hard-hitting and fearless') in their editorials, selective in their news reporting and, in their feature articles, aimed at a vapid, chatty, vaguely 'amusing' style with injections here and there of the necessary editorial self-righteousness. The Oxford piece I was looking at was signed 'Ralph Hunt'. Hunt? I had to think for a moment before recalling the fair-haired, rather 'tailor's dummy' man in my year, the one who prefaced everything he said with the little shrug that conveyed, 'What anybody thinks won't change anything.' Now that I had him focused, I could just see him getting a job in Fleet Street and turning out this stuff. He would have learnt the knack in no time. He was half-way there already, with his empty urbanity and his deep conviction that nothing mattered except making oneself comfortable.

Hunt's treatment of the question 'Will Oxford Still Not Fight?' started off like this.

To most of us, the word 'Oxford' conjures up a dreamy picture. We see fresh faces under flat mortar-board caps. We picture willowy undergraduates and their girl chums reclining in punts, to the sound of wind-up gramophones and the popping of champagne corks, through an eternal summer afternoon. Our fancy shows us crusty old dons in billowing gowns, stumping across wide quadrangles with armfuls of heavy calf-bound volumes. And all against a background of amusingly varied buildings of slightly grimy Portland stone, of many styles and many periods.

Portland stone? What the hell buildings in Oxford are made of Portland stone, I thought. It's a stone you see a lot of in London. In a few short months, Hunt had evidently taken to viewing the world entirely in London terms. I read on.

Does anyone in the outside world really care what happens in this enchanted playground? That's a hard one. Perhaps we ought to care, or at any rate to know. After all, the young men, and nowadays some young women, who spend three years there come from the top drawer of our society, from the families who rule this country and the whole British Empire. And for most of them, jobs are being kept warm, jobs in which they will have a lot of say in what happens to the rest of us.

Keep going, you scum, I thought. In a few short sentences you've managed to hold up the student population of Oxford University to (i) puritanical disapproval as they loll in punts and pop champagne corks, and (ii) class jealousy and hatred. Well, let's have some more.

Last February the Oxford undergraduates gathered in their Union Society and voted in favour of the notorious motion which declared that 'This house will never again fight for King and Country.' This motion caused dismay in many hearts. If the young men of the governing class had lost the will to defend our country, why – it was asked – should anyone else bother?
  Is that weary spirit still abroad in the City of Dreaming Spires? That question was in my mind when I set off last week-end to pay the place a return visit. I wanted to sample the prevailing opinion, talk with anyone I met, young or old, undergraduate or don. Except on rare occasions like that Union resolution, Oxford doesn't trouble to announce her thinking to the world. So the world, in the humble person of myself, would have to go to Oxford.

I liked that bit about the 'return visit'. It conveyed so deftly that the writer was an Oxford man, a product of the system with a right to pass judgement on it from the inside. Actually, as I well remembered, Hunt had been one of the failures of the system, a man whose view of the University had always been external and, at bottom, uncomprehending. Well, perhaps it was fitting that he should go back there representing 'the world'. It was what he always had represented. His was a common enough type in every university in the world. I read on.

On Saturday afternoon, with the bustling town full of people who had come in from the populous industrial suburbs to enjoy their weekly shopping trip, the colleges seemed immersed in their own business.
  But there were some undergraduates about in the first sleepy quadrangle I tried, including a pale youth with hair flowing down to his shoulders and a waistcoat in many strange colours who seemed to be stepping purposefully on some errand. I stopped him and enquired politely if he would mind telling me where he was going.
  'Oh, I'll tell anyone where I am going, my dear,' he squeaked. 'It's no secret

at all. I must get to the shops before they close, to choose some wallpaper.'
'Wallpaper?' I asked. 'Doesn't the College provide that?'

He gave a wince of distaste. 'The College wallpaper is too vulgar for words, my dear, and even if it weren't, I must have my rooms papered completely afresh because something very special has happened. Last summer, in the South of France, my parents bought me a painting as a present. A Georges Braque. Stunning, heavenly.'

'It's wonderful,' I said, 'how good the reproductions are these days.'

'Reproductions nothing, dear, it's an original. And I must have wallpaper that doesn't *fight* with it, you understand? It's only been delivered today, and as soon as I hung it I saw at once that the wallpaper was going to kill it stone dead unless I did something about it, *at once*. Excuse me, I can't stay.'

'Just a minute, please,' I said as he prepared to scamper away. 'I wanted to ask you about the King and Country motion. You know, that business about not being willing to fight?'

'Oh, that,' he said vaguely. 'Something to do with the Union, wasn't it? I never go there, my dear. The paintwork is so unbelievably dreary.' And he was gone.

What college could Hunt have been prowling in, I wondered, that he met an undergraduate whose parents were so rich that they could buy him an original Braque? And, presumably, give him an allowance big enough to enable him to do things like repapering his college rooms?

The next undergraduate I met was a burly young man carrying a Rugby ball under one arm.

A bit pat, wasn't it? Coming in just on cue like that? I began to see where this was leading. Hunt supplied, in the same playful idiom, a dialogue with this ball-carrying character in which he revealed his preoccupations as 'getting a good Fifteen together' and relaxing now and then by means of a good fast game of squash. 'And then of course, sport,' he had added, a good-humoured smile playing on his craggy face, 'there's always a good pot or two of beer in the evenings.'

I asked him whether the tradition of the harmless 'rag' still persisted.

'Certainly it does, sport,' he laughed. 'Nothing like a bit of pushing and shoving. Takes the jumps out of you. Besides, we have to be on our guard. There are always people about with, shall we say, a misplaced sense of humour. Got to be ready to give them tit for tat. Why, only last night those bounders from Trinity chucked half-a-dozen dustbins over the wall – full of rubbish from their kitchens.'

'Heavens,' I said, 'it must have taken a long time to clear all that up.'

'Oh, that wasn't our problem, sport; the scouts did that. Our responsibility was to get even with those johnnies. We collected all the dustbins and tonight, while they're all sitting in Hall having dinner, we're going to let them have them back, right over the wall where they came from. But they won't be empty. We've filled them with champagne bottles. Empty ones, of course. That ought to make enough din. Make them stop chewing for a moment, if you see what I mean. Ha, Ha!'

Like his fellow collegian the aesthete, he was beginning to move away, but

I stopped him with my question. 'Would you mind telling me what you think of the Union's King and Country motion?'

'The Union, sport? Can't answer that one, I'm afraid. I never go there. They haven't even got a Rugger team.'

'No,' I said. 'They're a debating society, not a college.'

'Well, if they're not a college they won't have a Rugger team or an eight on the river, so why should I go there? See you later, sport.' And he was gone.

By now, of course, I had realized that the article was fiction. I suppose I had been simple-minded ever to suppose that Hunt had been reporting an actual visit to Oxford, merely on his own assertion that he had 'gone there'. Well, he had filled in the two stereotypes; all undergraduates were either spineless aesthetes or brainless hearties. And of course I knew what was coming.

It was almost time to go, but strolling through one of the most beautiful and tranquil of the colleges, I saw a venerable figure whom I recognized as an eminent don who has known Oxford intimately since the reign of Queen Victoria. In the gathering twilight, I ventured to approach and greet him.

'Ah, yes, good evening, and how are you getting on this term?' He had obviously forgotten my name and thought I was one of the current crop of undergraduates. I thanked the professor and said I was getting on very well, but that I had a question I wanted to ask him to satisfy my own curiosity.

'Certainly, my boy, but don't let's stand about in this draughty quad. Come up to my rooms. I've just decanted a rather good bottle of port. I'd like your opinion of it while we discuss whatever it is you have on your mind.'

We climbed the stairs to his gracious panelled rooms. His scout had lit a coal fire in the Jacobean fireplace and we settled back in deep armchairs, each with a glass of ruby liquid.

'I think you'll find this something rather special . . . I don't drink it every day . . . a Taylor '07.'

I made appreciative noises, and indeed the port was superb, but it was not what I had come to Oxford for.

'Could you tell me, sir, your reaction to the King and Country motion at the Union Society a few months ago? Do you think it really means that this country won't fight back if attacked? And do you think foreign governments will get the impression from it that we're a safe target?'

The venerable old gentleman gave a chuckle. 'Bless you, my boy, I know more about the Second Punic War than I do about these present-day international squabbles. As for the Union, it may have been all very well when Gladstone was its president, but that was before my time and I have the distinct impression that it's never been much good since. Certainly, you can't get a decent glass of port at the bar there. Grocer's stuff, I'm afraid, most of it.'

I thanked him, finished my wine and took my leave. Sleep on, Oxford! I thought as the train bore me away to dear old dirty, rattling, wide-awake London. Oxford is always said to be the home of lost causes. Perhaps the defence of our country will have to become a lost cause before it will find a home among her dreaming spires.

I sat back with the paper on my lap, as I imagined Hunt writing this horse-shit and taking it along to his editor's office with a triumphant smirk. Like the toad he was, he had obeyed orders down to the last detail. No doubt the policy of the paper was to rubbish Oxford on every possible occasion, either because of some personal grudge on the part of the proprietor or simply because there is always latent anti-Oxford prejudice among the public and it's an easy popular response to touch off.

Hunt had played by the regulations (if a journalist mentions undergraduates, he must speak of champagne, and if he mentions dons, of port) and Hunt had got his reward. The piece was attributed to him by name. He had achieved – and so early in his career – the 'by-line' which every aspiring journalist is after. And in Fleet Street, too. It might have been nepotism, of course; he might have been related to a fifth cousin of the proprietor. Or his family might have bribed somebody. Or perhaps he knew something discreditable about the editor. (Something even more discreditable than *being* the editor, that is.) But it was just as likely that his success was genuine. Anybody as naturally slimy as Hunt would certainly rise, in a business like that, by his own unaided sliminess.

Why, I wondered, getting up out of my seat, is there so much social disapproval of a girl who goes out on the streets for a living? Isn't she an aristocrat compared with a man like Hunt, busily selling his integrity? Before leaving the Common Room, I unfolded the paper and took out that page. I wanted to keep it, because I had an obscure feeling that some day, somehow, I might be able to hit Hunt with it, show him up as a jackal. I shouldn't have taken it, obviously; it didn't belong to me, and the Episcopus Common Room conscientiously subscribed to a wide range of papers in order to get a 'balanced view'. But I didn't see why the balancing act had to include Hunt, and though I had this impulse to keep his article where I could get at it, I wasn't going to go into the town and buy a copy of the paper. If I had, I would have been playing Hunt's game, in that his contribution would have increased the paper's circulation by one whole copy. The only way out was to steal that page. I folded it and put it into my briefcase amongst a lot of documents about squalid political intrigue in the eighteenth century. It should be at home there. Dean Swift, thou shouldst be living. . . .

Those first two years in which I was a true academic passed quickly. Certainly, by comparison with the snail's pace at which my undergraduate years had gone by, they seemed to go in a flash. The explanation of this change of pace was, I suppose, that I was 'settled'. My life was no longer lurching from decision to decision; I could get on with my work and let time spool out, and when you do that it consumes itself very quickly.

Apart from the fact that Michael grew bigger and heavier and didn't keep us awake so much at night, I can hardly recall any major event till, in the spring of 1935, Brian decided to follow me into matrimony. He and Primrose were married from Doug's Speed Shop; that was the business Primrose's brother Doug Ravenscroft ran, trading on his fame as a motor-cycle racing star, and into which he had co-opted his whole family including his aged father. They had taken over a rambling farmhouse somewhere out near Great Milton. The place had once been in deep countryside, but it now stood near a busy main road along which customers could try out the fearsome machines – two- or four-wheeled, sometimes three-wheeled like Ivan Warmley's Morgan – which Doug and his relations sold to them, tuned for them, advised them on and encouraged them to drive in single-minded devotion to competitive haste. Doug's father was somewhat ga-ga but he was nevertheless the bride's father, and wedding etiquette was very strict in those days, which meant that Primrose had to be married from her father's home. We went to the local church, and then to a reception at the local pub. It was all a lot more fun than my wedding had been, with nothing fugitive about it, everything out in the open, the photographer getting people to stand in groups outside the church door and people drinking champagne in the sunshine (Doug had put down the money for a dozen bottles of a very decent vintage) and looking and sounding happy.

Heather and I took Mike along with us. At first we thought we were going to get away with bringing him into the church for the service, because he was sleeping peacefully, but as the ceremony got into its stride he woke up and began crying, a thin piercing wail that seemed to me (or was it just my imagination?) to convey a note of dismay, as if he were watching people walk over a cliff. In the end Heather had to take him out into the sunlit churchyard.

At the reception I managed to get near enough to Primrose to give her a kiss. It was a treat to have that excuse to get close to her, for once. She had changed out of her bridal stuff by that time and was looking very cool and composed in a linen suit; ready to set off with Brian for an undisclosed destination. She took my kiss with a kind of sisterly benevolence – to say that she responded to it would be altogether too strong – and I felt about her, as I always did, a slight quality of apartness. It was as if, although her body was standing among the wedding throng, her astral self had managed to remove itself to a few yards' distance and was looking on the scene with tolerant half-amusement.

When it was over, the couple had been seen off on their honeymoon, and the heterogeneous guests – the decrepit elders, the gnome-like uncles and aunts and cousins, and the assorted hot-rodders in, or more frequently on, their uncompromising powered contraptions – had been tidied away, our contingent found itself back at the Bargeman's. After the noisy crowd ours suddenly seemed a very small group, just the parents and Heather and me and Michael who, now that there was no nuisance-value in remaining conscious, was sound asleep. We did not reach the pub till seven o'clock, by which time it had been officially open for an hour, but the invaluable Mrs Warmley had been holding the fort.

'Don't go, Bessie,' my mother said to her in a rather entreating tone as she sank into a chair, still wearing her wedding hat.

'I had no thoughts of going, Katie,' she replied calmly. 'I shall stay and help you in the bar this evening, and I shall help you to get a bit of supper ready for your family after closing time, and I shall stay and help to eat it and wash up. And I daresay,' she looked kindly but commandingly at Heather and myself, 'that these young people will give us their company.'

'I'm afraid we have to take the baby...' Heather was beginning, but Mrs Warmley said, 'I see you've got a nice big basket with all the baby's things in it, my duck, so you won't need to take him home for his bedtime, the little mite. I'm sure Katie can find a room upstairs where you can put him down, and change him, and do anything else he needs.'

'Of course,' my mother said quickly. 'You can have Brian's room. It's quite empty now.'

She tried to speak in a calm, matter-of-fact way, as if Brian's room was just a room like any other, but when she got to the word 'empty' her voice quavered a little.

'Yes, we'll stay,' I said, feeling that for once I should answer for Heather. If she found it inconvenient, she would just have to put up with being inconvenienced. But, to be fair, her voice was warm and comradely as she said, 'It's nice of you to want us to stay.'

'Well, of course we do, dear,' my mother said. 'Of course we do. Family mean a lot at a time like this. I've always had two boys at home, and now, from today, I haven't got a boy at all.'

Always? I thought. How old was she when Brian was born? Twenty-one, something like that? Weren't those twenty-one years part of the always? Apparently not. Apparently you forgot them when the responsibilities of the world came. And I remembered her telling me once to my surprise that as a girl she often used to walk for hours in the garden at Episcopus. 'You don't seem to have the time after you grow up.' Time! Time! Would any of us ever have *time* again?

My father now took up his station behind the bar. In the living quarters, female solidarity took over. The two older women obviously found emotional release in ministering to Heather, and through her, to Michael. The presence of a girl of breeding age, accompanied by proof of her fertility, seemed to confirm their role as women. To be a woman, each one of them asserted wordlessly, was to guarantee in the face of every privation, every catastrophe, that there would be a tomorrow, that the endless lonely night need not come down.

In addition – and I had felt this very strongly from the moment we let ourselves into the Brian-less household – my mother was very glad of Mrs Warmley's presence; another woman who would understand how deep was her loss: a woman, what was more, of great openness and generosity. The three of them were needed in the bar for the last hour before the pub closed at half-past ten (thirty-five minutes extension in honour of Saturday) and then we all sat down in the kitchen for something to eat. This was no biscuits-and-cocoa occasion; we had bread and cheese and ham and pickles, with Guinness for Mrs Warmley and, very exceptionally, light ale for my mother. My father and I were on draught beer, which we kept going through and replenishing in pint glasses. It was a true send-off for Brian, even if in his absence.

Mrs Warmley was in a slightly emotional mood; caught from my mother, I supposed. When we had 'put away our desire of eating and drinking' (as Homer habitually puts it) she stifled a refined belch, stared reflectively at the opposite wall and remarked to my mother, 'Well, Katie, you know my thoughts are with you. No need to say any more, my dear, but you know they're with you.'

It was obvious that she did intend to say more, but I thought it natural that she should introduce the topic this way.

'Well, I can't pretend I don't know what you mean, Bessie,' my mother said with a sigh. It was touching to see how glad she was not to have to cover up her emotions.

'When the first-born leaves the nest,' Mrs Warmley said, 'it comes home to a mother. Really comes *home* to her, I mean.'

'What about a father?' Dad asked mildly, not disposed to make an issue out of it, just curious to know her views.

'Oh, men are different,' said Mrs Warmley. 'Their lives are out there in the world. You've only got to hear the things they talk about, when they're left alone together. Jobs, money, and after that football, and after that politics. When women are alone together they talk about weddings and christenings, and family things. Their lives are in the home. Men's lives are outside the home.'

'It may not always be like that,' Dad said. 'Some big changes coming up. From what I can see — '

'It may not always,' Mrs Warmley agreed, 'but it's like that *now*. And I know when your Katie lies down to sleep tonight, her thoughts'll keep turning to that empty room that's always been Brian's.'

'All right,' he said. 'Don't rub it in. You'll only upset her.'

'That's a man all over,' said Mrs Warmley. 'Women are all right as long as they don't get upset. Don't talk about anything that really matters to them or else they might get upset. Well, look, Jack, I'm not just talking for talking's sake. I know a lot about empty rooms.'

'I know you do, Bessie,' he said gently.

'A lot,' she repeated, nodding.

'How long is it now, Bessie?' my mother asked. Her eyes were downcast and she spoke very quietly.

'Fifteen years and five months,' Mrs Warmley replied promptly.

'I don't think I could have done it,' my mother said, turning and looking full at her friend. 'I don't think I could have found the strength, Bessie, if it had happened to me. To do without Jack all those years – God forbid I should even say the words. And with children to bring up.'

'Yes, you would, Katie,' Mrs Warmley said. 'You may think you'd never have the strength, but the fact is that when it happens the good Lord gives you the strength. He just – gathers it out of the air and gives it to you.'

Sitting silent beside Heather at our end of the table, I was doing some mental arithmetic. If Mrs Warmley had been widowed, which was obviously what they were talking about, I would have expected in a woman of her generation that it had happened during the 1914–18 war. But the dates were wrong. Fifteen years back from April 1935 took you to April 1920; five months back from that and you landed on November 1919, a year after the Armistice. Had Mr Warmley been demobbed from the bloodiest war in our history and shortly afterwards run over by a bus? It seemed too anti-climactic.

'Has it affected Ivan much, do you think?' my mother now asked.

'I think it made him grow up faster, what with him being the oldest. He's had to look after me and the two girls. That's why he's such a steady lad. Of course he could have gone either way. If it hadn't made him steady it might have made him wild.'

All of a sudden I saw Ivan's motor car, a snarling little Morgan three-wheeler, for what it was – the energy-outlet of a steady lad.

'He hasn't had to look after you, Bessie,' said my father.

'A tower of strength he's been, Jack. Nothing short. A tower of real man's strength.'

Then Mrs Warmley appeared to catch sight of me for the first time and smiled and said, 'But Peter here doesn't want to hear about my dull old troubles. He's young, he's got his life in front of him, he wants to think cheerful thoughts and so does his nice young lady here, with her little baby asleep upstairs. Life's always beginning again, isn't it?'

'No, tell him, Bessie,' my mother said seriously. 'He's never heard the story, why Ivan's called Ivan, all that. It'll do him good to know the kind of thing that happens to people.'

Silently, I made a note of my mother's opinion of my knowledge of life: that I was someone who saw human existence through books and had no notion of 'the kind of thing that happens to people'. Was it true? Perhaps it was. Was it my fault, if true? How could I answer that?

Mrs Warmley now told me the story in question. It seemed that her husband, who had joined the Marines in 1915, had elected to stay in the service a little longer, for reasons that were something to do with getting a better gratuity payment. Having secured his services, the High Command actually found him something to do: it sent him with one of the expeditionary forces that were, in the year or two after the war, despatched into Russia. I knew, vaguely, that most of the Allied Governments had sent similar forces into Russian territory, and I knew that there was the inevitable dispute about whether or not they were justified. Bolshevik propaganda naturally represented them as attempts by capitalist nations to overthrow the people's government, while the countries sending the expeditions tended to justify them simply as efforts to recover stores of weapons and other equipment which had not been returned after the Bolsheviks had taken Russia out of the war. Whatever the rights and wrongs of the matter, Charlie Warmley had been sent to Russia in 1919, never to return. His wife, anxiously tending her young children – a boy and two girls, in descending order of age – had received a few letters on the official military forms, heavily censored as to place-names and destinations; she had been confused by them at the time and had to some extent remained confused ever since. The Civil War was raging; Mrs Warmley knew and cared nothing about Russian history and politics, but she knew that there were the Reds and there were the Whites, and they had fought, and sometimes they had fought uncomfortably close to where Charlie was. Perhaps a stray bullet had struck him down. But she also knew that these warring people had been starving and ravaged by epidemics, so perhaps it was a bacillus that had taken her Charlie away from her, and what did it matter now anyway?

She stopped for a moment and dabbed at her eyes, but her voice was quite steady when she turned to me again and finished her story.

'I don't know much about what happened to him in those last months, when he was in Russia. Archangel they said it was, funny name for a place. They never let him say much in those letters and I expect he was saving it all up to tell me when he got home. But one thing he did tell me: he made a friend of a Russian fellow. His name was Ivan. I don't know how Charlie met him; he never said. He might have been a prisoner or a refugee or something. Or just somebody hanging about the place. But he mentioned him more than once. He said this Ivan fellow was a good friend to him and they liked each other very much. He was teaching Ivan a few words of English and Ivan was teaching him a few Russian words. He said he hoped he could stay in touch with Ivan after he came home, write to him and that, perhaps have him over to stay if we could manage it. It sounded to me like he was building up some really big dreams, but in any case he and this Ivan got on so well that Charlie said to me in the last letter I ever had from him, he said if we ever had another child after he settled down at home – and he wanted that, because he said next time he wanted to be there all along, instead of coming and going all the time like he'd had to all through the war – well, he said if we had another and it turned out to be a boy, he'd like him to be called Ivan.'

She stopped again, then, after a short struggle, recovered.

'Well, if we'd had another little son I wouldn't have minded what it was called if it was something Charlie wanted, but of course he never did come back and so we never did.'

She stopped again, her eyes brimming this time, and my father said, 'Don't upset yourself, Bessie.' He leaned over and refilled her glass with stout. She drank some of it, blinked a few times, and went on, determined now to tell the story to the end.

'So there was our boy, you see,' she said in a matter-of-fact voice, taking a new grip on the subject, 'our Bob, running about and playing in and out of the house and asking when his Dad would be back, and I'd have to tell him soon, and it suddenly came to me that when I did I'd change his name. I'd tell him that from now on he was going to be called Ivan because that was what his father wanted. It wasn't *exactly* what he wanted, of course, but it was still somewhere near. So I called Bob in from the backyard one morning about that time, and told him he was going to be Ivan because that was the name of a very nice man who was a friend of his father's. And he said, would his father be bringing this friend home with him when he came home, and then I had to tell him . . .'

'Bessie, Bessie, don't upset yourself,' my father said again.

'What's it all *for?*' Mrs Warmley whispered. 'What do we go through it all for?'

My mother looked down sadly at the floor and shook her head slowly from side to side; but my father, after a short considering pause, spoke:

'Who knows, Bessie, who knows? I certainly don't. It's not given to us to know. We just have to wait and then one day it'll all be clear – perhaps. Or perhaps not. But I do know this. We've got to carry on, that's all we can do. We have to see that life goes on. Just to see that the world keeps going round. That's all we can do.'

There was silence and then my mother said, 'Do we, Jack? Do we really have to do it? Won't it go round anyway, whether we do anything or not?'

My father turned to her. His face – broad and strong, Brian's face twenty years from now – was gentle and yet intensely serious. This was a side of him I rarely saw. This was different: he was expressing his deepest convictions.

'We have to help the world go round because there are people in it. Kids come into the world. They arrive and they're in the world and they've got to be looked after. Fed, brought up, taught how to know right from wrong. Taught a trade, how to make themselves useful. They've got to grow up right, and that's half of it. The other half is, to see that there's some decent sort of world for them to grow up in. If we can do these things, we can sign off then. If we can make some kind of shot at the first half of that *and* the second, we can breathe easier when we get old and forgetful. We can let go our hold then, when it gets too much for us. But if we *haven't*, if we've not taken our share in the work, well, I don't know how we're going to hold up our heads when we go down to the grave. Let alone how we shall look when we get to the other side . . . if there is another side. And we'll just have to wait and see about that.'

I heard the kitchen clock ticking in the silence that followed, and then Mrs Warmley said, 'Well, I just hope you're right, Jack. I just hope there's as much sense to it all as what you say there is.'

'Well,' my father said, 'we mustn't have long faces about it. There's some pickled walnuts here that want finishing up, and plenty more to drink.'

'I'll have another pint. Dad,' I said. 'I need it to wash down those words of wisdom.'

The pleasantry was my youthful attempt at offering him an easy step down from the elevation to which his experiences of life and solidity of character had lifted him. He understood this and gave me a conspiratorial grin.

'I don't know about words of wisdom, Peter,' he said, 'but you might as well fetch us another drop of draught each, and a couple of bottles for the ladies, and before we take Bessie home and go to our beds we'll drink a last toast to the happy couple. It's their day, after all.'

But it wasn't, it was my day; the day on which I took a giant step towards seeing my parents clearly as a man and a woman, bravely and thoughtfully battling along on this suffering earth; and when Mrs Warmley's story brought me closer to an acquaintance at first hand with 'the kind of thing that happens to people'.

When my father got out the old Morris and drove Mrs Warmley home, he

54

took Heather and me and Michael to North Parade on the same trip. When we got in there was the usual bedtime performance with Michael, who was at the stage of having to have his nappy changed and given a nightcap before settling down. It was my turn to change him, and I got through the job with practised skill, thinking as I did so that the faeces of babies were particularly revolting. Afterwards, as Michael sucked away at his bottle, Heather was in contemplative mood.

'Phew. Big day. So much *happens* in the world, doesn't it?'

'What particularly makes you say that?'

'Oh, you know, Brian and Primrose and all those racing-car people, and then Mrs Warmley's husband and the war, and going to Russia and the Reds and the Whites and him dying and all that. Such a crazy world to bring a child into.' She looked down pityingly at Michael's head.

'Well, crazy or not, it's a good thing to give him his chance. Let him have a shot at life.'

'So often it's just wasted, though, isn't it? I mean, that Russian chap, Ivan. What was the use of his parents bringing him up? He must have been just a young chap, the same sort of age as Mrs Warmley's husband when he was a Marine, and he just got snuffed out without trace.'

'Not quite without trace,' I said. 'Because that English friend of his liked him so much, there's a young man walking around today who bears his name.'

'I don't see why that should make the slightest difference.'

'Well, I can. I can very easily.'

'That's because you're always thinking about history and who's remembered and who isn't. Anyway, Michael's finished now. Come on, I'll put him down and we'll go to bed. Thank God at least you're here for once and not in that bloody college.'

The bull-nose Morris was very much a thing of the past by now, and, though one still saw quite a lot of them about, they looked decidedly old-fashioned among the more up-to-date cars of the middle thirties. Naturally, it didn't suit Brian's style to have his father driving around in one of these antediluvian contraptions, so – using his privilege as an employee of Morris Motors – he saw to it that Dad was provided with a featureless but spanking new twelve-horse-power Morris Oxford; not that they ever went very far in it, but appearances are appearances. It was this car that, to my surprise, I saw draw up outside our flat in North Parade at eight o'clock one morning in May, just after Brian's wedding and a day or two into the summer term.

I happened to be in the bathroom, shaving, and had opened the window in the cool balmy air, otherwise I would not have been looking down into the street. Hastily wiping the lather from the unshaved side of my face, I hurried downstairs to answer the old man's ring. No time to wait for Heather, who was feeding Michael, to get herself together and traipse downstairs! It must be something pressing to get him over here at this time in the morning.

'Yes,' he said in answer to my immediate question, 'it *is* something out of the ordinary. Just let me get sitting down and I'll fill you in.'

I made a pot of tea as he outlined the situation.

'Last night, we hadn't but barely opened, about ten-past six it'd be, and in comes your father-in-law.'

'Old Burrell? Been on one of his marketing trips to Oxford, had he?'

'No, nothing as ordinary as that. He was in a state. I wondered if he was ill at first. He kept flushing, going a deep red, then it'd all drain away and he'd look as white as a sheet. I asked him what he'd like to drink and he said a whisky. I poured him a big one; he tried to pay me but I wouldn't have it. Told him blood was thicker than water, and he was blood now. He thanked me but he hardly seemed to hear me. He just stood there and knocked it back as if it had been a thimbleful. I got a look at him and I thought, this isn't the first drink you've had this evening, mate. Early as it was. He was speaking a bit thick, like, but then he always does. Anyway, he collects himself and then he tells me what he's come for. 'I just stopped off,' he says, 'because I reckoned you might know the way to Uxbridge.'

'Uxbridge? What on earth — '

'He'd got the car outside and he wanted to drive to Uxbridge. He knew it was somewhere between Oxford and London but he couldn't be sure of hitting the right road. 'I've got no time to lose,' he kept saying. In a terrible hurry to be off. Well, I didn't want to poke my nose into his business but I was a bit worried. Well, more than a bit, really. First there was the drink he'd took. Then again, it struck me as funny that he was doing a trip like that without his missus. She'd be the type who'd take command on those sorts of occasions. If he was so keen to get to Uxbridge and he'd got the car out, ten to one she didn't know anything about it. Or it was something she wouldn't have let him do if she'd 'a' known.'

Heather, having appeased Michael and laid him down, had now joined us and was listening silently.

'In the end, after I'd tried to set him right about the way to Uxbridge, I asked him, "What takes you there, Mr Burrell, if I'm not being too inquisitive?" And he looks at me with his face all screwed up, as if he was biting hard on something, and then he said, "There's been a mistake." "Oh," I says. "A mistake?" "Yes," he says, "a very bad mistake and I'm going to see if I can get it put right. You see," he says, "my lad Tom's gone and joined up in the Air Force, and there's only me to work the farm and I can't manage by myself. They wouldn't have taken him if they'd known how I was placed, how much I depend on having him. One chap in the Air Force more or less won't make no difference," he says, "but a whole farm coming to a standstill, that's serious." "What are you going to do about it?" I asked. "Do?" he says. "I'm going to get down to Uxbridge and see his commanding officer. His adjutant or whatever they calls it. I'm going to tell him my boy joined up without a word to me and I can't let him go because the farm can't do without him." '

I looked across at Heather. Her face had become soft with pity, and as I watched I saw a tear well from the corner of an eye. The pathos of her father's position had touched her heart. It touched mine, too, but what could anyone do?

'So he sets off,' my father was continuing, 'and what with being very busy and a lot of people talking to me about one thing or another, I didn't get much chance to think about him all evening, though he was at the back of my mind. But then, about a quarter to ten, just when I was beginning to watch the clock and getting ready to call last orders, he suddenly comes in through the door again. But this time, there was no mistaking it. He really *was* drunk. He staggered over to the bar and asked for a double whisky. I suggested he should come back into the kitchen where he'd be more comfortable. I didn't say anything about not serving him or him having had enough or anything like that. I just said, "It's a bit crowded in the bar, wouldn't you like to come and sit by the fire with your drink? Just come through here and we'll make you comfortable." And then when we'd got him in the kitchen we made him a cup of tea. No more talk of whisky. He drank it all right and I hoped he might be able to pull himself together, but we couldn't get much sense out of him. He just kept saying, "They don't understand. They don't know what it's like."

Of course, I asked him if he got to see the commanding officer.

"No use," he says, shaking his head. "No use talking to a man who's never had to look after stock. Aeroplanes all his life, nothing but aeroplanes. Never had fowl pest. Never had to stand and watch grain sprouting in the sack. Work all year and then can't get a decent price for it at the mill. How could I stop it sprouting with the rain coming down all the bloody time? And it'll be coming through the roof now. No one to mend that thin patch now I'm too old to get up a ladder. They don't understand." And a lot more like that. Till in the end we put him to bed.'

'Put him to bed? He's been at the Bargeman's overnight, has he?'

'Is he there now?' Heather asked quickly.

'No. He's back home now. At High Cogges. I drove him out at about seven and then came straight on here. I can't stay. I've got to be at the Brewery.'

Christ Almighty, Dad, I thought. You could have done without all this.

'What about my mother?' Heather asked. 'Where did she think he was last night?'

'Oh, she knew he was with us. After we got him to bed I went out to the telephone box. I didn't know the number so I had to get it from the Enquiries. It took a long time; they always seemed to be engaged. But I got it in the end and rang through. It was pretty late by then.'

'Mother must have been grateful to you.'

'Not really. She let fly at me as if she thought I'd kidnapped him or something. Asked me why I was holding him in Oxford. Holding him. That's a good one.' My father laughed shortly. 'If she'd seen the state he was in. If we'd let him get into that car he'd have hit the first brick wall he came to.'

Heather stood up. 'Where's the car now?'

'Outside the Bargeman's, just where he parked it last night.'

'I'll take it out to the farm,' she said. 'They'll need it and it's the least I can do to help.' She turned to me. 'If Mike cries, get his wind up and if he goes on crying, change him. You can give him his lunch if I'm not back – mix some of that powdery stuff that's in the tin. It'll keep him going.'

'All right,' I said. It was the least I could do.

They went off together, my father to his morning's work at the Brewery, Heather to pick up the Burrells' Ford and drive it out to High Cogges. It was brave of her, I thought, to go home at this point, to face the storms that would doubtless be raging, but I could see that she felt easier doing something to help, rather than sitting in North Parade twiddling her thumbs.

As it turned out, she was back long before I expected her. I was just vaguely thinking about lunch when I heard her feet on the stairs.

'They didn't keep you long, then,' I said.

'They didn't get a chance. It was the flyingest of flying visits. I left the car in front of the house and just walked away.'

'Didn't anyone try to stop you?'

'I don't suppose they saw me. At least, Phil did. He was lurking about as usual. But he doesn't count. He'll tell them he saw me, of course, but in any case, when they see the car they'll know I must have brought it over. *You* don't drive. No, obviously, it's the dutiful daughter at work.'

'But not dutiful enough to dust your shoulder for them to cry on.'

'No, I'm not quite that dutiful. I talked it over with myself as I drove out, and I came to the conclusion that there was no usefulness in hearing my mother go on and on. Because of course it *would* be her and not him. I daresay he's lapsed back into silence. He'll just suffer, dumbly, and if it really does turn out that he can't manage the farm and he gets chucked off it and ends in the workhouse, he'll take it all without uttering a word. It'll be like watching an old horse go to the knacker's yard.'

'It won't come to that, surely? Not with your mother behind him.'

'My mother can't do a man's work on the farm as well as run the house.'

'No, I suppose not.'

'Well,' Heather said, 'we've got our own lives to manage. Tom cleared out because he'd rather be flying aeroplanes than managing a farm tenancy at High Cogges. He's living his own life, and it's an example I'm going to follow.'

I didn't answer immediately because I was thinking. Then I said, 'All this talk of his getting chucked off the farm . . . I suppose it could actually happen if he got too far behind with his rent.'

'Of course it could. It happened a few years ago to a farmer over at Ducklington.'

'Have you any idea who the landlord is?'

She looked at me quizzically for a moment and then burst out laughing.

'What's so funny?' I asked.

'Do you really not know who owns pretty nearly all the land, and pretty nearly all the farms built on it, from North Oxford right up to the borders of Warwickshire?'

'You're not going to tell me . . .'

'Of course I am. Your precious College.'

'You don't . . . you really mean it's an Episcopus property?'

'My dear sir,' Heather said with mock solemnity, 'it's time you realized that you are married to the daughter of an Episcopus tenant.'

'Well, I'll be . . .'

'So part of your salary, your stipend as you call it, is squeezed out of the slender bank account of my poor old dad.'

I was silent.

'Well,' she said, 'life has to go on. Has Mike been good?'

'He's been an angel,' I said. That much, at least, was going as it should.

After such an upheaval, I would have been glad to sink back into a normal routine. I was making a strong attempt to get on with some work just then, because this was the last Long Vacation I should have during the period of my Research Fellowship; already the next summer I would be having to look around for jobs, make arrangements for this and that and generally have an eye to the future. For the time being, I was safe inside the cocoon and, like a good silkworm, I had to regard the cocoon as a place of work.

The next afternoon, therefore, I was solidly at it in Bodley, sitting in the Upper Reading Room with a colossal stack of books in front of me, every one of which I planned to have read – or at least gutted – by the end of the month, twelve days away. It may sound like a recipe for reading oneself into blindness, but the fact is, anyone who deserves the name of historian will get through a lot of reading in a limited time.

All the same, I was blinking like an owl when I went down the broad shallow stairs, landing after landing, and came out into the quad in the thick, oily August

58

light. I needed a cup of tea, and the place to get one was Episcopus. It wasn't the nearest, but it was the best, and it was free, and it came with scones which helped my young appetite to last out until dinner. I went and had it and then, feeling much better, I looked into the lodge on my way out to see if there were any messages. There was one. Heather had telephoned: I was to go home, urgently.

I knew it must be something serious because she hated getting in touch with Episcopus. It reminded her that she wasn't supposed to exist; she couldn't say anything as straightforward as, 'Tell Mr Leonard his wife rang and wants to speak to him,' because Mr Leonard, officially, didn't have a wife. So the message, scrawled on a message pad in the porter's handwriting, simply said, 'Mr Leonard. Go home when you get this.' If he had thought at all, I presumed he thought it meant my parental home.

I went home. Heather said, 'You're too late.' She looked pale and tired.

'Too late? What for?'

'My mother was here. Come to make a scene. She set herself to give me absolute hell and my God, she succeeded.' Heather sank down on the frayed sofa, one hand vaguely pushing away strands of hair, trying to collect herself. 'Look, could you go out and buy a bottle of whisky or something? I need a stiff drink.'

'Well, yes, of course, but the nearest is way down in George Street, or over in Summertown. Before I go, can't you give me just a brief idea of what she's — '

'Well, obviously the first item on the agenda was to give me hell for not staying to talk to them when I took the car over.'

'Yes, I suppose that was to be expected.'

'I didn't bother to explain that the real reason why I hadn't stayed was because I knew when we started talking she'd twist things round till it was my fault Tom had left home – which of course she proceeded to do. That was stage two . . . Listen, are you going to fetch that bloody whisky or do I have to go myself?'

'I'll go.'

I went down the stairs quickly. I was pretty near broke but I could afford a quarter-bottle – enough for Heather to have a good slug and leave a bit over for me. I hurried back.

With three inches of the golden fluid in her hand, Heather talked more patiently.

'Basically, it was just that she wanted to pick a fight. It doesn't take much character-reading to see that she's been very deeply hurt by this business of having a daughter married to an Oxford don – which in her circles is considered a good catch – and having to keep it a deadly secret. The Women's Institute don't even know I'm living in Oxford. They think I'm still on that catering course in Birmingham . . . And that's another sore point. You know it was her pet scheme. She and I were going to run a posh restaurant, with me doing the work and her doing the organizing. She sent me to Birmingham and put down money for me to get trained, and we know what happened.'

'Yes. You jibbed.'

'Precisely. I couldn't stand it. I cut out and came back home, and she lost that money. So of course she brought that up again this time.'

'How much is it?'

'Two hundred and fifty pounds.'

'Phew.' That was a lot of money then, when a working man would slog his guts out for a year, five and a half days a week, for two hundred.

'Yes. And she's terribly bitter about it. Says that little fund was the only leeway she had.'

'Only one thing I don't understand,' I said, considering. 'Why didn't she kick up about it when we first got married, and had to borrow a wodge from your lot and my lot to put down on this place?'

'Because that wodge was different. It came from her *and* Daddy, out of the general family finances, if you can apply such a grand word as "finances" to our chicken-feed stuff. It was an obvious, conventional thing to do, and it was short-term. But the money she spent on me was risk capital, and I didn't even get as far as letting her risk it. I just threw it away. And now Tom's gone, and it's going to be harder to manage the farm – impossible, perhaps. I can quite see I've messed up their chances. But the only thing I feel ashamed about is that I *don't* feel ashamed. I mean I don't feel as if I ought to have finished that rotten course, and then settled down to be my mother's kitchen slave till I was middle-aged and haggard and not fit for anything else. When it came to it, I just didn't see why I should. That's why she hates me. Not for the things I've done or not done, but simply for being the kind of person I am.'

'Oh, come. That's a bit strong.'

'I tell you she hates me. You wouldn't have any doubt about that if you'd seen her this afternoon. She called me everything she could lay her tongue to. I was a whore because I'd been to bed with you before we were married, I was a thief because I'd stolen her money, I wasn't a fit sister for Tom, that's why he's gone off. And I wasn't a fit daughter for her because I'd married a selfish waster who wasn't even man enough to take me on in front of the world.'

'Poor love. You've had a bad time and the only thing in the situation that makes me feel a tiny bit glad is that at least you rang up and asked me to come home. You thought I might help you, and I'm glad you did. I'm sorry we didn't connect. But I'm here now. I'll go out to the box and ring College and tell them I shan't be in for dinner, and we'll have an evening at home.'

She brightened a little. 'A bit of entertainment would be nice. There's a girl I've met who says she'll stay in with Michael once in a while. We could go to the cinema. There's something with Katherine Hepburn on at the Scala. I'd like to see that, she's got style.'

'I've never seen her, it's time I got educated. You go and speak to the girl and I'll ring College.'

'I'll have to leave a message, she works in the day. But she'll probably come, and if she does we'll go and see Katherine Hepburn, and if she doesn't we'll stay in and have a bottle of wine.'

And fuck ourselves silly, I thought as I went down the stairs. I was really looking forward to a nice evening with Heather. It would be like the old times, before we got married.

I rang up College and cried off dinner, and then I went back and we messed about and did domestic things. About six the girl looked in and said she could baby-sit all right, and we fixed for her to come about seven. Heather began preparing her some food. She was a girl who worked in the public library or somewhere. Heather had met her in the last few months and done her one or two favours. It was all very cosy. And we were going to the cinema.

However, it was not to be. We had a light meal, settled the girl down to watch over sleeping Michael, walked down to the Scala in Walton Street, and happily

60

watched the titles and screen credits. But then, for the first and only time in my life, I had the experience of seeing myself paged on a cinema screen. It was quite simple technically; the projectionist merely inserted a piece of paper bearing the required message into the apparatus and it showed up, hugely magnified, on the screen. So there we were, and the rather illiterate, sloping handwriting was suddenly shouting at us: *Will Peter and Heather go to the foyer please, important.*

It was Primrose who had sent the message; she stood beside the box office and the display of photographs, waiting for us.

'I'm sorry.' Her voice was unnaturally calm, as if she were holding herself steady by a sustained effort. 'I don't like to spoil your evening out.'

'Well, I know it must be something important,' I said.

'I hope it turns out not to be important. I hope it's all just a silly mistake.'

Heather said, 'It's Brian, isn't it?'

Primrose nodded. 'He didn't come home from work and he should have been home at six. Nothing unusual in that, he's often out working till all hours. I had plenty to get on with – I still do the books for the Speed Shop. So I wouldn't have bothered, only it so happens that it's my birthday and we were going out. Like you.' She gave a brief, rueful smile. 'So when he didn't come home, I rang his work number. They said he left at five-thirty. It was six forty-five when I rang. Then I rang round a bit. No one had seen him, but one of his friends did say, "Try the pubs." "Pubs?" I said. "Brian's never been much of a pub man. He grew up in one, it's no novelty to him." "Never mind," he said, "try the pubs." Then he rang off. And when I dialled his number again, to try to get him to explain a bit more, I got the engaged tone. As if he'd taken it off the hook on purpose to stop me ringing back.'

'Has Brian had any trouble lately?' I asked. 'Any bad experience that might lead him to prefer an evening on the drink to coming home on your birthday?'

'Not as far as I know,' she said, and held my eyes with her own, steadily, for a second. I could see that was all I was going to get. If any tensions had developed between her and Brian, she wasn't going to let me see them.

'I want you to come with me to look for him, Peter,' she said. 'It's up to you whether you come too, Heather, and really I have to say again I'm sorry to disturb your evening. But if I'm going to go round the pubs, I don't know whether to start in Abingdon or the Cowley area where a lot of the fellows he knows would go. Or whether he'd go somewhere he *wouldn't* know anybody. I don't really know what to do, but I must do something. I can't sit at home by that telephone all night.'

'Of course, we'll both come, Primrose,' Heather said. 'I'm not due back for a couple of hours, someone's looking after Michael, and as for Peter, he's as free as a bird, aren't you?'

'As a bird,' I agreed.

'Let's get started then. You've got a car, I suppose?'

'Transport, anyway,' Primrose said, leading the way. It turned out to be a battered van with two seats in the front and in the dark, windowless interior some coils of greasy tow-rope and other impedimenta on which it was just possible to squat.

We worked out a plan of campaign. On entering any likely area, we would visit every pub we saw. Primrose, who was driving, would draw up and Heather would get out, followed by me; she would then go into the private bar while I went into the public bar. No drinking time allowed; once we had scanned the place and found no Brian we were out again, back in the van, off to the next pub. We got very fast at it. Even the biggest and most crowded pub rarely detained us for more than three or four minutes. As for the small ones, we were through them in sixty seconds.

I lost count of how many we visited. We started by going out to Abingdon and trying every pub there; then we came in and went all along the Abingdon Road, then headed for Cowley. My heart sank at the thought of visiting every pub in Cowley; fortunately, though, we did the ones in the Cowley Road as we went out, starting at the Plain, and well before we got to Cowley itself we entered a big barn of a place, and as I stood looking across the huge smoke-hazed room, with the door still hissing shut behind me, Brian was almost the first person I saw.

I went over to him. He was sitting by himself at a small table, with an almost empty beer glass in front of him which I supposed was his own. When I sat down opposite him he showed no surprise at seeing me, merely asked in a casual way, 'D'you live near here?'

He knew damn well I didn't live near there. He had been to the flat in North Parade.

'No,' I said.

'Can't see much point in coming to this pub unless it was the nearest. Beer's not much good. Pricey, too.'

'Would you like a refill?'

'Get me one if you're going over. Don't fancy the walk to the bar. Don't like these big pubs. Wrong atmosphere.'

'What is it you're on?'

'Red Label. Here . . .' He began fumbling in his trouser pocket. 'Have one on me. Give you the money.'

'I'll get them,' I said and turned to go over to the bar. As I moved away I heard a small crash behind me. Brian had pulled out a handful of coins and dropped them on the floor. Glancing back as I walked, I saw him sitting in exactly the same posture, staring at the coins scattered beside his feet, as if unable to work out how they got there.

My strategy was simple: to sit and have a drink with him – not that he needed another drink, but it was the simplest way of establishing a *rapport* – and find out, if I could, what was the matter. Then, and not before, I would hand him over to his wife. My non-appearance would have told her and Heather that Brian was found, and they would be waiting outside in the van.

Coming back with the beer, I said, 'Red Label, eh? I don't think I've had it before.'

'Do you live near here?' he asked again.

'You know where I live. You know where Heather and I live.'

'You must live near here. Why you come to this pub? No other reason anybody would come here. Bloody awful pub.'

'Why are you here yourself, for that matter?'

'No reason.' He drank from his glass and set it down. 'Why should I have a reason?'

'Well . . . people generally . . .'

'What's reasons got to do with it?' Brian was staring at me aggressively now. 'Have you come here to push me around?'

'No. I'm here because I live near here. It's the nearest pub or I wouldn't come here.'

'Damn right you wouldn't. Bloody awful pub.'

'Look, Brian, what's the matter?'

He took another swig, looked at his glass meditatively as if to make some pronouncement on the quality of the beer, then suddenly came back at me with, 'Did I say something was the matter?'

'No, but you look — '

'I look what? Don't give me your cheek, younger brother. What you come in here for anyway? You come here to push me around?'

'I care what happens to you, that's all.'

'Care what happens to me? That's a laugh. Nobody does that. Nobody cares what happens to any of us. Wouldn't notice if we went and shot ourselves.'

'Brian, I don't know what you're trying — '

'Where's your wife?'

'Heather? She's outside.'

'Outside? Outside here?'

'Yes.'

'Why isn't she inside?'

'My wife is outside,' I said, speaking very clearly, 'sitting in a van that's parked at the kerb, because she's keeping your wife company.'

'Primrose?'

'Yes, that's your wife's name, isn't it?'

He glared again. 'Don't start getting funny with me, boy. You know bloody well that's my wife's name. Primrose Ravenscroft. Primrose Leonard now. God help her. An unlucky bunch we are. I'm unlucky. You're unlucky.'

'How am I unlucky?' I really wanted to take this opportunity (*in vino veritas*!) of finding out how he saw things.

'Course you're unlucky. Knocking up that farmer's daughter. Having to get married. Didn't want to, did you?'

God, had it been that obvious?

'Different with me. I really wanted Primrose, really went for her. But makes no difference in the end. They've got me too. Taken everything.'

'*Who* have? *What* have they taken? Brian, I really need to . . .'

Primrose now appeared and looked at me over Brian's shoulder. Behind her, Heather watchfully took in the whole scene. Under their combined gaze I fell silent.

Heather stood still. Primrose came forward, pulled a chair close to Brian's, and sat down with her hand touching his as it lay on the table.

'Brian, would you like to come home? I've got transport outside. I borrowed Lou's van.'

'What you need to borrow Lou's van for?'

'You'd got the car and you hadn't come home.'

'No, hadn't come home.'

'Well, would you like to come with me?'

I liked the way Primrose was handling it. Some women would have started in straight away about its being their birthday and everything.

Brian looked at her. His eyes seemed to have gone smaller. 'I got the car. Our car.'

'Yes, but you haven't got it now, have you? It isn't outside.'

'No. Started to come home. In car. Then I thought I'd have a drink. Stopped at a pub, didn't like it. Rotten pub. Beer tasted off – don't look after it, some of these places. Dad wouldn't have served stuff like that. Never in his life.'

'I know,' she said gently.

'Always did a good job. All Leonards. Didn't make us lucky, though. Peter's unlucky.' He stared at me, trying to focus. 'Go on, tell her, Peter, you're unlucky.'

'I'm unlucky,' I said.

'Didn't like that pub. Went to another. Some blokes there I knew. Didn't want to talk. Came out. Went to another.'

'Brian, love,' Primrose said, 'we're going home.' She stood up, decisively. 'Come on. We're going home, now.'

He looked at her craftily, as if forestalling some clever move he saw coming. '*All* of us?' he asked.

'No, just you and me. We're going home, to be together. You don't have to talk if you don't want to. But it'll be better than sitting in all these pubs.'

'Car,' he said. 'Got the car.'

'I've got Lou's van outside. There's no need to worry about — '

'Yes, but the *car*,' he insisted. 'Must bring it, must bring it home.'

A long discussion ensued. Heather volunteered to follow them in Brian's car if he would say where it was and give her the keys. Primrose wanted to know how, in that case, she would get herself home. Finally it was settled that Heather should drive herself and me back to North Parade now, in Brian's car, which he finally revealed was only a short walk from where we now sat, and return it to them in the morning. Primrose reached into Brian's pocket for the keys, handed them to Heather, and said, 'Thanks for all this.'

'It's nothing,' Heather said lightly.

'I shan't forget it.'

'It's nothing,' Heather repeated and gave her a look that said, 'We women have to help each other with these impossible men.'

Heather was gone. Primrose was standing beside Brian's chair. Brian was sitting stiffly, looking ahead of him with a vacant expression. After a moment he slowly brought up his hand to his inside jacket pocket.

I knew what Brian was looking for. In his inside pocket, ever since he was a young apprentice, he had carried one invariable thing: his photograph of Old Number One, the first M.G. ever made. It had always been a symbol, a totem, a prayer object, for Brian, but it had become boundlessly more valuable on the day when Nuvolari had just won that T.T. race for M.G. and gave the pit crew his autograph, the signature of the world's greatest racing driver, on the back. TAZIO NUVOLARI, scrawled on the back of Old Number One! And at the winning moment, beside the dusty and boiling car itself, with the applause still ascending!

Brian's hand came slowly out of his pocket, holding the photograph. He brought up his other hand, his movements precise and deliberate. Holding the picture of Old Number One steadily in front of him, looking fixedly down at it, he tore it into two, then into four and then, with a last effort, into eight. Without speaking, he pushed back his chair, stood up and, letting the eight fragments fall on to the beer-shiny table, walked quite steadily to the door.

4

The next evening, I went down to the Bargeman's at my usual time, just after the place opened at six. I wanted to see if my parents brought up the subject of Brian, as they surely would if they had any news. But I found everything just as usual. Whatever it was that had hit Brian, he had not talked about it to them, and I knew better than to suppose, in that case, that he would talk about it to me.

All the same, I was worried. Heather and I discussed the possibility of going over to see him and Primrose, but decided against it. They lived at Horspath, which was too far away to drop in and make it casual, so it would be obvious that we were going with a purpose to investigate the situation, and that wouldn't do at all. If they had been on the telephone, we could have rung up on some pretext, but like us they weren't. So, not knowing what else to do, I did nothing.

Another twenty-four hours went by. I was very busy all that day, trying to get through my mountain of reading, and in the evening I had invited Harry Goodenough to dinner at Episcopus. The scholarship he was on did not give him any dining rights in his own college, so he was still living the undergraduate life of baked beans and spaghetti in a bedsitter. I thought I might as well share my good fortune by letting him get his legs under a good table every now and then, and with his hearty country appetite he made the most of it. After dinner, when we filed out of Hall and went into dessert, I couldn't sit next to him because of the obligatory re-shuffle and I lost him. I could see his big tousled head when he bent forward now and then, and I could only hope he was enjoying himself, though I was not very optimistic about this when I noted with misgivings that he was sitting next to Watson.

When it was all over, and we had adjourned to a nearby pub, I asked him how he had got on.

'Oh, fine. Many thanks! The wine was absolutely magical and I got hold of some delicious nuts. The best dinner I've had for — '

'I really meant the company.'

'Well, I just let that take care of itself. Spoke when I was spoken to, you know. Only one man made any effort to draw me out, and that was the rather pig-faced little chap next to me, Waterman or something.'

'Watson.'

'That's him. I rather distrusted his motives. A bit too keen to show off. Obviously very important to him to crow on his own dunghill. Be the witty presence in his own College.'

'You've got him right.'

'To make the time pass I just watched his mannerisms and tried to decide how I'd cast him. At first I thought he was a natural for Osric – you know, *this is a slight, unmeritable man.* But as the talk went on and I saw him dealing with one or two other people, I decided the character he most resembles is Malvolio. He could play that part without acting *at all.*'

I laughed, with a certain sense of relief. It reassured me to know that my estimate of Watson was shared by someone who saw life very much the same way as I did.

The next day was a Saturday and Heather and I walked out as far as the Bargeman's, wheeling Mike. We left him in the kitchen for half an hour while we had a drink in the bar, and once again everything seemed normal.

'I'm going to give up worrying about Brian,' I told her.

'Suit yourself.'

'Well, aren't you?'

'I never was all that worried,' she said.

'Really?'

'No. I think you Leonards will always look after yourselves.'

I digested this in silence.

On our way home it was agreed that she should go ahead with the pushchair while I went into Oxford market and did the weekend shopping. We were to have a half-shoulder of lamb, and Heather gave me instructions about what weight and what shop to get it from and the maximum price I ought to pay. I went into the cheerful, bustling Saturday-crowded market and almost the first person I saw was Ivan Warmley.

This in itself was no surprise. I was quite accustomed to bumping into Ivan. He had been a friend and work-mate of Brian's ever since they had both joined Morris Motors as apprentices; they had gone to M.G. together, and Ivan was a familiar sight at the Bargeman's. But now, since hearing his mother's story, I looked at him differently. He was a prosaic enough youth, lanky and good-natured, and yet, to my eyes, something of the majesty of history had rubbed off on him. The endlessly shuttling loom of time and place, strange, mysterious, terrible and beautiful. I just didn't believe Heather's dismissive, 'They just have their lives and that's that.'

There was, however, no time to give expression to these thoughts, standing in the doorway of a crowded butcher's shop in the market.

'Hello, Ivan,' I said. 'Still got the Morgan three-wheeler? I haven't seen you driving it lately.'

'Hello. No, I sold it last summer. I've moved up to four wheels. I suppose we all get older.'

'I'm just buying the week-end joint,' I volunteered. 'Talking about getting older, I expect you know I'm a married man now. Domestic responsibilities.'

He let this pass and asked, 'Have you seen Brian lately?'

'Well, I did run into him two or three nights ago.'

'What sort of shape was he in?'

I wondered how much to say, but decided to let him make the running and said only, 'Not quite his usual self, I thought.'

'His usual self,' Ivan said. He shook his head slowly. 'No. It's a fair bet that he won't be his usual self for a long time. All this is very difficult for him.'

'All what?'

'You mean you don't know?'

'Look,' I said, 'I could tell there was something the matter when I met him the other night. Very much the matter. But I didn't feel able to ask him point-blank what it was.' I didn't add that Brian had been drunk.

'Of course,' Ivan said thoughtfully, 'it hasn't reached the papers yet.'

'What hasn't, Ivan, for God's sake?'

'So you don't know. You really don't know why Brian's upset. All right, I'll tell you – you'll find out soon anyway, so there's no point in keeping it a secret. The Old Man's closing us down.'

'The old . . . ?'

'M.G.'s Racing Department ceased to exist three days ago. Billy Morris has axed it.'

'But . . .' I swallowed. 'Does that mean Brian's out of a job?'

'No. He'll be found something. M.G.'ll go on, but without the Racing Department. They won't race any more, they'll just build road cars. That's always been the bulk of their business anyway. People like Brian and me that worked on the racing cars will just work on the ordinary family runabouts.'

'Oh,' I said. 'I see.'

'I wonder if you do,' Ivan said. 'I wonder if anyone *can* see, whose heart wasn't in that game like Brian's was.'

I struggled to comprehend. 'But I thought they were doing so well. Success on success.'

'They were doing well. But it depends how you look at the accounting. M.G. were famous all over the world, and that must have been good for business. But if you look at the Racing Department on its own, and cost it out in pounds, shillings and pence, of course it costs money. Only a very few private entrants were rich enough to buy racing cars from us. Prize money would bring in something, of course – but pound for pound, the Department *cost* money.'

'Well, so does any form of advertising.'

'You can see that. I can see that. But Billy Morris couldn't see it. He always thought racing cars were nasty, noisy, dangerous things, and they didn't make a profit because they couldn't.'

'No, not directly, but in terms of reputation . . .'

'Try telling that to the Old Man. He'd just tell you to wrap your reputation up in a bit of newspaper and tie string round it and try selling it over the counter.' Ivan gestured towards the crowd milling about him in the market. 'How many of these people are ever going to buy a racing car? That's how the Old Man sees things.'

In my head, I heard my father's voice say, 'It must be having that approach to business that's put Billy Morris where he is.' For myself, I said nothing.

'Well, I'd better let you get on with your shopping. A married man and all.' Ivan began to move away.

'Just a minute,' I said. 'You're sure it won't mean the sack for Brian?'

'You can forget that worry. The Racing Department didn't employ many chaps and they were pretty high quality. They'll be absorbed into ordinary production work. Brian will. I will.'

'What about Brian's boss, Cecil Kimber?'

'Cecil Kimber's a director of Morris Motors and he'll stay a director. M.G.'ll go on, even if all they make is lawn-mowers. They'll be a body without a heart, but who cares about that?'

He walked away slowly, as if his own long body were already without a heart. I knew how he was feeling, and how Brian was feeling. They felt as Harry Goodenough would if he were given a theatre and told that he could put on anything he chose, except Shakespeare.

The war of 1914–18, by all accounts, seems to have struck most people as coming out of the blue. Right up to the summer of its outbreak, the population of most European countries had apparently based their lives on the assumption that peace and prosperity stretched unbrokenly ahead of them. People who watch the international scene closely, of course, had a different viewpoint, and quite a number of them are on record prophesying that there would be a war, what the line-up would be and when it would begin. But no one heeded them.

Things were very different in the run-up to the war of my youth. We all saw that it was coming. One could try to argue it away, but only by ignoring the plain rules of evidence and the lessons of experience. Everybody who remembers the 1930s has his or her own date when the war broke into their consciousness as a certainty. Mine, for what it's worth, was the day early in 1936 when the German Army marched into the demilitarized Rhineland. On the early afternoon of that day, just after lunch, I was strolling in the garden at Episcopus. It was chilly; the season had not yet begun to yield to spring and the trees had their pure winter beauty of bare twig and branch and a clear light on each strong, stark trunk. I was wearing my overcoat. There was no one else about except a man, also muffled in an overcoat, moving slowly along the path on the other side of the garden on a course that would ultimately bring him face to face with me. I noticed nothing about him at first except that he was tall and spare and moved with a thoughtful tread, his eyes mostly downcast. Then, as he approached, I saw that it was Nussbaum.

As he drew nearer he evidently recognized me, and his deep resonant voice came to my ears in the still air of the quiet garden.

'Greetings, my young friend. I am glad to see you in this beautiful place.'

'It is beautiful, yes. I feel I'm very fortunate in — '

'Ve must all imbibe beauty. Take it in to ourselves, appreciate it, falue it, give thanks for it, venever ve have the opportunity. There iss so little time left.'

Nussbaum's eyes, as they met mine, were doom-laden.

'You're referring to the likelihood of war?'

'To vat else should I refer? Ve must live for the day. It iss fatal at such a time to look ahead. But that is precisely our problem. Ve scholars cannot live for the day. Our vork must ripen over many years. That iss vy scholars are melancholy. I am melancholy. Even you, in your youth and vitality, are melancholy, my friend. I sense it – I divine it in your features. You are melancholy because you are a scholar. Only Hans Katz is not melancholy. This is inexplicable. He himself cannot explain it. It iss merely that melancholy vas left out of his composition. I suppose that on the day ven melancholy vas distributed, and every human being received a share, Hans Katz vas absent from the muster. Someone else received a double portion – perhaps it vas myself.'

He looked at me gravely as he spoke. In Nussbaum's discourse, even the little jokes were never exactly a laughing matter.

'Well,' I said, 'I hardly know what to say to all that, because I'm so totally in agreement with it.'

Nussbaum was walking towards the College buildings, I away from them. As a small courtesy, so as not to make him change direction, I turned back and walked beside him, falling in with his slow pace. The thin winter sunlight fell with an austere beauty on nature and art, on gravel, wall and stone, on grass, soil and wood. For some reason I thought how it must be shining in on the rows of leather-bound books in the library whose windows we were looking towards.

'You think war is inevitable?' I asked.

'You think it othervise?'

'No,' I said. 'As a matter of fact, today is the first day when I've actually known in my bones that it will come.'

'Vy today?' he asked, almost indifferently.

'Well, obviously . . . the invasion of the Rhineland. It's such a gesture of contempt for the democratic governments of Europe, such a naked statement that force is what Hitler believes in. And what Hitler believes in Mussolini believes in too, insofar as he's consistent enough to believe in anything. All those statements of his . . .'

I burbled on. Nussbaum let me finish, with the air of someone allowing a child to have his say, then gave a slight shrug and remarked as if to the garden in general, 'I have known that war was inevitable since the day Dollfuss vas murdered in 1935.'

'Dollfuss? Why that date more than any other?'

Nussbaum fixed me with a sardonic eye. 'I understand your field of study iss history.'

'Well, eighteenth-century history primarily. One can't take all — '

'An historian,' Nussbaum said as if to himself, 'and the significance of the murder of Dollfuss vas lost on him.'

'I didn't say it was lost,' I said, nettled. 'I read it as a storm signal, like everybody else.'

'Look,' Nussbaum said gently, 'Hitler has designs on Austria. Its existence as a state independent of Germany does not suit his notions. What he decrees, Mussolini vill in the end obey, because, as you rightly say, my young friend, ven it comes to actions, Mussolini vill do vat Hitler tells him to, simply because the weaker Fascist state vill obey the stronger rather than throw its lot in with the democracies.'

'Granted, of course, but I still don't — '

'Mussolini, in theory, wants to keep Hitler out of Austria because the settlement of 1919 gave Italy certain rights there. Mussolini is in no hurry for a complete absorption by Germany of Austria. It vill diminish his power. It vill humiliate him. So he plays for time. He puts in Dollfuss, a puppet of his own, to govern Austria. He tells Dollfuss to eliminate the Socialists. That vill appease Hitler for the time being. Dollfuss goes ahead. He arrests and executes Socialists. He exterminates them like mad dogs. So far, all is to plan. Dollfuss is a good servant. But –' Nussbaum held up a long, bony finger to make the interjection in the smooth progress of the story ' – there are Nazi elements in Austria and ven the Socialists are exterminated the Nazis flourish. Like a certain strain of bacteria ven the bacteria that resist it are viped out. What then? Mussolini is alarmed. He tells Dollfuss to suppress the Nazis. But Socialists are sentimental theorists, and have no state apparatus to support them, vile Nazis have a powerful and efficient state only next door. Barely has Dollfuss begun to murder Nazis than the Nazis murder him. Conclusions:' Nussbaum held out his fingers, counting them off. 'In first line, that the Nazis are in complete power within Germany; in second line, that they have no intention of staying vithin their own national borders; in third line, that their preferred method of dealing with those who oppose them is to kill. Once I am grasping these facts, I am understanding that var is inevitable and I live my life a day at a time.'

'That's what you're doing now, is it?'

'That is vat I am doing now. It is difficult – finally, perhaps, impossible – but one must try. Before going back to my vork of the afternoon, I am walking a little in this beautiful garden. Ven the Germans are ruling this country and are directing Oxford as they are directing everything else, this garden vill no longer be beautiful.'

'Even if it's physically exactly the same as it is now?'

'Precisely. Beauty has a spiritual dimension and it is the spiritual dimension by vich in the end it is judged. Plato knew that. Even your Jesus Christ glimpsed it in his fashion, as one sees in his reference to the lilies of the field.'

We walked on for a few paces more. I began to feel that I must get away from him. His absolute certainty of impending doom was beginning to bring me to his own level of calm despair. But, uneasily kicking against the constraints of his own logic, I said, 'You say *when* Germans are running this country. Don't you sometimes have moods when you say *if?*'

Nussbaum shook his head. 'The Germans vill attack this country ven they are confident of vinning quickly. They vill attack at a time and a place of their own choosing. They vill attack with discipline and planning. They vill be met with cheerful improvisation and gallant amateurism. There iss no example in history of the one combination of qualities losing to the other.'

I pondered. 'The Spanish Armada?'

'The Armada was a purely maritime invasion vith no territorial backing and its lines of communication vere impossibly long. The English sailors vere totally professional and their ships, though smaller and more lightly armed, stayed afloat in the unexpected storm that sent many of the vessels of the Armada to the bottom. There is no parallel here. You are thinking perhaps of the game of bowls? Yes, you may still play bowls on beautiful level turf, but this time there vill be a different outcome.'

'And the outcome will be defeat and enslavement?'

'You personally may be lucky. You are a young man and so vill probably be killed in the fighting that accompanies the invasion. You vill not live to see the swastika flying above vat used to be the Houses of Parliament. You vill not live to see the storm-troopers in their brown shirts terrifying the population. You vill not see Oxford colleges turned into training grounds for Nazi propagandists, Nazi historians, Nazi purveyors of their twisted ideology. Tell me this, my young friend. I have seen you with a beautiful blonde young voman and sometimes you are veeling along a child. This is your vife? Your child?'

'Yes.'

'And the child is male or female?'

'He's a boy.'

Nussbaum shook his head. 'If the child vere a girl, it might not matter so much. Women have tensile strength. They can exist under political tyranny and somehow live human lives, attending to vomen's skills. But a man . . . If the question faces you, vich vill you find preferable, my friend: to kill your son or let him grow up a Nazi?'

I stopped walking. My blood was freezing and my limbs halted of their own accord. In the afternoon silence a lorry rolled past, going along Parks Road, and the sound of its heavy engine made me think briefly of the movement of troops, here and there, across this frontier and that, endlessly moving across Central Europe. Why was I born in such an iron time?

'My God,' I said. 'That's an impossible choice.'

'Impossible or not,' Nussbaum said quietly, 'it iss the choice that vill face you.'

'Not if, as you say, I'm going to be killed trying to stem the initial invasion.'

'Ah, no. There is that. Ve can look on the bright side. There is alvays death. That iss vat I tell Hans.'

'And what does he say?'

'He agrees with me, of course.' Nussbaum suddenly gave a brilliant smile and

70

his hand rested for a moment on my shoulder. 'My so amiable friend, you are young and you have a beautiful vife and, I am sure of it, a beautiful child, and so you do not understand yet that there are vorse things than death. But you must reflect that classical scholars like Hans and myself vere brought up with the vords that Socrates uttered to his judges, after they had condemned him to death because he vould not stop asking questions and disturbing the *status quo.* "The hour of parting has come," he said. "Ve go our different vays, you to live and I to die. Vich is better, only the gods know." '

Obviously feeling that he had said all that there was to be said, Nussbaum walked slowly away, enveloped in his solitude. I went back to the Bodleian and tried to read, but I was in a leaden mood. If everything was headed for collapse, and so imminently, why fill my head with knowledge? After a while I gave up and cycled slowly back to North Parade. Michael had just woken up from an afternoon nap; he was at a demanding stage just then, too old to lie for hours in a cot like a baby but too young to go to nursery school. I offered to wheel him out for a while and when I took him back Heather and I sat around drinking tea while he played on the floor. I remember thinking what an idyllic scene of young domesticity we must have presented. Outwardly, that is. These effects are always easier to achieve outwardly than inwardly.

'Are you tired or something?' Heather asked as she poured me a second cup. 'You seem a bit down. Been overdoing the work?'

'It's not the work. But yes, I am a bit down. I've just had a very depressing talk with old Nussbaum.'

'Him? That old boy? What was he on about?'

'He was talking about the international situation.'

'Oh, that. Everybody seems to be going on about it.'

'Well, no wonder. I mean, it does look damned gloomy.'

'I don't see the point of worrying about it. A lot of foreigners who can't settle their affairs without getting excited and quarrelling.'

'You think that's all it amounts to?'

She stirred her tea impatiently.

'Well, what do *you* think it amounts to? I mean, it's quite possible they'll end up dragging us into their stupid quarrels, but there's nothing we can do about it. We'll just have to deal with it when it comes.'

'Look, Heather, both our fathers served in the last war. We're lucky, neither of them happened to get killed, but what about Mike? If it happens again, I mean.'

Heather thought for a moment. Her face was very composed. 'I don't see anything we can do about it,' she said at last, 'except let it answer a question I've had in my mind for some time.'

'Oh, what question is that?'

She nodded down towards Mike. 'Whether to let this one grow up as an only child, or whether to provide him with a number two.'

'And you mean . . .'

'I mean that if there's going to be a war, then our family circle, my dear husband, is emphatically, decidedly and finally going to stay at the number it now stands at. You, me and Michael. Three, no more, no less.'

'Well,' I said, feeling rather helpless, 'I see how your mind's working, naturally. It strikes me as rather a pity from Mike's point of view, but — '

'The worst pity from Mike's point of view will be if a war comes and something awful happens to you and me, separately or together. Little babies are so terribly vulnerable. You know the kind of thing that happens to people when war breaks out. They go hungry. Their homes are knocked to pieces by shells or bombs and they go trudging along the roads in long processions, trying to take a few belongings with them in barrows and handcarts, and then they get machine-gunned from the air. No child's likely to survive that for long, but a baby in arms wouldn't have a celluloid cat's chance in hell. My God, I get so furious when I think about it.' Pushing back her chair, she stood in the middle of the room, her eyes bright with anger. 'It's all men, bloody stupid *men*, wanting to be important, wanting to show each other how tough and aggressive they can be. They mess up the whole world.'

'That's what my mother thinks.'

She relaxed, managed a grin. 'Well, that proves it.'

'I agree.' I grinned back. 'My mother's a very sensible woman. But then, to be fair, my father's a very sensible man. It's impossible to imagine either of them starting a war. They're typical of the millions of ordinary people who *suffer* when wars happen.'

'All right. I can't imagine my father starting a war either, if it comes to that.'

'No,' I said incautiously, 'but I can imagine your mother starting one, if it suited her.'

Heather turned and looked at me very attentively. 'And what precisely,' she asked in the cool, attacking tone she used when she was really after my blood, 'is that supposed to mean?'

'Nothing at all, I swear,' I said. 'I can't think what made me say anything so stupid. It just slipped out.'

I grovelled for about ten minutes and then, having patched up some sort of peace, managed to slip away to the Bodleian. All the time, of course, I knew that my remark had been perfectly sensible. If Mrs Burrell had had, say, a territory dispute with a neighbouring farmer – if they had both laid claims to some useful resource such as an access gateway or a ditch for land drainage – and she had had a posse of armed men at her disposal, would she have hesitated to send them into action? Of course not. And if the dispute had been over a territory as large as Ethiopia or the Rhineland, and if the posse of armed men had been a national army, would the mere change of scale have made her see things any differently? Again, of course not. In fact, if the dispute had been international rather than merely local, she would have been even more likely to start shooting, because she would have the inducement of patriotism, which would allow her to wrap herself in the flag and utter stirring slogans while the band played.

I wasn't going to say all this to Heather because in her own mind she knew it already; she just wasn't going to have *me* saying it because she considered that I already did quite enough getting at her mother, and because she had a certain ingrained notion, derived from God knows where but quite ineradicable, that the Burrells were superior to the Leonards and ought not to be criticized by them. For that reason I also avoided pointing out that Tom, who had clearly inherited his mother's temperament and not his father's, was also the type one could easily imagine starting a war.

In the end the Second World War was started in Spain on 5 October 1936. From that fateful date onward, any democrat unwilling to wait his turn in the struggle against Fascism could jump the queue by going down to the south-west corner of Europe and meeting General Franco's troops, armed, trained and supported by Hitler and Mussolini. It was hallucinatory, this sense of living one's days in a background, while the foreground was somewhere else and not accessible except at second hand.

Even quite major changes in my life seemed to me like the episodes in a dream. At the end of September 1936, for example, I completed the three years of my Research Fellowship and although in theory there was no reason why Episcopus College should take any further notice of my existence, they in fact elected me to a Teaching Fellowship, renewable every seven years – in other words, metamorphosed me from a donling to a grown-up don. Bax had told me that this was likely, and during the six months or so before that autumn election it was more or less an open secret that from Michaelmas onwards, throughout foreseeable time, I would be the junior of the two full-time history tutors at the College, Bax being the senior. The College had never filled the gap left by the death of Gadsby, Bax's previous colleague; Bax had struggled unaided through those three years, overseeing the work of every student reading history, and necessarily sending many of them out to tutor in other colleges. The reason, it now transpired, was that the job was being held open for me. And the time would come, I was to suppose, when I too would pick a successor from among the bright and impressionable young.

At the time I first heard about this, the news did not trouble my conscience. It was an in-college appointment, so what? Bax knew that he could work with me and Bax was a solidly established historian; he had recently been elected a Fellow of the British Academy, and his published work was widely respected. The other Fellows of Episcopus were content to take Bax's word that I was competent professionally, and since they had had me living among them for three years they knew I didn't slurp my soup or pick my nose in public; nor was I the type, familiar enough in academic life, whom they could expect to find dead drunk in a flower-bed in the middle of the afternoon. *Oxford always chooses her own* – how often and how bitterly had I already in those days heard that charge levelled. And indeed, though it never did apply at professorial level, where the big international reputations were involved, in the humbler (and cosier?) world of college teaching it was still pretty much as true in the 1930s as it had been in Victorian times.

I had enough of a social conscience to worry about this, a little. Hadn't I, perhaps, fluked a little too easily into a job that, if I merely pulled my weight in an unspectacular way, could be mine for life? Weren't there men of ability equal to mine – greater, perhaps – in remote, inaccessible places – what we used to call in those days 'the provincial universities' – who would never get a look-in? And hadn't some of the steps I had taken to fit the system – most of all, the concealing of my marriage as if it were disreputable – been pretty degrading? Was I a fit person to carry the sacred torch of Learning?

All this disturbed me when in the autumn of 1936, the election duly went through – or I thought it ought to disturb me, or wondered if I ought to think so, and wandered into a maze of side-issues and arguments that could be used both ways and points of view that had something to be said for them, till one bright November day I put down the pen with which I had been doodling and walked out of my room at Episcopus, first into the quad, then into the street. I was tired of thinking the same thoughts over and over again, and wanted to take a turn or two in Christ Church Meadow; I had a tutorial to give at five, it was not yet four, and I had always found that my thoughts took clearer shape when I was walking about under the open sky than sitting in a room.

I never got as far as the Meadow, though, because as I went along Broad

Street I saw Geraldine and I made towards her at once. She was just the person I needed to talk to.

'Hello,' she said in response to my greeting. 'I'm fed up. Come and have a cup of tea somewhere.'

'If you hadn't suggested it I would have. I want to talk to you. If you'd like to walk around with me a bit and have tea at four, we can have it in the Common Room at Episcopus, with rather nice — '

'*No.* I don't want to sit with a lot of stuffy dons. I want tea now and I want to sit among ordinary people, even if some of them are students.'

So we went and had tea in a café in the market. Geraldine's face was screwed up into a resolute scowl that was just as schoolboyish as her grin. It struck me that she was like one of Thomas Henry's illustrations to the William books, which were very popular at that time.

'Cheer up,' I said. 'We can always go and play in the old barn.'

'I don't know what you're jabbering about,' she said disconsolately. 'Who but an oaf could cheer up with the world in the lousy mess it's in?'

'Which particular part of the lousy mess are you thinking about?'

'Spain, of course.'

'Oh,' I said, stirring my tea warily. 'I'd have expected Spain to give you . . . well, a bit of a lift, if you know what I mean.'

'Oh, yes, women are supposed to rejoice in bloodshed, aren't they? All their suppressed grudges against the male sex are supposed to come out when they get a chance to praise men for butchering each other in great bleeding heaps. Men ought to get what they deserve more often, is that it?'

'For Christ's sake, that's not what I — '

'Oh, I see, it's just that you think I'm a fire-eating Socialist woman. Up, Red Guards, and at 'em.'

'All right, if you're going to push me into a corner I'll push you into one. Aren't you glad, Geraldine, aren't you just a little bit glad that the evasions are over at last?'

'You mean glad that Fascist soldiers are actually shooting at non-Fascist soldiers instead of gunning down helpless Africans?'

'Well, yes, in a word.'

'In a word, no.'

'Why not?' I leaned forward. I really wanted to know. But when her answer came I hated it, because it fitted in too well with my own secret forebodings.

'Because our side are going to lose, that's why not. The Fascists are going to win in Spain because they're better armed, better financed, better looked after. And that'll give Fascism a pivot in that part of Europe. They'll be able to infiltrate France, and France won't get any help from us because we're too feeble and muddled and there are too many Fascists here already. Peter, it's all *awful.*' She drained her cup, banged it down into the saucer and, without waiting for me to say anything, burst out again: 'Then there's the waste of lives. Decent, brave lives thrown away. We've already started to get cancellations for courses at Ruskin. Young idealistic men who want to change the world. They're off to fight Fascism in Spain, push it back where it belongs, show the world that one Socialist country can survive and defend itself. And they'll be killed, of course. They'll be killed in the fighting or they'll die of wounds in some filthy prison camp.'

'They might not; they might win. They seem to be having a wave of victories already.'

'Yes, the first wave, when it's all popular enthusiasm and idealism. But they're pushing back professionally trained soldiers with home-made bombs and pitch-forks and broken bottles. How long d'you think that can last? Is there a single case in history where that sort of enthusiasm has been still winning after six months?'

'It depends on whether the other side are motivated.'

'The other side are motivated all right. The Fascists are convinced they're going to rule the world. And as far as I can see there's nothing to stop them.'

'The Russians might try to stop them, I suppose.'

'The Russians are too busy liquidating their own officer class and rewriting their own history to have any hostility to spare for outside enemies. If Stalin hated Hitler as much as he hates Trotsky, there'd be no world conquest by Fascism.'

I was getting restive; I wanted to talk about myself. 'The times are out of joint, Geraldine. No government, no political party, no corporate group of any kind seems to have a clear moral line any more. And that spreads down to individuals. Me, for instance.'

'You? What are your moral problems?'

'Well, I've just been confronted with one. Episcopus want to give me a proper job – to make me a regular Teaching Fellow.'

She looked disappointed. 'Is that all? You mean there's something morally wrong with that?'

'Well, it's taking advantage of privilege. I'm the insider, the man on the spot. They know they can get along with me and they know I'll fit in with their way of doing things, so they're putting me in the job. They didn't advertise it and they didn't interview anyone for it – not formally, at least.'

Geraldine was wide-eyed. 'And over this you're agonizing?'

'Oh, do take me seriously just for once. I'm allowing myself to be the beneficiary of a closed shop. Another Oxford man in another Oxford job. Outsiders keep away.'

'Will you make a mess of the job if you do it?'

'Certainly not. I'll do it as well as the next man, or better as far as I can see. But that's just it – how far *can* I see? Perhaps what's needed is somebody with a completely new approach to history and the teaching of history, someone whose presuppositions are so different from mine that I can't even imagine them. That might be the healthiest — '

'Look, Peter, if this hypothetical person has a set of presuppositions that you can't even imagine, my advice to you is to stop trying to imagine them. We're all only marking time anyway. The whole of Europe, and that means the whole of the world, is on the brink of such cataclysmic changes that you and I and everybody will change too, if we survive. So take the job and do your best in it from day to day, that's all you can do.'

I thought for a moment, then looked her straight in the face and said, 'It must all seem pretty trivial to you anyway, I suppose. You're too kind to say so, but you must be thinking that anyone who's a real man wouldn't be sitting around pondering history at a time like this, he'd be looking along the barrel of a rifle, somewhere in the mountains above Barcelona, doing his bit to *make* history.'

She returned my look just as straight and said, 'Wrong. You wouldn't be any particular use looking along the barrel of a rifle. I don't say you'd be *no* good, but you'd be no better than a quite ordinary person and there are plenty of those about. Whereas when it comes to weighing history, trying to get at the truth of what happened without being bribed or bamboozled into distorting facts to suit the purposes of any power group – well, you have it in you to be quite exceptional.'

'You mean it? Really, Geraldine? You think I'm . . .'

'I think you're honest, Peter.' She was not smiling now, she was looking at me gravely, gently, tenderly even. I knew there would never be sexual love between us, but this was something as deep: a declaration of faith in me as a human being and as a friend. 'You've managed to cram your head with a lot of information and stay sane and unselfconscious. You've carried your common sense all the way from Oseney Town without spilling a drop on the way.'

'Oseney Town isn't far.'

'It's a million miles from where you are now and you know it. You've done well.'

But something was still nagging me. 'Yes, but Geraldine . . .'

'*What?* You surely haven't got any more moral conundrums? And no personal problems, please. I'm not an Agony Aunt.'

'I just want you to know this. Who's doing the right thing – me by staying in Oxford and working on history at Episcopus, or your Ruskin men signing off courses to go and fight for the working class against the bullies and exploiters?'

She gave an imitation of a punctured balloon, sagging forward. 'Oh, Peter – everything's relative. They're doing the right thing for them, you're doing the right thing for you.'

I had to be content with that. We paid our bill and left; and only as we were going out of the door did I realize that this café was the one to which I had taken Heather to breakfast after our first night together. As Oseney Town was a million miles away, that exalted summer morning was a million years ago, and yet both of them were present, always and everywhere, as inescapably present as the beating of my heart.

So there I was, respectably established. The situation had its good points, and certainly one problem I had been dreading for years turned out to be no problem at all. Everybody had dispersed for the summer vacation in a mood of tension and uncertainty, and when they came back it was the same; nobody really thought about anything but the drift to war. I went to see the aged Salterton and notified him formally that I had committed matrimony, which was the due form between a Fellow of the College and its President, and though the courtly dotard received my news with the correct words of congratulation, poured me the inevitable glass of sherry, and said he hoped to be making the acquaintance of Mrs Leonard at a very early opportunity, he mercifully did not ask for dates in the matter. The good old man, born in 1855, was in the last years of his long, eventless life; all he was to see of the Second Word War was its declaration and its first few weeks, which was just as well because he would probably have referred to the enemy as 'the French', or even vaguely imagined them as Fuzzy-Wuzzies.

All I had to do now was to bide my time, and when someone happened to ask me at dinner whether I had been given a new set of rooms and if so on what staircase, I was able to reply, keeping my voice casual, that I had moved out of College altogether.

'Oh? Any special reason?'

'Yes, I've got married.'

'Really? When?'

'In the vac.' I did not say which vac.

And so the news discreetly spread. The Domestic Bursar grumbled slightly when he heard that I was leaving College without having given notice beforehand, but then he grumbled about everything, and it really made no difference to anyone because I used my new set of rooms for teaching, and storing my books; the only difference was that I didn't use the bedroom and so didn't need a scout to make my bed and bring my breakfast. The tiny gap left by my departure healed up instantly.

'So you're a married man,' Bax said in his dry way the next time we were alone. 'Quite out of the blue, was it?'

'Not altogether,' I stonewalled.

'Anyone I know?'

'No.'

It suddenly crossed my mind, for some reason, that he might be wondering whether I had married Geraldine who, as far as I knew, was the only girl he had ever seen me talking to. So, just to put him right, I said, 'It's pretty unlikely that you'll ever have seen Heather. She wasn't at the University; she's a farmer's daughter from the deep country.' I made it sound as if she had never had a pair of shoes on till she married me. Steady, I said to myself. You're getting nervous, and there's no need to be. If he does rumble what's been going on, so what? You've made it now, you're in.

'Well, do bring her in for a glass of sherry whenever you like,' said Bax, preparing to move away.

'Oh, we'd like you to come to us,' I said. 'Come and have a meal one evening, won't you? I've had so much of your hospitality through the years, it'd make a change.'

He smiled politely and said, 'Any time,' but in fact – as I had been counting on – the general leaden paralysis caused by the overhanging war seemed to affect him as much as it did me, and he never did anything about it. And since no one else from Episcopus came to see us at home during the three anxious years leading up to the third of September 1939, the question of Michael, curiously old for such recently married parents, never had to be faced. And when he was finally encountered, the exact year of our wedding was long forgotten.

Meanwhile, with more money coming in, we thankfully left the horrible flat in North Parade and rented an undistinguished but easily-run house in Marston. Rented, not bought; there were many houses to rent in those days, and with such uncertainty hanging over the future it seemed folly to own bricks and mortar.

So no one from Episcopus sampled our home life in Marston. Heather came to the usual bring-your-wife functions at College and mildly enjoyed some of them, but she didn't have to bring Michael with her. And if any of the other wives started trying to bring the conversation round to the topic of children, Heather was very good at changing the subject. We were not ashamed of Michael, on the contrary we were both fiercely proud of him, but displaying him was for obvious reasons impracticable.

If this hiding-away of my first-born gave me a slight sense of unreality at that time, it could fairly be said that almost everything did. Certainly the falseness of the peace disturbed me. Psychologically, also I was at odds. Internally I felt no different from when I had been an undergraduate, yet from the outside I knew I presented the appearance of a solid bourgeois citizen. I had a home, a wife, a child, a steady job, my foot firmly planted on the ladder of a career. Comforts and conveniences abounded, since with more money coming in there was no need to go on doing without them, and of course comfort changes one's nature more than anything. I began to feel that I really would turn into a different kind of person if this went on.

One of the things that changed our lives was that Heather pressed hard for a car. She said she was tired of going everywhere on a bike, with the groceries in a basket and Mike strapped into a seat over the back wheel. So, although I didn't much care one way or the other, I got us a Morris Eight, one of those little saloons with wire-spoke wheels that were obviously Billy Morris's answer to Herbert Austin's fabulously successful Austin Seven. I asked Brian if he could get me one at a discount, being an employee, but he said there was a limit to the number of cars employees could buy at a discount and he was already on that limit, having fairly recently got one for himself and one for our parents. It didn't matter much, you could buy one brand-new for £100. It seemed to do a lot for Heather, and she even made me learn to drive and take one of the new Ministry of Transport driving tests. I got through all right.

So there I was, driving around in a family-style car, living in a family-style house, teaching the young instead of just *being* one of the young and waiting for it all to make me feel like a totally different person, which so far it hadn't.

'Them polo ponies,' said old Trundle one night in the Bargeman's, wiping the wholesome beer-foam from his walrus moustache, 'is wicked little monkeys. Full o' tricks they is, as a barrel full of monkeys.'

'Thass all nothin' to do with it, nothin' to do with it at all,' said young Bob truculently. 'It don't matter whether the Duke's in his right mind or not. Meself I thinks 'e is, but it don't matter one way or the other. After 'e said what 'e said about that Mrs Simpson 'e was on 'is way out and that's all about it.'

'Aah,' said Trundle. ''Is grandfather'd never of got in this deep. Good ole Teddy. He'd of kept the woman round the corner. Nice 'ouse, mind. Proper posh set-up in the middle of Windsor Park. "Anythin' and everythin' you fancies, moy duck," it would of been. "Just say the word." But never nothin' like this, not the ole King. 'Is grandfather I'm a speaking of,' he added, looking round the circle of faces.

'Well, it's true most things skip a generation,' said Peake. 'If the father's a 'ard worker, the son's a idler, then 'is son's born poor and 'as to be a 'ard worker whether he likes it or not. Same with 'abits. Old Edward Seventh liked a drink and 'e knew a chorus girl when he seed one, an' 'e knew what to do with 'em, an' all. Then '*is* son, George Fifth, now 'e were different.'

'Yes,' said another man, a quiet-spoken fellow who joined the circle only rarely, 'and glad I am 'e didn't live to see this day.'

'That's as may be,' said old Trundle. 'But what's at the bottom of it? There's only one thing as it could be, to my mind.' He tapped his skull. 'A thump on the 'ead. Loosened his brain-box. Mark my words, there's nothin' else in the world as'd make him act so daaft. It comes of playing polo on them nasty little ponies.'

At the other end of the bar, I settled back luxuriously. I deeply enjoyed my early evening visits to the Bargeman's, which were becoming rarer now that I was in the business of teaching-loads and timetables. And I enjoyed them all the more when I happened to catch the *cénacle* in full cry.

'Many's the time I've stood there on Port Meadow and watched 'em,' Trundle said. 'The undergrads had money in them days. 'Tworn't nothin' to keep a string of polo ponies. Stabled 'em at Wolvercote. That's 'ow a lot of the folks at Wolvercote turned an honest penny. And fast! Them games was all gallop, gallop. I seen many a man get a taste o' the meadow. Often it was only the 'ard 'ats as

78

saved 'em. Well, stands to reason. It's been one of his favourite games. Always playin' it, 'e was. In India, and that.'

'Don't you believe it,' said Bob. He spoke quickly, like a man who has been biding his time for a decisive intervention. 'They been lookin' for a chanst. They wornts 'im out.'

'Why should they want him out?' my father asked. 'He's popular enough, and that's a good point for a King who's got to take over at a time like this.'

'That's just it. Him being popular makes it all the worse in their eyes, don't you see? They don't want the people to 'ave no leadership.'

I would have been tempted to break my usual rule of silence and ask whom Bob meant by They, except that it was unnecessary. To Bob, as to Edward Lear, They were Those over There, the ones who Got At You, who had power and would use it against you, the ones you Couldn't Trust.

'I could of told you,' he said with fierce emphasis, stabbing at the air with his smouldering cigarette, 'as they'd never rest till they got 'im out. Ever since 'e went down to Wales and seen the unemployed miners. Walked about in the streets and saw their little 'ouses and that and their 'ungry kids, Said 'e was going back to London to get it altered. That's when they decided to get 'im. A one-way ticket. They wasn't going to see the throne of England sat down in by anyone who could talk about changin' things.'

They continued for some time to discuss the abdication and speculate on the motives of the principal actors in that intimate but wide-ranging historical drama. In the bar of the Bargeman's Arms, no explanation was arrived at which had the support of all those present, and I myself had no theory to offer. Whether strangely or not, the only man I knew who was certain he had an explanation was Nussbaum, who adverted to the topic when I next spoke to him in our little pub in North Parade.

'Self-preservation,' he said, with a fatalistic shrug. 'It is impossible for him, in his position of vantage, not to see what is going to happen. He knows this country will be invaded and overrun. So he takes an American wife, which will conveniently leave him with no alternative but to emigrate to America and safety.'

'You think that's all there is to it? That he's saving his skin?'

'Most people in the world would do the same. Who would not choose to sit in the sun in California while European democracy is slaughtered?'

'But,' I persisted, 'is it so certain that he would be part of the slaughter? Heads of state and royal families weren't executed in the last war.'

'In Western Europe, no; the Kaiser simply moved to Holland. In Eastern Europe, it was different. The throats of the Romanovs were cut. You are thinking perhaps that the Nazis are more civilized than the Bolsheviks? Forget it, my young friend. Throw out your liberal illusions. You will find it lighter to travel.'

Yes, I thought. As I would without my clothes. Lighter, but so much colder.

I tried hard, during those leaden years, not to let the utterly chill hopelessness of the Eastern European world-view get too deeply into my bones, but certainly there were many times when it was difficult to go about one's normal business; there seemed always to be a small, metallic voice at the centre of my being, perpetually asking the one question: 'What's the point?'

This feeling was particularly strong, and this voice particularly audible when, being now a fully-fledged Fellow of Episcopus and therefore a member of the governing body, I took my seat at College meetings. Like most people, I had an attitude to these meetings that was distinctly ambivalent. On the one hand I found them a bore, consuming whole afternoons with discussion of such matters as pensions for gardeners, tenure of Research Fellowships and such. On the other hand, I approved in theory of the fact that an Oxford college was run by its Fellows, and for that matter the University as a whole was run by its academic work-force and not, like most other universities in the world, either by the state or by some outfit recruited mainly from business and industry. As long as a university was run by its dons, there was some hope of getting a balanced liberal education there. So I thought in 1936 and so I think now. Which is why, though they bored me, I turned up at College meetings.

At one meeting, early in 1937, I think, I was slumped in my chair, somnolently listening as the Land Agent made his report. He was a country landowner with experience of estate management who kept an eye on the College farms and saw that they were reasonably well run, and on this occasion he had to report that in two cases farmers on College property had failed to come up to scratch. One was in a place over in Northamptonshire, in some area where it was news to me that Episcopus owned any land at all. The other was – yes! – at High Cogges. Mr William Thomas Burrell of Jasmine Farm had been unpunctual in the payment of his rent for a year or two now, and the last quarter he had not paid at all, asking for more time.

I woke up. My *what's-the-point?* voice was silenced: suddenly there was a very good point.

The Land Agent, regretfully, was for slinging both these farmers off their land. In each case, a visit had revealed an ageing tenant who was simply less and less able to cope. Both farms were understaffed and managed in old-fashioned ways which, even if pursued with more determination, would bring in only meagre levels of profit. I can see him now: he was a high-coloured man who wore half-moon glasses and kept looking up over the top of them. There was no harm in him; he had a job to do.

Suddenly, though, I was holding up a hand in token that I wished to speak, and I raised my voice in the large, silent room.

'I'm against turning these farmers off. In normal times, yes, the case for handing their farms over to more efficient tenants would be overwhelming. But these aren't normal times. There's fairly obviously going to be a war, and when it comes land will be seized and managed by the government. Farmers will be told what to grow and they'll be supplied with labour if they need it. If they still don't make a go of it, then they'll obviously be pulled out and replaced.'

'All this, I take it, is conjecture,' said the Estates Bursar, a thin acidulated man whom I judged to be capable of selling his old mother into slavery for a suitable profit.

'It's what I believe will happen,' I said coldly, 'if a war breaks out and this country isn't immediately overwhelmed by an invader. You have a better theory?'

He shook his head silently.

'Perhaps,' the Land Agent said in his deep, measured voice, 'Mr Leonard is personally acquainted with one or both of these farmers?'

I sidestepped his question. 'I'm arguing from general principles,' I told him. 'I think it's quite possible that the country's agriculture is going to be reorganized from top to bottom within the next couple of years anyway, and it's a pity to put a man out of his livelihood on the eve of a shake-up that may well save the situation for him.'

'You mean, Leonard,' old Salterton put in, 'that it's an ill wind that blows nobody any good?'

80

'Yes, President.' I had not known he was conscious. But that is certainly what I did mean.

After a bit of humming and hawing, there was a vote on the matter. I shall never know whether it was my intervention that resulted in old Burrell being spared the Episcopus chopper, or whether they would have reprieved him anyway. But when I got home and reported the incident to Heather, I naturally took the credit.

'So at least,' I finished my account, 'I managed to talk them into letting him stay.'

'Well, you did yourself a good turn too. If the pair of them had been chucked out into the snow, they might have ended up living in our attic.'

'My God, I hadn't thought of that!'

'It could still come to it. You said they'd agreed to let him stay for the time being. But what makes you think he'll ever be able to pay the rent? They didn't offer to bring that down, did they?

'No, they reckon all their agricultural rents are at rock-bottom anyway. In fact they're wringing their hands because they didn't follow the lead of the colleges with clever financial advisers, who all got out into urban property long ago, or Consols. What are Consols?'

'I don't know, but I can't say my heart bleeds for them. The point is, what's going to happen to my father?'

'In six months' time anything may have happened. Land may be nationalized. And anyway, if it's Tom's going that's made him unable to run the farm properly, all he really needs is an extra hand.'

'Yes, he does, but he can't afford the wages.'

'That's where we come in.'

'We?'

'Yes, you don't mind if we put part of our income into paying the wages of a hand at Jasmine Farm, do you? How much would it take?'

Heather considered. 'Well, a really experienced all-rounder would cost a lot, but you could get a labourer who'd make himself useful for a couple of pounds a week. I don't suppose Phil gets any more. In fact, Phil's probably on thirty shillings.'

'Right, we find £2 a week, which is roughly £100 a year, which is about a fifth of my salary. You don't mind, do you? I mean, you and Michael wouldn't be going short of anything you really need, would you?'

'No, we'd just have to cut out a few frills. That trip to Italy you were talking about.'

'Or the car. We don't really need a car.'

'We don't *need* a trip to Italy.'

'We need it more than we need a car. Have you ever met an historian who's never seen Rome, Padua or Venice?'

'Well, I'm meeting one now and that's the way it'll stay. I'm not going to run your bloody household without transport and cart Michael about on the back of a bike. I had that for years.'

'And I had not going abroad for years. Look, you don't understand . . .'

We quarrelled, at fairly low intensity, for about three-quarters of an hour as to what we should give up in order to subsidize another labourer at Jasmine Farm. What neither of us doubted for a moment was that basically we could well afford it. Finally Heather, having gained her point about the car, fell silent for a moment or two and seemed wrapped up in thoughts of her own. Then, raising her head and giving me her straight, searching look, she said, 'One thing I don't understand. Why are you doing this?'

'I'm not quite sure,' I said. It was true that the offer had, so to speak, jumped out of my mouth before I stopped to give it any consideration. But now that I'd made it, I felt quite comfortable with it.

'I mean,' she pursued, 'what's it to you to rescue my parents from their awful difficulties? You can't say it's because you like them.'

'I don't mind your father. I think he's a decent man who's simply been caught on the wrong foot by the whole direction the modern world has taken. Food imports, falling land values and then his children leaving the farm – it's all overwhelmed him, and for no fault of his own.'

'And my mother? Obviously you can't stand her.'

'Well, that makes two of us, doesn't it?'

'I won't deny I'm going to be out of her clutches, but I'd like to see her self-sufficient. If I loved her I'd want to protect her and care for her myself, but I don't, so I'll be glad to see her able to manage. If the two of them were turned out of that farmhouse, God knows what they'd do. I don't want the guilty feeling that I ought to be looking after them.'

'What about Tom? You could unload most of the guilt on him, couldn't you? After all, you could always claim it's ninety per cent his doing that they're in this mess.'

Heather turned and looked at me, shaking her head. Whatever she was going to say on the subject of Tom, the gist of it was going to be No.

'I just don't want Tom involved in this, Peter,' she said. 'I'm sorry, but I want us to do this on our own. If it means too much of a financial sacrifice, I'll do something myself to earn the money. I haven't any training that'll put me in line for a decent money-earning job, but I'll . . . I'll take in people's washing or clean their cars or exercise their dogs or something. I'm strong and I can work. I'll –'

'Look, Heather,' I said, 'Episcopus College pay me a salary at least as good as I could get in a bank, and on top of that I get some privileges and free meals. I can absorb a loss of £100 a year as long as you don't mind adjusting to that – and let the neighbours do their own washing. All I ask is, help me to understand what's in your mind. Why shouldn't Tom help to pick up the apples, since he helped to upset the cart?'

She thought for a moment before she spoke. Then, as if formulating the matter for herself, she brought out her words deliberately. Her expression suggested that she was just as much listening as talking: listening to what her mind was coming up with.

'When Tom pulled out, he left the family cold. He's never been back. He writes once in a blue moon but he never shows much curiosity about how they're getting on. I'm sure he feels that part of his life is over and dead. He always hated being the son of a tenant farmer – just as Mother's always hated being the wife of one. Scrimping and saving and having to let all the decisions be made over your head, and never being able to answer back to the landlord. And she always knew that Tom looked down on her and the home she managed to keep going. It made her see red, Peter, and she hated him then.'

'Yes?' I prompted, making my voice as sympathetic and understanding as I could.

'What I'm trying to make clear is that it was a horrible atmosphere to grow up in. And particularly since my mother disapproved of me for not being a second

82

son. Tom took the same line. Deep down he always knew he wasn't going to stay around, and if there'd been a younger brother to take his place, he might have felt a bit easier in his mind about perpetually plotting his escape. But there I was, just a rotten old girl.'

'I'm sure you were as much use around the farm as any boy would have been.'

'Yes, and in a way that made it worse because it added insult to injury. After all, girls aren't real people. They aren't reliable. I mean, they couldn't take me round and introduce me to the Bursar of Episcopus and say, "She'll take over your farm." Colleges don't believe in women inheriting farms, or doing anything. They'd like to abolish women.'

I could only agree.

'Tom's solution to that was to boss me around and make me feel small all through the years I was growing up. And then when he got a realistic chance to leave the farm and go and do something else, he just took it. I don't suppose he gave his parents and me a backward glance; I think we've all just faded from his mind. Well, I'm not going to remind him of our existence by writing to him asking for money.'

'Well, it's only a matter of his parents really. He'd probably say his sister was reasonably well taken care of.'

'No, he wouldn't. He doesn't approve of dons and universities. What he wanted me to do was to marry some farmer in a big way of business, so that the poor man could absorb my parents, put them in a cottage on the estate or something and find them things to do. I might have solved all the family's problems at one swoop, just by catching the right man.'

'Instead of which,' I said gallantly, 'the wrong man caught you.'

She frowned, refusing to be side-tracked. 'The point I want to make, Peter, is that we do this alone. No Tom. If you think of it as something you're doing for me, so be it, and I appreciate it.'

'Only one condition,' I said. 'I don't want your mother to know I'm giving them the money. I still have hopes of a working relationship with her, one day. I don't want to go on being the Interloper and the Enemy for ever, especially as Mike grows up. And it's bound to make problems if I just give them £100 a year. Your mother loathes me as it is, and she'd do so even more if she had to accept from me what she'd probably think of as charity.'

'H'm. Easier said than done.'

'Can your father keep his mouth shut? I mean, could he at least avoid telling your mother where the money came from?'

'She'd find out. She keeps a pretty close eye on the books.'

'Well, it would have to be camouflaged of course. I'd get the bank to pay it into his account every month, and we'd just give it an official name like "Farm Fund" or something and tell them to keep my name out of it. She'd think it was some kind of government subsidy. I'd have a word with the manager; I'm sure he'd be understanding as long as they didn't have to conceal it from the account-ants and the tax people and so on. So what I come back to is, could he stop himself actually blurting out the truth to her?'

'Oh, I'm sure he could. Self-defence, if nothing else.'

So in the end that's what we did. The money was paid every month, anony-mously; the bank were very discreet, old Burrell was grateful, and he had no difficulty in telling his wife nothing. And Jasmine Farm got a new man. He was very good with machinery; he could assemble and repair anything, drive anything. He always seemed to be rather lost without a spanner in his hand; psychologically he was industrial, and at the end of each day he would get on to his motorbike and snort off to his home in one of the neighbouring towns, I think Witney. He suited the situation at Jasmine Farm perfectly. Old Burrell could leave the machines to the new man and take over the grain side himself. And, since it suited Jasmine Farm, that meant it also suited Episcopus College. This made me feel good. I was doing something useful: helping to pay the rent for a farmer who found he was unable to pay it himself. In fact, as a direct result of that marriage I had had to conceal as carefully as a crime, I was contributing to the College's prosperity, helping them to balance their books. So the whirligig of time brings its revenges. Meanwhile, however, the question persisted : why was I doing it? Did I, when the chips were down, really care about the Burrell couple? Hardly. There were the basic decencies, of course; whether I liked them or not, they were my wife's parents, and to see them actually turned out into the hedgerow without doing anything to help was not in my nature. If you are born with a few grains of human decency, you just have to put up with them as you do with any other slight disadvantage: poor colour vision, say, or faulty co-ordination that makes you no good at games like squash.

But deeper than that, there had to be other reasons why I didn't want Jasmine Farm to be simply snatched away by Episcopus College and rented to another tenant, and during the next day or so I dug around for them. I got them, finally, one morning as I was walking across the University Parks.

Living in Marston it was possible for me, if I set out early enough, to walk to Episcopus through the Parks, coming across the fields from the Marston side and entering the Parks by crossing the Rainbow Bridge over the Cherwell. It was spring now, the late spring of 1937, and I smelt the soft, inciting air as I walked. The hazel catkins were fully formed and there was a general greening of the hedgerows. For the millionth time I found reason to bless the semi-rural character of Oxford – the way, in spite of its growth in population, there was always a finger of countryside that reached to you wherever you were – the result, of course, of the rivers and their tendency to flood the low-lying flat fields. To grow up in Oxford is to have at any rate a few drops of country blood in you. Billy Morris, dumping a vast load of industry and commerce on Oxford, had gone a long way towards wrecking the lovely balance, but even he couldn't destroy it altogether; the rivers and reed-beds and the marshy fields had beaten him.

As I walked along I thought of Michael, now three years old, whose eager, puckish little face I had watched that morning grinning at me as he waved his spoon and pusher at breakfast. In my mind's eye I saw him as he would be at ten or twelve, and in this mental picture he was standing by a five-barred gate with what seemed to be corn-stooks all around him. I was seeing him in a country setting. An aspiration, an almost unconscious dream of what I wanted for my son was breaking through. Fool! How dared I have any plans for a growing child in 1937, with the troops drilling and the armaments factories pumping out smoke night and day in the European sky? And I heard the voice of Nussbaum. *It is the choice that faces you, my friend. Kill your child or accept that he will grow up a Nazi.*

Could that really be true? Perhaps, I thought (pacing on towards the barn-like outline of Keble Chapel), if the Germans did overrun us and the Nazi regime did take over, it might lie a little less heavily on people in the countryside than in the towns. The land is a great touchstone of truth. City populations can be manipulated and driven to hysteria, but country people know ways of surviving. A few eggs or a sack of oatmeal can quietly slip through the guard of the rationing system. A dead tree can be hidden away in a barn and then sawn into logs in a bitter winter. I knew, of course, that there had been instances where the cruel revenge of dictators had fallen on country populations and put them through unbelievable suffering. I knew (in outline – no one at that time knew the details) about Stalin's frenzy of vindictiveness against the peasantry of the Ukraine in 1929 to 1933, but I took these things to be exceptions. My instinctive feeling was that being in the countryside, having a root in the earth and a roof over one's head, gave one a better chance during desperate times. I wanted Jasmine Farm for Michael, not only as a source of happiness in his childhood – those weekends and summer holidays on the farm that always seem so golden when one reads about them in people's memoirs – but also as giving him, perhaps, a better chance of survival when the big crash came.

Of course, no one could realistically assess the chances of that. The people in the villages might be rounded up and herded into barbed-wire enclosures as easily as the town populations. And in any case, if the first wave of the invasion was as devastating as it threatened to be, no one could count on being alive, wherever they were. All this I knew. But that deep instinct still called out, keep Jasmine Farm, at whatever cost! Keep it for Michael! There may be so little you can do for him when the day comes that the landing-craft grate on the shingle of the Channel beaches and the bombs rain down on the cities: do that, at least!

The next time I had lunch at Episcopus, Watson looked at me archly across the table as I took my seat and said, 'Here comes our agronomic oracle.'

'If that's a reference to me, Watson,' I said, trying hard to stop myself becoming annoyed, 'I'm afraid it goes over my head.'

'Oh, surely not. I was referring to the totally unexpected depth of interest you showed the other day in the fortunes of the College's tenant farmers. Good, honest men, I'm sure, with good honest mud on their boots, but I hadn't known you felt such a personal involvement with their lives.'

Had the bastard heard something? I wondered. Was he probing to find out the truth of some rumour he had heard about me and Heather? A year or two ago, this probing would have terrified me. But now, if the worst came to the worst, I could simply say, 'My wife is from a farming background,' and as long as I managed to smudge over the actual date when we got married, I was home and dry. All the same, least said, soonest mended. I helped myself to potatoes without answering.

'I think I speak for us all,' Watson went on silkily, 'when I say that we saw a new Leonard in the eloquence with which you came to the rescue of those two farmers. Not a dry eye in the house.'

'You take an interest in agriculture, Leonard?' someone else asked me, a man with a straightforward, no-nonsense manner who (I suspected) had as little patience with Watson as I had.

'Not specially. But as a Fellow of a college with income that is partly derived from farming land ... and then, of course, as an historian of the eighteenth century, I can't help knowing a bit about people like Jethro Tull and Townsend, and I've had to wade through a lot of agricultural statistics – mostly estimates, of course, because in those days they didn't keep elaborate ...'

The talk drifted into historical chit-chat and I began to feel safe from Watson, but it must have been his day for needling me, because he suddenly fired in from another angle.

'I must mention you as an expert on country matters to my journalist friend Hunt.'

Hunt? Your friend; I might have known.

'Yes, he always drops in to see me when he's in Oxford. I think of him as our man in Fleet Street.'

I ought to have kept quiet, but I couldn't help saying, 'Well, he's certainly in Fleet Street, but I wouldn't want to acknowledge him as our man.'

'You disapprove of him, perhaps?'

'I don't think of him at all, but if I did I'd disapprove of him.'

'Being a bit hard, aren't you? But then you are rather a severe person, wouldn't you say, Leonard?' *In your terribly dreary way*, his expression added.

'I don't know whether I'm severe or not, but I admit to not admiring triflers like Hunt, who don't seem to have any beliefs they wouldn't cheerfully betray if they saw any advantage in it.'

'That's what I mean, you're severe.' In other words, dreary and humourless.

'I don't think Hunt betrays his beliefs.'

'His beliefs? You mean you think he's got some?'

'Certainly. I think he believes in civilized discourse.'

'You think *what*?' I could hardly believe my ears.

'Civilized discourse, with a dash of irony and an elegant style. For instance, I'm sure you remember that piece he wrote on the King and Country motion.'

'Yes, I remember it. I nearly threw up reading it. The man's a — '

'Oh, yes, I can quite see it wouldn't be to your taste.'

'It was a lie, to begin with,' I said. I could feel my face growing hot, and I hated Watson for putting me in this position, but I had to go on now. 'He claimed to have visited Oxford and talked to representative people. But it was perfectly clear that he'd made the whole thing up, doubtless sitting in his office in Fleet Street.'

'But my dear good fellow, there's no need to be so *literal*. Hunt had spent three years in Oxford, so it hardly matters whether he spent that particular Saturday afternoon here or not . . .'

'It matters if he says he did.'

'. . . and the important thing was that he conveyed something about Oxford that was perfectly true.'

'What was true? The stuff about the buildings being made from Portland stone?'

'The fact that hardly anybody took the slightest interest in that motion at the Union. There was a lot of cackling and squawking outside Oxford, but as far as people here were concerned, they were flooded with equanimity.'

Bax, who was sitting a couple of places down from Watson, put in, 'Not quite everybody. Some people were concerned.'

'Really, Bax? What concerned them?'

'They were afraid some European leaders might get the signal that England had lost any will to resist aggression.'

'And who in Europe was going to get this interesting signal?'

'Obviously Hitler and Mussolini, to go no further.'

Watson had been leaning forward, looking down the table at Bax. Now he sat back in his chair, wearily. 'Hitler I'm not concerned to defend, but I must put in a word against your expected denunciation of Mussolini.'

'I haven't denounced Mussolini,' Bax said crisply. 'I'm perfectly willing to, but it's unnecessary. His record since 1920 is sufficient denunciation in itself. Brutal repression at home, expansionism abroad, alliance with dictatorships across Europe, coupled with neglect of the real needs of the poor in his country, who are some of the poorest in Europe. Hitler's worse than Mussolini, but he's had to try pretty hard to achieve it.'

'As you know, Bax, I'm not much in favour of heavy political discussions over one's meals. But for once I don't feel in the mood to let you get away with all those *clichés*. Perhaps I've been infected with Leonard's earnestness of spirit.'

Well, I thought, a bit of earnestness of spirit wouldn't do you any harm, mate. Not that a mouthful of knuckles wouldn't probably do you some actual good.

'We'll leave Hitler on one side for the moment,' Watson was saying to Bax.

'You may find he's not willing to be left on one side.'

'Try not to interrupt me, please. I know it's difficult. But I have something important to tell you. Benito Mussolini is a force for good in the world.'

Bax had gone white in the face. But he said nothing.

'He's good for the world,' Watson went on, 'because he's good for Italy. I take it I don't have to argue that point with you, Bax, as an historian. You'll know that the Italian contribution to civilization has never been approached by another nation. The solid achievements of Ancient Rome; then when that finally shook to pieces, a profoundly interesting culture in the Middle Ages; then, as if that weren't enough, the *rinascimento*. A period of stagnation in the eighteenth century' – here Watson shot me a disdainful glance, as if anything that went wrong in the eighteenth century must be my personal fault – 'and then bang! Cavour, Garibaldi and the *risorgimento*. I submit, Bax, that once you see Mussolini against that background, you understand his logic and value his achievements.'

A good many Oxford dons, like a good many people of any kind, dislike discussions of highly-charged subjects at mealtimes. Furthermore, College lunch is very much an interval in a working day, a brief but necessary pause for sustenance. For both these reasons, the table was now emptying quickly as men finished their food. But Bax, Watson and I sat on amongst the wreckage of the meal, which the servants now began clearing away. I stayed because I wanted to see whether Bax would take up the challenge, and was pleased when, in his dry and patient way, he did so.

'Your defence of Mussolini, Watson, at any rate goes deeper than saying he's made the trains run to time, which is what apologists in this country usually say. But you see Mussolini as he wants to be seen – as the heir of the Roman Emperors, of the greater Italian medieval popes, of the Renaissance and the *risorgimento*. My distaste for him is precisely because he is an impostor who claims these credentials. He wears borrowed robes. I see no statesmanship in Mussolini, no vision. I see no genuine love of Italy, certainly not of the Italian people, whom he starves and oppresses.'

Watson had abandoned his normal expression, a superior half-smile, and was fairly glaring at Bax. 'He disciplines the Italian people because he's preparing them for a surge of endeavour. What was begun in the nineteenth century has still to be finished. Italy has a lot of ground to make up.'

'You give him the benefit of a great deal of doubt.'

'I'm not alone in that, Bax. Many people have faith in him.'

'Mostly people of rather shaky judgement. They may know their own business well enough, but they haven't much depth of acquaintance with Italy's business. Ezra Pound, for example, is an interesting poet, but his views on Italy are those of a deluded child.'

I pricked up my ears at this. I had never heard of Ezra Pound until a few evenings before, when Henry Goodenough mentioned him, remarking that he was like Coriolanus in being 'a natural leader who goes over to the enemy because he can't get enough support at home'. As usual, I hadn't known enough to argue, merely making a mental note to go and find out who Ezra Pound was.

'I suppose I should be flattered, Bax, that you bracket me, a humble bio-chemist, with such a literary celebrity. But I can't say that I do, since your object is so obviously to cut us both down.'

'I'm not concerned with cutting down either of you. But I would cut down Mussolini if I could. I think he's a small-town thug who's got his hands on political power by clubbing people and locking them up and driving them into exile. He's an Al Capone who stayed at home instead of going to Chicago. Al Capone does a lot of harm there, but at least they don't put him in the White House.'

'That's just name-calling. There's no connection at all between Mussolini and Al Capone.'

'Watson, we mustn't drag this out all afternoon, but let me just ask you if you've been to Rome lately.'

'Not in recent years; there's too much I want to see in other places. Last summer I went to Palermo because I wanted to visit the villas of Bagheria. And the Serpotta sculptures, of course. No other country — '

'The Italian contribution to all the arts is something we can agree to admire. But there are other things. You see some of the other things if you go to Rome, because that's where Mussolini puts on show his idea of the Fascist state.'

'Rome is the seat of political power. What better place to display the Fascist aspirations?'

'It's the aspirations themselves I detest. And if you haven't been to Rome lately, you won't have experienced *mussolinismo* at its height. The man's picture is on public buildings, it's framed in offices and shops, they carry it on huge banners in processions as they've been accustomed to doing with the portraits of saints. People who want to be seen as good Fascists even have his face on their personal letter-paper.'

'Isn't that just harmless identification with a symbolic force? If you go into a majority of English homes, you'll probably see a portrait of the King and Queen. People need these symbols.'

'I very much doubt that their natural need for symbols is as intense as Musso-lini's egotism would like it to be. Nothing is grandiose enough for him. If you haven't been to Rome you haven't see the Avenue of the Empire, but you should. It runs from the Colosseum to the Capitol. His object was to make an avenue through the centre of Rome wide enough for gigantic military parades. Since you go to Italy, Watson, since you delight in the art of architecture you find there, it ought to concern you that Mussolini knocked down eleven historic streets in the centre of Rome to make this vulgar avenue of self-aggrandizement. That meant demolishing fifteen ancient churches, not to speak of handsome houses and palaces. Not to speak, either, of the homes of ordinary humble citizens who were sent out to featureless apartment buildings on the outskirts of the city. Anything so that the big parade can go on, while the real problems of Italy are swept under the carpet.'

Watson parried with some flippant evasion, but it was obvious that Bax had annihilated him. And in any case it was time to go; the Common-Room servants were becoming frankly impatient, rattling cutlery and twitching at the tablecloth. Apart from my satisfaction at seeing Watson get a little of the drubbing he deserved, what interested me was to see, after all these years, another side of Bax. His ironic manner was in abeyance; he spoke quickly, fiercely, with emotion

88

even. His sympathy for the Italian people, smarting under the whips of Fascism, was memorable. I suddenly saw the central core of his humanity, and was moved by it to a new admiration for the man who had taught me my craft.

5

Katz and Nussbaum were sitting in the Rose and Crown at lunchtime on a bright October day. Everything was very beautiful outdoors. The brightly coloured leaves were falling, gently, in ones and twos, against the clear blue of an unclouded sky whose softness was in contrast, but not jarring contrast, to the slight chill that indicated the approach of winter's frost. Inside the pub, too, everything was agreeable. The old clock ticked on the wall, the amber beer glowed in the pint glasses, the motes of dust danced gently in the slanting sunbeams that came in through the window. A customer who was playing darts had laid down his half-smoked cigarette in a cheap metal ashtray and the smoke, ascending in a thick spiral, was a rich blue in the channelled sunlight. Only one detail was different from usual. Katz and Nussbaum each had copies of *The Times*. As a rule they shared a copy between them, passing it back and forth and commenting on anything in it that caught their attention. But this morning, for the first time I could remember, I saw them sitting opposite each other, at a small beer-stained table near the fireplace as usual, but each staring down at his own separate copy of the paper. They were reading about Chamberlain's visit to Munich, and the statement he had issued on his return to England.

'This passage is particularly rich in ironies, Hans,' Nussbaum was saying in his rich tragedian's voice, as I entered. 'Listen.' He shook any creases out of the paper, causing it to give a sharp crackle, and then uttered deeply and firmly the words of the poor deluded old politician: '*However we may sympathize with a small nation confronted by a big and powerful neighbour we cannot in all circumstances undertake to involve the whole British Empire in war simply on her account. If we have to fight it must be on larger issues than that.*' Nussbaum laid the paper down. 'One begins, I think, to read the man's mind in such a statement as that. He genuinely does not understand the issue. He thinks it is a quarrel between two foreign peasants over a duckpond. One is a big peasant, the other a small, but they both wear quaint costumes and they are a long way off.'

'Compare this similar passage,' Katz chimed in, searching with a blunt fore-finger down a column. 'Yes, is here.' He calls Czechoslovakia a small nation "far away" "of whom we know nothing". Katz spread out his hands in a gesture of stupefaction. '*Why* does this man know nothing of Czechoslovakia? Are there no maps in London? Does he not know where it is situated, what its frontiers are, why it is strategically important? And defensible?'

'And even,' Nussbaum took it up, 'if he were too stupid to look at a map, there is a Foreign Office. It is part of the British Government and it is staffed by men who have seen many maps. Some of these men employed in it are actually *in* this unknown country of Czechoslovakia. They even have telephones, connected if need be to London. He could have spoken to them . . .'

I sat down with a glass of beer and asked, really wanting to know, 'So you see this as a missed opportunity to stand up to Hitler?'

'A missed opportunity and worse,' Nussbaum said. 'The Czechs have no wish to be ruled by the German Nazis. They have seen them at close quarters. The

Czech army is well organized and would have fought. With the full support of Britain and France, the Germans could have been held for a long time. Perhaps even halted and turned back, perhaps not. But held. It would have been the first battle of the war. It was avoided because Chamberlain felt if he turned aside he could avoid war altogether. Not true. The war with Germany is here. It has started. Doubtless the Germans expected that they would have to fight over Czechoslovakia and destroy the country in the process. Now, they will destroy it without fighting. They will destroy its soul.'

'But perhaps,' I said, 'it's preferable for a country to survive physically even if its democratic institutions are extinguished. After all, if the people are still alive and the country's still there, the democratic institutions might be rekindled at some future . . . some future . . .' My voice trailed off. I wasn't much of a Bible reader, but my generation had a lot of the Bible shoved into us whether we wanted it or not, and the words suddenly came into my mind. *What shall it profit a man, if he gain the whole world, and lose his own soul?*

'My friend,' Katz said kindly (he always spoke kindly to me when he felt that my stupidity and ignorance stood in particular need of help), 'you are familiar perhaps with the name of Skoda?'

I wrinkled my brow and tried hard. Skoda? I was sure the name meant something, but what? It sounded like a kind of bread. I shook my head enquiringly.

'Skoda is enormous arms factory,' Katz said. 'Owned by Czechs, managed by Czechs, worked by Czechs. If there would have been fighting it would have been destroyed. So big a target! So important! It would have been bombed or shelled in first week. Or the Czechs would have destroyed it themselves. Now . . .' he shrugged. 'From this point it will be owned by Germans, managed by Germans, still worked by Czechs. And the Czechs will be slaves.'

I think that was the only time I walked out of the Rose and Crown without finishing my beer. It was good beer and I generally enjoyed it, but this time I was too preoccupied and upset. I left it standing there on the sunlit table in the pleasant quiet room and went back to my work – not that I was able to do any work when I got back: the sense of disaster was over everything. The brightness of the sun was stupidly artificial; it gave no warmth and even the light seemed false, meaningless, not able to reveal anything.

Katz and Nussbaum were of course perfectly right. The war had started, and the *Wehrmacht* had won the first battle without so much as squeezing a trigger. As for the Skoda factory, it was still churning out arms for the German war effort right into the spring of 1945. Not, of course, that I could have foreseen any such thing, that morning in the Rose and Crown. I think it would, on the contrary, have surprised me at that date to be told that the Germans would still be *needing* a supply of arms in 1945. I would have thought it unlikely, on the whole, that they would by then have had anyone left to fight.

Not everybody saw the writing on the wall, even after Munich. There was always the pacifist *chapelle*, while Bertrand Russell's recommendation, in 1938 and 1939, was that if German forces invaded England we should welcome them with cups of tea. Even people who did not descend to quite this depth of fatuity could still be remarkably self-deceiving; naturally, since the hard facts of the case were so bitterly unpalatable. Only a comparatively few people had the courage to face them; one, of course, being Winston Churchill, whose verdict on Munich was, 'The British Government have been offered a choice between war and shame. They have chosen shame, and they will get war.'

Watson, of course, was still keeping it up about Mussolini. During one of his lunchtime excursions into international affairs at about this time, he tried to heap credit on Il Duce's bullet head by pointing out that, according to widespread accounts, it was Mussolini who had persuaded Hitler to come down from his solitary peak of high resentment long enough to sit down at a conference table and accept the bound and gagged body of Czechoslovakia. 'That far-sighted statesman,' Watson called him. 'I refer of course to the generous-minded man of peace in Rome.' He brought out these phrases in a very distinct voice so that Bax, who was sitting several places away, could not fail to hear him. Bax, I was glad to see, having made his point once, did not trouble to make it again.

On that particular day I was glad to escape from the sound of his voice and get out of the Common Room. Winter was coming, in another few days the clocks would be put back and suddenly it would be dark at teatime, an annual ritual that always lowered my spirits. But we were still getting a gleam of that bright autumn sunshine which seems such an Oxford speciality, so I decided to take a turn round the garden. I headed that way, but as I passed through the quad that led into it I noticed an ancient, stooped figure close to the archway where one entered the second quad from the first. He was staring at something – entirely absorbed in what he was looking at, or in his own thoughts, or a mixture of both.

It was old Salterton. I went past slowly, without disturbing his train of thought. He was looking at the Episcopus War Memorial. Between 1914 and 1918 the College had lost enough men for their names to fill a sizeable panel, elegantly inscribed and headed by a suitable Latin inscription: dignity in death, or perhaps I should say dignity at last, after whatever tumult and agony their last moments of life had been passed in. The old man stood like a small column of weathered stone, leaning slightly forward towards the names on the wall. They would all be the names of men he had known. He was not elected President of the College until 1919, in time to greet the returning survivors and help them to mix in with the fresh-faced schoolboys among whom they would sit at table and in the lecture room, help them if possible to forget their recent wounds and their suppurating memories. And now – it was so easy to read his thoughts – they were asking him to tell them how it could possibly have come about that, only twenty years later, the current generation of young men were going to have to do what they had done.

Old Salterton had been at Episcopus since Victoria was on the throne. When he first got his Fellowship, wars were things that happened a long way away and were attended to by the Army and Navy. The last time England had been involved in a war so large-scale and hard-fought as to threaten her being overwhelmed by a foreign power had been the struggle with Napoleon, and even in Salterton's young days – ancient as he was – that was already so far back that it had faded almost into a folk memory.

I halted. Something about the spectacle of the good old man sunk in his grieving thoughts had stopped my feet in their tracks. He looked at me; it took him a moment to realize that I was a face from 1938 and not from 1918. Then he said, 'Ah, Leonard.'

I inclined my head in a vestigial bow, unable to find suitable words.

'I knew all these men,' Salterton said, indicating the memorial with a gesture. 'Many were my pupils. I was Dean of the College in the year when that . . . conflict began. Dean! In charge of discipline!' He was silent, then added, 'These men were going to a very different discipline, Leonard, were they not?'

I assented, standing in silence in the thin autumn sunlight. There still seemed

92

to be nothing I could say in answer. After a moment he nodded slowly several times and began to walk away towards the Lodgings.

I walked round the garden, but I couldn't settle my mind on anything. I had to start teaching at five o'clock, but it was only two now, and all at once I decided to go down to Oseney Town and see what was happening to life at the Bargeman's Arms.

When I got there the lunchtime session had just ended, and normally my mother would have been tidying up in the back. Instead, she was in the kitchen. What was more, my father was with her, and so was another man, whom I recognized to be Peake, of the *cénacle*. It took me a moment to recognize Peake because he looked different: he was wearing an armband that said 'A.R.P.' and he had a tin hat slung round his neck so that it dangled awkwardly down behind, bumping against his shoulder-blades. He was evidently unwilling to take it off, and hang it up, because of a belief that as long as he was wearing it he had authority; he had the Government behind him.

Peake was here for a purpose. The Government had given instructions that the entire population – men, women, children, even babies – were to be issued with gas-masks (civilian issue), and that these masks were to be distributed by Air Raid Wardens, who were also charged with making sure that everyone got the correct size and that they fitted properly.

Peake had attended to my father and now he was attending to my mother. She was sitting on a kitchen chair, pale and drawn, while he stood behind her like a hairdresser. My father had removed his mask and was eyeing it with distaste.

'Think we'll be needing these things, Peter?' he asked me.

'Highly unlikely,' I said. 'Issuing them's quite a good piece of psychology, but I don't see the Germans ever actually bothering. Gas isn't a very effective weapon; it can be blown the wrong way by any change of wind and it doesn't destroy buildings or supplies. Anybody getting into an aeroplane in Germany and flying it all the way to England isn't going to be bothered to carry anything as heavy and doubtfully useful as cylinders of gas. It'll be high explosives they drop on us.'

'That's what I think myself,' he said, 'but I'm glad you support me. Some of the customers in here have been expecting a gas attack every night since before old Chamberlain took his gamp over to Munich.'

'That's because they've been conditioned to expect it,' I said. For years the pacifist movement, whose aim was to whip up fear and revulsion against war, had been issuing a torrent of pamphlets about the horrors of poison gas and how impossible it was to defend civilians against it.

My mother took off her mask and exhaled vigorously. 'I was holding my breath,' she said. 'Is it all right? Have you finished now, Mr Peake?'

'No, no, Mrs Leonard. If you've been holding your breath you been doin' it wrong, moy duck. That's not the idea at all. You 'as to *breathe*.'

'I can't breathe with that thing on. It's like wet plaster sticking all round the sides of my face.'

'Come on, Katie,' my father said. 'Do what the man says, take a few breaths or else we'll never get this over with.'

'Have you got one, Peter?' she asked me.

'Everybody has. It's the law,' Peake said authoritatively. 'You been fitted in the street you lives in, I durst say,' he appealed to me.

'Yes,' I said to shut him up, although they hadn't come round to us yet in

Marston. 'It is a bit like wet plaster, Mum. But you can just about breathe if you have to.'

She allowed her face to be enclosed once more and I stood looking on. There were two types of civilian gas-masks. People who were taking any kind of active responsibility – Air Raid Wardens, auxiliary firemen, special constables – had a slightly more elaborate kind with two goggle-holes, like a diver's helmet. The basic issue, for people whose lives didn't matter quite so much, was equine in shape except that instead of a horse's moist, sensitive nose, they had a circular filter not unlike a tea-strainer, but with radial buttressing and a shiny black rim, and the eyes looked out through a one-piece visor. If you inhaled determinedly you could draw in enough air through the filter to support life, though since the filter also admitted cigarette smoke, the presumption was that a subtle enough gas would still reach your lungs. If you blew out vigorously enough, the breath forced itself through the clinging rubber at your jowls and made a noise like a wet fart. In the next few weeks, the entire schoolboy population of England became adept at producing this noise.

My mother now breathed vigorously in and out, under Peake's official scrutiny, about a dozen times. Satisfied, he stepped back and said, 'That's fine, Mrs Leonard, now let me see you take it off.' She took it off and he said, 'Not so bad after all, is it, moy duck?'

My mother shook her head from side to side as if to clear it of fumes or perhaps of persistent and unwelcome thoughts. Her eyes travelled from face to face : she looked at Peake, at my father, at me.

'I tell you one thing, Fred Peake,' she said. 'It's all men's nonsense, this is. Men! Not women! It's the men that spend their time inventing wicked devilish things like poison gas to burn people's lungs out. People they've never even set eyes on.'

'All right, Katie,' said my father soothingly.

'Don't all right me, Jack. Take notice of what I say. If the women ran the world there'd be no wars. Women respect life. They bring it into the world, with pain and trouble and suffering. They're not interested in fighting and killing people. War's a man's game.'

Silence followed her words. She got up and went out through the door that led to the stairs. We heard her go up to the bedroom and I imagined her sitting down on her and Dad's bed, staring in front of her, grappling with the thoughts that possessed her, picturing a world run by women.

Peake was packing up his stock of respirators, ready to move on along the street. My father invited him to come into the bar and have one for the road, though it was after closing time.

'Had any trouble getting these things fitted, Fred?' my father asked Peake.

'The only one as I 'ad trouble with,' he said, wiping his mouth with the back of his hand, 'was Job Trundle. An' even then you couldn't rightly call it trouble. Didn't make no fuss nor nothin' like that. Just refused, point-blank refused. I never got no further than the front doorstep. "You ain't comin' near me with that thing," 'e says, "an' that's all about it." "But if there's a gas attack, Job?" I says, reasoning with him like. "Don't waste my time with that there rubbish," 'e says. "If there's a gas attack an' it starts gettin' to my lungs, I'll walk into the river till my 'at floats," 'e says. "I'd rather choke on good clean river water than on some bleedin' gas dropped on me by a lot o' furriners," 'e says.'

We chuckled appreciatively. In my case, the chuckle was a tribute. What strength old age gives a man, I thought. Walk into the river? Of course he would.

I could see his body rolling there, moving downstream, fetching up against Oseney Lock and lying there with a triumphant smile on its dead face. He would have had what, in his last years, he liked best of all: the last word.

It was time for me to go back to my work. Trying to teach young men to understand history. To understand *what*?

November 1938 wore on, wearily. One sodden Sunday afternoon, with yellow leaves bunched in the gutters and rain-clouds chasing each other across the sky, I got out my bicycle and rode from Marston to Horspath to visit my brother Brian and his wife: no great distance, but not a trip I would normally have made on a drenching afternoon, particularly with the likelihood that darkness would fall before I got back.

On the other hand, Heather had received a royal command to take Michael over to tea at Jasmine Farm, and while I normally would have felt in duty bound to go, at this moment in history, with so much menace lurking in the air, I just couldn't sit with a cup and saucer in my hand and a plate balanced on my knees and go through the ritual of empty politeness that always seemed to be called for with Mrs Burrell. The old man, after greeting us, always had something to attend to on the farm and thankfully disappeared, leaving us in a room that always seemed to become stifling, so that one fought for enough oxygen to survive in: it was a physical effect of the sheer tension produced by our mutual hostility. Even after five years of being married to her daughter I hadn't even settled on a name that I could comfortably address her by. 'Mrs Burrell' sounded ridiculously stilted, but it was how I instinctively thought of her. Her actual first name, 'Alicia', simply froze on my lips. She, I noticed, would refer to me in the third person as 'Peter', but when compelled to address me directly she always just called me 'You'.

So I had told Heather frankly that this time I just didn't feel up to it. And since I wanted to put my Sunday afternoon to some use, not just loaf about at home, and I had had enough of College lately, I decided to cycle over and visit Brian and Primrose. They did occasionally go down to the Bargeman's for a ritual Sunday dinner, but I knew they were not going today. They would be at home. A brotherly visit, a cup of tea, a sense of virtue. I wheeled out the bicycle.

In the event, the visit was disappointing. It was not that I felt unwelcome; it was rather that Brian seemed incapable of enough animation to welcome anything or anybody. Looking at him as he sat beside the fire and gazed at the smoke disappearing up the chimney, it was difficult to imagine that he was the same person whom I had so often seen fired by enthusiasm and, when M.G. had pulled off some great master-stroke, flooded with joy. He was pleasant enough, but low-temperature, uninvolved.

Primrose, for her part, seemed much the same as ever, though what it amounted to for Primrose to be 'the same' was far from clear to me. The same as what? Who exactly was Primrose Ravenscroft, now dubbed by law Primrose Leonard, but so obviously unaltered? Where was the central citadel of her being, and what would it be like if one ever got to it? Did Brian ever get to it?

Their house was neat and rather bare, arranged for convenience rather than for character. Drinking my tea, I looked round. They had had the place for long enough to leave their imprint on it, and yet they hadn't. One thing was very clear to me, and it was a negative. Most people who have been passionately involved in a sport accumulate *bric-à-brac* to do with that sport – silver cups and trophies, photographs of people they were associated with or worshipped from afar. Brian's did not. No photographs, no souvenirs, no bulky album of press cuttings lying on a small table near the fireplace, nothing . . . it was as if Brian had scooped out the inside of his being and thrown it away. But was that possible? Could one scoop out that inside and go on living? But then – pushing it one stage further – was living what Brian was doing now?

I asked Primrose about her brother, Doug. Was his motor-cycle racing programme as full as ever?

'Fuller, if anything,' she replied laconically. 'He's gone into sidecar racing now. That's why he had a poor season last year.'

'Oh? Did he have a poor season last year? I'm sorry, I wasn't up with the — '

'There's no reason why you should be, don't worry. But he did have a poor season, didn't he, Brian?'

'Only to be expected,' said Brian indifferently.

'Yes, the riding technique's completely different, and then he had to try different passengers until he got one who brought out the best in him.'

'Oh.' I had a vague memory of seeing newsreel pictures of sidecar racing. The passenger crouched on a thing like a tea-tray with handles all round it and had to lean out from it at crazy angles on the corners. It looked like a sport for suicidal lunatics.

'I'd have passengered with him myself,' Primrose said, 'but I'm not heavy enough.'

Well, thank God for that, I thought, contemplating a vision of her bouncing around on one of those mad tea-trays, at ninety miles an hour.

'I can't get Brian to take an interest in it,' Primrose said, glancing over at him. 'He doesn't even come to watch.'

Perhaps that was her motive, trying to get Brian involved, to bring him back to life with *something*. But Brian didn't look up from the fireplace, he merely said, 'I'm out of racing now.'

'Well, you still make sports cars, don't you, Brian?' I asked.

'Toys,' he said. 'Toys for lads to play with. Designed to look faster than they are. No real poke in them. When you've worked on race-bred cars . . .' he gestured and fell silent.

I finished my tea and hoped it would soon be legitimate to escape. This seemed a house of the dead. But no, damn it, Brian was my *brother*. There must be something we could talk about. I tried several topics, but they guttered out for want of oxygen. Yes, he had seen Mother and Dad lately. Yes, they seemed all right. His own plans? Well, a war was coming: he agreed with me about that.

'Cowley'll be on war production,' he said. 'Tank engines and all that. So will Abingdon. I've seen the draft plans.'

'Will you still be working with Cecil Kimber?' I asked.

He looked at me with a kind of leaden curiosity, rather as an alligator in a vivarium might look at a passing human being. 'Cecil Kimber? Why d'you ask me about him?'

I had, in fact, merely been making conversation. Cecil Kimber's name had just popped into my mind. 'Well, I just remembered . . . how you always admired him.'

'I still do admire him.'

'And you'll still be working with him?'

There was a short silence and then Brian said, 'Nobody works with Cecil Kimber – because Cecil Kimber's been stopped from working.'

'Well, I see what you mean, but — '

'Making the kind of cars we used to make was work. Making toys isn't work. It's pouring your bloody life down the drain, that's what it is. Down the bloody drain!'

'Oh,' I said. Suddenly I was the younger brother again, trying to meddle in things too serious, too weighty, too tragic for me. 'I'm . . . sorry to hear that, naturally. But – well, I see it's getting dark and I've no rear light. Better be getting back.'

'Come and see us again,' Primrose said.

'Yes. Oh, yes. I will. Thanks for the tea.'

The ring road round Oxford had not been built in those days, though a beginning had been made, and to get back to Marston from Horspath I had to go a certain distance into Headington before turning west. So it happened that, hardly had I turned into a bleak street of terraced houses when I saw, a short way ahead, a determined-looking little figure, well wrapped up in a greatcoat, slapping up a poster on a vacant patch of brick wall.

I pedalled closer. The figure was Geraldine. The poster read: A VOTE FOR HOGG IS A VOTE FOR HITLER.

'What are you doing, Geraldine?' I asked.

She turned abruptly, peering, trying to make out through the rain-swept November dusk who had accosted her. When she recognized me she said shortly, 'Putting this poster up.'

'Well, I can see that.'

'I've got six more to do and then I've finished. I've been at it all afternoon. My patch was all the way from the Plain, right along St Clement's and up the hill as far as here.'

'That's a lot for one person. How many posters did you start out with?'

'About fifty. There aren't all that many spaces. And sometimes if people see you putting posters on their garden fence, they come out and scream at you.'

'Sounds tough.'

'You can help me with the last few, now you're here.'

It seemed churlish to refuse, though the conventional side of my nature objected that sticking posters was not the kind of activity suited to a Fellow of Episcopus. Addressing a political meeting, yes. Bill-sticking, no. Still, it was better than chalking up slogans.

'I suppose you think I'm wasting my time,' Geraldine said.

'Why d'you suppose that?'

'Because I can read your thoughts. I've always been able to.'

H'm, I thought. Aloud, I said, 'I don't think you'll stop Hogg from getting in.'

'In that case it's a protest vote, which surely has some value.'

'Under ordinary circumstances, yes. But today? What difference can it really make?'

There had been a lull in the rain, but now it began again. Geraldine stirred vigorously at her pot of flour paste. 'I think there's just enough left, doesn't matter if it gets diluted a bit. But we ought to get the posters up before they get sodden. What did you say? What difference will it make?'

'Yes, that's what I said.'

'Well, none, I suppose, but any decent person ought to support Lindsay, even if it's only a protest vote.'

'Why? Because he's Left?'

'Yes, you know all about it. He's a member of the Labour Party, but he's standing as an Independent for strategic reasons, so that Liberals and Labour people can sink their differences and get behind him.'

'But you aren't Liberal or Labour, Geraldine, you're a Communist.'

'I know I am, for God's sake, but all the Left-wing parties are combining against the appeasers.'

'I've heard about that too. It's called the Popular Front.'

'Yes, and about time too.'

'Look here, Geraldine, are you supporting Lindsay because you believe he's right or because the Party has told you to?'

'Both reasons. The Party's told me to *and* he's right.'

'But he's a Labour Party member, and their record in resisting Fascism has been no better than anyone else's.'

'At least he's not an appeaser. Here, you do this one.'

'No, he's not an appeaser, but on the other hand he's not a fighter. He knows as well as you and I do that Hitler's going to attack England and France some time in the next few months anyway. There's no chance that if we stand up to Hitler, he'll back down. Things have gone too far for that.'

'So? That still makes Lindsay right and Hogg wrong.'

'Empirically, Hogg may be right, for the simple reason that during the pacifist years we carried disarmament to such a point that we're simply not ready to fight. Selling Czechoslovakia to be turned into dog meat does at least give us a few months to introduce conscription and make some guns and dig air-raid shelters in the London parks.'

'Try saying that at a political meeting.'

'Precisely, and that's why Hogg's in a stronger position than Lindsay and why Hogg will get in. Look, there'll be war within the next two years anyway.'

'Put this up. It's the last one.'

'Where?'

'Over here.'

'All right, let's have it. Right. There'll be war within the next two years whether we appease Hitler or not. But the appeasers at Munich have bought us a little time. And they'll succeed at the polls because they can get the pacifist vote, which is still very strong in this country. Nobody can make a stand against appeasement who isn't prepared, if necessary, to go to war. So if Lindsay's asked that question at any of his meetings – *Are you prepared to see this country go to war?* – he has to hedge his answers. And every time he hedges he loses votes. Hogg's clever enough to see his advantage and he'll use it for all he's worth, that's why he'll get in.'

'Yes, he'll get in,' Geraldine said. The capacious basket at the rear of her bicycle was empty now, except for the brush and the cleaned-out can of paste that was ready to be dropped into a litter-bin. Her afternoon's work was over. 'He'll get in, but I'm still glad I've put up a few posters. A protest vote does count for something, you know.'

'And if, a couple of years from now, we're living under Nazi rule, will you still protest then?'

'I don't know,' she said, turning up her coat collar in preparation for cycling away through the rain. 'One never does know that kind of thing till the time comes, does one?'

Now the rain was coming down more heavily than ever. On a really wet day in Oxford one comes to feel that being a land animal is a mistake, that it would make more sense to be, if not a fish, at least an amphibian, spending at least the early part of one's life under water, breathing through gills and retaining webbed feet later. Geraldine was completely soaked. Probably, with that Party discipline they always rubbed into people, she welcomed it as an extra ordeal to be undertaken, an extra little service she could do for the Cause. I felt no such highminded doggedness. The rain had got down inside the neck of my mackintosh and soaked my shirt collar, so that I felt uncomfortably clammy. My hat, not waterproof, lay on my head like a sodden lump of cloth fished out of a ditch. My mackintosh itself, which was getting old and thin, clung to my body like wet paper. But I had not been out in the weather for anything like as long as she had: standing there on the pavement, she looked thin and frail. I felt a surge of protectiveness.

'Geraldine,' I said, 'what are you going to do now?'

'Go home.'

'And have a hot bath, I hope.'

She shook her head. 'There won't be any hot water. Sunday afternoon's family bath-time.'

'What family?'

'The one my flat is in the home of.'

'Well, I'm going to see you home.'

'To make sure I don't get lost, you mean?'

'I know it's not rational,' I said, 'but I can't just see you pedal off by yourself in this rain. You're soaked through and I'm sure you're cold, and you're going back to somewhere where you can't have a bath, and I'm damn' sure when you get there you won't be bothered to change out of your wet clothes and make yourself a hot drink.'

'I shan't have a hot drink. I shall sit by the gas-fire and have some wine. I've got some Spanish wine that's produced by a commune; it's from one of those areas where Socialists have had a chance to restructure society and the vineyards have been given back to the peasants who've worked in them for generations.'

'So it's correct to drink it. I'm glad to hear it. But I'm still going to see you home.'

'You can come in if you like, and have some wine, and see for yourself that I sit by the gas-fire. If you're so concerned about me.'

'Yes, by God, I am. It's time you stopped punishing yourself for coming from the property-owning classes.'

'And it's time you started to punish yourself for having gone over to join them.'

'Unfair!' I shouted through the blurring rain.

'I'm too wet to be fair,' her voice came back to me as she swung on to her bicycle, just as she used to after those History Discussion Club meetings, when I could never get her to linger and talk because the St Hilda's dons watched the entrance hall and pounced on any girl who was a few minutes late. Duty and discipline, duty and discipline! How her life had been ruled by them!

I pedalled after her and soon we were whizzing dangerously down Headington Hill. The last of the fallen leaves were still sticking to the soaked road surface and as my wheels slipped sideways under me for a fraction of a second, it flashed into my panic-stricken mind that I could easily get killed there and then, and know nothing about the approaching European blood-bath. Then the tyres gripped the road again, my danger was past and only Europe's remained.

Geraldine lived in a two-room flat above a little shop selling groceries and general provisions about half-way along St Clement's on the right-hand side as you came down into town. It was the kind of place that is called a flat only out

99

of politeness: she had a small sitting room facing the street and an even smaller bedroom at the back of the house, and shared kitchen and bathroom with the grocer and his wife and their numerous progeny. It was the sort of place that in those days the younger and less conformist members of the intelligentsia always seemed to live in. The staircase smelt faintly but decisively of gas-stoves and cats, the geyser in the bathroom made a terrifying noise, and the sash windows didn't fit their frames properly so the rooms were always draughty. But being 'less conformist' in that period meant being Left, and if you were Left you were supposed to be indifferent to your surroundings. Besides, the place was cheap. And, the most solid advantage of all, she could have Ruskin College men, whose background was industrial poverty, to visit her and sit around drinking instant coffee (Camp Coffee, in those days, out of a dark sticky bottle) and discussing class issues and the future of Socialism, and feeling at ease. If she had had a flat in North Oxford, even the tiniest flat under the rafters in one of those laughably dignified Victorian houses, they would not have visited her after the first time.

She now bent and lit the gas-fire, invited me to sit down and poured out two glasses of Spanish white wine, but instead of sitting down herself she stood in front of the popping and roaring gas-fire, glass in one hand, the other thrust stiffly into the pocket of her knitted cardigan. Without tasting her wine she stood there, scowling.

'What's the matter, Geraldine?' I asked, looking up from my low, collapsed armchair, willing her to come down and relax. 'You're very tense about something.'

'Oh, problems,' she said shortly.

Her tone sounded dismissive, but I knew that if she had really not wanted to talk she wouldn't have invited me to come up. I tried again.

'The state of the world is enough to be a problem to all of us,' I said. 'But I can't help remembering that Samuel Johnson said no one ever ate a spoonful of pudding the less because of the public situation.'

'I don't eat pudding anyway.'

'You would if you went to Sunday dinner in the home of a Yorkshire miner, and they offered you Yorkshire pudding. You'd force yourself to show solidarity.'

'Don't always mock. Besides, Yorkshire pudding's outside class, like bacon and eggs. My mother's a totally blinkered member of the smuggest and most reactionary middle class, but she makes beautiful Yorkshire pudding, as good as any miner's wife.'

'Better not let them hear you say that at Ruskin.'

'Oh, I'd be allowed to say things like that at Ruskin. I'm a token figure – our Middle Class Girl, our Young Lady Intellectual who never had to scrub floors or work at a loom. They're positively glutinous with tolerance. It's like a posh American prep school with one Negro student. They like being nice to me as long as there's only one of me because it proves they're liberal and open-minded.'

'All right, I get your point. During working hours I can see it might be trying. But I don't think it's what's making you tense and restless now.'

She gave me a penetrating look. 'You sound like a doctor. Some kind of analyst. *I don't think that's what's making you tense.*' She put her glass down, sat in a chair and set her finger-tips together in a parody of calm, detached reflectiveness. 'As if you were trying to help me from a position of superior wisdom.'

'God forbid!'

'I mean, Peter,' she said seriously, 'do you mean you're *not* tense and restless?'

'Is that what I seem to you?'

'No, no.' Her tone really was dismissive now. 'Don't play that rhetorical trick on me, answering a question with a question; it's a get-out.'

'I'm not trying to get out of anything. Please go on.'

'All right, granted – freely granted – that all of us live our lives in accordance with what's happening out there – ' her hand swept nervously in a half-circle – 'so that if you see signs of strain and weariness in someone, it's their personal life that's causing it, would you say that you always seem calm and that your personal problems have found a solution?'

'My God, no!' I meant my voice to be calm, but the words came out in a kind of yelp.

Geraldine was back on her feet now, her hands on her hips, looking down at me as if she had brought me to her flat to accuse me, to bring me to a sense of my own falsity. 'Most of our personal problems are sexual,' she said. 'If we weren't in our relatively favoured social class and in our – for the moment – relatively favoured area of the world, they might not be. They'd be more likely to concern food and shelter, and then perhaps finding some employment that gave us self-respect. But you and I, Peter, have those already.'

I nodded.

'Our problems usually concern the choice of mates therefore, in one way or another. And to enter into a relationship like that is a matter of making a decision . . .'

By now I was certain she had brought me there to tell me something. But she had stopped now as if not knowing how to find the next words. This wouldn't do. I had to give her a gentle push to keep her moving.

'What you say is true, Geraldine,' I said. 'And of course these decisions one makes, these big decisions that look so final and uncompromising, are very often just desperate attempts to smother one's personal problems. So talk, Geraldine. For God's sake, talk. We've all got things we need to express to people we trust. I'm listening.'

The sullen, irresolute look that had come into her face dissolved. This was it, she was going to speak, here came the words. I was attending to her so closely that I saw and heard her draw in her breath to begin. Then there was a tap-tap at the door, not loud, not heavy, but urgent, tap-tap, then a very short wait, then tap-tap.

Geraldine let out her breath again in a long exhalation. She went to the door and opened it. Craning, I looked past her: Harry Goodenough stood there. He was wet and his shock of hair glistened with heavy drops like a rough-coated dog's. He had on a soaked overcoat of check tweed. His face was tense and guilty.

'Geraldine,' he said.

'Harry, how did you manage to get up here? Wasn't the street door locked?'

'It was when I got to it, but one of the children came out just as I was lifting up my hand to ring the bell.'

'Quite a coincidence.'

'Not so much of one,' he said. 'I stood on the doorstep for about five minutes trying to get up the nerve to ring your doorbell.'

'Well,' she said, 'I'm glad you realize I've *got* a doorbell.'

'Of course I do, and I generally ring it, don't I? But I was nervous this time because you'd told me not to come round this evening.'

'Well, now you have you'd better come in for a moment.'

101

Harry Goodenough came into the room, dropping pools of rain on the carpet, and said, 'Hello, Peter,' in a dull, unsurprised voice.

I was about to say something about how I came to be sitting beside Geraldine's gas-fire, drinking her awful Spanish wine, when he had (it seemed) been told to keep away, but Geraldine took charge of the conversation.

'Harry, I did tell you I wanted to be alone this evening. Peter met me in the street and saw me to the door. I asked him in for a drink. But I'm still not entertaining guests.'

'Seeing me isn't entertaining,' he said with a kind of defiance, like a juvenile delinquent.

'You're damn' right it isn't. It's depressing. And you really must leave me some time to myself. I told you I was working this evening.'

'What's the work? I'll do it for you.'

'You can't do it for me, you ass, I'm preparing a lecture for Ruskin.'

'Well, that's no problem,' he said eagerly. 'Spend this evening talking to me, and in the morning ring up and tell them you're not well but they'll get a lecture from a brilliant colleague of yours, and I'll go instead.'

'Oh, Harry, why must you be so *impossible*? You don't know anything about the subject.'

'I'll think of a subject – I'll talk about Shakespeare and the Working Classes. That'll interest them.'

'Harry, I'm getting sick of your nonsense. The lecture isn't anything to do with Shakespeare; it's part of a course on Karl Marx.'

What else? I thought.

'The lecture's called, "The failure of the revolutions of 1848 and Marx's response to that failure in *Wage-Labour and Capital*." '

'Well, it's true I couldn't give a lecture exactly on that, but what I'd say to them would amount to the same thing. I'd just give them a new perspective.'

Geraldine's face set hard. 'No.'

'But what I wanted to say to you this evening was important.'

I got up. 'It's good to see you, Harry. Let's have a drink some time. And Geraldine, thanks for the wine and don't be too disappointed when Hogg gets in. I'm expected for family supper at home. I admit I'm a slave to domesticity, but everyone's a slave to something, as I'm sure Marx will affirm.'

Nobody tried to stop me going. As I went downstairs I heard shrilling and splashing from the bathroom, and a voice shouted. 'Move over, April, I'm right under the 'ot tap!'

It was pitch-dark now, and as the big raindrops came slanting down they looked golden in the lamplight. I found my wet bicycle, mounted the wet saddle and pedalled through the wet streets to my wet house. Would the world ever be warm and sunny? What would that feel like?

More urgently, what was going on in the mind of Harry Goodenough? It was impossible to mistake the hungry, beseeching quality of his appeal to Geraldine. I hadn't known she meant so much to him. Perhaps she never had till recently. I could remember the first stirrings of his excitement about her, when they were both undergraduates and he was directing her in a Shakespeare comedy, and her performance had suddenly brought home to him how sparky and attractive she was. But I thought all that had faded out of his life, after he had once tried and drawn a blank with her. Well, it must have revived. But her severity and exasperation just now hadn't seemed to hold out much promise for him. Poor Harry. I hated to think of him suffering. Also I couldn't see why, objectively, he shouldn't be a perfectly suitable match for Geraldine. They did share one quality: selfless devotion. And although they were devoted to different ideals, at least that gave them a common psychology. It was not like an idealistic person falling in love with someone who was completely selfish and frivolous.

Thoughts of this kind were still in my mind while I helped Heather to fold up some sheets she'd been ironing, read Mike *The Story of a Fierce Bad Rabbit*, then bathed him (keeping him away from the hot tap) and finally sat down to supper.

When Heather had been folding the sheets I had, as I so often did, noticed her hands: beautiful and womanly, but at the same time broad, strong, totally capable hands. It occurred to me now, how totally different from one another were the two women who had been closest to me in my life, and how the differences were summed up in their hands. Heather's were those of a country girl. Geraldine's – well, to think of Geraldine from now on would be to think of her quick, intelligent little hands at the end of her restless arms, wielding the paste-brush, slapping up that poster: A VOTE FOR HOGG IS A VOTE FOR HITLER. Women, and how they lived through their hands! If I were a poet like Lamont I would take it for a subject. But then, any poem written by me would be very different from one written by Lamont. Women and their hands! Paste-pots and politics, horsehair and harness. It was a good thing I wasn't a poet.

Hunched over my typewriter, scowling at the keyboard, I sat writing a letter to the editor of the paper Hunt worked for.

Sir, I wrote. I had to start like that instead of 'You lying scum,' which is how he should have been addressed.

Some years ago I read a report in your paper of a visit to Oxford in which the writer gave his views on the attitude of Oxford students towards the defence of our country, referring particularly to the much-discussed 'King and Country' motion at the Union in 1933. He reported that he had found the undergraduates he spoke to, and one solitary don whom he visited, totally indifferent to the question of national defence.

I did not add that Hunt's article was obviously no more than a piece regurgitating the paper's line, and that his claim to have visited Oxford was a transparent lie. One could hardly expect a paper like that to publish the truth about itself. Instead, I ploughed on:

Remembering this article, which was featured prominently, I naturally turned to your paper for some mention of a debate which took place last week at that same Oxford Union.

Like hell I did. Of course I'd known there'd be no mention of the debate.

Imagine my surprise, then, on finding that neither on the following morning nor on any subsequent day was there any mention of this recent debate. The Oxford Union has not changed. It still reflects undergraduate opinion as much as it did in 1933. (That is, patchily, but interestingly.) Why then, no mention? The motion carried in 1933 was, as everyone knows, that 'This house will never again fight for King and Country'. The conclusion in 1938 was the exact opposite. The motion before the House was whether the House did or did not approve of the way Mr Chamberlain, at Munich, had acceded to Herr Hitler's relentless demands. The principal speaker on the anti-Chamberlain side was Mr Christopher Mayhew. He denounced the Government's policy of appeasement, and the House voted with him.

In other words, sir, the young men at Oxford, who after all represent the generation which will have to do the fighting if and when war comes, have just declared, through their principal debating society, that, having had a few more years to think over the alternatives, they *are* now prepared to 'fight for King and Country'. Why, in that case. was this year's debate ignored by your paper? If the opinions of a set of students about foreign policy and war and peace were worthy of your attention in 1933, why are they not worthy of it now, in 1938?

Could it be that news from Oxford is never printed in papers like yours unless it is of a kind that can be used to stir up popular dislike of Oxford?

The 1933 motion, though it was popular with the pacifist lobby, did the University a lot of harm among the population in general. If, now, the Oxford young are in a mood to show courage and determination, and if their mood were to become widely known in the country at large, a lot of that harm could be undone. I hope I am wrong, Sir, in my suspicion that there are people on your Editorial Board who don't want to see it undone. Please put me right if you can.

Yours, etc.,

After I had written this I sat back and read it. I knew, of course, that the letter had about the same chance of being published in Hunt's paper as an arthritic toad has of winning the Grand National. But to have got the words down on paper was one of those tiny symbolic actions that one performs not because they are going to make the slightest difference but simply as an expression of one's feelings. Like putting your tongue out at the portrait of a person you hate.

I knew that as soon as it got to the office the letter would be thrown in the waste-paper basket, but I wanted *someone* to read it, however low down in the chain of command. So, to make sure that some kind of record of its existence remained, I had made a copy, and that meant carbon paper, which I never got the knack of putting in the correct way round, which usually meant – as in this case – that I began by duplicating the letter on the back of the top copy, so I had to do the whole job again. I also got my fingers grubby, again as usual. But even these annoyances did not dim the sense of relief I felt at having written the letter. I hadn't affected anything, but I had at least put out my tongue.

Hogg was elected. It made no difference. That winter of 1938–39 was sheer hallucination. I remember nothing about it, and the only thing I recall from the spring that followed is a conversation I had with Bax during one of the last days of the Michaelmas term. He came up to me as I was leaving the library bowed down with books, and asked me to go and see him in his rooms that evening if I possibly could. He wanted to discuss practicalities, he said. 'Do come,' he added, 'even if it's not very convenient. I don't think it'll wait.'

I went in to see him about nine o'clock that evening. He had recently moved to new rooms, better than the old – more elegant, less poky. They were reached by a staircase within the archway between the first quad and the second; the second quad had fewer rooms and they were more select: of the dons, only the senior and bachelor ones, who made the College their life-long home, lived there.

Bax's moving to the passageway – poised, as it were, to be the next in one of the best sets of rooms – had been a mark of his advancing seniority and status. Not that it seemed to have put him in a cheerful mood – he was obviously oppressed and worried. He was sitting at his desk, not by the fire, looking grave and moving papers about. He had had a visit, he said, from a man who worked in Berlin as a correspondent for Reuters: an Episcopus man, one of his own former pupils, someone whose judgement he trusted. (Why not, I thought, if he helped to form it?) This man was convinced war was coming in the summer of 1939, or the autumn at the latest. His sources were reliable, his information was confidential, and unless Hitler succumbed to a sudden attack of sanity the course was now set.

'The question is,' Bax said, looking at me through his round, scrutinizing lenses, 'what do people like you and me do about it?'

I thought for a moment. 'It depends, I suppose, on how long the country holds out. As long as it does, we ought to join in and do what we can to keep the Germans at bay. And if they're too much for us, and the country's defeated, we must see what we can do to help the population to survive that defeat.'

'Or to fight on unofficially,' he said, so quietly that I scarcely heard him.

'Or to fight on unofficially, if there's any kind of resistance movement that looks half-way convincing.'

'Oh, there'll be that,' Bax said. 'There'll be that. In fact . . . from what I've heard, it's being set up already.'

We were both silent, pondering the implications of this, but not for long. Bax sat up briskly in his chair and said, 'Meanwhile, we must deal in such certainties as we can muster.'

'Agreed.'

'Speculation, as I spent enough time trying to teach you, is usually an unfruitful use of one's mental energies.'

'Agreed.'

'What the mind needs to work on is certainties.'

'Or, failing that, probabilities.'

'Just so,' Bax said. 'Now, you, I think, are twenty-six years old.'

'Twenty-seven next June.'

'Right. The chances are that you'll be twenty-seven when this thing actually starts. A borderline age, the sort of age at which there's probably a certain amount of room for personal choice. If, at twenty-seven, you positively *want* to get into the war as a fighting soldier, no doubt it'll be easy for you to do so. If, on the other hand, you feel you could be more useful behind a desk, using your trained mind to overcome some of the very difficult administrative problems the war is bound to throw up, you can probably do that too.'

'Won't it be purely a mechanical process? Up to a certain age, into the Army. Over that age, into an office.'

'Not by any means necessarily. I don't think that's how they'll approach it this time – "they" being our masters in Whitehall.'

'No? You're in their confidence?'

I did not mean the question sarcastically, nor did Bax so take it. 'Up to a point. I have a few contacts. One can't be an Oxford don for as long as I have without knowing a fair number of people who've gone on to work in government.'

'And what do they say?'

'Well, one thing's pretty clear. Last time we fought the Germans, there was a terrific slaughter of young dons. Chaps who'd got through everything with flying colours and been elected to Research Fellowships, or started on teaching ones like you, and in most cases were beginning to build up pretty effective structures of investigation and ideas generally, were just sent over in wagon-loads to the trenches and were killed within a few weeks. Clearly it must have struck somebody as a waste of resources, so this time they're going to be more careful. Most men in academic posts, certainly over about twenty-five, are more likely to be given a chance to fight the war with their brains rather than their bodies, simply on the grounds that they'll be more effective.'

'Well, it's certainly true in my case. I wouldn't be much use with a gun. And I'd probably go to pieces if I were in a battle.'

Bax looked at me thoughtfully, the way he had sometimes in tutorials. 'You might or you might not. Military discipline might keep you together. That's what it's for.'

'So I believe.'

'The point is at the moment that unless you definitely choose to volunteer I don't think it'll arise. But if you feel you'd be more use behind a desk, as I certainly feel about myself, that probably means London, which is likely to be as dangerous as most battlefields if half of what they tell us about aerial bombardment is true.'

I thought briefly of aerial bombardment: the flying glass, the blazing streets, the people buried under toppling buildings.

'They're starting something called the Ministry of Supply,' Bax was continuing. 'They've asked me to be in it, and to recommend people. It seems quite useful work. The assumption, surely justified, is that everything's going to be scarce once war starts, so that the free movement of goods and services will be out of the question. It'll all have to be allocated.'

'Sounds like a position of power,' I said facetiously. 'I'm not sure that I'm cut out — '

'Oh, I don't think you and I will be doing any actual allocating. More like finding out exactly how many pairs of leather boots were stored in some warehouse in Northampton at the end of a certain month. Going there to count them ourselves, I shouldn't wonder. And then making decisions about where they're needed and whether there's transport to take them there. And all the time keeping an eye out for the kind of profiteering that went on last time.'

'It sounds like the sort of thing I could do,' I said.

'Shall I send in your name?'

'Please.'

Going down the stairs I had to fight down a wave of hopeless incredulity. There we had been, sitting calmly in Bax's handsomely-proportioned room, talking in civilized tones ... about what? War, and the roar and scream and rubble and blood and flying splinters. Standing still in the middle of the staircase, I suddenly saw Oxford under aerial bombardment. Of all cities it was surely the least able to survive the total destructiveness of twentieth-century war: so much of its character was embodied in stone buildings which, once they were smashed down, could never be replaced. I saw Magdalen Tower dissolving into a column of rubble at the speed of a slow-motion film, the tons of masonry falling into the bed of the Cherwell, while the river itself, baffled in its attempts to flow through the heaped mounds, spread and spread, a bed of cold water for the corpses. I saw the millions of books stored in and underneath the Bodleian smouldering among the ashes, with sad survivors picking their way through the pyres of murdered intelligence. I saw St Mary's Church – headquarters of the University in its medieval beginnings and still symbolically its centre – broken and burning, its stained glass lying on the stones like spilt blood. I saw my father's cellar at the Bargeman's Arms taking a direct hit, the beer welling up through the fractured bricks and timbers, and there in my vision was old Charlie the drayman, standing amidst the rubble, lifting the remains of a barrel to his whiskered mouth in those huge arms, swallowing down the ullage and saying to me, 'That's where the goodness is, my boy, that's where the goodness is.'

I knew what I ought to do next. I ought to go straight home to Heather. She must need me in these doom-laden days, though she never put that kind of need into words; perhaps that was because of the years with me in which she had had to summon all her pride to bear her frequent loneliness, so that not to express her needs had become a habit, a dangerous habit which I ought to try to break down if I could. I ought, I ought, I ought . . . and one of the things I ought to do was to get home now, immediately. But I couldn't bring myself to do it. Soon, yes, but not immediately. I could not yet break free of that nightmare of destruction. Even to go through the main quad of Episcopus, at this moment, would be to pass that spot where I had seen the flames of the bonfire flickering and the smoke twisting upward, as the contents of Walters' room were burnt. I shrank back from walking past that spot, shrank from hearing in my brain a voice from my past, the curt, authoritative voice of Kent: 'Hold him! We'll do it here.' A little boot-polish, that was all, a single infliction of the whip of indignity, something to teach a lesson to a man who was 'too stand-offish'. It was nothing, but it was everything because it was a taste of what, when the *Luftwaffe* and the *Wehrmacht* had done their work, we were in for at the hands of the *Schutz-Staffel*.

Forcing my legs into motion, I went down to the bottom of the staircase. To the left lay the main quad, the lodge, the way out into the street. To the right lay the calm, elegant inner quad and beyond it the garden, dark and mysterious, not locked away but folded and hidden in rain and cold, a background to thought rather than a place to go. I ought to have turned left; I turned right. The lamplight threw the slanting shadows of the slender colonnades in a calm, still pattern. From one of the staircases came the sound of music: a gramophone playing something I recognized but could not quite place: one of Chopin's *ballades*, I decided, the pianist playing from his heart, the frail, passionate music spilling out in a soft tumult oddly at variance with the austere winter air, the calm light, the ordered finality of the stonework. Then I saw that there was a solitary figure walking round the quadrangle towards me, not straight down the central aisle but following one wall in the way a cat does, pacing meditatively. When this figure got nearer I saw that it was hatless and wearing an overcoat, loosely thrown on and not yet buttoned, indicating that the wearer had just emerged from indoors. And I saw that it was the poet Lamont.

I stood still under the archway. He smiled as he approached me and said, 'Hello, Leonard. I heard you were a Fellow these days. D'you live in College?'

'No, I live out. I'm married.'

'Congratulations on that too.'

'And you? Are you in Oxford for long? Could you come to — '

'Just a twenty-four-hour visit. The fact is, I discovered I had some books belonging to the library. I don't know how I came to hang on to them – just carelessness, I suppose. So, having come south for a quick visit, I thought I'd drop them off and apologize in person. They were pretty nice about it – glad to see them back at all, I expect. People are pretty ruthless about library books.'

107

'Come south?'

'I'm living in a village in Yorkshire. A tiny place, you wouldn't have heard of it.'

Something in his tone suggested that he didn't want me to start making polite conversation by asking him what he was doing in this village in Yorkshire. He need not have worried. As I saw it, a man like Lamont had a right to meditate in undisturbed privacy if anyone had a right to anything. I determined to let him go, not hold him with idle chatter; I knew I could never say anything that would really interest him. But, because of the profundity of my respect for him, an impulse made me reveal to him just one tiny corner of the terrified landscape that filled my mind.

'Bad times to be living in, these, Lamont,' I said.

'Internationally, you mean?'

'What else? I don't know what it feels like in the emptiness of the Yorkshire Moors, but in Oxford . . .' I gestured about us. 'It's hard to get away from the thought of all the destruction that's bound to follow if a war breaks out.'

'Universities,' Lamont said, 'are instruments of a civilization. If that civilization is destroyed by its enemies, the only question worth discussing is: What did it leave behind it? What kind of legacy for mankind? If the University disappears, we shall just have to rely on the legacy to have enough vitality to pass itself on, by one means and another.'

'But what kind of means? I can't envisage — '

'Yes, I agree it's not imaginable from the point we're at now. But if Oxford and Western civilization generally has managed to create something, then that something ought not to have to depend on any one stone standing on another or one book being shelved next to another. Greek poetry went on being influential after the expulsion of the scholars from Alexandria in one forty-five, you know.'

'This is nineteen thirty-eight,' I said. 'But you think my mood is appropriate to the year one forty-five?'

'To both equally. But that's just my point. Greek poetry went on being important to the world after that date. Euhemerus — '

I felt glad and reassured that Lamont had brought up the subject of Euhemerus. It showed (i) that his preoccupations had not changed, (ii) that he was willing to share them with me, if only in a short conversation. He talked for some minutes about Euhemerus, during which I paid virtually no attention to his discourse but basked in his presence. Then, courteous as ever, he wished me good-night and said he hoped we would meet again before long.

After he had gone, I stood alone in the windy quadrangle for a moment. The order and beauty of the place seemed created to draw to themselves the presence of a man like Lamont. I even wondered whether I had met Lamont in person at all, or had merely communicated with the *idea* of Lamont. Had he really been there, or had I been confronted with a hallucination, a vision that embodied my notion of Lamonthood – the Platonic idea, as it were, of Lamont, the gentle and meditative poet whose presence was sorely needed and would be needed even more in the iron time that was coming upon us?

A few days later I received a summons to London to be vetted for the Ministry of Supply job. I went up and was interviewed in a bleak narrow office somewhere near Victoria Station by a terrier-like little man with a brown moustache, whose chief concern seemed to be to stop me from getting a toe in the door of a Civil Service career. I told him till I was black in the face that all I wanted was to make myself as useful as possible in the event of a war, and that at the conclusion of such a war my intention would be to resign from any position they might see fit to put me into and go back to my own world – always assuming that my own world still existed. Obviously he had never in his life met, or imagined, anyone who had no wish for a permanent, secure, pensioned job in the Civil Service. Only when, towards the end of the interview, we were joined by a man much higher in the organization and more intelligent, did I feel that I hadn't after all strayed into the pages of a novel by Dickens or Gogol.

At about this time I happened to go into the Common Room one afternoon for a cup of tea and found a conversation in progress. Usually men just sat quietly imbibing their tea and glancing at the newspapers for anything they might have missed in the morning, but on this occasion several of them had actually begun to discuss something. I didn't join the group, but from where I was sitting I could hear a lot of what was being said. 'It all depends on what Hitler decides. He could go for a spring offensive.' 'So you'd put it in 1940, would you?' 'I hardly think that's likely. The historical evidence is all in favour of autumn. Most wars are started in September, when the harvest is in. Or August at the earliest.' 'Like last time.' 'After all, it's a rare society that can afford to go to war with a lot of its men needed out in the fields.'

When they had got to their feet and disappeared, with one of those abrupt group movements that remind one of a flock of birds leaving telegraph wires, one was left thoughtfully behind, and after a moment he came over to me. This was a man named Ransom, a plump cannon-ball of a fellow with a spherical torso and sturdy legs and arms; he had a round, good-natured face and curly brown hair just beginning to turn grey. I always used to think he was more like a popular, easygoing master at a public school than an Oxford don. He stood looking down at me for a moment, as if unable to break his train of thought.

'Do you think we're in for a war, Leonard?' he asked me.

'We're in it already,' I said. 'It started in Spain in 1936. Our bit of it started when Chamberlain handed over Czechoslovakia. We didn't start shooting then, but we acquiesced in the use of force to gain territory.'

'All right,' he said patiently, 'but when do you forecast that the first bullets will actually hit us?'

'As I heard someone say just now, it depends on Hitler and when he decides to invade Poland. Myself, I'd say that, having got all ready to launch a war in September this year, he might perfectly well launch it at any time now. Unless we can persuade the Poles to lie down and die too, of course, and I doubt that. It's not their tradition.'

'H'm,' Ransom said. 'If you really think our present state of, as it were, eggshell peace, is just holding on from week to week, then there's not much point in planning ahead.'

'I don't know. It might be useful to lay in some supplies of tinned food. And things like whisky that might become unobtainable. A bunker of coal . . .'

'I was thinking more,' he said, 'of College functions.'

That was typical of Ransom. He was a great College man; he loved all the meetings and the reunions and dinners and clubs for this and that. When I was an undergraduate I despised people who fussed about those things. Now I didn't. It was one of the ways I could tell I was growing up.

'What I'm thinking,' Ransom went on, 'is that your generation would be due for a Gaudy in 1940.'

And bless my soul, so they would, I thought. It was the sort of thing I would have gone my whole life without thinking of. But now I came to think of it, Ransom was right.

Every Oxford college invites back a group of its former students for a Gaudy, a reunion dinner and an overnight stay, once a year. The dinner takes place every year, but one's own invitation turns up in rotation. Colleges differ, but at Episcopus it was every five years. In 1920 they would invite everyone who entered the College in 1915, 1910, 1905 and so on back, mixing the generations in five-year bands. The response to the invitation was always patchy. Some people love to keep in touch; others take the view that the fact of having been at College at the same time as someone is no reason why you should like to meet him again. Also, memories of undergraduate days may have a rosy glow after fifty years that they don't have after five.

Ransom, of course, was a natural Old Boy, and a Gaudy really was his idea of a happy evening. And here he was, looking solemn and telling me about my generation being due for a Gaudy in 1940.

'I wouldn't put money on it,' I told him. 'By 1940, institutions like the Gaudy may have become a thing of the past.'

'That's just what I was thinking. I suppose you were at the 1935 one? I don't recall seeing you there, but I suppose — '

'No,' I said, 'I skipped it.'

Ransom looked slightly hurt, as if I had trodden on the grave not perhaps of a loved relative of his, but of a favourite dog. 'Ah, well,' he said, meaning that it took all sorts to make a world. 'And now you think that there may not be a 1940 one.'

'No. I mean yes, that is what I think.'

'Well, I've been thinking along the same lines,' said Ransom. 'And I've decided to do something about it.'

Do something? Tell Hitler not to start a war until after the 1940 Gaudy at Episcopus?

'You know I run the Episcopus Society. We don't wait for a Gaudy, we have a dinner every year. Of course it isn't as lavish as a Gaudy and the College doesn't foot the bill. But they're cosy little affairs. Good fun. Helps the men to keep in touch.'

'Yes?'

'I shall make a point of having a membership drive for the Society,' Ransom said, 'and have a dinner for as many chaps as I can get to come along.'

'When?'

'Oh, pretty early in the year. About March. Just about the end of Hilary term.'

'Well,' I said, 'that gives it a better chance than waiting for the Gaudy.'

'Much better,' he agreed.

The usual time for a Gaudy at Episcopus was November. And who felt confident, as the winter of 1938 closed down on us, of arranging anything for November 1939?

6

Uncle Ernest sat in the bar of the Bargeman's Arms, wrapped in the calm majesty of age and experience as in an embroidered mantle. Leaning against the bar, I contemplated him with pleasure. I liked Uncle Ernest, not merely as a person but as an idea. I was glad that there existed in the world such an institution as Uncle Ernest. He typified in his small, slender, erect person the immense dignity of service, service fully comprehended and willingly performed. As surely as myself, he was a product of Oxford University. The University had called his type into being. There were no Uncle Ernests in its earliest days; it had caused them to evolve, by providing the appropriate eco-system. The rabble of thirteenth-century students – poor, rowdy, usually ragged and dirty, often hungry – had existed in holes and corners and in fetid, cramped dormitories. There had been no Ernests to tidy their rooms, make their beds, see to their simpler alimentary needs and generally set them free to live a studious life. Ernests had arrived in the centuries when the crowded, undisciplined halls had given way to stately colleges. Something of that stateliness had entered into the breed of these men. It was there in Ernest, sitting watchfully beside the bar.

It was the last week of the Michaelmas term. December had come in, daylight was short, the air bleak. Ernest was wearing his winter hat. It was a grey tweed cap, and he wore it absolutely level on his head, without the faintest hint of a tilt to either side. He carried it as a badge of rectitude and regular habits.

I had called in for a glass of beer and to see my parents, after walking along the towpath from Folly Bridge to Oseney, on my way to Episcopus for lunch and an afternoon's work. The reason I had joined the towpath at Folly Bridge was because I had been at Christ Church, where I had heard a lecture on Roman law by Canon Jenkins. He, like Ernest, was an old gentleman for whom I felt a great respect. But even that respect would not have been sufficient to draw me into attending a lecture on Roman Law, a subject in which I had only a subsidiary interest. It had arisen in this manner: Canon Jenkins, with his immense range of knowledge, lectured regularly on four quite separate subjects: English Puritanism, the theology of the Church Fathers, Roman law, and the interpretation of the Hebrew scriptures. Such was his physical resilience that, in order not to let these lectures take up too much of his time, he was able to concentrate them into a very few days, and sometimes found that he had arranged to give four sixty-minute lectures on the same morning, at 9, 10, 11 and 12 o'clock consecutively. Not surprisingly in an ageing man, he sometimes fell a prey to patches of vagueness in which he gave the three lectures in the wrong order, holding forth for an hour on Subject A to a bemused audience many of whom only grasped towards the end of the hour that they were not being lectured on Subject B, C or D.

So it had been with me. I had intended to hear Jenkins on English Puritanism, a subject on which he had unrivalled knowledge, particularly in its literary outcroppings; and I knew that although his lectures were designed for undergraduates they would contain a great deal that was new to me. At the beginning of the term

111

I had been to the opening lecture and, finding it richly rewarding, decided to attend the whole series of eight. I had recommended several of my Episcopus students to do the same, and during this final lecture I had seen their increasingly baffled expressions as they tried to make notes on Roman law and relate them to the other seven they had attended on English Puritanism. I didn't feel guilty; it was all part of the broadening effect of an Oxford education, and privately I thought Jenkins had done well to lecture on the right subject seven times in a row.

And now here was Ernest, a man as worthy of respect as Canon Jenkins, and as pure an expression of the traditional essence of Oxford.

He was saying to my father: 'I don't go to see a team win, I go to see them play football.'

'Well, there is that,' my father conceded. He gave the bar a wipe with a cloth and pursued, 'But it gets depressing, week after week, if they never wins.'

'They started the season with a poor patch,' Uncle Ernest admitted, 'but they've played football and that's what I goes to see. Winning isn't everything. In fact I'll go this far, Jack. Winning's nothing at all if you has a dogfight instead of a football match. When Coventry come down here, two Saturdays ago, all right, they won. They went home with a win in their pocket. But it wasn't football.'

My father now deserted the conversation for a moment in answer to some summons called through from my mother in the kitchen. When he returned he said, 'Katie wants to know if the Fred Couling as you're waiting to have a little talk with is the same that used to live in Bridge Street.'

'One and the same,' Ernest said, nodding.

'They were the ones,' my father went on, 'whose daughter got into that bit of trouble.'

'A lot of trouble, Jack, a lot of trouble.'

'But that's no reason why you shouldn't give the lad this job,' my father said, nodding in his turn.

'I've told the bursar I know them as an honest family,' Ernest said, 'and the boy's been brought up honest. I never heard nothing against any of 'em except for that girl. And it's my belief, Jack, as she was not quite right in the head. Nothing seemed to do her no good. She went to one of them special schools, but she come back just the same.'

'But the rest of the family was different.'

'Different as chalk and cheese,' Ernest said. 'I never heard nothing against Fred Couling, nor any of his brothers that lives over at Headington.'

'What time was he bringing the boy here?'

Uncle Ernest consulted his large, solid silver watch, drawing it out of his waistcoat pocket and snapping open the lid. The operation, including the replacing of the watch, took some ten seconds. The pub clock was staring Ernest in the face from the wall behind the bar, but he came of a generation that despised pub clocks, holding it as an article of faith that they were always ten minutes fast on purpose.

'Half-past eleven,' he said. 'He's late already.'

'That's not a good sign, for a lad that wants to take up that kind of work,' my father said.

'I'd soon train him when I got him. It's the father as I blames, not the son, if they comes in late. And for all we know, they might have got held up by something as wasn't their fault.'

Ernest drank up his half-pint glass of beer and courteously accepted the refill my father offered him on the house. They resumed talking about football. Ernest followed Oxford City. In those days Oxford's two football clubs, City and United, were more or less equal in reputation, both semi-professional teams and neither of any importance nationally. But United (Headington United, as they were then) were already more aggressive, more obviously destined to climb to the vertiginous heights of the Football League and become a magnet for rancorous partisanship, venomous boardroom feuds and all the other blessings of soccer success. Ernest, even in those days when the differences between the two were minimal, preferred the more decorous atmosphere of the Oxford City ground on the south bank of the Thames just beyond Folly Bridge. He liked to spend his Saturday afternoons with about 250 other people, watching pleasantly hard-fought matches between players who during the week were postmen, railway workers or bus conductors, matches whose outcome would leave no one angrily resentful or spitefully triumphant.

As they talked, I watched the door for the arrival of Fred Couling with his son. Ernest, presumably, was going to take on the son as a 'boy'. Scouts in those days had 'boys', usually aged from fourteen to about sixteen, who ran errands and did the simpler parts of the job. It was still the epoch when the college servant was the aristocrat of Oxford working men; his wages were not high and he had to endure being laid off at the beginning of July and not re-engaged till October, but on the other hand he had lifelong regularity of employment, and the generally higher status of Gown as against Town tended to rub off on him. Families who wanted to give a son a good start in life would do their best to have him taken on as a 'boy'. The college paid the 'boy's' wages, but the scout whom he was to assist played the major role in vetting him for the job. Most scouts had started as 'boys'.

Ernest took out his silver watch a number of times in the next half-hour or so. Finally, at 12.15, he snapped it shut, slid it back into his pocket and got down from his bar stool.

'I can't wait no longer, Jack. I have to be in Pembroke Hall at a quarter to one, to lay up. If Fred Couling comes in, tell him he'll have to get the boy round to Pembroke at two-thirty and I can give him a few minutes then. If he can't manage that, well, the lad's missed the job. The College won't wait any longer and I'll have to take the next on my list.'

He made his usual quiet, purposeful exit. I knew I must follow soon, but I lingered a few minutes to talk with Dad and to go through into the kitchen to greet Mother.

'Why didn't this Couling boy turn up, have you any idea?' I asked Dad.

'Search me. If he comes I'll send him up to Pembroke.'

'I could see Ernest was pretty fed up.'

'I'm not surprised. He went out of his way to come in here and have a talk with the lad.'

I drank up. 'What did the girl do? The black ewe of the family?'

'Shoplifting,' he said briefly. 'She did time for that after a couple of offences, and when she come out she went on the game up and down St Ebbe's. Got arrested for that one night, and then disappeared. Nobody knows where. London, I 'spect. That type mostly ends up in London.'

I learnt later that Fred Couling and his son never did come looking for Ernest. The son had been told that there was the chance of a job on the assembly line at Cowley, building Morris cars. The pay was about twice what he would have got as a 'boy' at Pembroke or any other college. In the end Ernest had a lot of

113

trouble finding a 'boy' to assist him; it was nearly Easter before he could fill the vacancy, which meant that for about ten weeks he had far more work to do than was at all suitable for a man of his age. For instance, one of the 'boy's' duties was to clean out the grates and lay the fires in all the rooms on the staircase, at six o'clock in the morning. For ten weeks Ernest had to do this himself, and trudge round on a good many errands in addition to his staircase work. Ernest at this time was aged sixty-four. He had been at Pembroke College since 1891.

What with Ernest, and Canon Jenkins, it seemed that I was going through a time when the venerable elderly were in my thoughts. Looking back, I am sure that this was not mere chance. Inwardly, just under the surface of consciousness, one was perpetually aware that a certain phase of civilization was ending. What lay ahead no one knew, but for the time being it looked like nothing more than a bottomless black pit, and the lives of men and women who had reached their old age seemed now, though they had contained the horrors of 1914–18, to be bathed in a gentle glow.

The young, by contrast, seemed doomed and pitiable. There were times when I could hardly face my pupils at Episcopus. The Oxford tutorial, seated by one's study fire with one's student, seemed in those months like some kind of ritual performed over a sacrificial victim. Here I am, I would think, working to fill these chaps' heads with knowledge and to enable them to set that knowledge in order: and in a few months – a few weeks, perhaps – they will find themselves flung into a roaring pit of violence. How will they look back, from the depths of that pit, on what I am trying to do for them now?

In the event, it turned out that these feelings were unduly pessimistic. Still, they were the feelings I actually had, and I don't want to falsify them in memory. The result was to make me, in 1938, much more at ease in the company of the old than of the young. In particular, I valued such glimpses as I had of our venerable President at Episcopus. The notion that heads of colleges should be subject to a compulsory retiring age had taken a long time to be adopted in Oxford. Like most such measures, it had not been imposed from any central authority but had made its way slowly from college to college, for the old decentralized Oxford kept as much power with the individual colleges as it could. Certainly by the time Episcopus got round to accepting that the President should follow modern custom by retiring at seventy, Salterton was well past that age, and since Oxford tradition does not permit rules to be applied retroactively he stayed on. I was glad of this. I knew that when he died I would lose my one living contact with the England of Florence Nightingale, of John Henry Newman, of T. H. Huxley and Matthew Arnold. Not that I was merely using him as a walking document. I felt genuine love and respect for the old man, with his fine honest eyes and slow, thoughtful voice.

My wish to have a little of Salterton's conversation was the main reason why I occasionally stayed in College for dinner rather than going home. As a rule, I preferred to have my evening meal with Heather and to see something of Michael before he went to bed. But it didn't do to be too anti-social, and in any case there were some among my colleagues whom I genuinely wanted to see and talk to, and the ritual of dinner, then dessert, then coffee in the smoking-room, gave me the best opportunity. I used to look at the list in the morning before half-past ten, when it closed, and sign on if there was anybody I specially wanted to see. Tonight I signed on because I saw the President's name down. He dined with the rest of us rarely, never more than once a week; his frail health and great age led him to prefer a light meal on a tray by his fireside, in the company of his almost equally venerable spouse. He made the effort about once a week, though not on a set night.

On this particular evening, we were a large company at dinner, and I sat a long way from Salterton, but when we went into dessert I managed to dodge nimbly round the table and get myself a place only two or three away from him. Not everyone stayed for dessert, so we were a smaller number anyway and general conversation was possible.

Someone who had come in from another college – a guest, as it happened, of Bax – was talking about the appeal for funds which the University had launched some twelve months previously. In the August of 1938 the fund had been declared closed and the proceeds counted up, and since that had been in the middle of the Long Vacation, it was still a topic of conversation in the autumn. It had realized a sum that was considerable in those days.

Bax's guest knew the exact total, he had it in a newspaper cutting which he took from his pocket; evidently he was a stickler for detail. He intoned the figures: 'Four hundred and sixty-three thousand, one hundred and twenty-one pounds.'

'Any shillings and pence?' someone asked facetiously.

'They were not mentioned,' the man said, unsmiling. It was all intensely serious to him.

Old Salterton, who had been engaged in trying to crack a walnut and meeting with no more success than if it had been a cobblestone, now raised his eyes from his plate, looked round with his usual benign expression – I thought, for the thousandth time, how incredibly fine and silky his snow-white hair seemed, lying still quite thickly round the edges of his ancient head – and spoke.

'The University's finances, yes,' he said. 'A subject not without interest and not, I fear, without its latent elements of foreboding.'

'Yes, President?' said someone encouragingly.

'Foreboding,' Salterton repeated. 'Foreboding and melancholy.' He looked round the table, from face to face, as if wondering whether it was worth trying to make us understand something he had in his mind. 'I've been reading the Vice-Chancellor's Annual Report, which as you know is largely concerned with the University's finances. Such documents make fusty reading, but for the Head of a house they must always be obligatory.'

How like him, I thought, to use a word like 'fusty'. It was the perfect word for the job, as Salterton's words generally were. He had grown up in a good period of English, the period of *The Yellow Book* and Robert Louis Stevenson, of Skeat, Furnivall and the great philologists.

'My attention was arrested in particular by the startling figure of the contribution from the Treasury, without which, as the Vice-Chancellor tells us, we could not survive. The time has been, as you all know – and as I remember from my own experience – when the University, both considered in the concrete as a collection of individual colleges and in the abstract as a University, had enough resources without having to ask anyone for a penny. I know that times change and that such a fortunate state could not go on for ever. We teach far more students nowadays and we teach them far more expensive subjects.'

'Still,' said Bax's guest, 'some pretty generous help seems to be forthcoming. Not only the Government but private donors. There's quite a lot we can do with four hundred thousand.'

'Generous enough, I grant you, at present,' Salterton conceded. 'My forebodings are not precise. I don't particularly envisage the day when Oxford hasn't got the resources for this or that specific activity. Nevertheless I can't but remember that there was a time when the University could, if necessary, snap her fingers at Whitehall – when she received not a penny that had to be voted from the public purse and dispensed by officialdom. When she could go her way in total and splendid independence.'

'It would be worth looking up the numbers,' Bax said, 'in the last year when that kind of independence was possible. I suppose, President, you're talking about 1914 or not much later?'

'The body of students was indeed much smaller. I was elected President of this College in the year you mention, Bax, in 1919. For four years our numbers had been very low, but immediately after 11th November 1918 the pressure for admissions became so high that virtually every college doubled its numbers. But size is only part of our difficulty. The real change is in the nature of our studies. The sciences, to which the modern world increasingly demands that we turn our attention, cost infinitely more than the subjects traditionally studied here. History, languages, theology, philosophy, literature – they cost little enough to study. A supply of books, a few libraries, provision for teaching and private study, and the task is done. The Treasury can keep its distance, Government can stay away from the affairs of the University, we can be left alone to do what we are good at.'

'But assuming Oxford was good at the study of history and theology and philosophy and those other traditional things,' Bax put in, 'wasn't it a laudable impulse to set ourselves the goal of trying to become good at science as well? Isn't excellence always a good thing to aim for?'

'Any object can be laudable,' said Salterton mildly, 'and yet the price for it can be too high.'

'But surely, President,' I spoke up, 'knowledge and understanding must be the prime objects. Science gives us knowledge of the physical world, history and the arts tell us what man has made of life in that world – how can we say that one of them is more important than the other, or more affordable?'

'We don't say so,' Salterton returned patiently, 'but we might take leave to doubt whether Oxford is so organized, and so situated by her history and circumstances, as to be able to undertake the study of both of them simultaneously. This amounts to nothing less than the attempt to take the whole of knowledge for her province. Don't you sometimes feel that is hubristic? These questions, Leonard, rarely occur in their purely theoretical form. They abut on matters of circumstance and adaptation. The physical sciences are very young at Oxford. The first degree courses in them were initiated only in 1850, less than a century ago, less than a seventh of the life-span of the University. Already one dire result has followed. We are delivered by Delilah into the hands of the Philistines. This is a tendency that can only continue. Our independence may be safe for the moment. But what will become of Oxford if a government should attain to power that had no tincture of respect for the values of scholarship?'

'You mean some rabble of Bolsheviks,' Watson's voice came in on a high note.

'Not necessarily,' Salterton rejoined quietly. 'There might be the same dangers in say a government of totally materialistic tendency, any creed that respected money and power and had no goodwill towards anyone not possessed of them. It would be a government that despised a poor man, whether his poverty arose from simple incompetence and failure or a deliberate choice on his part to put his energies into other channels. A scholar is often a poor man.'

116

'Individually, yes,' I heard McLennan pipe up. 'But Oxford University isn't poor, surely?'

'Oxford University is poor in terms of the enormous tasks she has seen fit to undertake. Hence the cap in hand to government, the bated breath while decisions in Whitehall are awaited. Financially we are in the power of politicians, and politicians disappear and are replaced by other politicians. My own life is nearly over, but I grieve for the future of the University.'

'It seems to me, President,' Watson added testily, in the tone of one about to lose his patience, 'that you really believe, and are half trying to persuade us, that the decision of 1850 was the wrong one – that we ought to have left science alone, if only to stay within our own financial limitations.'

'I do believe that,' Salterton said calmly.

'But knowledge! The sacred obligation to pursue knowledge – surely we couldn't duck out of that.'

'All knowledge?' said the old man. 'Knowledge simply as knowledge: knowledge of any kind and pursued at any cost?'

There was a brief silence while everyone waited for someone else to speak.

'The motto of the University,' Salterton said, 'is not "Knowledge above all". It is "*Dominus illuminatio mea*". To be guided towards truth by the light of religion is not precisely the same thing as the headlong pursuit of information, regardless about what and at what cost. That pursuit was the motive of Faustus in selling his soul to the devil through the agency of Mephistopheles. His thirst to *know* was stronger than his moral nature. When the question of whether or not to include the sciences in the range of her concerns was before the University, many worthy men, with the interests of the University and of England at heart, were against it. Jowett was against it. The tide might have been held back for a good few years longer, even if it had to break in sooner or later, but for the circumstance that Acland managed to win the support of Pusey and Pusey rallied the Tractarians to the support of the scientific party.'

Salterton broke off and took a sip of his claret. He rarely drank anything alcoholic, but on evenings when he dined with the rest of us he sat through dessert with a glass of claret beside him and occasionally took a sip to fortify him. I watched him with sympathy. He was obviously driving himself beyond his usual limit, trying to get his message to us. His face had become grey and papery, but as I watched a faint trace of colour appeared in it, and his eyes lost their dullness, as the glow of the wine began to spread through his system.

Watson, meanwhile, had taken advantage of the pause in Salterton's discourse to say silkily, with the air of one playing with an opponent not worth his skill to oppose, 'But surely Acland and Pusey and those other Victorian heavyweights were right, President – simply *right*?'

'They represented modernity,' Salterton admitted, 'and it would be argued by most people today that Jowett's party were simply obstructive and reactionary. But they had a vision of what Oxford could achieve within the national life. They saw this place as the centre of a certain kind of study and contemplation, the study of human institutions, human languages, human thoughts, and of the relationship of the human to the Divine. They foresaw, correctly, that the changes proposed by the scientific party would be no mere matter of widening the scope of the University's work but of changing its nature. In my opinion it remains very much an open question whether those changes will prove beneficial or, in the end, ruinous. One thing is already clear: they have put us into the power of the politicians.'

117

Bax's guest, whom I conjectured to be an economist, spoke up now with an edge of protest in his voice. 'With respect, my dear sir, but to do anything else would have been to become a backwater. It's easy enough for a stream to be tranquil if it isn't going anywhere. By choosing to involve in the study of science, which was obviously going to be such an essential concern in the modern world, the University was deciding to stay in the main current of the world's life.'

'If we had turned aside from what some saw as that current,' Salterton asked, 'what accusation would have been brought against us?'

'Of turning our backs on the world. Of turning our gaze inwards, cultivating our own garden and not making our contribution in areas that urgently concern the majority of mankind.'

'If this country is ever ruled by the kind of government I most dread for it,' Salterton said quietly, 'that accusation will be brought against us in any case. Oil and water will never mix, and neither will a totally materialistic attitude mix with any degree of intellectual idealism. If such people come to power, they will parcel you up and sell you over the counter.'

'President,' Bax said earnestly, 'if we were to take what you have just said as a solemn warning, and decide to act on it, what action could we take?'

Salterton held his eye for a moment and then said levelly, 'I have to tell you, Mr Bax, that I do not know.'

As we broke up that evening, I happened to find myself with Bax as we hung up our gowns in the corridor. 'An interesting moment,' he remarked, looking at me with his usual half-quizzical expression.

I didn't have to ask what he meant. 'Highly interesting,' I said. 'But I'm not sure that I agree with what was quite obviously your guest's attitude.'

'Henderson? Oh, yes. A worthy fellow, but quite without any imagination. To him, Salterton would just come over as an old dodderer.'

'He wouldn't see,' I said, 'that the question raised by Salterton is actually a very real one. Was the decision in 1850 really inevitable?'

'You know,' Bax said, 'there's only one thing I regret about tonight – that Weatherby wasn't dining. It would have been good to have the thoughts of a really distinguished man of science.'

'Presumably Salterton wouldn't deny that Weatherby, and people like him – if there are any people like him – have brought great honour to Oxford?'

'He would approve of Weatherby's work, no doubt. The question in his mind would be whether it ought to have been carried on somewhere else and not in Oxford.'

'But surely,' I said, 'it's good for all of us, whatever our discipline, to have a really good scientific mind like Weatherby's in our midst?'

Bax gave me the kind of look he used to give me when he was my tutor and I said something he didn't think I could substantiate. 'Isn't that just something we say to each other? I mean, how true is it *actually*?'

'That's an imponderable,' I said. 'Presumably a scientist, like an artist, affects the atmosphere he lives in just by being the kind of person he is. To have people among us who weigh evidence in the way scientists weigh it, and speculate in the way they do, must surely release some vitamin that the rest of us can take in.'

'It is, as you say, an imponderable,' Bax said carefully.

'Of course.'

'And there's no arguing with imponderables,' he said as he turned away. 'That's what makes historical work so difficult.'

*

118

Christmas was a nightmare, but then Christmas so often is. That year there were all the usual reasons why it should have been a difficult time, fraught with possibilities for tension and suffering, but on top of that there was a dreadful blend of menace and irony in the atmosphere. 'Peace on earth, goodwill towards men' seemed obscenely out of place as a slogan and offensively fatuous even as a pious hope. I must have been one of many thousands who were heartily glad when it was all over.

Not that the long, black mid-winter months that followed were much better. The only positive thing about life was that one felt the fragility of normal things, ordinary routines, commonplace habits, with such poignant intensity that they became precious. It seemed, often, like a glorious privilege simply to go into a shop and buy 5lbs of potatoes. To be allowed to walk down the street to the shop in peace, to find it open and go in, to find that they had potatoes for sale, to buy some and walk out unhindered, it all seemed so valuable and so doomed. For how long? we kept asking ourselves, those who were capable of thinking, how long can it last? We expected the end of everything. A great wave of catastrophe and destruction and death.

Apart from this incessant consciousness of waiting, life seemed to stand absolutely still. I never knew a time like it for sheer stagnation. History hung unnaturally still, like a wave just before it breaks. The only thing I can remember from that spring is something so trivial that in normal times it would have been a non-event: my seeing (I can hardly say 'meeting', though I did speak to him) a newly arrived philosopher.

It stole up on me unawares, as a non-event naturally would. I was in the King's Arms one mid-morning having coffee, and while I held my coffee-cup in one hand I held in the other a book I was reading. It was Geikie and Montgomery's *The Dutch Barrier*, a superb contribution to eighteenth-century international history, and I was getting particularly good value from Chapter IV, 'The Repudiation of the Townshend Treaty'. The book was published in the year I had entered Episcopus College as an undergraduate, and Bax had repeatedly told me to read it, but I had never got round to it, and now it was filling gaps for me by the minute. Keeping my eyes on the page, I moved my left hand to set down the cup, in which there was still a little coffee. I was more or less aware, at the edge of my field of vision, of the position of my saucer, but failed to see that instead of waiting for my cup, it was occupied by someone else's. My cup clinked against the one already there. In slight irritation, I looked up. Had I made a mistake? No, that was my saucer. The man sitting next to me, who had been issued with a perfectly good saucer of his own, had put his cup down in mine. I opened my mouth to point this out, courteously. 'Excuse me,' I said. But the man appeared not to hear me. He was staring fixedly in front of him and he continued to stare fixedly.

'I wonder if you'd mind – ' I began, but I was interrupted by a voice which came not from the man himself but from the woman on the other side, who was, I now saw, Molly Whitworth.

She fixed me with a coldly appraising look through her round rimless lenses and said, not to me but into the air generally, 'There is evidently a problem of spatial relationships.'

'No, there isn't,' I said. 'I have a saucer. This gentleman has a saucer. He's simply put his coffee-cup down in mine and not his own. No problem. All he needs to do is — '

'Stephen,' she said, 'your next-door neighbour wants *Lebensraum*, my dear.'

119

I didn't particularly relish the small quip. *Lebensraum*, in those days, was a particularly loaded word. It was a key ingredient in the German vocabulary of threat and blackmail.

'*Lebensraum*, no, Miss Whitworth. A saucer, yes – that and nothing more.'

Instead of answering, she leaned across and took the man's cup from my saucer and put it in his own. Her expression said, 'I am humouring this peasant before he turns nasty.'

I nodded in acknowledgement, though the gesture was wasted because she was not looking in my direction. But the spell of Geikie and Montgomery was broken, and I only stayed the few minutes it took me to see if any of my acquaintances were there. Molly Whitworth, it was plain, did not consider herself one of these. She had made it perfectly clear to me, long ago, that I was not important enough – or was it just, not *intelligent* enough? – to come within her field of recognition.

The small incident had the effect of breaking my concentration on Lord Townshend's treaty and its fate at the hands of the Dutch, and I turned to look for an instant at the man she was so protectively in company with.

He was a broad-built man; his body was broad and so was his face, with wide cheek-bones and a broad forehead, so that overall his head measured more from side to side than from crown to chin. I don't think it actually did so, but that was the impression it conveyed. He had thinning pale hair, already sparse on top though he was probably not yet thirty; his eyes had a distant look and his brow was marked with deep furrows of thought. Obviously, a man whose gaze was focused inward. He and Molly Whitworth were engaged in intermittent conversation, and when my hearing became attuned to the buzz and clatter of the place I began to pick up his words. This was no easy matter because of his idiosyncratic delivery. He spoke in rapid instalments, punctuated by long pauses. He would sit as motionless as a statue, staring into that distance, then suddenly open his mouth and emit a cluster of words that, as far as one could make them out, formed a grammatical sentence. The sentence would be – I can't remember one exactly between the difficulty of following what he said and the unfamiliarity (to me) of the kind of thing he talked about – but it would be something more or less on the lines of, 'Since reflex paradoxes are so apt to occur, people are right to have a recurrent doubt whether "is R to itself" does express a genuine form of predicate, though I personally don't think these paradoxes necessarily arise in ordinary first-level predicate calculus.' When he had finished rattling off such a statement, at well-nigh incredible speed, he would briefly stretch his features into a smile. It seemed a genuine smile and not a mere grimace or facial spasm, since it extended not only to his mouth but to his eyes, which beamed momentarily with something that seemed like genuine benevolence and good humour. But it came and went so swiftly that the effect was entirely mechanical. He looked like a clockwork doll that has been wound up to smile charmingly, but was running too fast.

I only spent a couple of minutes listening to their exchange, but before I got up and left it so happened that three other people came in, greeted the couple, and sat down to join them, perhaps by prearrangement, and I heard Molly Whitworth say, 'This is my husband, Stephen Fishman.' So her mission was completed: she had, as reported, got married to a Cambridge philosopher and brought him back to Oxford. The question had barely reached my consciousness when I heard her say, in an explanatory tone, 'We managed to lure him away from the Cambridge philosophy faculty – to their fury, needless to say.' I felt it was slightly unnecessary to add those last words. If the Cambridge philosophers were really furious at losing Stephen Fishman as a colleague, it would have been more becoming to let them say so and show themselves good losers; for an Oxford person, particularly an Oxford spouse, to say it seemed a little like gloating. On the other hand, there was, I knew, the possibility that the statement was just window-dressing. Cambridge might have been perfectly willing to see the back of him; how could an outsider judge these things?

My cup was now empty, but I lingered beside the table because I was beginning to find a certain fascination in studying Molly Whitworth (a.k.a. Molly Fishman)'s attitude to her husband. It was obvious that she was stage-managing him as the Genius on a pinnacle, the Great Abstract Intelligence who was above the Mundane. Personally I had, and have, every sympathy with absent-mindedness. I know the effort of intense concentration, and I know how Tmesic (I'm sorry to use so pedantic a word, but there really is no other) can be the interruption of concrete reality at a jarringly two-dimensional level. But it's also quite healthy, and quite good conditioning for the mind, to have to struggle with these interruptions for oneself and not get too much into the habit of floating above them in some kind of stratosphere of abstraction. That way lie self-indulgence and solipsism, and a serious intelligence, seriously engaged with real problems, cannot afford either.

Molly Whitworth obviously did not agree with this attitude. Her own policy was based on the assumption that her husband's mighty intellect would flourish best when everybody within a wide radius was suitably awed – awed, that is, by her – into not interrupting his train of thought and not spilling grit into his finely-adjusted mental machinery. To point out his simple mistake about which cup went into which saucer was just one piece of grit: ergo, I was a grit-scatterer, a pest, a Philistine.

So be it. It was the husband I felt rather sorry for. He was so obviously being manipulated as part of some complex power game she was playing. Looking across at her as she talked to the people who had joined them, noticing her quick, calculating glances from face to face, I saw her as first and foremost a schemer, planning her life like a chess game, three, four, five moves ahead. It suited her, in some way I couldn't bother to guess at, to be the wife of the Supreme Philosopher.

As I walked out into the sunshine I wondered, idly, how her husband fitted in with her sexual life which, I had been credibly told, was never sleeping and omnivorous. I couldn't, somehow, see him as a great lover. The chances were, I decided, that Molly Whitworth was like the champion chess player who can take on almost any number of opponents simultaneously.

Well, Stephen Fishman's fate, driven by his wife's all-purposive will, was not my affair. Another matter that might have been of some slight interest, had I the prescience to recognize it, was the man's way of expressing himself. There is widely supposed to be something called 'the Oxford accent'. To the population in general, it stands for the accent and speech-habits of the super-cultivated. In Edwardian England this manner was languid and drawling, and as late as the 1930s there were still older people in Oxford who spoke in this manner, their leisurely enunciation falling on the ear like the murmurous ripple of a gentle stream under summer boughs; it suggested, not at all unconsciously, a background of leisure, of complete economic security, of immunity from the pressures of day-to-day competition, of habits of quiet thoughtfulness and assured authority. What I was hearing from Fishman was the new Oxford accent, developed first among a knot of philosophers and shortly to take root throughout the academic community: a stop-and-start, tumultuous manner, its abrupt silences indicating that the speaker was lost, however briefly, in labyrinthine thoughts, its breathless word-clusters eloquent of ideas that poured from the fertile brain so fast that they jammed in the doorway of utterance. A superficial change: but, like many such, an indication of much greater changes working beneath the surface.

One freezing March night the Episcopus Society dinner finally happened. I thought I might as well go: a glance at the list of acceptances showed the names of several men I really did look forward to seeing again; it was only six years since we all graduated, but that was long enough to get thoroughly out of touch with them. And here, as I went into the well-lit, warm, welcoming room, they were. One of the first faces I recognized was that of Fred Armitage. His appearance had subtly changed; he was still the lanky, raw-boned lad I had known, but his face had begun to smooth out, some of the hollows were filled in, his bony wrists didn't seem to protrude so much beyond the cuffs of his jacket and his voice, when he greeted me, was still Yorkshire but with some of the edges worn away. His hair, too, was a little longer and a little sleeker. But his eyes were just as honest and candid. He had, I learnt, become a chemistry master at a well-known public school

'How d'you like it?' I asked him.

'Not bad. The work's pretty easy, but it isn't so elementary that it bores me too much. I have a Sixth Form and I prepare them for University entrance. Cambridge, a lot of them.'

'And the people you live and work among?' I asked. 'What's the human side of it like?'

'They're pretty easy to work with,' he said, though whether he was aware of how unrevealing his answer was I couldn't decide. 'They know how to get on with it.'

At this point we were interrupted by someone else joining us, but afterwards I found my mind quite often going back to Fred and his public-school job. It was easy enough to see what had happened. As a Yorkshire miner's son he had, of course, to react one way or the other once his talents got him over the threshold of a place like Episcopus, either going forward or backward. Fred Armitage had gone forward. Not that he had ever disowned his family or his origins. He had merely, in his harmless old-fashioned way, fallen in love with the venerable beauty of the place, its graceful buildings, its stately trees, the long avenue of history that stretched back behind it. When the time had come for him to go back to Yorkshire – well, perhaps not actually there, but to somewhere similar, somewhere just as workaday and prosaic, making his living as an industrial chemist – he had shied away from the prospect. He had wanted, at the very least, ivy-clad buildings and immemorial elms. His academic attainments had not been sufficient to keep him at Oxford, but to an Oxford science graduate the most august of the public schools, even back in those days, were wide open. So there had been no need for him to leave that atmosphere of traditions and stately ceremonies, even if the price he had to pay for it was schoolmastering which, however much you glamorize it, will always be a job with a lot of frustrations and not a few downright penances. Fred had stayed within in a world which, at any rate now and then, contrived to reproduce the atmosphere of Episcopus. The men he worked with were graduates; the atmosphere he lived in was the same atmosphere that he was in now, standing in that panelled room with a glass of sherry in his hand. And yet, I was as sure as I was of anything in the world, the man was not a snob. He was totally lacking in the punitive side of snobbery, the impulse to thrust down and humiliate anyone

122

he felt was of a lower social position. One knew, for instance, that if he had in any of his classes a scholarship boy who had struggled there from a poor home, he would be specially attentive to that boy; but the attentiveness would be very discreet, careful not to draw attention to itself, because he would not want the boy to feel he was being treated differently from the others.

I circulated. In a few minutes we would be called into dinner, and I wanted to say a word or two to as many men as I could. It was good to see Wilmot again, with his spiky hair and round glasses, always cheerful, always inoffensive, the first man I had exchanged words with when I had gone into Hall for dinner on that first evening, a million years ago, wondering if I should ever get to know anyone among this crowd of roaring and barking strangers. Wilmot had sat next to me and had opened a conversation; I had never known, and I never would know, whether he had realized that I was lonely and insecure, or whether in his innocent middle-class way he would have started a conversation with whomever he happened to sit next to, but I had loved him for it, and I still loved him now. He, like Fred Armitage, had gone into the schoolteaching business, but not at a public school; he was at a large grammar school in some south-coast town, rising in responsibility and doubtless to be a headmaster by the time he was forty, liking his work, a round pin in a round hole. He had married his Grace – we laughed gently together about his getting me to take him out in a punt and give him some rudimentary instruction on how to handle it without making a fool of himself, when he had first arranged to take Grace on the river. It had been a purposeful step in his life: to equip himself with a girl-friend at Oxford, whom in due course he could marry and settle down with, and now they had a family, and his life was so settled, so buttressed. In fact, it had already been settled and buttressed back in those early days, when he was making plans to get on with his courtship because he could see beyond courtship to marriage and a family and a future: whereas I, at the same stage in life, had only one thought in my fevered head – to get inside Vinnie's knickers.

There was also Norbert, who represented a type of man entirely different from either Armitage or Wilmot – a third type also to be met with at the ancient Universities: the man born into a family of people with authority, occupying responsible positions. It was in Norbert's face, in his carriage, in the tolerant and yet appraising look he gave you – the assumption that it was natural and expected for him, and for people like him, to carry part of the weight of the world, to make decisions affecting other people *en masse*. He was being genial and relaxed this evening – I heard his rich laugh ring out – but it was there in him, watchful and not to be escaped by himself or others: the sense of his being there to take charge if and when the need arose.

But perhaps of all the men there it was Knowlton I was most glad to see. Exactly why I had always liked Knowlton so much it was hard to analyse. He had always been very amiable and pleasant, just as amiable and pleasant as he was to everyone. He was – or seemed to be – never out of temper, never sulky, never flustered or confused about anything. I sat next to him at dinner and we chatted about what we had been doing in the last five years. Since I was, essentially, doing what I had been doing ever since my first day at Episcopus, there wasn't much for me to tell him, so he mostly told me things. I had always assumed the existence behind Knowlton of some comfortable family business in which he would take his prearranged place on leaving Oxford, but I had never known what it was, or known anything specifically about his background. Now, I gathered some details. His home area was Dorset. The family's business was printing, on a fairly large scale but mostly traditional, country-town kind of printing – local newspapers, parish magazines, auctioneers' catalogues, centred mainly in towns like Dorchester and Weymouth. The family also owned some land. Knowlton had grown up in an Elizabethan house. He was so obviously a child of privilege that I, a child of the people, felt almost guilty liking him so much. Surely I ought to feel, if not personal envy of his good fortune, at least a noble generalized indignation on behalf of all wage-slaves, all the over-driven and dispossessed, that Knowlton should simply float through life, encountering none of its tribulations and frustrations. But I couldn't, I liked him too much, liked his ease and geniality, liked his manners which, though casual in the modern way, were always perfect, liked his tact and kindliness. His Oxford education – three years under the sardonically perceptive eye of Bax – had not transformed him into an essentially reflective or scholarly person, but it had nevertheless added a touch of depth to his thinking, made him a more interesting person to talk to, and this was all part of his attractiveness. If an unjust economic and social system could produce only Knowlton himself and not a single further specimen, then at least it had achieved something. And certainly it was hard to imagine a Knowlton being produced in an entirely egalitarian world, desirable otherwise as such a world would be.

Of course he was a friend of Norbert's. It was interesting to see how, within the broad general equality imposed by the University – any Oxford undergraduate was ostensibly the social equal of any other Oxford undergraduate – the classes tended in fact to settle into the same stratification that they would have had in the outside world. You got along reasonably well with everybody, but you chose your circle of close friends from among people whose background you were easy with. Norbert was a natural companion for Knowlton, just as Wilmot had been a natural companion for me. Just as the great oceans of the world have currents within them, invisible to anyone looking at the broad surface, so the broad surface of a great University has currents within it, moving its inhabitants along towards their appropriate zones of climate and food sources.

But wait! What was Knowlton saying to me? 'Your brother,' he was saying. 'Your brother was there.'

Knowlton had, it appeared, recently spent a week-end at the house of the man he called 'Fergie Kingswood'. I knew the name, of course, and remembered the man. He was rich and titled, he was at Magdalen during my undergraduate days, and one of his hobbies had been to run an M.G. racing car. He had competed in various events at Brooklands and Brian had been deputed to service his car and see that it was properly tuned, and to look after him generally. What more natural than that now, only a few years later, Kingswood had kept up his hobby of motor-racing and that the M.G. company, in the person of Brian, should be giving him the same support? Brian had told me that they still provided a racing service for private owners, a ghostly after-life embalming the great memories.

'He's a martinet,' Knowlton said with his easy-going grin. 'We all had to get up at some unearthly hour to be down at Brooklands by eleven in the morning, even though the first race wasn't till two in the afternoon. He had Fergie doing a lot of practice laps, not just warming up, tearing round as fast as ever he could go. I was afraid he'd break his neck before the day's racing had even started. Your brother wanted him to try all sorts of different . . . what was it?' He wrinkled his brow. 'Oh, yes, carburettor settings. Apparently the carburettor setting has to vary with the weather. Or perhaps I've got it wrong. Anyway, he had me timing them, sitting in the pit with a stop-watch and then working out the speeds with a slide-rule.' He laughed in self-mockery. 'And I thought I was going to Brooklands for a nice relaxed day out and to watch old Fergie do his stuff.'

I could imagine how Brian would keep them all down to it. And how the effort and involvement would have given them a far more interesting experience, and more lasting memories, than any number of nice relaxed days out.

'Of course Fergie has these enthusiasms,' Knowlton was saying. 'If he takes something up, you've got to show a healthy interest in it. It's not so much that he's offended if you don't, it's more that he's puzzled. While he's in the grip of something, whether it's deep-sea diving or mountaineering or exploring the Amazonian jungle, or gliding, or roaring about in racing cars – well, he can't get it into his head that there are human beings walking the earth who don't take an interest in these things.'

'So you have to go along with it,' I said.

'Well, he's never got me to go to the Amazon jungle, or down on the seabed in a diving helmet, but he did take me over to Dunstable once and got me up in a glider. It was quite pleasant, except that I thought it would be beautifully quiet, floating up there above the landscape, but actually it makes a deafening noise. It's like the flapping of the sails on a yacht.'

'I'll take your word for it,' I said, pouring out sherry for him and myself.

'The whole thing took me completely by surprise,' Knowlton said. 'Fergie never tells you anything ahead of time; you never know what he'll drag you into. It just so happened that Philip and I were spending a week-end with Fergie down at his place, not far from Sevenoaks.' (I had never even known before that Norbert's first name was 'Philip'. To me he had always just been 'Norbert'.) 'And he'd just bought this racing car, an M.G., and it seems your brother works with them.'

I liked 'works with them'. It had a dignified ring; it suggested collaboration: the M.G. company and Brian Leonard, the eminent engineer, who worked with them. It was all a long way from that spring morning in – what? 1927 or '28, when Brian had gone off on his beaten-up old bike, with the strips of cardboard stuck into the rear wheels so that they rattled against the spokes and made what he hoped was a sound like an engine, up to Cowley to get a job at Morris Motors. From there it had been a long haul, with a lot of string-pulling, to get into M.G. and bring himself to the notice of Cecil Kimber and finally become part of the Racing Department. But at the end of that road he had found a landscape far more interesting than mere assembly-line work.

'How did Fergie Kingswood get on in his race?' I asked.

'Pretty well, I think. The big race of the day, the one he was in, was a handicap job, so there was no reason in theory why anyone who started shouldn't have been the eventual winner. Fergie was something like seventh overall, but what I remember pleased your brother was that he came in second in his class.'

'You don't remember what kind of M.G. he was driving, do you?'

'Yes, it was one he'd just bought and he was very thrilled with it. It had a number, let's see now . . . oh yes, K.3.'

'Yes. Brian says they're the best.'

'I wouldn't know,' Knowlton said with his humorous, resigned air. 'I was out of my depth all along. But it certainly went like a bat out of hell. If excitement's what Fergie wants, he'll certainly get plenty of it zooming around in that thing. I wouldn't even have the nerve to sit in it and start the engine.'

The main course of this dinner consisted of enormous beefsteaks smothered in mushrooms. At this moment mine was put in front of me, and the task of consuming it occupied me for the next few minutes. Not talking, I had the leisure to muse for a while on the curious relationship between Brian's life and mine. His involvement with racing cars had brought him into contact with Norbert and Knowlton. Had he mentioned to them that I was his brother? It seemed unlikely.

'How did you know that the man who looked after the racing car was my brother?' I asked Knowlton when I had established ascendancy over the steak.

He seemed surprised at the question. 'He's called Leonard and he looks like you.'

'But didn't you think it odd . . .' I began, but stopped. What was there that he should think odd? Was it odd that a man who had read History at college should be the brother of another man who concerned himself with racing cars? The question was absurd.

That last thought reminded me of the poisonous Carshalton, the one man I had known as a student who was quite plainly ashamed of his social starting point and determined to leave it behind and obliterate it. He'd gone to America, I'd heard. I looked round the table to see if he was there, but to my relief he wasn't. Evidently, America had got him. And, as far as I was concerned, America could keep him.

It was good to find that one absolutely poisonous character from my generation, who might conceivably have been present, was not; but inevitably, there were one or two flies in the ointment. No social gathering, from the highest to the lowest, is complete without its pests, and that department was well taken care of by Watson (representing Pests: Oxford division) and Hunt (Pests: London division). Ever since Watson had mentioned that Hunt was a friend of his I had uneasily wondered whether fate held in store for me any exposure to the two of them together. Now it had come, and though I did my best to steer clear it turned out that Ransom in his innocence had seated them both fairly near me at dinner.

Without entering into conversation I couldn't help taking a certain amount of notice of Hunt. He had, if anything, become more repulsive still during his years in Fleet Street. His face had always worn an expression of aloofness, but now the aloofness had hardened into something definitely cynical, definitely hostile to the human spirit. His pale eyes looked out at the world as if in ceaseless watch for something he could turn into profitable ridicule. Of course he would be a friend of Watson's; or more precisely, an ally, since friendship would not exist in the mental world they both inhabited. Seeing things from the same angle, playing the racket for the same kind of advantage, they would naturally co-operate.

From such snatches of conversation as I couldn't help overhearing, I gathered that Hunt was pumping Watson for funny stories about the oddities and eccentricities of some of the elder dons. Watson enjoyed telling a story provided it was at someone's expense, and was not a bad hand at it. I heard scraps of recalled dialogue in which he was evidently mimicking the voices of men I knew, some of them at Episcopus – Weatherby, I remember, and in particular the Arabic scholar Tonson. I thought of Tonson's round, innocent face, his guileless eyes, his shy gentle voice, and finally, in the middle of what the pair of them evidently saw as an excruciatingly funny anecdote about Tonson's gullibility in dealing with some swindling customs official in Cairo (I think it was), I couldn't restrain myself from calling down the table, 'Hunt!'

He turned to me smoothly and said, 'Yes, Leonard?'

'Have you really come all the way to Oxford to sit around pulling Tonson's character to pieces? What harm has he ever done to you?'

'None, but then I'm not doing him any harm either,' he said blandly, conscious of occupying higher ground. 'You must realize, Leonard, that the endearing absurdities of Oxford dons are a legitimate source of amusement to the wider world.'

'What you mean is that scholars are there for people like you to laugh at.'

'You have to make allowances for Leonard,' Watson remarked to anyone near enough to hear him. 'He has these sudden rushes of pomposity to the head.' He leaned towards me. 'You're very *solemn*, aren't you, my dear Leonard?'

'There are some things I'm reasonably serious about. To you, that probably amounts to the same thing.'

'Well, my dear colleague,' Watson said, 'since I'm quite sure that a man's right to earn a living is one of the things you're most serious about,' he paused long enough for me to wonder why he didn't call me working class and have done with it, 'you might feel more kindly about our conversation if I tell you that Hunt is collecting material for some articles he's writing.'

'I'm sure he is,' I said.

My face felt hot with rage. I knew Hunt and his articles. A few funny stories about absent-minded professors and doddering old dons – pay your tuppence and come and have a laugh at the freak show! For a moment I felt words rising to my lips that would have opened the flood-gates of a denunciation of Hunt. But at the same time I noticed that heads were beginning to turn towards our part of the table, and knew that if the evening were spoilt by a disagreeable scene it would be hard on the men who had taken the trouble to get here and wanted a pleasant dinner. Perhaps there would be a chance to deal with Hunt later.

At a deeper level, of course, I knew that there would never be a way of dealing with Hunt. Huntism, so to speak, would go on even if Hunt himself lay buried at a crossroads with a stake through his heart. As long as an institution like Oxford University exists, with its particular set of ideals and aspirations, there will be a range of cheap minds who see it as merely a target for easy ridicule, and easy ridicule as a path to easy money. Hunt! Who cared? If it wasn't Hunt it would be Schmunt or Dunt or Kwunt.

Ransom had taken a lot of trouble over the organization of the dinner, and it was set up in the proper fashion, with dessert as a separate event. Since we didn't have the use of two rooms, that meant having to clear the room for a few minutes while the scouts rearranged the table and laid up for dessert. When Ransom rose to announce this he took the opportunity to make a short speech. His speech, which was quite an able one, followed predictable lines. His main theme was that there was obviously going to be a war in the near future and therefore he had got up this dinner as just about the last occasion when we could count on seeing one another. But he never actually mentioned the probability of war in so many words. One encountered this everywhere, in the spring and summer of 1939. It reminded me of what they used to say about the wrapper on an old-fashioned laxative – 'It mentions constipation fifteen times and never uses the word.' All of us there, Ransom said, had enjoyed the privilege, the advantage of an Oxford education, and in the trials that lay ahead it was going to stand us in good stead, and when we were uprooted and scattered all over the place we were likely to come across other Episcopus men wherever we went, probably in the least auspicious places (I suppose he meant hospitals and prisoner-of-war camps), and this would help to give us *esprit de corps* and all the rest of it. But, of course, Ransom went on admonishingly, a privilege like that carried its responsibilities and he was quite sure we didn't need to be reminded of that. From those to whom much had been given, much would likewise be expected. And now would we step out into the quad for a little fresh air and give the scouts a chance to get at the room?

Out in the quad I found myself standing with Knowlton. We strolled a little way, out of the immediate range of the yellow light from the windows, and the deep blackness of the sky above us became so intense as to claim our attention. The stars, strung out across the sky in their familiar northern hemisphere pattern, were sharp and glittering. You could see every individual star and even the vague but powerfully exciting nebulous stripe of the Milky Way. Unexpectedly, Knowlton said, 'It reminds me of a line by that old chap my family used to know quite well. Wrote poems. You know – Hardy. Our local literary gent. My governor was quite a friend of his.'

'What line does it remind you of?' I asked.

'The full-starred heaven that winter sees,' Knowlton said. He did not fumble for the line, but brought it straight out as if it were familiar to him. I didn't, at that time, know Hardy's poetry and I had never heard the line.

'Got it right, didn't he?' Knowlton said half to himself. 'He was a good old boy. Not as difficult to get on with as some people said. My governor got on with him all right and he was pretty crotchety himself. They used to get into the back room at the local beer-house and swap yarns, funny things that had happened to people round there that they'd known in their younger days. Old Hardy used to laugh until he cried sometimes, and I gather he wasn't much of a laughing man. But then my old man could tell a good story. He only died last year. Didn't live as long as old Hardy, of course, but not far off.'

'I'm sorry,' I said, meaning I was sorry his father had died.

'I'm not,' Knowlton said, suddenly blunt and unceremonious. 'I reckon he picked a good time to die.'

We both knew he was talking about the coming of war. There was no escaping the subject. But, once again, Knowlton had mentioned it and yet not used the word.

We went back into the room. At dessert I sat between Armitage and McFarlane. McFarlane appeared the least changed of all the men there. He had always seemed incredibly young. As a first-year medical student he had looked like a fifth-former. By the time he had graduated or done whatever it is that medical students do before going off for their hospital experience, he had come to look more or less like a first-year undergraduate. Now, in his late twenties, he was just beginning to look like a man you could almost trust with the care of other people's health. What made him seem still so youthful was his physical smooth-ness, his fresh skin and complexion, his air of guileless goodwill. What would McFarlane look like at forty? At fifty? At sixty? Would I have the chance to find out, or would I never see him again after this evening? If I never did, he would have to remain in my memory as McFarlane the Youthful, just as certain kings are preserved in history as Charles the Bald or Charles the Fat.

Ransom's speech, I found, had put me into a reflective, stocktaking mood. He had sounded, and indeed was, so certain that having one's student years at Oxford, and at a place like Episcopus, meant something; that it put one in touch with Higher Values. I realized, slightly to my surprise, that I had never really considered this question as it bore upon myself. I had come to Episcopus because it was here: it lay on the broad highway of my life, its main trajectory; it was the obvious way forward. As an adolescent, I was in love with history – really in love, smitten by the goddess History as a young man can be smitten by a girl. (I had

128

been smitten by a girl, too, but then my life had had room for both passions.) So of course I had beavered away until a path opened up that took me from the Bargeman's Arms, Oseney Town, to Episcopus College, Oxford University. It was a convenient way of going where I had the encouragement of more seasoned worshippers, men like Bax and old Gadsby, bless him. Had I ever slowed down long enough to think about Higher Values and whether I was getting enough of them? I had not.

I glanced at my neighbours on either side. No point in asking Fred Armitage what he thought he had gained from Oxford. Starting from Back Mill Lane, Hopton, in Yorkshire, the road to Episcopus had been upward all the way, into a landscape that grew wider and brighter and more green with opportunities. As a child, the only adult life he had had a chance to contemplate had been his father's. Walking to the pit gates, going in, getting into the cage with a squash of other men, then the sickening drop into the blackness, emerging into the underground city of tramways and cables and passages and shale dust underfoot, bending double and working his way along a narrow passage, finally getting to the coal-face and slogging away for seven hours, kneeling or lying on his side, breathing coal-dust, with millions of tons of earth and rock ready to drop on him at any moment; then back up in the cage, aching with weariness, and back to his little terrace house – still covered with coal-dust which his wife had to scrub off in front of the fire. And all for a wage that kept him, by every social measurement, poor and downtrodden. To the growing boy Fred Armitage, this must have seemed like a grim sentence he would do anything, anything at all to avoid. And it had been the local grammar school and the scholarship ladder that had been his means of escape, a whole social machinery which in his father's boyhood was only just being put into place.

So I turned the other way. 'What made you decide to come to Oxford, McFarlane?' I asked. 'Was it anything in particular, or did it just happen?'

'My parents wanted me to,' he answered in his lilting Edinburgh accent. 'For myself I didn't care one way or another. My training was vocational. If it was educational, that was only in the sense that everything that happens to you is educational. I wanted to be a doctor, and if I'd stayed in Scotland at one of the medical schools there it would have been just as good. But my mother and father had the idea that a few years in England would be broadening for me. So I ended up here.'

'Are you glad about it, in retrospect, or sorry? Or neutral?'

'Neutral. As a medical student you don't have much in your life except medicine, wherever you are. The training's very long, and when you're not having tutorials or demonstrations you're usually up at the hospital.'

'So what would you say Oxford has done for you?'

'Trained me. But if you want me to say whether it turned me into an educated man or not, I can only say no. I'm neither an educated man, nor an uneducated man. I'm a medical man, which is a strange in-between species, with its own way of looking at things. A real Third Estate, if you like.'

These questions were still in my mind when we moved to a small common room that had been put at our disposal, where coffee was being kept hot for us and there were decanters of whisky and brandy. Everybody settled down, some lighting cigars. An atmosphere of gentle self-indulgence filled the air. The time, and the occasion, were right for talk.

As Norbert sank into a comfortable chair I slid into another beside him, but to my annoyance Watson, with Hunt in tow, immediately came and stationed himself on a sofa facing us. I looked round to see if escape was possible, but Norbert was saying something that interested me and I didn't want to miss this rare chance of his company. Almost at once, though, Watson began talking, addressing Hunt and the two of us indiscriminately.

'Well, the decencies have been observed, wouldn't you say, gentlemen? I thought our worthy Ransom struck all the right notes and made all the expected points. A little earnest, of course, but then it's nice when someone behaves totally in character.'

I knew Watson well enough to understand that 'earnestness' in his eyes was a grave social *gaffe*. Everything had to be handled deftly, lightly, and above all with an unspoken assumption that it was slightly ridiculous. One of the things that bored me most about Oxford was the convention that however important the subject you were discussing, you had to keep tittering all the time.

I kept silent, but Norbert said levelly, 'I found myself agreeing with most of what he said. It would be hard not to, I suppose.'

'Oh, impossible not to,' Watson rejoined, his voice solemn but his eyes gleaming sarcastically. 'He provided just that ballast of moral earnestness that one needs on a social occasion like this, wouldn't you say?' When Norbert had nothing to add, Watson looked across at me and said teasingly, 'I'm sure Leonard agrees with me. He's a stickler for his ration of moral earnestness. Won't be done out of it.'

I leaned back. Let him get on with it, I thought. If he wanted to demonstrate his superiority by being flippant at my expense, let him get it out of his system. I determined not to be drawn; and I would have managed perfectly well if Watson had been the only gobshite I had to deal with. But Hunt was a different proposition. He aroused in me a dislike I had much more difficulty in keeping stoppered up. Watson represented the collective mind of Oxford at its weakest and most unattractive. Hunt, on the other hand, on his excursions into Oxford, came as the emissary of a world that felt threatened by the atmosphere of high endeavour which Oxford existed to promulgate. If, by constant jeering and patient undermining, the interest that Hunt served could bring about the collapse of the ancient universities and then make short work of the modern ones, and so finish up with a world in which careful thought and devoted study were no longer present even as concepts, they would be pleased and satisfied.

I looked at Hunt, forcing myself to take him in. I had read somewhere that people who had a phobia about spiders can sometimes cure it by trapping a spider under a glass and forcing themselves to make a drawing of it, noting the delicate intricacy with which the creature is constructed, losing their horror in the interest of study. I tried to do the same with Hunt, but soon decided that I was not comparing like with like. There was no delicate complexity in *his* construction.

'Old Ransom's speech made me want to laugh,' he said, his eyes moving from my face to Norbert's and back. 'Perhaps I should have given way to it. If I'd started a general laugh at the absurdity of the whole thing, it would have been more useful than all just sitting there like stuffed penguins.'

'Useful to whom?' I was fool enough to ask. As I spoke I cursed myself for letting him draw me out.

'Useful in doing the one major thing that needs to be done around here,' Hunt said, leaning forward slightly. 'I wouldn't expect you to know what that is, Leonard. You're too far gone.'

'Encouraging Oxford people to laugh at themselves, I expect you mean,' Norbert said. 'But don't you think they already do quite enough of that?'

130

'Not nearly enough. Too solemn and self-congratulatory.' He pointed at me with a long white forefinger. 'Holier than thou. Always representing the place as a nest of high ideals when in fact it's just an elaborate structure for mutual self-advantage.'

'Big words, Hunt,' I said. 'Let's hear how you justify them.'

'No need to. Boot's on the other foot. It's all these posturing Oxford types who need to justify themselves and the claims they keep making.'

'The problem is,' I said, 'that if we did, we'd have to use words like "scholarship" and "dedication". Then you could still accuse us of trifling, and of defending ourselves by spouting hot air.'

'Those words are all right. Only I put a different interpretation on them.'

'I've no doubt you do,' I said.

'Scholarship, now,' said Hunt. 'The way you roll out the word it's sort of . . . liturgical. Well, most of what you call scholarship I'd call self-indulgence, and so would most people. The self-indulgence of chaps who've turned their backs on the real world and retreated into a little nest where they have a lot of nice comforts around them and spend their time playing elaborate games, pushing counters around.'

'By counters, Hunt,' Norbert interposed, 'you'd be referring to . . . what exactly? What are the counters that Oxford chaps push around?' He leaned forward attentively, as if really wishing to know. 'You mean facts? Or ideas?'

'Facts, ideas, theories, all concerning things that either happened so long ago that they can't possibly affect the life of today or are so utterly trivial . . .'

'Hunt,' Norbert said patiently, 'I'm willing to meet you at any time and in any place that we can settle on as mutually convenient, to have a really serious discussion of these issues. If you're going to take an entrenched position, that the values of Oxford University aren't real values and that it's all a sham to cover over an organization devoted to privilege and self-interest, I ought to warn you that I believe the opposite and that my position is just as entrenched. But we can't really thrash it out here. It's impossible at a dinner party.'

'And most undesirable, surely,' Watson put in silkily, 'even if it were possible. One gets few enough opportunities to relax and talk in a reasonably light-hearted manner.'

'Granted,' Norbert said, 'which is one reason why I suggest that sniping is just as out of place as a full-scale engagement. If we're going to have peace, let's have peace.'

'Oh, a dig or two won't hurt Oxford,' Hunt said savagely. It was as if a real impatience, a real hatred, were suddenly flaming out from under his veneer of indifference. 'Everybody round here's armoured at least a foot thick in complacency.'

'Well, Hunt,' I said, 'you're looking at one man who isn't. I grew up, as you probably know, in a working-class pub in West Oxford. I had a passion for history and I wanted to spend my life studying it. Oxford gave me a chance to do that and I took that chance. So today I'm an historian. Perhaps you'll tell me I ought to be working at the brewery all day and pulling beer behind the bar all evening, like my father.'

Hunt gave me a cold, appraising look-over as if deciding which part of my body would be most hurt by a sudden sharp blow. 'I have to admit you might be more use doing that.'

'Setting aside the insult, is utility the only standard you bring to bear? What about your own trade, if you judge everything by its usefulness?'

'Oh,' Hunt said, recovering his square manner, 'I'd be the first to admit that being a journalist isn't as useful as working in a brewery. Still, it has its uses: opening people's eyes, exposing sham and hypocrisy – that's not quite useless, wouldn't you say?'

'If everything that you, or rather your employers, think of as a sham and a hypocrisy were swept away tomorrow,' I said, 'I dread to think what a desert our society would be.'

'Being pompous again, Leonard.' It was Watson's voice: whose else? 'It's so reassuring when people behave in exactly the way one expects of them.'

In that case, I thought, I ought to find *you* reassuring, but I don't. Aloud I said, 'Glad to oblige, Watson.'

'I'm really interested in your point of view, Hunt,' said Norbert. 'As I say, I don't want to get into a heavy discussion, but I don't want to just drop the subject without asking you, are you really serious?'

'Course I am.'

'Do you actually *believe*,' Norbert said, 'that a place like Episcopus,' he gestured with his hand, indicating the College all about us, 'is actually built on a foundation of mutually supporting vested interests, that it's just a set-up for mutual benefit – that it doesn't correspond to anything that matters in the real world?'

'Course I do,' said Hunt again.

'Well,' Norbert said, 'I read Greats myself, and I can imagine what you would say about that. It meant that I spent four years studying first Latin and Greek literature and history, and then philosophy in general. I suppose you'd call those just wasted years.'

Hunt's face was a mask of cold insolence. 'Presumably you wouldn't?'

'Not at all. As it happens, I've found it all useful in a perfectly down-to-earth manner. Most of the ideas that still rule people's minds were born in the Graeco-Roman world, and you might as well get them at source. Democracy, for instance – I suppose you'd say that was alive as an idea? – was invented in Ancient Greece. Linguistically, I don't see how anyone could deny that those languages are useful. All the Southern European languages – and they're also spoken now by enormous populations in the New World – are Latin-based. Reading Greats gave me a lot of practical skills.'

'And it made you a member of the right club. You found it easier to get a job at the F.O. because you were a Greats man.'

Norbert kept his temper. 'If the F.O. tends to choose men who've been educated along certain lines, there may be reasons for that and they may not all be discreditable reasons. If we ever have that serious discussion I'll try to explain them to you. Though I must admit my hopes of that discussion are fading as we sit here. I don't really think a serious discussion is what you want.'

'There's no need for it. You've only got to look at a place like Episcopus for half a minute to see what a put-up job the place is. It's full of people just indulging their hobbies and living on the fat of the land while they're doing it. It's far less use than a bicycle factory.'

'Well,' Norbert said, 'I dare say there are enough bicycle factories without turning Episcopus into one. But could you give me an example of someone at Episcopus whose work is absolutely useless? Just a hobby?'

'I've no doubt he thinks I'm one,' I said.

'Yes, I do, but even you're not the worst. There are worse cases than yours. There's . . .' He searched his mind for the ultimately damning, the ludicrous name. '*Tonson*', he finally ejected.

132

'Yes,' Norbert said, 'I overhead some of what you were saying earlier and I know you make a special target of Tonson. It seems to you just plain funny that he studies Arabic.'

'Well, I ask you! Arabic! Who the hell's going to — '

'Arabic,' Norbert said a little more sharply, 'is a language of enormous historical importance. Millions of people speak it.'

'Yes, but not millions who count for anything. These days the Arabs are just mouldering. The Arab nations will never count for anything any more. They've been outstripped completely by the scientific and mechanized Western countries and they're subject populations who have their decisions made for them, over their heads.'

'To begin with, Hunt, I don't like your implicit assumption that might is right,' Norbert said. His body stirred as if he were about to get to his feet, which I wouldn't have blamed him for. 'You obviously think that if people no longer have material power their traditions are without interest and their language not worth knowing. For a start I don't agree with that. I think it's to the credit of any University that it should study a language and a tradition because they're interesting in themselves. And secondly, one thing that you ought to have learnt in your three years here is that history is a very surprising subject. I've noticed that journalists very often make the assumption that a state of affairs which obtains today will also obtain in the future. If the Italians have overrun North Africa, the Italians will always be in North Africa. If Nazi Germany and the Soviet Union are mutually hostile, they'll always be mutually hostile. If the Arab nations are of no account in the world, they'll never be of any account in the world. I gather from what you said just now, Hunt, that you know I work in the Foreign Office and I wish I could say that there are no traces of that kind of thinking there. But I'm afraid there are. At least, though, it's not accepted as a law of nature, as it is in Fleet Street.'

Hunt remarked blandly, 'I knew that sooner or later you'd start running down Fleet Street.'

'Well,' said Norbert, 'you've been running down Oxford pretty wholeheartedly. Perhaps I should have left it to Leonard to put up the defence, but it didn't seem quite appropriate for a don to defend a don's way of life. A bit like having a Highlander to defend kilts.'

His tone was affable, almost comradely, as if he were unwilling to let Episcopus men go on brawling while on Episcopus territory. I remembered the trouble he had taken, when he was President of the J.C.R. years ago, to smooth over that dreadful business which had arisen of Carshalton's claiming that a valuable watch had gone from his pocket and that McFarlane and Armitage were the only ones who could have stolen it. One thing was certain: that Norbert was infinitely more tolerant than I. He was even more tolerant towards a man like Hunt.

As I formulated this thought I was aware that someone was standing beside the back of my chair. It was Bax. I thought he was going to sit down and join us, which would have been a relief. Any contribution from Bax, I thought, would tip the balance on the side of reason. I looked round for a chair that I could pull over and place conveniently near; but he was standing and obviously intended to remain so.

'Won't you join us, Bax?' I asked him.

'Thanks, but it's getting late. I shall go and turn in.' It was in fact barely midnight, and I could see several of the men were perfectly willing to sit there for an hour or two yet. But Bax was obviously tired – with, it seemed to me, a

133

tinge of something deeper than the fatigue that always comes over a college tutor in the seventh or eighth week of term. He looked grey and strained; something was wearing him down.

'I was just about to ask you,' he said, bending slightly forward and speaking in a low voice that reached my ears only, 'if you'd care to join *me*.'

Join him? Weren't we in the same room already? Bax was quite clearly asking for a few minutes of my company. He wasn't feeling sociable, he was off to his rooms, but he didn't want the emptiness and solitude that would encompass him there. As soon as I understood this I was on my feet. I valued and admired Bax, and if there was anything I could do for him I was going to do it. After a rapid circuit of the room, making routine farewells, I joined him in the doorway and we went out into the freezing blackness.

Bax was silent as we walked rapidly over towards his staircase and up it, silent as we entered the room and sat down. He switched on a powerful electric fire and we sat in its glow. On the table stood a bottle of whisky with about a third gone. Without asking me whether I wanted any – after all, I had accepted his invitation and the invitation included a drink – he fetched two glasses and poured out two generous portions. Generous? They were prodigal. When I held mine in the glow of the electric fire and looked at it, I opened my mouth to protest, then thought, what the hell and took the first gulp. Normally it would have gone down like liquid fire, but I must have been anaesthetized by the amount I had drunk already, for it settled into place as gently as a cup of cold tea.

Bax sat opposite me, already well into his whisky, still without speaking. Then, as if speaking aloud a string of thoughts that were moving in his head, he said, 'You came up in 1930, didn't you, Leonard?'

Even as informal as we were, he still called me by my surname. He was a surname man through and through. I knew, as an intellectual fact, that his initials stood for Robert Sidney Charles, but who called Bax by his Christian name? Did his mother? Had he got a mother?

When I confirmed the date he had given, he said, looking at me reflectively, 'So if we all live another year or so, you'll have engaged in the study of history for an entire decade.'

'Yes,' I said. 'It's a beginning.'

His eyes behind those round lenses went down to his whisky glass and then back to me. 'In retrospect,' he said, 'd'you feel satisfied with what you've done with ten years of your life?'

'Satisfied? Well, hardly. I haven't done enough work, of course, haven't achieved any serious — '

He cut me short. 'I didn't mean that; we all have that kind of dissatisfaction with our own performance. I mean, are you glad you spent the decade in history? Wouldn't you rather have been doing something else?'

'Not for a moment,' I said. 'It's the only thing I know how to do and the only thing I want to do.'

He sat silent for a little. 'Doesn't it ever seem to you a drawback that we never make anything *happen*?'

I was taken aback. I never expected to hear a man of his intellectual subtlety come out with such a bald, take-it-or-leave-it postulate.

'Who knows what makes anything happen?' I said, thrashing about for words. 'What about the arts, for that matter? Does a painter, or a lyric poet, look at his work and say, "That'll make things happen!" '

134

'Painters and lyric poets stir people's emotions,' Bax said. 'What does historical research stir?'

'People's minds, for God's sake,' I said. 'Their understanding of the world they live in.'

Bax took another swig at his whisky. 'Do you really feel that the world has been any different, over the last decade, because of the presence in it of people like you and me?'

'Before I could answer that,' I said, 'I'd have to have a clear idea of what the world would be like if people such as ourselves *didn't* exist and had never existed. Surely historical consciousness is a part of civilization, and surely civilization counts for something?'

'That's just it.' Bax put his glass down, very carefully, on the table. 'That's just it. Does civilization count for anything? Has civilization, in the last ten years, counted for anything?'

'If I were to say no to that,' I responded, 'would you conclude that the history departments of all universities should be closed down, that historical libraries should be dispersed or pulped, and that the whole idea of history should be abandoned by the human race?'

'I don't know,' Bax answered. 'I don't know.' His voice sounded flat and hopeless.

'Well,' I said, 'it's too late to worry about it now. Whether or not the civilization of the 1930s has been in any way enlightened or improved by the study of history, we're just about to enter a war. It can't last for ever, and what the world will look like when it's over I don't think one can foresee. And personally I don't waste my time in trying to foresee it because I don't expect to survive it.'

'You anticipate death?' Bax asked incuriously.

We have been through all this before, said a voice in my mind. Sitting there with Bax, the man to whom I had had to defend and justify my opinions during these formative years, I had the sense of making a second circle on a carousel that we had recently ridden together. When, a few months ago, he had talked to me about what I intended to do when the war came – volunteer to fight or buckle down to a war job – we had discussed the matter coolly, spelling out what we thought the situation to be, and we had been in no mood to deceive ourselves one way or the other. But the civilized veneer of rational discussion had been left in place. There were stark realities that we had chosen not to speak of directly. We had felt the cold movement of the air about us and we both knew it was made by the wing-beat of the Angel of Death. But it had not seemed the occasion to speak directly of matters so intimate and so ultimate. Now, late at night, our guard lowered by hours of slightly sentimental good fellowship, our blood loaded with alcohol . . . now was different. Now was the occasion. We knew that Death was standing in the corner of the room watching us and listening to our talk. There was no longer any reason to mince matters or gloss over anything.

What was more, I needed at this moment of crisis to live up to my faith, especially with the man who had instructed me in that faith. I was an historian, and more specifically an historian of the eighteenth century, a time when men believed that the dignity of life depended largely on the human being's ability to throw away bolstering myths and comforting illusions. And I thought of the noble words of Joseph Butler in that great tract of 1736. *Things are what they are: the consequences will be what they will be: why then should we desire to be deceived?*

So, turning my face full towards Bax, I said calmly (let me be calm now, at least! – whatever panic will doubtless seize me in the hour when all this comes true), 'Yes, I assume I'll die, and I think it would be rash of anyone in our situation to assume anything else.'

Bax showed no reaction. He hardly seemed to hear me. Something very fundamental was going on inside him and only a part of it, if any, concerned the general situation. But he had started me now, and there were things I had to get said.

'Reckoning simply by the probabilities, I expect to be killed in the first wave of the invasion, or rounded up and interned in the period immediately following it. Obviously I'd rather be killed straight away, because the Germans aren't in a mood to treat people like us with any gentleness. From their point of view, we're subversive. We've spent years cultivating intellectual detachment and they won't want anybody like that in the nice new colonized, sanitized British Isles they'll be running. At best it'll be a model farmyard, at worst a slaughterhouse. But in either case there'll be no future for people who've trained themselves to be sceptical. Historians are argumentative because they have to be. And we know what happens to argumentative people under that form of tyranny. Athenian democracy was a pretty lenient kind of dictatorship by majority opinion, but lenient as they were they still made Socrates drink hemlock.'

'So,' Bax said, 'you're ready for your hemlock.'

'Perfectly. I don't say I'm looking forward to it, but I've crossed that psychological bridge and I'm no longer trying to run away from it. I'm not as brave as that – not brave at all, actually. I'd willingly go along with their system if I thought I could, but I know I couldn't. I'd try to repeat all the slogans and join all the right movements and wear the right uniforms, and persecute the people they told me to persecute, and for a while it might work, but pretty soon I'd give myself away. I'd open my mouth and the truth would come out, instead of some smooth lie to save my skin. I'd *want* to save my skin but I wouldn't be able to do it. You're partly responsible for that, Bax. However much I'd like to be a slave, you've made a free man of me.'

'So,' Bax said, 'I'll have that on my conscience.'

'It's not the worst thing you could have on your conscience.'

Bax poured some more whisky into his glass. He offered to do the same for me, but I held up my hand. He put the bottle down on the table, then he said, 'If it's of any interest to you, Leonard, my forecast of the immediate future is the same as yours. The only point where we differ,' he went on, 'is that you seem to have escaped the mood of disillusion which has come down on me. At least,' he corrected himself, 'I don't know whether it is a mood, or a bleak realization of the truth.'

'It's a mood, Bax,' I said. 'I'm going home now. I'm sure you want to go to bed.' I meant, of course, that it was damn' well time he did go to bed. 'I'll get along home,' I said. 'Good-night. Thanks for the whisky.'

'Good-night.'

I left him but I did not get along home. That giant slug of Scotch had robbed me of my co-ordination. I found that I couldn't walk straight, and it was as much as I could do to weave across the quad to my College rooms. The bed was made up as a matter of routine, though it was horribly unaired. I had not slept in it once in the last two years. But needs must, and with that load of alcohol in me I fell down on top of it and blacked out. When I woke up in the morning I was very cold and stiff and had a terrible headache. I went and rang up Heather and explained that the dinner had gone on too long for me to get home at a reasonable hour.

'You mean you got drunk,' she said.

'Yes,' I agreed.

'I bet you're regretting it.'

'Yes,' I said again and replaced the receiver. Then I stood staring at the telephone, with a strong mental image of Heather putting down the instrument at her end with a gesture of exasperation. Well, the way she felt was justifiable enough. Obviously it's boring to have a husband who stays out all night and rings up in the morning in a weak, suffering voice. I would just have to put things right as I went along. And meanwhile I had indeed all the classic signs of a hangover: blinding headache, parched throat, evil-tasting mouth, a general feeling of being poisoned. Also, my eyes felt stiff in their sockets. And I had a day's work to do! Oh, confound Bax and his mysterious problems!

I went over to Hall. It was twenty-past nine and the last stragglers were just coming away from breakfast. I suddenly knew that all I really wanted in the world was coffee – strong coffee, hot coffee, large cup after large cup. I went eagerly up the steps and into the Hall. There was nobody left at High Table, and the two scouts on duty were just clearing away the dishes. But I could see there was a coffee-pot and I went towards it like a man in the desert – dying of thirst, delirious, walking step by step towards the mirage of a clear pool bubbling up out of the earth.

I got to the dais, stepped up to it, gained the table and closed my hand round the handle of the coffee-pot. As I lifted it I knew at once, sickeningly, that it was empty. One of the two scouts came up and said in a reproachful voice, 'I'm afraid the coffee's finished, sir.'

I lifted the lid and looked inside. It was a pewter pot and I could even see the faint burnish on the metal as it reflected the light. It was good and empty. It also felt cold, as if it had been empty for some time.

'Couldn't you . . . isn't there . . . ?' I said piteously to the scout.

He shook his head. 'Sorry, sir. I'm afraid the kitchen staff are very busy this morning. They've had a lot of extra breakfasts in guest rooms – the dinner last night.'

I had forgotten. The men who had been at the Episcopus Society dinner. Why weren't they here, having breakfast in Hall? Obviously Ransom, in his desire to give them a good time while the state of the world still permitted it, had had breakfast brought up to them in their rooms.

Knowing that my life depended on being able to find some coffee, I went over to the lodge and out. There, facing me, was the Randolph Hotel. Their dining room would be in full swing. I went across, not caring that I was hastily dressed and unshaven. I saw the head waiter hesitate briefly, but I put on such an authoritative governing-class voice in demanding a table for one that his resistance melted away. Installed at a corner table, I kept up the voice while waiters kept coming towards me with menus and with trolleys of things like grapefruit and cereals, and I insisted that I would order breakfast but that I wanted coffee *first*. And finally I got some just before my endurance crumbled. I verily believe that if it had been another thirty seconds in reaching me, I would have collapsed forward over the table in a dead faint. But the first cup gave me the strength to demand more . . . then more. After that I even toyed with some breakfast, enough to justify my going into the dining room in the first place.

By the time I got through the whole business, settled the bill and was making my way towards the entrance, it was nearly ten o'clock. I had to give a tutorial at ten and it occurred to me that if I went to the men's washroom and emptied my bladder and splashed my face with water I might begin to feel almost up to it. I did so, which was why five minutes to ten found me standing by the reception desk, just about to make my exit. I stood there for an instant, still trying to get myself together, one hand brushing the front of my trousers to make sure I was buttoned up correctly, and as I did so I happened to turn my head to the left, looking along the hallway and into the lounge. And that's how it happened that I saw Hunt and Molly Whitworth having coffee together. They were sitting on a sofa with their heads confidingly close. I thought they were taking a bit of a risk, what with her being so recently married and Oxford being such an echo-chamber of gossip, but then it occurred to me that ten o'clock was actually a very safe time. The mid-morning coffee drinkers very rarely got to the Randolph before half-past, and anyone who had stayed overnight had usually departed. And in any case, they were only having coffee together. Who could see any harm in that?

Term ended. Heather and I had decided not to go anywhere during the Easter vacation. There was nowhere within the British Isles we felt the heart to go to, and it seemed foolish to go abroad in case war was declared and we might be unable to go back. A lot of the people I knew thought exactly the opposite – that this was the time to go, to take a last lingering look at France or Italy or Greece while it was still possible. In the event their optimism was justified and my pessimism wasn't, but I couldn't help how I was made.

One evening I went into the lodge at Episcopus and found a message awaiting me. 'Please telephone Mr Carshalton at . . .' and then a number. The poisonous Carshalton? Why the hell should I want to telephone *him*? I thought he was safely in America, but this was an Oxford number; an hotel, probably. To get it over, I dialled straight away. It was an hotel. The Clarendon, no less. He must have been one of the last people to stay there, it closed before the end of the year.

'Dominic Carshalton.'

'Leonard here.'

'Oh, thanks for calling. The fact is, I have a little favour to ask you.'

Surprise, surprise.

'I'm here with my wife. I got married in the spring.'

'Congratulations.' And my condolences to the girl.

'I'm showing her Oxford and naturally she's interested to see Episcopus. Is there any chance I could bring her to dinner tomorrow night?'

'Not a hope, I'm afraid. We'd have to wait until there's a Ladies' Guest Night and they only happen three times a term.'

'But that's ridiculous.'

'Look, Carshalton, I happen to agree with you that the absence of women from the social life of Oxford colleges is a thoroughly bad tradition. But I can't change the statutes of Episcopus College overnight, or even the rules of Common Room. Damn it, ten years ago there wouldn't even have been the occasional Ladies' Guest Night. Progress does happen. But in matters like this, it happens with the speed of a glacier.' I got ready to ring off. 'So there it is. Enjoy your trip.'

'Just a minute. Don't be in such a hurry. Hannah's come a long way and it's natural for her to want to see what she can. Couldn't I bring her in to lunch?'

'Look,' I said, 'if it makes that much difference to her, bring her to the Senior Common Room for tea tomorrow afternoon.'

There was a pause. 'Well, if you're sure that's all you can manage.'

Yes, and it's all I feel like managing too. Go away and leave me in peace. 'Four o'clock tomorrow.'

'I'll bring her to your rooms first, shall I?'

'Come straight to the Common Room,' I said. I had a suspicion that if Carshalton once got into my rooms he would be hard to get out. 'I'll be waiting for you,' I said cheerfully and rang off.

Precisely at four o'clock the next day, Carshalton turned up in the Common Room with his bride, a wealthy American who, I quickly gathered, had been one of his students – though after their wedding she had not bothered to stay at college the few more months needed to complete her degree course. Obviously at her level of income it made little difference whether she had a degree or not – she would hardly be needing a job, I thought.

I enjoyed meeting Hannah Carshalton. She was something new in my experience. To begin with, the mere fact that she was American made her interestingly different. The world was very different in those days from what it was to become, America was not at that time in the mainstream of world history; and I had reached the age of twenty-seven without having met many Americans. And if Americans in general were an interesting novelty to me, the particular sub-species that Hannah belonged to, New York Jewish, was something quite unfamiliar. It was from her lips that I first heard the New York Jewish accent whose intonations were to become so dominant in Manhattan in the following decades as to constitute the New York accent *simpliciter*, though across the water in Brooklyn the Liverpool-Irish influence still persisted.

I liked Hannah from the beginning, largely because she seemed disposed to like me. In fact she was very much disposed to like everything. The Common Room at Episcopus seemed to her gracious and charming, as did the whole College. She admired everything – the tall windows looking out on the quad with a great chestnut tree in bloom just outside; the silver tea-pot and milk-jug, the elegant design of the cups and saucers. Turning to her husband, she asked him to make a point of seeing that they got to a store where they could order some of exactly that pattern for their home. Or was it their several homes? She was obviously very rich – her clothes alone demonstrated that, and without knowing much about such matters I would have hazarded a guess that just the accessories she wore – handbag, shoes, casual jewellery – would have cost more than Heather had to spend on dressing herself for a whole year. In response to the point about the china, Carshalton merely said, 'We'll have to be fairly quick about it. We shall only have one morning in London.'

'But one morning's enough, you slow old dinosaur,' she cried. 'Back home, I could go into Macy's or Balaban and Katz and in less than half of one morning I could . . . I could furnish a whole apartment.' She turned to me with a confiding smile. 'It's just a matter of knowing your mind, isn't it, Mr Leonard?'

'Peter,' I said.

'Isn't it, Peter? You know, on this whole trip, Dom's been leaving all the decisions to me. Where we go, what we do – the whole schtuck. He says it's my trip and he's not gonna interfere. Before I got married' – she pronounced the word to rhyme with 'varied' – 'I was warned not to try to dominate my husband, but I don't think Dom feels pushed around. I think he's quite glad not to have to take any decisions. It's a rest for him after all that teaching.'

'How's the teaching going?' I asked Carshalton.

'All right,' he said dismissively. His tone indicated that he rather despised me for asking the question. Obviously, his teaching post had come up to expectations, if it had enabled him to fish a rich young woman out of the Sarah Lawrence bran-tub. What else was there to go well or ill?

139

'Of course,' Hannah was rattling on, 'I jumped at the chance. I've never been let off the leash before. My parents were always so protective; they wanted me to stay where I could be under their eye. I know it was sweet of them and all, but they never go anywhere. They go to Florida in the winner and in the summer they go to some fancy resort in the Burrkshires, where my father doesn't have to feel too far away from his office. And that's it, Florida, the Burrkshires. I got to the age of twenty and I'd never been out of the golden ghetto in my *entire* life.' Her face was a self-parodying mask of tragedy. 'But of course a married woman can go anywhere. Boy, have we ever hit the opera trail this summer! Paris, La Scala, London – we've seen so much opera I even ask Dom to pass the salt in recitative.'

'Hannah has a passion for opera,' Carshalton said drily. I could imagine the marathon he'd gone through. But willingly, I supposed, as all part of a package that had made a rich man of him. Or perhaps I was being unfair, and he'd married for love.

It would in any case be no penance to find oneself married to Hannah. She was of a pleasant temperament, with none of the arrogance I had expected from the rich. She had a genuine curiosity about the world, like that of a puppy tumbling and sniffing around on its first outdoor excursion, and a genuine love for at least one of the arts. And she was physically attractive. Her rather wide face, framed in brown hair, was pleasant to look at if only because it habitually wore a pleased expression. Though she did not have the deep, haunting black eyes that make so many Jewish women irresistibly beautiful, her brown eyes were handsome enough. She spoke with a slight lisp, perhaps accentuated by the fact that there was a tiny gap between her two central front teeth. Her hands were expressive, and she had a need to use them, not merely in gesture but also to touch the person she was addressing. She also needed to stand close to you and lay her hand on your wrist or forearm every few seconds when she had a point to emphasize. It is a habit I have met since, always in her sex, often in her race, and as a rule in her nationality, and I have never found it anything but attractive and reassuring.

To cap it all I noticed – at some moment when she happened to have her back to me, having turned to examine a painting on the wall – that she was broad-hipped. With the passage of years she would fill out into a true Jewish matron, finding her fulfilment in ruling over a large brood. Exactly how Carshalton planned to fit into this pattern was not clear to me and probably not clear to him either.

We chatted on for about half an hour. A change, I noticed, had come over Carshalton's manner of speech. It had become more clipped and there was the hint of a wide-open vowel in words like 'nevah' and 'clevah'. I fancied I could account for this. In the Hollywood of those pre-war days I knew there were certain English actors, permanent residents of the film colony who were on call whenever English roles were to be filled. They were screen Englishmen and, rarely visiting their home country and being unaffected by the inevitable slow change in fashions of speech and mannerism, had become perfectly fossilized. C. Aubrey Smith was one prominent example; Carshalton, if he went on as he had begun, would soon be eligible to become another. He must have made the discovery, by no means confined to him alone, that in America an English accent fascinates many more than it repels.

At the end of the half-hour Hannah slipped away to do some shopping before they had to leave Oxford. The couple were on their way to London and then, a day later, to Southampton and a stateroom on one of the big Atlantic liners. Hannah had bought a pair of slippers at Elliston and Cavell's, and after some soul-searching had decided she ought to have chosen another pair which were shown to her at the time. She wished now to return the first pair and pick up the other.

'It's all right, honey, you don't need to come with me. I'll go straight back to the hotel. Well, thank you, Peter, it's been so lovely meeting you and seeing your beautiful college. I'll leave you two old friends together for a while – don't say bad things about me when I'm gone.'

And then she *was* gone. Carshalton and I looked at one another. At least we didn't have to pretend that we had any shared happy memories to bask in. I wanted to see the back of him, and he wanted to go.

After a moment or two I asked, 'What time's your train?'

'Train?' He reacted to the word almost as the car enthusiast Brian would have done. 'I haven't been in a train since I met Hannah.'

Of course, I thought. Hannah would use cars, hiring them as necessary.

'Where's your house?' he asked.

'Marston.'

'Can I give you a life there?'

'No, thanks. I'm not going home just yet.'

'Well, there's plenty of room if you change your mind. And it's a nice car. We rented it through an agency in New York and it was waiting for us on the dockside at Southampton.'

I meanly didn't ask him what kind of car it was. Instead I said, 'Sounds like quite a grand tour you've had.'

'Yes. You've put your finger on it there. It's very much Hannah's Grand Tour, to see everything and then go home and chew on it.'

'I dare say a lot of these places are new to you too.'

'Yes, though it's not so important to me, of course. If you've had your education in a place like Oxford, you feel that European civilization has touched you already.'

If I thought this place existed to foster complacency like that, I thought, I would work for its abolition.

'But of course,' Carshalton went on, 'there's always the time factor. European civilization obviously won't be there much longer. Better to see it while one can.'

I didn't want to get drawn into discussing any serious matter with him, but I couldn't help asking, 'If and when a war starts, d'you think America will get involved?'

'Hard to say. It's so much easier, over there, to let the future take care of itself. There just isn't the sense of urgency, the pressure. It's something to do with the sheer size of the country. We spent a month out in California just recently, house-hunting. When you're out there, sitting by that blue ocean, it's impossible to feel disturbed about Europe. It's like a fairy tale far away.'

'That could be a dangerous feeling.'

'Maybe. But we're buying that house in California when we get back. Santa Barbara.'

'I thought you worked somewhere near New York.'

'Oh, I'm chucking that.'

'Will you keep any link with academic life? There's a University in California, isn't there?'

'Well, nominally there is, but it's just an undergraduate college. There aren't

141

any jobs worth having there, and anyway I don't want a job.' He stood up. 'Sure you wouldn't like that lift?'

'Quite sure, thanks.'

I walked him over to the lodge. When we halted under the arch, he turned to me and said, 'Leonard, why do you stay here?'

' "Here" being Oxford?'

'Oxford, England, this side of the water generally. You could easily have got a job in America. If I could do it with a Second, you with a First, well . . . you could possibly have got to Harvard or somewhere.'

'And you want to know why I didn't?'

'I'm just curious about what makes you stay. Is it just sentiment?'

'I don't know whether it deserves such a big word as sentiment. It's simply to do with the kind of animal I am. Why do threatened species not move out when their environment starts being destroyed? Why do they stay and go down with the environment, rather than survive somewhere else?'

'They'd move out if they understood the issue.'

'Perhaps that's it,' I said. 'Perhaps I just don't understand the issue. I'm that kind of animal.'

He looked at me from those deep-set eyes and said, 'Goodbye, Leonard.' Then he turned and walked out of the lodge, his face towards Southampton, then the Atlantic, then New York, then California. I knew he never expected to see me again.

7

'We know how much the German people owe to their Fuhrer.' I stared down at the words. Molotov speaking in Berlin. August 24th, 1939, on the subject of the non-aggression treaty he had just signed with Ribbentrop. This was one newspaper report I had never, in spite of all my misgivings about the Soviet State, in spite of all my intuitive, personal conviction of Stalin's cruelty and treachery, expected to find myself reading. And now it had come. I thought, briefly, of all the people it would affect, all the good and decent people who had seen the Left as the way forward. In particular, they had seen it as the only defence against the rising tide of Fascism. Well, now Stalin, the Great Leader of the Left, the father-figure, the Pope of that world secular church which rejected original sin and had written out a new theology of social justice and equality, had betrayed them to the Fascists, handed them over bound hand and foot, and done it with a smile and a compliment.

I went out of the house. There was nothing to go to Episcopus for, in the August doldrums of the Long Vacation, and I certainly had no intention of going to the Bodleian. But I couldn't sit at home and look at four walls. I might have discussed the situation with Heather, but she refused resolutely to take any interest in a political topic, however large and general or however small and of immediate concern – whether it was the collapse of a political ideal or an agitation for a new bus shelter, it was all hot air and probably stage-managed in somebody's interest.

I could have pointed out to her, of course, that the news of an alliance between Russia and Germany meant that the outbreak of war was now inevitable. But instead I went out. I spent the day performing routine tasks, or wandering about (I walked round Christ Church Meadow for about two hours in the afternoon, just round and round). I had lunch at Episcopus, largely because I had already arranged to do so, and it seemed too much trouble to telephone and cancel it. There were only half-a-dozen men there, and they all seemed listless, almost somnambulistic. The news from Berlin was mentioned, but not discussed with any animation. Nobody, really, had anything to say. There it was, flat, heavy, ugly, immovable, lying across our future.

At six o'clock I found myself walking down to the Bargeman's. I needed, suddenly and intensely *needed*, to hear the matter discussed in the idiom of the public bar. I wanted to know what the *cénacle* would say about it: how it would strike Trundle and his mates.

The first thing I heard as I impatiently pushed open the door was Trundle's voice saying, 'Well, it's gorn up now. Gorn up fair an' square. They won't shift it this time. George Trubshaw told me 'e was a-passing an' 'e see it nearly done, an' that were three o'clock.'

'Never,' said Peake. 'That company, they won't never give up. They'll send their fellows round and knock it down again.'

'Ah,' said Trundle, 'that must a bin a sight to see. A sight for sore eyes, that must a bin.'

By this time I was standing at the bar. My father and I exchanged greetings, quietly, and he drew a pint of beer and pushed it towards me. I produced the coins to pay for it, but he waved them away with, 'Not this time.'

'What are they talking about?' I asked him *sotto voce.*

'Cutteslowe,' he said.

Of course! The wall! That was why Peake had said something about the company never giving up. The litigation had been dragging on for years; the City Council, advised by Stafford Cripps, seeking authority to pull the wall down, the company invoking every legal sanction to keep it in place and preserve the refined seclusion of Carlton and Wentworth Roads. Cutteslowe! The ultimate *exposé* of the English class system that had made a Communist of Geraldine! The ironies of world history! I should be able to enjoy them: but somehow I couldn't enjoy them.

'Honest, you'd a died laafin',' Bob said. 'I nearly dropped me bloody bike. I was tryin' to lean it up against the kerb and I were laafin' too much to do it.'

'And they was both at it, was they?' Old Trundle prompted.

'The boogers was both at it as hard as they could go,' Bob told him.

'Nor they didn't try to stop each other?' someone asked.

'Never once. They just keeps on as if the other lot woren't there.'

'Well,' Peake said. He took a long pull at his pint of mild, set it down and said again, 'Well. I never heard nothin' like it.'

'How did you come to be standing there, taking it all in?' my father asked.

'I'd been down in the estate, doin' the meters.' My father nodded. Bob was employed to read gas meters, or was it electricity, from house to house. 'I'd done me Cuttleslowe meters and I was ready to move off. I generally goes round on my bike. I gets an 'lowance for it. Threepence a mile. Makes it cheaper nor — '

'Right, so you'd been doin' your meters.'

'I was going to take the long way round, like you 'as to with that wall there, but I 'appened to glance up Carlton Road, and my eyes nearly come out of me 'ead. Two bloody great lorries drawn up. The wall down to four or five rows of bricks, not that much in some places. Two work gangs, about, oh, five yards apart. So I goes up to have a look. A lot of people was standin' about.'

'Council house people?'

'Both sorts. Everybody wanted to see what was going on. And there it was. The council lot had been sent round to knock the wall down, and the one from the company'd been sent to build it back up. As fast as one lot puts a row of bricks in place, the other lot knocks it off. There was some lads there was cheerin' like a football match.'

'Did you ever,' Peake asked of the room in general, 'in your life 'ear of anythin' so bloody ridiculous?'

'I tell you what it reminds me of,' Trundle said, 'Gilbert and Flanagan.'

'You means Gilbert and Sullivan.'

'No, I doesn't. I means Gilbert and Flanagan. They was two fellers as used to do an act at the old Empire in Didcot. That'd be in, well,' he wrinkled his brow, 'nineteen-ought-five. Crockery-breakin' act, it were. The things them two fellers got up to with a packin' case full of crockery!'

'What'll 'appen now, d'you reckon, about the wall?' someone asked.

'It'll go back up an' stay up, you mark my words,' Peake said. 'The council won't keep spendin' the rates money on sendin' workmen round to pull somethin' down as is goin' to be put straight up again. They just done it to show willin'.'

'What I can't understand,' Trundle mused, 'is why there worn't no trouble between the two sets of 'em. I mean to say, if I was buildin' up a wall and a feller alon'side o' me was knockin' it down, I'd take a swipe at 'im with a shovel.'

'Well, I took that up with one of 'em,' Bob said eagerly. 'I says to 'im, "Why d'you let 'em do it? You blokes is buildin' up a wall and they're knockin' it down, where's the sense in lettin' 'em do that?" I says. An' 'e says, "I'll tell you where the sense is, lad," 'e says. "It's a wage-packet," 'e says. "We'll come along 'ere every day for a year and put one brick on top of another and they can come along and take it off again, and at the end of the week we'll all get a pay packet an' we'll leave somebody else to figure out what it were all in aid of," 'e says. "But there ain't no sense in it," I says. "It's a job, sonny," 'e says, "an' that's sense enough for me." Then 'e looks at me and 'e says, "Where d'you work, laddy?" "On the meters," I says, "reading 'em, like." "Well," 'e says, "you stick to it. You read them meters an' don't ask no questions. If you got a job, do it. Since what they calls this De-Pression started," 'e says, "I been in work three years an' out three. An' the three years out wasn't no bloody fun. No bloody fun at all, mate." And then he bends down an' puts another brick on the bottom row, and a council bloke comes along an' smashes it off.'

There was a brief moment of silence now. It was Trundle who finally spoke. 'Aye,' he said. 'It's a bloody funny world an' no mistake. And if you wants to know what I thinks, that wall's going to stay where it is, for the rest of our lives.'

The *cénacle* received his words in thoughtful silence, noses disappearing into beer-mugs. On me they had an opposite effect. I wanted to ask them, *The rest of your lives? How long do you imagine that will be? Don't you hear the tramp of thousands of boots, don't you hear the roar of engines? Don't you hear the guns already opening up?*

They didn't, of course. What I heard in my mind, they, with their different mental organization and their different tradition, did not hear in theirs. But, I realized as I stood looking across at them and listening to their desultory talk, that didn't make me feel isolated from them. On the contrary, I felt very close to them. They were still my people, I was still one of them. The Dance of Death was moving towards us across Europe, and the fact that on that 24 August 1939 they did not look towards it, or listen to its gathering and approaching sound, was trivial by comparison with the immensely larger and stronger fact that very soon now, in a few days or a few weeks, it would be upon us all.

Amid all the turmoil caused in me by this sudden cataclysm, this final proof that perfidy ruled the world, I found I could still spare a thought for Geraldine and how it must be affecting her. I would dearly have loved to go to her and try to bring her some comfort. It was bad enough for the rest of us to learn that the Soviet Union had abandoned its policy of opposing the advance of Fascist power and actually signed a treaty of formal accord with the principal Fascist leader. But for a devoted, card-carrying Communist like Geraldine, the betrayal must seem as a personal one. She must be feeling that Stalin had betrayed, not only the human race, but in particular her and people like her.

Being so fond of Geraldine, my impulse was to hurry to her and tell her that generous, idealistic people are often deceived: their idealism lays them open to the promises of creatures who climb to power precisely by exploiting generosity, idealism and the love of one's fellow men. But this impulse died on reflection. It was overborne by the impulse to leave her alone. If I knew Geraldine, she was probably going through a stage of wanting to be left alone to straighten out her own thoughts and emotions. And of course she would be having to endure a dreadful amount of self-righteous and superior gloating from people who had told her she was mistaken in becoming a Communist in the first place. In particular I saw her parents, in my mind's eye, as I had seen them on the only occasion when we met, outside the Sheldonian on the day of her, and my, graduation. I saw their well-scrubbed, well-manicured, well-dressed bodies, their faces which conveyed so complete an amiable assurance of being right, of having always been right, of belonging to the right social class and being the kind of person within that class who were always, unshakeably right. Never wrong under any imaginable circumstances. And I could imagine what Geraldine, a compassionate and loyal daughter, must be going through at their hands. I wouldn't even put it past them to descend on her, to get into their clean shiny car and drive over to Oxford for the purpose of making sure she now fully realized the error of her ways. Poor Geraldine! She must be so bruised that even an encounter with someone like me who loved and wanted to support her would be painful. I stayed away from her, except in my thoughts.

I did, though, make the mistake of mentioning to Heather the following morning as we were drinking an early cup of tea in the kitchen, that I felt sorry for Geraldine over this business. It was unwise of me to say so. It brought out the least attractive side of Heather, directed partly at the absent Geraldine but also, I couldn't help feeling, at the present Peter Leonard.

'If Geraldine's suffering because some foreign politician has done something even more swinish than usual,' she said, 'all I can say is it'll be good for her. It'll teach her not to get in a tizz about bloody stupid politics. She ought to grow up.'

'But it's her job, Heather. She teaches politics. And she's involved with a lot of people who care about it very deeply.'

'Well, let her sort it out with them then. Let them get on with it.'

I had the sense not to pursue the subject any further. And there was, after all, a certain usefulness in getting Heather's instinctive reaction. It was the reaction of nine out of ten English people: anybody who got steamed up about political ideas was ripe for the mental hospital.

After she had finished with Geraldine, Heather went upstairs and presently I heard her in the bathroom, splashing around in the shower. I sat at the table drinking another cup of tea and thinking how beautiful she must look, standing naked with water flowing over her. She would be soaping herself, and then she would be just standing there, turning this way and that, as the warm water laved her body, and then just before stepping out of the shower she would turn the knob and bring the temperature of the shower down to cold. She would gasp, goose-pimples would appear on her skin, her flesh would glow with warm health, and her nipples would stand out, pink as shrimps and hard as pebbles. And I thought, although worrying about the fate of the world is legitimate enough, how foolish I would be to neglect the sources of happiness that actually lie about me, real and available. I have a beautiful wife and a delightful young son: having them shouldn't make me neglect the problems of the world, but neither should those problems make me neglect *them*.

I looked out of the windows, at the fields that sloped down towards the Cherwell. It was a perfect late-August morning. The leaves on the trees, the long grass at the edges of the fields, were absolutely still. The variegated greens of May and June, of every tree and shrub, every hedge and reed-bed, had faded into the dark and uniform green of August: but that too had its particular beauty, especially when brooded over by a pale blue August sky which promised strong, mature sunlight once the high haze had melted. Late summer! How long was it, I asked myself, since Heather and Mike and I had shared that magic together, taken time, slowed down long enough to enjoy it and know we were enjoying it? And *together*?

Mike, at four years old, presumably didn't make much distinction between the seasons. But he had the intuition of childhood, the ability to tune in to the unspoken dialogue of his elders. If Heather and I could seize today and really enjoy it, he would enjoy our enjoyment as well as his own. And his happiness would make us happy, and ours would make him the more happy, and so round in a glowing and rising circle.

I went upstairs and knocked on the bathroom door. Heather said from inside, 'What is it?'

I said, 'Have you got any social engagements today?'

'You mean have I arranged to meet anybody?'

'Yes.'

'Not particularly. I was rather planning on running into Jenny Winslow over coffee in Fuller's. I want to ask her about the — '

'Do you have to have coffee in Fuller's?'

'Course not. I just go there when I'm in Cornmarket Street.'

She opened the door and stood looking at me in crisp clean shirt and needle-cord trousers, her casual clothes. 'What's it all about?'

'It's about a picnic.'

'Have we been asked to one? You might have told me.'

'I'm asking you to one. You and Mike.'

'Who's giving it?'

'We are. And it's just for the three of us. Don't look so surprised.'

'Well, of course I'm surprised. You, suddenly wanting to go off on a picnic! You never do a thing like that.'

'Well, I'm doing it today.'

I got out the bicycles while Heather went into the kitchen and made a pile of sandwiches. My bike needed air in the tyres. I pumped away conscientiously. Heather's bike had a little passenger seat on the back for carrying Mike, but I saw how it could be unbolted from Heather's bike and put on to mine. That would mean I took the extra weight of Mike, which was only fair since the picnic was my idea. Heather could carry the sandwiches in her basket.

By the time we had got everything ready, and corralled Michael, it was nearly ten o'clock and the dew on the fields had dried off. It was already hot, and the August languor was over everything. Michael, who had reached the stage of incessant questioning, wanted to know where we were going for our picnic. I told him it was a mystery ride and he must wait and see. We went into Oxford. I was aiming for the Thames north of the city, and we soon got on to the Witney Road. When I had first taken to cycling out in this direction, my motive being to get to High Cogges and somehow scrape an acquaintance with Heather, this road had not been built; one progressed by way of a tangle of lanes, taking in places like Eynsham and Ducklington.

We pedalled for a time along the Witney Road, forced now and then to get into single file as cars overtook us. There was much less traffic in those days, and for minutes at a time the road was quiet, even a well-used highway like this one. We moved along steadily with the humped green line of Wytham Woods over to our left. The tall, slender spire of Cassington Church came into view on our right and a minute or two later I said, 'We're there.' We stopped and I opened a gate to the left of the road. Beyond it a track led down towards a line of willows beside the river.

We closed the gate behind us, mounted our bicycles again and rode the last bit. When we got to the river bank we saw that we were opposite King's Lock. To our left was Duke's Cut, linking the canal just north of Wolvercote with the Thames. Across the river was the lock-keeper's house, the lock cut, the lock itself with its procession of boats. But here, where the river curved away towards Duke's Cut, we were secluded. The boats passed on the other side of the artificially-formed island and at the nearest point they were fifty or sixty yards from us.

The water was dark and shining. It flowed with a strong, peaceful current. Anyone who doesn't understand how a current can be strong and peaceful at the same time has never seen the Thames in the vicinity of King's Lock. This had been for centuries the recognized bathing place for the boys and young men of Yarnton village. On the bank, at exactly the right point, a sturdy tree grew with a branch thrust out over the water. From that branch there hung, by ancient custom, a stout rope.

It was a place that must always have been beautiful, but it can't ever have been more beautiful than on that August day, with the hot pallor of a dog-day sky spread over it, the quiet green fields about, the dark line of the woods up ahead, and the smooth dimpled surface of the river sliding by with such tranquil, unchangeable purpose. Or perhaps, and I could just as easily believe this, it was just an ordinary unremarkable August afternoon, remarkable only in that the eye of the beholder, my eye, Heather's eye, looked out from a mind that knew this moment for what it was. And then I remembered, briefly, how Nussbaum had spoken of the beauty of the perfectly proportioned buildings of Episcopus as seen from the garden: how he had said that, without changing at all in their measurable characteristics, they would not be beautiful any longer when they came to be looked at by people who lived under the rule of the Nazi Party.

But the bathing place was beautiful *now*, which was all that mattered, and we lay down in the soft grass on the river bank and cupped our chins and gazed down into the water, trying to spot fish. It was impossible to see them in the deep, unlighted parts of the river, but at the sides, where the slanting light of the sun struck down on the yellow clay of the bank, the water was lit up like an aquarium and you could see any fish that idled there or darted past, shoals of minnows and sticklebacks that floated almost motionless and then suddenly, moved by some collective impulse, shot away into the blackness. And after a while I saw a huge pike, with those saw-teeth lying along its big undershot jaw, cruising at leisure no more than a foot beneath the surface.

The sun grew higher and hotter. Across the river the lock-keeper came out and put up a notice that said the lock was closed for lunch. The slow procession of boats halted, each new arrival having to moor by the bank and wait till the lock-keeper came back on duty. Heather had brought bathing costumes for herself and me, and now she slid into the water from the warm soft grass, splashed around in a vigorous circle to get used to the cool of the river, and then came back, holding on to tufts of grass, and had me sit Michael where she could take him with one arm and swim on her back. He sat joyously on the grass with his feet in the water, like the little naked frog he was, and I delivered him gently into her keeping. As she swam out into mid-stream I watched with a momentary spasm of anxiety, but immediately I decided that this was unworthy: Heather was no more likely to be careless of Mike's safety than I was myself, and I got into the water and swam after them.

After we had swum we got back on to the bank and dried ourselves and warmed up in the sultry air. Then it was time for sandwiches, and for languid reflectiveness. Drowsy insect-hum filled the wide afternoon. As we lay side by side I confessed to Heather that I had been anxious about her swimming with Mike.

'Well, *he* wasn't,' she said. She rolled over and looked at him. He was plucking blades of grass, holding them firmly in his chubby fingers, up to some immensely serious business of his own. 'He loves it here, doesn't he?'

'Yes, it's wonderful to see him.'

Heather gave me her level look. 'And d'you think he'd love it just as much if we put fears into his mind, if we said to him, keep away from the river, it could kill you?'

'No, but it remains an objective fact that the river *could* kill him. It kills people every year.'

'It won't kill Mike, because as long as he's too little to swim we'll always be with him when he's close to the river and because he's growing up full of love for the river and trust in it, he'll learn to swim very quickly. You'll see, as soon as his limbs develop a bit more he'll swim as naturally as he got on his feet and started walking.'

'Yes, you're right,' I said. 'You really are right, my love.'

Heather was silent for a moment, looking at the river, and then she said, 'In any case . . .' and stopped.

'In any case what?'

'If you really love a child,' she went on slowly, 'it's more important to teach them to love life than to fear death.'

'I'm still agreeing with you, my darling.'

"Everybody will die some time,' she said, almost as if to herself. 'But not everybody will love life.'

I looked at her. She was so beautiful, and she seemed so natural just where she was, beside the river, amid the cool dark grass, under the time-rooted tree. And the child she had borne out of our love-making was beautiful too, and seemed natural there. They were both the right human beings in the right place.

Looking down at Heather as she lay there, my mind went back to the first morning I had ever spent with her, after the night of the Episcopus ball when she had finished up in my skimpy bed. We had made love that morning, on the river bank out near Eynsham. The strong association of the river bank with sexual happiness, which was so rooted in my mind and perhaps in hers, must have been rooted in the minds of thousands of young men and women in the crowded centuries of those Thames-side settlements: the river had murmured placidly by Anglo-Saxon lovers, Norman lovers, lovers under the Plantagenets and the Tudors. Cavalier lovers, Roundhead lovers even! As an historian, I had an emotional need for things that connected me with the past, and here was such a connection, living and breathing and beautiful, lying close to me.

Michael now put down his bundle of grass blades, carefully, as if the secret game he was playing involved remembering where they were and going back for them later. Coming over to Heather, he seated himself astride her belly and said in a matter-of-fact tone, 'I want a ride.'

Heather, in accordance with the accustomed routine, began to jerk her midriff up and down, at the same time chanting:

Ride a cock horse
To Banbury Cross
To see a fine lady
Ride on a white horse.

She stopped and lay flat, pretending to be exhausted, but Michael's insistent little voice prompted, 'Wings on her fingers!' so she groaned theatrically, and then began jigging him up and down again.

Rings on her fingers,
And bells on her toes,
She shall have music
Wherever she goes.

The shadows were slanting now. Over towards the road, on a line of telegraph wires, I saw some swallows beginning to gather. In the distance, on the Wytham side, a man was driving a herd of cows towards the farm to be milked. In the still air the rope hung down from the branch, waiting for the next group of boys to exult in the strength of their arms and the agility of their bodies. She shall have music wherever she goes. I leaned my back against the tree, savouring the scene, possessing it, photographing it on my memory. And just before my outstretched feet, the eternal river flowed on.

Molly Whitworth (now Fishman), she of the high-handed manner and the coolly penetrating stare, may have been open to sexual advances from all comers (for it was ludicrous to imagine Hunt as the kind of idealistic, chivalrous *cicisbeo* who would ever have any demand on her that was more than casual), but whatever side-activities she went in for didn't prevent her from spending plenty of time with her husband. It was rarely that I went into the King's Arms for coffee in the middle of the morning – a habit that, owing to the increased demands of teaching, was now more or less confined to the vacation – without seeing the two of them sitting together discussing some such question as, by what means the mind can understand a statement it encounters for the first time. At such moments her face would convey stern, authoritative concentration; his, beatific raptness. The English Tourist Board had not been formed in those days, I believe, otherwise the pair of them would have qualified on the spot for substantial cash grants. After all, a busy pub in the heart of the classic academic area of Oxford was bound to be frequented by many day trippers who were wanting to absorb its atmosphere without loss of time; how convenient to have two people who so prominently announced, as if with sandwich boards: WE ARE OXFORD INTELLECTUALS. Looking across at them, drinking my therapeutic coffee, I used to be visited by a frequent urge to break into the ditty one of whose verses goes:

Oh, the clever men at Oxford,
Know all there is to be knowed
But they none of them know half as much
As intelligent Mr Toad!

One morning towards the end of August, a few days after our picnic, I spotted Geraldine in there, sitting with the Fishmans and evidently sorting something out with them. At least, Molly was sorting something out; she was bending forward, talking rapidly, making brisk gestures, while Geraldine, at her side, kept nodding in a rather listless fashion: it was the first time I had ever seen her looking listless, nor had I ever imagined that she could. Her eager, expressive little face was not made for it.

The only empty table I could find was quite close to the three of them, but of course, though I was plainly in view, Molly Whitworth-Fishman didn't spare me a glance of recognition. I was prepared for this, since she thought of me as so achingly tedious. But that Geraldine too should avoid my eye was slightly surprising. She was, doubtless, still hiding away from anyone who might bring up the dreadful topic of the pact. If she had been alone, I would have gone straight over to her, and gathered her – metaphorically speaking – into my arms. Literally, too, if I thought it would do any good! I cared deeply for Geraldine; and not the least of my grudges against Josef Stalin was the suffering he had inflicted on her and on people like her everywhere, the generous and idealistic Left.

I finished my coffee and their conference was still going on. As I left my seat I gave the briefest of glances over towards where Geraldine sat, quite prepared to see her deliberately lower her eyes. But I was wrong. She caught and held my look, and signalled me with her hand to delay my departure a moment.

I went over to the door and stood there, waiting. She spoke a couple more sentences to Molly, obviously wrapping up their conversation and perhaps agreeing some future arrangement. Then, nimble and quick as ever, she was out of her chair and over to the doorway to join me. 'Are you in a hurry, Peter?' she asked.

'Well,' I said, 'I've got things I was going to do, but if you want to talk for a while, or go for a walk somewhere, I can be free for a bit. After all, it's pretty important. I haven't seen you for ages, and this is a time when — '

But she was not listening. She simply went ahead through the door and stood for a moment on the pavement outside in the thin morning sunlight. When I joined her, she said, 'We're going for a short walk. It won't take long.'

I didn't ask questions. I knew it wouldn't be just an aimless walk. There was something very purposeful about Geraldine's face and manner. Her mouth was set in a straight line of determination, and her springy little body seemed poised for some kind of action. Moving a couple of steps ahead of me, so that what I saw when I looked at her face was its three-quarter profile, she conducted me rapidly across Holywell Street, past the front of the Indian Institute under its somnolently wise stone elephant head, and away down Catte Street. We crossed the High, turned right when we got to the other side, and almost immediately plunged into one of the side lanes that led down to Merton Street. Was she taking me to Christ Church Meadow? Not quite. We went along to the gates of Peckwater Quad, across the leisurely immensity of Christ Church and emerged in St Aldate's. Still without pausing, she hurried me down to the left, past diminutive Pembroke, across the road and down Brewer Street. Finally we stood at the point where Brewer Street ran into St Ebbe's, just down the slope from the old church. Geraldine stopped and looked at me as if she expected me to say something.

'Well?' I said expectantly.

'What d'you see?' she asked, gesturing around.

'Come on, Geraldine,' I said. 'There's no need to play games. I see St Ebbe's Street. I grew up in Oxford. My home streets are less than a mile from here. I've always seen St Ebbe's whenever I've walked along here.'

151

'That's just it, Peter, you've always seen it.'

I felt exasperated. 'What're you trying to do, Geraldine?'

She stood on the street corner like a small traffic policeman. 'Look around, Peter, and tell me what you see. *Exactly* what you see. Particularize.'

'I see,' I said, 'a working-class street in central Oxford, composed of small two-storey terrace houses, not very different from East Street, Oseney, where I grew up, only more run down.'

'Correction. *Much* more run down.'

'Agreed,' I said. The houses on either side needed a coat of paint and the insides, if one could have seen them through the yellowed net curtains, probably needed just about everything. The putty that held the window-panes was dried and old, and in many places it was breaking away in lumps. Many of the roofs had tiles missing, and of the tiles that there were a good few were cracked. The gutters needed renewing. As I watched, two very dirty children came out of a house two or three doors along from where we were standing, a boy who looked about five and a girl who looked about eight. The boy was barefoot and the girl had wrapped a shawl round herself, a very grimy shawl that covered her from shoulder to knee. On her feet she had worn-out gym-shoes that flapped open. They moved away along the pavement, arguing shrilly. I caught some words that in a more privileged neighbourhood would not have been in their vocabulary.

'Peter,' Geraldine said, 'how long did it take us to walk down here from Christ Church?'

'I don't know. Two minutes? Three minutes?'

'And Christ Church is the most magnificent of the colleges, wouldn't you say?'

'Certainly it's the biggest. And it says to you, *I was built by rich and powerful people.* You get that message as soon as you step inside it, if that's what you call magnificence.'

'It'll do. Three minutes from magnificence to this.' She indicated the poor little houses. 'Have you ever been inside one of these houses?'

'No,' I said, feeling ashamed.

'If you had, you'd know that they're infested with rats. And the sanitary arrangements consist of one W.C. to an average of eight or ten people. Quite often two families share one. And it's usually defective.'

I was silent for a moment and then I said, 'I think I have an idea where this is leading.'

'Well,' she said, 'I credit you with enough intelligence for that.' She turned her face towards me, intensely, almost fiercely. 'You've been a friend of mine for a long time, Peter. I didn't succeed in carrying you with me into the Communist Party at the time when I myself made that move, partly I think because you have a dislike of wearing a definite label that might restrict your freedom of action. You want to have unfettered individual scope.'

'Something like that.'

'Well, I presume you realize now that after what happened a few weeks ago it's impossible for me to stay in the Party.'

'Yes. I didn't suppose you'd want to march under Josef's banner now he's publicly declared himself a friend of Adolf's.'

'Obviously that's true as far as it goes. I've torn up my Party card and although they've sent people around to see me I haven't let them talk me into going back. As far as I'm concerned, that side of it had got to be over. But there's another side to the whole business that isn't over and can't be over.'

'What side is that?'

For answer she simply asked, 'Why did I bring you here, Peter?'

'To recall me to a sense of social realities,' I said. 'Did you think I was drifting away from them? Being claimed by comfortable middle-class don-hood?'

'Not quite that. I wanted us to talk to each other *here*, in the heart of Oxford, amid this wretchedness and injustice, because I'm interested in keeping your friendship.'

I felt a surge of warmth towards her. What I saw in her face contained so much eagerness, so much goodwill towards the world, and also so much vulnerability. I thought of all she must have been suffering in the last few weeks from the insensitivity of some of the people she knew.

'Geraldine,' I said, taking hold of her elbow, 'you must know you could only lose that if you committed some squalid act of betrayal, and *you*, as you couldn't do that. It isn't in your nature. You wouldn't be you if you did.'

'All right. I'm glad to get that clear. You've always been very nice to me, Peter.'

'I've always liked you, that's why.'

'Thank you for liking me, then. But let me make the point I was coming to. All right, I'm out of the Communist Party. But it's the Party I'm giving up, not the deeper values of the Left. If I didn't believe that the Left existed, the Left as a state of mind, an attitude, a faith as to how human beings ought to live in the world, I couldn't go on. I'd just lie down and turn my face to the wall and die.'

'I hear you, Geraldine,' I said, 'and I believe you.'

The two children, who had disappeared down the length of the street, now came back. The boy was carrying a large bottle of one of the very cheap gaseous mineral waters you could get in those days. It was a quart bottle and its size emphasized how small he was, with his skinny little arms wrapped passionately round his burden as if it were some immensely valuable prize. I noticed, now that they were facing towards me, that the girl had a skin disease breaking out on her face, just below the corner of her mouth: a big dried scab with a yellow area in the middle. They went into the house.

'The Left has to exist,' Geraldine said, 'because it's the mind and voice of the more generous and idealistic half of the human race. To the extent that people have generosity and idealism, they're on the Left – that's all there is to it.'

I tried to imagine a generous and idealistic right-wing person, but that had always been difficult in Geraldine's presence.

'So where does that leave you?' I asked.

'It leaves me an interior Communist,' she said gravely. 'Just as a person with a deep faith in the values of Catholic Christianity might have been an interior Catholic in the Middle Ages, in spite of the cynicism and wickedness of bad Popes.'

We moved off. As we walked along between the cramped, comfortless little houses with their cracked panes and peeling paintwork I reflected that if there were people living in them who still looked to Stalin as their Pope in spite of the Molotov-Ribbentrop pact, that might be better than having no Church at all. But then the thought came, could I really be content with so simple a solution? Is it, after all, so simple a matter to give one's allegiance to a Church, to build a life on its values? I glanced from side to side. The houses along this street were probably seventeenth century, and in any case the housing in this district, where the ground fell away between central Oxford and the river bank, had immemorially been the dwelling-space of the poor, the district in which one found not only crowded, insanitary houses but evil-smelling trades like the tanner's and the skinner's. When there were epidemics, they generally started first, and eased off last, in this area. What of my own ancestors? Was it not likely that some of them, as the generations went by, had been unsuccessful enough for one reason and another to be forced to seek their habitation about here, perhaps in this very street? And then I thought, as indeed I never went for long without thinking, of the St Scholastica's Day riots, when the fourteenth-century townsmen turned on the University, brought in reinforcements from the surrounding villages, and three days of bloody fighting left everyone terrified, a large number injured and six killed outright.

Geraldine and I, as students, had discussed this very topic, the likelihood that some of my ancestors were involved in that ugly violence, and of course I knew on which side. So much for acceptance of a common faith – so much for building one's life on the rock of a Church! Those medieval students, with hardly any exceptions, had been candidates for the Catholic priesthood, most of them already in orders, already the Lord's anointed; the citizens, too, had been Catholics at least in name. The answer, I decided after thinking a little further, was clear. The inhabitants of St Ebbe's might feel a warm, imprecise benevolence towards Stalin's Russia because they thought of it only as a large country that had thrown off its aristocracy and declared itself a People's state. Not being theorists, they would need to experience Stalinist tyranny in their own bodies before they saw it for what it was. Then it would be the fourteenth century over again: actual face-to-face contact would produce actual emotion, and it would be hostile.

Our slow, meditative pace had taken us to the top of St Ebbe's and we stood facing the end of New Inn Hall Street.

'Which way are you going?' Geraldine asked.

'Well, to Episcopus, ultimately.'

'I'm coming that way too.'

We walked a certain distance along the street and then Geraldine stopped and said, 'Peter ... are you terribly busy just now?'

'No. I've always got work to do but there isn't anything absolutely vital in the next few hours.' I could see, plainly, that she needed me for something.

'It's just that ...'

'Yes?'

'Oh,' she said, trying to sound careless and offhand. 'It's not really anything in particular, it's just ...' She finished in a rush, 'I do so terribly feel like talking to someone and most of the people I could talk to are, well, not ready for it or not right for one reason or another, and you're somebody I trust. With you I'm never afraid of giving myself away or saying the wrong thing.'

'I'm glad,' I said. 'And I'd like it if you talked to me.'

'Dear, dear Peter,' she said, 'I do love you.' I knew that wasn't anything much in the way of a compliment. She could look at me and say,'I love you,' and we both knew the words couldn't get us into any trouble. She loved me as she might love roast chestnuts. But after all, roast chestnuts are a fine thing.

'Geraldine,' I said, 'we'll go somewhere and you can talk and I'll listen and only give my opinion if I'm asked for it.' Then I stopped. 'The only trouble is, where can we go? Oxford's such a place for being *interrupted*.'

'I know what you mean.'

'Well, my dear, it's August, the air is warm and for once it doesn't even look like rain. All through my life, whenever I've wanted to think anything out, I've always gone to the same place. Wytham Woods.'

'Can we get in there? It's private property.'

'Geraldine, you're speaking to a local yokel who grew up within sight of Wytham Woods. I've been trespassing there since early boyhood. I know every path among the trees, every way in through the fence, every cosy little depression in the ground where the ferns grow thick and you can lie full length if you want to.' As I spoke my mind went back, as inevitably it must, to that summer evening, the last one I would see as a bachelor, when I had gone up into the woods with a girl called Vinnie, tingling from head to foot with a savage determination that we would fuck, and how I had come down again with that wish still unfulfilled. I shook my head as if to clear it. 'Where's your bicycle?' I asked.

'At Ruskin.'

'If you start walking towards Ruskin, I'll go and get mine, which is at Episcopus, and I'll catch you up when you're just about getting there. Then we'll ride over to Wytham and have some lunch in the pub there.'

So we did that. And the beginning of the afternoon found us deep within those blessed 2,000 acres of woodland, sitting side by side on a felled tree trunk coated with bright green lichen. Everything was still. Once, a jay screamed from among the high branches. Apart from that, there was only Geraldine's voice.

'Peter,' she said, 'it's a time of endings for me. Endings and beginnings. I feel so much crashing down around me that it puts a kind of desperation in my soul. Then I think, well, why not make a virtue of necessity and co-operate with it?'

'What do you mean exactly? What does co-operating with it involve doing?'

'One thing above all,' she said, turning her head to look straight into my eyes. 'Finding the courage to break off a very, very deep-rooted relationship. One that, in spite of its deep roots, was never going to flourish and bring real happiness.'

I waited.

'Do you remember,' she said, 'having coffee with me one morning years ago, and asking me if I'd like to come away with you on holiday in the vac?'

'Of course.'

'Since it's so long ago and it doesn't matter now, may I ask you whether that invitation was meant to be, well, a first step?'

'Certainly it was. If you'd come to France with me, I'd have tried to move the pieces across the board a bit.'

'I'm afraid I was vain enough to think so. So instead of just making some polite excuse, I told you the truth, that I was going abroad with someone who was very important and very permanent in my life.'

'You don't have to remind me. I know. It just seems like yesterday.'

'Well, it wasn't yesterday, it was years and years ago and I'd been involved with Robert for years already at that time.'

'Robert . . . ?'

'Robert *Bax*, for God's sake,' she said impatiently.

'Bax!' I nearly fell off my log. I couldn't speak: for a moment or two I couldn't even get my breath.

Geraldine's voice still had that slight impatience as it said, 'You mean it never crossed your mind?'

'Never for an instant. And I wouldn't mind betting that if you asked all the people who knew you and him, you wouldn't find one who . . .'

'It isn't really so wildly unlikely, is it? I mean, I know he's about fifteen years older than me, but that's not very extraordinary when you look around.'

'Well, no. It isn't that. It's just . . .' I sank into silence. *What* was it? Why, for that matter, had I never speculated about Bax's personal life, his sexual needs and what did he do about them? I realized that if I could have answered the

155

second question I could probably have answered the first. It was just that Bax . . . Well, he always seemed so self-sufficient, so . . . Then I remembered things that ought to have given me a clue, if I had been on the look-out. I remembered, for instance, how at meetings of the History Discussion Club he would sit watchfully on the back row and would never intervene except to head Geraldine off, even to shut her up, if she seemed in danger of burbling on. With hindsight, I saw it all. She was his darling, and he didn't want her to look silly.

'And all this time you were lovers, the two of you,' I said.

A certain blankness, a non-expression, came over her face and she said, 'You could call it that.'

'And now it's over?'

'I'll tell you how it was. On the morning I heard about the Pact, I knew I had to get out of Oxford. It was absolutely vital to get away somewhere by myself, away from all the people who'd be wanting to talk to me about it. They'd either be comrades trying to react to it from within the movement, wringing their hands over the way we'd been betrayed or coming up with various contemptible arguments for whitewashing it – which needless to say the *Daily Worker* did immediately – or they'd be people who'd told me all along not to get mixed up with those nasty ill-bred Communists. I wanted to scream when I thought of either set of them.'

'I don't blame you. I kept clear of you myself because I knew we couldn't avoid the subject, and there just wasn't anything I could say that would have helped.'

'Well, that was understanding and kind, and just about what I would expect from you, and that's why we're friends. So anyway, I got on a train and then another train and then another little single-track branch-line train, and I finished up at Fairford.'

'Fairford? In Gloucestershire? Did you book to there?'

'No, I just got out when we stopped there. I saw the name written up and I remembered reading or hearing that it was a beautiful old country town with a fine church.'

'Yes, indeed. Famous stained glass.'

'So I got off and paid the excess fare and there I was, in Fairford. I went to an inn called the Bull, right next to the church, and checked in. I stayed there for two days and walked about by myself and lay on my bed by myself and just got away from the sound of voices. And the people at the inn didn't think it was odd that I was there because I was a recognizable type. The spinster intellectual doing a tour of the Upper Thames Valley, looking at picturesque villages and historic churches.' She snorted. 'They probably thought I was a schoolmarm.'

'So then?' Fairford was all very well, but I wanted to hear about Bax.

Geraldine looked down at the rough lichen-coated bark of the log. She scratched at it with a finger-nail. Then she looked up at me again.

'After a couple of days of that, I knew what I had to do. I telephoned Robert and told him I had to see him. I said I'd be in that afternoon at five and if he had anything else fixed, would he please put it off. I knew there was nothing for it but to get it over. Such awful things were happening that I had to get down to bedrock. You can't face a world that's full of madness and evil unless your own life has its basic simplicities out where you can see them. I sat in the train going back and I deliberately kept my mind a blank, in case I thought about how much it was going to hurt him. And at five o'clock I went to his room at Episcopus. He'd got tea ready. Tea!' she laughed, a hard echoless sound. 'We'd got beyond tea.'

156

'I suppose he was just clinging to some ordinary bit of routine to give himself hope. He must have known something awful was coming.'

'Well,' Geraldine said, 'I didn't even sit down. I just stood there and told him, gently but firmly, that it was no good any more. The me and him business wasn't going to work, however long we kept on trying.'

I said nothing, waiting for her to continue. I was puzzled, wondering what had gone wrong between them. Presumably that was a question she'd answer when she was ready. Instead, I prompted her with, 'How did he react?'

'At first he didn't show any reaction at all. He just sat quite still and I actually wondered whether he'd heard me. Then he got out of his chair, still without speaking or looking at me, and went over to his desk. He took something out of a drawer and held it out to me. I didn't take it.'

'Could you see what it was?'

'Yes. It was a wallet with the name of a travel agent on it. Then he said, "Our tickets have come." We were going to the Hebrides for a month. We'd decided it wasn't the time to go to the Continent but it would be nice to explore the Western Isles, and Robert had rented a cottage on Mull for the month of September.'

'My God. He must have been all packed to go.' I knew Bax's methodical habits, his forward planning.

'I just said, "No, Robert. No Mull. No cottage. No nothing. It's over. I'm terribly sorry, but that's my decision." At least I think that's what I said. At a moment like that, you just open your mouth and say *something*, just to move the situation along.'

'And how did he take it?'

Geraldine turned her head. Her face was hidden from me now. I just heard her voice, as she sat beside me on the log.

'It was terrible. He cried.' She gave a slight shudder. 'I turned and went to the door, but when I had my hand on the knob to open it, something stopped me. I just couldn't bounce straight out after all that we'd . . .' She paused, then continued, her face still averted. 'I looked back at him and he was sitting in his chair with his back very straight, you know, how he does, and tears were running down his face.'

'Oh, my God.'

'Yes,' Geraldine said. 'It was terrible. Worse even than you think, Peter.'

'How d'you know how bad I think it was? I know it must have been hell.'

'It's worse than you think, Peter, because I haven't yet told you the whole bloody story.' Her voice rang out with sudden loudness in the quiet wood. I didn't reply. I'd known all along there were crucial things she hadn't told me.

'Have you ever seen Robert with a woman?' she asked. 'Not just with me, I mean, but with *any* woman?'

'Now you come to speak of it, no.'

Understanding broke in on me. 'You're telling me that . . .'

'Yes. He isn't inclined towards them.'

'Well,' I said, 'I've seen a lot of him and I've never seen any sign that he's inclined the other way.'

'You wouldn't see that, either. Robert's always very tightly controlled. That's part of his problem.'

I said nothing. I didn't want to go down that avenue.

'But there was an episode, years ago. When he was an undergraduate. It seems he had an affair with a bloke in the town, a clerk on the railway or something.

And of course when it all came out that made everything worse. You know how obsessed they are with keeping up the barriers between Town and Gown.'

'My God,' I said. 'It sounds like a major row, but no memory of it survives at Episcopus – not that I've heard, anyway.'

'It was a pretty well-kept secret. They went right to the brink of sending Robert down, but when it came to it old Gadsby made a fuss and supported him, and said he wasn't prepared to lose the most promising young historian he'd ever had, and they just smoothed it over.'

'Whereas,' I said bitterly, 'if it had been a *girl* from the lower orders he'd been knocking it off with, they'd have thrown him out without hesitation.'

'Of course.'

'After all, a monastic society devoted to learning isn't seriously damaged by homosexuality. It's letting women in that really does the damage. It leads to really destructive practices like marriage.'

'Well,' she said quietly, 'it didn't in our case.'

I felt ashamed of letting my tongue run away with me. I wondered if I would ever get over, really *get over*, the grudge I bore the University for having made me keep my marriage a secret, as if it had been something shameful.

Geraldine said dully, 'If we'd been happy together even for a time, it would be so much easier for me now to stand letting go of Robert.'

'But you will stand it. You made a decision and it was a wise one.'

'Oh, it's so easy to *say* that. If only you knew how I feel inside.'

'But Geraldine, you're free now. You can start new things in your life.'

'Are you thinking of anyone in particular when you say that?'

'No. I wouldn't have the right to poke my nose into your business, but I can't help knowing that Harry's in love with you.'

'Yes,' she said. 'That's all part of it. I've known for a long time that Harry's in love with me. And there's always been a part of me that responded to it, and loved him. But I was so confused. My feelings were all in a terrible mess – you just wouldn't believe.'

'Yes, I would. I would believe it.'

What she did next took me completely by surprise. She suddenly burst into tears and fell against me with her head on my chest and clung to me while great sobs racked her. I did the only thing I could do – locked my arms around her and kept her there. I felt the spasms go through her slender body and the thought came to me – a thought highly unwelcome in the circumstances – that she was built like a boy. No wonder Bax had tried to use her as a bridge to cross from one sexual continent to another. The poor bastard! I thought. And I held Geraldine tenderly, firmly, until her sobs died away and she finally straightened up and said, blinking, 'Have you got a handkerchief?'

I gave her mine. She got herself sorted out and then started talking about Harry. It seemed they had all sorts of ambitious plans. Breaking with Bax was only part of it, even if it was the most convulsive part. She had a whole series of radical changes worked out. She was giving her notice in at Ruskin. Harry's Shakespeare research scholarship had run out, and even if it hadn't he would be finishing with academic work. He felt he had waited too long to get into the theatre. Jobs were terribly scarce, but he was going in with a tiny, barely visible outfit, which nowadays would be called a 'fringe theatre'. They were going to do experimental (and Left-wing) new plays in an abandoned shoe warehouse in some unreachable south London place. Geraldine was very proud of Harry. Her notice at Ruskin would not be worked out until Christmas, but in the new year of 1940 she was going to join Harry in London – 'if London's still there,' she added gaily.

It all sounded pretty harebrained to me, but then I knew that happiness is never harebrained, so I encouraged her up to the hilt, and we got off the log and walked through the sun-dappled woods and I felt grateful to her for sharing her life with me, if only in words, because I truly loved and admired her.

I admired Bax too, of course, and now I thought I understood better why he had seemed so tense and lost on that evening of the Episcopus Club dinner, and I wished more than ever that it had been possible to help him in some way. But then I realized that evening had been months ago now: and Geraldine had cast him off only in the last few days.

'I'm sorry to bring up the Robert business again, but there's one thing I would really like to ask you. Was last spring a bad time in your relationship? About March, perhaps?'

'Why d'you ask?'

'No mystery. It's just that I had some contact with him at that time, of a personal kind, and he seemed terribly gloomy and stressed.'

'It was an awful time,' she said in her brisk, matter-of-fact voice. 'If I told you the details you wouldn't thank me. Satisfied?'

'Of course. And I promise never to speak of the matter again unless you do.'

'I won't. But thanks for letting me pour it all out. Come back and let me give you a cup of tea and then I'm going to send you on home to that wife of yours. I feel I've taken too much of your time and attention away from her and I have nothing, absolutely nothing, against her; in fact I feel a great kinship, a sisterhood, with any woman who's been cold-shouldered and pushed outside the circle of the Oxford camp-fire.'

'You must do.'

'It can't have escaped your notice,' Geraldine said as we picked up our bicycles, 'that my position in the last God-knows-how-many years has been like a distorted parody of your Heather's. And what makes me particularly bitter is that if I'd been a boy, Robert could have taken me everywhere and let people think what they liked. When has Oxford, or Cambridge, for that matter, ever cared about homosexuality between social equals?'

'But you said you'd always been very careful. What were you being careful about? After all he was of an age to please himself. Even marriage would have been forgiven him, at his level.'

'Yes, and that's where I came in. I didn't want to be known as one of these trollops who go to bed with dons. They do exist, you know.'

'I never met one.'

'Well you haven't known as many girls as I have. Not for want of trying, I dare say.'

'You're damn right. Why, in those days, if we got as far as even speaking — '

'All *right*, Peter. For God's sake don't get on about it. That subject really is your King Charles's Head.'

'Exactly. It concerned something they were trying to cut off.'

'You needn't be *coarse*.'

'Yes, I need. A bit of coarseness is what they — '

'Anyway, I wasn't going to have it known that Robert and I were having a sexual relationship until I felt confident that it was going all right, and when I did I was going to make him marry me. It was as simple as that. I knew I'd be good for him and make him a good wife.'

159

'Yes, I'm sure you would.'

'But it didn't work out. Never at all. It never *looked* like working out. It never *felt* like working out. It never — '

'Geraldine, please!'

'Please what?'

'Don't upset yourself.'

Fortunately we arrived at her place just then, and she repeated her invitation to come up and have a cup of tea, and I accepted. As I followed her up the stairs I thought, *Don't upset yourself.* I remembered that those were my father's words to Mrs Warmley, when she was re-living the tragic history of how she had lost her husband and why her son had grown up with the name Ivan. *Don't upset yourself!* Perhaps that was what all men said to all women. Perhaps what men wanted of women, most of all, that they should not upset themselves. That they should take whatever came their way, in a world planned and set up and operated by men, and never be upset.

At home that evening, I peeled the potatoes for our meal, read a story to Michael, carried in some coal and made a fire, and discovered that I was enjoying these things. Having a home and a family was good; being married was good. I thought of the endless succession of persecutions and uprootings that had marked the lives of such people as Katz and Nussbaum. I thought of the agonizing frustrations and bafflements and trailing silences, the desolating spells of loneliness *à deux*, that must have been the lot of Geraldine and Bax during the years of their doomed relationship. She had said, with grimly resolute matter-of-factness, that I wouldn't thank her if I had to contemplate the details of their sexual fiasco, and I had no doubt it was true. How fortunate I was by contrast! My own marriage, in comparison, was good. Obviously it was not perfect, obviously there were areas of less than perfect compatibility, but it had happened, it was there, we had a marriage and a home and a child. And if, as now seemed inevitable, the world was about to step in and pull down the structure we had made together, at least we had made it.

After Michael was in bed and asleep, Heather and I had our meal. Then we sat by the fire and listened to some music on the radio. It was a symphony concert. The orchestra was English but the music was German. The conductor was an Englishman with an Italian name, Barbirolli. It seemed to me, as we sat close together in the firelight listening to that wonderful music, that we were receiving a message from the greatest civilization the world has ever known, the civilization of Europe, sending out a last chorus of music before going down in a tide of blood and destruction.

We listened to the end of the concert. Then we went to bed, made love, and slept. My dominating emotion, throughout, was one of gratitude. I felt grateful to Heather for being my wife, for being dependably there, for sharing my bed every night without having to be persuaded, for living with me in our house. I had spent so many years trying to buck the system, and trying to get my needs satisfied in the teeth of obstacles of one kind and another, that I loved Heather among other things for her legitimacy. My last thought, as I sank into unconsciousness, was, again, that I was glad I was married.

On Friday, 1 September, at least two important things happened. The first was that the German Army invaded Poland. The other was that my mother telephoned to say that Uncle Ernest was very ill in the Radcliffe Infirmary. She did not say that Ernest was dying, but from the anxiety in her voice, and the mere fact that she used the telephone to inform me – still something her generation did only in an emergency – I guessed that this was the case.

'Dad's up there now,' she said.

'Have they let him in?' I asked. It was mid-morning, nowhere near visiting time.

'Yes. They said it'd be all right, just for a few minutes, as he's the nearest relative.'

At that, I knew Ernest was dying. My mother wanted to ring off, but I made her put some more money in the slot and go on talking. It seemed that since the spring Ernest had been complaining intermittently of a pain in his side, and tests and diagnoses had proved steadily depressing, but she hadn't wanted to worry me. Listening to her quietly anxious voice, I knew that, unless some miracle intervened, the good man's life was over.

An exploratory operation was, I gathered, horrifying in what it revealed. The surgeon had opened up his thin, brittle old body and what he found there caused him to close it again hastily and advise Ernest's immediate relatives to come and say their farewells. I went at once.

My father had always said of Ernest, 'If we all do as little in our lives that we regret, we'll be able to face death calmly when it comes, and that's how it'll be with Ernest.' It was an article of faith with him: Ernest was the eldest brother and he had set the example. Looking down at him now, I couldn't decide whether he was facing death calmly or not. His mind was wandering. He seemed pathetically anxious that I should visit someone further down the long ward. He himself was near the door, but he kept gesturing, weakly, towards the far interior.

'Don't bother with me, Peter,' he said in a thin, urgent voice. 'Get down there and see 'im. He 'asn't got long. You might not catch him unless you goes now, right away.'

'Who hasn't?' I asked. 'I came to see you, Uncle Ernest, not some – '

'Bettington, o' course,' he said. 'Hotchkiss was burnt with the plane. They never had no chance of pulling him out alive. He was the pilot and he went down with the craft. But Bettington, 'e was thrown out. Clear over the tops of the trees. Broke a lot o' bones when he landed, but he was alive when they picks 'im up. Get down there to his bed, Peter, he might 'ave some last words.'

It did not surprise me that Ernest should feel the presence of Bettington in the ward where he lay dying. Bettington and Hotchkiss had been present throughout Ernest's life. They were the two R.F.C. fliers who were killed coming in to land at Port Meadow in 1912. The deaths of these two young officers had affected Ernest more than the hundreds of deaths of young airmen that followed in the next four years. It was personal to him. He remembered when their crash had been the talk of Oxford. He had been present at the unveiling of their polished granite memorial beside the Meadow.

Nothing would do but that I must go to see Bettington. I walked down to the end of the ward, stood there for a couple of minutes, and came back to Ernest.

'Well?' he demanded.

'Lieutenant Bettington thanks you for your care and interest,' I said. 'He's sitting up, quite clear-headed.'

'What'd he say?' Ernest insisted. 'Any last words?'

'Yes,' I said. 'He said he knew there was going to be a war with Germany and he hoped not too many airmen would be killed in it.'

'Tworn't no Germans as killed Bettington and Hotchkiss,' Ernest said. 'That were an accident. A wire hanging down. A catch come open.'

161

'I know.'

'Always seemed to me funny,' Ernest said, 'as it was the junior officer at the controls, like, and the senior officer was just the observer. You'd a' thought it'd a' been the other way round. But no. Hotchkiss was a Second Lieutenant and he was the pilot. Bettington was a Lieutenant and he was the observer.'

Ernest lay back among the pillows. Suddenly he looked waxy, papery, almost dead already. 'What was that he said to you, Peter?' he asked in a voice that was hardly above a whisper.

'He said he hoped not too many airmen would be killed when England and Germany start fighting each other again.'

Uttering these words, standing there with the long rows of beds stretching away down the ward and the hazy sunlight coming in through the tall windows, I knew that on that sultry, threatening August day my thoughts were inevitably reaching forward and back at the same time; that my sense of past and future was as scrambled as Ernest's.

'Are they going to fight each other, Peter?' Ernest asked.'Has Jack joined up?'

'No.' I said, 'my Dad joined last time. He's too old now.'

'Too old?' Ernest said wonderingly. 'How can Jack be too old? He's going to be taken on as a "boy". I seen to it. I went to see Mr Partridge.'

I would never know, I realized, who Mr Partridge was. Some college bursar, or senior bursary clerk, back in the early years of the century, when all the world was different, back when the ladies' dresses trailed on the floor and the hansom cabs went *clop, clop, clop* along Broad Street.

A nurse came and bent over Ernest and took his temperature and told me to go away. 'Short visits are best,' she said firmly.

'I'm going to have another word with Bettington, Uncle,' I said to Ernest.

'We haven't got anyone of that name,' the nurse said to me severely.

'Yes, you have,' I said and moved away between the beds. Goodbye, Ernest. Goodbye, Bettington and Hotchkiss. Goodbye, so many who have died and so many who are about to die.

Saturday came in, 2 September, a fine day. Hitler's troops pushed on faster and faster into Poland. The British and French governments delivered their ultimatum: halt this invasion or we declare war. No one expected it to be halted.

At about ten in the morning I knew that Ernest was dead. Nobody told me, I received no telephone call (that came later), but I knew he was dead. When his time came, I felt it in my own body.

We had got up late, but not too late because Heather planned to take the car and drive in to Oxford market for the week-end supplies. Michael was going to play with other children at a neighbour's house. We were peaceful and close together, looking forward to meeting again at lunchtime and being together for the rest of the day. It was not a time to be apart, and besides, she and I still felt in our bones the warmth and closeness of our love-making of the night before. When I knew – somehow, from somewhere – that Ernest's spirit had left his body in the Radcliffe Infirmary and was moving away over our heads, I drew Heather towards me and kissed her.

'I shall go out for a bit, while you're in town,' I said.

She seemed to understand; at any rate, she nodded a simple assent.

I went out. The sun was shining. If the world had been peaceful one would have thought, 'We're going to have a lovely autumn.' I walked quickly over the fields to the Rainbow Bridge and across the Parks. I had never seen them looking more beautiful. Then I walked across the Banbury Road and got to the Woodstock Road. By the Horse and Jockey I waited for a bus, and when it came I went as far as the turning for Wolvercote, then I walked again. I wanted to get on to Port Meadow and do the walk that Uncle Ernest used to take me on when I was a little boy with short legs. We had always ended up by the little toll-bridge, and he had always halted me in front of the memorial stone and told me about Bettington and Hotchkiss and how it had been on Port Meadow when hundreds of people turned up to watch the stone's unveiling.

That crowded scene, so etched on Ernest's memory, had been unusual indeed in the quiet thousand-year history of Port Meadow. It was crowded again today. But today the figures were all of one kind. They were all young men, all dressed in khaki. They had rows of tents that stretched away to the far end of the meadow, and they had high-built khaki lorries drawn up in a long line down the Godstow Road.

I went up to the top of the bridge that carried the road over the railway and the canal, the bridge between Upper and Lower Wolvercote. From there, you could see the whole huge extent of the encampment. There were other people lining the bridge too, a lot of them, and I asked the man next to me if he knew what unit the soldiers were from. He looked at me sharply, as if he thought I might already be a German spy, and said he didn't know.

From my vantage-point on the bridge I saw soldiers going across to the houses on the other side of the road, carrying empty fold-flat canvas buckets. On their return the buckets were full: of water, doubtless. It would be their chief problem. Back and forth they went. I could see the water splashing out of the nearest ones' buckets when they swung them.

I moved on over the bridge. As I passed by the gate just before the duck-pond I saw two or three men, civilians, putting up a structure that had no military look about it. It was painted dark green and was in fact a stall, open in front. As I went past they were just fixing the counter. No doubt some enterprising local firm was hoping to sell some kind of refreshments to the soldiers.

I walked on through Lower Wolvercote. I had a date with three dead men. At the toll-bridge I stopped and read the memorial's inscription for the thousandth time, as a way of being with Ernest for a moment. I knew that life would carry me away from him very swiftly now. He belonged to my boyhood, as did Bettington and Hotchkiss. They, like him, had lived their life and died their death. Of course, I thought, looking at their names and at the year, 1912, those two fliers had been lucky. They had died at a time when the death of two young men like them was still news, still an event, still a cause of shock and grief. Another year or two and few would be interested enough to listen to the names as they were read out; how could they be? So many and so inexorable were the announcements, the slow march of sorrow that had gone on for four long years.

My farewell was over. I turned and walked back to Wolvercote Bridge, passing under that row of chestnut trees which, always the first to turn in the autumn, had begun to show an edge of brown on a few broad leaves here and there. I threaded my way through the lower village and passed the duck-pond again. The refreshment stall had been erected now and an urn had been hoisted up on to the counter. The comfort that was being dispensed was of the simplest kind, just tea, straight from the urn, with a dash of milk from a metal jug, in cardboard cups that were stacked up on a shelf running along the back of the stall. It cost a penny a cup, and at that price the men wanted it, hot and sweet and reviving.

They were two or three deep round the stall and I was walking along the road on the other side of the fence, but as it happened the clustered bodies and heads moved apart for a moment as I went by and at that exact second I was looking towards the stall. I could see right into it and I knew I was not mistaken. There were two women serving the tea. One had her back, momentarily, towards me as she reached for a supply of cups. The other was facing me as she handed some out and collected the pennies. The one facing towards me was Vinnie.

I saw her so clearly that she might just as well have stood still for half an hour and let me gaze at her with time to take stock of every detail. I *saw* her, not as she had been when I last set eyes on her five years earlier, but as she was now, on this actual day. She was exactly the same except that she had begun to fill out slightly. Her sleek brown hair was the same colour and it fell forward in a neat fringe in just the same way. In the instant when my eyes rested on her face, she lifted her eyes, those hazel eyes I remembered so agonizingly well, to look into the face of the soldier who was handing her his coin.

I couldn't tell whether she had seen me. But I had seen her, and I knew her. I don't just mean I recognized her: I mean I *knew her*, in a deep, interwoven, inseparable way. Whether or not she ever wondered about me, whether or not she had ever bestowed a single thought on me during those five years, I didn't know, but I knew her and I always would. I remembered so much about her and it was of such a close-textured nature, all the way through my student days till our knowledge of each other reached its culmination in the insane multiple fuck, beginning in the upstairs room of that cottage in Wytham Village and ending in the reed-bed beside the Thames at Botley, opposite Fiddler's Island, with the public-address system of Oxford Station sounding in our ears and a swan taking off from the canal. I had walked her back to Jericho afterwards, though, unsteady on my legs, I could have done with someone walking me back to Oseney Town, and after that it was over and I never saw her again. The very next day, I had been married to Heather, in the presence of the Archangel Michael and the souls of the lost and the saved!

Never again, that is, until this moment. I was seeing her now, handing a cup of tea to a soldier. She was deep into a new chapter in her life. I was deep into a new chapter in my life. Our whole society was just about to be engulfed in a war that would make ordinary private life seem an irrelevance. For Vinnie and me, there was nothing. Nothing before, nothing on either side, nothing behind except memories, and I would never know if she even shared those. But surely she would. Surely she couldn't forget the kind of thing we had known together.

But of course I knew she could. Forgetting would be something Vinnie was good at. She lived the kind of life that is easiest if you have no memory.

My feet didn't want to move. They wanted to stay where they were, holding my body there to look at Vinnie. But I made them move. I made them walk on. As I came down the other side of Wolvercote Bridge, turning my back on the meadow and the rows of tents and the long green ridge of Wytham Woods across the skyline, I made my mind as blank as if I had gone over it with a damp cloth. I must get home, I thought, in time to hear the radio news at six o'clock. That will tell me whether the war has started.

8

'No such assurance has been received, and therefore a state of war . . .' The poor old voice came over the radio in a thin, sharp bleat, its exhausted *timbre* saying more about Chamberlain's heartbreak than any words the man could have found for himself. Certainly it was no tone to inspire a nation to pick up the burden of war and carry it forward victoriously. What it spoke of was dismay, disillusion, the crash of hopes.

Heather and I were listening in the kitchen. Michael was outside; I could see him through the window, throwing a tennis ball up against the side of the house. He had only just arrived at the age when his hands were big enough, and his co-ordination of hand and eye good enough, to bounce a ball off the house wall and catch it. As I watched, he dropped it and went after it into the shrubbery, diving and scrambling.

Heather and I listened to the end of Chamberlain's broadcast and then switched off.

'What's your chief feeling?' I asked her.

'Relief.'

I nodded. 'You're glad the waiting's over.'

'Of course. Aren't you?'

I was, and yet I wasn't in the least looking forward to what we had been waiting *for*. Most of us expected the sky to be dark with German aeroplanes as soon as our declaration of war was issued. One half expected to hear the old boy's last few sentences drowned in the roar of bombs; and indeed, in London by some ghastly mistake, the air-raid sirens were sounded all over the city within a few minutes of the broadcast.

I wandered out of the house. The back lawn looked much the same, and over the fence the cows were cropping as if nothing had happened, but I wasn't fooled. Everything had changed. Hitler had not said, and few had expected him to, that he and his battle-primed Nazis would leave Poland alone. Already, as I stood looking out at those grazing cows, German troops had been killing Poles – men, women, children, old people, babies – for two days. The onslaught was not to be halted until 16 September, and then only because there were no Poles still able to defend themselves. On 19 September Hitler, broadcasting from Danzig, would claim that the German drive against the Polish forces, now successfully completed, was 'one of the biggest battles of extermination of all time'. When I read those words in a newspaper, I thought of Bertrand Russell and his cohort of still unpersuadable pacifists, all armed with cups of tea. How many cups of tea, I wondered, does it take to stop a battle of extermination?

For me, that morning was the start of a frenetic period of non-stop activity, a whirlwind of decision-making and step-taking that gathered up not only me but just about everyone I knew. Right away, there was my Episcopus Fellowship to be put away in cotton wool. Contingency plans had already been drawn up for about half of the College buildings to be occupied by the staff of a ministry evacuated from London, and one of the rooms they took over was mine; I hastily moved my books into store in a basement and said goodbye to College for the duration. Then there were interviews with Army recruiting boards to confirm that I was in fact to be 'reserved', and accommodation in London to fix up.

But meanwhile, even before all this was properly under way, the evacuees had hit Oxford. They came out actually on that first Sunday, trainload after trainload of them, whole schools with their teachers, and the inhabitants of Oxford were cajoled, browbeaten, shamed, blackmailed and bribed to take them into their houses. The old provincial Thames Valley isolation of Oxford finally died that night. What Billy Morris had begun with his car works, Adolf Hitler finished. That wave of children, nearly all working class (the middle class could make their own arrangements for removing their children to safety) arrived, welcome or not, in the homes of Oxford householders, nearly all middle class (it was they who had the spare accommodation), and before the calendar could register 4 September, fortress Oxford had ceased to exist. I did not mourn its passing.

No member of Heather's family attended the funeral of Uncle Ernest, which took place when the war was three days old. This caused no surprise. Mrs Burrell (I still couldn't think of her as 'Alicia') would have felt insulted at being invited to attend the obsequies of a college servant; old Burrell would not have come without his wife, and in any case was too dazed to remember who Ernest was. His son was away about other business and his daughter – the one who bore Ernest's surname and who had seen him most often – gently dismissed the idea when I put it to her.

'Well, no, darling, I mean, really, *no*,' she said. 'I'd have to take Mike because there just isn't anyone I could leave him with, everybody's so busy, and, well, it's just not on.'

She was sitting at the kitchen table, and she put her elbows on it, interlaced her hands under her chin and looked at me.

'You don't think Mike should go to his great-uncle's funeral? You understand, I'm not saying he ought to go. I'm just – '

'To dress him up in clean clothes and take him to the graveyard, and make him walk behind the coffin and watch it be lowered into the grave and have earth dropped in on to it, and all that traditional stuff said and sung, don't you see what I mean? It'd be saying to him, "This is death. This is something you have to stop and look at." He's never had to think that up to now. He's known death as an ordinary fact. He had that white mouse that died. He finds dead birds. He knows people die. He cried nearly the whole night when Buster died.' Buster was a dog belonging to the people next door. 'But he's never had to take death *solemnly*. He takes it as just one of those things that happen. And this is a bad moment to start him thinking any other way.'

'I see that. You've convinced me.'

Heather unlaced her fingers. She stood up and put her hands in her trouser pockets like a boy. 'Besides,' she said, 'from now on death has simply *got* to be just something that happens, like the weather. Either you're caught in it or you're not caught in it. But either way – *no fuss*.'

I stood up too, and kissed her. 'My love,' I said, 'I shall go to Ernest's funeral by myself, and bless you for being the best mother our son could possibly have.'

Ernest's funeral turned out to be unexpectedly moving. My parents were there, of course, plus Ernest's poor old wife, very frail now and leaning on my father's arm; she didn't, in fact, survive him for long. Brian and I were the only representatives of our generation: Primrose was not a funeral type. What really did surprise

166

and impress me was that Ernest's colleagues at Pembroke made it an important occasion. No fewer than six of his fellow scouts turned up, in heavy blue suits, two or three even with bowler hats, and they carried the coffin on their shoulders down the gravel path to the waiting grave. Looking at them as they lowered his worn, weightless old body into its final place, I though that their lives, like his, had been spent doing exactly this – moving things about, lifting them up and setting them down again; they had gone up and down staircases with trays, with bed-linen, with buckets and brooms, they had carried ships and shoes and sealing-wax across quadrangles and along passages, and everything had ended up in its appointed place, as Ernest had now.

Afterwards my father provided beer all round for these honest men at the Bargeman's, and I was interested to talk to them. Not one, it turned out, but thought Ernest had chosen the right moment to die.

'A pity,' I ventured, 'for him not to live to have his retirement.'

'Ah, sir, a few years ago I'd have said the same meself,' one of the older men returned gravely. 'But not now. Not the way things 'as turned out.'

A rumble of assent ran round the group. I thought, He calls me *sir*. That's because he knows I'm a don; he couldn't call a don anything else. Uncle Ernest would have called me *sir* too, if he hadn't known me since birth as Peter.

When they left there was hand-shaking all round. Some of the Pembroke men said, 'Goodbye, Jack,' to my father, but to me they said, 'Goodbye, sir.' I wondered what they would have said to Brian. But he had gone off straight from the funeral. He had to get back to the works.

About the middle of September the letter came which informed me that as of that day's date I was an employee of the Ministry of Supply, and set out my conditions of employment. So it was here. My 'war service'. I looked across the table at Heather, who was spreading honey on a piece of toast – we had one last jar of lovely thick, cloudy honey that tasted of clover, and it was to be years before we saw another – and said, holding up the letter, 'This is it. You're married to a civil servant.'

She smiled calmly. 'I suppose it's a change, but you don't look any different.'

'It's not very heroic, is it? You know, I'm half inclined to chuck it up even now and try to get into one of the fighting services.'

'I'll settle for the Ministry,' Heather said. 'Do a good job in your London office and dodge the bombs when they start coming down, and I'll think of you as my warrior in shining armour. Will they let you come home at all?'

'They're talking of week-ends. We work from Monday morning to Saturday lunchtime. A day and half's leave a week – it's long enough to get down here.'

'If there's any transport.'

'Oh, there'll be trains. Unless everything collapses, there'll always be a few trains on the main lines. We'll see each other for twenty-four hours a week, from early evening Saturday to early evening Sunday when I'll have to start thinking about getting back.'

'Such luxury. Hardly like wartime at all.'

So it was settled. The Ministry had given me a week to put my Oxford life in order before I reported for Monday-to-Saturday duty. It was going to be an impossibly full week, and some colossal areas of the job would fall more or less entirely on Heather. Still, she seemed to thrive on it; so much so that it crossed my mind that the previous six years of doing nothing very much must have been against the grain of her nature.

Well, that epoch was over now. Indeed, the following evening she informed me crisply, 'We're going for a drive tomorrow afternoon, to Mulberry Hall.'

I wrinkled my brow. 'Mulberry Hall? Let's see . . . I've heard of the place — '

'Of course you've heard of it. The Acheson-Fiskes' place.'

'Good Lord, yes. But I didn't know you knew the Acheson-Fiskes.'

'Well, I know the girl a bit, Diana. From pony club days. She once lent me a pony at a gymkana. She was a nice girl, not spoilt at all. If anything, that battle-axe of a mother brought her and her brother Robin up rather severely. Anyway, horses were the link between us then and that's the link now.'

'And may I ask why horses are bringing us together tomorrow afternoon? In the middle of a week when we can hardly find time for — '

'We're doing it,' Heather said, 'because this country has no oilfields.'

'Without disputing that statement, what has it to do with us and Mulberry Hall?'

'Agriculture needs traction. Things have to be dragged to and fro. Tractors burn oil. Horses eat oats. We can grow all the oats we need in this country, without sailors having to risk their lives bringing them here.'

'So?'

'I had a talk with Diana Acheson-Fiske over the telephone today. There's going to be a pool of Shire horses that can be used by Oxfordshire farmers, not to replace their tractors but to back them up. You can't fight battles with horses these days, but you can cultivate the land with them. It may mean some re-training for the farm workers. Quite a lot of the older men used to handle horses when they first started their working lives, but anyone who came into farming since about the mid-twenties will have to be trained from scratch. And of course the horses will have to be selected, and bought, and stabled till they can be taken to the farms they'll be working on. It's going to be what you might call a Shire-horse pool, and it's going to be run by Diana and me.'

'So that's going to be your war work.'

'As a start, at any rate. Have you a better suggestion?'

'On the contrary. I couldn't come up with one half as good. Will you be able to live there?'

'Of course. And Michael too. That's why you're coming out there tomorrow afternoon. Diana wants to vet you.'

'To vet me? But I'm not a Shire horse.'

'No, but you'll be in her house when you come down for week-ends. So of course she'll want to see what you're like.'

Mulberry Hall was a beautiful place. I had often seen pictures of it, but until we arrived there the following afternoon I had never engineered myself an *entrée*. I was glad to be there. Not only was it a pleasure to be in such a place, a beautiful house in a beautiful setting, but I also felt that Mike's early impressions of life would be coloured by the graceful harmony between its buildings and the landscape. I was also interested as an historian. The house was a perfect example of Carolingian architecture; the place derived its name from the attempt by Charles I, following the example of James I, to foster by legislation the cultivation of mulberry trees, the object being to provide food for silkworms and so build up a thriving industry. The attempt had met with only indifferent success, but Mulberry Hall was a happier monument than is usually left behind by ill-judged economic ventures.

Diana Acheson-Fiske received us in a friendly manner and showed us the stabling for the horses and also the couple of rooms up in the rafters, with a tiny kitchen and bathroom, which would be home to Heather and Mike, and at week-ends to me. In itself the accommodation was nothing much, but it seemed that there would also be the prospect of some domestic help, a commodity that had abruptly disappeared when the munitions factories opened their gates to women and the housemaids, parlourmaids, nurserymaids and kitchenmaids of England, glad to be rid at last of their hated servitude, went streaming in. But Mulberry Hall had become home to a Polish refugee woman, an ample blonde named Lisa; and Lisa, severed from family and friends, beamed with satisfaction at the thought of having a little boy to look after.

And there we were, into our war. That first week in the office at the Ministry of Supply revealed my work for what it was going to be, presumably for the duration: intellectually within the capacity of a child of twelve, but needing all a mature adult's patience, perseverance and ingenuity if the delays and frustrations and bureaucratic imbecilities which cropped up every day were to be surmounted. And then, at about one o'clock on Saturday afternoon, the taxi ride to Paddington, its huge acreage of glass roof meticulously painted black, the train with heavy blinds pulled down over the windows, and the small, weak light-bulbs not enough to read by.

When I got to Oxford Station I was by no means home. Heather was still running our car – there was a basic petrol ration for a year or two yet – but I didn't telephone and ask her to fetch me because it was already unpatriotic to use petrol for personal transport if there was any way of avoiding it. So I waited for the rattling little country bus that would take me to within half a mile of Mulberry Hall, and then finished the journey on foot, walking up the stately drive with my little case like a brush salesman. And when I missed the bus, I thumbed a lift instead. You soon got used to that sort of thing in wartime.

Of all those homecomings, the one I remember the most clearly is the first. I hadn't altogether been looking forward to the business of settling into what was to be a long-term temporary home, and of pushing into a space already occupied by Heather and Mike, and that slight uneasiness revealed to me something I had for years been determinedly looking away from: our relationship flourished best if left undisturbed, its rather fragile roots not stirred up. We had been man and wife for six years, we had produced a child whom we both loved, yet there were thickets of Heather's character in which I had no wish to go exploring. Nothing precisely focused, just a general atmosphere of caution, of never being quite able to relax, and I'm willing to admit that its source was probably in me just as much as in her.

In spite of a determination to be rational and businesslike, then, as I opened the large, imposing front door and stepped into the equally imposing hallway, with high-ceilinged rooms opening off on either side and a sweeping staircase confronting me at the far end, I felt a distinct sense of anxiety.

The first voice I heard was that of Diana Acheson-Fiske. She called my name as I went past the open door of a handsome room just inside the front door, now turned into some kind of all-purpose junk-room. Halting in the doorway, I looked in and saw her standing at a table sorting over a mass of second-hand clothing.

'I'm to tell you,' she said, 'that Michael's having something to eat below stairs, and that Heather won't be long but she's busy just now in the stables, giving some of the girls a lesson in harnessing. Trying to get them to tell the difference between a snaffle and a crupper, I expect.'

'Perhaps I should join them.'

169

'And that you've got a visitor.'

'A visitor?' I had hardly told anyone that I was moving out here.

'Yes, he's waiting for you upstairs.'

I thanked her and went on up to our quarters. As my footstep made itself heard the door of our little sitting room opened and a bulky figure came out, a soldier, in battledress and boots.

'Harry!'

'Had to take this chance to see you,' Harry Goodenough grinned, enveloping me in a bear-hug. 'I've only got leave until tomorrow morning.'

'Why aren't you with Geraldine, then?' She'd taken the plunge, I knew, and they were engaged to be married.

'I'll be with her when I've seen you. She's busy for a few hours.' He grinned. 'You're up with everything.'

'Yes, she filled me in. Congratulations! It's what I've always wanted for you.'

This *always* was a slight untruth. Some years ago, there had been a period when it had been what I wanted for myself. But Harry had made the more determined approach, stuck to it longer, and now he was there. And I had Heather.

Harry had brought some sloe gin, and I mixed it in two glasses with water and some blackcurrant juice which I vaguely hoped Heather wasn't saving for Michael to make sure he got his vitamin C. I excused myself, as I sloshed it about, by thinking that since Mike was now living in the country, he could spend his leisure time collecting enormous harvests of blackberries and wild rose-hips. We settled down and drank some of the gin and blackcurrant. It was good, so we drank some more. It loosened our tongues. I felt a leap of joy at seeing Harry; my friendship with him had been one of the best things in my life. Harry was in a class of his own: there was a selflessness about his passion for Shakespeare that was humbling. It went naturally with his outgoing, gregarious, generous nature. He was not a man to hug things to himself. No wonder he'd been planning to go into the theatre. For him, to be fired by the poetry and wisdom of a Shakespeare play was to feel an immediate need to bring that poetry and wisdom into the minds of other people, to invite them in and set that feast before them. It was the side of his character that, unpoliticized as he was, joined up easily with Geraldine's Socialism; it was one of the reasons why they would be so good together.

And here he was in his battledress and great clumping boots, his face red with exposure to the open air, his great thatch of hair trimmed down to matchstick length. He was Private Goodenough, an infantryman, the lowest form of life in His Majesty's Forces.

'What's it like?' I asked.

'Bloody awful,' he said and burst into a roar of laughter. 'Spit and polish, square-bashing and being yelled at. But I'm hoping not to stay in that state for ever. I've put in for training in a tank regiment. I fancy the idea of driving a tank.'

He had, he said, set his mind on that kind of soldiering from the start. But you couldn't just walk in off the street and join an armoured regiment; you had to be accepted for training and then get through a lot of tests. If you failed them, it was back to the P.B.I. 'But we'll hope for the best.'

I poured out more gin and blackcurrant, and we talked. Just as Diana Acheson-Fiske was standing at the table downstairs sorting out garments, we joyously rummaged amongst our common stock of memories. Then, the first afflatus dying away, we became graver.

'How d'you feel about being at war, Harry?' I asked. 'Really *feel*, I mean?'

'Dreadful, of course. I'm frightened out of my wits. Most of the time I avoid thinking about it, but underneath everything I do there's a layer of cold fear. I so much don't want to die.'

'Yes, I feel like that too. It's so much the wrong time to die, just when we've completed some kind of apprenticeship and started to take up the slack of our lives.'

'Yes.' Harry thought for a moment. 'Of course, in my case there's one real benefit, of a back-handed kind, but still a benefit. The disruption . . . the way I've been jolted out of my rut. It's made me realize I needed to get out of it, more than I ever knew.'

'Really? I thought you were happy in your theatre group.'

'I was happy, but the theatre's a world on its own. And if you love Shakespeare it's because you're responding to a great playwright, and if you're responding to a great playwright you must be the kind of person who'd be keen to foster the possibility of more great plays being written and produced. We're not just curators. We're shielding a flame – keeping something in being that could flare out again. Trying to create the right conditions, so that if another Shakespeare was born he wouldn't be wasted.'

'The actual Shakespeare, Harry, was lucky. He was born at a time when this country had a population of five million. It was a small, daredevil, thrusting country, reaching out for a lot of new horizons at once. At the same time as Shakespeare it produced Raleigh and Drake and Bacon and William Byrd and Inigo Jones.'

'Yes, and it had a heavy censorship enforced by a secret police under that swine Walsingham, and it had outbreaks of plague because they hadn't worked out what to do about sanitation. Though it wasn't overcrowded, Shakespeare's England certainly wasn't all peaches and cream.'

'I see all that, Harry, but in either its bad sides or its good it's not a society you could recreate today.'

'I don't want to replicate Tudor society, I just want to clear an avenue for major drama. If we don't do that we'll never know whether we might have had any or not. Damn it, Peter, suppose there'd been a Shakespeare born in 1920. What would he be doing with his energies? Would the West End theatre have seemed the right setting for his work? Never – he'd have been sickened by all that tinsel and varnish. The sort of experimental theatre I was in? No – too self-conscious, no tang of the people's sweat, no deep national roots. Hollywood? Hardly.' He paused, staring ahead of him as if lost in thought.

'What then, Harry? What would you do for a twenty-year-old Shakespeare?'

He was silent for a moment or two longer, then began to speak more slowly, assembling his thoughts.

'It depends on how we survive the next few years. A captive nation doesn't get drama. It doesn't get adventurous plays because they have to be rehearsed and staged and publicized, and none of that would be allowed. But if we manage somehow to be the victors in the war – if that happens, we'll be poor in resources but high in spirit – and that's what I want, Peter.' He turned to look at me, his eyes bright with emotion and purpose. '*That's what I want*. We need to strip off all the flab. Shakespeare doesn't need scenery, doesn't need elaborate lighting and stage-effects – he just needs actors who can speak and audiences who can listen, and that's a combination you can get in a barn, or even in the street if you have to. And where a revived Shakespeare could go, a whole new drama could follow. I tell you, Peter, I'm glad the war's come and jolted me out of my furrow. I may never get back to dramatic work, I know that. I may be dead in six months' time. But if I do get back to it, I want to work with *people* – actors and audiences. Scholars? Yes, certainly, they can tell us things, but when they've told us the things we've still got to act on them. My aims will be — '

At this point the door burst open and Mike entered, his head enveloped in a cardboard box on which he had stuck pieces of putty in a pattern recalling the shape of a triceratops's skull, and he had draped a roll of brown paper along his back, secured with string tied though scissored holes, which he had coloured with chalk so as to represent scales. He rushed towards us, but as he did so the eye-holes in the cardboard box slipped. No longer able to see where he was going, he tripped and fell sprawling, and in the ensuing commotion the thread of Harry's disquisition was lost. I never did hear what his precise aims were to be.

Mike now suggested that we should go and find his mother. I agreed on condition that he remove his triceratops costume, because it would frighten the horses. Harry helped him to roll it up and stow it away, at the same time offering some practical suggestions for greater realism.

The stables were red brick, nineteenth century. They spoke of solid, accustomed things, of great wooden wheels and iron axles and grooms and ostlers in leather gaiters. I suddenly thought of Charley, the drayman, when I was five years old, lifting the almost-emptied barrel to his great whiskered mouth: *That's where the goodness is, my boy, the goodness.*

Dusk was falling when we finally located Heather in a corner of the great shadowy stables. Her lesson to the girls was over and she was tending a fine large chestnut mare and her foal. The foal must have been born some time during the previous week. Though clearly marked out for growth into tremendous size and strength, the little creature was still unsteady, teetering on its already large legs as it nuzzled and sucked for nourishment, safe under the canopy of that great bronze belly.

'You're a good girl, aren't you, Judy?' Heather said, patting the mare's neck. 'She's just stood perfectly still and let me give her an injection.' She went on patting the huge animal. 'She's very young. This is her first foal.'

'She doesn't look particularly young to me. But then to me all horses look about the same age till they get really old and spavined.'

'That's what they think about us, I expect,' Heather said.

Harry Goodenough put in, 'I wonder what sort of horse Shakespeare kept? He must have had a reasonably good one, for those journeys between Stratford and London.'

'You think he was a good judge of horseflesh?' I asked.

'Well, he was obviously a good judge of most things, and it's clear he admired horses. He liked their energy and spirit. Remember . . .

> Think, when we speak of horses, that you see them,
> Printing their proud hoofs in the receiving earth.

That's good writing. It conveys the idea of strength and speed without — '

'Come and eat with us, Harry,' said Heather. 'I'd hate to make you late for your train.'

'Well, if you're sure . . . that's terribly kind of you.'

She turned and went with us into the house.

Some *apparatchik* at the ministry had found me accommodation – a dark, musty little rat-hole of a place where I only went to sleep at night. At the same time it was suggested to me by one of my superiors (virtually everyone, except the typists, was my superior) that I might find it an advantage to join a club ('Life in town gets pretty rootless without one, you know') and he indicated that he would put me up for the one he belonged to, the United Universities Club. Its premises in Mount Street were certainly quite pleasant. I ate there, spent time there, formed acquaintanceships there, and very soon developed the habit of having all my messages and letters sent to me there. On mature reflection, perhaps, it was all a device for keeping an eye on me. Well, if so it did me no harm. I was neither a spy nor a *saboteur*, I was not even using my London life for a hectic sequence of extra-marital affairs, which was fairly standard form among my colleagues. All I did was move dully and dutifully in a triangle formed by the office, the club and my unpleasant digs.

It was, then, at the United Universities Club that I found – on going there for a drink after work, early in my second week – a telephone message, 'Please ring Flying Officer Burrell', and a number.

Flying Officer Burrell now, was he? Promotion had come Tom's way and I was sure enough that it was merited. He and the R.A.F. were obviously made for each other. I rang the number immediately, puzzled that he should ask me to, and wanting to get the small ordeal over. It turned out to be an hotel: he must be on leave.

'Peter Leonard here. You left a message asking me to — '

Oh, yes. Thanks for ringing. The fact is, I'd like a few minutes' talk with you. Could you fit me in tomorrow morning? My leave's nearly up. I've only just got to town. I'd be obliged.'

'Well, it'd have to be in my office, which isn't very private. People come in and out all the time.'

'What I have to say won't take more than a couple of minutes. I expect they can leave us alone that long.'

'All right, shall we say eleven?'

'Done. See you tomorrow then. Goodbye.'

I derived no comfort from his tone which, as it always had been when he spoke to me, was remote and tinged with hostility. And when he turned up in my poky little office the next morning I read the same qualities very plainly in his face.

'Do sit down,' I invited.

'Thank you, I'd rather stand. This won't take long.'

'Oh, for God's sake sit down, Tom,' I said in sudden irritation. 'This isn't a parade ground.'

'No,' he looked at me icily. 'You wouldn't be on it if it was, would you?'

For a moment I didn't grasp his meaning, but then I saw that he was telling me he despised me for being a non-combatant.

I swallowed and said, 'Very well, now you've got that said, is there anything else?'

'Of course. I didn't actually come here just to say that. It just slipped out, actually. I suppose I ought to apologize.'

'Oh, please don't do that. Just sit down. It makes me nervous to have you standing over me like that.'

He was, indeed, a terrific presence. His uniform, in that smoky grey-blue with the silver wings and the badge of his rank, became him as if he had never worn anything else, though beneath its tailored lines one could sense his burly shoulders trying to burst through the stitching. And he had the correct R.A.F. moustache. It was not yet so fully developed as to be visible from behind, but I guessed he was working on it.

He sat down, majestically. 'I won't keep you long. There's just something I think we should clear up.'

'Go ahead,' I said.

'Just recently, I applied for a few days' leave on compassionate grounds.'

'Compassionate? Why? Has somebody been ill?'

'Not physically. But word reached me that things were getting . . . what shall we say . . . a bit snarled up.'

'Things at Cogges, you mean?'

He looked at me for an instant before replying, as if debating inwardly whether it was any business of mine to know that. But he must have decided that it was, because he said shortly, 'Yes.'

'So you went home to sort it out?'

'I went over to Cogges,' he said, 'spent a night or two there, and took stock of the situation, and on my third day I rang up Episcopus College and talked to the Estates Bursar. He invited me to lunch and was very forthcoming.'

'Oh yes?'

'Yes, he showed me the files and talked about the financial position of the farm, and the tenancy, and how the College saw things.'

'Did your father know,' I asked, 'that you were making these investigations?'

Again that slight pause, then, 'As a matter of fact, he didn't.'

'I expect he just thought you'd come home to see something of him and your mother and bring them some comfort.'

'I don't need to explain myself to you, Peter, but as a matter of fact I did intend it as comfort. Taking a look at how my father was getting on and having a frank talk with the landlord of the farm.'

I felt myself disliking him intensely and I could see how Heather had always hated having him as an elder brother. But I did my best to keep my feelings out of my voice as I said, 'And what did your frank talk bring to light?'

'It brought to light something that gave me quite a surprise.' He stopped and looked at me.

'I can't wait,' I said, knowing all too well what he was getting at.

'Don't let's beat about the bush, Peter. This payment that goes into his bank every month. That's you, isn't it? You've been helping him.'

He said the last words in the same tone which anyone else would have used to say, 'You've been robbing him.' I nearly laughed out loud. 'Yes,' I said, 'I've been helping him. What d'you want me to do, apologize? He's my father-in-law, no matter how little you may approve of the fact, and I couldn't stand by and see him — '

'That maybe, but he's not on your pay-roll.'

'That's a silly way of putting it. The plain fact is, he was having a thin time and he wouldn't have got by without it.'

'Well, that's as may be. But if I'd known he was in such trouble I wouldn't have stood by and let him accept help from someone outside the family.'

'I'm in the family now, remember? I married your sister.'

He ignored that and went on. 'It wouldn't have been easy. I'd have had to raise a loan or something. But now I'm a Flying Officer and I'm better off. So as soon as I heard they were falling short by a hundred a year I arranged to pay it. And all I'm here for now is to request that you cease your quarterly payments into my father's bank account.'

'Very well. I'll do that.'

'I gather my mother doesn't know about it either.'

'No. They're both in the dark.'

He stood up. 'I do understand,' he said with an effort, 'that you meant well. But please try to realize that my family don't need to be supported by you.'

'You mean you don't want them to be.' He had his pride. I understood that. But there should still be some sort of truthfulness between us.

'No,' he said. 'I mean they don't need to be.'

Now it was my turn to stand up. A cold rage had taken possession of me. It was an effect I associated with Tom: I knew I was about to say something I would probably regret, but I knew also that I would regret it more if I let his lie go unchallenged.

'I'll tell you why I paid that hundred a year. Because I thought it was time somebody did something for your father.'

'Did something for him?'

'Yes, something, anything except disappoint him and sell him down the river. You walked out and left the farm too short-handed to be workable, because you wanted to live your own life. Heather had already gone because *she* wanted to live her own life, which happened to be with me. All very understandable. But even his wife was planning to live her own life too, though it would be the finish for him as a farmer.'

'What on earth are you — '

'That *chic* little restaurant she was planning to open, with Heather as kitchen-maid, in Witney or somewhere, probably saddling herself with a huge bank loan. And with her away, he'd have been finished as a farmer. He'd have had to get out, and live out his days making himself useful at the restaurant: driving a van around, peeling potatoes, emptying the garbage. Not much dignity in that for an ageing man who, whatever his troubles, had always had the status of being Farmer Burrell. I didn't want to see that. So I gave him the money to tide him over.'

He stood silent for a moment, then said, 'H'm. Well at least we understand each other.'

'I wouldn't say that. But I feel fairly sure that I understand you. You want to go on looking down on me and that doesn't square very well with the thought that I'm keeping your parents in business. So you come in here, ordering me to stop meddling in your family affairs. That's fine with me. I don't care where they get the money from as long as they get it and stay at Jasmine Farm, because it's the only life your father wants.'

Mentally I made one reservation. There was something I had no intention of telling him: the particular place I gave Jasmine Farm in my thinking about Michael. But that was none of his business.

Tom started to walk to the door. I stood behind the desk, looking at his big shoulders and the neat line of his haircut on the strong column of his neck. But after a few steps he halted and turned round.

'I don't know if it's worth bothering to answer all that. Some of what you say is true anyway. I ought to have done more for my father. But whether I ought to have stayed on the farm instead of going off to learn to fly . . .' He shrugged. 'There isn't only my father to consider. I had a duty to him, but there are other duties too. I got some flying experience in. Not many chaps did. All the years we were messing about, the Germans were training pilots. Even the Italians were getting in practice, dropping stacks of bombs on poor bloody Abyssinians. What ought I to have been doing? Hanging around on a tenant farm, driving a worn-out tractor, baling hay and taking sick calves to the vet?'

It was a good question. He turned back to the door, went through it and was gone, but his face stayed in my mind: the eyes were so incredibly like Heather's. I was linked, genetically, to this man. I had fathered a son who was half his stock. Ought I to feel sorry about that, or glad?

As usual, I was unable to answer. I didn't seem to know the answer to any fundamental question concerning my personal life. But at least I could act on a practical, day-to-day level. That lunchtime I went round to my bank and cancelled the standing order in favour of my father-in-law.

September, October, November, December . . . that strange period of inaction, the 'phony war', ticked along. The children had been evacuated from their city homes in readiness for the air raids that had not yet come; troops were being hastily trained, munitions feverishly turned out in government factories, and still the fighting hadn't started. People began to wonder if the war were all an illusion: some ceased to believe in it. There were even calls for a negotiated peace.

For the time being, however, the life of the Leonard family had achieved a balance and a routine. Brian, I knew, was extremely busy with war work – no talk of military service for him! While nominally still an employee of M.G. at Abingdon, he had been switched back to Cowley, scene of his working life back in the days when he and I were both living under the roof of the friendly old waterside pub, and he used to pedal over there on his ramshackle push-bike to do his apprentice training. Now, his business was to repair damaged R.A.F. 'planes. Times had changed indeed, he reported to my father. Billy Morris, 'the Old Man', had become Lord Nuffield, the very firm itself had ceased to exist and become merged in an amorphous growth, spreading out far and wide to the east of the city, called 'the Nuffield Organization', now entrusted with all R.A.F. repairs for the duration of the war, with the Old Man himself as 'Director-General of Maintenance, Air Ministry'. The floodgates of work had not yet broken open, but some damaged 'planes had been coming in since 1939 and Brian, with his years of experience on racing-car engines, could repair an aircraft engine with the best of them in those simpler pre-jet days. As for Primrose, she had a typical wartime job, something to do with delivery driving, that took her off on cross-country journeys, often at night, My parents carried on at the pub. I slogged through the week in London and took that blessed Paddington train every Saturday afternoon. Heather divided her attention between slow, patient and sagacious horses, and human beings who as a rule lacked these qualities.

Even little Michael had made his wartime adjustment. Mulberry Park was now his home, the village school his place of education. He seemed to get on all right there. One benefit – or at any rate I decided to treat it as a benefit – was that a good many of the children at the school were evacuees from working-class areas of London, who brought with them a range of experience and a saltiness of speech not hitherto found in the placid village community.

'What does "fuck" mean?' he asked me once. (He was five and a half.)

'It's something men and ladies do.'

'Is it rude?'

'Not specially. But it's best if the people who do it are grown-up. And they usually wait till they get married.'

'Is that why men and ladies get married? So they can fuck?'

'Yes,' I said. It seemed the only answer that was reasonably simple without being altogether untrue.

'Is that why you and Mummy got married?'

'It's one reason, yes.'

'When do you do it?'

'At nights, mostly. When you're in bed and asleep.'

'But you're only with Mummy on Saturday nights and a bit of Sunday.'

'Yes, but that isn't the way we want it. It's because of the war.'

'What's the war?'

'A lot of people have decided to fight us. So we're going to fight back and do our best to drive them off.'

'Why have they decided to fight us?'

'Well, some people are like that. Doesn't anybody come up to you in the playground and start hitting you for no reason?'

'Yes, David Wild does.'

'Is David Wild big and strong?' I asked carefully.

'He's big, but I don't think he's strong. He likes to pin little kids down. But I can fight him. He never hits me when he's by himself. He has a boy that goes round with him called Martin Graham; he gets Martin Graham to jump on your back suddenly when you're not ready, and then he holds your arms behind your back and then David Wild comes and laughs and hits you in the face.'

'Well,' I said, 'you see what I mean. Some people are just like that. They like hitting other people and then the only thing the other people can do is fight back. That's what wars are.'

'Why do the first people like hitting the other people?'

'Because they're bastards, I suppose.'

'What's a bastard?'

'A person like David Wild.'

'What are Germans?' he suddenly asked me.

'Germans are the people who are coming to fight us. That's what they're called. They're people from Germany.'

'Are Germans bastards?'

'Not all Germans, but the ones who are coming to attack us are.'

'Do Germans fuck?'

'I expect they do if they get the chance.'

'Does everybody fuck if they get the chance?'

'Yes. Now it's time for you to put your toys away and wash your hands before supper.'

Would the fighting ever start? As the 'phony war' went on, it became possible to believe that the German army was not going to attack us after all. On the fourth of March the luckless Chamberlain declared, 'Hitler has missed the boat.' Anything said by Chamberlain, particularly anything in the nature of an analysis or a prediction, was certain to be proved wrong. In this case, the proof took just over one month. On the ninth of April the Germans invaded Norway and Denmark, countries which had hoped to stay clear of the war by declaring themselves neutral, and swept through them in a few days. On the tenth of May they attacked through Belgium and Holland, and by that route struck at France.

177

On the evening of that day, Neville Chamberlain ceased to be Prime Minister and was replaced by Winston Churchill. 'A vote for Hogg is a vote for Hitler', Geraldine's poster had said. Well, that was over now. And to be fair to Hogg, he, like many others who had made an honest mistake and supported Chamberlain's party and its policies, was now expiating his mistake in the Army. The mood of the whole country changed. It hardened. The Emergency Powers Act, passed into law on the twenty-second of May, gave the authorities power to take over any resource or equipment that might be useful in fighting the war, and also to direct labour where it was needed. Our workload at the Ministry of Supply suddenly towered higher, I was lucky to get home one week-end in three; I often slept in the office and began work again at first light. Holland collapsed; Belgium surrendered; it seemed that nothing could stop the *Wehrmacht*. On the twenty-second of June, France fell; Churchill made his 'finest hour' speech; we prepared to sell our lives dearly. If we had to go down, we would do a lot of damage as we went.

I remember those summer weeks as punctuated by deaths. The British Expeditionary Force was pushed back and back. I looked at *The Times* every day and there were names I knew among the columns of deaths; the Honourable Fergus Kingswood, I remember, was one; I wondered what would happen to his K.3. M.G. Other deaths did not get into *The Times*. Doug Ravenscroft, a despatch rider, never returned from his last ride; even his whirling speed could not outpace the bullets. Yet life had to go on. Everyone who has lived through such a time knows the paradox, how the smallest concerns coexist with the greatest, how the trivial jostles with the numbingly tragic. Wherever heroic sacrifices are made, every few hours the survivors also have to have something to eat. They have to sleep, ease their bodies of waste material, sort out their clothing, talk. Even laugh, even make love.

One lunchtime, for instance, I remember encouraging my thoughts to ramble as, sensing a nervous breakdown looming ahead, I made myself stop working, leave my cluttered desk and go out to lunch by myself, avoiding any company. I chose Soho. Solitude and Soho: that was the combination I needed.

'Soho' used to be a huntsman's call like 'Tally-ho', and in the days of Charles II the marshes north of Leicester Square were much resorted to by sportsmen, particularly for wild-fowling. The thought gave an ironic tinge to my mood as I picked my way through its narrow streets. Hunting, quite obviously, still went on in Soho; not of the kind which had earned the district its original name but nevertheless of a kind which Charles would have well enough understood. Personally, I was hunting for nothing more exciting than lunch. In those days Soho had delicious little French and Italian restaurants where a succulent meal and a half-bottle of wine could be bought for prices that, when one mentions them today, don't sound like prices at all. Prices? They don't even sound like *tips*.

One little French place I was particularly fond of looked cool and inviting on that glaring August day, with a couple of tables shaded by striped umbrellas on the pavement outside. There was no room left at these pavement tables, so I stepped straight inside, and the waiter beckoned me to a corner table. The sudden plunge into shadow made my eyesight uncertain and it was not until I was sitting in my corner, looking at the menu, that they adjusted well enough to see people's faces across the room. When they did, I became aware that a couple on the opposite side of the room, sitting with their heads together, were known to me. Instinctively, I raised the menu, which was on a large sheet of cardboard, in front of my face. I felt it would be embarrassing to be noticed by either of these two.

They were not people I liked or wanted any contact with. One was Hunt. The other was Molly Fishman.

As I watched over the top of the menu, Molly threw back her head and gave a long peal of laughter. Her frizzy hair caught a beam of sunlight and shone palely; she looked, for a moment, almost attractive.

Wanting to enjoy my lunch, I shifted my seat to avoid having to look across at them. But I couldn't help reflecting again that Soho was still a sporting area. Hunt and Molly had tracked each other down to these discreet thickets – though which was the hunter, which the quarry, it would have been hard to say. I had no doubt they were both equally carnivorous.

I wondered, idly, how the war had affected their lives. Hunt was still in civilian clothes, but of course he might have been awaiting call-up or even on leave. As for Molly, I had no idea what she was doing. The King's Arms was the only place where I had ever seen her, and I never went there nowadays. Where was her husband? Did it matter? It did not. I dismissed the subject from my mind, and enjoyed my lunch.

Later, going out into the street, I was halted at a road intersection, the point where the Strand becomes Fleet Street. Everybody was halted. Police were on point duty. Traffic was reduced to a single line and pedestrians were permitted to keep moving only if they stayed on the pavement and did not try to cross the road.

So I waited, and now I saw that a brown tide of soldiers was flowing towards the corner where I stood, coming across the bridge from the direction of Waterloo Station. On all sides, from the people about me, I heard the word 'Dunkirk'. This was a unit of the British Expeditionary Force which had been despatched to France in the closing months of 1939. What I was witnessing, by pure chance, was the final stage of their retreat and withdrawal.

There had been a few ragged cheers from the bystanders, but as the soldiers drew level the townspeople fell silent. This did not seem like an occasion for cheering. I was never before or since in the presence of such fatigue: it came off the soldiers in cold, heavy waves. It was in their hollowed eyes, their dead expressions, and most of all in their heavy clumping gait, each foot dragged forward as if that effort must be the last. These were the men, I discovered later, who had lain on the beach at Dunkirk for day after pitiless day while the German aircraft thundered endlessly in. They had seen their comrades killed and maimed all around them. They had despaired of rescue, despaired of life. And now here they were, somehow alive after it all, still putting one foot in front of another, carrying pack, rifle, rolled-up greatcoat and water-bottle, moving over Waterloo Bridge, presumably on their way to Knightsbridge Barracks.

A fringe of onlookers three or four deep had gathered. Since I was one of the first, I was on the edge of the pavement, just on the corner. As the soldiers came past, hardly in step but keeping more or less in rank, four abreast, the nearest man in each rank passed very close to me, near enough to touch, if I had stretched out my hand. But I did not stretch it out. Physically close to me as they were, these men were removed from me to an immense distance. I had not the presumption to try to reach across the gulf between what they had known and what I had known.

One after another, they came past me, some strained, some inert and flaccid, but all exhausted, all pale with a pallor that seemed impossible ever to replenish with the blood of life. I stood on that corner, rooted, hypnotized, staring. And then a face I recognized came slowly past me and was gone: a face which had

179

been buried deep in memory, but within that memory was indelible, so that I knew the man at once. It was Chucker.

Immediately, without ceasing to be aware that I was standing on that London pavement, I was equally conscious of being in a time and place far removed: in Oxford, ten years ago, on a sweltering summer night in the dormitory of the Gryphon School. In all the long row of beds only three people were awake: myself, rigid and fearful, and in the end bed, next to mine, 'the beast with two backs', now and then visible as a black shape against the indigo of the summer night beyond the window, always audible in its dual breathing and whispering, its steady threshing movements, its convulsions and gaspings. The components of the beast had been Vinnie and this same Chucker. Vinnie I had never seen before that evening, standing in a circle of lamplight in a Jericho street and beginning the process of being picked up by the Herculean Chucker, but she was to obsess me for years – her slender body, impudent hazel eyes and fringe of brown hair unsettling my reason and bringing a cloud of madness into the centre of my adolescent world, exacerbating and magnifying the lusts that were natural to my flesh. Him I never saw again, not until this moment as he walked past me wrapped in his mantle of fatigue, newly come from some unimaginable ordeal. I knew that I was nothing to him, that in all the years he had never recalled my face or my voice, that I had passed immediately from his attention. There had been no thought of me in his mind as he lay on the beach at Dunkirk, any more than when he lay with Vinnie in that narrow bed ten years ago.

To me, recognizing Chucker was a deep, savage jolt. To him, if he had been told who I was and where he had met me, it would have been nothing. So what is history? I thought. History is in the mind. No mind, no history.

During the next couple of months, I had virtually no time for personal things; it was work, work, work, and when I got home for a week-end at Mulberry Hall there was always so much to be seen to. Sleeping one night a week with Heather did at least keep us in touch sexually, and it was not a time when one could think of anything beyond the meeting of immediate needs. History was moving so fast that one's personal life became like a speeded-up film. For once, the public events really did overshadow the private.

To take the biggest example of all, the Battle of Britain was launched by the *Luftwaffe* on what their High Command dubbed 'Eagle Day', 10 August. Wave after wave of German fighters came over; and the same few squadrons of Spitfires and Hurricanes, manned by the same few, daily fewer R.A.F. pilots, went up to intercept them over the fields of Kent. It seemed impossible that the defenders could hold out day after day, but in fact they held out week after week, until finally flooding the watching nation with a mood of exultant triumph and putting them in a receptive mood for Churchill's famous dictum, part epigram and part purple prose, about the many and the few.

I remember it well, that Sunday 15 September; a long, glorious hot day, with the cornfields a brilliant yellow, the leaves on the chestnut trees a clear burning gold, and the fish gliding timelessly in the streams. I had seen the fish because I had taken Michael on an expedition to collect sticklebacks. We used a net and managed to get about a dozen fiery little fellows with shiny red bellies and the aggressive spines along their backs that made him shriek with mingled horror and pleasure when he managed to touch them with a finger.

It was a long, happy day in the sun, far away from the war, and all the time we were hanging head down on the steep gravelly banks of the stream with our

180

net, the Air Force and the *Luftwaffe* were fighting it out in the perfect blue sky, not so very far away.

We got back, well satisfied, and set up an old glass accumulator tank as an aquarium in one of the garages at Mulberry Hall. (There were two.) Then I ran a bath for Mike and got him into it with the soap and his wooden boat. Then, to give myself a rest for a few minutes I went into our sitting room. Heather had been busy all through the middle part of the day, leaving Michael in my care, but we were all three going to eat together about six, which would give me time to go for my train from Oxford at a quarter to eight. First, though, we would listen to the six o'clock news on the radio; now a ritual in our household as in most across the land. The announcers had begun giving their names, getting us used to their individual identities so that no German invader could come to the microphone under the guise of the B.B.C. We knew them all, Bruce Belfrage, Alvar Liddell, Stuart Hibberd, Wilfred Pickles. It was familial, and comforting.

I switched the wireless on now and waited for Heather. But she did not appear and the announcer's animated voice, telling us of the enormous toll of *Luftwaffe* planes that day, sounded odd in the low-ceilinged room with only myself to hear it. I walked over and stood by the window. Down below in the courtyard a car was drawn up, its deep blue colour indicating it was the property of the Navy. As I watched, the driver, a Wren, got out, a trim figure in white shirt and dark blue skirt. She stood waiting for a moment and then three figures came from the house and stood in conversation beside the car. One was Heather; the other two were Diana Acheson-Fiske and her brother, Robin. He was in the uniform of a naval lieutenant. He looked, I thought, very debonair, in what must be the original French signification of that word, *of good air*. I watched while brother and sister, with their long aristocratic faces almost comically alike, stood beside the car and talked with Heather, just come from her stable work in her rubber boots and corduroy trousers; she had an old check overcoat thrown round her shoulders like a cape, though the weather was so warm, and I wondered if she was hiding some more than usually torn or stained shirt.

As I watched, Lisa came out of the house and went over to the group. She said something to Heather, who stood perfectly still, almost rigid, for an instant and then, without speaking to her companions, began to walk quickly back towards the house. She disappeared into the door below me. Lisa stayed on for a moment, then the lieutenant gave his sister a kiss on the cheek and got into the back of the car. The unseen Wren started the engine and they drove off. Lisa and Diana now came into the house.

The news bulletin had finished with the Battle of Britain and was saying something about North Africa. I went along to see how Mike was getting on in the bath; he said he wanted to come out. I told him to wait a minute or two, then began to go down the stairs, thinking to meet Heather on her way up. I went down the narrow upper flight of stairs without meeting her. Then I reached the broad lower stairs and met her just beginning to come up.

'There's some wonderful news,' I said, but she walked straight past me, her face totally without expression. If she had not had her eyes open, I might have thought she was sleep-walking. Clearly something terrible was stalking among us.

Downstairs I found Diana Acheson-Fiske. Her face was serious and compassionate. 'You've seen Heather,' she said.

'I've seen her. But I couldn't tell whether she was seeing me.'

'She didn't tell you?'

'Tell me what?'

'Look,' she said, 'she had a telephone call just now. From her parents.'

'They do ring her sometimes.'

'Not like this,' she said, 'not with this kind of news.'

'Is it one of them?' I asked. And then, of course, I knew. 'It's Tom, isn't it?'

She nodded. 'His commanding officer rang the parents.'

All I could think of to say was, 'I thought they usually did these things by letter.'

'That was in the last war. In this one they ring up. At least they do if it happened in this country.'

'And it . . . happened today?'

She nodded again.

'I'll go up to Heather,' I said.

'Well, it's your decision, but perhaps I ought to tell you that she said she didn't want anyone to try to speak to her for a bit.'

'I have to go to London,' I said. 'I shan't see her for another week. I must try to say something to her before I go.'

I went up the stairs. When I tried the handle of the bedroom door, it was locked.

'Heather,' I said gently, knocking. 'Heather, darling.'

There was silence. It took a lot of knocking and saying her name before her voice came out, sounding almost smothered. 'I have to be by myself.'

'I just want to say I love you. I just want to help you.'

There was a silence and then she said, 'Tell Diana to give Michael his supper.'

That was all I got out of her. I listened and the silence from the other side of that door was worse than the most agonized sobbing could ever be. I went and got Michael out of his bath and dried him, and then I told him his mum was resting because she had had a very long day with the horses and Diana was going to give him his supper.

'What's she going to give me?' he demanded suspiciously.

'What she has herself, I suppose.'

'I don't mind as long as Lisa cooks it. Diana can't cook worth a fart.'

'Michael, if you must use language like that keep it for school. This is a respectable house.'

I took him downstairs and passed on Heather's message to Diana, who said it would be no trouble to give Mike his supper. He asked if Lisa would be cooking it and she said she expected so.

I went up to our sitting room. The radio had finished with news and gone on to dance music. I switched if off in the middle of a number called 'Corn Silk'. It had a nice catchy tune but it didn't survive the war and you never hear it now. In fact I don't think I have heard 'Corn Silk' since that moment on 15 September 1940 when I switched it off in the middle. Odd, the things one remembers! Then I packed my little overnight case. Before leaving I went along to the bedroom one more time. The door was still locked and there was still silence beyond it. I drew in my breath to tell Heather I was going and I would telephone her from London, but I let it out again without speaking. Instead, I went downstairs and found Michael. He was in the kitchen waiting for Lisa to dish up his high tea, which seemed to consist of meat balls and spaghetti. I picked him up and gave him a hug.

'See you next week-end, old pal,' I said. 'Look after the sticklebacks.'

Sometimes he resisted when I hugged him, but this time he didn't. I put him

182

down again and he smiled up at me. 'Can we go sticklebacking again next Sunday?'

'I hope so.'

'Grown-ups always say that. It doesn't mean yes and it doesn't mean no.'

'That's right. It means they hope so. Grown-ups aren't always free to do just what they like any more than children.'

His face expressed disbelief. 'If you wanted to go and get sticklebacks nobody could tell you not to.'

'May be no*body* could, but there might be *things* that could. Happenings.'

'To do with the war?'

'Mostly that. But I can tell you one thing *for certain* – I'll always go out and do things with you, as often as I possibly can, until the day when you don't want me to any more.'

'I'll never not want you to any more,' he said.

Then I went quickly out of the big front door, down the drive and through the gates. I started thumbing and got to Oxford in two lifts. By eight o'clock I was on the train to London. Like all wartime trains it was slow and unpunctual. Dusk fell as we started out and the train kept stopping in the middle of dark fields; it would run for a quarter of an hour or so, grind to a halt and stop for twenty minutes. I was stiff, tired, dirty, thirsty. Finally I must have fallen into a wretched slumber, because I had a dream: I was back at Uncle Ernest's funeral, following down the path as the six Pembroke scouts carried the coffin. Only this time there was a knocking from inside the coffin-lid and Ernest's voice calling to be let out. The scouts put down the coffin on the path, carefully, keeping it level, and at once Ernest flipped open the lid and sat up, in his ordinary clothes and looking just as he used to. He got out and said to me, 'Come on, Peter,' and I followed him out of the graveyard and we moved rapidly along the pavements towards Binsey and then on to the towpath. Ernest was a little ahead of me, and despite my best efforts he was always just in front. When we got to Godstow and went over the bridge by the Trout Inn, he put out his hand behind him as if waiting for me to catch up and join hands with him, which I did, putting my right in his left. Another few strides took us across the old toll-bridge, and we stopped with Port Meadow on our right and, on our left, the memorial to Bettington and Hotchkiss. Ernest stood between me and the memorial, so that I couldn't see it, but I heard him muttering the inscription to himself as we stood there; and then he turned to me and said, 'There's been a change.' He showed no surprise; it was merely a statement of fact. 'What change is that, Uncle?' I asked. 'There's one more now,' he said and suddenly flew up through the branches of the trees into the sky and disappeared.

I awoke to the knowledge that we were crawling into the huge bleak cavern of Paddington Station, with its cowled lights and blacked-over glass roof. For a moment, as I struggled back to consciousness, the station was no more real to me than the toll-bridge, Port Meadow, the polished granite slab, and Ernest flying up into the sky. One more! I thought. There'll be many more than one more, many more, many more, and as the train ran resignedly into the station its wheels kept time with those words, forming themselves ever more slowly in my head, many more men, many more men.

9

So there I was, back in church with the Archangel Michael and the exoskeletons and the ministers of grace, and the lost and saved souls, and the flames blasting out of Hell's mouth, on the walls of St James the Great, South Leigh. I had last seen them at Michael's christening, and before that on the day of my marriage to Heather; now it was the memorial service for Tom, on a Saturday afternoon in October with the sun streaming in through the windows. Heather and Michael were beside me; the rest of the congregation was pretty much as expected – the Burrell parents, Phil lurking at the back, an imposing Air Force officer (I think he was a Group Captain), one or two local farmers who had known Tom as a boy and, up in the pulpit, the faintly scholarly, faintly doddering vicar in charge of proceedings.

I didn't, as it happened, find the experience edifying. Perhaps I had entertained too great hopes of it. I had hoped, perhaps naively, that the loss in which we all shared to some extent might have brought us together as a family. And in particular it might have made Mrs Burrell – Alicia, as I must try to call her in my mind and even to her face – more ready to move towards a relationship with me. After all, if she no longer had a son she had at least a son-in-law, and I would try to ... try to ... what? There was no way I could replace Tom in her life; I hadn't any of his qualities. But why did she detest me so much? Oh, for every reason – for not being a farmer, for not having enough money and land, for not being of the right social class.

It was obviously impossible to do anything about all these things, so I tried instead, as the service wound its way along, to think about Tom: to think about him positively. But of course it was hopeless. If his death was not drawing the family together, well, why should it? He had not been a drawing-together kind of person; he had been a loner. Why, I wondered, was there no young woman among the mourners in these pews? Had Tom had a girl-friend? Had he ever thought of marrying, of starting a family? It seemed unlikely. He had been less like a man than a dedicated bird, and a bird of prey at that. The first time I had met him had been when I was innocently walking across the farmland and he had told me I was trespassing and threatened me with a shotgun. That was what his nature was adapted for – to repel intruders. And so it had been to the end. The German pilots had intruded into the skies above Kent, he had threatened them with a Spitfire, and he had downed some of them, not a doubt of it, before one of them downed him. And here we were to do honour to his memory. A hero's death.

Heather, beside me, was moving her lips soundlessly to the words of a hymn. She seemed to have willed herself out of the situation altogether. This came as no surprise to me. She had been barricaded inside herself ever since the news of Tom's death. When, on arriving home at the end of that week, I had tried to bring up the subject, she had laid a hand on my sleeve and simply said, 'No, Peter. D'you mind?'

'No, I don't mind, but hadn't you better ...'

'If you're going to say hadn't I better talk about my feelings, get them out in the open, no. Just leave everything alone. Just leave it be. That's what I'm going to do and it's what I want you to do. It's the only thing you can do for me.'

Naturally, I let it go at that. I had enough sense to see that it was going to be a terribly difficult package for her to handle. She had hated Tom, and therefore couldn't wholeheartedly mourn his death; this in turn made her feel guilty. In the three or four weeks which had gone by since his death the population as a whole had grasped the fact that the turning back of the German air attack had been decisive; the *Luftwaffe* had been sent over to soften up the country in preparation for a full-scale invasion, and when the air assault failed the invasion was halted. We were saved. The R.A.F. had bought us another six months of life, in which anything might happen. A wave of gratitude swept through the country. I shared this general feeling, and I knew that Heather did too. I knew she admired courage. And none of this changed the fact that she had hated Tom for the way he had treated her during the years of their growing-up and she still hated him. I knew that this guilt spiral would go on and on, and where it would all come to rest there was no knowing.

Meanwhile the only crumb of comfort lay in the fact that Michael was only six years old and still at the stage of being absorbed in marbles and conkers, in trying hard to keep the sticklebacks alive, and some caterpillars that he hoped would become swallow-tail butterflies, though it was so late in the season. 'If I can get them to pupate,' he said to me as we went home from the service, 'I can keep them warm and there's no reason why they shouldn't live through the winter.'

'Who taught you the word "pupate"?' I asked him.

'Miss Marshall.'

I was impressed. But even the impressive Miss Marshall only occupied the top layer of my mind. Further down, I was busy with the thought that owing to the efforts of Tom and his fellow pilots, there was no reason why all of us shouldn't live through the winter.

After the Battle of Britain, the Blitz. In November the air raids on London and other cities began, and went on for the rest of 1940 and most of 1941. In London, 40,000 people were killed during the war, the majority of them during those two years. So what? I was alive. That was the state of mind you settled into, surprisingly quickly. (*Horribly* quickly.) What else was there to do? We had decided to go on with the war, and going on meant going on. The fact that bombs were falling on streets and squares, on people's houses, on hospitals and old people's homes and orphanages and on gasworks and sewage farms, and that most of the bombs which fell killed somebody or at the very least smashed up their life – all this was just a rumble in the background, a steady, monotonous accompaniment to life. The stuff stuck over the windows of the tube trains so that the glass wouldn't splinter in an explosion, the surface shelters at the street corners, just brick boxes with slit entrances to protect people from flying splinters and debris, the eternal blackout, the sirens and the tin hats and the ambulance crews everywhere and the people wandering about with street-maps in their hands looking for streets that had disappeared in a sea of rubble. It was all rather like a low-level infection, which doesn't make the patient ill enough to give up and stay in bed, just enervates and depresses him.

The sirens were always going off. I went through the usual stages. In the first few weeks I went down into the air-raid shelters whenever they sounded, thus losing about half of each day's work, until it piled up and there was just nowhere

185

to put all the pieces of paper. After that I just shrugged and worked on. If they went off while I was still in bed, the same applied. At first I got up, threw some clothes on over my pyjamas and took shelter, but after a few weeks of dragging myself up out of a warm cocoon of sleep I just snored on, like thousands of others. Brave? Of course not. Foolhardy? Not even that. After all, 5 million people lived in London, and the chances of living were far greater than the chances of dying, and what more could you ask for in the darkest days of a total war?

Nor do I have, looking back, any feeling of being particularly hard done by. We had bargained for this when we declared war, and when it was our turn to have the upper hand, when we bombed German cities in 1943, '44 and '45, we showed not a glimmer of pity for them. How could we? The early and middle 1940s were not a time for pity – though I have to add, as an historian, that if such a time has ever occurred in human history, I have never heard of it.

During this period, in the darkest days of the war, I very rarely saw Brian. I knew he was working terribly hard repairing damaged fighter planes, and when I thought of him I often recalled his remark to Tom, as the two of them had stood confronting each other like young turkey-cocks. 'You talk as if you don't realize that the engine of a racing car is very similar to an aero engine.'

However, one day in February 1941 my Ministry of Supply job required that I go to Oxford and Cowley. The outfit Brian worked for, which was called No. 1 Civilian Repair Unit, had been much praised in Whitehall, and I had been able to give my standing in the Ministry a perceptible boost by letting it be known that I had a brother who was a key man in it. I had no doubt that this information lay behind the decision to send me to Cowley. Before going I managed to get Brian on the telephone. I told him I was coming to Oxford for the day and would have to have lunch somewhere, and why not with him?

'Why not?' he agreed. 'As long as you can eat a canteen lunch.'

'Yours can't be worse than ours,' I said.

'Don't bank on it. Anyway, half-past twelve?'

'I should be finished by then.'

I was finished by then, and we had lunch, and chatted, and caught up with such meagre news as we had. I told him what Heather was doing and he told me what Primrose was doing. Then, when we had each consumed our time and our shilling's worth of food – a tenpenny lunch and a twopenny cup of coffee – he said he had to go over to the Dump Reception Office and sign in a load. 'You can come if you like. It's on your way back,' he said.

'What's the Dump Reception Office?' I asked.

'You'll see,' he said, and when we got there I did see. Just at that point where the Garsington Road ran out into the main road past the factory there was a field about an acre and a half in extent. Beyond it other fields stretched out in the same direction, all of them filled up with metal shapes of every kind; all they had in common was that they were either broken (if large) or well-worn (if small).

'Most of this is just ordinary M.P.R.D. stuff,' Brian said.

'I'm sorry, I don't — '

'I'd have thought it was part of your job to know about this Metal and Produce Recovery Depot,' he said severely; I was the younger brother again.

'I never was any good at acronyms; I suppose it's all stuff to be salvaged.'

'Yes. The drivers go out all over the south of England and bring stuff in and pile it up here. Goodness knows how much there'll be in three or four years, if the war goes on that long. But the part of it that concerns me is this bit here.

Just at the corner.' He indicated the nearer field. I could see it was his pride and joy.

'I see,' I said. 'Aircraft.'

'Not just any aircraft, either.'

I looked more attentively. Every machine there was broken, some merely crumpled, others twisted and shattered, not a few blackened by fire, and all of them German. Wherever a wing or tailplane showed an insignia, it was the black cross of the German Air Force. I turned to Brian with a question on my face.

'Yes,' he said. 'Brought down over England, somewhere within Southern Command. Every single one of these set out in first-class trim and with a highly-trained and battle-ready pilot, and every one finished on the ground. Shot down by fighters or potted by ack-ack.'

'You study them?'

He shrugged. 'Not much. Once you've looked at one you've looked at them all. I keep an eye on them, though. There might be some bit somewhere that's had a modification we could learn something from. Mostly they're just here because we've got to put them somewhere. But we keep the German jobs all together, and close to the road, because it's good for morale for people to see them and to see the pile growing.'

We began to walk towards the site hut. 'I suppose,' I said, speaking carefully, 'that if there were chaps killed in them when they crashed, the . . . bodies would be taken out before you get them?'

'When possible. Quite often we have to clean them out.'

'Clean them out?'

'When a plane's been hit by an explosive shell like the ones that come from a Spitfire's cannon,' he said over his shoulder, 'if the shell happens to hit a bloke who's in the plane it doesn't usually leave much of him. I mean he's there all right, but it's hard to find him.'

'Oh.'

'So we have to clean them out. We can't have them going bad in there and stinking the place out.'

'Oh. No.'

'What we usually do is hose them out.'

The sun was shining brightly and I had a thick overcoat on, but for a moment I felt cold. 'What a horrible job. Having to do that.'

'Well,' he said, 'it's not a job we have many volunteers for.'

I looked at the scarred and twisted remains. 'D'you think there's a field somewhere in Germany,' I asked, 'where they keep the R.A.F. planes they've brought down?'

'I doubt it. They wouldn't have enough to fill a field yet. As far as we're concerned the air warfare up to now's all been defensive. We simply haven't sent any significant numbers over Germany. If we ever do and they bring enough down, they'll put them on show. It's natural enough.'

'You think that's why these are here? To be on show?'

'Well, I wasn't consulted, but that's what I would expect. In fact, one day last summer, right in the middle of the Battle of Britain, we spotted a bloke taking photographs of the field. Walking all round it doing shot after shot. And who d'you think it was?'

'I don't know. Some forward-looking citizen who wants to go into the scrap-metal business when the war's over?'

'Not a bit of it. It turned out he was an Official War Artist. Planning to use the snaps to make into an immortal canvas. Funny what they'll do, isn't it?'

'Well,' I said, 'I suppose it's what he's paid for. And you can hardly say that this' – I gestured towards the unearthly scene in front of us – 'isn't worth a canvas.'

'Daresay you're right. Anyway, we left him in peace when he showed his permit. Actually with the Air Ministry, he was. You can't get more official than that.'

We walked on towards the site office. A driver had brought in a long-loader with twisted girders and wings on it. Brian went into the office, followed by the driver. I stood outside, gazing at the field of broken pterodactyls, and as I watched an aeroplane, obviously a Spitfire, appeared in the sky, coming in from the direction of Buckinghamshire. It was one of those crystalline blue-and-gold winter afternoons, when you can see every detail from miles away. The R.A.F. markings on the Spitfire's wings glowed festively in that clear sunlight. While I looked, the pilot suddenly dived it towards me, then took it up again steeply, vertically, at the same time rotating in a corkscrew motion. As I stood rooted to the spot, gazing upward, Brian appeared at my side.

'That one looks sound enough,' he said evenly.

'Sound . . . ?'

'He's testing her, of course.'

The aeroplane had disappeared beyond the line of buildings, but now it reappeared, flying at ninety degrees to the vertical, passing over our heads at about 500 feet.

'It certainly seems to be sound,' I said.

'If I'm not mistaken,' Brian said, 'that's the one I was working on yesterday. It didn't need much. A few holes in one wing, but enough to damage the wiring.'

'Oh?'

'Yes, there's a lot of wiring in a Spitfire's wings. There has to be, with eight guns all carried in there. And the radiator, of course. She's so sleek, first sight you'd think she hadn't got a radiator at all, but actually if you look closely there's a little slot under the starboard wing and that's all the radiator she needs.'

'Well, fancy that.'

'Of course, Reg Mitchell always was a dab hand at solving those heating problems. He spent all those years on racing aircraft, remember?'

I didn't remember. But the word 'racing' alerted me to what it was that had loosened Brian's tongue. One racing man was saluting another.

'Yes, that Reg Mitchell,' he said, shaking his head slowly in admiration. 'He was a designer and a half. Those Schneider Trophy seaplanes were the fastest things in the sky, and why? Because they were packed from end to end with Mitchell's original ideas. For instance: he put a false skin on the wings, and d'you know what for? To cool the fluid for the cylinder jackets! That's where he carried it!'

'Can you beat that?' I said. 'Where is this Mitchell now? Have you met him?'

'Dead,' Brian said laconically. 'Died about three years ago, barely a year after the first Spitfire had taken off. Knew his work was done, I suppose.' A wistful expression came over his face. 'Just think,' he said, 'if Billy Morris had given Reg Mitchell a thousand pounds that he'd never have missed, and got him to design a racing car, what an M.G. world-beater we could have had!'

With that thought I left him and pushed on into town. I had a couple more official errands to do in Oxford to salve my conscience about not getting back to

188

London straight away, and early evening found me in the vicinity of the Bargeman's. I timed myself not to get there earlier because I knew that my father would be getting back from the job he still had at the brewery, setting up to open the pub at six and then sitting down, tired, to relax and have a much-needed meal to keep him going for the next four hours. I didn't want him to have to cope with me as well, and besides there was always the danger that my mother would insist on my sharing their meal and giving me food they needed for themselves. I managed to get some sandwiches made with unidentifiable meat paste in a cafe, swilling it down with dishwater tea, and when I got to the pub it was half-past six, and the place was bright, cheerful, swept and dusted, the fire burning brightly, and my father behind the bar just as in peacetime. He greeted me and we chatted easily, like old friends. I thought he looked well; not much older, not much more careworn; he was standing up well to these difficult years.

When I told him I had seen Brian, he asked, 'Did he tell you anything about that bit of fun and games?'

'What bit of fun and games?'

His eyes widened slightly. 'He didn't say anything about it? All that rumpus with the racing car?'

'He said absolutely nothing about any rumpus or racing car.'

'Well,' my father said, 'he must be keeping it on the dark side.'

'Go on, then,' I urged, but at that moment two customers came in and had to be served. I had to wait. Then he came over to where I was perched on my stool and said, 'Ivan Warmley told us, but it didn't matter because Brian told us himself the next time he was in. They've de-reserved Ivan, by the way. He's going into the Navy.'

'O.K., now tell me about Brian.'

'Well,' said my father, 'you know Brian's been given this racing car.'

'Given a racing car? No. It seems a funny time to — '

'There was a chap he used to mention now and then. One of your fellow students, he was: Fergus Kingswood.'

'Oh, him? The last I heard, he'd been killed with the B.E.F. in France.'

'That's right, he was killed before Dunkirk. Well, it seems he left Brian this car in his will.'

'The K.3.? The one Brian used to look after for him, groom it for races?'

My father nodded. 'He left a will before he went off to fight. People do, in those sorts of families, with estates and that. Well, this Fergus made a will and he said in it that Brian was to have his racing car.'

'What does Brian want with it?'

'Well, I suppose Fergus thought someone ought to have it that'd look after it. And Brian was glad to get it all right. I think he was touched, you might say, to be remembered in the chap's will.'

'Well, I can quite see that.' More customers, another pause, then I went on, 'All clear so far, but where do the fun and games come in? What is there for Brian to keep dark?'

'Just this funny little pantomime a few days ago,' Dad said, a reminiscent smile on his face. 'It made your mother and me laugh when we heard about it, it was so typical of Brian.'

'Well, let me in on it. I could do with a laugh just now.'

'In a way,' Dad went on, his expression becoming conspiratorial, 'I shouldn't be telling you this because you're Ministry and Brian broke a regulation.'

'I'm shocked.'

189

'He broke a very serious regulation. P'raps you *will* be shocked when I tell you.'

'If you ever do,' I said. 'I never knew such a slow man with a story.'

'Well, Brian's one of the people in charge of the transport that goes out bringing in these crashed 'planes and that. And it seems he fixed a big lorry with a trailer to go down to wherever it was that these Kingswood family live. Where the M.G. was, in the garage, just as young Fergus had left it. He'd given the driver all sorts of instructions, how this racing car was to go on the trailer, *by itself*, and to be roped up in a special way, and he drew it all with diagrams and everything, and that it had to be covered with a tarpaulin. Anyway, the driver does everything just like he's told, and the load gets back to Cowley just at a time when Brian's busy in another part of the factory and they starts unloading it without waiting for him to turn up. It's about three o'clock in the afternoon and they gets it round to the tip and gets the tarp off it. Then they stand around and scratch their heads a bit, because they can see it's not broken or anything, but they reckon someone must have donated it to the war effort, so they get it off the trailer, and just at that moment Brian comes rushing down the road on a push-bike, yelling *"Leave it alone! Stand back from that bloody car!"* so they could hear him from about 500 yards.'

Brian's face, his yelling voice, his straining legs, the racing car beside the scrap tip, the bewildered workmen, all grew from my father's story. I could well agree with him that it was typical of Brian.

'Anyway, he just chucks the bike down and runs over to 'em and then it starts. The foreman of the gang that's unloading the stuff starts asking awkward questions. If this is just a load of salvage, by what authority was it given special treatment? Is it salvage or isn't it? If it's salvage, they're going to throw it straight on the tip with the rest of the stuff or he'll know the reason why.'

'So how did Brian handle that?'

'Well, as far as I can make out what happened was this. First Brian tries telling the foreman to mind his own business and giving him a sniff of his fist. When that doesn't work, he comes out with a whole string of official reasons why they'd been looking everywhere for an intact specimen of that particular car because they want to carry out some tests on the engine to help them to improve the performance of the Spitfire engine, and of course you know Brian, he makes it sound very convincing. The foreman melted away, but that still left Brian with the problem of getting the car away out of sight because he'd used Department transport, with their fuel and their labour, to do a private job for him, and if it'd all come out they'd have made an example of him. Well, it seems there's a lock-up garage he can put it in, at the back of his office, where it could stay till he can organize some way of towing it home. It's a good long stretch down the road, half a mile at least, no short cuts. So he did the only thing he could do. Set off pushing it.'

'All that way?'

'Well, you can push it along with one hand. It wasn't the weight that bothered him, it was the thought of somebody seeing him. He said he was praying for luck every inch of the way. And I'm glad to say he got luck.'

I thought for a moment. 'It was quite a risk for him to take, wasn't it? Why didn't he leave the car with the Kingswoods till he could get it comfortably?'

'I asked him that. He said he wanted it where he could see it. He said it was entrusted to him and he owed it to Fergus and to M.G. racing to look after it.'

I could see it. I thanked my father for telling the story and we chuckled together

190

at the thought of the mad bicycle ride, the fearful trundle along the road, the bluff, the machinations.

But when I took the rest of my pint into the kitchen to have a chat with my mother, I found she wasn't amused by the story of Brian's escapade.

'I'm just glad it turned out no worse,' she said. Her fingers were busy with something as she sat at the table – when were they not busy? She was, if I remember rightly, cutting a piece of cloth into thin strips for some unguessable purpose. 'He could easily have got into such serious trouble, and all over nothing.'

'Well, an M.G. racing car isn't nothing to Brian, Mum.'

'You don't have to tell me, I know his wits are turned when it comes to that particular subject. It was a bad day when he first got all that foolishness into his head.'

'His interest in racing cars, you mean? It must be donkey's years ago.'

She shook her head sadly. 'What a nice peaceful life he could have had, if he'd just done a normal job in the factory and made ordinary cars for ordinary sensible people.'

We looked at each other across a huge gulf. But I understood and sympathized with my mother's position. In her world, men were big children who had to be supervised and kept in order; and in addition to being unruly they were also fanciful and irrational.

'Racing cars!' she said witheringly, more to herself than to me. 'Who'd be any the worse off if every single racing car disappeared from the world?'

Brian would, I thought. But I didn't pursue the matter. I had only a short time with my mother before I had to put on my overcoat and go out into the black freezing night and take a horrible train to horrible London, where the German Air Force would probably arrive again and try and kill me. If they succeeded, I didn't want my mother's last memory of me to be of someone who argued with her.

I had always known that I was fortunate in being fond of my parents, but these years of London exile – perhaps it was their one beneficial result – brought my love for them into sharp relief, largely because it was much more difficult to get to see anything of them, so that when I did I was the more appreciative of their combined personality.

In fact those years reinforced my love of my family and of my home setting generally.

It always seemed funny to Heather that I arrived home every weekend hungry for news. 'Anything been happening?' I would ask, as soon as I had set down my bag and taken off my overcoat. 'What the hell ever happens here?' she would ask. 'Around you in London all week bombs crash down on you, people get killed, big decisions are made, and you come out here in the middle of these fields and ask what's happened?'

However, I did not see it that way. Living and working in London through the Blitz was mostly a matter of boredom. People who live safe lives imagine that danger must be exciting; what it actually is, most of the time, is just rather numbing. I remember a man who served in the 1914–18 war, doggedly surviving years of the trenches, summing up the experience in three words: 'dull and dangerous'.

Real life to me was what went on back home, the things that concerned Heather, concerned Michael, concerned Mulberry Hall and district, even what concerned Jasmine Farm. I devoured everything. One story I particularly relished

191

was the tale of how Phil had suddenly appeared in the unexpected guise of a knight-errant to Mrs Burrell, rescuing her from a highly unwelcome situation.

The word 'evacuee' had fallen with a particular menace on the ears of my mother-in-law. She lived in the deep countryside, her house had once been home to four people and was now home to only two, and she was consequently a sitting target for the billeting officer. Needless to say her patriotism, vocal enough when it suited her, did not stretch as far as putting up with inconvenience and disruption; besides, the children arriving in Oxford came from London, and in nearly every case from working-class areas of London. Depressed by years of unemployment and bad housing, they knew nothing of table manners or folding their clothes away neatly or treating antique furniture respectfully; they had not learnt how to leave the bathroom in a dry and tidy state, because in most cases they had never in their lives seen a bathroom; in Mrs Burrell's opinion, they were not Jasmine Farm material at all.

When the first wave of evacuees hit Oxford and the country towns round it – Witney, Faringdon, Banbury – she made a hasty appeal to Heather to come home and live there with Michael for the duration of the war. On the telephone she painted a glowing picture of the advantages, the good food for our son, the safety, the affectionate care of his grandparents while his mother was doing her war work, the immunity from the spread of possible epidemics among the local children. Mrs Burrell had seen a glimmer of hope here. But Heather was adamant, and within a week Mrs Burrell had two little girls from Haringey billeted at the farm.

She fought back. Some instinct made her insist that, if children there must be, they should be girls. Boys, she argued, were too apt to run into danger on a farm, being fascinated by machinery and tools, and more likely to provoke the animals into attacking them. So girls it was, and before long an unexpected saviour appeared in the person of Phil. The children were ten and twelve years old respectively, not an age at which girls usually inflame lustful passions, but it seemed that their presence had been enough to awaken Phil's need to exhibit his intimate equipment to any available female onlooker. The maidens had scarcely inhabited Jasmine Farm for a fortnight before Phil came towards them one evening through the autumn mist, unbuttoning his trousers and fishing out his already stiffening truncheon. One of the children had been merely puzzled but the other, who had an uncle given to the same recreation, burst into shrilly voluble protest.

The billeting officer, called in to deal with the crisis, suggested that the Burrells might get rid of Phil, but before the words were well out Mrs Burrell had firmly declared that Phil was an experienced worker and essential to the running of the farm. 'Haven't we been told often enough,' she demanded, 'that for us country people, food production must come first?' The billeting officer had wilted and removed the children.

All this had happened in the early weeks of the war. What I didn't know – because she didn't reveal it to me until her plans matured – was that Heather had been busy for months behind the scenes trying to get Land Girls billeted at Jasmine Farm. Mrs Burrell moved in a perpetual and infuriating atmosphere of self-approval, of smugness even. She was a farmer's wife, she was involved in the essential work of producing food; what else could be asked of her? Without mentioning it to her mother, therefore, Heather put Jasmine Farm down on her Land Girl training project list to take three. 'It'll be a bit of a squeeze,' she said to me, 'but one can have my room and the others can double up in Tom's – he had a bigger room than I did.'

Needless to say, Mrs Burrell squawked, but this time it stuck.

'What about Phil?' I asked. 'If little girls of twelve can set off his propensity, won't grown-up girls set it off even more?'

'Not necessarily. But anyway I've taken care of that in advance. Before the girls go there I'm going to put them in the picture, tell them they have a fellow worker about the place who's got some pretty disagreeable habits. But he's not dangerous, he won't do them any physical harm, and as far as being shocked and annoyed, well, they can just put up with it. If they don't like having to look at Phil showing himself off, let them go and volunteer as stewardesses in the Merchant Navy. They'll find anything Phil can show them isn't as bad as being torpedoed in the North Atlantic.'

'Do they have stewardesses in the Merchant Navy these days?' I asked. 'And if it comes to that, did they ever have them?'

'Don't split hairs. You know what I mean.'

So life rumbled on until the next big turning-point, which was of course the twenty-second of June in that year, the German attack on Russia. By a curious succession of chances I must have been one of the last people in England to learn of this event. My London lodgings, horrible as they were, at least had the advantage of being near enough to the office for me to walk to and from work, so I didn't see the headlines in people's newspapers as I sat in the tube; and, since the radio in my lodgings happened to be on the blink, I didn't hear it before setting out. As a matter of fact, the first person I actually discussed it with was Geraldine. She telephoned me at work, about ten o'clock that morning, full of excitement, suggesting that we have lunch together. She had come to London at the end of 1940 to join Harry, but apart from speaking to her once or twice on the telephone to make sure that they were all right, I had been too busy to make any contact with her. I was free for lunch that day, and met her in a pub.

I could see as soon as she pushed her way through the door that the news had acted on her like Aquavit. Her eyes were glowing and her normally pale skin was tinged with pink as if the blood were glowing keenly just under her delicate skin. 'So it's come,' she said, without wasting time in superfluous greetings, as she dropped into a chair opposite me.

'What d'you mean, it's come?' I sparred. 'You're not trying to tell me you saw it coming all along? They were *allies*.'

'I knew you'd throw that at me. All right, let's get it over. The Pact was a disgrace. But the shame of the Nazi-Soviet Pact was Stalin's personal shame. All right, so Stalin appeared to betray the Left – '

'*Appeared* to? By Christ, he – '

'All right, perhaps he did actually betray it. Certainly he took a lot of the heart out of the struggle against Fascism *at that time*. But when everything comes out it'll probably be revealed that he knew Hitler was going to attack him, and wanted to buy time just as we bought it at Munich. He betrayed the international Socialist movement, we betrayed the Czechs. What's the difference? The fight's *on* now. And I'll tell you something. The shame was never on the Russian people themselves. They were just the workers and the peasants who are trying to carry the burdens of a Socialist state and make it succeed. And now they've got to defend it against attack, and they'll do that.'

'Yes, of course they'll do it, because Russians, like everyone else, love their country and won't stand for having it invaded. They're not doing it out of loyalty to that mob in the Kremlin.'

'They'll fight,' said Geraldine, leaning forward in her seat. 'Whether it's for an old-fashioned virtue that *you* can approve of, like patriotism, or whether it's for progressive ideals, internationalism and economic justice, they'll *fight*. . . . But what I chiefly want to say to you is this, Peter. Today's news means that the *essential* clash between Communism and Fascism has come back into the open. The Pact had the effect of letting people say that Communism and Fascism were the same thing under the skin. But the reality of a situation has a way of forcing itself to the surface. Communism and Fascism are opposing forces, and now that they're actually at one another's throats that opposition is there for everyone to see.'

I said nothing, beyond asking her what she would like to drink, and announcing my intention of trying to get us some sausage rolls. The belief that Communism and Fascism were the same thing under the skin was exactly the belief I held myself, and I saw no reason to change it merely because one bloodstained tyrant had launched an attack on another. But to say so would have been to start a quarrel, so I got some sausage rolls instead and very terrible they were. In those days nobody could afford to be fussy, however. Between 1940 and 1946 I never refused a sausage roll, and since then I have never eaten one.

In retrospect, of course, it became clear that the German invasion of Russia was the first great turning-point of the war. The onslaught launched by the German Army was terrific, unimaginable, appalling. Even a country the size of the Soviet Union, one-sixth of the earth's land surface under a single authority, only just succeeded in surviving it; though supported by the heroism of the populace and with very useful support from ourselves, the Russian forces were pushed back, on a 1,000-mile front, almost to within sight of the towers of the Kremlin. If the fury of that onslaught had been thrown against the British Isles, defended only by its sketchy little army and backed by civilians fighting with broken bottles, it must surely have succeeded. The German decision to turn and attack Russia was in fact what saved us. I assumed at the time, naturally enough, that it was a decision of the German General Staff, who after all had been waging the war pretty successfully up to that point. I didn't realize – how could I? – that it wasn't their decision at all, but merely an outcropping of Hitler's madness. Whatever form of mental derangement he suffered from was beginning to take a new and (to his own side) disastrous form.

The very next week-end there was a rare occurrence at Mulberry Hall; the telephone rang and it was for me. The deep, sonorous voice of Nussbaum asked me, 'Have you any time of leisure tomorrow?'

Tomorrow was Sunday. 'I shall be coming in to Oxford in the evening, to take the train. Otherwise transport is difficult and I tend to have things to do here. But it would be good to see you. Is Katz around? It's been a long — '

'What time leaves your train?'

'There's one about eight I usually try for. But the nine-fifteen is a possibility, just about.'

'You appreciate slivovitz?'

'I've very rarely had any, but I remember it as pretty delicious. And fiery.'

'Precisely, my friend. Delicious and fiery. Hans is, as you say, around. He has bottles of slivovitz, the last of a stock he brought back from Dubrovnik during his last visit there before the war. Now, we have decided to open them. May we

194

invite you to savour a glass? It will be many years before you have another opportunity.'

I saw at once that an important change had occurred in Nussbaum. In 1938 and '39 he would never have said, in however casual a context. 'It will be many years before this, that or the other happens,' so ingrained was his conviction that we weren't going to have a future. Now, the casual remark betrayed that he had got rid of this conviction of doom. No wonder he felt like celebrating. It was an occasion for slivovitz if ever there was one.

I arranged to spend an hour *chez* Katz on the way to the station on Sunday evening. (Nussbaum had rung up because it was he who had the telephone.) Heather was invited too, but she declined ('I've got too much to do to sit about talking to two old clowns who can't discuss anything but Greek dustbins. You go, you'll enjoy it'), so the following evening found me standing alone on the doorstep of that thin gaunt house in Walton Street with a real sense of pleasurable anticipation. Nussbaum! Katz! I valued them and I had missed them in the scurry of the past couple of years.

It was Nussbaum who opened the door and greeted me. 'Ah, my friend! Too long since I had the pleasure! The war has separated many people. But us it has not succeeded in separating. Hans and I were together even in the Isle of Man, where we spent a few months at the urgent invitation of your government. Now we are both back in Oxford. He was allowed back a few weeks ahead of me: perhaps they decided he was the more harmless animal. We are both back now, and some friends have joined us for our modest celebration of homecoming.'

He led the way up the rickety stairs. 'Please to follow me. My eyrie is in the topmost branches of this stout old tree.'

'Anybody I know?' I asked. 'Apart from you and Hans, that is.'

'Perhaps not. They are mostly fugitives like ourselves.' He opened the door on Katz's long narrow room, filled with smoke. 'Mr Peter Leonard!' he announced like a footman. 'Of Episcopus College!'

Of the Ministry of Supply would be more like it, I thought, but I nodded affably as I confronted the assembly and heard Nussbaum reel off their names, which I failed to retain, six or eight people, women as well as men, all obviously foreign and all obviously intellectuals, with that keen, penetrating look which seems to sit naturally on the European intellectual countenance; it isn't so uniform in England, where the intelligentsia do not make common cause and form a separate class but merge in with the professional middle class, and English society both gains and loses from the fact.

The conversation, which fell silent as I entered, had sounded German to me as I climbed the stairs, but now, perhaps from politeness, it started again in English, more or less heavily accented.

I felt intensely *apart* from these people, though I felt sorrow and indignation for the various disasters that had befallen them. In such company, an Englishman always does feel intensely apart. If he is complacent, with a provincial outlook, he feels superior; if he has a healthy streak of self-mistrust, he feels uneasy and slightly inferior. They always seem to be so devouringly intelligent and so concerned with absolutely fundamental questions; they brush aside small-talk and go straight for the big issues. And then the Englishman thinks, but of course they do! They live their lives in a permanent atmosphere of crisis. How different is the atmosphere of England, where 300 years have passed since any man lay dead for an idea.

Hans Katz now came beamingly towards me. His bouncing, Jack-in-the-box optimism seemed this evening to be justified. 'We have much to be grateful for, my friend,' he said, pouring slivovitz into my glass, and we clinked glasses and I smiled back at him. I had always liked the way both he and Nussbaum called me 'my friend'.

Nussbaum now appeared at my other side. 'Hans is always mentally prepared for good news. I am mentally prepared for bad. Of course logically I am right. In this century, in human history as a whole, which has predominated? Good news or bad?'

'You can't put that kind of question to an historian,' I said, laughing. 'Everything that happens is good news for some and bad for others, because people have opposing interests. The Battle of Lepanto — '

'There is no need to dig all the way back to Lepanto. Was the Battle of the Somme good news or bad news?'

'Well, the fact that the Battle of the Somme happened at all was a disgrace to European civilization. But I suppose you could say that on the whole it was a good thing that the last war didn't end with the German Army dominating the whole of Europe.'

'Why? What difference would it have made?'

'Well, Germany had pretty elaborate plans for wholesale expansion, if not actually world domination. It's all in the record. You remember the September Programme, that they brought out when the war was only about a month old, stating their war aims? It's just as well they didn't succeed, surely?'

Nussbaum looked at me with his great bloodhound's eyes. 'What difference would it have made? France has been weakened anyway, only twenty years later. The Russians are being pushed back at this moment. It is clear that Hitler thinks German military power can seize now what it failed to seize twenty years ago, and he may still be right. And if he is right, what is twenty years in the time-span of history?'

I noticed that another man was listening. He had a white moustache and a distinguished, sensitive face, and I had a vague impression that his name was Helmut something.

This man now joined in. 'There is one thing you are forgetting, Otto. The last war was the cause of the rise to power of the Russian Bolsheviks.'

'Without doubt it was. First it produced a war-weariness in the people which made it easier to lead them into an uprising, and in second line, the military defeat of Germany removed any military threat from outside.'

'In fact,' I put in, 'you might say that the Englishmen and Frenchmen who died in such numbers in 1918 – yes, and the Americans too – were making the world safe for Lenin.'

'And now,' this Helmut said in his gentle, precise voice, 'if there is a second defeat of Germany – and we must all pray that there will be – it can only strengthen the regime in Russia. In fact, with Stalin and Hitler now at war, we shall ultimately be the losers, because whichever of them is defeated the other will be strengthened.'

'Well,' I said, 'I suppose most people in this country would say that it would be better to strengthen Stalin than to see Hitler victorious.'

'Most people in this country,' remarked Helmut quietly, 'are still living mentally in the reign of Queen Victoria.'

'Probably they are wise,' said Katz fatalistically. 'Why should they be pulled against their will into barbarism?'

'Certainly,' said Nussbaum, 'the age of Victoria was a time when democratic

196

institutions all over Europe were quite secure. Even Tsarist Russia showed some signs of a leaning towards democracy. Whereas today,' he made a gesture of resignation, 'democratic institutions are very shaky in most European countries.'

'And,' Helmut rounded off, 'if Stalin takes command in Europe there will be no trace of democracy left anywhere.'

This was beginning to sound like a pretty funny kind of celebration, but I had to make allowances for the amount that these people had suffered.

'So you think,' I said, looking round the circle of faces, 'that this war can only end with the strengthening of a tyrant. Personally, in the long run, and taking in the whole globe, I'd say that the picture is less black-and-white, and that perhaps there's some room for hope.'

'Hope of what?' Nussbaum asked. 'Please continue. I have a genuine desire to hear this.'

'I'm sorry,' I replied, 'I simply can't be an oracle. I don't see enough and I haven't experienced enough. But it's impossible to have considered these matters at all and not to have *some* point of view. And it seems to me that the fight for world power is on, with three systems competing. Two of them are totalitarian, one Fascist, the other Communist, and both pretty fully defined. The third force competing for mastery of the world is less cut and dried. But it's pretty all-embracing none the less. If I had to give it a name, I'd call it pluto-liberalism. Most of the power gets into the hands of the people with money, but there's a token show of deference to other values. It's a mixed system, as I say, but at least it isn't monolithic. There's some room for light and air in it, even some capacity for change. It's better than the other two systems. And these are the three that are going to spend what's left of the twentieth century – if there is anything left of it – in competition.'

'You really think,' said Katz, looking intently at my face as if he were trying to guess my inmost thoughts, 'that this third system of yours, the one you describe as libero-plut – '

'Pluto-liberalism.'

'That this pluto-liberalism has a chance? That it can survive the onslaught of a victorious Stalinism, for example?'

'It may not be able to withstand it in Western Europe. But it could in America, and perhaps even in Asia.'

'So how do you think this war will end?' Helmut asked me. 'What will be the state of things, in your opinion?'

'Ultimately,' I said, 'the best thing is to hope that the fate which is coming to European civilization will come slowly, so that we can have a bit of our allotted lifespan in the meantime. After all, that's all human time ever is – it's always in the meantime.'

'Ladies and gentlemen,' Helmut cried out suddenly, 'I give you a toast.' He raised his glass, in which there was still a tiny remnant of the nectar. 'To – the meantime!'

'The meantime!' a dozen voices echoed. And I thought, did I mean that? Is that what I really think human life is, a permanent meantime? Certainly it seemed true of the people closest to me. Brian waiting for Cecil Kimber to get back into some creative relationship with motor-racing; me, waiting to exercise my skills as an historian. But the intelligent, fine-drawn alien faces I saw around me – they were another thing; they were the faces of people to whom anything like normal life had ceased to be attainable, who could never go home because in their lives the very idea of home had vanished, who had only the one bleak choice, either meantime or nothing.

For me the autumn months of '41 settled into a dead, monotonous routine, backwards and forwards between London and the country, sitting down to my dreary office desk with a pile of papers in front of me and wearily getting up again, many hours later, with the desk (more or less) cleared. I had a certain full consciousness of utility, but none of excitement. The fear of the threat that menaced my country had receded; even at moments when the war seemed to be going badly, one never had those days when a grey-clad wave of invading troops seemed to be just over the next ridge.

During this dead period, I actually looked forward every week to my train journey back to London on Sunday evenings. It was the only link I had, nowadays, with the larger world of the University. Many academics had London war jobs and of those who did, a high proportion spent the weekends in Oxford. Sometimes as I waited on the platform I would look down its length and try to spot the recognizable faces; there were times when it looked like one of those nineteenth-century political cartoons which assemble all the members of a political party in one drawing.

One chill and uninviting Sunday night, with a river mist beginning to thicken into fog and a discouraging raw dampness settling over everything, I was particularly pleased to fall in with Tonson, the Arabic scholar from Episcopus. Tonson was so unobtrusive a man, so shy and unassertive, that one very easily lost sight of him, and indeed I had scarcely thought of him since the war had descended on us all; but I was glad to see him now. He was a voice of calm thoughtfulness amid all the madness and violence.

He told me that he was employed at Bush House, in the Strand, writing and delivering news broadcasts in Arabic to a range of Middle Eastern countries. 'It's rather strange,' he said, 'to find oneself suddenly in demand in the active world, to have people with clipboards and schedules asking one when they can have this or that ready. You know, people in pursuit of some urgent practical objective who actually *want* one around, are actually glad that one knows Arabic reasonably well. There aren't nearly enough of us in fact – there are always a lot of people about who speak and read Arabic, but most of them of course are Arabs, and I'm afraid their notion of what constitutes a news bulletin from London can be a bit idiosyncratic.'

'So anyway, there you are in the mainstream of the busy world. Not much flavour of the cloister these days.'

'No, I could do with a bit of it. Actually, I'm looking forward to the day when we can all get back to work. I'm a ruminating animal, I'm afraid. Study's what I'm adapted for.'

'Even though it's a study that tends to attract only a few people? You don't mind having a minority subject? I mean, I'm not saying that you *should* mind. But some people could find it a bit – well, lonely. Just a very small circle to discuss things with.'

Tonson spoke in a resigned, gentle voice, only just audible above the rumble of the train. 'I know how my subject is regarded by the majority. They can't understand how a man can spend his life studying the language and culture of nations which don't cut any figure in the world. If you say that an Islamic civilization reached a very high peak in the tenth and eleventh centuries, and made a channel for Greek ideas to flow down into the Western Europe of the

198

Renaissance, they just brush that aside as history, the past. That was then, this is now – why bother about it? That's their attitude.'

'I meet it myself,' I said. 'Even about matters that quite obviously bear very directly on present-day life. A lot of people resent an historian because he asks them to think, and thinking gives them a headache.'

'And even if I stick to the present day,' Tonson said, 'and remind them that millions of people speak Arabic as their first or only language, they say, "What does it matter? They're not people who count for anything." It's all rather horrible, the underlying cynicism – it's like Stalin, you know: *How many divisions has the Pope?*' He laughed shortly. 'It makes your blood run cold, rather.'

'And of course it fuels their dislike of scholars and scholarship. They enjoy thinking of a place like Oxford as a nest of idle privilege where people sit around indulging in frivolous hobbies, enquiring into things that can't possibly be the slightest use.'

'Oh, they think that all right. When I'm introduced to people as an Oxford don, and they ask me what my subject is and I tell them Arabic, they practically burst out laughing. Yet you and I don't see it like that. Why is there such a big difference?'

'How wise Oxford was,' I mused aloud, 'to set up a Chair of Arabic, your Chair, in the seventeenth century, just at a time when the Islamic countries were beginning to sink out of sight. They didn't say to themselves, "Is this the coming thing?" They saw it as a valuable study and they set it up.'

'And one day,' Tonson said, 'the world may come to recognize the wisdom of that.'

'You mean one day there'll be a demand among so-called practical people for a knowledge of Arabic?'

'Yes. And for an understanding of the Islamic mind.'

I didn't want to contradict him, but I really couldn't bring myself to believe any such thing, and I suppose my disbelief must have shown in my face.

'Islam,' Tonson said, 'is a concealed force in the world. But I wouldn't be prepared to say that it'll stay concealed for ever.'

'Well, I'll stick my neck out and say that it will,' I said. 'It's based on a religion, and it seems to me a religion bound to go down. It's too uncompromising. After all, Christianity, which has always been its chief rival, has managed to adapt to the modern world. It survived the Reformation, when the whole of Northern Europe became Protestant. It survived the splitting into East and West and the decision of the Byzantine Empire to use the Cyrillic script and become unintelligible to Westerners. It even survived Darwinism, which for a time in the middle of the nineteenth century looked like being fatal to it. Where's the Christian now who loses any sleep over Darwinism? They've simply managed to adapt to it – they say that the notion that God created the world in six days in 4004 B.C. was simply a manner of speaking and that God actually worked through evolution. Hey, presto! Darwin is dead, long live Darwin! But Islam can't adapt like that. What do Islamic theologians do about Darwin, to stick to that example?'

'Nothing. They just brush him aside as a benighted Western unbeliever.'

'Well, there you are. Islam can break but not bend.'

'Perhaps it won't have to bend,' said Tonson. 'If civilization gets as far as a twenty-first century, the chances are it'll be a century of fanaticism. Marxists are fanatical – they brush aside arguments from reason and evidence. So do Muslims. Christians tend to be reasonable. Not a good formula for surviving what the twenty-first century will probably be like.'

199

'If that's true,' I asked, 'what on earth is going to happen in the Soviet Union, where there are millions of Muslims? What's going to happen when they and the Marxists really come face to face?'

'I have no idea.'

Later, when the train slid in under the great round arches of Paddington Station and halted, Tonson and I went our separate ways. As I watched his small, erect form disappearing into the maw of the District line, I longed, suddenly, for the war to be over, for the day when at last, and however hesitantly, the life of the mind could begin again. Until then, I shared the fate of Katz and Nussbaum and their friends; I was a person of the meantime.

When I got to the office one morning my secretary said to me, 'There's a man waiting to see you.'

'Waiting to see me? At this hour? Who is it?'

'He didn't say.'

I told her to bring him in. I had only just finished hanging up my coat when he entered. It was Brian. He looked exhausted, his face had a yellowish tinge and beneath his eyes there were dark bruises of fatigue. He hadn't shaved for a day, or perhaps two days.

I checked the exclamation of surprise and horror that was my natural reaction. 'Sit down, brother,' I said. 'I believe I can get us a cup of coffee if I bend the rules a little.'

At that time, it was frowned on if you paused in your work before a woman came round with a trolley at eleven o'clock, but my secretary and I had some bottled coffee, some powdered milk and an old tin kettle hidden in a little pantry that also had a gas-ring. We had a long war to get through and we were going to get through it.

'O.K.,' Brian said. He did not speak again until he had accepted the coffee. It was in a cardboard cup that gave it a bad taste, the kind you used to get at football matches before plastics were developed. He swallowed half of it in great gulps. 'Thanks. I needed that. It's piss, but I needed it.'

The weather was cold. A gritty wind blew through the cracks in the window-frames and under the doors. The world seemed a hostile, tiring place. 'Is there something I can do for you, Brian?' I asked.

'No,' he said. 'It's just a social visit.'

'You mean,' I stated, 'that you just needed somewhere to sit down.'

'You could say that.'

'Why didn't you go home last night?' I asked.

'How d'you know I didn't go home last night?'

'Because I'm not a fool. If you'd gone home you'd probably have shaved. So even if you'd got up early enough to get the kind of train that'd land you in my office at a quarter to nine in the morning, you'd be looking . . . better than you do now.'

Brian drank the last acrid inch of his coffee and dropped the cardboard cup in the waste-basket. 'I didn't go home last night because I didn't go to work yesterday. And I knew they'd have been after me. Ringing us up. I wanted Primrose to be able to tell them she didn't know where I was.'

'I suppose she could have told them that anyway.'

'No, she couldn't,' he said quickly. 'She doesn't like telling lies. She never says anything unless it's true.'

I digested this in silence. Inwardly I was wondering what life would be like, actually like on a day-to-day basis, if one never said anything unless one were sure it were true. Aren't some of our statements just things we say in the hope that by saying them we will help them to become true?

'I suppose,' I said, 'that you're going to tell me why you didn't go to work yesterday.'

'They've sacked Kim,' he said.

'Sacked...' I had known that Cecil Kimber had been prevented by Billy Morris from continuing to build racing cars; but still, I knew he had been kept on at Morris Motors as a Director. It came to me now that Directors can be sacked like anyone else.

'What is he sacked for?' I asked.

'You'll never believe this.' Brian leaned forward and stared into my face. 'Cecil Kimber has been sacked by the Nuffield Organization,' he said very distinctly, as if recording the words for an incredulous posterity, 'for arranging for the M.G. factory to go into aircraft production.'

'Air...?'

'Since 1939, when we had to stop making sports cars and the factory suddenly became unused, we've been trying to find something to do that would help the war effort. We've been farting about doing a bit of this and a bit of that. Do you know what we were doing at the beginning of this year?'

'No, I don't, though in my job I probably ought to have known, if it was anything I could have — '

'*Frying-pans*,' Brian said, his voice heavy with disgust and irony. 'We were making bloody frying-pans. For a local Forces catering unit. I know it's hard to believe. The men who put together the K.3. Magnette were standing around making bloody frying-pans. And all the time the natural thing for us to be making in a war was aircraft engines. Well, Kim went out and fixed it. He got sick of watching hand-picked men making frying-pans and he went out and fixed us an aircraft contract. Then he comes back all smiles and tells the Directors he's got it in the bag. And what do they do? They sack him!' He stood up and began walking about the room. 'Those are the bastards I've been working for all these years, and I'd be working for now if I hadn't been seconded to this 'plane repair work. Company men. Boss's men. They hate free spirit, they hate anyone who makes decisions and *acts* instead of just writing little minutes. Frying-pans! With a hundred million people trying to kill us, they want to go on making frying-pans!'

'Sit down, Brian. You're below the age that's normally associated with strokes and heart attacks, but you'll have one as sure as fate if you go on like this.'

'You'd have a stroke yourself if you could grasp the absolute...the absolute...' Brian was fighting for words, but gave up and gestured helplessly. 'It's impossible to convey it to you, to *anyone* who's outside the way these things are...' He stopped again, choked. 'Look, that's why I didn't go to work yesterday. I couldn't, that's all. I *couldn't* go and fiddle about with aircraft in Cowley while there was so much going on at Abingdon. I had to go over to the works and be with the lads. You realize they all feel the same way as I do? There was a very strong move to bring everybody out on strike and just refuse to work until Kim got his job back. If they had struck, I'd have stayed away from work too. I know it's wartime and it's a crime to stay away from work. Let them send me to prison – the case might get a bit of publicity and it'd show these buggers up for what they are.'

'Well,' I said dubiously, 'I know how you feel, but really I do wonder — '

201

'But they didn't go on strike and d'you know why? Because he told them not to. Yes, Kim got up and spoke to them when they were all in the canteen, and said it was the most important thing for the factory to keep going, the war had to be won and never mind what happened to individuals. I tell you, that man's *big*. He's only a little bloke, but he's big in his mind, too big for the people he's been trying to work with.'

'This aircraft contract,' I said. 'Did the other Directors throw it out? Or will it go ahead?'

'I dunno. Probably it will go ahead. It's to make the nose-cones for Albemarle bombers. That's a very complex piece of assembly, you can't just let any peasant loose on it. And that'll be Kim's legacy to M.G. – that he got them on to bombing planes and off bloody frying-pans.'

I looked at my brother. I knew all these events had their significance in large, impersonal matters, but with the two of us here, this morning, in my shabby office, I saw it as something that affected Brian, and affected me because of the way I felt about Brian.

'How long have you known about this?' I asked.

'We've known for about a month. They gave him that much notice, to clear his desk and everything. It's taken us that long to believe it. I've been numb. I didn't know what to think or what to do. I kept dreaming at night that it wasn't true. Peter, it may seem nothing to you – '

'It doesn't seem nothing to me.'

' – but that man had the loyalty of the chaps who worked with him, real solid deep-down loyalty. We had a whip-round at the works, to get him a present. I chipped in of course, but the jig and tool makers decided to give him something they'd made with their hands. They thought he'd rather have a bit of their skill to remember than just something they'd paid money for. So they made him a pipe and tobacco cabinet. The rest of us got him a silver candelabra. There isn't a lot you can buy, these days, and that seemed more or less the kind of thing.'

'Was he pleased with them?'

'Well, of course he was very grateful and everything, and his wife was too; she was there of course and the daughters were coming in and out as well. The lads had made a really beautiful job of the smoking cabinet, with perfect tongue-and-groove work and some nice inlay, though they're not trained as woodworkers. They've always been used to doing the impossible for Kim and they did it one more time. It was their way of saying all the things they hadn't got words for. Kim ran his hand over the lovely smooth finish and said he never knew you could get a finish like that – it had the precision of an engineering job. Typical of him.'

'Did you get a chance to talk to him?'

'Not one to one. He made a little statement to us, just a few words about how he'd be sorry not to be working with us any more and he wished us luck. Then he went round and shook hands with us. That was when I'd been going to say something to him, just personal to us, just a few words, but when he shook my hand I . . . well, nothing came. I just had to keep quiet. I was afraid for a moment I was going to make an exhibition of myself.' Brian paused and then added with sudden vehemence, 'You know what I wished in that moment? I wished we'd all been a lot of bloody foreigners, Eye-ties or Spaniards or something. Then we could've let the tears just roll down our faces. I've seen 'em. When they won a big race . . . or lost it. Whatever it was, joy or disappointment, quite often they'd have tears pouring down. And nobody thought any the worse of anybody for it.'

'Aeneas weeps several times in the *Aeneid*,' I said.

202

'I don't know who he is.'

'He was an Italian,' I said, 'and no one thought any the worse of him for having a good cry sometimes.'

'Well, they bloody would of me. This is bloody England.'

I pushed him towards a chair in the corner.

'Now,' I said, 'sit down and just let your mind go blank while I do an hour or so's work. Then we'll go to a pub for a drink and I'll stand you lunch in our canteen, and then you'll get the afternoon train back to Oxford. I'll ring Primrose and tell her the score.' A sudden thought struck me. 'You never used to be on the telephone at home.'

'Just recently. They made us ... everybody in the works at a certain level of responsibility.'

'There you are,' I said. 'You're a key man; they need you. And after all it isn't the chaps at Cowley who've sacked Kim. You ought to get back there and help with the job. What's your 'phone number?'

'There'll be no one there,' he said.

'Give it me all the same,' I told him. 'I must write it down while I think about it.'

So he gave it to me, and after that I worked, and Brian sensibly decided not to sit on a hard chair and watch me but to take himself off and meet me at noon in the pub. As soon as I was sure he was out of the building I dialled his home number. I knew Primrose had a war job, but all the same it was possible she might be at home, the circumstances being what they were.

Primrose answered. I said, 'Primrose, it's Peter here, speaking from London. I've got Brian here.'

'Does he want to speak to me?'

'I didn't mean he was here at this exact moment. He's gone out for a bit. I'm seeing him at twelve o'clock and after lunch he's coming back to Oxford.'

'Oh,' she said. 'Thanks for telling me.' Her voice was expressionless.

'I'm surprised I caught you,' I said.

'I'm on a funny shift, ten o'clock at night till two in the morning.'

'Oh,' I said. 'That means I've woken you up.'

'I was awake. I was just lying there thinking about getting up. You haven't disturbed me.'

'When he took off yesterday,' I said, 'didn't you know where he'd gone?'

'No. He just put up a little note.'

'A little note? What to say? If I'm not being too inquisitive,' I added, feeling the lack of response coming down the line from her and deciding I probably *was* being too inquisitive – but after all, damn it, I was his brother.

'I was in bed and I thought I heard him moving about downstairs, but I just assumed he was going to work at his usual time. Then when I came down at about twelve o'clock I found this piece of paper saying he'd been called away suddenly and he'd be in touch.'

Called away suddenly? It sounded so sinister. 'Were you worried?'

'I try not to let things worry me,' Primrose's cool voice came back. I understood that it was a rebuke – she was telling me to mind my own business. If she *had* been worried, that was a matter to be settled between her and the Fates.

Sitting there at my battered desk with the cigarette burns on it and the untidy mess of official papers, I suddenly had the thought that only one person apart from Brian himself could have got away with asking her that question. My mother.

'Well,' I said, 'he'll be better than just in touch this afternoon, he'll be home.'

'You think he's ready to come home?'

'I know he is,' I told her. 'What he . . . had to do has been done.'

'You say you're seeing him at lunchtime?'

'I'm seeing him at twelve o'clock for a drink and then we're having lunch in the canteen here.' Trying to sound natural and unrestrained, I added, 'Shall I get him to ring you?'

'If he wants to.'

I made a few conversational noises and then we rang off. But when I met Brian for that lunchtime drink, I couldn't resist saying to him, 'I spoke to Primrose. She was quite calm, outwardly at any rate. But I must say I was surprised to gather that you hadn't told her where you were going.'

He said nothing. Just looked at me, his glass in his hand, untasted.

'I know it isn't any of my business,' I said.

'No,' he agreed. 'It isn't.' He looked at me very coldly. 'Do I tell you how to run *your* marriage?'

'I'm not telling you how to run your marriage. It's just that I'm worried about you. Get that? It's just that I, Peter, am worried about you, Brian.' As I spoke I stabbed my forefinger towards myself and then towards him. '*I* want *you* to come out of this without losing too much flesh.'

'Well, if you want to know,' he said, 'though I agree with you that it's none of your business, this whole thing about walking off the job and coming to London and going underground for thirty-six hours is to do with not telling Primrose things.'

'Really? How so?'

'I wanted to sort this Kimber thing out in my mind, to make sure I could face it without going to pieces. This bit of running away and hiding – yes, even talking to a know-nothing like you, Peter – it's done what it was supposed to do. I've digested it, somehow. I can live with it.'

'I'm glad to hear it,' I said. 'I know it's none of my business, but I'm glad to hear it.'

He looked at me across the rim of his beer-glass. Then he set the glass down and said, 'Primrose, you see . . .'

'Yes?'

'Primrose . . . isn't the kind of girl you want to go to pieces in front of.'

'Yes. I can understand that.'

'If you're going to do any falling apart, you want to do it where she can't see you.'

'Precisely.'

'And afterwards, when you've got yourself together, you go back to her and then you find it was all the more worth getting yourself together. Not to let her down.'

'Say no more,' I said and grinned.

'I wasn't going to say any more,' he said and grinned too.

I lifted my glass, which was not quite empty. 'I give you a toast,' I said. 'To Cecil Kimber and his big, wide, wonderful post-war world.'

'I'll drink to that.'

All these things happened in the autumn, as the Germans pushed on into Russia, the bombs slammed down on London and the world moved towards the Japanese attack on Pearl Harbor, which rounded off the year. I was seeing a good deal of Bax in London, especially during the evenings I spent at the United Universities

204

Club. It was always good to see him, and interesting to discuss world events with him. The only times I headed him off from a subject were when he tried to up-date me about wartime life at Episcopus. Being a bachelor to whom the College was his home as well as his place of work, he naturally went there a good deal, often spending the week-end. Oxford University did not close down in the Second World War as much as in the First. Most of its teaching work went on at a reduced volume, and in the case of medicine and many of the sciences not reduced at all. Bax had plenty to say, but for some reason I was unwilling – obstinately, totally unwilling – to make room in my mind for wartime Oxford. I wanted, if we all survived the war, to go back there one day and start a full-time life, but I couldn't bear to contemplate the patchwork arrangements, the wartime degrees awarded on a few months of study, the military training that bit deep into the time at the young men's disposal, half of Episcopus itself given over to a Ministry evacuated out of London. No, it was all bewildering and distasteful, and I was determined to leave it out of my consciousness.

And in that list, of course, I didn't mention the strongest reason of all: the trickle of active-service deaths rising every now and again to a torrent, dwindling to a trickle again, but never ceasing. Bax told me that a number of the men I had taught had been killed, and I knew that many more would go before the war ended.

'Please leave me in ignorance,' I said to him, some time during this year of 1941. 'When it's all over, I'll sit down somewhere quiet, and read through a list of all the men who've been killed, and think about them and remember them, and speculate a little on what they might have become and the things they might have achieved. I'll spend as much time as it takes – a day, a week, a month – till I've assimilated the list and come to terms with it. But not in dribs and drabs.'

'The choice, of course, is yours,' said Bax, looking at me through his thick round lenses as if I were still his pupil and he was giving me the choice of several essay subjects.

I made that choice and I stuck to it, for which I have always been glad. It is an often repeated statement – a *cliché*, almost – that except on the Russian Front and in certain very bloody engagements in the Pacific, the Second World War was not as blindly wasteful of lives as the First. Broadly speaking this is correct. But at any Oxford or Cambridge college, the Second War memorial has quite as many names on it as the First. That is because the Second World War was fought at a higher technical level and fell with particular force on the educated, the trained, the intelligent; and their names are up on those walls to prove it.

Episcopus College seemed, at present, incredibly distant from me; only sixty-five miles even from my London office, barely fifteen from Mulberry Hall, yet like a place in another world, a place in a dream. A dream of peace? No, of completeness rather. The past, in which Episcopus had its deep roots, had never been peaceful. No human epoch was peaceful; there were always hostilities, oppositions, people trying to get their way by force. Episcopus College was a place of study and quiet reflection, a place for the nurture and increase of wisdom, but war, violence and death had made themselves felt within its graceful quadrangles and panelled rooms. Had not its most famous building been planned and reared under the storm-clouds of a civil war that was just about to tear the country apart? Of the long line of its past Presidents, had not the greatest and most celebrated taken his last breath with his head on the executioner's block?

10

Sunday was not a regular evening for Job Trundle and his friends, the *cénacle* who gathered in the Bargeman's Arms. All through the rest of the week they were reliably there at six o'clock, as soon as the place opened; most of them, being college scouts, would be enjoying a pint and a few minutes' talk on their way in to the evening session of work, which would begin with serving in Hall at 7.15 or 7.30. Old Trundle himself, long since retired, took his six o'clock pint of beer as an apéritif before walking the few yards to his own house in East Street. A few others, working at various trades in the town, had finished for the day and were on their way home.

But Sunday evenings were hit and miss, as far as the *cénacle* was concerned, and since my visit to my parents usually happened in the hour just before I boarded the London train at the end of my day-and-a-half break, I saw Old Trundle and his mates only in rare and fugitive glimpses, and seldom all together. I regretted this. It was, to me, one of the privations of wartime. Without realizing it, over the years I had built up a dependence on these gnomic citizens and their portly chairman. They were one of the touchstones against which I tried my own reaction to the unfolding events of life. Not the only one, of course. I had grown up too close to the working class to think of it as a source of infallible wisdom, unflinching realism or incorruptible honesty. It was the function of expensive boarding-schools to produce an intelligentsia who thought of the working class in these terms, idealized it, yearned over it, longed to identify with it, but I saw old Trundle and his mates for what they were, and it didn't prevent my liking them. I missed them during the long spells when I had to do without them. But now, as the year 1942 dragged on through spring and summer and autumn, I had to do without them most of the time.

On one particular evening in early December, though, I was lucky. Old Trundle himself was sitting in his usual corner seat; attended, it is true, by only one member of the circle, and that the youngest, Bob. Bob was in uniform, some outfit like Signals. Presumably he was on leave, so it was more than ever a lucky chance that he was there, talking to Trundle. What was more, he was not just talking to Trundle but pouring out some story so compelling that in normal times he would probably have held it back until there was a full house for it.

'Not a word of a lie,' he was saying. 'I was with this bloke yest'day dinner-time. At the Jolly Postboys in Cowley, we was, an' 'e'd only just knocked off from doin' the job.'

'Brickin' it up?' old Trundle asked slowly. He picked up his beer-mug, took a draught, set it down deliberately and asked again, 'Brickin' it *up?*'

'Them was 'is instructions,' said Bob flatly. He lit a cigarette and looked round with satisfaction, his gaze moving from Trundle to my father, who was taking advantage of the fact that no other customers were present and had his elbows on the bar, giving the story his full attention.

'Who gave the order to brick it up, did he say?' my father asked.

'Superintendent,' Bob said non-committally.

'Seems a funny thing to order, that's all. Brick up a store-room doorway when they're using the site office all the time.'

'Not no more, they en't,' Bob said. 'Thass the 'ole point. Not one o' them fellers as works there won't go through the doorway. They won't set foot in there if you was to offer 'em five 'undred pounds.'

'Did this mate o' yours *see* anythin',' old Trundle demanded, 'while 'e was a-brickin' of it up?'

'Nothin'. O' course it was broad daylight. Not that that's ever stopped 'im before. They say as 'e comes through any time. No knowin' when 'e'll come through.'

'And what do 'e do? When 'e comes through, I means?'

''E just walks. Just walks straight a'ead of 'im through the door, an' out. In 'is flyin' 'elmet and all. Goggles round 'is neck.'

'And they're sure as 'e's a Jerry?'

'Well, o' course they're sure,' Bob said impatiently. 'Anybody can see the difference between one of our blokes an' a Jerry.' Leaning forward, he pursued his advantage. 'An' why would it be one of our blokes? It en't our blokes as is in there, it's all Jerries, ennit?'

I had realized by now that they were speaking of the site office into which Brian had disappeared for a moment on some errand, when he had shown me the field full of wrecked German aircraft.

'Let's get this straight,' my father said in his judicial way. I remembered now, all the way from my boyhood, that when these tap-room discussions were in progress Trundle was the chairman but my father was Ultimate Authority. After all, it was his pub. 'Let's get this straight. What do they keep in this store-room?'

'Bits of everythin', like,' Bob said. Obviously he felt his position would be undermined if he admitted to any areas of ignorance. 'Boxes o' papers an' that. Some tools. First Aid . . .' he trailed off vaguely.

'And they took this Jerry pilot in there when they found him in the 'plane?'

'A bomber, it was. They thought they 'ad all the bodies out an' then they found this chap. Not all smashed up like some of 'em. Just dead with a couple o' bullets through 'im, like. Radio operator or somethin'. They brings 'im in and rings up for instructions about 'im. In the meantime they puts 'im in the store-room.'

'So then,' my father asked, 'they took him away and buried him?'

'That's just it,' Bob said. 'The blokes as 'as to work there, they see 'im taken away, but 'e's *still there*.' His voice sank, impressively, to a hoarse whisper.

'Still there?' Old Trundle demanded. ''Ow can 'e be still bloody there?'

''E comes through that doorway. They never knows the time when 'e won't come walkin' through that doorway, with 'is flyin' 'elmet — '

'Yes, and his goggles round his neck,' my father interrupted. 'I suppose he comes through even when the door's shut?'

'Well,' Bob said with an attempt at sarcasm, ''e don't knock an' wait till they opens it.'

'So why bloody brick it up?' Trundle demanded fiercely. He seemed resentful, as if the story had somehow disturbed him. 'If 'e's goin' to come through a bloody wooden door, surely to Christ 'e can come through a brick wall?'

'Well, don't ask me,' Bob said. 'All as I knows is, they've 'ad it bricked up, an' I knows because I 'ad a pint o' beer yest'dy in the Jolly Postboys with the bloke as bricked it up.'

'Perhaps,' I suggested, 'they're hoping the ghost'll take it as a hint that his company isn't needed. A brick wall must surely be even more unwelcoming than a sported oak.'

I could see from their expressions that this remark was regarded as being in poor taste. But at that moment a group of four or five fresh customers entered, talking animatedly, and a general conversation started. Through its interstices, I could see Bob biding his time, waiting for a chance to get their attention and begin his story again. It was a story I was to hear many more times, over the years, though in one respect the various tellings never settled down into a single, generally accepted version: it was never decided whether the airman's ghost did, or did not, cease to come through the doorway after it had been bricked up.

Still thinking about the German airman (Was the poor fellow buried now? Was he at peace?) I took my haversack over to the station to get the 8.20 to Paddington. It was a bitterly cold night, and as usual the black-out made it seem worse. Every lamp that could possibly be taken away had been, and the rest were fitted with demure little bell-shaped funnels which directed the light downwards in a neat circle. The object was to achieve such a total darkness that from 25,000 feet it would be impossible, looking down, to distinguish between a town and an area of countryside; an impossible objective, but I dare say it came somewhere near to being fulfilled. Meanwhile, people stumped around, wrapped up to the eyes, feeling their way with sticks and umbrellas. If you had an electric torch and happened to shine the beam straight ahead of you some indignant patriot was quite likely to strike it down. To try to read a door number in a strange street amounted almost to signalling to the enemy.

Little clumps of people were converging on the station, and for the last few yards I found myself walking just behind a tall, shambling figure whose loose-knit body movements seemed somehow familiar, and who bent over as he walked to bring his ear closer to the head of his companion, female and not very tall. As we got into the subdued lighting of the booking-hall I saw that it was old Tarrant, the Professor of Arborology or Dendrology or whatever is the correct academic name for tree science. This Chair is attached to Episcopus and its holder is always a Fellow there, which accounts for the fact that a non-scientist like myself knew Tarrant at all. He was a vague, dreamy old man with long, unco-ordinated limbs, but his faded blue eyes took on a keen, scrutinizing intensity when he was brought within range of a plant of any kind, and I believe he was pretty good in his field.

I had the return half of my ticket and so passed straight through the barrier and got on to the platform, but as I went I saw that Tarrant went over to the machine to get himself a platform ticket, from which I gathered that the person with him already had a ticket, but that he was not travelling himself. I decided that if he spotted me and wanted to introduce her, whoever she was, I would encourage him. I had never been fond of meeting strangers, but the slow, clanking journey back to London on those Sunday nights was deadly boring, and it might be pleasant to have someone to chat to. So I stayed exactly where I was and Tarrant's dim blue eyes picked me out straight away. He came towards me, ushering what I now saw was a slender, dark-haired girl. She was bare-headed and had on a grey mackintosh and black leather gloves.

'Ah, Leonard,' he said. 'Going up to town, eh?'

'That seems to be the idea,' I replied.

'I'm glad,' he said. 'You'll be company for my guest. Peter Leonard is one of our younger Fellows, Mairead,' he said to her. 'Leonard, this is Mairead Hoey.'

I write down that name confidently now, but at that moment, standing on the

208

cold, blacked-out Oxford Station, I was not quite certain that I had registered it clearly. I heard 'Hoey' all right, but would have been slightly puzzled if asked to spell it. As for 'Mairead', though it is a perfectly normal Irish equivalent of English 'Mary' it was not very familiar to me; I had encountered it a few times on the printed page but never met anyone whose name it was.

'How d'you do?' the girl said to me. I noticed at once that her voice was musical, with a soft Irish lilt perceptible even in those few syllables – but then both the 'oo' and the 'ow' sounds are infallible indicators, so it is a good test phrase in spite of its brevity.

I mumbled something and old Tarrant smiled at her with avuncular fondness. 'Mairead works at the Irish Embassy. She's a real live diplomat.'

'Tenth grade,' the girl said. 'I'm just there to empty waste-paper baskets.'

'Her father's one of my oldest friends. Works at a laboratory not far from Dublin somewhere. I have a certain amount to do with him even in these days, when either one of us can get across the water for a day or two, or find a telephone that works. He's a plant virologist – done some very interesting work on marine algae that might have practical results one day, especially for agriculture.'

'His laboratory's at Newtownmountkennedy,' the girl said. 'It's not on any Official Secrets list.'

'Oh, well, glad to hear it. It's just a habit one seems to have got into these last few years, never mentioning places or people by name – eh, Leonard?'

'I just keep my mouth taped up,' I said, 'not that I know anything the Germans'd be interested in.'

'One never knows, that's the problem. Well, here's something that looks like a train, Mairead. It was good of you to come down and see me. I daresay you don't get much time off.'

'I enjoyed it,' she said. 'I'll tell my father you're looking well.' She kissed him on the cheek before turning and getting into the compartment, where a door now stood open immediately in front of her.

'Look after her, Leonard,' he said, and I followed her into the smoky light of the compartment, settling down beside her on the bench seat.

At first there was nothing but the little preliminaries of a wartime railway journey in winter, better-keep-your-coat-on and so on, but as we slowly clanked out of Oxford I had time to take stock of her a little and also of the four other people in the compartment.

Mairead was young but not schoolgirl-young; mid-twenties, I guessed. Her body was compact and neatly put together, with instinctively graceful movements, and she had that very striking combination, black hair and blue eyes. High cheekbones. The whole bone structure of her face was as clear and delicate as a cat's. I decided that would probably do to be going on with. It would probably be just as well, for a married man, if I stopped there and didn't analyse her qualities in any more detail.

As for the others, they consisted of a middle-aged lady in a fur coat, an R.A.F. sergeant slumped in a corner with his eyes sternly fixed on the pages of what looked like a training manual, and a citizen with a bony face, slightly protruding eyes and a ginger moustache, who looked abut fifty years old and was wearing a duffel coat. The duffel coat caught my attention because it was the first time I had ever seen one worn by a civilian. They were, of course, naval issue and hardly reached the population in general until after the war, when they became fashionable because they were warm and you could get them from military surplus stores.

209

There was a fourth occupant – a private soldier with a rifle, pack, overcoat and enormous polished boots, who seemed to take up about half the available space – but fortunately the train had only got as far as Didcot when he laboriously gathered the whole lot and took himself off into the black-out. We all expanded slightly, and I decided that since I was doubtless never going to see her again I would take the opportunity to learn something about how the diplomatic world is run.

'I don't often meet diplomats,' I began.

She smiled. 'Bit of a fancy name for me. It's a long training, and I'm very much at the beginning of it.'

'Did you come into it from some other kind of work?'

'No, I set my sights on having some sort of international career while I was still at University and I managed to get taken on in the Diplomatic Service as soon as I graduated.'

'T.C.D.?' I asked with routine academic interest.

'No.' She smiled again. 'Do I look like a T.C.D. type?'

'I don't know what a T.C.D. type is supposed to look like,' I admitted.

'They look like English gentry. Trinity College Dublin is a Protestant English foundation. Village Irish like me go to the National University.'

'Oh.' I felt vaguely put down.

'I served in Stockholm at first,' she said. 'I was there when the Emergency started.'

'The Emerg . . . ?'

'The war, to you.'

'Let me get this straight,' I said. 'You were in Stockholm in 1939 and you didn't stay there? Did you have a choice in the matter?'

'Yes, I could have stayed. But I thought it would be more interesting to be in a combatant country.'

'Good God,' I said, genuinely amazed.

'I don't see what's so astonishing. It *is* more interesting.'

'So you chose to come to the Embassy here.'

'Let's get one thing straight, Mr Leonard,' she said, turning her face straight towards mine.

'Peter.'

'Let's get one thing straight, Peter. There's no such thing as the Irish Embassy here.'

'Well, Tarrant thinks there is, for one. He introduced you as — '

'Yes, and I didn't correct him. But he just doesn't realize, very few English people do, that the British Government hasn't yet got round to recognizing Ireland as an independent country.'

'Oh. I thought all that was settled in the twenties.'

'That's what you're encouraged to think, but it's very far from settled. In terms of formal diplomacy, the whole thing is still up in the air. You talk about the Irish Embassy in London, which leads me to believe that you probably think there's a British Embassy in Dublin.'

'Well . . . at least a legation.'

'As a matter of fact there's neither.'

'What is there then? There can't be just *nothing*.'

'Look,' she said, settling back in her seat. This was certainly helping to while away the journey. 'If you actually do want to know, I'll tell you, though you'll probably find it deadly boring. When De Valera gave us our constitution in 1937,

210

which the British Government accepted because they had to, we abolished the office of governor-general But when we said we were no longer members of the British Commonwealth, that was too much for them and they said yes, we were. So they still won't concede our right to have an ambassador accredited to us. That leaves an administrative gap, and you know how they've solved it? By calling back from retirement old Maffey, Sir John Maffey who was the governor-general till he retired some years before the Emergency, and making him British representative in Ireland. The perfect British solution! You have to give up the office of governor-general, but you keep the man and he keeps everything in the same shape it always used to be.'

'And where does that leave the Dublin government? Have they appointed an ambassador in London?'

'Of course not, how could they? What's happened is the same thing the other way round. Keep the existing man on, and let him manage as best he can. I work for Mr John Dulanty, who since 1930 has been looking after Irish interests in London with the title of High Commissioner for Ireland. That's the — '

At this moment there was a loud, explosive sound from the other side of the compartment: it was the throat-clearing and attention-gaining detonation that is customarily represented in print as 'Harumph!'

It came from the bony man with the ginger moustache and the duffel coat. 'Harumph,' he said fiercely, and glared fixedly at Mairead.

'You must excuse me speaking to you, miss, without being introduced.' His tone of voice announced clearly that his intention was to pick a quarrel. 'But would I be right in supposing that you are of Irish extraction?'

He spoke the words distinctly and woundingly. When he said 'extraction' I had a sudden vision of a fierce, tangle-headed child, barefoot and in a ragged shirt, being dragged out of a thicket with an enormous pair of tongs. I wasn't actually sitting close enough to the girl to be touching her and yet it seemed to me, perhaps because of the intensity with which I was following the situation, that I felt her body stiffen against the dusty seat-cushions.

'I am of Irish nationality, sir,' Mairead returned levelly, 'and of Irish extraction, also.'

'Then I have just two words to say to you, young lady.'

'Come now,' I intervened. 'Just two words? What — '

'And who might you be?' he enquired, switching his angry gaze to my face.

'A passenger in this train like yourself. But the young lady you addressed was talking to me, which gives me some right to — '

'I butted in from nowhere. That was a breach of etiquette. I admit it. But there are times, sir, when etiquette has to take a back seat. There are times when other things might be more important. Do you take my meaning? Do you follow me? Eh?'

'I'm sure he follows you,' said Mairead gently, 'so may we hear these two words that you've got to say to me?'

'Certainly; with pleasure. They are: *North Atlantic*.'

He packed the words with a hostility that made them into curses.

A brief silence fell. Then Mairead said, 'I suppose I know what you mean.'

'I suppose you do,' he said.

The R.A.F. sergeant turned over a page in his instruction manual, and settled down to his study of it in what seemed a silent avowal of determination to keep out of any row that was brewing. The lady in the fur coat glanced, with a wary expression, from face to face.

211

'Will you expand a little on your two words, sir?' I invited him coldly.

'There's no need,' said Mairead. 'He's obviously talking about the Treaty Ports.'

'I am talking, young lady, as everyone in this carriage must be perfectly aware, of the Irish refusal to allow the British Navy, that is protecting Irish lives and Irish food supplies, to operate out of the West Coast of Ireland . . .'

'Yes, the Treaty Ports. I understand perfectly well.'

'. . . and thus effectively reducing the range of our North Atlantic patrols by 400 miles.'

'You object to Irish neutrality?' I asked him.

He glared at me. 'Object to it? Of course I bloody well object to it. It's costing lives, the lives of our men, every day of the week. How the hell can any English person not object to it, unless of course they're a sympathizer with . . . unless they've got some reason for wanting to stab this country in the back and throw their lot in with Hitler and that gang. If that's what you want, just say so, just let us know it in plain language and then we'll all know where we stand. Object to Irish neutrality? When they're sitting there, being protected by us, and letting our ships go to the bottom every day of the week? That's what you want, is it? That suits you, does it? My God, I don't know where some of you people get the—'

'Irish neutrality,' said Mairead in a clear voice that cut through his tirade and silenced him for the moment, 'was a decision taken by the elected government of the Irish Republic under the leadership of Éamonn de Valera. As for your point about food supplies, the Germans do not sink the ships of neutral countries where these are plainly marked, and in any case Ireland is very largely self-supporting in food. No, it isn't the food supplies that bother you, it's the fact that Ireland isn't involved in the war on England's side.'

'Why the hell shouldn't they be in it on our side? They know damn' well what would happen to them if Hitler won the war.'

'You'll excuse me, but that's one of the issues which look rather different seen from Dublin than seen from London.'

'*What*? You're surely not going to give me all that stuff about, it doesn't matter who wins the war because they're both as bad as one another . . .'

'I happen to believe, personally, that England is very much to be preferred to a Germany under the rule of the Nazi Party. But that still doesn't give me the psychology of an English person. The English have been absolutely certain, since the beginning of time, that they're right and the other country is wrong. God is on their side and so they have to win in the end. Anything else just isn't thinkable. If England went down, the universe would cease to exist. That isn't quite how things look to the world in general.'

'So you want the Germans to win.'

'Did I say that? Haven't I just said that I—'

'No, you didn't say it, but it's damn' well what you mean, isn't it?'

The lady in the fur coat stirred fretfully in her corner and said, 'The Irish wanted the Germans to win last time. I was only a young girl but I remember it. They were signalling to the submarines and all kinds of things. Of course I was *very* young at the time, but I remember it quite clearly.'

'When you say "the Irish", ' Mairead told her coldly, 'it's not clear to me whom you are referring to. If you mean the Irish people, you have to explain why thousands of Irish soldiers gave their lives fighting on the British side. If you mean the Irish Government wanted the Germans to win, the short answer to that is that there wasn't an Irish Government. Ireland was administered as a colony of England, as it had been since Tudor times, and understandably a lot of Irish wanted to get rid of their colonial masters.'

'Well,' the lady said, 'you've got a very clever line of talk, my dear, and I'm sure some people would be very impressed by it, but you won't change my mind because what I know I know. The Irish wanted the Germans to win in the last war and I don't see why they should be any different now. I was only a young girl, but I remember it.'

'Never mind last time,' said the duffel-coat man, leaning forward in his seat. 'Last time can take care of itself.'

'That's the trouble,' Mairead pointed out, 'it didn't take care of itself. The consequences of that war went on and on. When the Black and Tans were sent to Ireland—'

'Never mind the Black and Tans, that was when I was a schoolboy. I'm talking about *now*, nineteen forty-two, the third year of the present war, *this* one, d'you understand? My son is serving his country, and his country happens to be England. Not Germany, not Ireland, but England. Or, if you prefer, Great Britain.' His voice became louder and harsher as he reached the final words.

'Steady on, mate,' the R.A.F. sergeant said to him. 'The girl can hear you.'

'I hope she can. Because I don't think I'm infringing any official secrets if I say that my son is serving with the British Navy. That means he's a sailor. He goes on the sea. The North Atlantic. Remember those two words?'

'Yes,' she said, and I could feel, physically feel like a tremor running through me, the effort it cost her to keep her voice steady. 'And I remember the Treaty Ports too.'

'Four hundred miles,' he said in a quieter voice, sinking back in his place, his face now drained of colour. 'Four hundred miles of open sea without any battle-ship escort. When a convoy's going across, the battleships have to turn back four hundred miles short of where they can be met by ships coming out from Newfoundland.'

'Yes,' she agreed. 'That's the difference it makes not being able to use those western—'

'They have to waste fuel coming all the way round from ports like Falmouth or Pembroke Dock,' the man said.

'Steady on, mate,' said the R.A.F. sergeant again. This time he got a reaction.

'What d'you mean, steady on?' the duffel-coat man demanded.

'Naming names,' the sergeant said. 'Not supposed to come out with a lot of facts in railway carriages.'

'Facts!' the duffel man snorted. 'The North Atlantic has to be patrolled to protect the convoys that keep us alive. And we have to leave the job half done because the blasted Micks won't let us use the ports that look straight over the sea. You don't have to be a German spy to know that Falmouth and Pembroke Dock are westward-facing ports, my friend.'

'All the same,' said the sergeant.

'All the same what?'

'I think you should give it a rest. It isn't the girl's fault.'

'I'm surprised to hear you talk like that. A serving man.'

'Well,' said the sergeant mildly, 'you are hearing me talk like that, so what are you going to do about it?'

'Do you, or do you not believe,' the duffel man said coldly and deliberately, 'that British seamen's lives are being lost in those 400 miles of undefended water? In other words, that the action of the Irish in closing those ports to the Royal

213

Navy has increased the number of our men who are now at the bottom of the sea?'

'Increased them? It could have. But I don't see that you make it better by yelling at this girl.'

I interrupted them. 'In any war the number of casualties can be increased or decreased by all sorts of factors.'

He looked at me with concentrated loathing. 'What kind of bloody silly talk is that?'

I didn't like his answer, but deep down inside me there was a part that took his side. It reminded me that if Michael were serving in the war, and if his duties led him to sail the North Atlantic and particularly those 400 miles, I would talk – or at any rate think – not very differently from this man.

Mairead was speaking now, getting back to her attacker. 'When de Valera negotiated the Anglo-Irish Treaty in 1921 he conceded British control over three ports in the north. But when in 1938 Britain became obviously involved in preparations for a European war, he brought the Treaty to an end and got the ports back into Irish hands. After all, no nation can control its own destiny without controlling its own seaports.'

'Controlling its own destiny? Excuse me, did I hear you correctly? You're talking about Ireland controlling its own destiny?'

'Certainly, and that's just what seems to be annoying you so much. You think we're a colony that should be dragged into the war at England's heels. Well, we've had enough of being dragged about by England. The Irish Government's decision to stay neutral in 1939 had the support of the Irish people.'

'I'm sure it did. It's always easier to let other people defend your liberties for you. I dare say it had the support of the German people too.'

'Cheap sarcasm. Why don't you exercise it on the Swedes or the Portuguese?'

'Because the Swedes and the Portuguese don't put my son's life in danger.'

The lady in the fur coat now said, 'Roger Casement. That was his name. I've been trying to remember it. Roger Casement. He wanted the Germans to win. He was on their side. They even landed him in Ireland from a submarine.'

'The U-boat commanders,' the duffel man said gloomily, 'must thank their stars Ireland exists. They must have done then, and they must be doing now. Thanking their stars they can come ashore and pick up fuel. The I.R.A.'s always waiting with plenty of fuel for them.'

'Isn't that just a rumour?' I asked him. 'Have you any hard evidence that the I.R.A. – or for that matter anybody in Southern Ireland – has any U-boat fuel?'

'Why shouldn't they have it? They get it from the Americans.'

'You seriously mean,' I said, trying hard to believe what I was hearing, 'that the American Government ships U-boat fuel across the Atlantic to the I.R.A., and that American sailors carry it?'

'Not the Government exactly. It'd be some well-organized contraband chain. These Irish Yanks are all anti-British.'

'If they are,' said Mairead, 'have you ever wondered why?'

'Setting that apart,' I said to the man, 'I really don't think you ought to spread a rumour like that without hard evidence.'

A long silence fell. The sergeant went back to his instruction manual. The duffel man took a crumpled newspaper from his pocket and began reading it, or at least kept the same page open in front of him for the rest of the journey, as a shield. I didn't blame him. For that matter, I didn't blame him for his attitude to the Irish Treaty Ports either. All opinions are valid from the point of view from which they are seen. If his son was unfortunately killed in the war, he would be consumed with bitterness for ever. Nothing would alter that. It is the legacy of every war.

Mairead, for her part, seemed to have retired inside herself. I made a few hesitant conversational overtures, but she replied with monosyllables. She clearly didn't want to talk, and seemed too exhausted even to read. She folded her hands in her lap, closed her eyes and put her chin down on her chest. Whether she actually willed herself into sleep I couldn't tell, but that was obviously what she wanted.

The train stopped at Reading, then Slough. At Slough it seemed to wait for an eternity, and when we did slowly get going again the guard came along the corridor, saying that there had been a telephone message at Slough Station to the effect that we were going to arrive in London in the middle of an air raid.

Exactly what use the guard expected us to make of this information, I couldn't guess, but I did know from experience that it meant one thing for sure: there would be no taxis at Paddington. Taxis in London didn't disappear during air-raid alerts, but they did go where they were likely to be desperately needed, which meant that, since there were two tube stations at Paddington for passengers needing to travel, the taxi drivers simply cleared off to all the long lonely stretches of road where people would be longing for the approach of a friendly yellow-lighted *For Hire* sign.

The train stopped and we all stiffly got out. 'D'you have far to go?' I asked Mairead, as she settled into her overcoat and put on her black leather gloves.

'I live at Tufnell Park.'

I searched my mind. I'd forgotten, if I had ever known, where Tufnell Park was, but I did remember it as a station on the Northern line. So she could go virtually all the way home in safety. My duties were at an end.

Was I glad that my duties were at an end? I was not. I had decided that Mairead was, to put it at its least emphatic, a person it would be easy to like. It gave me pleasure to look at her face. She was pleasant to see and interesting to talk to. That was all, wasn't it? There was no need to make too much of it. No need at all. And if I chose to walk down the platform with her towards the tube entrance, chatting of this and that, damn it all, I had been introduced to the girl by one of my senior colleagues at Episcopus, and that gave me not only the right to, it was even a kind of *duty* . . . if my wife could see me being courteous and attentive to this slender Irish girl I had met on the journey, I had no doubt at all she wouldn't mind – not only wouldn't mind, would actually be *glad* to see that I . . .

'Is your . . . place actually near the station?' I asked Mairead. I didn't know whether she lived in a flat, rented a room in a house, or for that matter had pitched a tent on a piece of waste ground. I was reaching out for any scraps of information so that I could have a basis for a conversation with her. And she wasn't helping me. 'Yes,' she said in answer to my question.

I could see what she was conveying, of course. She was telling me that she wasn't the kind of girl it was easy to get to know, or at least easy for *me* to get to know.

We were going down the stairs now, towards the ticket window and beyond, the corridors and escalators and finally the platform. Soon she would be swallowed up in the vast, impersonal city. To find her again would be as hopeless as to find an individual grain of sand on a beach. It would have to be goodbye.

By this time we were getting our tickets. Thinking quickly, I realized that by going a long way round I could travel via Baker Street. I got my ticket, by which time Mairead had taken hers and moved away. I caught her up by the barrier.

'You go via Baker Street, don't you?' I asked.

'Yes.'

'I go that far too.'

Her eyes didn't light up with joy at the information, but neither did she appear downcast. I decided to take the same attitude. By going as far as Baker Street with Mairead, I could give myself another brief spell of looking at her, noting particularly the combination of blue eyes and black hair set against the soft pallor of her skin, and then the little episode would be over. By the time I got home and went to bed in my dingy bedroom, she would have become a memory, and within a week or two not even that.

So, as the train rattled and stopped and started, I observed her attentively, to make the memory a bright one for the short time it lasted, and then at Baker Street we parted – as I thought, for ever – and I began the weary, rattling journey to the station I ought to have made straight for in the first place. When I got there I came out and stood for a moment in the street before beginning the short walk to where I lived. The air-raid alert was still on, I was told. And indeed, during a lull when the traffic thinned out and the silence of the night asserted itself I could hear the engines of German bombers going over, somewhere about two miles off I supposed. Those German aircraft engines had a very distinctive sound, quite different from that of our own. They droned, of course, as any aircraft engine does, but along with the drone one heard a definite *thrum – thrum – thrum*, like, as someone said, a nasty headache. Standing there on the pavement breathing the damp night air and listening to that sound, I wondered what was the distinguishing feature of those engines that caused them to make that throbbing sound. I must ask Brian; perhaps he knew. And that thought took my mind to Cowley and the great dump of broken enemy aircraft, and I found myself hoping that some of the 'planes I could hear at this moment would be brought down, before the night was out, and would find their way, ripped, crumpled, shattered, to lie there in that field at the corner where the Garsington Road ran into Cowley. If they were brought down, there was at least a strong possibility that the men in them would be killed. So what? I thought, staring fiercely up at the cloudy sky. They were trying to kill me, weren't they?

1942 had been something of a settling-down year. From being a crisis, the war had become a fixed state. Intellectually, one knew it must necessarily end with victory or defeat or simply with an exhausted stalemate; but, though everyone constantly used the phrase 'after the war', it wasn't actually possible to imagine in any detail what 'after the war' would be like. One thing changed in 1942; the nightmare of an out-and-out German victory, with England being overrun like France and reduced to a state of serfdom, moved to a distance. We couldn't, yet, automatically assume that our side would win; but at least there was an even chance of it; better than an even chance – a majority chance, if we could get through the next year or so.

The first of those getting-through years was 1942. And my own life curiously paralleled the national situation. I, too, got through 1942. Nothing much changed. I was now used to my work, and my colleagues, at the Ministry of Supply. Living in London was no longer a desperate adventure; the *Luftwaffe* had unleashed its fury on the civilian population in 1940 and '41, but the bombings had now shrunk to a routine trickle of short-term alerts, so that an uninterrupted night's sleep had become the rule rather than the exception.

My marriage, too, and my domestic life generally – shrunken as it was to a day and a half a week at Mulberry Hall – hung in equilibrium. Every Saturday afternoon saw me on the train down to Oxford and then on the bus out into the country, and every Sunday evening saw me on the same journey back. The rural landscape was amazingly pristine and tranquil in those days. Technically, of course, it was 'fully mobilized', with every scrap of land turned over to food production and every hand employed in some kind of work for the war effort. But in practice, with so little traffic on the roads, the early summer loud with the carolling of birds along every hedgerow and the middle months of the summer heavy with the drowsy hum of insects, it didn't *feel* mobilized. We still had hedgerows in those days; the heavy machinery that demanded their destruction had not yet come in; the combine harvester, for instance, was still unknown, and the harvest workers still gathered the sheaves of grain and stood them up in wigwam-like stooks, which may have been time-consuming but *looked* very pretty.

In this landscape Heather was a natural queen, always healthy, always radiant, always seeming to be in her right place and busy; and when Michael was frisking around her like a long-legged colt she carried with her a suggestion of a young thoroughbred mare. By contrast, I felt the week-end intruder, pale from bad food and indoor living, always slightly fatigued, slightly jumpy and irritable, even though I tried consciously to relax and bring down my nervous pace to match Heather's.

Our sexual activities, needless to say, took place on Saturday nights. I didn't mind this. At thirty-one, I was beginning to find that a habit-based life suited me. Our weekly joust was perfectly satisfactory – we both had plenty of energy for it and slept very contentedly afterwards – and as months went on I began to congratulate myself on the fact that being a faithful husband was turning out, in my case, to be no very difficult business. During my late adolescence, in the Sixth Form and then as an undergraduate, I had assumed that I was over-sexed by nature, that all through life I would always want more the more I had. But since my marriage, since getting used to sliding into bed beside Heather, my needs had settled down. One of the things I liked (or loved, perhaps?) about Heather was her legitimacy; I enjoyed the fact that she was my wife, I enjoyed going down to her every week-end, and in the other six days I was quite willing to wait and to give my energies entirely to the work I was trying to do for my country.

In this I differed, I knew, from a good many of my colleagues at the Ministry. Certainly there was a good deal of casual sex going on in wartime; the sexual revolution of the 1960s was not even dreamt of, but the general fracturing of the regular surface of life was sufficient to breed promiscuity, as it always is in wartime. Many of my colleagues, including a good few from Oxford, evidently welcomed this as a harvest to be reaped, and it made me smile to think of the monastic ideal, the insistence on sexual abstinence as the natural duty of a scholar, which was the outward face of Oxford University. A strange development that I, Peter Leonard, condemned and browbeaten by the likes of Dick Kent as 'a womanizer', giving my best energies for years to outwitting this same monasticism, should end up feeling placidly superior to the skirt-chasers I saw around me!

It was in this mood of self-satisfaction that I accepted, one day in the spring of 1943, an invitation to a social evening from, of all people, Brian. Always rather badger-like, preferring solitude when he could not have the company of his racing colleagues, my brother had never made the first move towards any meeting. But now he telephoned me from his place of work, on a mid-week afternoon, and suggested an outing for the following Saturday evening.

'I don't suppose you get to go out much, you and Heather,' he said. 'Fact is, Primrose and I have got an invitation to go to the American Servicemen's Club at Chipping Norton. I've got transport and I might be able to pick you up.'

'That's all right. Heather gets a bit of petrol for her van. We could manage the trip to Chipping Norton, it isn't far.'

'But you couldn't get in without us, anyway. And we can't get in without the bloke who's taking us. We'll have to liaise.'

'Oh, you've got a tame American, have you?'

'Yes. Primrose met him first, through her work. Seems a nice enough chap. Anyway, he says he can get four guests in.'

'I'm impressed. He must be an officer.'

'Well, he's air-crew.'

I accepted, and we named a pub in Chipping Norton where we would meet. Feeling that if I hesitated Brian would ask someone else, I took the risk of accepting on Heather's behalf without consulting her – it would be impossible to get hold of her at that time of day – but when I telephoned her that evening and told her we were going out on the Saturday night, she was unenthusiastic.

'The American Servicemen's Club? What on earth for?'

'A change of wallpaper and to fraternize with our gallant Allies. Have you any objection?'

'No particular objection, but it'll be a waste of time, surely.'

'Well,' I said pacifically, 'there wasn't a lot I was planning to do with the time except have a rest from my work and be with you, and I thought perhaps you'd see it that way too.'

'Be with me? You won't do much being with me, will you, with a great crowd of Yanks around?'

'Oh well,' I said, still pacifically, 'we can discuss it when I get home on Saturday.'

But of course we never did discuss it. When I got home it was too late to change our minds, and we just asked Lisa to keep an ear out for Michael, changed our clothes, got into the van and drove over to Chipping Norton. We arrived at the agreed pub on time, but the other party were slightly late and Heather was in an impatient mood.

'Is this going to be a wasted evening?' she muttered, when we had got ourselves two glasses of something and settled down in a corner of the dimly-lit little bar.

'Well, it won't be for me,' I said, 'because it'll be an evening out of London. I just hope you haven't decided in your own mind that it was a mistake to come along, and that you won't sulk and ruin the evening for everybody else.'

'I didn't get much chance to *decide* anything,' she replied. 'You accepted for the two of us and I was simply informed that I was coming along.'

'It won't hurt you to have a change for one evening, and come out to a different place and meet some new people.'

Over her shoulder I saw the door open and Brian came in, then Primrose, then a young man I didn't know but who was obviously our host. He was short, fair-haired and chunky and he wore American Air Force uniform.

'Hello,' Brian said. 'Sorry if we're late.'

'You're not,' I told him. 'We were early.'

'This is Chet Cummings,' he said.

218

Chet said, 'Hi,' and held out his hand. Chet's hand was very strong and very broad, with short fingers and a hard, dry palm. You can tell a lot about someone from their hands. He was short, not even as tall as I, but in width he would have made two of me. His hair was fair and looked very soft, and his eyes were a mild blue. But the most noticeable thing about him, to me, was the skin of his face. It was lightly tanned by the sun and wind, but underneath the tan it was pale, and it looked extraordinarily clear and unblemished. There were no lines on it, a few freckles around the nose, and no chin stubble. It was like the face of a boy of about twelve. And his eyes – there seemed to be no guile in them, no complications. I felt that this was a young man whose life and character were spread out like an open book for anybody to read at a glance. He had absolutely nothing to hide.

Heather, who had clearly taken a rapid decision not to sulk, gave Chet a welcoming smile and managed to be affable to Brian and Primrose too, though she had often told me she found them difficult to talk to, and once we got inside the Servicemen's Clubroom I was soon relaxed enough to give attention to my surroundings. The presence of Americans in large numbers was still at that date a novelty to the English populace, myself included; for that matter, even the American accent was still a relative novelty to the majority of English people; until the cinema began to talk in 1930 or so, most of them had simply no idea that Americans had 'an accent' at all. So here they were, the speakers of this language, the ambassadors of this classless society, and as I looked round that room in Chipping Norton and saw that throng of men in U.S. Army and Air Force uniforms, I realized that these were our allies, brought here by the necessities of a global war to join us in the effort to batter the Germans out of their stronghold in North-West Europe, and I did not have to be any kind of crystal-gazer to know that many of the men I was looking at would never see America again. Waiting for them on the other side of the cold, grey Channel was an enemy, fully trained, briefed, armed and watchful, who would make them, as well as us, pay a terrible price before the Nazi flag came fluttering to the ground.

I became so absorbed in just staring and thinking my thoughts that, for a quarter of an hour at least, I must have been a very bad guest. I was trying to compare the men I saw about me with anything I could have expected in a similar gathering of British forces. There were two differences that stood out at once. The first was the racial diversity. The British are of course a mixed race, as much as the French, but centuries of dwelling in a small island have processed the social classes into something like facial similarity; an English working man does not cease to be a working man when you put him into uniform, and he does not cease to look different from someone brought up among the governing classes. Nothing of the kind held good in the scene before me. Huge long-boned Scandinavians stood side by side with compactly built men with expressive faces who, if set down in a crowded street in Rome or Naples, would have vanished instantly in the *mêlée*. Stringy men who looked as if they had been kippered in the sun of some desert region stood talking to apple-cheeked fellows who had clearly grown up in some region of rolling, fertile dairy country. About a quarter of the men were Negroes (as we called them then), and these seemed to range all the way from faces with a slightly African cast to full-blooded Congolese-looking types who seemed to have no tincture of Europe at all. But the one thing I simply could not tell, and determined not to ask but try to deduce from observation, was whether this club was for officers or for other ranks, or for both together.

As a matter of fact I never did succeed in guessing, and in the end forgot to ask. It was my first experience of a citizen army, and of a society that has social democracy, which is a distinct thing from political democracy and could even survive its demise, though probably not for long.

After a while I became aware that Heather was giving me a look that was the equivalent of a kick under the table. Realizing that I was being unmannerly, I wrenched my mind away from the scene about me and tried to concentrate on the conversation at our table. At first I was mystified by it, until I realized that Chet, back in his pre-Air Force days, had been a racing driver. Brian and Primrose were drawing him out about what this involved. His smooth, open face turned from one to the other; he seemed so young, so confident, so totally certain of what he was good at and what he wanted to do, that one could not help wishing him well.

'I only had two seasons since I went pro,' he was saying. 'Forty-two would have been my third, but Uncle Sam said he needed me. I was all ready to move into big-car racing. Those two seasons, I'd been in midgets. I had a lotta fun and learnt a lot, but it ain't the same.'

'What kind of tracks do they race the midgets on?' Brian asked.

'Concrete mostly. Sometimes a little banking, sometimes flat. Quarter-mile or half-mile circuit. Cinders now and then.'

'Do they still use board tracks?'

'No, that went out when I was a kid. I saw one or two of the last of them – at County Fairs, mostly. They were trash. The boards used to warp. Sometimes holes'd break out in 'em right in the middle of a race. Too many guys got killed. It was never good racing, on boards.'

'So you were all ready for big-car racing, Chet?'

I was silent, listening, because I had no contribution to make. Heather was silent also, her eyes moving from face to face. The big-band music, pumping out from the radiogram, drifted between us like smoke. Through it I heard Chet describing his world.

'All ready? You better believe it. I was in business with two other guys. They ran a garage and sponsored me. We had the car and everything. I was going to start trying to qualify for Indy. Everybody wants to qualify for Indy. Some guys, they go down there every year they live, and pay their fee and do their qualifying laps and they never turn in a good enough time. They never see the starting grid at Indy and yet they're real race drivers, professionals. Boy, it's tough. But I was serious about trying. I figured I had a good chance. We had a car that would do it if I was the right driver.' He laughed suddenly, as if he had said something funny.

'What kind of speeds d'you have to turn in, to qualify?' Brian wanted to know.

Chet told him. It was some fantastic figure, I can't trust myself to remember it.

'How does that compare with the winner's overall time for the whole race?'

'Pretty close. They don't slow up much.'

Brian thought for a moment, drank from his glass and said, 'Funny. It never seems to get much attention over here.'

'What doesn't?'

'Indianapolis. Track racing just isn't our tradition,' Brian said. 'Racing in all the European countries started city to city. Later, when it got too fast for the open road, they put it on enclosed circuits, but they had to be road circuits with gradients up and down, and fast corners and slow corners, and turning different ways, and changing gear. It all tests the car much more thoroughly.'

220

'Maybe,' Chet said. 'But maybe racing isn't about testing cars. Maybe it's about going fast.'

'The European public,' Brian said, 'just don't think it's motor-racing to put your foot down and keep turning to the left.'

'Well,' Chet said evenly, 'I guess the American public thinks racing's about going fast. What makes a car a race car is that it goes fast. And if it goes faster than the other cars it starts out with, it's the winner. Sure, to drive at Indy you have to keep turning to the left for 500 miles. But there ain't no other race in the world that's as fast as Indy, and to us that's gotta mean it's the best.'

For a moment I wondered if they would really confront each other, and I prayed inwardly that Brian's competitive streak wouldn't come to the fore. Clearly my prayer was answered, because he smiled easily and said, 'I see a lot of empty glasses around me. Am I allowed to get a round?'

An amicable discussion followed, in which it turned out that neither Brian nor I were allowed to buy anything from the bar, but Chet pointed out that at the kind of prices the drinks were being supplied at from the P.X., and with the high level of U.S. servicemen's pay, this was no hardship for him. Heather was drinking gin and lime, Primrose was sticking to soft drinks, but we men were drinking American beer, which I for one had never tasted before. The brands available had different names, all the German breweries in Milwaukee, Schlitz, Pabst, Budweiser, but I formed the opinion during that evening that you could sell any kind of beer in America as long as you made it cold enough. I decided to keep this knowledge from my father who, as he moved deeper into middle age, was already convinced that the world was going to the dogs.

Brian was now asking Chet about the car in which he had been hoping to launch his career.

'We built her,' Chet said. 'My buddies got all the parts and we blue-printed her and built her. Basically she's a Miller. But we put in an Offy mill.'

'What capacity?'

'A hundred and seventy-five c.i.'

Brian nodded as if satisfied and they moved into a discussion about the technical requirements of American racing with regard to fuel and supercharging. Soon afterwards Chet went up to the bar to get cigarettes or another round of drinks or something, and I took the opportunity to ask Brian, 'If you tried hard enough, d'you think you could make me understand what you and Chet were talking about?'

He gave me his patient look and said, 'What didn't you understand?'

'Well,' I said, 'what's Indy?'

'The Indianapolis Five-Hundred-Mile Race. They only hold one race a year at the Indianapolis Speedway, and to Americans it's more or less like the Grand National.'

'Thanks. And what's an Offy mill?'

'A mill is his word for an engine. His car has an Offenhauser engine, that's all he's saying.'

'Is an Offenhauser a good kind of engine?'

'It's a professional racing engine. Chaps who have Offenhauser engines are usually pretty serious contenders.'

I thanked him and drew back as Chet returned. Primrose was still interested in what Chet was saying, as Brian was, but looking about me, I noticed that Heather was showing signs of boredom. About half the area of the large room was cleared for dancing and had a wooden floor with a passable polish; and the radiogram was playing, working its way through a stack of the twelve-inch 'V-Discs' that the GIs brought with them, and which amazed us natives by being flexible and unbreakable, the first such records we had ever seen. The discs were mostly of Glenn Miller, with a sprinkling of Goodman and Artie Shaw. It was good enough. Leaning over to Heather, I asked her if she would care to dance.

'*Dance?*' She seemed genuinely surprised. 'D'you know how long it is since you asked me that?'

'About ten years, at a guess. In the Hall at Episcopus College.'

We stood up and moved over to where the dancing was.

The music stopped and then a new record started; a Bob Crosby number, as I recall. We were lucky to have arrived in time to get that one. It was exhilarating and we danced well. Heather, I thought again, was dancing as she had danced at the Episcopus Ball, all those years ago. My God, ten years, a whole decade, and she was still as tireless and springy as she had been then, moving her limbs so gracefully and with so much pleasure. And I acknowledged it in my heart as we glided and pivoted and flowed, and was grateful

Why then, I asked myself with a flash of annoyance, did I have to spoil it by wondering, suddenly but very intensely, what it would be like to dance with Mairead?

Summer came, that hot breathless summer of 1943. As the rising sap stirred in my veins I sometimes caught myself eyeing the prettier of the girls who worked at the Ministry. But it went no further than eyeing and I was content that it should go no further. I liked my uncomplicated life. Sometimes, too, I thought of Mairead. Not that she, I told myself sternly, came into the same category as the pretty girls one glimpsed in lifts and corridors at the Ministry. My velleities concerning her were not sexual (I told myself). Or not sexual simply (I told myself). She was, of course, beautiful, but that was just the point – a person who has all those things didn't need to be thought of as attracting one 'sexually'. All right, she was a beautiful woman, and how many beautiful women could I number among my acquaintance?

In this kind of reverie I was making my way along Greek Street one mid-day, having decided to take my lunch in Soho. Though of course it had always had its raffish side, Soho had not yet become merely the hub of a huge international vice market. It was still 'foreign' in the sense that perfectly ordinary, unassuming French and Italian provision shops and little restaurants were everywhere, and it was still Bohemian, with shabby little flats where poets and artists could live at low rents. I had acquired a little knowledge of this quarter: I had had characters like Tambimuttu, Julian Maclaren-Ross, Nina Hamnet and Dylan Thomas pointed out to me in the bars they frequented; I had seen Louis MacNeice, saturnine and ironic, coming and going from his work at the B.B.C. Normally fairly unobservant, it had become something of a game with me to keep my eyes open when I walked on these particular pavements, to see which of them I could spot. So it was with a sharpness of observation that I saw coming towards me, along Greek Street and at that moment just about level with the Budapest Restaurant, a stocky figure whom I knew I recognized but couldn't, at that moment, quite place.

That sensation always means that one is seeing the person in an unfamiliar context, and so it was now with Hans Katz.

'Ah, my young friend!' Did he simply not know my name, or did he call everyone younger than himself his young friend? It didn't matter. I was very glad to see him, with his thick stumpy body and huge head, his balding cranium, his eyes beaming behind round lenses. I bore him off to the Dog and Duck for a drink. ('These names of drinking-places in England – such unashamed rural nostalgia! How long is it since there was a dog or a duck here? Hunting – *ach*, yes, hunting, but how long ago was that? We all know it was once for hunting about here. Do you think every European city is not built on what was once wild marsh or open heath?')

'Yes, they were,' I said. 'But tell me – what on earth are you doing down here in London?'

'Well, cheerio, my young friend, you see I know your English customs.' And he took a swig at his beer that would have done credit to one of Trundle's *cénacle*. 'What am I doing in London? Oh, I have a job now. Press business, the fetching and carrying involved in running a learned publishing house.' Katz's English was very creditable now, but he never quite mastered the respective roles of *v* and *w*. 'Are you in search of food? Shall we have some together? I have a little allowance of money.'

In the end we had the sandwiches they could offer in the pub. It seemed too much trouble to move, and I took pleasure in the fact that the small, intimate Dog and Duck reminded me of Oxford's Rose and Crown, which I thought of as Katz's natural habitat. Mostly, as usual, he talked and I listened.

'My young friend, I have a wonderful anecdote I am telling everybody. No, not everybody. Just those who will appreciate it. Connoisseurs of the English quality. Those who can appreciate the flavour of Englishness.'

'Does that mean English people? Or does it very definitely mean *not* English people?'

'The dividing line is not so simple. Some English people are too insular to be aware that there is an English quality. They think their attitudes are normal attitudes and the rest of the world is subnormal. They think so in a kindly spirit, but that is their opinion and it is unshakeable. And some Continentals are insular in their own way. They see Englishness simply as stupidity. Those who become connoisseurs are those who can see that Englishness is different, often valuable, sometimes obstructive, usually endearing. Because the English do not fear competition from foreigners – who fears competition from an inferior species? – it does not occur to them not to be tolerant and humane.'

'Well, some of them are pretty intolerant.'

'Yes, some of them are, but they are the exception. Attend now to my anecdote. As you know, I was one of the enemy aliens who had to be hastily rounded up and put on the Isle of Man where they could do nothing to sabotage the war effort.'

'Yes. I was very glad to see you back, you and Otto. We all felt a bit uncomfortable about — '

'There is no state in the world that would not have interned nationals of a country with whom they were fighting. Whether it was done intelligently is another matter. I have no bitterness. Neither Otto nor I would ever sabotage the British war effort, because we hate and fear the German Nazis, but that is also what an enemy agent would say if he were questioned. So they had no choice. I now proceed.'

'Do.'

'I was not held for very long because I am not a young man and any official could see that it was highly unlikely that I would assist anyone to do anything, except examine papyri. On the Isle of Man I spent eight months only. Some were not so fortunate. Recently I spoke with a good friend, an electrical engineer from Leipzig, who may have been more suspected than myself because he had technical knowledge. Be that as it may.' Katz sighed and took another pull at his beer. 'Because this man was still there in December 1941, he saw the captive population of Man Island increased by a fresh nationality, the Japanese.'

'Yes, I suppose so.'

'The Japanese who were interned were in a separate encampment, not far away. There was another difference. Many of the internees of German nationality were like myself, poor in the goods of this world. But the Japanese – mostly they were bankers, financiers. This made their imprisonment much more tolerable because they were allowed to use their wealth to bring in comforts and delicacies. We listened enviously to rumours of their champagne, smoked salmon, *und so weiter*. They also had parties, with loud music and merriment. Their morale was very high. One night there was an extra racket from the Japanese encampment. They were having the party to end all parties. The noise continued till dawn. The next morning we sent a deputation to the camp commandant, a benign old British Army colonel who last saw action at Ypres or some similar place, demanding an end to these noisy Japanese parties. He replied that he would be stricter in future about noise after midnight. But, he explained, on that particular occasion it seemed to him only right that the Japanese prisoners should be allowed a special celebration. And why? You ask why?'

'Yes, I ask why.'

Katz leaned forward on his bar-stool till I thought he would tumble into my lap. He stabbed the air with a forefinger. 'Because, my young friend, he thought it was only fair play to let them celebrate the fall of Singapore.'

We looked at each other.

'Yes,' I said, 'that's Englishness.'

Katz was thoughtful again. 'And this Englishness? What do you make of it, as an Englishman yourself?'

'I don't know. It's for you to say, rather than me. You see it from the outside.'

'But you must know,' Katz insisted, 'whether it expresses your values or not.'

'Yes, it does express my values. I like the English tolerance and the easygoing way they accept different points of view, even though I know it springs largely from mental laziness. And even that comic old colonel who let the Japanese internees kick up a row because he thought it was only right that they should celebrate the fall of Singapore is an admirable figure in some ways. He's living up to an ideal of Fair Play, and that's such a rarity in the world that it's become rather valuable. I can't foresee what the world'll look like after the war, nobody can, but it's bound to be ruled by big power conglomerates and their motives are bound to be cynical to a greater or lesser extent. There won't be much time for fair play.'

'Or for amateurism,' said Katz, nodding, 'that other English fetish.'

'Well, no, except that the amateurism sometimes has strange fruits. After all, we've only survived this far because those young R.A.F. pilots won the Battle of Britain. And they won it not only by being good pilots but by having a good aeroplane. And the Spitfire, as it happens, evolved out of a series of racing seaplanes which were built to compete for something called the Schneider Trophy – in other words, for a race. The Victorians used to say that the Battle of Waterloo had been won on the playing fields of Eton, and I think we could say the Battle of Britain was probably won in Italy, competing for the Schneider Trophy.'

Katz shook his massive head. 'Nothing English can really be brought into the

224

light of rationality. One has to be born knowing it. This, my young friend, is what makes me uneasy.'

'I suppose so. But there's no point in being gloomy about it. We're here now, so let's have another drink.'

'Sometimes,' Katz said, immersed in his own thoughts, 'while I was on the Isle of Man I was with other men, younger, who did not expect to settle back in England at the end of the war. I am an ageing man but there were others – younger, better able to turn keys because of what they knew and could undertake – who planned to go to Canada or perhaps Australia.'

'You wish you could go too? You'd like to be uprooted from Oxford, and your work and your friends, and set off for Canada or Australia?'

'The world that is coming in,' Katz said in a hoarse undertone, 'will be unknowable and hostile, I fear it. Europe will be in ruins, but Stalin will not disarm. There is an iron time coming. When I think of North America, when I think of Australia, I think of secure, undisturbed lands. It is selfish, but I have been through enough disruption, enough upheaval and fear. England bought me a few years of life. But a shadow is coming again, and now I wish just to live out my last years in peace in some safe corner where I shall be given a desk and a lamp and time to proceed with my work. But,' he said, suddenly sitting very upright and speaking in a normally raised voice, 'my friend, I rely on you to keep the words I have just uttered as a confidence between us. Tell no living soul, if you please, that I spoke in this fashion about leaving England.'

'Certainly, if that's what you want, Hans, but I can't think anybody would think the worse of you for it.'

'I would think worse of myself,' he said firmly. 'I am European. My thoughts, my wishes, my memories are European. To come to England is not totally to leave Europe. But the New World is not Europe. To go there would be to cut my cable with everything that nurtured me. It would be a gesture of despair.'

'Do you speak of these things to Nussbaum?'

'To Otto? To him, least of all. He would think me a traitor.'

'Well,' I said, 'that's something no English person would think.'

'No,' he said sadly. 'They would take it as harmless talk. To them it would be without significance. Like the Japanese inmates of the Isle of Man internment camp celebrating the fall of Singapore.'

We spoke briefly of other things, then finished our drinks and I went back to the office. But for months afterwards I was haunted by that image of Hans Katz, standing huddled in his overcoat against the driving mist of the Isle of Man (somehow I always imagined the scene as one of driving mist), staring out over the flat grey Atlantic, looking at the monochrome water, dreaming of that desk, that lamp, that safe corner.

11

Mairead worked for Mr John Dulanty. She had mentioned the name to me during our conversation in the train and I had stored it away in my memory. (Why?) So I knew I had only to look in the telephone directory and there would be a number that would find her, during work hours. There would be no difficulty in getting in touch with her if I wished to know how she was getting on.

I could think of a number of reasons why I should want to find out how she was getting on. After all, she was a young girl, alone in a foreign city, away from her family and friends. (Well, not all that young, but a girl. And presumably alone.) After all, old Tarrant, as he turned away into the gloom of the blacked-out station platform, had tossed to me over his shoulder the words, 'Look after her, Leonard.' Would a man like Tarrant, a man of his integrity, have uttered such words lightly? 'Look after her, Leonard.' How could I refuse the old man's request? What was I, a cad? No, no, I must fulfil my obligations. We Episcopus men must stand together at this crisis in the nation's history.

What I actually wanted, of course, was another look at Mairead, another whiff of her exciting, restless, fine-balanced personality. And why not? I demanded fiercely of myself. My intentions were innocent enough, surely? Especially by the standards prevailing.

What I wasn't prepared for, when I finally got in touch with her and we spent a lunch-hour together in a pub in Kensington Church Street, was how forcibly I would be struck by the contrast between her and Heather. I had had no such thoughts as I made my way towards this *rendez-vous*. It never entered my mind that I would find myself comparing Mairead with Heather. But so it was. Heather was unquestionable, assured, queenly. Now, I discovered with an inward shiver of excitement that this thin, nervous Irish girl, like me, was pale and rather tired; she, like me, was suffering under the endless shabbiness and difficulty of wartime London. Her eyes, quick with sensibility and intelligence, looked back at mine from a face that was a little too meagre to be perfectly in proportion with them, and for some reason this prompted in me a quick surge of feeling towards her. Yet what I felt for her was not pity; there was no trace of pity in it. Mairead was too quick, too energetic, too various, resourceful, mercurial; she was on top of her experience, just as I hoped I was on top of mine. We were fighters together, sufferers and participants.

I can't remember what we talked about, that first lunchtime, though I've often sat down and tried very hard to recall it. Obviously the psychic effort of setting up the occasion absorbed all my attention, at any rate at the deep level where it would be likely to leave a deposit in the memory. I had, I know, invented some lying pretext for wanting to see her, but anyway she seemed to accept that it was quite natural that we should meet for a friendly talk. For the rest, all I remember about our conversation is that I really enjoyed being with her; I determined to go on seeing her. As I walked back to the office afterwards, I made myself face the question of my motive. What was I after? With an innocence that I clutched about me like a robe, I answered that I found her a very likeable person and very

226

interesting to talk to. Her slant on things was . . . well, it was interesting and likeable. Besides, she was an Irish citizen and wouldn't be in London for ever. Well then! I held my robe firmly, and simply avoided looking sufficiently ahead to ask whether it would one day slip from my shoulders.

Evening hours in the pub were shorter on Sundays. My parents and I could take our time over our six o'clock meal and have it all together as a family, because the Bargeman's did not open its doors to customers till seven. At two minutes to seven my father went through into the bar to put the lights on and see that the fire, lit an hour earlier, was burning brightly; then I heard him drawing back the bolts. Then, once again, the Bargeman's Arms was open and Jack Leonard was on duty.

One Sunday I stayed in the kitchen another few minutes, checking to see that my bag contained the usual few necessities I carried to and fro, and seeing that Michael, who'd come with me that evening, was settled by the hearth to occupy himself quietly and not get in his grandma's way till his mother arrived to pick him up. He settled down readily enough; a boy relishing a story about boyhood, he was reading *Tom Sawyer*, so I went into the bar for a drink before going out into the night to face my journey. Old Trundle was already there, behind his accustomed pint in his accustomed corner, and for once the rest of the *cénacle* drifted in over the next ten minutes. The circle had changed slightly; some of the younger men, such as the round-faced Bob, were missing, doubtless on war service; and where was Peake? Once as immovable a member of the *cénacle* as Trundle himself, he was not there. Trundle, for his part, had changed only in becoming, if it were possible, still bulkier, still more ponderous and authoritarian, and still less penetrable by any opinion coming from outside his own mind. To me, watching him stealthily from farther along the bar, none of these seemed like deterioration; they only made him more Trundellian, more Trundle-esque. Only when, later on, he hoisted himself on to his feet and set off in a slow, laboured walk to the plumbing in the back yard, did it come home to me how much he had aged. His breathing, as he went past me, was loud and stertorous; cardiac, perhaps. I hated that. I wanted him to live for ever.

That revelation, however, was still half an hour in the future. For the moment Trundle, ensconced as the great corner-stone of the *cénacle*, was still Trundle. My father, by way of ritual courtesy, made one or two routine enquiries about matters that concerned them both. But the meeting really came to life when the door swung open and Peake hurriedly entered. He had on the full panoply of his Air Raid Warden officialdom and was actually wearing his steel helmet rather than carrying it. Everything proclaimed him as the bearer of tidings. He went up to the bar while a chair was hastily cleared for him next to the presiding Trundle; and still he did not speak.

'Busy day, Fred?' my father asked promptingly, pushing his usual towards him – dark mild beer with its creamy lace of foam.

'First minute I've drawn breath,' Peake said. He took an immense draught, put down his glass and looked round at the company. 'Been on that bloody exercise since eight this morning.'

If there was anyone there who didn't actually know *what* exercise, he was unwilling to lose face by admitting it. I did know, more or less. That day at the beginning of 1943 marked just about the last full rehearsal, in the Oxford area, of the procedures for resisting a German invasion. Regular forces and Home Guard units were involved, and just about everybody had been mobilized. All week-end the countryside had been buzzing with rumours of tanks, artillery, aircraft.

'Didn't know as you blokes was mixed up with it,' was Trundle's comment.

'Mixed up in it? Air Raid Wardens mixed up in it? Do you think as if Jerry tries summat on, he won't start by sendin' a wave of bombers over?' Peake took off his steel helmet, as if at last conceding that he had reached a position of comparative safety, and laid it on the floor beside him. Then, suddenly, he looked round, grinning.

'Something to laugh at, was there?' asked one of the other men.

'Depends who you are, I s'pose,' Peake said. 'There's some as won't think it's as bloody funny.'

'Well, tell us what it is, and we can 'ave a go at seein' for ourselves whether it makes us laugh,' Old Trundle instructed.

'Them as lives on one side of it, they'll think it's a good laugh,' Peake said. 'And them as lives on t'other side'll be bloody up in arms about it, you mark my words.'

'Other side o' what? Come on now, spit it out,' encouraged Trundle.

'The 'ole idea,' said Peake, recovering his solemnity, 'is that Jerry'll come in east to west. He'll be pushin' over from London way, and that means from 'Eadingon, from Marston, from Elsfield where 'e's got a bit of 'igh ground.'

'Well, Germany *is* east of 'ere,' said another of the circle sagely. 'Makes sense – go on.'

'So we've got a line strung out at the edge of the city over beyond the Banbury Road,' Peake went on. 'And we're defendin' the Cherwell.' He pronounced it, town fashion, Churr-well. 'We has a real armoured position strung out along the Churrwell as far up as Kidlin'ton. I was down in the council estate that's nearest to the river.'

Suddenly I knew what he was going to tell us. Of course! The Cutteslowe wall! It must have been breached, or demolished; blown up, perhaps. On purpose? By accident? If on purpose, on whose orders? I leaned forward, listening.

'There was tanks,' Peake said. 'Armoured personnel carriers and tanks. I'm not rightly sure how many, but a hell of a lot. Thirty or forty, I shouldn't wonder. Well, like I say, I was down in the council estate, tellin' the people about the A.R.P. arrangements. And a kid comes down on a bike, flyin' along. About three o'clock it was. There was some people standin' near us and he shouts to 'em as he goes rushin' past. *They've knocked it down!* he says. *Gone right through it with a tank!* So we stepped up the road a bit and there it was, a big 'eap of bricks layin' in the middle of the road, and people standin' about, and takin' snapshots, and kids and dogs runnin' back and forth through the gap.'

'What about farther up?' someone asked. 'Wentworth Road, Carlton Road, all up there? Did you go up there too?'

'Course I did. It was very quiet. People lookin' out from behind their curtains.'

'You say,' said Old Trundle, 'a tank done it?'

'Yes. I got the whole story. This tank driver, they was tellin' me, 'e was a local lad. Growed up round there. Never liked the wall. It'd cut the street in two when he was a nipper and made 'im go a long way round to school every day. Well, it was during a lull, like. Everybody havin' a bit of an easy. An 'ousewife'd taken out cups o' tea to the crew of this tank. ' "Ow long you lived in sight of this thing, Missis?" the driver says to her. "Ever since it went up," she says. "Are you used to it yet?" "No," she says. With that 'e just nods. 'E and the others finishes their tea, they gives back the cups to the 'ousewife, thanks 'er kindly, and goes back into their seats and fastens the lid down on their tank. A few minutes later she's in the kitchen at the back of the 'ouse when she 'ears an almighty bang-crash and rumble. Dashes out into the road, and there's this bloody great gap, bricks all over the road, and the tank careerin' away with 'alf the Cutteslowe wall lyin' on top of it!'

As he finished his story Peake dissolved in laughter, joined loudly by the other members. Even Trundle was grinning with stately satisfaction.

During Peake's recital the door had opened and a man in a khaki Home Guard uniform had entered, moved quietly over to my father and ordered a drink in an undertone, before leaning against the bar and listening to Peake. When the laughter had dissolved into gurgles and finally into a short, contented silence, the Home Guard man spoke.

'Was you there when it happened?' he asked.

'Well, o' course I was there, didn't you hear me?'

'Only thing is,' said the Home Guard man, 'that's not the way I heard it.'

'Well, I can't help that, mate. I can't help that. If you just step along to Wentworth Road, you'd see for yourself that what I'm sayin' — '

'Oh, yes, knocking the wall down, that happened all right. You got that bit right, warden, no offence. It's the other bit that's different from the way I heard it. The way I heard it, the driver was from Yorkshire. The whole outfit was from Yorkshire, and this one'd misunderstood the orders he was given. He saw that a wall'd been built across the street and he thought it was something they'd built as part of the exercise. He thought he was *supposed* to knock it down. So he done it.'

His words ran out into silence. After a moment, Peake said calmly, 'Well. You got your story, I got mine.'

'That's right,' agreed the Home Guard man.

'Neither one of us,' Peake went on, 'was a fly on the side o' the tank.'

'Very true,' said the Home Guard man.

'So if it's all the same to you,' said Peake with subdued venom, 'I believe I'll stick to tellin' the story the way I heard it, and me not three 'undred yards from the very scene.'

There was a rustling movement among the *cénacle*, and several heads nodded. No one liked the Home Guard man's story; Peake's had the right shape and the right ring. It was a story of retribution, of how the war had given the working class a chance to strike back against privilege.

The Home Guard man, feeling disapproved of, finished his drink and went out. There was a brief, triumphant pause, and then Old Trundle said derisively, 'Yorkshire!'

He made the word itself sound ridiculous.

'Is it likely,' he demanded, 'as they'd fetch a lot o' blokes down all the way from Yorkshire to take part in an exercise defendin' the Churrwell?'

'Course not,' was the murmur.

'While they're messin' about by the Churrwell, 'oo's lookin' arter 'Ull and that? Lookin' right across at Germany, 'Ull is. I knows me geography. I done me map-readin' when we was into it with Brother Boor. 'Oo does 'e think we are?'

Being in London, I was for ever running into people I knew. So many people had been uprooted from their homes and their normal occupations and sent journeying hither and thither, and London was the great transit point. Not a week went by in which I didn't meet someone I had either known at Episcopus, or even earlier than that, at school. One day I came round a narrow street corner and literally bumped into one of my earliest friends, Tupper Boardman.

We hadn't met for some years, but I would have known him anywhere. He was still the absolute archetypal member of the Lower Fourth, big and clumsy, not fat but getting there. We had been pretty good friends at school, on a larking-about level, then I had lost touch with him when I left to go to University. But his father ran a boat-hire business at Folly Bridge, and one Easter vacation when I was desperately scratching about for money I had taken a job with him for a few weeks. Ah, those days! The smell of paint and river water, the gentle rocking motion of the long row of tethered punts as one walked along them. The ripple of spring sunlight on the surface of the water!

We greeted each other – apparently he recognized me as instantaneously as I recognized him – and then, as one always did on these occasions, dived into the nearest bar for a drink. Not until we were standing there with glasses in our hands did we look at one another attentively. He was in uniform, of course: R.E.M.E. said his shoulder flash, Royal Electrical and Mechanical Engineers.

'What kind of a war are you having, Tupper?' I asked.

'Not bad. Better than mooning about with a lot of bloody punts. How are you?'

I noticed that his speech had changed. In his boyhood he had an ordinary local Oxford town accent. He had talked the way Brian and my father did, and as I did before influences began to rub off on me. But now he had obviously made an effort not to sound so Oxford-town. He had been commissioned, I noticed, and he had clearly tried to bring his voice into line with what would be normal in an officers' mess.

I told him briefly what I was doing – it was so boring I could never bring myself to spend more than about twenty-five seconds telling people about it – and then gave him his turn. While he told me his story, which was pretty well as boring as mine, I leaned against the bar and regarded him with affection. Just to look at him released a flood of warm, life-giving memories. He could posh up his accent as much as he liked, I knew it was just old Tupper Boardman. He and I went back a long way. I beamed at him fondly.

'I have such good memories of looking after those punts,' I said. 'How's the business? Still going, I hope?'

'Oh, yes,' he said indifferently. 'But who wants to spend his life looking after a string of punts and rowing-boats?'

'What are you planning to do then, after the war?' I asked.

'Stay in the Army. There's a career for me if I want it, and I do want it. It's a hell of a lot better than messing about with a few wooden boats. Repairing and painting them all winter and standing about hiring them out all summer. No, thank *you*. I dare say I'd like it if I'd only got the memories of doing it for three or four weeks in a nice spell of weather. If I remember rightly, you were just trying to earn a bit of pocket money.'

I nodded. It was easy enough to understand his attitude, but I couldn't feel, inside me, any sympathy with it. My whole imaginative current was running the opposite way. Seeing Tupper, and talking to him, had brought back such sharp, fragrant memories. I could remember the punt-pole in my hand, I could remember the gentle tremor that passed along it as the metal claw bit into the gravel of the river bed. Though a punt moves so slowly, it is in fact possible to steer it very precisely. The secret is to combine the strength of the forward thrust with the delicate balance of stress and weight as you pivot on the fixed point of the in-driven pole. And here was Tupper, with his new-found officer-class accent and his almost hostile suspicion of me, tipping out the whole lovely, multi-faceted experience with one flick of the wrist as 'messing about with a few wooden boats'.

Well, I reflected, if I were to put my money where my mouth was, I would resign my Fellowship of Episcopus and go to work for Tupper Boardman's father after the war. And since I knew I wasn't going to do that, I had no right to feel critical of Tupper for not doing it either.

The last time I had dropped in at the Bargeman's, on my way to the station, my father had leaned across the bar confidentially and said, 'You know, Peter, your mother would like to see the whole family round the table for Sunday dinner one of these week-ends.'

'Sounds feasible enough at our end,' I said, 'if only Heather can get away. See if you can fix it on the telephone. I'll fit in with anything. At this stage in the war there's hardly likely to be a sudden crisis that keeps the likes of me in London on a Sunday.'

So telephone calls were made, Brian and Primrose no doubt did some juggling with shift-work, my mother must certainly have given hours to planning to scrape together the necessary food with contributions from Jasmine Farm via Heather, and finally, one bright day in March 1943, we were all sitting round the table in the kitchen at home. Sunday dinner! Once the great pivotal point of the week, when decisions were announced, policies hammered out, praise and rebuke distributed, and the great heavy machine of family life measured off another turn.

Whenever people met in those days to eat together, the conversation always turned, initially, on food and its availability. A Sunday joint was out of the question, the meat ration for civilians being not only too small but organized in such a way that it would have been impossible to pool the resources of people living at different addresses. My ration-book was in London, with the landlady who fed me during the week, and Heather's was required in the kitchens of Mulberry Hall. But my mother, by whatever miracle of organization, had managed to put on the table a fairly substantial stew, and there were apples and cheese to follow, and bottled beer from the bar and lemonade for Michael.

'A grand effort, Mother,' our father said, leaning back in his chair and lighting a cigarette. 'I wish everybody could have a dinner like that, this deep into the war. Let's see, how long has it been going on now?'

'We're in the fourth year,' said Brian.

'Fourth year! What a thought! It'll have been going on as long as the last one soon, and not an end in sight.'

'No, the end isn't exactly in sight, but it's coming,' I said. 'We know now that however long it takes, our side'll come out on top. We didn't know that two years ago. And three years ago things looked exactly the opposite.'

My motive in taking our minds back to 1940 was harmless. I was simply trying to strike a positive note about the war, but I saw at once it had been a mistake. 1940! I was sitting at a table where two women of my own generation also sat, whose brothers had been killed in that very year. I was not ashamed of not having been killed in the war, nor did I feel ashamed on Brian's part that he had not. And yet, certainly, it was a subject that should not have been raised, even indirectly. A silence fell.

All this distracted me and I did not hear the next few things that were said at the table; when I got back Brian was saying, evidently in response to some question from Dad, 'It all depends where Kim ends up.'

'You'll go where he goes, then?'

'The minute he's got something going, I'll be with him.'

Our father said, in a considering tone, 'I s'pose you mean something to do with racing.'

'Not necessarily, straight off. I don't know what he'll find to do when anything like ordinary motor engineering gets going again. If he can get straight back into racing, so much the better. But if he has to start a company making runabouts and build up the economic base for a racing programme, I'll make runabouts with him for a year or two.'

'What's a runabout, Uncle Brian?' Michael asked.

'A runabout, young Michael, is a kind of little putt-putt car that looks pretty but isn't meant to do anything except just roll around the streets. It's what we had to start building when Billy Morris in his wisdom made us stop building real cars.'

Heather was sitting at the other end of the table from Brian. Down its length she said to him in her clear voice, 'You're bitter, aren't you, Brian?'

Brian thought for a moment before he answered. Then, looking steadily at her, he said, 'Calling somebody bitter makes it sound as if it's their own fault – that they oughtn't to be like that. But – '

'Michael,' my mother suddenly said from her place at the far end of the table, 'would you be a kind boy and run upstairs and fetch me something off our dressing-table?'

I had noticed, ever since Michael was quite small and just able to handle language, that my mother was too sensible to refer to herself in the third person when speaking to him. I never heard her say, 'Please bring Gran the milk-jug.' In such details she revealed her wisdom and her inborn cultivation: I had never met anyone I respected as much as my mother. Certainly, I realized afresh at that moment, I felt much more respect for her than for my wife.

Michael slipped down from his chair, and in a moment he was back, handing to my mother a shiny and gaily-coloured, but not new, biscuit tin. It would have been impossible, in that year, for my mother to have bought a new tin of biscuits, but she had managed to fill the tin herself with odds and ends of fruit and nuts and one or two sweet biscuits she had scavenged from somewhere. She must have been working at it for weeks, and now she was rewarded by being able to use it to head off the trouble that was otherwise coming from Heather's carping mood.

I had no idea why my wife was in this mood, and I couldn't challenge her openly because it would have provoked a spat between us right there at the table, something I was determined to avoid. I stole a glance at her face as she sank into silence. It was withdrawn, sullen. What had happened? I cast my mind back to see if there was anything I might have said, during the last few hours as we drove over from Mulberry Hall, to cause her resentment. But I could think of nothing. All I could conjecture was that sometimes, when my family were all together, the total impression was somehow affronting to her. Perhaps it contrasted painfully with the unhappy atmosphere in her own parents' home.

When we had cleared away the dishes, we moved our chairs into a rough semi-circle facing the hearth and poked up the fire into a bright blaze; the day had been bright, but the afternoon was sinking into a cold evening. With my parents installed in armchairs and the rest of us leaning back comfortably, blinking at the fire, the scene looked like some conventional wall-calendar picture of domestic contentment. But I could feel that in Heather the tension was still present.

Primrose, meanwhile, had been quietly answering when spoken to, placidly

232

taking part in the domestic ritual, and as usual not quite fully present. I knew I would never understand her. Where did it come from, that separateness? I looked at her face with its high cheekbones and unfathomable, untroubled eyes: basically, a gipsy's face. Why was her allegiance given to something as meaningless as speed, to merely rushing about in or on highly tuned machines? Was it, I reflected, simply a matter of the culture she had been born into? A family tradition pulling her into something that was, at any rate, reckless and stylish?

My father now tried to brighten the conversation by asking me about my life in London. It was not a success. I couldn't give him any real idea of what I spent my days doing; it was too remote from his experience. Come to that, it was remote from my experience too; it involved such a limited part of my mind, though that part was used intensively and indeed exhaustingly. I knew for a fact that when the war was finally over and I left the Ministry of Supply, I would have to write down any memories I wanted to preserve about it within the first three months, because by the end of that time they would have faded.

There was, perhaps, another reason why I found it hard to talk in a relaxed way about my London life. It contained an area of secrecy, a large and indeterminate but immensely important area called Mairead. If my tongue were to begin to gallop, it might bring me up to one of the boundaries of this area and I might, before I could stop myself, take a few paces into it. And there, unthinkable disasters lurked. I was in love with a girl in London – I admitted it now – and here I was, sitting by a fireside in Oxford talking about my London life, and my wife was at the same fireside. The thought froze me. I kept such a strict guard on my tongue that I turned to personalities. I was, I told my father, constantly running into people in London, mostly doing Civil Service jobs or with the B.B.C. sending out Allied propaganda, whom I had been accustomed to meeting in Oxford.

'There's Harold Wilson from Univ.,' I said. 'An economist. He's about my age. With the Air Ministry now, I believe. And there's Herbert Hart, and — '

I could feel the company growing bored. The names meant nothing to them, and why should they? I tried to change the subject, and floundered; I just couldn't think of anything else to talk about. But Dad would not give up. He wanted conversation; as an innkeeper, he spent his life providing the conditions for people to sit together and talk; and surely now that his own offspring and their spouses were about him, it wasn't too much to expect the same from them? I perfectly sympathized with his wish. But I could do nothing to bring it about.

So he too fell back on personalities, talking to Brian about various young men, friends of his, who were on war service, and asking what news he had of them. Some of the names he brought up raised no echoes in my mind, but others I knew. Ivan Warmley was in the Navy, and, when last on leave, had told his mother he expected to be on convoy duty, escorting ships carrying supplies to the Russian ports within the Arctic Circle. Like father, like son, I thought.

That topic in its turn ran out, and Father turned his attention to local news and asked me what I thought of the University's acquisition of Wytham, which had been announced in the newspaper a few weeks before.

'The whole lot,' Dad said. 'The village, the woods, the farms, the Abbey, everything.'

'Yes, I saw it.'

'You reckon the University'll know what to do with it all?'

'Well, there's plenty they can do with it,' I said. 'It just depends on whether they tackle the job responsibly. But the former owner's made his wishes clear enough. They're not to use it for profit, they're to keep it as an island of peace and quiet, and they're to let the public have access to the grounds on those terms. I think ffenell's a good old boy. He's given them something that no one else could have done.'

My father was silent for a few moments, obviously pursuing a train of thought. Then he said, 'There's some people don't think it right for one man to have all that land.'

'Well, he hasn't got it now,' I said. 'He's given it to the University.'

'Well, but it was his to give away. He got it from the Duke of Abingdon and now he's given it to them. But it's all private ownership, isn't it?'

'The University isn't a private owner in the old sense. A lot of people will have access to the land.'

'Yes, but they'll be University people, won't they? What about the people who say it ought to belong to the common man?'

'If the common man got hold of it,' I said, 'in five years' time it wouldn't exist any more. People who talk like that just don't understand what's involved in looking after 2,000 acres of woodland.'

'That's not what Bert Finstock thinks. He wants to see the day when there aren't any private owners of land – says it ought to belong to the people.'

'Who's Bert Finstock?' I asked.

'The local Comrade. Sells membership cards for the Communist Party. A big friend of Abe Lazarus, at least if you believe him.'

'I don't believe half the things Bert Finstock comes out with,' my mother said.

'Well, if you believed fifty per cent you'd be going quite a long way. Often comes in here. I'm surprised you don't know him, Peter.'

'I know him,' said Brian. 'Makes a lot of trouble up at Cowley. Tried it on at our place once, tried to bring the lads out. But they didn't listen to him.'

'Why not?'

'He hadn't got a good enough case. It was trouble for trouble's sake.'

'What do you think, Brian,' I asked, 'about this private ownership business? D'you think it was wrong for Colonel ffenell to own Wytham?'

'I don't care one way or the other who owns it. The important thing is looking after it. Once a place like that's gone, it's gone and you can't bring it back.'

'Bert Finstock,' my father said, 'would say the common man'd look after it.'

'That's because Bert Finstock's a fool. It wouldn't *be* the common man, it'd be some government department, and they wouldn't look after it half as well as a private owner. Old ffenell's taken care of it and spent his money on it. If those woods'd had the wrong owner twenty years ago, they wouldn't be there now.'

'What d'you think would have happened, Brian,' I asked, 'If Billy Morris had owned Wytham instead of old ffenell?'

'He'd have knocked the village down and built a factory on the site – with an arterial road running to it, slap through North Oxford from Cowley to Wytham, and a four-lane suspension bridge over the Thames at Godstow.'

'And the woods?'

'He'd have had the trees wired up for fairy lights and turned it into an amusement park for his work-force.'

'You're joking,' Dad said.

'You think so? You think he couldn't do that because Wytham's a nice little place? Come off it, Dad. He doesn't think like that. Blackbird Leys was just as nice as Wytham, and so was Horspath. Have you taken a look at *them* lately? Why should Wytham be any different?'

'Well, that's what Peter thinks, I know,' Dad said. 'He thinks building those factories in Oxford was a mistake.'

'Yes, I do,' I said. 'I think the place was already serving two purposes. It was a University city and it was a market town, a centre for rural industries and the retailing of produce. It's a perfect market centre – look how wide the streets are. It was doing two things at once and doing them perfectly well, and you can't ask more of any place than that.'

'Is it very old, Peter?' my mother asked. 'The Abbey, and all that? It's beautiful, isn't it? I used to go there so often when I was young.'

'The Manor House as it stands is only about 300 years old,' I said. 'But the manor itself existed before 1066 because it's in the Domesday Book. It had pretty much its present boundaries in the days of an Anglo-Saxon king, Edward the Confessor.'

'I've always wondered about him,' said Heather. 'Did he go around confessing all the time? What did he confess to? Did he misbehave an awful lot?'

'Quite the reverse,' I told her. 'It just means he was very pious.'

'How boring,' she said indifferently.

'D'you think good people are boring?' I couldn't help challenging her.

'Mostly, don't you?'

'Not particularly. No more boring than bad people. Anyway, do you actually know a lot of people – I mean genuinely *good* and not just respectable?'

'I expect I could think of some.'

'Name one.'

'All right, I will.' She thought hard for a moment. 'That chap who took us to the club at Chipping Norton. You know – I can't remember his name. That funny little American.'

My parents, not knowing who she was referring to, naturally said nothing to this. Brian also said nothing, but then Brian said nothing most of the time. Michael said nothing because he wasn't listening. I said nothing because I was thinking, wondering whether 'funny little American' was a good description of Chet. Short in stature, yes. American, undoubtedly. But funny? What was funny about him?

There was, then, a moment of silence and in it Primrose's quiet voice sounded very distinctly.

'Heather,' she said, looking directly at her sister-in-law, 'why d'you think Chet's funny?'

'Chet?' Heather seemed confused. She gave an impatient shrug. 'I mean, Americans just *are* funny, aren't they?'

Primrose got up and moved towards the little scullery that opened out of the kitchen. 'I'll make a start on the washing-up,' she said to my mother, and left the room.

Heather looked vexed. Her face took on an enquiring expression, as if asking 'What was all *that* about?' I thought it was time I came in. 'Let it go, Heather,' I said. 'Please just let it go.'

Heather shrugged again, but in that same instant Brian spoke. 'Before Heather lets it go, I'll just tell you what I think Primrose has in mind. Chet's air-crew, you see, in a Flying Fortress, a B17. If you've ever seen a Flying Fortress you'll know that it's the biggest bombing plane there is. It has to operate beyond the range of fighter escort, so it's the most heavily armoured.'

From the scullery I heard splashing of taps and the rattle of plates and dishes, as if Primrose were trying not to hear what Brian was saying.

'One of its guns is underneath the aircraft, about mid-point. The gunner sits in a thing like a plastic bubble, sticking out underneath this huge 'plane, just to the rear of centre. Now. Usually the 'plane flies through a lot of flak – ack-ack fire and cannon fire from other aircraft. One of the things most likely to be damaged in that kind of fire is the winding equipment which raises and lowers the tail gunner in his bubble. If it gets hit at all, it usually jams so that the man can't be wound up. He knows it and he just has to sit there. When the aircraft lands, and it has to land sometime, the tail gunner is just smeared off against the runway. There's nothing left of him. Not even as much as when a car runs over a hedgehog.'

The rattle and splash from the scullery had ceased. Brian, too, was silent.

There was no need of more words. What was clear to me was that Primrose was already grieving for Chet, the young driver of an Indy special with an Offy mill. His survival over the next year or so was so unlikely that she had accepted his death as if it had already happened, and had begun to mourn.

I spent a good deal of time in the summer of that year worrying about my relationship with Mairead: worrying, that is, about whether I was going to have one.

It was one thing to tell myself, after that brief and enjoyable lunchtime in Kensington Church Street, that I saw no reason why I shouldn't get together with her quite often. But my nerve always seemed to fail me when I approached the telephone with the object of dialling Mr John Dulanty's office and asking for her. I tried, very frequently, to analyse this failure of nerve. Was I afraid she would bite my head off? No, assuredly. She was, for all the fighting spirit she could show on occasion, too gentle and courteous to do that. It was rather, I ruefully concluded, that I might bite my own head off, so to speak. What I feared was my own self-accusation. Because, for all my defensive bluster, there was a little hard nutshell of truthfulness at the centre of my mind. And I knew if I broke open that nutshell it would contain a message, and the message would be: *Getting to know Mairead Hoey is playing with fire.*

Did I mind playing with fire? Was I willing to risk it? No. Yes. Yes. No. Weeks, months, went by.

At last, one sultry day in August, I felt so desperate that I decided to go for a defined and limited objective – a whole day in Mairead's company. At the end of that I could think again, take stock of the situation. It would involve, of course, getting her to come out with me on a Sunday. Immediately, without giving myself time to get cold feet, I telephoned her at the office, and asked if she happened to be free on the Sunday following. Sounding a little surprised, she said she had no particular plans, so – still terrified I would lose my nerve before I could get the words out – I asked her if she would come out on an excursion with me to Richmond Park.

I hadn't known I was going to say 'Richmond Park'. The words just formed themselves. I said one could see deer there and she said that would be very pleasant. So we arranged where we would meet, at the ticket barrier on Baker Street station.

I was sweating slightly as I replaced the receiver, and my chest was constricted with anxiety. I knew the reason for it. By making that arrangement, I had committed myself to ringing up Heather and lying to her, something I had never done before.

I couldn't ring her there and then, though I wished I could get it over, because she would be out at work. I had to wait till evening and then ring her from a coin telephone in a pub, telling her I was tied up at work that Sunday. I gabbled out my invented story over the rattle of pub conversation, then hung up and drowned my agitation in double whiskies. It was a bit unfair, I snivelled to myself, it really was. All I wanted was a change in the unvarying routine of my life, didn't I? A break from the iron routine of Mulberry Hall every week-end. See some deer! When did I last see a deer? Harmless enough, wasn't it?

So if it was that harmless, why didn't I tell Heather the truth, instead of inventing a pack of lies? Well, there were some things women just don't understand. Better not to give her a chance to get the wrong impression.

So I took Mairead to Richmond Park. It was a soft autumn day, and the sky was blue, with one or two masses of high-piled cloud moving slowly across it, and the sunlight came and went on the bracken that was turning to russet and gold, and the deer duly allowed themselves to be glimpsed at the end of moss-grown rides. I think I was a little dazed by everything that was happening; which would account, perhaps, for my remembering so little of what happened that day. Mairead was wearing a dress of some green material, shot through with purple; she said it was Donegal tweed. When the sun came out it shone on her rich black hair, and when it went in again there was still the piercing light of her eyes.

In case I ran out of things to talk about, I had determined to bring up the subject of Yeats, whom I was reading at the time. I still believed that poets wrote for their fellow human beings and not for word technicians in white coats, and at the time of Yeats' death in 1939 I had gone out and bought his *Collected Poems*, a plum-coloured volume which was soon to become unobtainable. I used to read it on those long, blacked-out train journeys; in fact I had it in my bag on that first occasion when I travelled with Mairead. Strange to think of that now, the old Irish poet and the young Irish woman, together filling my consciousness.

'It must be wonderful for a nation to have a great poet,' I said to her now. 'It's something that hasn't happened to the English for a long time.'

I was rather startled when she replied, 'The bulk of the Irish nation, the overwhelming majority, don't care a fig about Yeats.'

She was getting over a stile as we spoke; she stepped lightly down from it and went on, 'They live in the here and now. They don't see Ireland as a vague misty place where everything happens in a story-book.'

'Well, that's hardly how Yeats saw it either.'

'Yeats,' she said firmly, 'had to stand aside from the great questions of his lifetime. He was a Protestant, with his roots among the country gentlefolk, whereas the decision-making Irish were Catholic and urban. When the Easter 1916 Rising was planned, he knew nothing about it till it happened.'

'He wrote a great poem about it all the same. He made it the material for great literature, which means it'll be remembered for the same reason that the quarrel between the Greeks and Romans is remembered. Surely that's something?'

'His poem about the Easter Rising is exactly the kind of thing that annoys Irish people. He says it's up to heaven to decide when the Irish will get their freedom and we don't believe that, we believe it's got to be in our own hands.'

'Does he say it's up to heaven? I don't remember that. It seems to me the poem's full of Irish patriotism.'

'That's because you've got an English view of Irish patriotism as something merely picturesque. When it issues in political demands you just find it irritating.'

'No, I don't. I've never said any such thing.'

237

'All right, not you personally. But on that specific point about the poem, look it up and you'll see I'm right.'

As a matter of fact I was sufficiently interested, when I next got back to my Yeats, to look up the poem. She must, I concluded, have been thinking of the passage:

> Too long a sacrifice
> Can make a stone of the heart.
> O when may it suffice?
> That is Heaven's part, our part
> To murmur name upon name,
> As a mother names her child
> When sleep at last has come
> On limbs that had run wild.

To base a rejection of Yeats on lines like these seemed to me a bit heavy-handed; all the same, I couldn't pretend that I didn't know what Mairead meant. And to that extent her point was made.

All the rest of our conversation in that September landscape, with the drabness of war forgotten and the richness of autumn glowing before our eyes, has faded from my mind. Except for one fragment that I do remember. As we rested our backs against a split-log fence, basking in the afternoon sunshine, she suddenly asked me, out of nowhere, 'What do you usually do on Sundays?'

This, of course, was my cue to tell her that I spent Sundays with my wife and son, and to go on to talk about Mulberry Hall and all that.

'In peacetime,' I said instead, 'I used to use Sundays to catch up on my reading. But since I've been coming to town and working in an office, I generally try to spend Sunday in the country. Like this.'

I gestured to the scene around us, and the moment of danger was past. It wasn't that I exactly wanted to avoid telling Mairead that I was a family man. It was just that . . . well, all that side of things belonged to decision-making, to planning for the future and taking account of the past, and just for this one afternoon I wanted there to be no past and no future, only today. I wanted to be at peace with the sunshine, the bracken, the distant glimpses of deer, and Mairead's company.

I kept everything in the lap of the gods and the gods duly obliged, making the evening turn out in a way I couldn't possibly have foreseen.

It fell out this way. By about half-past six we were both hungry, though we had had a meagre picnic in the middle of the day, and we left the park and began to hunt for food. The pubs didn't open till seven o'clock because it was Sunday, and the few cafés we sighted turned out to be firmly closed. (The English Sunday was one institution that came through the war with no sign of change.) And when the pubs did open their doors at last, we went into three in a row without finding one that had anything to eat except potato crisps. I had a glass of beer in each, so as to soften up the landlord before getting round to the request for food, though Mairead refused to drink anything until she knew whether she was going to get any food to go with it. By the time we came out of the third, I had rather a lot of beer in my stomach and it felt unpleasantly acid.

'Oh, damn this,' I said. 'Let's get on a train into London. We're bound to find something open in Soho.'

'That'll be very expensive.'

'It can't be, it's against the law to charge more than five bob for a meal.'

'On the meal itself, yes, but I've heard about these cover charges they slap on. And I couldn't pay my whack. It's near the end of the month and I'm broke.'

'There'd be no question of your — '

'So I've got a better idea. A member of my family paid me a visit last week, all the way from Cork, and brought me a ham.'

'A ham? A whole one, to yourself?'

'Yes, disgraceful, isn't it? That's why I have an obligation to give some to the beleaguered, underfed English. Like you. Come to Tufnell Park and I'll give you a supper of ham. And probably boiled cabbage; I think I've got a cabbage I didn't finish. There, is that traditionally Irish enough for you?'

Traditionally Irish or not, I was very much more than willing to go to Tufnell Park with her, even though the journey by tube all the way across London from south to north was interminable.

Her place, at the top of one of those big Victorian houses in Laurier Road not far from Tufnell Park station, turned out to be not quite self-contained: a bed-sitter at the top of a couple of flights of stairs, with a shared bathroom on the floor below but its own little pantry-kitchen. Quite a comfortable place by the standards of those days; a lot better, certainly, than the rat-hole I myself was living in from Monday to Saturday.

We went up the stairs to her place (worn carpet, but no more than you would expect in a rented house after three years of war) and she led the way in.

'I haven't, as you see, anything that could be described as a dining room,' she said as I stood there taking the place in. 'I'll give you the choice of eating in the kitchen, which is small and cramped, or in here with the plate on your knees.'

'In the small and cramped kitchen, please.' I've never liked balancing a plate of food on my knees, and besides that, Mairead was not the kind of person I minded being in a small, cramped room with. If the narrowness of the space caused us now and then to brush against each other, I thought I could bear it.

'Well, you can at least sit down in an armchair while I go and put it out,' she said. 'It's just cold ham, but I can heat it up with the cabbage.'

She disappeared into the kitchen. I called after her, 'Can't I come and chat to you while you get the stuff ready?'

'No, you'll be in the way. Stay there for a bit. Put the wireless on if you like, I think there's a news bulletin coming up.'

I switched it on, but she must have been wrong about the news bulletin, because what came out seemed to be a variety programme, transferred wholesale from the old twice-nightly music halls, and consisting simply of a succession of turns. At the moment when I switched on there was a comedian just finishing his act. He told a last couple of jokes, eliciting a few scattered laughs from the invited audience, and then, as comedians were very apt to do in those days, in conclusion sang a glutinously sentimental song. Even that song, however, was not quite so glutinous as the repertoire of the next performer, one of those Irish tenors without whom no English variety programme ever seemed to be complete in those days. This character launched immediately into one of the old standards of his profession, 'The Mountains of Mourne', and as I listened idly I became aware that Mairead had come to the doorway between the two rooms and was standing there, also listening. She didn't fidget or make any exclamation, but I knew from the waves I was picking up that she was feeling very impatient.

The first verse of that much-loved song, most people will remember, runs (spelling it out in ordinary English and not attempting to represent the professional brogue):

> Dear Mary, this London's a wonderful sight,
> With the people here working by day and by night,
> They don't grow potatoes, nor barley, nor wheat,
> But there's gangs of them digging for gold in the street.
> At least when I asked them that's what I was told,
> So I just lent a hand with this digging for gold:
> But for all that I found there, I might as well be
> Where the mountains of —

Before the mellifluous songster could get as far as the remaining words, 'Mourne sweep down to the sea', Mairead had abruptly walked past me to the radio and, with an angry, decisive movement, flicked up the 'off' switch.

'I'm sorry if you were listening to that, but I'm afraid I just can't bear another second.'

'No, of course I wasn't listening, it was just what was happening to be . . .'

She stood in front of the fireplace, tense, holding in her temper. 'I'm sorry. I ought not to let that kind of rubbish annoy me. But when an entire people is insulted, incessantly, on and on, and these insults then become the justification for political discrimination, I simply can't — '

'Steady on, surely that's a lot of weight to put on a slightly sentimental song.'

'Not at all. Let me write a nation's songs and I care not who makes its laws — I forget who said that. But whoever said it, it's true. Songs and jokes, they're the means by which the English view of the Irish is spread around and accepted. Oh, Paddy may be charming but he's a fool, he's slow-witted and credulous, he'll believe anything. You can't let him run his own affairs or he'd get into a frightful mess. If he demands his independence that must be because he's been listening to Agitators. Only Agitators would tell him that kind of stuff. No, he'd do much better to let us run his country for him, and fleece him and bleed him white into the bargain. Save him from himself out of pure benevolence. And don't imagine that *you're* specially privileged. It's a disease that affects the whole English nation. They all have Ireland-blindness.'

'Look, I'm an historian. It's my job to — '

'Oh, yes, Peter, you're holy, aren't you? You're *an Oxford historian*.' She spoke the words with mock, wide-eyed reverence. 'You're clever, and every breath you draw of the air of Oxford makes you cleverer.'

'For Christ's sake, what's come over you? All I'm saying is that at least I'm a professional — to that extent it's got to be my business to disentangle — '

'What do you tell your students about the Irish Rising of 1641?' she flung at me.

'1641?' I was thrown for a moment. 'Well, I start by making sure they understand it was basically an episode in the English Civil War. Charles — '

'There you are! A mass movement of desperate people, fighting to regain a little of their freedom, and to you it doesn't even exist in its own right, it's an episode in English history!'

'Mairead, you can't rule lines down the page like that: this is English history, not Irish history. Was the Norman victory over Harold's forces in 1066 an episode in the history of England or of France?'

'Don't set your Oxford traps for me. A gang of Normans won the day over a

240

gang of Anglo-Saxons. It would only be a parallel if the Saxons, all the way down to their modern descendants, had never been allowed to get up off their backs from that day to this.'

She turned on her heel and went into the tiny kitchen. I hesitated a moment and then followed. She had her back to me and was stirring a saucepan on the gas-stove.

'Look, Mairead . . .'

'I'm sorry.' Still she did not turn round.

'I just wanted to say that I understand perfectly how you feel. If I were Irish myself I'd feel just . . .'

She turned round to face me and I stopped short under the full blaze of those eyes.

'One of the things I hate about the whole business,' she said more calmly, 'is that it makes me behave out of character. I'm not, actually, a mass of resentments and wounded feelings. I don't enjoy lashing out and being unfair. I'm perfectly well aware that you didn't write the words of "The Mountains of Mourne" and I don't suppose you even go about singing the damn' thing. Still, in a way I don't regret that you saw me having that fit of temper. It comes to every Irish person now and again.'

'You don't have to tell me that. I've heard Irish jokes all my life and yet I've often noticed that the Irish people I actually *meet* are pretty clever.'

I checked myself. Mairead was such a straightforward, down-to-earth person. She had invited me to her home after we had spent the day together because she happened to have some food that she was willing to share with me. There was no need, once I was over her threshold, to stand around flattering her. So I changed the subject and we ate some delicious thick slices of ham, all the way from Cork, very tender and moist, boiled exactly right, with fragrant hot cabbage and that grey wartime bread, spread with a very little margarine because she had only a tiny amount, and I felt like a cad taking any of it at all.

The evening went by very decorously. I was determined to behave myself and make a good impression. I wanted Mairead to think of me as someone who could be given a meal and a couple of glasses of wine and allowed to sit in front of her gas-fire without the feeling that complications might start up.

Was this because I, Peter Leonard, considered it a racing certainty that if I could arrange to see Mairead fairly regularly, complications *would*, sooner or later, inevitably start up?

Indeed it was.

What, then, had become of the state of mind I had so carefully cultivated only a few hours earlier in Richmond Park, when I had enclosed myself in a soap-bubble of the present and managed to avoid thinking of what might develop in the future?

The soap-bubble had burst.

I helped her with the washing-up. Not very seriously; my actual motive had been simply to come into the tiny kitchen with her. I wanted to be near her. I wanted to be very near her. A wave of longing for her swept over me and I moved forward to take her in my arms. But she deftly put the milk-jug into my hands and said, 'Dry that, then you've finished.'

There is something about drying a milk-jug with a tea-towel that simply doesn't go with sweeping a girl into a passionate embrace. I dried it and put it down and we stood for a moment looking at one another. I knew that if Mairead had wanted to be in my arms she would have come towards me. But she didn't.

'Am I going to see you again, Mairead?'

'I expect it depends more on you than on me.'

'Why d'you say that?'

She turned her blue eyes full on me and said, 'You're married, aren't you?'

My immediate thought was that she must have been checking up on me. And, pitiful as it sounds, in that instant a tremor of hopefulness ran through me: she is sufficiently interested in me to *want* to check up!

Fencing for a little time, I asked, 'How d'you know that?'

'It's the first thing a single girl learns,' Mairead said. 'If a man doesn't mention his background it's because he's married. Anyone who's single and free lets you know in the first ten minutes, if he's interested in you. And if he isn't, you don't see him a second time anyway.'

'But you have seen me a second time,' I said. 'And a third.'

'Yes. And you still haven't mentioned your wife, so I know you've got one. Any children?'

'A boy, nine years old.'

'Nice for you,' she said.

'Does it make any difference to you,' I asked, 'my having a wife and son?'

She shrugged and said, 'Why should it?'

'If it doesn't make any difference to you, why did you bring it up?'

'Because you'd put a blanket of silence over it. And I don't like blankets of silence.'

There seemed to be nothing to do but go. At the door I paused. 'Thank you for spending the day with me.'

'Thank you for asking me.'

'Am I going to see you again?' I asked once more, plunging in, driven by desperate needs.

'Depends,' she said.

I knew that was all I was going to get, so I turned and went down the stairs and into the street. At least, I assume I did, though afterwards I didn't remember doing so. The next few minutes have vanished from my memory – everything is just a dark space until the moment – which must have been about ten minutes later – when I stood in front of the ticket window at the tube station. As I handed over my fare I had a sudden vision of the deer cropping quietly in the glades of Richmond Park, and I thought how much I envied them.

I gather that inveterate Londoners, who are inclined to be sentimental about their city, even develop in time an affection for its underground railways. I can't say I developed any of that affection during my London years. I disliked, and still do, the noise, the harried and preoccupied crowds, the nagging advertisements, the lonely, *angst*-ridden platforms along which, for no accountable reason, cold winds rush every now and then at gale force.

Still, even in tube trains a good thing happens now and then; and one day in the middle of 1943 I had a welcome surprise: I met Knowlton on one. I forget where I had been, but I was coming back into central London at about six o'clock, and when the doors slid open at Victoria and a crowd spilled in, I saw at once that Knowlton was among them. What was it that made him so instantly recognizable? There was his height, of course, that raised his head and shoulders above crowd-level, but somehow it was Knowlton's brand of amiability and pleasantness that marked him out as unique. He spotted me at once and, being immovably stuck in the rush-hour crowd, began to send me messages. His features conveyed gratification with a tinge of surprise in the raised eyebrows ('Fancy meeting you! I'm glad!'), humorous resignation ('You can see I can't move') and what I read as ironic self-mockery ('Don't think I don't know how odd it must look to see me, of all people, dressed up as a soldier'). Finally, as the train ground to a halt at Green Park, he looked towards me enquiringly and mimed the action of raising a glass to his lips. I rose and joined him on the platform, and in another few minutes we were comfortably sitting in a pub in Piccadilly called the Yorkshire Grey, which I remember because I had never been in it until that time with Knowlton, and have never been there since.

We talked easily; one always did talk easily with Knowlton. He passed on such news as he had of men we had known at Episcopus. Norbert, it seemed, was 'doing something in Intelligence'. That didn't surprise me. Lamont – and this did surprise me – was, Knowlton had heard, 'at sea somewhere'. At sea? Lamont? Was he in the Navy? Knowlton had no information. He asked me about myself, but I rather fobbed off the question; my life seemed to be so boring, I didn't want to spend our few minutes talking about it. I preferred to move the conversation over to what had been happening to him.

'Pretty easy, so far,' he said. 'I wouldn't actually have a rooted objection to doing a bit of fighting – after all, it's what one joins the Army for – but so far it hasn't happened to me. I wasn't called up till October '39, so I wasn't trained in time for Dunkirk. After that for a bit there wasn't much fighting one could do. I got as far as Crete, but the outfit I was in was pulled out before we actually saw a German. I believe that was all pretty much of a mess-up. Then we all expected to go to North Africa, but that hasn't happened either.'

I said, tritely, 'Well, I suppose once you're a serving soldier you can't forecast what might happen to you.'

'Not forecast exactly,' Knowlton said, 'but insofar as one does get any choice, I've gone through this war so far on the principle of trying to be with chaps I like being with.'

'Good principle.'

'Very often you don't get any choice at all, but sometimes there's a tiny bit within a limited area. I mean, you can volunteer for this rather than that – at any rate once you're commissioned. And when I've had a choice, I've gone with chaps I've enjoyed being with, and it's been the only good thing that's come out of the war for me. Apart from the fact that I'm still alive, of course.'

'Yes,' I said. 'Survival is definitely a good thing.'

'It's a good thing if one can arrange for it. But if one makes it the only thing, one ends up with some horribly boring types.'

If the speaker had been anyone but Knowlton, I would have felt that those words were intended as a criticism of me. Certainly, if so, they were justified. I was a horribly boring type and I knew it. Knowlton was the kind of man in whose presence I felt myself definitely inferior. But he was too kindly to be aware that he created this impression in me, or he would have tried to correct it. I felt certain of that.

Knowlton now began to tell a funny story about the commanding officer of the unit he had recently left. He was not the type who bombarded you with funny stories, but on the rare occasions when he did tell one he told it well, and though I have forgotten the story I remember that it amused me. But before long he was back on the subject of chaps he really liked being with: it seemed to be in the forefront of his mind just now.

'For instance, in that outfit I'm talking about,' he said, 'there was just one man

243

I really could make a friend of. Felt I was on his wavelength, you know? And yet I didn't feel as if we were equals exactly. I always looked up to him a bit. He was the chaplain, actually.'

'The chaplain? Is that why you looked up to him?'

'No, no. I don't think I've ever taken that stuff with a lot of seriousness. I mean, they've got a right to their opinion, you know, but so have I. No, what I liked about this fellow, apart from the fact that he had a good sense of humour and was nice to have around, was that on top of that he was very brave, I've never known anybody with so much in the way of guts.'

'How did that show itself, if he was the chaplain?'

'Well, that's just it. He'd been in action a few times, and he'd always insisted on going in with the men. He didn't carry a weapon, he just went in with them. Said if he was their chaplain he should be out there where they were most likely to need him. And he was more exposed than they were, in a way, because he hadn't got a weapon to defend himself with. As a matter of fact he very nearly bought it at one point. In Crete, it was. A piece of shrapnel or something shaved so close to the side of his head that it took his ear off. Sliced it clean away. He was self-conscious about it – hated you to look at where the ear should have been – grew his hair long on that one side.'

'The men must have respected him,' I said.

'They did. Everybody did. I did. I used to wonder if I'd have done the same, but I don't think I would. I mean, I wouldn't have volunteered. I don't mind taking risks if I have to, but I'm not the volunteering type.'

It was strange, I thought, to hear Knowlton musing on courage. He had always appeared to me a man whose life contained no danger, no stress, very little effort even. A man who had never been tested. Perhaps this was how Knowlton saw himself, and why the example of the volunteering chaplain with his shrapnel-sliced ear seemed so much to fill his thoughts.

'And yet,' I said, 'your view of yourself as not being a natural volunteer can't be entirely true. It conflicts with your other principle, of being with chaps you like being with. Sometimes that must have an element of volunteering.'

'Well, I suppose so.'

'In any case,' I said, 'judgements on matters like that wouldn't come very fittingly from me, because I'm a non-combatant, fighting the war from behind a desk, and the less I say about volunteering and risk-taking the better.'

'Oh, I wouldn't say that, old man. Pretty high civilian casualties too, aren't there?'

'There are, and yet everybody knows that's a different thing. Being hit by a bomb is about the equivalent of being run over crossing the road in peacetime, whereas a battle's a battle.'

Knowlton shrugged. 'Mostly luck, I suppose, in either case.'

'I'd guess, though it's no business of mine, that it has some personal motive in your case, and I don't mean buying a bit of Civvy Street time either. I mean something to do with choosing your company. You don't have to tell me whether I'm right, but I just have that intuitive sense.'

Was I preternaturally alert to these small mannerisms, or did I discern a very slight hesitation, a mere fraction of a second, before Knowlton answered casually, 'You could say that.'

Soon afterwards, he left to keep an appointment. As I watched him walk out through the door with a last grin and wave, I thought that Knowlton seemed as little damaged by the war as a man could possibly be. By taking him into a military life and away from his corporate civilian existence just at the end of his twenties, the war had postponed what would have been, in peacetime, the beginning of his slide into middle age. He looked, I felt sure, younger than I did.

As summer turned to autumn and moved on into winter, I began to invite Mairead out on a regular basis. I wanted to begin by getting it established as a matter of course that we saw each other regularly. I invited her for an evening out, not quite as frequently as once a week, but a little more often than once a fortnight. I offered no excuses or explanations: I simply rang her up and made the suggestion, the implication being that if she didn't feel like bestowing her company on me she could always refuse. In that spirit I telephoned soon after Richmond and asked her out to the theatre. She accepted. The play was a witty comedy and we both laughed a good deal. Soon afterwards I asked her to something else and she refused. Then to something else and she agreed. Now and then to lunch. It became standard, accepted. We were people who saw each other, spent time together.

And I tried to avoid hypocrisy, and at least be honest with myself, if with no one else, about my motives. The first essential was to recognize frankly that I was 'in love' with Mairead, whatever that blanket term may mean. I was obsessed with her. I couldn't get her face out of my mind or her voice out of my ears. Obviously this was inconvenient for a married man, and the only thing that made it possible for me to live with the situation was that my marriage to Heather was, during those years, in suspension. We had one night together out of seven; I had long since ceased to miss her very acutely on the other six, and I would guess fairly confidently that she felt the same.

What I intended to do about my obsession with Mairead was quite simple. I intended to involve myself as closely with her as I could. My object was to try to burn out my obsession, to smother it under a fantastic weight of fuel. Right, I said to my rebellious instincts, you want Mairead? Very well – if I can manage it you shall have her, and not only have her but devour her, revel in her, inhabit her, put her on like a second skin. We'll see who gets tired first!

And what if the obsession didn't burn itself out, but on the contrary burnt its way more and more deeply into the centre of my being?

I would cross that bridge if and when I came to it.

And what if the passion we were going to stoke up between us should burn itself out in me but not in Mairead? What if a time came when I was willing to part and she was still deeply enmeshed and unable to face life without me?

She would have to cross that bridge when and if she came to it.

Was I satisfied that this was an acceptable moral attitude? Was I pleased with myself for holding it?

I was not satisfied to this effect and I was not pleased with myself.

Did my moral self-disapproval affect my decision-making and cause me to alter my conduct?

No.

The summer of 1943 was long, and hot, and close. Oxfordshire lay in a fitful sleep, like a toad in a greenhouse. On my week-ends at Mulberry Hall in July and August, I wandered about the somnolent countryside, lapsed as it was now into the uniform green of late summer, and dreamed impossible dreams. Everything was trance-like; the air went into my lungs like the fog of opium. I could remember nothing like it.

One Saturday evening, with Heather busy over a supply of horseshoes and Michael off on a search for newts with a boy of his own age, I wandered out for a walk in the fields before dinner. With very little traffic on the roads, it hardly mattered which direction I turned in once I left the gates of Mulberry Hall, and I found myself in a gravel lane that led gradually down a slope into a wooded stream-valley.

This lane was bordered on one side by a high thick hedge, largely impossible to see through; on the other by a fence, across which one saw a vista of fields and hedges, with the occasional coppice, and here and there a farm building or a cottage. Although farmers were producing food with desperate intensity, we were still in the epoch when it was possible to do this without turning the countryside into an industrial wasteland dotted with concentration camps for animals and birds. The huge machines which demanded the rooting-out of hedgerows had not arrived yet; fields were still small and variegated; the landscape was still beautiful.

There was a gate in the thick hedge to my right and I leaned against it thoughtfully, looking over at the more sloping field which lay beyond, sweeping down to a willow-fringed stream where a group of Friesian cows stood meditatively, a sure sign that the day had been hot. Even now, towards seven o'clock, as the shadows slanted and a cool mist began to rise along the valleys, the air had not yet cooled enough to tempt them out of the knee-high water.

As I leaned gently with my forearms resting along the top of the gate, I became aware of a pair of male legs sticking out of the hedge a few yards to my left. I regarded them with interest. They were lean and muscular, as I could see all the better because they were clad in faded and rather too wide khaki shorts, with woollen socks and stout brogues: an outdoor man, obviously. Leaning a little further over the gate, I was able to pin-point more exactly the *kind* of outdoor man he was: the Scholar Gipsy, the type who loved to retire from the bustle of the world to dream, and think, and pore over some well-loved page, amid the surroundings that matched the perfection he dreamt of:

> Till all his Greek and Latin learning seemed
> A long blast on the horn that brought
> Nearer to men's thought
> A measureless consummation that he dreamed.

On the grass beside the legs lay what looked like a cheap exercise book. Leaning forward another inch, I could see that on the man's lap, obviously being read, was a small leather-covered volume. As I watched, a long, thin, rather saurian hand reached down and picked up the exercise book, spread it out on the knees above the leather-bound book, and wrote a line. Then crossed it out. Then wrote it again. Then sat perfectly still for what seemed like at least five minutes. Then crossed it out again.

I now knew that I wanted to see the rest of this man. I wanted to know what was in the leather-bound book. What was the nature of the thoughts that so possessed and anchored him? Was he a philosopher, stretching his mind over Plato or Bergson? Or was it Gibbon who stimulated him to profound reflections on history and the affairs of men? Or was he some harmless nut-case, happily immersed in speculations about ley-lines or the Lost Tribes of Israel?

I clambered over the gate. The sound I inevitably made in doing so would have attracted the man's attention, so there was no point in stealth. As I set out

246

to walk boldly past him, he looked up with a nervous start. He seemed partly to be making an effort to recall his imagination from distant realms and partly to be apprehensive, as if he anticipated being sent packing.

'Good evening,' I said casually, conveying that to find a man sitting deep in a hedgerow was an everyday occurrence.

'Good evening.' His voice was abrupt, rather staccato. 'I hope I'm not in anybody's way.'

I smiled, halted, and said reassuringly, 'Well, I don't farm this land, but I can't see any reason why you should be.'

'Ah,' he said, and as if reassured settled his back comfortably against the tree-trunk he had been leaning against. 'It would be a sad day if one . . . couldn't take one's ease in the countryside.'

'Undoubtedly.'

'It . . . aids reflection.' He glanced down at the book on his lap.

'You're at work on something?' I prompted. I wanted to encourage this man to tell me something about himself. I liked him.

'Well . . . yes and no. "At work" would be perhaps a grandiose term for what is essentially a recreation, though perhaps a recreation that might, in time, minister to . . . minister to . . .'

He paused for so long that I came to the conclusion that he was not going to finish his sentence. During the silence his arms stiffened until they pointed down towards his feet as straight as broomsticks, and his fingers twitched rapidly. I began to speak, when he abruptly rapped out, '. . . something more substantial that is as yet unformulated.'

By this time it was clear that I was dealing with an eccentric, though my years in the academic community prevented me from immediately writing him off as a mere mental casualty who would doubtless soon be reclaimed by whatever Bedlam he had wandered from.

I looked at him with real attention. Fundamentally he had a handsome appearance. His nose was aquiline, his brown eyes piercing; the skin of his face was deeply tanned, with the ingrained colour of years of habitual exposure to sun and wind. His hair was dark, not beginning to recede or thin, and would have suited him well if it had not for some reason been parted in the middle, a fashion that had gone out in the 1920s. He wore old clothes of expensive quality, but in an undefinable way there was a comicality about them. Were they just old-fashioned? Or, when he stood up, would they be revealed as ill-fitting also?

Beside him on the grass lay a curved briar pipe, much scorched and blackened. The man now picked this up, put it into his mouth and produced a large, unwieldy flint-operated lighter. At this he struck several times with no result, then he adjusted the wick with minute care, then struck it again with no result. Muttering in annoyance, he shook it vehemently, and this perhaps activated the fuel to permeate the wick more effectively. Immediately, a fierce flame shot up to the height of almost a foot. With exaggerated rigour, his cheeks hollowing, he sucked almost the entire flame into the bowl five or six times before extinguishing the device by putting back the top section, which did not hinge or open but pulled right off like the roof of a beehive.

Acrid smoke poured from the man's mouth and nostrils, and enveloped his head. Even standing a couple of yards from him, I felt a coughing fit coming on. But almost immediately he allowed the pipe to go out, and during the rest of our conversation he used it as an aid to gesticulation, reinforcing his remarks by prodding the air with its stem. He was not a thin man in general, but his hands and feet were long and slender; in a man who cared for his appearance, they would have attracted the term 'elegant'.

'It's always been my experience,' he said, fixing me with his brown eyes, 'that a rural solitude and a fine day are ... hmm ... the most auspicious setting for an encounter with any poet whose terms and complexities I'm trying to bring over into English. Do you ever try your hand at translation?'

I liked him for the direct way he assumed that I was a literate person.

'I haven't,' I said. 'But I've had to do plenty of reading in Latin, French, German and Spanish, so I can see what you're up against if you're trying to translate poetry.'

He handed the leather-bound book up to me. Taking it, I saw that its leather binding had been added to an original modest, even cheaply produced little volume. The title page said: *George Trakl, Gedichte*. 1913. I forget the publisher.

'You know Trakl?' the man asked me.

'He's just a name to me. One of that generation killed in the last war, wasn't he?'

' "Died" would perhaps be a more cautious term than "killed", if one were concerned with literal accuracy. He was one of that company of poets who are caught up in war and die as a result, though not actually in battle. Like Byron or Rupert Brooke.'

'Where did Trakl die?'

'In Silesia. He was a pharmacist by profession. When war came he was made a reserve officer in the medical corps, and in that capacity,' he stabbed the air with his pipe, 'he found himself one of the pitifully inadequate team trying to deal with the sudden flood of wounded and demoralized thrown back at the Battle of Grodek. He broke down, was sent to hospital in his turn, and died there of an overdose of cocaine.'

'Did he mean to kill himself? Any suicide note?'

'Nothing of that kind. The question is insoluble. His poetry shows an agonized awareness of suffering, his own and other people's.'

'I see.'

'Trying to give Trakl a voice in English, to carry over his awareness and compassion, his knowledge of pain ... it has helped me, during these dreadful years.'

'Of course.'

'All the poets are valuable; they have so much to teach us. But there is surely a special value just now in a German poet.'

He got up. Standing, he was taller than I was. The eyes, in his tanned face, looked out across the valley where the sun was going down.

'These are terrible years for Europe,' he said, speaking as much to himself as to me.

'They are,' I agreed. 'But at least we've a chance of a new start.'

'You read German?' He looked at me now.

'Just for utility.'

'Well, try Trakl when you have an opportunity,' he said, putting the leather book in his pocket and beginning to gather up his belongings.

'I'm not driving you away, am I?'

'Oh, no. I have to be back in Oxford. I'm staying in College.'

A don! I might have known.

'Staying ...' I was prompting again.

'Yes, at Episcopus.'

248

'Really? But that's my College. I'm surprised we've never — '

'I don't work at Episcopus. I'm not a Fellow. I'm just staying there, that's all.'

Feeling I should not be too inquisitive, I contented myself with 'oh'.

The man now lit his pipe again, as fiercely as before. He still didn't put any fresh tobacco in it, so that the material in the bowl, compounded of ash, dottle, shreds of tobacco and a glue made of saliva, must have been lethal. Snorting out smoke, he said, 'If one has any kind of connection with the College, and at least I have that, they let you stay there for nothing in the vacation.'

'Really? Do you have to do anything to earn it?'

'Yes, I have to spend one half of every third night up and dressed. Fire-watching. I don't object to that.'

I could imagine him looking out over the dark quadrangle, hearing the sough of wind among the trees in the garden, pondering Trakl.

'May I know your name?' he asked me, ready now to stride off.

'Leonard. Peter Leonard.'

'James Garrity.' We shook hands, rather formally. It struck me, suddenly, that he would have been quite at home at a German university, particularly in the earlier years of the century, the years of Trakl and Doderer and Rilke. Being a shy man, perhaps a recluse, he would have felt safe with the all-pervading formality of German manners in those days.

Garrity was almost ready to move off. Bending, he picked up the last remaining objects from his scatter on the grass, which were, I now saw, a couple of small bottles. In colour they were dark brown; in shape they were tapering, rather like miniature hock bottles.

'Your liquid lunch?' I asked, nodding towards them.

'I always have a supply with me when I go out on this kind of expedition. It never fails to help my . . . lucubrations.' He pronounced the last word with relish, enjoying its amplitude, its resonance.

'What is it?'

'Morrell's College Ale,' he said with solemn emphasis, as if uttering a rune. He put the two empty bottles carefully in his capacious pocket, then stood looking at me for a moment as if uncertain what to do next. He seemed one of those shy people who have difficulty in ending a conversation, so to make it easier for him I walked with him to the gate and into the lane, and for something to break the silence I said, 'Yours is an Ulster name, if I'm not mistaken.'

'Ancestrally, I believe. But I have no personal connection with Ulster. I was brought up at Burnham-on-Crouch.'

Moving a few yards along the hedge, he lifted up a bicycle he had tucked so deeply into the foliage that I had not even seen it as I walked past. It was large and heavy, with a huge metal carrier, and the handlebars drooped slightly, as if they had set out to be the dropped handlebars of a racing bike but had lost their nerve.

'This is my touring machine,' said Garrity. 'We've had many adventures together. I've pushed it up those gang-planks a few times, I can assure you.'

'Gang-planks?'

'On to the Channel packet. Across to Calais or Boulogne and then on to a train. Yes,' he slapped the saddle of his cumbrous bicycle as if it were the shoulder of a brother, 'we've had some adventures together. The Pyrenees. The Harz mountains, the Black Forest . . . my last few expeditions were all to Germany. It was essential to talk to my friends there who were increasingly intimidated by the odious regime. I did it as a means of satisfying myself that the heart of the country was still beating.'

As he spoke the last sentences, his voice rose in pitch and in volume and he also increased the pace of his utterance: the hesitation ceased and the words came out like a stream of machine-gun bullets. I was to get to know this, as time went by: it was in Garrity a sign of excitement, of being possessed by his subject.

Then, suddenly, with no indication that he was about to cease (another sign I was to get to know, meaning that he had uttered his fill about something important), he seized the handlebar grips, gave two or three rapid skipping motions, mounted and pedalled rapidly, almost furiously, away down the lane. I stood and watched as he rode towards the main road to Oxford and Episcopus. The level sun picked out his outline in sharp relief, the creases in his clothes and the slight bulge made in the hip-pocket by the small volume of Trakl that he had obviously had bound in leather because it was dropping to pieces from use. He knew, and had considered a thousand times, what every word in those poems 'meant'. No wonder there was, in his other hip-pocket, no corresponding bulge made by a pocket dictionary. Garrity was a serious man.

I turned back towards Mulberry Hall, immersed now in thoughtfulness. It wasn't every day, I reflected, that one met a serious man.

All through the summer I continued to buttress my relationship with Mairead. I was in absolutely no hurry. Having reached the stage of honestly admitting to myself that I wanted as full a relationship with her as I could get – as close and as important to both of us – I worked away at it patiently. I knew it was like building a bridge. Not until I was convinced it was strong enough would I trust it with my full weight.

And then, of course, as generally seems to be the case with matters concerning one's innermost emotions, events took over.

Christmas was upon us. We were actually going to get a few days off from the Ministry; the best part of a week, if I remember rightly. And on the evening before we departed there was to be the inevitable office party. Where on earth they got the food and drink, I don't know, but supplies were procured, and everybody was to meet in the lounge of a neighbouring hotel and have a Good Time.

I rang up Mairead and asked if she would be interested in coming. She replied that she couldn't do anything on that evening because she was going to be busy packing.

'A journey?'

'Yes, Dublin. It's a lovely bit of luck. I'd made up my mind I wasn't going to be able to go home and see my parents this Christmas because there's just no chance of getting a sea passage, and even if I could, the break we get's so short. But suddenly today I was offered a seat in a 'plane.'

'A 'plane? I hope you'll be careful.'

Her quick, gentle laugh came down the wire. 'Well, I'm not piloting the thing. It's a twelve-seater aircraft that's used for high-ranking diplomatic staff and V.I.P.s, and it's plastered all over with Irish national colours. Somebody couldn't make it at the last minute and there's a seat going. So I'll see you when I get back after Christmas.'

'What day will that be?'

'The twenty-ninth. I'll be at home on that evening and the next morning I'll be in the office. Now have a reasonable time yourself and don't *fret*.'

'All right. See you then. And look after yourself.'

'You too.' She rang off.

I didn't, though, wait till the twenty-ninth before seeing her again. I meant to, but things didn't work out that way. It was rather as if, as Wordsworth says in a crucial passage in *The Prelude*, 'I made no vows, but vows were then / Made for me.' I went along to the hotel on the evening of the party; I set out punctually and was one of the first to get there. And right from the beginning, as I was checking in my hat and coat, I knew I wasn't going to be staying long. I went into the lounge and had a few drinks and made some affable conversation. Then I returned downstairs again. The hotel had a coin telephone in a glass kiosk. I went in and dialled.

When I told Mairead I wanted to come and see her, she said, 'I thought this was an evening when you had to go to an office party.'

'Well, I had to stay up at the party, but I've done my duty and now I want to come and see you. It's important.'

'Why is it important?'

'It just is.'

There was a brief pause. I said, 'Have you got someone else with you or something?'

'No. I told you, I'm just packing. And ironing my — '

'I'll come then,' I said and left the 'phone box.

When I got out on to the pavement I realized that I was in an extraordinary mood. It wasn't the drink. As a matter of fact I had hardly drunk anything. It was just a – well, 'state of mind' seems altogether too weak a description. State of *mind?* It was a dimension of being. I began walking in the general direction of the tube station. Tottenham Court Road was the nearest one, and just inside its entrance there was a flower-seller. On this December evening, at about seven o'clock, someone had thought it worth while to set up a small stall and sell bunches of flowers. Perhaps they were intended for people who were having an evening out in the West End, going to a theatre and then on to a restaurant. The bunches of flowers were an outrageous price. I bought carnations for Mairead, a large bunch, more like two bunches.

Then I hailed a taxi. I wasn't going to wait on a dingy platform and sit in a slow, clanging underground train. To go from Tottenham Court Road to Tufnell Park was a long way and would cost a lot. I didn't care. The ordinary clogs and burdens of life seemed to have dissolved before the penetrating sun-rays of the happiness that possessed me. I was free. I was in a world that wasn't the ordinary hampering, judging, restricting, punishing world. The reason I was in that world was because I was innocent. I felt love, and only love. For months I had been plotting, tensely and sweatily, to get my penis into Mairead. Now, moving through the dark streets towards the small lighted space that held her, I knew that for tonight at any rate I didn't care whether I achieved any such thing, tonight or in the future. I had, for this one evening at least, no lust. I had no feeling towards Mairead except an immense tenderness, an overwhelming gratitude towards her simply for existing. Whatever she did would seem right because she did it; whatever she was would seem right because she was it; I could imagine no other order of things.

I paid off the taxi at Tufnell Park, emptying my pockets, and went across the road. It was a muggy, mild evening, such as you often get towards Christmas. I stood on the pavement, drawing in the damp air, feeling happy because I knew I was going to see Mairead. There was no street-lighting, but moonlight filtered

251

down from the sky, shining through a layer of cloud, enough to outline the dark mass of houses I was standing in front of. Behind those curtained windows there were lighted rooms, and in the rooms were people, living their unguessable lives. I felt whirled aloft on the fierce updraught of human existence, the sheer multitude of passions and experiences.

I rang the bell. Above my head Mairead's window went up and her voice called, 'Coming.' The window closed again. I waited, and sooner than I had thought possible she had the door open. She was wearing a thick chunky jersey and trousers. I was taken aback by the speed with which she had got downstairs. Eagerness? No, I then remembered, simply a need to get to me before her landlady did. She bounded up the stairs, I following her at my best pace.

The door of her room stood open. It certainly looked like the room of someone preparing for a journey. There were garments strewn about or hung over chairs, and an ironing-board occupied the centre of the room with the iron standing up on it. On the divan was a suitcase with the lid open. There were some books too, but they were beginning to disappear under the layers of clothes.

Mairead's jersey was black and it suited her well. The trousers made me think for a moment of Geraldine, who had gone about in trousers in the Oxford of 1931 as a deliberate gesture of unorthodoxy, a challenge to the College authorities at St Hilda's: disobedience to an unwritten rule. Nobody thought that about trousers now.

Not that such matters were uppermost in my mind. I still felt that preternatural lightness, that extraordinary relief from tension. I sat down and waited for the evening to begin. I loved her so much that she made everything perfect just by existing where I could see her.

I gave her the flowers and she said, 'Oh, how beautiful. What brightness to come out of a black December night! But you shouldn't have.'

'Yes, I should.'

'I shan't be here to change the water.'

'They wouldn't last more than a day or so anyway. Let them look beautiful for us this evening. That's sufficient.'

She found a vase and said again that they were beautiful. 'And I haven't got anything at all for you. I can't even offer you a drink. I didn't know anyone was coming and I've got nothing in the house.'

'I don't want anything. I came to see you, not to drink.'

'Have you eaten?'

As a matter of fact I hadn't eaten anything since lunch, but I told her I had had some food at the party. I thought that if she got the idea that she ought to feed me she would waste time hunting around for food. To me, anything at all that stopped her from just sitting and talking to me was a waste of time. It was the most delightful conversation I have ever had. Not that we talked about anything very important. We just reminisced and speculated and chatted and laughed and let our thoughts flow in whatever direction they wanted to. She was happy at the prospect of going home for a few days. She spoke affectionately of her parents, but obviously the strongest pull was that she loved Ireland. I drew her out. Would she go about at all, make many visits? What sort of places were there in her part of the country?

'We'll probably go out for the day in the country,' she said. 'Galway's not all that far and it has a lovely coast. So peaceful and remote. It's like another world. When I'm there I just can't believe the war is happening.'

Her imagination was caught now. She began to speak of Ireland. 'It's no good trying to describe it to you. Great long sandy beaches and breakers rolling and blue hills and an enormous sky over it. And long narrow roads with maybe just the odd cart going along them and the little white houses with cow-sheds. There's a place called Buncrana we sometimes go to.'

She was silent, remembering. Buncrana! I thought. What can Buncrana possibly be like, in what fold of the land, in what inlet of the sea does it lie? How can Stalingrad mean anything in Buncrana? Or El Alamein, or Hamburg? What does Tufnell Park look like when viewed from Buncrana?

But Tufnell Park, I thought, has Mairead in it, and that is everything, Buncrana included.

We sat for a while, just talking. She told me about the Ireland she loved and I told her about the England I loved, mostly in the Upper Thames Valley. Where she had just put Buncrana into my mind I put Lechlade, and Kelmscot, and Newbridge into hers. I told her about willows shading the deep pools, and swallows skimming the water on the broad open stretches, and fish rising for insects and making plopping circles as the sun began to slant down.

At last, remembering that she hadn't quite finished her packing, Mairead got off the divan and moved about fetching garments and putting them into the suitcase. Finally she brought out a towel, folded it, put it into the case and closed the lid. Then she fastened the catches and said, 'There, that's finished.'

She picked up the suitcase and carried it over to the side of the room.

'Let me do that,' I said, half getting up from my chair. But I wasn't quick enough.

'It's all right. It's not a very big case and I'm quite strong. I'll have to do plenty of carrying tomorrow, anyway.' She sat down on the divan again, facing me.

'I don't like to think about tomorrow,' I said. 'You'll be away in another country, where I can't see or hear you.'

'No, but you can think about me.'

'I do that anyway, because I love you.'

'Funny,' she said, 'you've never said you loved me before, and I've known it for a long time.'

'Of course you have. It's been very obvious.'

She thought for a moment and then looked at me and said, 'Is it nice, loving me?'

'It's wonderful.'

'It makes you feel good, does it?'

'It makes me feel that the world is basically an all-right place.'

'Some people don't find it so.'

'Mairead, I know there's a terrible lot of suffering in the world, and believe me I'm not without compassion for it. But since I got to know you and realized that I love you it's made an absolutely fundamental difference to me. I mean, I know intellectually that the world's full of evil and suffering, but the fact that it contains you is evidence that it's pretty solidly right somewhere.'

'Isn't that just a bit of an exaggeration?' she asked, but she was smiling gently. 'Just an elaborate way of saying you find me attractive?'

'No. It's a statement of approval of the universe.'

Mairead laughed softly. 'The universe didn't do too badly either when it produced you, Peter. Come her and give me a kiss.'

I went there and gave her a kiss. She fell back on the divan and I went with her. We lay together for a moment. Her arm was underneath my body, and after a moment she drew it free and put it round my neck. We were now frankly in each other's arms. I was silent. She was silent. Then she said, speaking softly with her mouth close to my ear, 'Peter, you don't have to think of me as being in another country when I go to Ireland tomorrow. I'll take you with me.'

With my lips close to her ear, and my voice quiet, I said, 'How do you propose to do that?'

'Like this,' she said and suddenly sat upright. 'I'll show you how I'll take you with me,' and she stepped lightly off the bed on to the floor and began to shed her clothes.

Hypnotized, dragging at buckles, tearing off buttons, I did the same. We were back in the same position, lying together with our arms round each other, but now her smooth naked body was pressed against mine and in that instant my ethereal mood melted away: I was a man, and I needed to possess her urgently, immediately, before my whole being exploded in a fountain of molten lava. It had to be now, *now* – I was maddened beyond the possibility of finesse. Boldly I reached down and explored the neat little thicket at her crotch. With a surge of relief I found it as heavy with dew as the sweet grass of the meadows beside the Cherwell, when one walks out in them early on an April morning. There was no longer anything to wait for. I waited no longer.

12

Half-way through the following week my father telephoned me at the office, the only time he did so during the whole war.

'Any chance you could get down to Oxford a bit earlier than usual this Saturday, Peter?' he asked.

'How much earlier?'

'Well . . . If you were here about half-eleven that'd be about perfect.'

'Not a chance,' I said. 'I'd have to take the whole morning away from the office, and as it happens we've got a load of stuff that's just been dumped on us and we've got to — '

'You see,' he said, 'it's Job Trundle.'

'Been taken ill, has he?'

'No,' Dad said. 'He's been taken dead. He had some sort of attack yesterday afternoon and they rushed him to the Radcliffe, but he was dead when he got there.'

Good old Trundle, I thought. It was so like him to act decisively. Just his autocratic style.

'We've been arranging his funeral,' Dad said. 'It mostly fell to us, with a bit of help from Fred Peake. There don't seem to be any relations. Of course there was his sister.'

'What sort of shape is she in?'

'Bad. It was too much of a shock to her. Can't seem to get herself together.'

I had known that Trundle was a bachelor, or perhaps a widower of many years, and that he lived with an aged sister. She appeared very rarely in the street and never in the pub, a tiny wizened saurian creature, nothing like the mountainous Trundle. And now she was alone.

'The old Bargeman's won't be the same without him, Peter,' my father said. 'Six o'clock every evening, regular as clockwork, and he'd been doing it since well before I had the license. Last night was the first six o'clock of my working life that I didn't see him. It's right that he should be buried from here.'

Strangers will sit in his chair at the end of the bar. For a few evenings it will be empty, but as time goes by newcomers will enter, and sit in Job Trundle's chair as if it were just a chair like any other. And they will be right: it *is* just a chair like any other. O world! O life! O time! On whose dark steps I climb!

'Isn't there any chance you could stretch a point and get down by half-past eleven, Peter?' my father's voice went on, with a note of appeal in it. 'Saturday at twelve's the funeral, at Hinksey, and it's the only time the vicar can do it. We have to be ready to move off from here at quarter-to.'

I could see the whole scene in my mind's eye. It would be like Ernest's funeral, without the college scouts. Or perhaps there would even be some of them too, solid dark-suited men. Dust we are, into dust we shall return.

'I'm really sorry, Dad,' I said. 'If I don't handle this shipment, a lot of people's plans will go sky-high. I'm not trying to make out that the war depends on me, but I do have a job to do. You know I'd come if I could.'

255

'I understand,' he said. 'Come and see us when you can.'

He rang off and I sat for a few minutes tasting his disappointment and picturing the change in his life. Being the youngest of the family, he had been a child when his own father died, and for thirty years of his adult, responsible working life, Job Trundle had filled that gap. Trundle was obstinate, he was opinionated, he was comically wrong-headed, but he had sat in the same place at the same time every evening and he had been a father-figure to my father. At second hand, even I would miss him.

By the time Mairead and I emerged into the full sunlight of our happiness, there was already a dark clump of shadow moving into position, ready to pass over it. And this shadow, by a sad irony, had gathered itself out of material that should have gone to the making of a rainbow. The war was manifestly beginning to wind towards its end. No war, no London job. No London job, no regular contact with Mairead; and, concurrently, a full resumption of my responsibilities and duties in Oxford – to my work as an historian, my teaching fellowship, my family. Mairead would at one stroke become what I knew she would never consent to be: the tawdry centrepiece of that shabby, unsatisfying thing, a Double Life.

No, when the war went Mairead would go. This produced a strange state of mind in me. Whenever there was a step forward in the war, I genuinely welcomed it. Even before Mairead and I became lovers, Italy had capitulated, the population so weary of the war that the Anglo-American invasion of September 1943 was hardly more than a formality and was followed by Italian surrender within a week. (Sicily had been a very different story, but then Sicily had been defended by Germans.)

The Atlantic was cleared of U-boats, or nearly so. Churchill, Roosevelt and Stalin had met at Quebec and issued a demand for unconditional surrender. And every road in England was humming with American trucks and troop-carriers, as the assault on Western Europe was prepared week by week. For the population, all these things could be put in the Plus column. In the Minus column there was one unadmitted entry, and it was steadily increasing: exhaustion. We were in the fifth year of privation, disruption, fatigue, monotony. And just as everyone hit their lowest point, in 1944 the first 'flying bomb', a relatively home-made affair, essentially a pilotless aircraft, landed on English soil, to be followed, after the June Allied invasion of Normandy, in September by V2 rockets. No warning could be given against them: they suddenly dropped from the sky, unannounced, wiping out a fish-queue here, taking off the roof of a church there, smashing into a hospital wing somewhere else. This engendered a tension so unceasing and so deep that, even when one was no longer conscious of it, it surfaced as irritability, lack of concentration, tiredness, tiredness. Even I felt all these things, and I was one of the lucky ones, with a refuge out in the peace of the Oxfordshire countryside which I could get away to almost every week-end.

That was just the trouble. To me, Oxford wasn't peace, not any more. I was away from Mairead and worried about her, spending her week-ends in London.

So the sands of the war ran out (good). And the sands of our wild, joyous, guilty, beautiful love affair ran out also (bad).

Sometimes, when I was away from her, I would think over the ecstasy, the intensity, of our love-making. What fuelled it? Love, yes. Joy and passion, yes. But was there, at its centre, something else – a desperation which made it all the more powerful? Had my desire, like the flame of a candle, a core of shadow that seemed to intensify its brightness by the contrast with its own darkness?

In this atmosphere, 1945 came in. The Allied invasion had gone well. There were setbacks, but it was now obvious that the war was going to end quite soon, possibly this year. Even so, there was many a weary step still to be taken. Many a man now walking about would be dead, a plain military cross over him, before this job was finished.

One dark, sullen afternoon in the early part of February I had a totally unexpected visitor at my office in the Ministry. Primrose, of all people. I knew straight away that something unusual must have happened, and probably something disastrous. She wasn't the type that made social calls.

'Sit down, Primrose,' I said, hastening forward with the rickety office chair. 'Let me organize you a cup of tea.'

'I won't stay long,' she said.

'Well, stay long enough to have a cup of tea and tell me how things are with you,' I said. In other words, cough it up: what's happened? What's wrong?

Primrose looked in a bad state. As a rule she was so contained, so securely packed away in her own dimension somewhere, that one felt the ordinary stresses of life didn't affect her. But today she looked as if things had been getting at her. There were signs of fatigue in her face; the skin, which seemed to be stretched tightly over the bones, was sallow rather than pale and beautiful as it normally was, and at the side of her mouth was a little cluster of what I took to be period spots. She wasn't in good shape. I felt protective, the first time I had felt any such thing about Primrose.

She accepted the awful office tea I gave her, and sat there holding the cardboard cup between her two hands, as a child does, and looking across the desk at me. I waited for her to speak.

'I've got a funny reason for coming to see you,' she said at last. 'Not much like me, really. A bit out of character.'

I nodded encouragingly.

'You see, Peter,' she said with an obvious effort, 'the next time you see Brian he's likely to be pretty unkind about me.'

'Unkind? About you?'

'Well, about something I've done. Or not done, rather. He thinks I've let him down.'

'It doesn't sound like Brian,' I said, 'to tell his younger brother that he feels let down by his wife.'

'He might not, of course,' she said. 'But I know he's very angry with me. It's something I made a sudden decision over. I just couldn't go through with it, I'd have felt so false.'

'Look, Primrose, you'd better say what it is, because as long as I'm just guessing I can't — '

'He wanted me to go to Cecil Kimber's funeral with him, and at the last minute I wouldn't go. I let him go by himself.'

For a moment I genuinely didn't register the words.

'Cecil who?' I said. 'Whose *what*?'

'Well, you must know Cecil Kimber is dead.'

'Of course I didn't know. I never saw a word about it.'

'Well, there wasn't much in the papers. I think the *Oxford Mail* was the only one that carried it. I mean, he wasn't exactly in the limelight.'

'But *dead*? Surely he was quite young?'

'Yes, just in his fifties. And he wasn't ill or anything. It was one of those silly railway accidents. Two trains just brushed each other and one carriage fell over on its side. One passenger got killed and it had to be him. Happened at King's Cross Station, I think. He'd got a job with some engineering firm in the north and he was just going up there after a trip home.'

'A railway accident.' I was silent. Brian had always so despised railways, seeing them as dinosaurs that went on cluttering up the earth, claiming resources that ought to be channelled into motor cars. And now one of them had killed his idol.

'So he went to the funeral,' I said. 'And you didn't.' I kept my voice gentle. After all, it was her choice whether she went to a funeral or not. Heather hadn't come to Uncle Ernest's, and I had accepted that she had a valid reason.

Primrose hesitated a moment and then the words came out in a rush, 'I just couldn't go. I'd said I would, and then at the last minute I just found I couldn't do it.'

'Any . . . assignable reason?'

She looked away. Then came another rush of words. 'It isn't anything to do with not having sympathy for Brian. He's always built his life round Kim and what they'd do together after the war. This is a very bad blow for him, and I want to help him to get over it if I can. I tell you, Peter, I came downstairs this morning ready to go to the funeral and there was Brian standing in the hallway with his hat and coat on ready to go. But then I just stopped where I was on the bottom stair and I looked at his face. It seemed so *closed*, somehow. As if he was telling himself that he was facing a brick wall and wouldn't ever be able to climb over it. As if his life was over.'

'That's probably just how he was feeling at that particular moment.'

'All right, fair enough, but what I was feeling at that moment was that I wanted to get into the light and air and out of this tomb that seemed to have been built around us. It was closing right in. I felt I could have touched it with my hands. And I stood there and said to him, "Brian, I don't know if you're going to understand this, but I don't want to come with you to the funeral. I want you to go by yourself and get all that grief and hopelessness out of your system before you come back to me." '

'What did he say?'

'He just gave me a look without any expression in it, and then he turned straight out and went through the door and I heard him drive off.'

'When was this?'

'Today, about ten o'clock.'

'So you haven't seen him since?'

'No. I came here.'

I didn't know what to say to that. It was hardly for me to tell her that it had been her duty at least to wait at home till he got back and she saw what state of mind he was in. I just looked at her across the desk and said, 'Well, I hope it's been a help to you, seeing me.'

'It has, a bit. At least I know now that if Brian comes and tells you what he thinks of me for letting him down you'll have heard my side of it.'

'Primrose,' I said, 'I would never take sides between you and Brian.'

'You might not be able to help it.'

'I just wouldn't do it. I'm sure Brian isn't the easiest person to live with.'

'Well,' she said, 'I don't want a man who's the easiest person to live with. I just want a man who's alive.'

Preparing to make her departure, Primrose now said to me as she got up from her chair, 'By the way, one nice thing did happen lately, just before that awful business of Kim's accident. We had another evening at the club in Chipping Norton.'

'Oh? Who took you this time?'

'Chet, of course. The one you remember.'

'Oh,' I said. 'Oh. Really? Is Chet still . . . around?'

'It sounded as if you were going to say, "Is Chet still alive?" ' she said with a small, quizzical smile.

'Well, to be honest I was. His job didn't exactly put survival first in its scale of values.'

'Well, as it happens he is alive and in all probability he'll stay that way. He completed his recognized number of missions. You know, because it's so hazardous they only give everyone a fixed number of missions to fly, and if you survive that number you're pulled out and made an instructor. That's what he's doing now.'

'Is that so?' I said. 'Well, good for Chet. He took his risks and he came through. Does that really mean that combat flying is over for him?'

'As far as anyone can foresee. If the war were to go on for another two or three years he'd probably have to take another tour of combat duty, but I don't think it will.'

'No, I don't think it will either. Well, say hello to Chet from me when you see him.'

'That's if I see him,' she answered, and then she was gone. Except that in the doorway she turned and said, 'Thanks for letting me talk, Peter.'

'Any time,' I said. I sat down at the desk again and thought about Brian, and the long series of disappointments his life was turning out to be. No wonder, I reflected, that the goddess Fortune is depicted as having a wheel, which she spins at random. Chet signs on as a ball-turret gunner and flies all those missions and comes out unharmed. Cecil Kimber takes a train from King's Cross and gets killed. And Brian goes to the funeral, alone.

Mairead and I were talking in bed. It was a quarter-past seven in the evening. At about nine we would get up and go to a restaurant for a meal, then I would go down to the tube station and take the train back to my lodgings. This is how we generally handled our evenings together.'

'What does your wife look like?'

'I'll show you some photographs of her.'

'That's not what I asked you, Peter Leonard. You can't tell what a person looks like from a photograph. The only way you can tell is to get someone to describe them.'

'Am I the ideal person to do that?'

'What stupid questions you do ask to be sure. I didn't say you were the ideal person, but you're the only person I know who's ever seen her, so what's she like?'

'Quite tall. Straight back. Fair hair, blue eyes,'

'Does she look like a German?'

'She looks like a Northern European, but not specifically like a German. She could be Dutch. She could be a French blonde from Normandy.'

'Blue eyes, you say?'

'Yes.'

'What kind of blue?'

'Cornflower. Not electric like yours.'

'Stop comparing us.'

'I'm sorry. I wasn't.'

'You said the blue of her eyes wasn't like mine. I don't want to know about that. If you come to anything else about her that's like me or not like me, keep it to yourself, d'you hear?'

'All right.'

'What's her voice like?'

'Middle register.'

'Does she like to sing?'

'Not specially. She has no ear for music.'

'What art does she like?'

I thought for a moment. 'Equestrianism.'

'When she was a girl, did she want to be a ballet dancer?'

'If she did, it was trampled out of her pretty damn' quick.'

'Are her parents poor?'

'Depends how you view poverty. Tenant farmers. Tightly stretched, I'd say, rather than actually poor. They can't sink into the working class and yet they haven't the resources to compete for a middle-class standard of living.'

'You analyse them very dispassionately, don't you? Is that how you analyse me behind my back?'

'Of course not. I never talk about you behind your back, for one thing.'

'But you think about me behind my back.'

'I think about you when you're not with me for exactly the same reasons as I think about you when you are with me.'

'Sounds as if you never think about anything else, much.'

'I don't, much.'

'Why?'

'Because I love you.'

A pause devoted to non-verbal activities, then:

'D'you think about your wife when you're with her?'

'When I'm with her, I attend to her, yes.'

'And when you're not with her?'

'I don't think about her much when I'm not with her.'

'Why?' .

I moved her into a position where I could look her straight in the eyes, and said, 'What d'you want me to say to that? D'you want me to say it's because I don't love her?'

'I just want you to tell me the truth. Whatever feelings you have I want you to tell me about them. If you want to. Otherwise don't bother.'

'You're getting huffy now.'

'I'm not. For your information, I don't get huffy. It's too petty.'

'It's just that you're digging so hard, taking so much trouble to get me to say whether I love my wife or not.'

'Yes, and after all I can't do it, can I? I can try as hard as I like, but you're not going to bloody well tell me whether you love your wife or not. You might at least tell me the truth now you've fucked me a few times. I thought men only lied to women when they were trying to get them into the net. Well, you've got me, you've made it, so why not tell me the truth?'

'What makes you say I'm not telling you the truth?'

'Because you're not telling me anything. That's usually a sign that a lie's being covered up.'

'Mairead, *you* speak, *you* tell *me*. What lie am I covering up?'

'That's for you to say.'

I raised myself on one elbow and looked down at her face on the pillow, determined to utter a passionate remonstrance, to beat off these attacks once and for all. What did she want of me? To renounce Heather formally, to give an undertaking in so many words that I would never go back to her? No, surely not. Or if yes, it revealed a deep contradiction in her. She never talked in this strain when we were out of bed. Up and dressed, the controlled and self-possessed Miss Mairead Hoey, she was perfectly willing to speak coolly of our relationship as temporary, a radiance that had come out of the clouds and would go back into the clouds, a beautiful game which would accept its end when the whistle blew. These murmurs of insurrection against our self-limiting ordinance, these sudden whiffs of steam from some deep-down sulphurous spring, only came when we were stripped of our daytime personalities and our professional masks, reduced to nakedness, anonymity, mutual helpless need and overwhelming impulse, the poor bare forked animal.

I opened my mouth, drew in my breath to deliver the strong, authoritative answer that I felt was needed. But as she lay looking up at me, her breasts were uncovered, and they began to hypnotize me as my recently spent forces began once more to muster to the flag. In a word, I found myself sidetracked. Or perhaps it was the flat, boring, obvious truths I was about to utter that would have been the sidetrack.

The next evening we again went to bed before going out to dinner and had, at about the same point, a rather similar conversation, terminated in the same way. And the next, and the next. And many times thereafter, as the weary and blood-heavy months of 1945 dragged their way forward towards that scarcely-to-be-imagined goal we thought of as 'peace'.

About now, one of the carapaces of my life developed a serious crack: I discovered that the odious Hunt had joined the United Universities Club. I saw his smooth, expressionless face at the end of the bar one evening, and for a moment did not recognize him because he was in uniform. The United Universities was not a Service club and most of the members wore civilian suits; Hunt's pale eyes looked out over the collar of a well-cut, well-pressed khaki tunic. It was, as I saw when we happened to be in closer range, the official uniform of a War Correspondent. What was he doing here? Something, I was certain, that I would distrust if I knew about it. I was totally antipathetic to him and had been so ever since our undergraduate days. He saw human beings as funny little puppets, and he picked out whatever aspects of their show he was told to pick out, and wrote little pieces which he then handed over to nourish part of a news empire. These 'pieces' were like bowls of gelatine, a neutral substance but capable of taking on any flavour if that flavour was stirred in at the right stage. Hunt, before composing a piece, knew what flavour he had been instructed to add, the object being to make the consumer like or dislike the mixture when it was doled out: to find it amusing, or pathetic, or contemptible, or frightening, or even – in very, very rare cases – admirable. Hunt had no opinions or attitudes of his own; it was always the Someone Else, the faceless figure with the cheque-book, who dictated the flavour that went into the gelatine. And for Hunt, the word 'betrayal', though he would have known where to find it in the dictionary, did not exist in the full sense in which words can be said to exist. It was a sound. If he had been accused of it, he would have felt no shame, for shame arises from having values and Hunt had none.

I avoided him, as I always had avoided him. I didn't know where Hunt had spent the last two or three years, but he appeared now to be based in London, because to my annoyance he took to haunting the United Universities Club. It mattered the less to me now that I was spending so many of my evenings with Mairead, but I still dropped in there when I had nowhere else to go, and I saw him on a depressingly high proportion of those occasions. One lunchtime I went in and found him sitting in a corner with Molly Whitworth: so *that* was all still going on. As I passed near them I caught her clear, penetrating voice above the general hum of conversation: 'Ultimately I suppose all that stuff comes out of Heidegger.' Heidegger? I thought. What the hell is Heidegger to Hunt? Was anyone going to tell me that *he*, of all people, was interested in modern German philosophy? Well, he must have had *some* reason for picking the Whitworth brains. Hunt never did anything without his eye on some sort of main chance. Heidegger, yet! What was going on in his little brain?

In the summer of that year, the Allied forces roared across Germany. And as they went they burst open the gates of the concentration camps, Belsen, Buchenwald, Auschwitz, names to be accursed for ever, and the survivors crawled out. Most of these were Jews. A tiny minority of homosexuals who had not been discreet enough to escape notice; a pathetic fringe of gipsies swept up from the roadsides; but mostly, and overwhelmingly, Jews, Jews, Jews, six million Jews, men, women, old, young, even tiny children.

We had heard of Nazi anti-Semitism for years before the war, the world's press had carried photographs of Jews being mocked and humiliated; in academic circles stories were told of brilliant Jewish scholars being dismissed from their posts, of racial-origin questionnaires being circulated at even the most august German universities. And we had known of the existence of the camps. But somehow it had been possible to hold on to a few shreds of reason-saving incredulity. Pacifists and other groups opposed to the war had pointed out the tradition, observed in every country, of exaggerating the enemy's cruelty in order to stiffen people's will to fight: all these horror stories about what went on in concentration camps – the children in the gas-ovens, the dreadful experiments performed by Nazi doctors – were (they derisively declared) exactly the kind of thing the propaganda machine *would* come out with, and when peace returned we would see that the reality was very different.

What we did in fact see when those gates were burst open was that the reality was even worse than the stories.

'I don't know what to do with this knowledge,' I said to Mairead as I lay with my arms round her, holding her close to me so that the human warmth of her body would be something to set against the chill in the marrow of my bones. 'I can't deal with it – I can't get my mind round it.'

'You've got to try, Peter,' she said. 'You have, I have, everybody has. Because there has to be a future.'

'But what kind of future is imaginable . . . now that we know, *for certain* and not just in our worst nightmares, that people can do things like that to other people?'

She was silent for a moment and then said, 'But look, Peter, you must always have known that people were capable of monstrous cruelty to one another?'

'Yes, but not on this scale.'

'Is scale the really important thing? After all, if one human being is sickeningly cruel to one other human being, the principle's established – people can be like that.'

'But Mairead, these things went on with the permission of a whole society. They were *government* decisions.'

'I don't suppose the worst excesses were particularly well publicized among the German population. It's usually the case, isn't it, that when a government behaves with really desperate cruelty towards some identified group, they don't tell the population much about it. The decision not to relieve the suffering of the Irish in the potato famine a hundred years ago, so that a million of them starved to death – that was a result of government policy in England. But it wasn't announced as such, was it?'

'I don't see that it was comparable with – '

'On the contrary, it was strictly comparable because it was genocide. Those people were killed because they were Irish. These others have been killed because they were Jews.'

'Yes, but if you're looking for a shred of justification for the apathy of the English populace, you could point to the fact that Ireland's a different country, separated from England by water. These Jews were citizens, they were people's familiar neighbours.'

'Well, if you want an example of people who were known as individuals, what about the Jews who were driven out of England in Edward the First's time? You know all about things like that, it's your job to know.'

'Well, of course I know that when Edward dispossessed the Jews and threw them out of the country, there was no backlash from the population as a whole.'

'*Backlash*? You really do go in for understatement, don't you? The people behaved like an Arkansas lynch mob.'

'Oh, come, that's a bit – '

'What about all the sailors who offered to help them to get away to France, and then just took their money and landed them on some island in the fog?'

'Well, of course some individuals – '

'What about the bastard of a ship's captain who took a cargo of Jews and told them he'd take them to France, and then landed them on a spit of sand that was going to be covered by the tide. You've read the story – as he shoved off he shouted to them to pray for another Moses to come and divide the sea for them. Don't say there weren't children and old people among his passengers, yes, and pregnant women too. He was a natural Nazi, and he was in the thirteenth century.'

'I still think this is different. I still think it's to do with scale.'

'That's because you're English. You'd feel different if it were possible for you to become an Irishman for a year. The Irish are the Jews of the British Isles.'

I had never considered the matter in that light. But then, after every conversation I had with Mairead, I seemed to end up considering some matter in an unaccustomed light. I realized, now that I came to think about it, that Irish peasants dying of starvation in the Great Hunger can't have looked much different from inmates of Belsen, except that they didn't have numbers tattooed on their wrists and that no one took their photographs.

Germany was now fighting desperately in what was clearly the last phase of the war; fighting not with any idea of winning, but to try to be in a better bargaining position at the conference table. It was no use. On 23 March British forces crossed the Rhine. On 2 May the German forces in Italy surrendered, followed three days later by the surrender of all Germans in North-West Europe. The few isolated pockets in other parts of the world could be cleaned out at leisure. The war with Germany was over.

And bells were ringing, minutes being exchanged, urgent meetings set up in the world of diplomacy, and Mairead finished her day's work later and later: at seven, at eight, nine, even ten sometimes. I hadn't seen anyone work such hours since Brian's days with the M.G. racing cars.

'Well, at least we'll have a celebration,' I said to her when the announcement came that 8 May was to be set aside as an official day of celebration, V.E. Day for Victory in Europe. 'I know a place where we can get a bottle of champagne, if we eat a meal with it.'

'Not possible, I'm afraid.'

'Not *possible*? But Mairead, for God's — '

'I have to go to Dublin that week. Please don't make me feel bad about it, Peter. After all, there's a lot to be getting on with there too, you know.'

Dublin! Could there be a better illustration of the fact that Mairead had come into my life on loan? That her strength and intelligence, her idealism, yes, even her beauty and her lissom body belonged to the land that had sent her out and would always have the power to call her back?

So it was that on Tuesday, 8 May, I was in London and, amid a city of joyous, carolling, brawling, sprawling gregariousness I was alone. In preparation for a day with Mairead I had pitched some yarn at Mulberry Hall about how I couldn't get home till the week-end because the end of hostilities had caused us a final burst of work (which was true enough), and now I was stuck with it. I stayed at the office a long time in the afternoon, clearing up odd jobs. Then I went to my lodgings and had a bath. Half-way through getting dressed I paused and looked at myself in the mirror in my bedroom. Peter Leonard, historian, civil servant, preparing to face the rigours of peace. I looked sallow, pouchy, middle-aged and rather bad-tempered. Some time during the previous five-and-a-half years, my youth had dribbled out through my toenails. What the hell, I thought. What can it matter any more? I even felt quite cheerful. It was one of those times in one's life when the situation is so bad that it's good. I went down the stairs and onto the street which now, towards six in the evening, was full of people.

Normally I stay away from crowds. They make me feel slightly claustrophobic, so that I catch myself looking round for hand-holds to climb up the nearest building and at least get my head above the sea of other heads. And they make me feel that the real trouble with the human race is that there are just too damn' *many* of them. Not a good feeling, that.

In fact I think that the evening of V.E. Night was the only occasion in my life when I have voluntarily gone amongst a crowd. I actually *wanted*, for once, to feel myself one with the people of England and particularly the people of London. Yes, I felt proud of them, and proud of myself to the extent that I was one of them. They had endured so much, for so long, and had carried their burdens in such a positive spirit, with so much humour, so much courage, so many instances of self-sacrifice. And the cause for which it had all been undertaken had been so obviously worth pursuing.

Yes, just for once I wanted to be out in the street with the people, to swirl along with them, to sing with them, dance with them, shout for joy with them. But inside my mood there was folded a tight bud of loneliness. I was glad to be part of this national scene, but I would have loved to have someone to be part of it *with*. Well – I forced myself to be honest – not just someone. Mairead. Why on God's earth did she have to be away in Dublin just at this moment in the history of the world?

Wouldn't Heather have done? Better still, Heather and Michael together? I felt close to them, didn't I? Yes, undeniably. But I didn't feel the need of them this evening. I was sure there would be a celebration going on at Mulberry Hall, a turn-out of villagers and drinks all round, and I had in fact spoken to them on the telephone and ascertained that they would be part of it. But to me, V.E. Night in London was a climax to the war – to most people there the only climax that mattered, since the European war had impinged on their lives infinitely more than the Japanese conflict – and to me celebrating its victorious end meant being among Londoners.

But the end of the war also meant the end of Mairead, the end of our relationship, and at that thought I shivered. That she should be away from me tonight, when I most wanted her, was a portent of the sundering that was, now, so soon to come.

Hurrying to get from under the bat-shadow of this knowledge, I plunged into the excited throng that moved around the streets of central London, and my memories from that point on become slightly blurred. I don't think I was drunk, though of course I went in and out of pubs and each time I went into one I had a glass of something. Beer, mostly. You couldn't get wine in the average pub in those days, and spirits were virtually unobtainable. I just drank beer, quite modestly, in half-pint glasses.

As it happens, I met an American before the evening was out, an officer in one or other of the fighting services. It's the details I don't remember with any clarity: what service he was in, his rank, or how, for that matter, it happened that I got talking to him at all – except that on V.E. Night you just talked to anybody. He was, and again I don't know why, one of a knot of seven or eight men I happened to find myself gathered up and swept along with, and I do remember that the others were all British naval officers. They were very smart in their shore-going uniforms and I felt lowly in my shabby make-do-and-mend wartime jacket and baggy trousers. But it didn't matter. They were wonderfully affable, and though they obviously didn't know me from Adam, nor how they came to be talking to me, they joked with me and slapped me on the back and kept standing me drinks.

I recall the occasion best as a series of pictures. I see us all in an upstairs room, looking down through tall windows on the crowded street below, with the long summer dusk just giving way to darkness. There were, as I say, seven or eight of these naval officers, and I remember three of them in particular. One was tall and nonchalant and reminded me somewhat of Knowlton. (Where was Knowlton? What was he doing this evening? God bless him.) The second was a slight, thin-faced fellow, sharp as a needle, whose interjected comments showed a real turn of wit. The third, who happened to be standing at my elbow, was a shortish, thick-set man with brown curly hair and an expression of imperturbable good humour. He looked immensely strong, and though his face was not particularly intelligent it spoke of character and determination; you felt that once he started to do a job he would finish it, carry it through. He struck me as a good man to have on one's side in a tight corner.

The American, for his part, was much more taciturn. He was in any case a specimen of the taciturn kind of American, long-shanked, with a bony jaw, economical with words, whose humour, when he has any, tends to be of the laconic variety. It was this character who remarked to me, with a nod at the capering multitude below us on the pavement, 'All a bit previous, ain't it?'

I knew what he meant. 'They think the war's over,' I said, nodding. 'They're mistaken, of course, but you can't really blame them.'

'Can't blame 'em, eh?' he said musingly.

'No,' I said. 'The Far East has never been a reality to them, they can't really imagine it and most of them have never even seen a Japanese. It's all just a never-never land to them, unless of course they have some personal — '

'I wish it was a never-never land to me,' he interrupted. 'I didn't have but one brother and I was mighty fond of him. His name was Charlie and he was two, three years younger'n me.'

'Yes?' I said, but I knew what was coming.

'Charlie was on the Bataan March,' he said. 'Leastways, he was on it at the beginning. He wasn't still on it at the end.' He drained his glass, suddenly, and turned to look me full in the face. 'We still got those bastard Japs to settle with,' he said quietly.

I was silent. I knew, as everyone knew who followed the war news even as sketchily as I did, that American and Filipino soldiers had put up a desperate resistance at Bataan; that they had finally surrendered, exhausted and in many cases wounded; that they had then been marched forty-five miles to a rail-head at San Fernando, then de-trained at Capas and marched twelve miles to the prison cages that awaited them. These were not long marches by military standards, but a great many of the men had not survived, and I knew, in general, why. I did not know the particular details. I did not want to know the particular details. But I wondered why the man I was talking to was out on that evening in London, listening to the cheers and whoops and laughter. Perhaps it was better than sitting in a room by himself.

Unable to continue the conversation with the American, I deliberately let myself be sucked into the swirl of geniality from the R.N.V.R. men, which was at my other elbow.

At that moment one of them was rather insistently launching the suggestion that they (or we?) should all go to the Something-or-other Club; I forget its name. 'Get some female company there. Could do with a bit of female company,' he repeated several times; the drink was beginning to affect his diction. 'All these chaps. Jolly good chaps. But chaps all the same. Get a bit sick of chappery, eh? Need a bit of femi . . . feminin . . . Well, girls, eh?'

'What are these girls,' the man who resembled Knowlton asked, 'The ones at this club?'

'Hostesses.' It came out more like 'Hoe steshes.'

'You mean whores, I suppose,' said the sharp man.

'You can take it that way or not. Take your choice. Hostesses will . . . fall in with your wishes. Depends what your wishes might be. I didn't say anything about whores, now did I? All I said was, appreciate a bit of femininin . . .' He looked round. 'Come on, let's go round there. It's only a couple of streets away.'

'I should have thought, Bob,' the thickset man said, 'that if you want female company this is one night when you could have it for nothing. Just walk out into the street and go up to any girl you like the look of and start talking to her. That's female company right off, and who knows what it might ripen into – eh, sport?' He brought me into it.

Bob shook his head. 'Can't do it. Haven't been introduced. Can't speak to woman I haven't been introduced to. Had a strict upbringin'.'

'You must have done, old son,' the thickset man said. 'Still, I don't suppose it was any stricter than mine. Brought up in the country, I was. Place called Ducklington in Oxfordshire. Had to make our own amusements, I can tell you, only there weren't any to make. If you didn't ride a horse there was nothing, absolutely nothing, you could do.'

An enormous hunch was stirring in my mind. I decided to try a running shot. It was very much of an outside chance but, after all, what would it matter if I missed?

'I was just wondering,' I said, 'whether, growing up in that district, you ever met a man I used to be acquainted with?'

'Well, let's have his name, sport.'

'Tom Burrell,' I said.

'Tom B. – Well! That's odd! Fancy you knowing old Tom!'

'I didn't know him very well.'

'He and I were very thick. Grew up together, you might say. Used to get up to all sorts of things when we were schoolboys. Lost touch a bit later on. He got the flying bug. Never would talk about anything else. I was interested up to a point, but with Tom it had to be hook, line and sinker. At one time he even had a scheme that he and I were going to buy a 'plane together. He was so persuasive he nearly talked me into it.'

Just to distance it a bit I said, 'But you didn't go along with it.'

'In the end, no. I mean, what would I be doing with an aeroplane? Even a half share of one? Actually Tom just wanted me to write the cheque. It would have been his 'plane all right, but I'd have bought it. I quite understood, but I wasn't really in a position to do it. I mean, I had a bit of cash, but not that much. My old man was still alive then, and he kept me on a pretty short lead. Good for me, I don't doubt.' He laughed imperturbably.

Yes, I said to him silently, he made you go to Birmingham for a spell on the shop floor in the factory. That was when you were knocking it off with Heather, weren't you? Remember Heather, Tom's sister? Remember how he wanted you to marry her so that some of your money would be channelled into the Burrell family? I'm sure you remember a lot about Heather. I know a lot about her myself, too, as it happens.

'You're completely different from how I imagined you,' I said to him, aloud.

'What was that, sport? I didn't quite catch — '

'You're hardly how I imagined the typical inhabitant of Ducklington,' I said. I spoke fairly quietly, and my words were probably difficult to catch amid the mounting swell of conversation.

'What's that about Ducklington, sport? You been there?'

'Look, Dick, are you coming or not?' The 'femininity' man, who was now finally making up his party, confronted the thickset man aggressively. 'Are you going to come and have the next stage of the evening with us, or just stand about here drinking and talking to civilians?'

'Drinking suits me all right,' Dick said easily, 'and some civilians are all right.'

'All right, come or don't come. Suit yourself.'

'Oh, I'll come. Only I don't know whether I want much to do with these hostesses of yours. They sound a high-risk proposition to me, sport. Now that I've managed to get all the way to the end of the war without catching . . .'

They moved through the throng towards the stairs. I stood quite still by the window, looking down into the street, and watched the group of them emerge and move off.

267

As I pulled my eyes away from the scene outside and turned back to the interior of the room, I saw the lantern-jawed American officer leaning against the wall a few yards away. I fancied he had been looking at me. Thinking what? I wondered.

Glancing down, I saw that I was mechanically holding a glass with quite a lot of beer still in it. Carefully, choosing a clear spot on a nearby table, I laid it down without drinking any more. For me the evening was over. For the American, probably it had never started.

13

I don't think my parents left Oseney Town, even for the length of a day, throughout all the war years. The brewery was short-handed, and so my father worked longer hours at his job there, which put my mother behind the bar for correspondingly longer. Apart from Mrs Warmley, they had no help, and the general fatigue and monotony of the war must have seeped into their bones as into everyone else's. But they always kept up a staunch front. When I managed to get in and see them, they always assured me that they were 'getting along fine'.

'What I look at, Peter,' my father said one Saturday afternoon, when I had dropped in before making my way out to Mulberry Hall, 'is that our family's been just about the luckiest in England. I did my bit of service in the last lot, and I used to get worried sometimes when you and Brian were growing up and the rumours started flying round about another war coming and that. Of course by the time it arrived you were pretty well grown men, but that didn't stop me worrying. You were of military age and you were fit. Just the type they might have made a meal of.'

I was looking out of the window. The willows that fringed the river had put on their early summer green, there were soft colours everywhere in the earth and the sky, and life seemed precious, precious.

Dad was clearing up the bar after the lunchtime session. He had forbidden me to help him, so I was sitting with a glass of illegal beer – illegal because it was after half-past two – and watching as he emptied ashtrays into a bucket, swept the floor, moved chairs back and forth.

'Of course, it's not as bad as last time,' he said, 'but it's been bad enough. We never seem to go a week without hearing that some chap from round here won't be coming back. Now I think of it, there was one only a couple of days ago that you'd have known. It was Brian that really knew him, very good mates they were. It'll have been a very nasty shock to Brian. I haven't seen him since, and to tell you the truth I'm not looking forward to that. You knew the lad as well, if I'm not mistaken.'

'Who was it?' I asked.

'Ivan Warmley.'

I stood quite still and went on looking out of the window. The colours over the world outside were still soft and gentle, but a darker filter seemed to have fallen over the eyes with which I looked at them. Ivan Warmley! Tall, smiling, unassertive; loyal friend to Brian; and now he was gone from life. From his own life, from Brian's life, from everybody's life.

He'd been serving in the Russian convoys, I knew. His poor mother. First her husband, then her son. Bessie Warmley had lost them both, one on the very soil of Russia, the other in the freezing waters of its northern shores. The very name 'Ivan' had been an act of homage to the spirit of Russia, to a high-hearted friendship his young father had found there among the scattered victims of a smashed and starving society. And now Russia had claimed back the name she had lent, and with it the life of the young man who had cheerfully answered to it.

And with his life, the woman's life too. For surely Bessie Warmley would never again be the woman we had known.

My mother now came through the communicating door from the kitchen, into the space behind the bar, carrying several clean cloths for wiping glasses. Her face was pale and set.

'Have you told him, Jack? About the Warmley boy?'

'Yes, Katie.'

My mother looked at me with such fierce concentration in her eyes that it was as much as I could do to hold her gaze and not flinch away.

'*Men*, Peter,' she said. 'Remember. All this is men's work. Wickedness and foolishness.'

I could not speak.

'If it was the women ran the world,' my mother said, 'nobody's son would have to go to a country he'd never seen and maybe never even heard of, a place he had no business in, and leave his bones there.'

'I suppose . . .'

'A woman's life is at home. Among people she knows and loves, and people she's brought into the world. A woman isn't interested in poking her nose where she's got no business. Women attend to what concerns them.'

I could only nod, though I knew that 'concern' varies from person to person. The Nazi-Soviet pact had concerned Geraldine.

'And women don't kill,' she said, still speaking with that clenched intensity. 'Remember that, Peter. Remember it when I'm dead and gone. Women don't kill. Their business isn't death, it's life.'

My father took her arm gently. For a moment I was afraid he was going to ask her not to upset herself. I think that, unaggressive as she was, she would have flown at him.

A little later, when I took my leave, I went round a longer way to the Botley Road. I wanted to avoid going past Mrs Warmley's house in case she came out and I had to speak to her. I hoped I would not meet her for a long time. I knew this was cowardly, but I thought it better to face my cowardice and call it by its name.

As it happens, I can remember in detail my circumstances on the afternoon of 6 August 1945. Why 6 August? Because the bombing of Hiroshima was one of those dates on which history takes a new turn: it was perhaps *the* once-and-for-all date, when a man as a social and political animal entered a new phase of his existence.

I was sitting at my desk half-way through the afternoon, puzzling over a minute that concerned a shipment of metal desks for the use of the R.A.F. I was staring at this minute with slightly unfocused eyes, having had one of my occasional Soho lunches, when Dillinger, the man in the next office, put his head in at my door and said, 'Heard any news today, Leonard?'

'I heard the eight o'clock news on the radio. Nothing since then.'

'Oh,' he said. 'So you wouldn't have heard about this Japan business?'

'Japan business?'

'Yes.' He came fully into the room and stood in front of my desk. I can see him now, looking at me rather solemnly with his pouchy eyes. I had always attributed this pouchiness to his attending to the needs of a red-headed Aberdeen girl in London as well as of his wife at week-ends, but perhaps I was wrong and he just stayed up late at night reading Ministry documents. 'It seems,' he said, 'that they've dropped some super-colossal bomb on a Japanese city, and destroyed the whole place in one explosion and killed everyone there.'

'I thought we'd finished with those wartime rumours,' I said. 'Where would they get a bomb that big? One bomb, one city? It's just another of those wild – '

'It seems the thing works on a new principle,' he interrupted me. 'It's called nuclear fission.'

I thought for a moment. 'Isn't that the stuff Rutherford got up to in Cambridge?'

Dillinger shrugged. 'Well, apparently it's led to a bomb so powerful that just one of them can wipe out a city.'

'What city was it?'

'Some place in Japan I never heard of.' He moved towards the door again. 'I've got a portable wireless in my office. I'll leave it on in case there are any more bulletins.'

I thanked him. In those days, before the invention of the transistor, portable radios took large batteries and were heavy, and their reception tended to be poor. At six o'clock, though, I was listening with Dillinger to his portable wireless gratefully enough, having stayed on at work for an extra half-hour. Together, we learnt that the race had entered the era of extinction weapons. We listened in silence, exchanged a few meaningless remarks, picked up our belongings and went out into a new world. I headed for the United Universities Club. When things like this happen, things that change every perspective there is, my first instinct is to want to discuss it – preferably with men who *know*, in the sense that they can separate the reality from the mass of mushy sensation that is bound to blow up round it.

When I got to the club the first person I saw was the physicist Weatherby. What a chance to get a real opinion on this business, I thought. Weatherby, as a Nobel Prize-winner, would know, if anyone did, what truth there was in the report of an all-time super-bomb.

He was in fact just leaving as I was entering. He came down the stairs in a slow, deliberate fashion, walking almost as if hypnotized. His eyes were looking straight ahead, but obviously their gaze was inward.

'Good evening, Professor Weatherby,' I said.

He passed me, not speaking, and went down the staircase. Turning, I saw that he was just pushing the door open to go out into the street when the club porter came forward with his hat and umbrella. Since Weatherby made no move to take them, the porter hooked the umbrella over his forearm and, after a moment's hesitation, reached up – for Weatherby was a tall man and towered over him – placed the hat on his head and settled it correctly. Weatherby tilted his head down and stared briefly at the porter.

'Your hat, sir. You'll be wanting your hat,' I heard the porter say.

'Thank you,' Weatherby said. 'My hat, yes. Thank you.' He resumed his progress through the glass-panelled door into the street.

I went on up the stairs. Predictably enough, I found that no one at the club was willing to talk about anything else but the event in Hiroshima. Even so, there was a dearth of hard information about it and its background. Many of the members were scientists, and they were naturally to the forefront of the discussion, but only the physicists had anything particular to say. And even from them I

271

learnt only that the bomb resulted from something called 'the Manhattan Project', which they had all known about as utterly confidential.

'It was a dark horse, anyway,' a man from Imperial College was putting it, as I hovered on the fringe of his group. 'Obviously any government has to choose where to put the money and the resources, and they put it into things that are most likely to hurt the enemy and to do it soonest. The Manhattan business was a long shot, an outsider.'

I thought of Weatherby. Had he been actually involved in producing this device, and was that the reason why he had seemed so shattered, so deeply indrawn? I had to know. Interrupting someone who was asking a much more intelligent question, I asked, 'Were there any native English scientists working on it, d'you know?'

'Only Weatherby. They couldn't very well leave him out. He'd pushed the theoretical work so far. He didn't talk about it, of course. He wouldn't have been allowed to anyway, but I don't believe he wanted to.'

Weatherby! I thought. You wanted pure science, you wanted to contemplate the beautiful intricacies of the physical world, and you got this!

Various scattered opinions continued to float about in the crowded bar. It wouldn't have been dropped on a white race. The war was nearly over anyway. (The war wasn't nearly over anyway.) Churchill didn't know about it. (Churchill did know about it.) The Emperor of Japan had been warned. (The Emperor of Japan had not been warned.) It was really aimed at the Russians – a warning to them not to carry too far their obvious hostility to the West. It was to rescue the men from the prison camps.

I went into the dining room and had something to eat. The reality of Hiroshima was sinking in and the air seemed heavy with a terrible menace – terrible even when measured against the menace we had all lived with for a decade now.

On my way out I met the Imperial College man, putting on his mackintosh in the cloakroom.

'In view of today's news,' I said, 'how long d'you give the human race?'

'Eighteen months,' he said. 'Could be two years.'

'Of course,' I said desperately, 'these weapons may not actually be used.'

He stopped with his raincoat half done up and looked at me as if I were the stupidest of his students.

'Give me one instance in history,' he said, 'when a new weapon, once it existed, *hasn't* been used.'

I nodded slowly and turned away without answering.

'What do you think about it?' I asked Mairead, later.

'About what?'

'About It, of course. There's only one thing that everybody in the whole world's thinking about tonight.'

She brushed the back of her hand across her forehead in a gesture of weariness. 'What can I think about it? It's the worst thing that's ever happened.'

'Morally the worst? Or just the worst as a catastrophe?'

'Both. As a catastrophe *and* morally.'

'Morally is it worse than the concentration camps?'

'Equal.'

'They're just as wicked as one another?'

'When you get to that pitch of wickedness you stop making distinctions. It was just pure evil.'

272

I pondered. 'I share your recoil of course.'

'What kind of pompous remark is that?'

'I'm not being pompous, I'm saying I feel the same way about it as you do. But I have a lurking difficulty. I wonder how I'd see these things if I were a Japanese. They don't have a religion that teaches compassion, you know. They just worship the Emperor and that's that.'

'And us? You mean we *do* have a religion that teaches compassion? We've got a funny way of interpreting it, haven't we?'

'Yes, but our religion also teaches that it's a moral duty to fight against an evil enemy. Bombing's just a form of fighting. Or does it become something else when the bang gets big enough?'

'Yes, that's exactly what it does, it becomes something else. Something evil. And I won't have you sitting there and telling me it's all right to drop that hellish thing on people. It makes me angry. So just get out of your chair and come here. If the human race is going to kill itself, we might as well try to be happy for a little while before it happens.'

6 August 1945, as I have said, is indelibly branded on my memory. Two days on from that date, because I also have reasons for remembering that exactly two days had gone by, I went round again to the United Universities Club after leaving the office. Mairead had told me that she would not be home till nine. I had three hours to kill, dreaded my own company, didn't want to sit in a pub in case I got drunk, so the club it had to be. But damn it, when I walked in I saw Hunt standing at the bar with a figure in American uniform who, to my surprise, waved at me in greeting. Who could this be? I didn't know any American servicemen personally, unless it was Chet, and it obviously wasn't. This man was bigger, and his face had a plumped-out and smoothed-over quality that was nothing like Chet's broad honest features. Who on earth . . . ? Wait a minute, could it possibly be . . . No! I didn't believe this. But there it was, inescapably. The man was Carshalton, another of my less-than-favourite people, last heard of with an American wife, teaching at an American college.

I ordered a drink, but before I could pay for it Carshalton was at my side. 'Here, have this on me, be my guest,' he said. 'We haven't met for a long time.'

The barman asked him if he was a member. Carshalton said he wasn't a member. The barman told him that in that case he couldn't buy a drink. During this exchange I had silently taken out the coins required to pay for the drink. He saw them and served me.

'Sorry about that stupid rule,' Carshalton said. 'I'd have liked to buy you a drink to celebrate meeting again.'

'I'll take the will for the deed,' I said.

'You know Ralph, of course,' he said, nodding towards Hunt. 'Let's all sit down and catch up with things.'

I had no wish to sit down with Hunt, and to be fair to Hunt I was sure the feeling was mutual, but I couldn't see how to avoid spending a few minutes with the two of them. Quite obviously Carshalton was busy rebuilding his lines of communication in England, brushing up contacts, reintroducing himself to people who might have forgotten him. He briefly explained why he was in uniform; he belonged, apparently, to one of those innumerable surveys that the American Government was launching at that time, heaping up information about all the countries that were being opened by the German retreat, information that would be used in Washington as the basis of decisions. He was off to Germany in a

273

week's time, then back home. As he talked I looked at him. Five years of living in California had put a layer of flesh on him that wasn't there in 1940, but there was no other change that I could see. The watchful eyes set deep in his head, the lack-lustre dark hair, overall the impression that there was a calculating brain whirring away behind that façade, were all just as I remembered them.

Having given me the minimum of information that would make it obligatory for *me* to tell *him* something, he launched into a routine questionnaire: what I had been doing, where I'd been working, whom I knew. Had I kept up contacts at Oxford, at Episcopus? In a word, where could I be fitted into his filing system?

As he queried, and I mechanically answered or parried, Hunt sat back in his chair and watched us with his usual amused, half-contemptuous air. I also noticed that his gaze travelled very often towards the door. Once he even got up from his chair and went out on to the landing; I saw him standing on the balcony, looking down at the entrance hall and the stairway.

Returning from a second such expedition, he said to Carshalton, his voice showing for once a certain liveliness, 'He's here, Dom.'

'Here? Where is he, downstairs?'

'Yes, he's just gone to hang his coat up. He generally comes in here for a sherry.'

My first reaction was of relief. If they were waiting for someone, I could seize the diversion created by the man's arrival and get away. I picked up my now empty glass, meaning to get a refill and go over into a far corner. I could even read the evening paper; it wouldn't take long, because in those years the newspapers consisted of a single folded sheet, giving four pages of print. But I could spin it out. Four pages would keep me going till it was time to go and see Mairead. Ah, Mairead, Mairead.

As the thought of her filled my mind I saw Carshalton stand up and move towards the door to corral someone who had just entered. I turned my head. It was Weatherby.

I watched as Carshalton went up to him and began speaking, then fell silent and concluded with a gesture of invitation, obviously asking Weatherby to come over and join him and Hunt. Because he was not as tall as Weatherby (very few people were as tall as Weatherby), he had to stand with his head tilted back to look the old man in the face, and thus they stood now, the one upturned and coaxing, the other motionless, obviously with a deep need to be left alone, just as he had been the last time I saw him. Something had him fast. His thoughts bound him like a coil of rope.

Fresh drink in hand, I prepared to move away. But then it struck me that perhaps I had a duty not to abandon Weatherby to the mercy of those two piranha fish, with their combined rows of teeth capable of stripping the flesh from his old bones in five seconds flat. I stayed within earshot. They settled Weatherby into a chair and stationed themselves on either side of him. Then the questioning began. He had been involved in the Manhattan Project, correct? In which case they wanted his opinions as a distinguished man of science. They wanted to know if his involvement in this mass slaughter troubled his conscience. They wanted this, they wanted that. I could understand Hunt's motives, he wanted a journalistic package he could take away and sell; what I couldn't see was why Carshalton had got himself into it, but no doubt that would become clear as time went on.

Weatherby looked at them, but I could read nothing in his expression. It was just blank. I couldn't even be certain that he was hearing what they said. It was like the time the porter had spoken to him about his hat.

'While you were conducting these investigations, Sir Thomas, did you know what your work would be used for?'

Sir Thomas! I had completely forgotten that Weatherby had been knighted. His title was scarcely ever used at Oxford, where people just called him Professor Weatherby.

Weatherby slowly raised his eyes. 'A scientific investigator never knows with any precision what his conclusions will be *used for*.' He spoke the last two words as if uttering a quotation. 'To the world, scientific thinking only becomes real when it results in a practical invention. To those engaged in it, scientific thinking is real from the beginning, real by its very nature.'

'Yes, but I'm sure you can sympathize with the way the ordinary man sees things. Pure science doesn't affect him any more than people playing chess affect him. But when an atomic bomb falls on him out of the sky, that affects him. So what I'm asking is whether, when you're engaged in the one, you spare any thought for the other?'

Weatherby folded his hands in his lap. 'I am a physicist,' he said. 'Nuclear physics is an extremely important area of my field. When I had an opportunity to be funded to do some work on stubborn questions in that area, I accepted it. I knew that the funds came ultimately from the military effort. They had been made available because in wartime it is easier to get money out of politicians if you tell them that there may be military advantages to be gained. Personally I don't believe anyone thought so. They gave us a little money because in wartime one will try anything, but we were very much a second or third string. Our political masters did not imagine that we would win the war for them. They thought the rocket engineers would do that, and most of the money that was made available for scientific work went into the development of rockets. We had a little of what was left. That our line of work was the line which ultimately led to a new weapon was just a chance.'

Carshalton leaned forward. 'Are you happy about that chance, Sir Thomas? How d'you feel about the way things worked out?'

Weatherby now took out his enormous heavy-rimmed glasses. The sight gave me a stab of nostalgia. I remembered the evening so many years ago at Episcopus, when Lamont had read an essay to our little discussion club on 'Symbol and Impulse in Art', or some such theme, and how Weatherby had been present and had joined in the discussion with such seriousness, such tolerance, such courtesy, totally accepting that the youthful poet, forty years his junior and entirely unknown to the world, might have thought that would be really helpful to him. Weatherby was a truly civilized man.

'The relation of cause and effect in scientific work,' Weatherby said in his deep, slow voice, 'is always unpredictable in the initial stages. Work that is undertaken with a definite practical purpose in mind is very often wasted effort. Work, on the other hand, that is undertaken purely in a spirit of enquiry – what the world would probably consider the merest idle curiosity – has many times borne fruit in technology. The case of Michael Faraday will be familiar to you. He was the first man to penetrate the mystery of electricity and explain its nature. Yet his curiosity was purely intellectual. When he had an audience with Queen Victoria, she asked him why he didn't concern himself with work that could have a practical purpose. And he had nothing to say in reply, except that he wasn't that kind of scientist.'

'But the game's different now, Sir Thomas,' Carshalton said. Evidently he thought that by sticking doggedly to one point, the destructiveness of modern weapons, he would jolt a statement out of his prey, something that Hunt could write down and in due course serve up with garnish. 'That bomb altered the whole nature of warfare. The question now is whether anything could justify its use against human beings.'

I moved in. I had realized suddenly that although it was Hunt who was chasing up this story, most of the top men who had worked on it were in America; but Weatherby happened to be in England and Carshalton was coming to England anyway and happened to know Weatherby, so between them they had decided they could turn in a neat little job, getting the old man to make a saleable statement about Hiroshima. 'Look,' I said, 'the pair of you, drop it. You're trying to make him feel guilty about his personal responsibility for this business. Is he responsible for the war? Did he tell the Japanese to knock the Chinese about all through the thirties, and then in the forties to go for us and the Americans? It was their decision to expand into South-East Asia by military means. It all led to war and war led to this appalling demonstration of blind force. Why is it Weatherby's fault?'

'Who made it possible, what you call this appalling demonstration?' Carshalton came back. 'The team that developed this weapon. And a leading member of that team was Weatherby. So why not ask him what he thinks about it?'

We had raised our voices, and the club members were becoming restive. Behaving like gentlemen, however, instead of storming over and telling us to shut up, one of them approached us in a casual, all-in-this-together fashion, and started a topic of conversation intended to take our minds off whatever we were arguing about and lower the temperature.

'You chaps hear the news just now?' he asked, nodding in the general direction of the smoking-room, where the club had a radio. 'The six o'clock bulletin?'

None of us had. Even Hunt, whose business it was to keep abreast of the news, had been too occupied in the wait for Weatherby.

'Rather interesting,' the club member said. 'Seems the Russians have declared war on Japan.'

There was a moment's silence and then I said, 'What a gruesome moment to choose.'

'Rather a good moment, from their point of view. The Japs are bound to surrender in the next few hours. The piece of paper containing the surrender, with the Emperor's seal on it and all that, hasn't landed on the table yet, that's all. By declaring war while the Japs are still technically our enemies, the Russians have got themselves a seat at the peace conference. They've got territorial claims to the Kurile Islands and Southern Sakhalin, and that's when the spoils'll be divided up.'

The man produced a tortoise-shell cigarette-case, snapped it open and offered me one. Since cigarettes were very hard to get, it was a friendly gesture and, though I refused, I did so with thanks. He nodded affably and, satisfied that he had imposed some order on our turbulence, moved away.

Carshalton, for his part, said nothing, but I caught for an instant a gleam of admiration in his eyes. I had no difficulty in understanding that admiration. The government of the Soviet Union, in contrast to most governments across the world, had managed to do something of which Carshalton whole-heartedly approved.

Mairead, it seemed, was due for another of her trips aboard the twelve-seater aircraft. She was to go on a mid-August Monday to Dublin, returning on the Thursday.

'You must be an important person, if they have to have you there in the flesh.' I was resentful. The dreaded day of our final parting was now so imminent that I grudged a great slice out of what must now be one of our last weeks. She presumably would stay in London, but I wouldn't. Already our office was buzzing with speculation about when we were to be closed down.

'Mr Dulanty's going and he wants me with him.'

'Why the hell can't he go over at the week-end?'

'You're being silly now, Peter.'

'Yes, I'm being silly. Love makes people silly ... so when can I come round again and see you?'

'The first evening I'm home. Thursday.' And I had to be content with that.

On the Thursday evening I rode over to Tufnell Park, my heart pounding. I opened the gate, went up the steps and rang the front-door bell. Mairead did not have a personal bell. Instead, one rang three times to bring her down. I now, therefore, stood on the top step, breathing the refined air of Laurier Road, and rang three times. After a moment I heard footsteps approaching. Mairead! At last we would be together and would throw off our clothes and dive into bed. Always we did that first, then, when we had cooled our raging physical need, we spoke of other things.

The young woman who stood regarding me, holding the door about three-quarters open, was not Mairead. I had never seen her before.

'Hello,' she said guardedly. 'Did Cyril send you?'

'Cyril? No, I . . .'

'Is it to see the flat?'

I was so banjaxed that I literally could not speak. I opened my mouth and not a sound came out.

'Don't tell me the advert's appeared already,' she said in a more friendly tone.

'Erk,' I said.

'Well, if you want to see the flat you can come straight up. It's all cleared. We weren't thinking of starting to let till next week, but we could manage Sunday. Afternoon, anyway; we'd need Sunday morning to give it a bit of a going-over.'

She was closing the front door behind me as she spoke, and now began leading the way up the stairs. As I went up behind her my whole being began to be flooded with dread. We mounted to the first landing, and moved on up to the second.

Mairead's door was standing open. It wasn't Mairead's door any more. It was the door of an empty room. She had gone. Her furniture had gone.

I stood there, looking round the bare room. And the girl stood there, looking at me looking at the room. She didn't speak, and I couldn't.

Then there was the rattle of a door opening on the floor below, and the mother's voice yelled up, 'Doreen!'

'Yes?' the daughter called down.

'This might be the gentleman the note was left for. Is his name Leonard, ask him?'

'Is your name Leonard?' the girl asked me.

'Yes.'

'Well, my mother seems to think there's a letter for you.'

I followed her downstairs. I had only just come up these stairs, and now I was going down them, but a whole lifetime had gone by. Everything was changed. A

277

final glance round: farewell, room where I have been happy. Go down the stairs now, *one, two, three*, to what fate I do not know.

The mother, standing in the oblong of light from her door, handed me a letter with my name on it in Mairead's writing. I took it, thanked her and walked on out of the house. I wasn't going to open it with the two of them watching me. I wasn't even sure, yet, whether I was going to read it at all.

I walked over to the beginning of West Hill that went up to Highgate. Just across from one of the entrances to Parliament Hill Fields there was a pleasant enough pub: Victorian: an interior that was empty. I got a drink, though I wasn't thirsty. My throat felt so tight that I didn't think I would be able to swallow. But I bought a glass of beer and set it down on the table beside me. Then I took the letter out of my pocket and looked at it. Well, go on, open it. I turned it over in my hands. Go on, go on, open it.

When I finally did tear the envelope open my hands were shaking and I tore the paper inside. But it didn't matter because there wasn't much on it. Just a London telephone number. Immediately, because I knew if I hesitated I would never do it, I went over to the coin telephone just inside the entrance to the pub. I got the number. It rang and rang.

Finally a girl's voice answered, a very young voice; she sounded about sixteen. For some reason I had a very clear vision of her, with a Marcel wave, as they were called in those days, and wearing her first lipstick.

'May I speak to Miss Hoey?' I said.

'Miss Hoey's gone out,' she answered.

'Oh.' I wondered, dully, whether to leave a message. But what message? As I hesitated, I heard a faint swishing, rustling noise at the other end and Mairead's voice came to me. She was obviously turning her head away, speaking to someone else. 'I'm sorry, Elsie,' I heard her say. Then she asked, 'Is it Peter?'

'You know it's Peter, my love,' I said.

'Look, I'm sorry,' she said. 'I know this is the wrong way to do it. But there isn't a right way.'

'Do what?' I said, but I knew.

'You know what. Pull away from you. We both know it's come now, and I just couldn't bear to be face to face with you when we had to say goodbye. You may think it's cowardly. But if I had to look at you I'd just cry. I don't want you to remember me like that – just crying and crying . . .'

As she spoke the last word her voice faltered and I knew the tears were coming. I heard some sobs and then 'Goodbye, Peter', as she put the telephone down. I heard the clonk as it settled back into its cradle; then the thin, continuous snore of the dialling tone.

A man in an Army greatcoat came and stood within four feet of me, waiting to use the telephone. I hung up, and moved out of his way. There seemed to be nothing to do but go outside. I went across the road and into Parliament Hill Fields. People were playing tennis on the courts just to the left as you come in, making use of the last hour of daylight. I stood and watched them for a while. There seemed to be nothing to do but stand around and watch people do things. The war was over.

14

The Ministry of Supply released me from my wartime duties in the second week of September 1945. From the point of view of my duties at Episcopus College this wasn't a day too soon. Tired as I was, there was no question of taking a holiday. Term would be starting in October, and the College was already preparing for an enormously swollen intake. Now that the war was completely over, the servicemen were impatient to get home. A trickle of demobilization began immediately after the Japanese surrender, and rose within a few days to a flood. Considering what awaited them in civilian life – food shortages, lack of living space, hardly anything in the shops, and businesses too preoccupied with the big changes they had to make to be ready to take on employees – the haste with which everyone got out of uniform and off the parade ground says a lot about the basic attractions of home and family.

I did that return journey from London to Oxford for the last time, with a large suitcase of dirty washing and a heart full of mixed emotions. The journey, as usual, was a slow clanking one – all the trains seemed too worn out, by the end of the war, to get up a speed of more than about thirty miles an hour, and liked to stop at as many stations as possible – and I determinedly made use of the journey time to point the headlamp of my spirit forward. What was done was done. I would carry Mairead in my mind for ever, as a man who had been wounded might carry shrapnel in his body. The memory of our love would always be with me, and there was nothing more to be said.

Now my life was to be Heather and Michael, and there was cheerfulness in that prospect. Heather had not been idle since the end of the war: she had been house-hunting. Before I arrived back she had already made up her mind that the post-war era should not find her living in Oxford itself. No, ours was to be a country setting. Before the war she had made sporadic efforts to fit in with North Oxford social life, even to the extent of going to dinner parties where the other guests had mostly been dons' wives, but the years at Mulberry Hall had got her out of this and she was determined not to go back to it. She was stalking a house at Chinnor. This attractive village, about half-way between Thame and Watlington, lying at the foot of a range of chalk hills, had always appealed to her, and she knew a couple who intended to go and live overseas as soon as the husband could find a job. Any day now might bring the right vacancy, and on that day their house at Chinnor would go on the market, with Heather getting (she had been faithfully promised) an early tip-off.

'It'll suit us perfectly,' she told me. 'The right size of house, flint construction, very handsome, nice garden, and lots of room all round. I can ride, you can walk at week-ends and get some fresh air, Michael can grow up a country child. And we'll be away from all that stupid old Oxford clutter.'

'It'll mean a lot of driving.'

'There's a bus. And it won't hurt you to do a bit of driving now and then. I'll probably end up doing most of it, anyway. I know how good you are at being too busy to do anything you don't like doing.'

That, as my memory records it, was the total amount of discussion we had about the location for our new home. The fact is, I suppose, that if I had really been set on living in Oxford town I could have dug my heels in, but it didn't seem worth fighting over. I was quite drawn to Chinnor myself.

Meanwhile, the house at Marston had been let during the war, but Heather now busied herself with getting rid of the tenants and clearing enough space for the three of us to settle back in while we waited. By the end of September we were there, though whether for a few weeks or many months we had no means of knowing.

So life went on. But it was a strange life. The end of the actual fighting was something to be grateful for, but what the world had emerged into, after the fog and noise of five years of war, didn't seem much like anything that could be called 'peace'. There was so much conflict, so much menace, so much anxiety still in the atmosphere. During the war, when the sense of being marooned and shut off from the international movement of ideas had been particularly oppressive, I had longed for the day when a free wind would blow across the frontiers and carry with it the seeds of new thinking. Now that the fighting had stopped and the frontiers were in theory open, the only wind that blew across them seemed to be the melancholy soughing that one associates with a ruined building. The ideas that reached us from the Continent, in that first autumn and winter of peacetime, were the notions of *Angst* and its formalization into the hybrid thought system called Existentialism.

It was not a happy time for anyone, and it was not made any happier by the brooding sense that huge forces were building up to attack us. The hard face of totalitarianism seemed to be graven on the clouds that floated in towards us from the east.

'In due course all those with whom the Soviet authorities desire to deal must be handed over to them, and we are not concerned with the fact that they may be shot or otherwise more harshly dealt with than they might be under British law.'

I had not, back in June 1944, known that these words had been written in a Foreign Office minute by Sir Patrick Dean, and the Thirty Year Rule effectively kept the lid on them until they had been robbed of any possible urgency. But everybody knew – everybody who took the slightest trouble to look into the matter – that many Soviet citizens who found themselves outside the borders of the U.S.S.R., and expressed the strongest possible wish to stay outside them, were nevertheless packed off home under armed guard, to be duly slaughtered or consigned to the unimaginable hell of concentration camps within the Arctic Circle. We couldn't see the wheels go round, but that they *were* going round was horribly obvious.

The thinking that lay behind Sir Patrick's minute formed a strand in the texture of English behaviour that followed, and as such has a natural interest for me as an historian. Quite simply, in the first few years after the guns fell silent in 1945, it was a strand of peace-at-any-price submissiveness. Whatever Stalin demanded, he was to be given. The Russians had fought heroically in the war; the defence of Stalingrad was possibly their greatest epic. Who would want to oppose such people? They had been our gallant Allies, and if they now didn't seem to be behaving much like allies, we had to be understanding. Left-wing opinion, which was the general opinion in England at that time, held that not to be friends with Russia would be not only wrong but inexcusable.

Thus the attitude that only a wicked person, or at best a short-sighted one, would oppose any Russian demand was very strong in those days. It was behind the farce enacted at the very first meeting of the United Nations at San Francisco in the autumn of 1945, when the Soviet delegates refused to take their seats until the Polish delegation, chosen by the elected representatives of the nation, had been turned out and replaced by Kremlin puppets. It was behind the weary acceptance of the Soviet refusal to allow free elections in any of the territories occupied by the Red Army, which were simply to be annexed. It showed clearly when normally sharp-tongued commentators refrained from poking fun at the Communist-inspired Waldorf-Astoria Cultural and Scientific Conference for World Peace which managed to parade such venerable innocents as Pablo Picasso, Charlie Chaplin, Albert Einstein and Frank Lloyd Wright to utter resounding platitudes about Peace while, behind the scenes, the killing in Stalin's labour camps went on. We had got rid of Hitler, but only at the cost of strengthening Stalin, and the countless other miniature Stalins who radiated out from him, all the way from Vladivostock to Leipzig.

One soft September evening I had Nussbaum to dinner at Episcopus. He was a good guest, impeccably courteous and willing to find something to be pleased about in everyone he met; while the melancholy irony of his spirit looked out through his eyes, the gentle eyes of a St Bernard dog.

It was an evening when Heather didn't need the car, so I had the use of it, and I sat comfortably in the Common Room after dinner until I judged Nussbaum had had his talk out. He had got into conversation with a young classicist, just returned from the war, whom the College had taken on as a Research Fellow, and obviously they were interested in one another because after the meal was over they sat together with their coffee. They motioned to me to join them, but they had become so engrossed in discussion of matters concerning their world that within a few sentences their talk left me behind. I was content, therefore, after a few minutes to steal away and leave them to it while I talked to other men I had business with.

Ultimately the young chap had to go and keep some appointment of his own, and I had the pleasant sense of having given Nussbaum a stimulating evening without having had to flog my own brain. Thus it was with a sense of contentment and good fellowship that, as men drifted away and the room emptied, I asked Nussbaum if he would care for a lift home.

'Under normal circumstances, I would decline your kind offer,' he said. 'It is so short a walk and the activity would be good for my sixty-year-old limbs. But tonight, yes please, I will get into your car and ride to my lodging – but I must ask you as a favour to stop there for a few minutes. I have something that I want to show you.'

I supposed he was talking about a coin or a medal or a fragment of manuscript that he wanted the pleasure of showing off to a fellow scholar, even one not in his own field. And when we got to his place I parked the car, which in those days you could rely on doing at almost any point in any street, and went willingly enough up the stairs to his eyrie.

'Sit down, my friend . . . a small stirrup-cup of something? I have a fine liqueur here.'

'Well, I've had quite enough to drink, really . . . one always does at Episcopus.'

'As you wish. I shall take a very small one because I have something to celebrate.'

'Oh, well, I'll have a small one too. Just moisten the bottom of the glass. Thanks.'

It was one of those sweet, strong, fruity liqueurs, kümmel or something. I'm not a liqueur man, but it went down all right.

'What is it you've got to show me, Otto?' I asked.

'This,' he said, swivelling his chair to face his desk. He opened a drawer and swivelled back to face me, now with something in his hand. Since I had expected a book, or a sheaf of papers, I was startled when he actually held out to me a revolver. A large, business-like revolver.

Had Nussbaum gone mad? Had he invited me round here to kill me? No, he was smiling benignly and holding out the gun as if he wanted me to take it.

'It is harmless,' he said. 'Not loaded.'

I took it. It was heavy, and the handle fitted perfectly into my palm. It felt incredibly purposeful; I had an impulse to pull the trigger. It gave me that evil, fleeting thrill of thinking that it must be rather fun to shoot something. Or someone.

'It is an English make,' he said. 'A Smith and Wesson. I bought it in nineteen thirty-seven.'

'How long had you been in this country?'

'Three years. I had delayed. I was reluctant to buy it, even after I realized I should. I could not banish from my mind the time when I had thought I would never again need to handle a weapon.'

I looked at him, down at the Smith and Wesson, up at him again. 'And you knew by 'thirty-seven that you would want to buy this?'

'I expected to use it,' Nussbaum said.

'Against whom?'

'Myself.'

I was silent for a moment.

Nussbaum took the gun back. 'Beyond question, my friend, you understand me.'

He put the revolver back in the drawer and slid it shut. 'It will not have to stay there much longer,' he said.

'What are you going to do with it?'

He shrugged. 'Sell it. I am not sentimental. It will pay a fortnight's rent. There is no corrosion. It has been cleaned regularly.'

'And now,' I said, 'you feel justified in getting rid of it. The Nazis are no more. We're going to live in peace for ever and ever.'

'Did I say so? I would be a fool to say so. From nineteen thirty-five I knew that war with Germany was coming, inexorably. Quite probably the next war will be with Russia. Adolf Hitler is gone, but Josef Stalin remains. He has exactly the same motives for going to war as Hitler had. Both have made slaves of their population. Slaves have to be kept in order by the carrot and the stick. War is at the same time the most effective carrot and the most effective stick. You terrify the people with images of a devouring enemy who will eat them up if they do not work and fight. That is the stick. You dangle before them foreign conquest, wealth, power, ease. That is the carrot.'

'And for all that,' I said, 'this seems a time when you can get rid of your revolver.'

'My friend,' Nussbaum said, 'I have something else to show you as well as the revolver.' He opened another drawer and took out a flat box which he opened. Inside was a plain iron cross on a ribbon. 'You know what is this?'

'The Iron Cross was the German Army's decoration for bravery in the last war.' We still called it 'the last war' then.

'Precisely, my friend. The Iron Cross. Awarded to me, to Lieutenant Otto Nussbaum, in 1917. Why did I keep it? When Germany turned into a land of hatred and persecution for me and for my race, why did I keep the simple decoration I had won by helping to defend her?'

'You had every right to keep it. It was Germany that had changed, not you.'

'No, I had not changed. And even Germany had changed only on the surface. I came away because the criminal riff-raff who had come to power would have killed me, but I brought away my Iron Cross as a pledge that wherever I wandered on the earth's face I would represent the Germany of Goethe, of Höldelin, of Kant, Beethoven, Schubert. I would speak with her voice, think with her mind.'

'You do, Otto. That is what you do.'

'It was not death I feared when I came away from my home and my tradition. I have not been a man with an abnormal fear of death, only the ordinary fear that we all have, which can be conquered when there is need. But the death they had prepared for me was a death that denied humanity. The death of an animal in a slaughter-house. And if they had taken over this country I would have blown out my brains on the very day I knew they were here. But you know what happened.'

'Yes, I know what happened.'

'This country kept them away. This blessed country. Partly by luck. Partly by courage. Partly by stupidity and unawareness. Partly by brilliant improvization. Later, with massive help. There was a special hand of Providence over this island. I do not know what those words mean, but I utter them and I believe them. And because I believe them I shall part with my revolver.'

'But you'll keep your Iron Cross.'

He laughed. 'Pacifists speak as if there were only one kind of death. But there are many kinds. That is why I keep my Iron Cross. If the Russians kill me, I shall die with it in my hand. And I shall die in England, which will be a good and comely thing to do because England gave me back my life. England, with all her faults and all her quaintness . . . So now we will drink a little more kümmel and that will finish the bottle.'

Outside in the street, walking towards the car, I felt that I didn't know what to do with the statement Nussbaum had just made. It was as if he had put into my hands a bulky package that I wasn't ready for and didn't know where to put down. In a sense, I never have known where to put it down, how to fit it in with my political world-view. All I do know is that to think about the war, and particularly of the year or two before and after 1939, is inevitably to imagine Nussbaum, sitting in his high room above Walton Street, taking out his revolver, checking the safety-catch, making sure, with all the meticulousness of an old soldier and a scholar, that he could use it to kill himself if ever the Nazis looked like getting hold of him. He was a civilized and tolerant man: but them he would not tolerate. Into their hands he would give only his dead body, with its tall skull broken into pieces.

'If you'll eat the white of that egg,' I said to Michael, 'scrape it out and show me the empty shell when you've finished, I'll come down to the model shop with you and we'll buy a complete new Airfix kit.'

He made a face. He was sitting opposite me at the breakfast table, in a shaft of autumn sunlight that brought out the shine of his pale hair and the blue of

283

his eyes. That year had seen his eleventh birthday; already he was well-grown, evidently set to inherit Heather's tall, straight frame. But his face was screwed into a frown as he looked down at his boiled egg.

'I don't *like* the white.'

'I didn't say you had to like it. I said you had to eat it. This isn't a time to waste good food – there still isn't quite enough to go round for everybody.'

'I've eaten all the yolk. I thought that was the good-for-you part.'

'Well, you thought wrong. Everything inside an eggshell is there to feed the chicken as it develops. But the white is pure nourishment. The yolk's mainly just fat, and there are plenty of sources you can get that from.'

Heather was standing at the sink, washing last night's dishes. She said over her shoulder, 'What nonsense are you filling his head with?'

'It's the latest nutritional wisdom.' To Michael I said, 'What Airfix model are you planning to build next?'

'A Lancaster.'

'I thought you'd done all the bombers.'

'No, I haven't done a Lancaster.'

'Well, eat your white of egg and you can build it this week-end.'

He picked at a shred of it.

'I bet you don't like it any more than me,' he now accused me. 'If you did, you'd be eating one now.'

'No, I wouldn't. I've told you my reasons for that.'

I had, in fact, told him some, but not quite all, of the reasons why I so seldom ate eggs. They concerned my relationship with Mrs Burrell, his maternal grandmother. She did not like me and never would, but she had too much practical sense to have no dealings with me at all. And, fortunately for her pride, she was now in a position to play Lady Bountiful. With each year of the war, the mounting food shortages had moved farmers rung by rung up the ladder of importance. In a world where just about everything was difficult to come by, farmers had Resources. And one of the commodities that virtually every farmer had within his gift was the humble chicken's egg, still as heavily rationed in 1945 and '46 as during the war – which meant, for an adult, a maximum of one a week. Since the Burrells could keep us supplied with eggs, if they chose, they did choose, and if I personally decided not to consume any of this *largesse* because of the bad feeling between us, there was no reason why I should. And I could always decline gracefully since I took a fair number of my meals at Episcopus and so escaped the worse effects of rationing; it was only natural that such food as came into our home should mostly be eaten by Heather and Michael.

So I ate my one government egg per week, and occasionally had an omelette made from reconstituted dried egg, which tasted like egg-flavoured chalk. And Michael formed his young bones on seven eggs a week, or at least on seven yolks. It was a contest between us, but a relatively good-humoured one, and one I was ready to let him win sometimes.

One of the reasons why it would have been unthinkable to enter into actual warfare with Mrs Burrell was that Michael was so fond of spending time at Jasmine Farm. He was always asking to be ferried out there, and ever since he had had his first bicycle he had been loud in his demands to be allowed to cycle there by himself; fearful of the long miles over main roads, I put my foot down and said he would have to be turned thirteen before he pedalled there on his own. This meant that he was driven out there pretty often, and I might as well admit that I sometimes went along too when I might perfectly have left it to Heather. There was always the factor of Phil. That horrible creature had certainly become no less horrible during the war years. After his rebuff by a Land Girl who had burst out laughing at the sight of his brandished bludgeon, his sexuality seemed to have become even sicker and more twisted. One Saturday afternoon when we were out there, and old Burrell had gone off in the van on some errand, taking Phil with him, it so happened that we needed a screwdriver, and when one could not be found in the house I was sent out to the shed where Phil spent the bulk of his time, to see if I could see one lying about. I couldn't, and during a desultory search I moved a layer of old sacks and found underneath them a yellowed collection of pornographic magazines: pre-war French ones, it seemed from a rapid flick-through. I put everything back exactly as I found it, and I never mentioned the existence of Phil's hoard to anyone: but sometimes in the night I was tormented by visions of his showing these things to Michael, setting his young mind downward and inward rather than, as it would have naturally gone, out into the sunlight of his natural instincts. I feared and distrusted Phil even more after that Saturday afternoon, and if Michael, during the slack times between diversions, showed signs of wanting to go and hang around in the shed with Phil, I was quick to suggest some expedition or game.

For all these reasons I was at Jasmine Farm much more often than I would naturally have been inclined, and it was on one such afternoon that Mrs Burrell let fly on a subject obviously close to her thoughts: Michael's education. She meant, of course, his social conditioning, not the development of his mind and interests. We had taken our places beside a bright log-fire in the farmhouse parlour for the ritual tea from the best china: fingers of toast with Mrs Burrell's home-made blackcurrant jam, little cakes also made by her. Was it ungallant of me to feel, as I always did, that these little marks of privilege were not so much a sign of welcome as of warfare, significant weapons for attacking Heather's housekeeping skills? Perhaps the suspicion was an unworthy one, but it all struck me as an attack, and as an attack I received it.

We were three plus Michael; old Burrell was pottering somewhere on the farm. The master of the house was never included in these tea-table enclaves; it was always assumed that, with his muddy boots and muddy complexion, his place was somewhere out of doors and out of sight. I tried, sometimes, to imagine what his life must be like. About like that of an ox in a stall, I decided. Quite relaxed, quite comfortable; if you were an ox.

After Mike had polished off as much toast and jam and as many cakes as he was allowed ('You'll be sick!' 'Me! You must be joking, Gran!') he was packed off to one end of the kitchen table with his modelling kit. He had assembled two aeroplanes in plain plastic and the next job was to paint them. Satisfied that he had it all set out on a thick layer of newspaper, I went back to the mother and daughter, who were discussing the latest addition to the room's furnishings, a handsome grandfather clock that stood in the corner.

Mrs Burrell was explaining that it was an antique, made just after the end of the Napoleonic Wars. She had bought it at an antique fair in Burford. For the time being its function was purely decorative, but she knew of a man in Witney who was marvellous at fixing up clocks and was sure he would be able to start it going without charging much. Her eyes as she spoke played over its warm dark wood and bright face, and I had a sudden vision of what her life would increasingly be. They had turned the financial corner; agriculture, for so long a way of life that had been pushed into the economic shadows, was steadily emerging into the sunshine. No one could have foreseen, in 1946, the way showers of gold from Westminster, and later from Brussels, would cascade on to farmers, but it was already obvious that they were going to be front-runners in the race for subsidies. I even had a silent bet with myself: that Mrs Burrell's next purchase would be an estate car, one of those wood-panelled jobs that had doors which opened at the back like a van (without, of course, being as common and tradesmanly as a van) and she could carry antique pieces from places like Burford home in it.

Sitting back in the warm glow of the fire, drinking up my last cup of tea, I looked across at Mrs Burrell with (reasonably) benevolent feelings. But it is always a mistake to lower one's guard. She returned my look with a little smile that had the brightness and also the hardness of a diamond; and moved on to a subject that was obviously, as I ought to have foreseen, very much in her thoughts at a time of upward change in her fortunes.

'Michael's getting a big boy now, isn't he, Peter?'

'Yes, he's growing well. Must be all those wholesome eggs.'

'I suppose you're planning hard for his education.'

I saw the ground opening before my feet. 'Well, obviously he's getting on with his lessons.'

'Have you decided on a school for him?'

I shot a glance at Heather to see if I could count on any support from her, but her face was composed, like that of someone idly listening to a radio programme. Clearly she was going to be a spectator at any contest that developed. Her general attitude towards Jasmine Farm, and it was one I sympathized with, was that it was enough for her to be there now and then and simply breathe in and out while she gave her mother the chance to see Michael, on whom she doted.

'Well,' I said, 'he's fine now, and there are several schools within walking or cycling distance of the village we're planning to move to.'

'*Day* schools?' She made them sound like Borstals.

'Yes. Day schools.'

'But I should have thought — ' She gestured helplessly. 'I should have thought you were looking beyond that.'

'Beyond? Well, if he's going to go to University he'll have to go to school first.'

'No, of course, I mean beyond the ordinary local day schools. To a public school.'

As an historian, I have always found it mildly funny that the English refer to a handful of expensive fee-paying private schools as 'public'. The reference of course is historical: when, in the sixteenth century, grammar schools were set up for clever boys from families in modest circumstances, they were known as 'public schools' because they were for parents who couldn't afford to have their sons educated at home by private tutors, which was the only alternative. But when people like Mrs Burrell breathed with reverence the words 'public school' they weren't thinking of Henry the Seventh or traditions of sound learning: they were thinking of the right contacts, the right opinions and alliances formed early in life, the right accent and manners.

Accordingly, she now said, 'I think it's a pity you've only the one child. But at least that does put you in a good position when it comes to paying for his school fees.'

I felt my pulse accelerate, and my heart seemed to grow in size and try to force itself up into my windpipe, the familiar symptoms of rage and alarm.

'Yes, I can afford it,' I said. 'I don't suppose there's any school in England that I absolutely *couldn't* afford to send Michael to, if we skimped and scraped a bit. So the reason why we're not going to send him to that kind of school has nothing to do with — '

'You're not *going* to? May I ask whyever not?'

'It's a matter of principle, Mrs Bu — Alicia,' I said, forcing the name out in an effort to keep the conversation familiar. 'I don't approve of boarding schools because I don't believe that other people can bring up my son better than I can myself. And because their social results are divisive. A boy who goes to a boarding school doesn't know the boys who grow up in his own neighbourhood, so in the holidays he's bored and lonely. And if, like most boys who are at all sensitive or original, he doesn't like school, he's caught between being unhappy at home and even worse at school. Don't tell me *that's* a good thing.'

Her expression was enough to show me that she wasn't listening to a word, merely waiting till I paused to draw breath. When I did, she cut in.

'But the public schools are *better*, aren't they? I mean, they have such a tradition behind them.'

'Very few of them are as much as a century old.'

'And the brilliant men they've produced! Well, I mean, look at them! Just about everybody who *is* anybody.'

So our talk persisted, in an atmosphere of distrust and weariness, drawing parallel lines that never met and never could meet, while Heather stared at the flames of the log-fire and thought her own thoughts, and Michael in the kitchen coloured in his models, and the handsome grandfather clock waited for the day when the clever man in Witney would set it ticking once more.

Finally, as the autumn dusk descended and the white river mist began to creep across the fields, the time came when we could decently go. We went out to the car, uttering the ritual salutations. Old Burrell was standing just inside the gate, talking to Phil. His round, brick-red face turned towards us and he waved a hand to speed us on our way.

'Goodbye, Grandad,' Michael called. Then he said to me, 'Just wait a minute. I want to show Phil my Lancaster.'

I was going to refuse, just on principle, but after all it seemed fair enough. 'Well, don't be all night about it,' I said. I got into the car and started the engine. In the driving mirror I could see Phil turning the plastic model over in his hands and grinning and saying something to Michael. I started to back the car out, and called to Michael to get in.'

'What's the hurry?' Heather asked.

'He's had plenty of time to talk to Phil if he wanted to. We have to get back.'

'That's not fair. He couldn't talk to Phil because he was in the house and Phil was outside.'

'All right, it's not fair.'

Michael now joined us and we moved off.

'You're in a funny mood,' Heather said.

'Well, I suppose I'm always in a funny mood when I'm confronted with the way your parents never seem to feel the need to get rid of Phil. Surely they could find someone better.'

'My father feels some kind of loyalty to him, I suppose.'

'In that case it's a loyalty that's very bad for the atmosphere of the farm. Surely he could get somebody more generally capable. He doesn't *have* to employ a degenerate like that.'

'Generally, capable people come expensive.'

287

'Even a young apprentice would be better than a near-idiot like Phil.'

Michael, who had been immersed in some business of his own on the back seat, put in from behind us, 'What does denegerate mean?'

'It means someone who's falling apart at the centre,' I said.

'Is Phil falling apart at the centre?'

'Yes,' I said bluntly.

'You just don't like Phil,' Michael said. 'You don't want me to like him because you don't like him.'

'Well, that's true enough. I'd be very sorry if I thought you were getting close to Phil.'

'Leave the kid alone,' said Heather.

'Well,' I said quietly, staring ahead at the road, 'I never thought I'd hear *you* defending Phil.'

'It's Michael I'm defending, not Phil. Michael's right to live his own life.'

'Let me get this straight – do you think it's a mistake to try to safeguard a child?'

'Safeguard me what from?' came the insistent voice from the back seat.

'Let's leave it,' I said to Heather.

'Yes, let's.'

The next thing to hit my life was a heavy wave of routine teaching, as the University got down to the job of coping with the huge post-war intake. I think I was fortunate in the first crop of pupils I had after the war, starting in that first October. One heard on all sides of returned servicemen who found it very difficult to settle down.

I heard about these, but among the men I actually met face to face I found only one. His name was Williamson and he had originally come to the College early in the war as a 'cadet' – one of the young men accepted by the services as officer material and then given six months at the University in which they partly studied the subject of their choice and partly did military training. The cadets were, academically, a mixed bunch, and when, after the war, the colleges honoured their promise to take back any cadet who had once enrolled with them, a few awkward cases came in with the rest. But I never heard any Oxford don complain about this. The prevailing attitude was that if the returning cadets were sometimes difficult to turn into the kind of men who could earn Oxford degrees, the difficulty of the task was good for us; we put on muscle through it.

I certainly put on muscle in my effort to make a history student out of Williamson. Most of the time he was just naturally not adapted to this kind of work and lacking real interest. But occasionally he had moods of hostility to the subject itself as if he were accusing me, and through me the Faculty of Modern History and the entire University of Oxford, of trying to pen him up in an artificial enclosure. On one occasion I had set him an essay on a very straightforward subject, 'The changes in the relation of Crown and Parliament brought about by the Revolution of 1688', and he had produced a farrago of half-digested information and shallow, contradictory generalizations. After pointing out a few specific failings I had no option but to tread on him a little.

'You obviously wrote that essay with only half your attention, Williamson,' I said. 'I don't hit the ceiling if a pupil of mine writes one bad essay, but in future do take more time and try to think more carefully about the subject. You'll enjoy your work more if you manage to find some interest in it.'

He looked at me mutinously. 'I take plenty of interest in it.'

288

'Well, your interest seems to have run dry on this occasion. People who take an interest in a subject usually manage to think a few consecutive thoughts about it. All you managed this time was random jottings.'

'I did my best,' he said sullenly.

'Look, Williamson, you've read me a number of essays and they've all been better than that one, so you must know it wasn't your best.'

Williamson pushed his chair back and stood up and said, 'There's not much point in discussing it then, is there?'

'No, there isn't. But I'm supposed to give you an hour's tutorial, and there are twenty minutes of it left, so if you'd like to sit down again we'll discuss any historical topic you want to bring up.'

'I don't want to bring any up. I don't want to talk about history. I feel discouraged.'

'Well, do another essay for next week and turn in a better job and we'll start from there.'

I gave him an essay title and told him a few things he might read. Then I said, 'I needn't keep you.' He went off with no form of salutation, but at the door he turned and said, 'I expect the College will be glad to get rid of us cadet riff-raff.'

'You expect wrong,' I said. 'Every one of you is worth a place, and some of you are among the best men we've got.'

He went out as if he hadn't heard me. This one was going to be difficult, I thought. I was slated to be his tutor until the summer of 1947, when he took his Schools and went down, but he didn't have to stay with me if he really disliked me so much. I decided to ask Bax what to do.

'Persevere,' Bax said. 'Let him work out his bad feelings on you. If you absorb them without getting offended he may surprise you by beginning to work really well. I've seen it happen.'

'How long shall we give it?'

'A couple of terms. If he's still unco-operative with you by about next Easter, we'll send him out to someone with a completely different approach.'

In the end, Williamson did get over his bad patch. It took the whole two terms, and I was just about to ask Bax to send him to someone else when he suddenly seemed to decide that it was time to straighten up. He became a perfectly sound student and when it came to his Schools he got a creditable Second.

One cheerless December afternoon with the light almost drained out of the sky by about four o'clock, I was sitting in the Common Room having a cup of tea and contemplating the approach of Christmas, that first peacetime Christmas that so many thousands had looked forward to, when the Common Room telephone rang with an enquiry for me. The porter had taken a call for me in the lodge, put it through to my room and, not finding me there, had started to ring round. I told him I would go back to my room and take the call. I went over and, when it rang again, picked it up. It was my mother. I felt a stab of anxiety. She so rarely used the telephone. Had something happened? Was it my father?

'Peter,' she said, and I could hear the tension in her voice, 'I want you to do something for me. It's important. I want you to go and see Brian.'

'Go and see him? He'll be at work, won't he?'

'No. He's not at work. He's at home, at least that's where he said he'd be when he left here about an hour ago.'

'Look, let me get this straight, Mother. It's not half-past four now, so you saw Brian as recently as three o'clock?'

'Yes. He came in just before we shut at half-past two, and he stayed till about three.'

'Well, that was nice, wasn't it? You always like either of us to drop by.'

'It wasn't very nice this time. He seemed . . . look, I don't want to waste time, Peter. I want you to go and see him. You've got your car, and even if you haven't it's not all that far in a taxi to Horspath. I'm not asking you to go to the ends of the earth to see your brother.'

'To see him?'

'Yes, to see if he's all right.'

I thought for a few seconds. I had two tutorials to give before dinner, one at five and the next at six.

'Look, Mum, will it do if I cancel dinner and go out and see Brian at seven o'clock? I could ring him up now and tell him I'll go round at seven. You see, I've got rather a lot of — '

'No, it *won't* do. Peter, how often do I ask you to do anything for me?'

Oh, Christ, I thought. Scratch a woman and you'll find an emotional blackmailer. 'You know what I'm going to say to that, Mum,' I said. 'I'll do it. I'll just give him a ring first, to tell him I'm coming.'

'That's just it, he's not answering.'

'You've been ringing him?'

'After he left here, I gave him about twenty minutes and then I rang him at home. He'd said he wasn't at work today and he was going home. But when I rang he didn't answer the telephone.'

'Well, that just means he hadn't got home yet. He'd gone shopping with Primrose, I expect.'

'Primrose isn't there.'

'How d'you know that?'

'Brian told me. She's away in London for a day or two. Peter, will you go to see him or won't you?'

'I'll go,' I said, 'and as soon as I've seen him I'll give you a ring.'

'Please go *straight away*,' she said.

I said I would and put down the telephone. Then I asked the porter to put me through to Brian's number. It rang and rang.

I gave up and wrote a note I could pin on the door for my two students, saying that I had been called away. Then I went to the rank outside the college and took a taxi way over to Horspath. It would cost the earth, but today was one of Heather's days with the car. Oh, blast Brian! Why did he have to go down to the Bargeman's with a long face and upset Mother? And I wished, too, that she wasn't so protective of him. He was a grown man, wasn't he?

At last we got to Horspath. Brian and Primrose's house was at about mid-point in a little loop that came out of a slightly bigger road and went back into it after describing a half-circle.

As the taxi drew up, the headlights briefly caught a figure standing on the pavement. It was a skimpy figure: a boy of about twelve or thirteen, just at that age when they start to grow out of their clothes. In that momentary flash I saw his wrists sticking out of his jacket sleeves. Then he moved to one side, and was swallowed in the blackness.

I got out and paid off the cab. Whether Brian was there or not, I wasn't going to use it for the journey back, because my money was nearly all gone. If there was no one to give me a lift back I would have to do the journey in slow stages by bus. Sullenly, I strode up to the front door, knocked, and rang the bell for good measure. There was a light coming through the small opaque windows of the door from the bulb in the entrance hall. Presumably that meant someone was in. Or did it?

I knocked and rang again. A voice on the path beside me said, 'Mister.' I turned. It was the boy who had appeared in the headlights; he pointed past the house into the unlit depths of the back garden.

''E's in there,' he said, and bolted away.

I went round to the side of the house. Brian had built himself a large garage there which had to house not only their current car but the K.3. M.G., and it took up most of the garden. The doors were closed but, once again, there was a low-powered light coming through the windows. Was he in there? Doing a job of some kind? The garage seemed silent as I walked up the concrete drive towards it, but as I approached I did hear a sound, the steady drumming of a car's engine. I went up to the doors. They were closed, and locked. I rapped smartly on the door, hoping to attract Brian's attention. Nothing happened except that the engine continued its steady drumming. Then I began to smell the exhaust fumes.

I raced round to the side of the garage. It had a window, formed of two fairly large panes, joined by a strip of wood down the centre. I looked round. There was a spade leaning against the fence. I grabbed it, and swung it with all my strength at the window. The central wooden strip proved unexpectedly strong, and I had to hit it about four times before I finally had it smashed away. Then I was into the tall oblong gap, wriggling, pushing with my shoulders, getting one knee up and then the other. Some glass was lodged in the frame at the bottom and it cut my knee. Then I was inside, beside the driver's door. It was Brian in the car. In the faint light that filtered into the garage from the lit windows of the house next door, I saw that he had his arms crossed over the steering wheel and his head was down on them. There was a length of hose-pipe running from the car's exhaust and coming into the interior through a slit of window that had been left open beside the driving seat. All the other windows were wound up and the doors were closed.

I snatched at the door handle. It opened and Brian fell against me, unconscious, a dead weight. I leaned over him into the car, reaching for the key to turn the engine off. It was not where I expected it to be and I had to search the dashboard with my eyes, dizzying as I did so. My head swam and I knew that in another few seconds I would collapse across Brian's motionless body and we would go together. I wasn't ready to go, and I wasn't ready for Brian to go either. Please God, I had to find that bloody key. I found it. I gave it a turn. The engine fell silent in the same instant that I ceased to hear it.

I don't suppose I was unconscious for long, probably just a few seconds. When I came round it was to the knowledge that I was about to be sick. Terribly giddy, I swung my head back and out of the open door of the car and managed to get the tidal surge of vomit out on to the garage floor.

I slumped on the floor, my back against the open door of the car, facing towards Brian where he leaned motionless against the steering wheel. Unconscious or dead? As soon as my head stopped swimming I pushed back his sleeve and felt for his pulse. It was ticking. He was alive. I shook him violently: he stirred and lifted his head. His eyes opened. His face looked ghastly, corpse-like.

'Can you walk?' I asked him. I didn't feel strong and his stocky body, I knew, would be heavy.

He said nothing, but began slowly moving over. I helped him. As we left the garage the door swung closed behind us and I heard the latch click into place.

As Brian and I walked slowly towards the house I had a sudden vision of my first student getting to my room in Episcopus and finding the note on the door: 'Called away'.

We got into the house. Brian sat down heavily on a chair beside the kitchen table. I filled the electric kettle and switched it on. Only a few minutes ago, Brian had been standing on the other side of a bridge, in a different kind of territory. A territory where there were no next times. By crossing that bridge he had said goodbye to the very idea of next times. And now he was back.

He shivered and said, 'I'm cold.'

'It's chilly in here,' I said. 'Come into the front room.'

I shooed him along the passage to the living room and he sank on to the sofa. There was a large gas-fire, which I lit. Why, I wondered, had that boy been hanging about outside the house? Why, for that matter, had he been snooping around when Brian had gone to the garage to commit suicide? If he hadn't been, Brian would be dead by now. I would have gone round to the back door, rattled on windows, wasted precious minutes. I might have heard the sound of the car's engine, but I would have heard it only very faintly, muffled by the closed doors, and I would have assumed it was coming from a distance.

The boy had saved Brian's life. Who was he? Just an ordinary neighbourhood boy? No doubt: though if I had had a totally different mental make-up, if I had been a medieval man, for example, I would have concluded that the boy was an emissary from the world of the normally unseen, Brian's good genius, the spirit assigned to protect him.

What was the truth? How could I ever know? It would remain a mystery, lying in my mind amid all the other mysteries, and I knew I would never speak of it to anyone.

As I took an armchair beside Brian, my eye fell on two pieces of paper lying on the floor. An ordinary sheet of typing paper, quarto size, folded once across the middle, had been torn in half: just one decisive tear. It was easy to get the two halves into line and read the message written on it, in a neat, clear hand.

I know I should write a long letter, Brian. Perhaps I will, when I get there and think back over our life. Then perhaps I'll be able to find the words to tell you why it was going wrong. It was just drifting further and further wrong, didn't you feel that too? Don't bother looking for me. I'll be in America. Going to be with Chet. It isn't that I'm not fond of you, though you may not believe me. You may do one day, when you have time to think it over. Keep going, Brian. Make a new start – that's what I wish for you. Thanks for all the good things.

It wasn't signed. I looked up: Brian was watching me read it. We just sat there looking at the flames of the gas-fire, listening to the faint roaring and occasional popping sound it made. Now and then a car swished by along the road outside. There was no other sound in the room.

Finally I said, 'Well.' Just that one word.

He said,'Yes. Well.'

'Bit of a shake-up.'

'Yes. Too much of one.'

'No, Brian,' I said, turning in my chair and looking straight towards him. 'No. Not too much. You can come through it.'

'Don't say any more,' he said. 'Not yet anyway. I'm just not taking it in. If you want to do anything, make a good strong pot of tea.'

I had forgotten switching the electric kettle on. Fortunately I had filled it full and it was only just coming to the boil as I got to it. I made a pot of tea, then carried a tray into the front room and gave Brian a cup and had one myself. He drank it and then sat on the sofa for a long time without moving. At last he said, 'Peter.'

'I'm here,' I said.

'Peter,' he said again. 'Well, fancy old Peter. Of all people in the world. Nick of time, eh?'

'Looks like it,' I said.

He was silent again and then asked, 'How did you know?'

'Know what?'

'How did you know to come round just then?'

'Mum told me to.'

'Mum?'

'Yes. She rang me up. She was worried about you and she told me to get round here. I was busy and didn't want to, but she wouldn't take no for an answer.'

'Good God,' he said and passed his hand over his eyes.

We sat silent for a few moments and then I said, 'She knows things, doesn't she?'

'How extraordinary. How absolutely bloody extraordinary.'

'Not really, when you think you spent nine months inside her body. In some very deep areas of your being you go on being the same person, I'm sure of that.'

He turned now to look at me, a deep gaze as if he wanted to take me in properly for the first time. 'So if in some deep place I'm the same person as Mum, and in some deep place you're the same person as Mum, we must be a bit of the same person too, you and me.'

'Yes.'

'But I don't know you. We've never really known each other at all.'

'With our minds, no. But with our bones we must have. It's like Mum knowing what you were going to do, with her bones.'

'Didn't do it, though. You came out and stopped me.'

'Well, I hope you're not going to tell me I did the wrong thing.'

'No, I'm not going to tell you that.'

'Let me get this straight, Brian,' something in me made me insist. 'You do want to live, don't you?'

'I don't say I want to, but I'm going to.'

Then I said, 'You know what you've got to do now, don't you? Now, straight away?'

'No, what?'

'Ring Mum, of course. Go straight to that telephone and speak to her.'

'I'll do it when I've had another cup of tea. I still feel a bit groggy.'

'Do it now while I get the second cup. If you sound groggy and she asks you what's the matter, you can say you've got an upset stomach or something.'

I sat with my eyes fixed on him till he got up and went out into the hallway. I heard him speaking to Mum. I went past him with the cups, to refill them in the kitchen. I must have rattled the cups or made a noise of some kind, because he said, 'No, it's Peter. He came over to see me. We're having a cup of tea.' Then he said, 'Yes, Mum, of course. I'll drop over soon. The week-end, probably. Say hello to Dad. Take care of yourself.'

He went and sat in the front room again. When I came in with the tea he said, 'She wanted to know who it was she could hear in the background. Wanted to know if it was Primrose.'

'Ah,' I said. 'Her intuition doesn't go as far as knowing exactly what's happened, then.'

'Perhaps she does sense something. Perhaps that's why she asked.'

We sat and drank tea in silence. Brian did not speak for a long time. I was just casting round in my mind for something to say when he broke the silence. 'Peter, are you superstitious?'

'Yes, very.'

'How does it show itself?'

'I'm very affected by signs and symbols and portents. Things are always seeming to point ahead in some way.'

'What way?'

'I can't be more precise. I just think that . . . things that are going to happen seem to send out waves before they actually surface, which one can often only read in a very general way.'

He sat for so long without speaking that I began to think he had done with the subject. But at last he said, 'That's why I did it.'

I waited, but he said no more. But I couldn't leave it like this, just in mid-air. '*What's* why you did it? Portents? You mean something pushed you?'

'It's the signals I'd been getting,' he said. 'They started coming true. I didn't know where it'd all end. I felt I didn't want to be around for more.'

'You got that part of it wrong, old Brian,' I said. 'One must always be around. Then things have got a chance to come right again. But please go on. I want to know how things look to you. It's as you say, we've never got to know each other, not with our minds. Talk and I'll listen. There isn't anything else I'd rather do.'

'If I'm going to talk,' he said, 'we both need a drink.'

'I'm agreeable to that.'

'There's that off-licence – but it's half a mile and I frankly don't feel much like driving.'

'No,' I said. 'You feel like walking instead. The fresh air's what you need.'

He grumbled a bit; perhaps he had wanted me to get the car out and drive over myself, but I didn't want to go near the accursed thing. I felt, for the moment, a dread of cars. Also I had a lingering headache – after all I had breathed enough of the gas to make me black out – that fresh air would put right.

When we got back with the whisky we sat in front of the gas-fire and had a glass each, to start with, generous measures that were good news. They cradled in our hands comfortably.

'Speak, Brian,' I prompted. 'Omens. Superstitions.'

'It'll mean talking about Primrose,' he said.

'Sure you don't mind that?'

'No. I want to get it out in the open. You know . . . when I first met her I saw at once that she was the kind of girl . . . exactly the kind to be the wife of a racing driver.'

I nodded. The thought had in fact occurred to me also. Primrose had a steely steadiness, something at the centre of her being, that would be needed in a woman who had continually to watch her husband screaming past her at 180

294

miles an hour, and who might at any moment be catapulted off the track into Kingdom Come. No normally constituted woman could stand that.

'It certainly isn't a role most women would want to take on,' I said.

'You know how Primrose seemed to me when I first met her?' Brian turned his whisky glass carefully in his hand, round and round, studying the way the light came through it. 'She seemed like a . . .' he struggled for the right words, 'like a woman and not like a woman. She seemed to . . . have all the things about her I was after and yet to somehow stand apart from it. I don't suppose I'm making this clear at all.'

'Keep trying.'

'There she was, right in the middle of that world. Speed, racing, competition, all that striving to get past the post in front of the next man. Everything narrowed down to one effort . . . the excitement of it! I suppose any sport's a bit like that. But motor-racing – all the noise and the speed . . . and dangerous, even though nobody ever mentioned danger. And there was Primrose, right in the middle of it. In one way she was the spirit of racing, she in herself. Look, you know how easy it'd be to learn to walk the high wire if the thing was stretched out eighteen inches above the ground. You'd just practise till you could do it, and there'd be no nervousness to interfere with your judgement. But as soon as the high wire goes up really high, nobody can walk along it except people with no fear of heights. A normal person would fall off. Speed's the same. Well, Primrose was like that. She had no nerves, and she belonged with people who had no nerves. They were her natural circle. In that way she was the classic person who belongs in that racing world. But in another way she seemed quite apart from it. She was so calm, you see – there was so much noise and bustle and tension about, but she never seemed part of that. She could act quickly, but she couldn't get excited. It was like fear – it hadn't been built into her.'

'Yes?' I said. 'And?'

'Well, imagine me trying to live up to that. She was like a kind of Spirit of Speed. A kind of . . . of . . .'

'Presiding genius.'

'Yes, something like that. When I first met her, I thought I was in that world for life. I never made the mistake of thinking I could ever develop into a racing driver, but I could handle the cars, test-drive them and all that. I could take Primrose into a world she liked to be in. And although I wasn't Nuvolari, I was at least on the inside. . . . Then . . . well, you know what happened.'

'Yes.'

'Billy Morris spoke and from then on I was on the outside.'

'That wasn't your fault, Brian.'

'It wasn't my fault but it put me in a world that just wasn't right for Primrose. For a while I hung on and just lived on hope. I thought Kim might still do something with M.G., if Billy Morris would just see reason. Then it was wartime and the factory was taken off cars altogether. And then blam! A train kills Kim, a lousy bloody train! Peter, do you understand what I'm telling you?'

'Yes. You thought all these disasters were messages from Fate addressed to you personally. I'm sure you were wrong.'

Brian shrugged. He took a long swallow of whisky, emptying his glass.

'But every time one of those bombs dropped on me it threw me further from any life I could have made for Primrose. After each awful let-down I had less in my life that I could share with her.' He poured himself another slug of whisky. 'Well, it's all over now anyway.'

'What will you do?'

'Nothing. I'll just leave it to Primrose. If she wants to get married again she'll have to organize the divorce. I'm just going to do nothing and let it all happen. I don't care if I'm married to her on paper or not. If she's not with me she's not with me.'

I reflected. 'Arranging that kind of thing, from one country to another, and in the absence of any co-operation from you – I can see it putting some good money into lawyers' pockets.'

'I'm not going to bother my head about it. She'll have dollars.'

This talk about arrangements and money brought me back to mundane things, and I remembered that I hadn't telephoned Heather. I did so and told her I was at Brian's and I was staying on for a while because he was alone in the house and had been taken ill.

'What's the matter with him? I was counting on you to — '

'He just needs someone with him for a few hours, that's all, and as it happens Primrose is away.'

She saw through it at once. 'You're trying to tell me something, aren't you?'

'No.'

'Well, you're trying to keep something from me, then.'

'Yes.'

'Why don't you come out with it?'

'I can't.' Brian could hear my side of the dialogue, and I wasn't going to start discussing him with Heather. She would just have to take it or leave it.

'Well, when shall I see you back here?'

'I'll see how things work out. You'd better go to bed if I'm very late.'

'Go to *bed*? Look, what the hell is going on over there?'

'See you later, then,' I said and rang off.

I sat down with Brian again in front of the gas-fire.

'Here we are, then,' I said. 'And this, for the moment, is it. No more talk now of plans for the future and of things in the past and how they might have turned out differently. Just for tonight, we're going to shut the world out and be Brian and Peter, brothers.' I might have added, 'Getting to know each other,' but there was no need to.

'I can't think of a better idea,' Brian said.

We had some more whisky and then we started to feel drunk and realized we ought to have something to eat. We went into the kitchen and found some bread, which we toasted, and two tins of baked beans, which we heated up. There were some bananas slowly going bad in a paper bag; we salvaged two that were still eatable. There was some instant coffee and some milk. Sitting at the table, the grill and the gas-rings warming the room, we had an excellent meal. We even washed up. And all the time, we talked. Mostly, we reminisced about our boyhood. We laughed over the great old comic characters who peopled it: Charlie the drayman, Old Trundle, some of our teachers who seemed in retrospect like Dickensian grotesques. And – I can't help it if this sounds incredible – we were happy. We let the years slip away. All the effort and struggle, all the things that had gone dreadfully wrong, even all the successes that had to be paid for in such hard currency, we let them all blow away. The past, as a subject for meditation, has one great advantage over the present or the future: you know you have survived it.

After eating and washing up we went and sat by the gas-fire again and started on what was left of the whisky. At first our mood of irresponsible happiness stayed with us, but inevitably as the evening lengthened out it began to ebb away. Part of it, of course, was the boomerang effect of the alcohol: whisky on an empty stomach gives you a powerful lift, but it drops you just as far. And quite apart from the whisky, there were hard, cold fingers of truth poking through our rainbow-coloured wall of dreams. I was sitting with my brother, who had just been deserted by his wife and had tried to kill himself. My own situation was not as extreme as that, but it was certainly not a good one; I was married to one woman and trying by sheer will-power to get over a passion for another. Finally, after a particularly long silence, he stood up and said, 'I don't want to stay here.'

'In this house, you mean? You'll put it up for sale, I suppose?'

'No, I mean tonight.'

'Tonight? But what — '

'I'm going to get on the road.'

'*What?* You can't mean driving. You've got a skinful. You'll have a smash.'

'No, not driving. I'll just get out on the ring road and thumb a lift. One of these all-night transport drivers'll probably pick me up.'

'What?' I said again. 'You can't mean it. Where would you go *to?*'

'Oh, just anywhere. What I can't face is staying here. It's the house. I can't spend a night here.'

'Yes, but Brian. Just wait till it gets light in the morning. Look, there's no need to go to bed, we'll just sit here. I'll be with you and we'll make coffee. Then as early as you like in the morning you can pull out. But that'll give us a chance to talk it over and perhaps we can hit on some more practical arrangement.'

'You don't understand. I have to get out.'

'In the *morning*, brother. I don't care if it means quarrelling with you, I'm not going to have you standing on the edge of the ring-road in a freezing December night, waiting for some lorry-driver to give you a lift to God knows where.'

He looked at me stonily, and for a moment I wondered if he was going to shove his way out of the house by force. Then he went out of the room and I heard him in the kitchen, putting the kettle on. 'We'll make coffee,' he called to me, and I knew my suggestion was accepted.

I hardly remember much about the next few hours. We drank coffee in large cups, and that prevented us from actually falling asleep, but it couldn't be said to keep us actually awake. We were in a drugged state, emotionally and physically exhausted. Slumped against the back of the sofa, my mind crammed full of indigestible thoughts till it was like the stomach of someone who had eaten a large pork pie, I must have sunk into a coma, because when I opened my eyes there was a faint border-line of light round the edges of the curtains. Brian's chair was empty. Had he bolted? Angry with myself for losing consciousness, I scrambled to my feet and went quickly through the other rooms. He was nowhere in the house. He must have gone! I ran to the front gate and looked up and down the road. A milk-float was making its leisurely way round the crescent, stopping every few yards while the driver made his deliveries. I asked him if he had seen a man on foot. 'No,' he said. 'It's too early for the postman,' and laughed as if he had made a joke.

I turned and went back towards the house. There was a thick white frost over everything and it was terribly cold. I shivered, trying to get back through the front door. But then I looked past the house and saw that the garage door was open. There was a scraping noise coming from inside it.

I went to the garage and looked in. Brian was in the part furthest from the door, where he kept the tarpaulin-draped shape of the K.3. racing car. The tarpaulin was off now and the projectile stood there, greyhound slim and beautiful. He had the engine cowling off.

'Brian,' I said.

He looked up and said, 'Hello. I've been checking the tappets. And it's a bloody nuisance not to be able to start the engine.'

'Why? Won't it start?'

He grinned and said, 'Have you ever heard it?'

'I don't think I have.'

'Well,' he said, 'it isn't the kind of engine you start at six o'clock in the morning in a thickly populated neighbourhood. I may be leaving this district for good, but I don't see why I shouldn't let the poor sods sleep on my last morning.'

'How long have you been messing about in here?'

'Not messing about. Attending to the K.3.'

'How *long*?' I insisted.

'Oh . . . an hour or two.' He was shivering.

'Come in the house at once,' I said. 'That's an order. You're not fit to look after yourself.'

'I'll come in and get warm. But I'm moving out with the K.3. and I'm just making sure she's in trim.'

'You don't mean you're going to drive her.'

'Of course not, imbecile. A single-seater racing car with no lights or mudguards? She's coming on her trailer.'

We went into the house and had hot tea. If there had been any food I would have made him eat some. I felt terrible. He must have felt even worse, fumbling about in an unheated garage in that freezing dawn. Tappets! The poor man had needed to find reassurance and comfort in touching his beloved, the only beloved he had left.

After we had drunk the tea and made ourselves more or less presentable (I knew I would have to go home and wash and shave, but at least I could put a comb through my hair), Brian moved straight into action, throwing a few articles into a small suitcase and then going out to the garage again. In a moment I heard the engine of his workaday car. He backed it out of the garage. I thought of the broken glass still on the floor among the streaks of my vomit. What a mess!

'Could you give me a hand, Peter?' Brian called. He was wheeling out a trailer, which he deftly attached to the rear of the car. 'We have to get her up on to this. You see the spaces are all marked out. There are straps for holding the wheels.'

'I suppose you've got to do it now? You can't do it at a more sensible time?'

'This *is* the sensible time. I'm leaving here. I'm not coming back. There's only one thing I'm interested in taking and that's her.' He patted the car's muzzle.

I helped him to roll the K.3. up on the trailer. It was very light, but it still took two of us to get it up the steep ramps. Then Brian secured the wheels and made a tour of inspection.

All ready, he pronounced. We went back into the house and I followed him. We stood in the sitting room, facing each other. The gas-fire had been on since I lit it the previous evening. The room was warm and stuffy after the winter air outside.

'This is it, Peter,' Brian said. 'I'm leaving here. I'm going to put the house into the hands of an agent and just sell it. There's a mortgage, of course, but I'll clear that off with the proceeds.'

'But you can't do it all without being here.'

298

'Look,' he said, 'if I went out on the main road and fell under a lorry the house'd have to be cleared and sold without me. So it can be done.'

'Yes, but who's going to do it?'

'I won't beat about the bush, Peter,' he said. 'It's something I'm hoping you'll do for me.' He took from his pocket a ring with two keys on it.

'Me? But where the hell will you be?'

'Towcester, I hope.'

'Towcester? Wait a minute.' I thought for a moment. 'A little place between here and Northampton? What on earth are you going there for?'

'To live. For some time, at least. You needn't look so puzzled, it's not really a mystery. There's a village called Silverstone just outside Towcester, and it's had a wartime airfield beside it, and now that the airfield isn't going to be used for flying they're going to turn it into a motor-racing circuit by linking up the runways. It's not perfect, but it's a way of getting circuit on the cheap, and we've lost Brooklands because the shareholders sold it while most of the racing types were away at the war, and we've lost Donington Park because Lord Whateveritis wants his park back, and we've got to race somewhere. Well, a friend of mine lives in Towcester, he moved there to be near the circuit and generally get involved from the beginning. I thought I'd go over there and look for a house. I was thinking of it before . . . this happened. Now there's every point in doing it quickly. Takes my mind off things.'

'So,' I said, 'you're off to Towcester with a change of underwear in a suitcase and your racing car on a trailer, and you want to give me the job of selling this house and everything that's in it?'

'There are people who clear houses. But it won't come to that except for the odds and ends. I'll send a van for the furniture when I've got somewhere to put it.'

I looked round at the house, the furniture, the whole awful chore.

'I'll do it,' I said. 'But don't expect me to do it efficiently.'

'Oh, no,' he said. 'That'd be too much.' He grinned, suddenly. 'Come on, I'll give you a lift home and then I'll be on my way.'

Michael was just setting off to school when we drew up in Marston with the racing car on its trailer behind us. His eyes almost popped out of his head. I couldn't talk fast enough to deal with his torrent of questions, and told him to get on and go to school and everything would be explained when he got back. He hung about in the roadway, goggling at the K.3., till I finally chased him towards the bus-stop.

Brian didn't come into the house. He just dropped me and waved to Heather when she appeared at the front door.

'Now,' she said, 'you can just tell me what you've been doing.'

'Drinking coffee,' I said, 'and loading a racing car on to a trailer.'

After that I had a bath, shaved, dressed and had breakfast. And while I ate I told her the story.

Winter had now really set in. Winter always does set in, of course, but the first two or three after the war seemed particularly gruesome. One could tighten one's belt when it was a matter of defeating the Germans or Japanese; but what was it to defeat 'shortages'? Vague resentments floated in the air, and were attached to scapegoats who were distrusted for any reason. 'The Government', of course, was one: the landslide Labour victory in the 1945 General Election had kept a Socialist party in power, which gave the popular press, overwhelmingly Conservative-owned, a target for orchestrated grumbling. 'The Americans', too, were useful as an Aunt Sally. Lend-Lease, the favourable financial arrangement whereby Britain had been supplied with war materials and fuel without having to pay on the nail, ended in the autumn of 1945 and this was widely believed to be the result of American hostility to Socialism. It was vaguely linked in the popular mind with Truman's policy of countering the world expansion of Communist power, as if the two were in some way the same thing. Actually the continuation of Lend-Lease was hardly the kind of thing that would have been likely once the war was over, but it certainly caused a hardening of the discipline imposed on the British population. Bread, for instance, which had never been rationed throughout the war years, was rationed in 1946, and pretty strictly too.

None of this would have been serious in itself – after all, no one was actually starving, and there were hopeful signs in the air that society might be slowly turning in the direction of more social justice – had it not been that, like all times of shortage, it produced horrible creatures who exploited it. At the milder end of these stood the Spiv, that street-corner character with pointed shoes, padded shoulders and a hairline moustache, who had managed to corner a consignment of something or other and was busy selling it off with one eye out for the approach of a policeman. The Spiv could be lived with. But at the extreme end was the gangster who kept the black market supplied. With the melting away of wartime restrictions and controls, expensive restaurants could afford to open their doors to a prosperous *clientele* who liked fillet steak and had no intention of accepting whale-meat or frozen mutton. These people could pay; the expensive restaurants saw to it that they did pay; the black market saw to it that the expensive restaurants had plenty to serve; and the gangsters pulled up after dark in unmarked vans and made deliveries to the restaurants. Money changed hands. Organized theft occurred. And if the theft was resisted, then it was backed up by violence.

Anyone who farmed beef cattle during the winters of 1945/6 and 1946/7 would usually admit that in the morning, doing their rounds, they would often discover that an animal was missing. It happened to sheep as well as cattle, though naturally more often to cattle. The customers of expensive restaurants are not as a rule fond of mutton, even with the chef's best caper sauce.

There were cases of this kind of cattle-rustling in Oxfordshire. But to the best of my knowledge only one farm worker was actually killed, and the evidence indicates fairly enough that his death was an accident.

About the most surprising death of an Episcopus man during the war was that of the College's Fellow in English, a dour, seldom-spoken man named Warren who had always kept himself to himself, rarely engaged in conversation, and appeared to have taken some kind of sacred vow never to make any reference, overt or otherwise, to English literature. He never published anything, though he was said to be engaged on a vast collection of the letters of Thomas Love Peacock. When his papers were gone through after his death, no trace of these documents was discovered; perhaps he was keeping them in a secret hoard somewhere else. Being of military age (just about) but too old for combat duty, Warren had, by one of those quirks of wartime administration, found himself working for the information services in, I believe, Ankara, and, succumbing to a rare form of infection, had left his bones in that city in 1944, uncommunicative to the last. There was, I remember, a brief and acrimonious wrangle at an early post-war Fellows' Meeting to decide whether or not Warren's name should go on the Episcopus College war memorial. The diagram of the argument was roughly this:

Position 1: the memorial should only contain the names of those killed in combat with the enemy. Position 2: Warren had been fighting the enemy with his brain, by being in the service of British propaganda. Position 3: his catching this disease was presumably an accident; the bacillus was not of German or Japanese origin. Position 4: the bacillus inhabited Ankara rather than Oxford, and Warren had been in Ankara in the service of his country; therefore, he had died on active service. This proposition squeaked through on a narrow vote, and Warren's name became one of those commemorated in sonorous Latin in the quadrangle that led to the garden.

That left the problem of how to fill his vacancy. 'English', after a timid beginning when it was under the cloud of not being regarded by many people in Oxford as an academic subject at all, being domestic and accessible, was in 1945 gathering pace and attracting greater numbers. The choice of someone to handle the subject could be an important matter for the College. Reading the material that was circulated to the Fellows before the question came up at the next College meeting, I was interested to see that Garrity, the man I had encountered in the hedge near Mulberry Hall, deep in the poems of Trakl, had applied for the post; and to notice, too, that he had the recommendation of several senior figures in the English Faculty.

'I know this man,' I said to Bax.

'Do you? He was quite a lot senior to you. He'd gone off to work at Exeter, or wherever it was, long before you came up.'

'Yes, but I met him during the war.'

'During the war? When you were never here, on principle?'

'Well, as it happens I met him out in the country. I stumbled on him one week-end afternoon, sitting by himself with a book of German poetry, almost hidden by a thick hedge.' I smiled as I recalled the scene. 'I liked him. He was . . . a bit like the White Knight, you know, in Lewis Carroll. Completely wrapped up in his thoughts. His thoughts, not himself. Self-forgetful, actually. He was reading Trakl.'

'Who?'

'George Trakl. I'd never heard of him. But Garrity said he was fascinating and had a lot to say to the present moment.'

'He does,' Bax said drily, 'have these enthusiasms.'

'I'm not surprised to hear that, but I'll bet, even on ten minutes' acquaintance, that they're not half-baked enthusiasms. I expect he knows a good deal *about* the work he gets entranced by.'

'Oh, yes, he does. He's a good scholar.'

'What's his background? I'm afraid I didn't read the hand-out very carefully.'

'Well, he's pretty much my generation. He was still a little senior to me as an undergraduate, but then he stayed a long time. He read Mods, and then Greats, and I think he did reasonably well. Then he read the English School and got a good first. He's always been very well-read. Knows languages too. Seems to learn a new one every year, just to keep his hand in.'

'Did he look for work here?'

'Yes, he put in for a lot of things, but nobody in Oxford felt quite ready to take him on. You know how conventional they can be. When it came to the pinch no college was quite ready to vote Garrity in as a Fellow. He's a bachelor, so he'd be living in College, and I suppose they felt if they had to see him at every mealtime they might find him a bit much.'

'I'm sorry to hear that,' I said. 'I can't think that he would have made himself unpleasant in any way.'

'Unpleasant, no. But he seemed a bit odd to the conventionally-minded people, who are always in the majority. He grew his hair down to his shoulders, for a time, and that didn't do any good.'

I could imagine Garrity's narrow, aquiline face peering hawk-like from between two curtains of brown hair, and perhaps his foul-smelling pipe clenched in the middle. Personally I would have welcomed the sight. But I knew quite well that there were those, and a majority, who wouldn't.

'Well, I think it's a damn' shame,' I said. 'What happened to him?'

'Oh, he got a University post. But not in Oxford, which must be what he wants because he's trying again.'

'Well, of course you can see that a man like that would be happier in Oxford. The completely dedicated scholar who hasn't got much of a social manner is a traditional figure here, and God help us if that ever ceases to be true.'

'It was truer in the old days of Life Fellowships,' Bax said. 'Up to 1924, when a man was elected to a Fellowship at Oxford he was in it for life, and people could develop richly crusted characters without bothering to measure themselves against ordinary standards. But not now. The modern don is more like an ordinary bureaucrat. I'm a bureaucrat. Even you are, though you're too irascible to be much of a success at it.'

This last sentence took me aback. Was that how I seemed? I had always thought of myself as rather tolerant and patient, but I now suddenly realized, in a flash of illumination brought on by my old tutor's calm candour, that this was an illusion. I knew that feelings of irritation welled up in me fairly often; when I thought of Hunt, for instance, or when Watson's supercilious tones floated towards me across the Common Room. But surely those would be the normal reactions of a human being? Irascible? I, Peter Leonard?

Bax, whether or not he was aware of having delivered a telling blow to my illusions (it would be typical of him to do it without any outward signs of knowing that he was doing it), was talking levelly on about Garrity.

'He's always had his partisans. Ransom likes him and never loses a chance to state his case.'

'Good for Ransom,' I said.

'And for that matter I shall vote for him myself. He's a considerable scholar. I've been looking up his work. He's done a very valuable edition of the Parnassus plays.'

'What on earth are the Parnassus plays?'

'It's a trilogy of plays written by some gang of Cambridge undergraduates in about 1600. They deal with a character called Philomusus and his cousin Studioso, who set out on a journey to Cambridge to get themselves an education. They meet all sorts of allegorical figures on the way, who try to dissuade them. You see them on their way back to London and it becomes a satire on various contemporary issues. You have to know a whole lot about England in 1600 to edit those plays, and it's obvious that Garrity does. I was impressed. Quite apart from his wide reading in all these European literatures, the man's a whale in his own pond. And he's an Episcopus man who'd like to come home. I shall vote for him.'

'Well, I shall too, that's for certain. I'm glad he's coming up for an interview. I look forward to seeing what he looks like with long trousers on.'

'Ah, yes, you saw him in those khaki shorts, did you? They're famous. They're as much part of him as that stuff he drinks out of those nip-size bottles.'

'Morrell's College Ale,' I said.

'That's right. You have a good memory.'

'Not particularly. It's not very long since I heard him name the stuff, and his way of uttering the words is intensely memorable.'

I gave an impromptu imitation of Garrity saying, 'Mor-rell's Coll-idge Ale.' emphasizing each syllable separately, and gestured with my hand as if I were holding a pipe and pointing with the stem. Bax gave one of his rare chuckles.

Settling into the house at Chinnor was a terrible sweat, and of course took much longer than we had anticipated. We started moving our chattels in about the end of October, when the people vacated the house, and the winter overtook us long before we got settled. In the winter of 1945–6 just about everything was scarce, or unobtainable, or old and worn-out, or too expensive to contemplate. Central heating was very rare in those days, and the vast majority of houses were heated by open coal-fires; there was never enough coal to go round, and sometimes there were outbreaks of industrial unpleasantness in which the supply died out completely. The one good thing, to me, about our move to the countryside was that it became easy to get logs. I built log-fires morning, noon and night. I carried logs, stacked logs, sometimes spent half a day sawing up logs to make them small enough to go into the grates. But a life of academic calm, uninterrupted scholarly seclusion, it wasn't.

Christmas came and went; another good point for the move was that we had, genuinely, so much to do at home that we could duck an invitation to Jasmine Farm. I went over to Oxford to have a Christmas Day drink with my parents and Brian in the bar of the Bargeman's before they opened at twelve o'clock, and that was just about it for our first peacetime Christmas. I think our parents were glad not to have to set up an elaborate family celebration. They felt keenly the departure of Primrose. They had grown up in an epoch in which marriages were indissoluble. Even unhappy marriages were indissoluble; even marriages that drove people to despair were indissoluble. This notion underlay the Victorian notion that murder, as a way out of an impossible marriage, was just about preferable to divorce. It caused less rocking of the social boat to destroy a human body than to destroy a marriage.

As for Brian, he drove over on that Christmas morning from Towcester, bringing with him the friend who was putting him up while he went through with the purchase of a house in the town. The friend's name was Fred. He was a burly, jovial man in a tweed cap; when he took off his tweed cap he revealed a large egg-bald head. He had been, Brian told us, a frequent competitor in races at Brooklands in the 1930s, and the racegoers had made something of a pet of him and given him the nickname of 'Curly'. He and Brian were full of plans, though Brian was going back to his old job at Abingdon for the time being.

The short school holidays flashed by, with Mike getting to know the area and pronouncing himself satisfied with what he found. We had solved the school problem because, while it was now too far for him to go to Oxford to school each day and I was still determined he wasn't going to board, there was an excellent day school at Thame, which was accessible. That at any rate had worked out well.

He went back to school on the morning of 6 January or thereabouts. On that first morning I took him in the car, though it was agreed between us that from

Day 2 he would get himself there on the bus as befitted a well-grown man of almost twelve. It was a cold, dark morning, with the countryside deep in the sleep of mid-winter. Our side of the earth had just begun to tilt back towards the sun, but only the first signs of the tilt were visible, a moment or two of extra light in the afternoon, a sharp glitter over the frosty fields in the morning.

I went with him into the school and released him into his new life as one might launch a fir-cone on to an unknown stream. Good luck, young voyager. May something, if only my love and thoughts, guide you safely through the difficult years ahead. Then, sobered by such a momentous occasion, I turned the car round and drove back. When I got into the house Heather was on the telephone.

'My God,' she was saying. 'My God ... My God,' over and over again she spoke the words softly into the mouthpiece. 'Oh, my God.'

I went and stood next to her and put my arm round her. She seemed hardly aware of it. Her body was rigid, unresponsive. Something utterly horrifying was being said to her over that telephone. 'Shall I come over? Well, later on then? Look, I can't just sit here and do nothing at a time like ... you must need me for *something* ... can I speak to Daddy?' Finally, her face hardening into determination, 'Look, I'm coming over. Now. I just don't believe there isn't something I can do.' She rang off and turned to face me.

'What is it?' I said. 'Heather, for God's sake, what is it?' Her face had gone paper-white.

'Phil. They found him dead in a hedge this morning.'

'In a hedge?'

'Down at the bottom of the half-acre field. The one with the stream at the end of it. My father went out at first light and he was expecting Phil to join him. They had to feed the stock and do some milking. When he didn't find him he looked round. Phil's body was ...' she stopped and a shudder ran through her, '... lying along the hedge at the bottom of the field. He was cold, he'd been dead for hours. There were two sheep missing. There was ... blood on the grass. They don't know yet whether it was the sheep's or ... Phil's.'

'Phil's blood? Was he ... did someone — '

'Murdered,' Heather said flatly.

I led her over to a sofa and made her sit down. I did it as if I were protecting her, and indeed I was perfectly willing to protect her against the impact of news like this, but the fact is that by the time we reached the sofa and sank down on it together I knew it had come only just in time for me. My knees had suddenly gone weak. Blood on the grass? Wounds, murder? Was death stalking these quiet fields? Had he penetrated even *here*?

'Let's get a strong cup of coffee inside us and get over there straight away,' Heather said. 'We needn't kid ourselves that we'll get any kind of welcome, we'll probably be given the impression that we're a nuisance, but personally I couldn't live with myself if I wasn't around when they've had a shock like this.'

'Me too, of course.'

She made coffee. I telephoned Episcopus and put off whatever it was I had to do that morning. We drove over to High Cogges. Petrol was very strictly rationed, and I remember having the unworthy thought that this one trip would clean us out for the rest of the month. I would have to go everywhere by bus. I repressed the thought, sternly, ashamed that it had intruded.

When we got there the place was swarming with policemen. They were measuring everything, examining everything, taking statements about everything. One of them even took a statement from me.

304

Old Burrell was more or less continually with two of them. I didn't get a word with him that morning, hardly had more than a couple of glimpses of him through a half-open door. Alicia Burrell was, as one would have expected, pale but composed. Our visit was – again as one would have expected – something of an anti-climax. If I had thought that this shattering blow might have drawn us all closer together, I had got it all wrong. It seemed, if anything, to isolate us further in our different compartments.

Phil's body had been taken away. Apparently the injury that killed him was a dreadful sight. Old Burrell, who had found the body in the first chill daylight, had seen Phil's legs sticking out of the hedge and gone over to investigate. What he found had made him incoherent. It was his wife who had telephoned the ambulance and the police; then she had telephoned Heather.

We wanted to do something to help, but there seemed to be nothing. Heather offered to cook lunch, but her mother said she was not hungry and wouldn't be having any lunch. We hung about till after mid-day; then, with promises to keep in touch, we drove off.

We had lunch in a pub and tried to get our minds round what had happened. But we still had so little information. We didn't even know, at that stage, how Phil had been killed. Only later did we learn that he had a hole through his throat, clean through from front to back, and the police had found, in the grass under him, an object they did not immediately recognize. They took it down to the police station and there it was identified as a bolt from a crossbow.

It flashed into my memory that at the end of the fifteenth century there had been a serious international attempt to outlaw the crossbow as a weapon too horrible to be used among civilized nations. It had gone the way of all attempts to outlaw weapons. And now Phil – Phil! – had been smashed to death with a crossbow bolt.

'What are the theories about it?' I asked Heather. 'Presumably they were thieves after sheep. Does anybody know how he to came to tangle with them?'

'Nobody heard anything. It was a completely successful crime. Just two sheep missing and Phil's body in a corner of the field.'

Yes, I thought, it would be in a corner. I could see it clearly in my mind's eye. He must have been doing what he was always, most characteristically, doing: he must have been lurking in the shadows. Even on a moonless night there would be some patches of darkness that were darker than the rest, where the hedge was tall and dense. He must have been there and they must have been startled to come suddenly up against him. But what was he doing out of doors at all? If he had heard a van drive up, park in a quiet spot and switch off the engine, he may have thought there was a couple inside making love. Something worth peeping at. That would have been enough to make him pull on his boots and trousers and come soundlessly out of his den, even if he had been in bed. If so, he wouldn't have been the first *voyeur* who had got killed more or less by accident. But however ignoble the impulse that had drawn Phil out into that field on that particular night, it had drawn him to his death.

'My father had to go and identify the body,' Heather was saying. 'He couldn't talk about it coherently, but apparently the bolt had gone through Phil's neck from one side to the other.'

'Are they sure it was a crossbow?'

'Perfectly sure. The police have seen a lot of them this winter. Only all the others had been used on animals. After all, how d'you steal a bullock? With luck you might drive it into a van, use the crossbow to slaughter it inside the van, then butcher it and fling out the bits you don't want.'

'They smash its skull in, you mean?'

'Well, that's how it's done in a slaughterhouse. They have a special kind of pistol, which these chaps either can't get hold of or wouldn't want to be caught with. And besides, a crossbow is silent.'

'Good God.' I was horrified.

I tried to stop thinking about it, but the images wouldn't go away. Even after a war in which one had got used to the idea of violent death, it still harrowed me to think of Phil – or anyone! – being killed by having a tunnel smashed through his neck with a crossbow bolt. It didn't help, either, to think of this terrible thing on sale as a 'sporting' weapon: that there were men in this world who thought it fun to go out and let these things off at beautiful wild animals. Who *were* these people who took such pleasure in the act of killing? How could we get rid of them before it was too late? Not by killing them, because that would breed more killing, but by educating them, helping them to grow into a new humanity.

But whatever happened, it would be too late for Phil, as it was too late for all those millions in the war.

The dreadful fate of Phil cast a gloom over our spirits, Heather's and mine, in those early weeks of 1946. They would have cast an even worse one over Michael's, but we managed to keep the story from reaching his ears for the time being, and that gave us a breathing-space to decide on what to tell him.

It was a low, dark, sad time, and when we unexpectedly had an invitation to go to a party in somebody's rooms in Christ Church, I worked hard to persuade Heather to come with me in spite of her aversion to Oxford social life. I knew the man who was giving the party only slightly and was rather surprised that he had asked us, but that in itself meant that he was out to give a large party, and as he was a wide-ranging character whose life was to some extent London-based there ought to be a chance of Heather's finding someone she would like.

When we came in out of the intense blackness of the January night, it seemed that I was going to be proved right straight away. As Heather, with the first glass of the evening in her hand, began to move across the room, I saw another young woman of about her age detach herself from a group and go towards her, welcomingly. But this welcome was clearly not something that Heather wanted. I didn't hear what passed between them, but I saw plainly enough that Heather kept on walking at exactly the same rate, turning the girl's greeting aside with some perfunctory response.

After that I lost track of Heather for a while, button-holed by a man I knew only slightly, a philosopher from Trinity, with whom I fell into an acrimonious wrangle about Jean-Paul Sartre, then just coming to the height of his post-war vogue. The Trinity chap was all for Sartre as the only person saying something new and stimulating; I, having been disappointed in *La Nausée* before the war and not much impressed by *L'Être et Le Néant* since then, was maintaining that Sartre's was largely a spurious reputation whipped up by modish Gallophils, though to be fair I modified this opinion slightly when *L'Existentialisme est un Humainisme* came out the following year. Anyway, we fairly went at it, and the next time my eyes searched out Heather she was standing rigidly in her corner listening to the maundering of a chap with a receding chin who was obviously failing to hold her attention.

306

She shot me a look that presaged trouble, so I started to make my way across the room to see if I could mix her in with some lively company, but once again I was derailed, this time by a man with a grievance: he had written a book on what seemed to him a red-hot historical subject (Swiss troops in European wars in the sixteenth century) and submitted it to the University Press, which had been sitting on it now for some months. Did I know anyone with whom I could put in a word? I didn't, but he obviously disbelieved me when I said so and launched into a passionate recital of the useful purposes served by his book. I groaned inwardly, shifting from foot to foot, and by the time I got to Heather she was hardly in a mood to speak to me.

'Why did I let you talk me into this?' she hissed, as the receding-chin man went off to get her and himself a refill. (It was the beginning of the epoch of mulled Algerian wine at parties.) I whisked her away – let him find her gone when he came back, who cared? – and settled her with a couple I knew to be friendly and cosy, a man who did something obscure in the Music Faculty and his wife who was a pediatrician. Between them I knew they'd find something interesting to pass the time.

But obviously it was no more than passably interesting, because only another forty minutes or so had gone by when she came thrusting towards me through the crowd and said, 'I'm going home.'

'Home? At a quarter to eleven? Not giving it much of a chance, are you? We didn't get here till half-past nine.'

'I didn't say we were both going, I said I was going. You can stay if you're finding it all so enchanting.'

'We've only got one car,' I pointed out.

Well, get a taxi or go round to your College and kip – I'm sure you'll think of something.'

Obviously Heather was fed up; I wondered if boredom was enough to account for it or whether someone had actively annoyed her. But who? Had the receding-chin man been as awful as all that? Then I remembered the girl who had spoken to her at the beginning.

'Haven't you met anyone you know?' I asked, probing cautiously.

'No.'

'I thought I saw a girl speak to you.'

'I can't help it if people speak to me. It doesn't mean I know them. That's what people do at parties. You ought to know, you're such a mad party-goer.'

A rather reclusive person by nature, I had never before been called a mad party-goer, but the extravagance of the phrase seemed to sum up Heather's irritation. She was simply seething to be out of there. All the same, a little defiant streak made me unwilling to go home myself right at that minute. 'Well, if you're sure you'll be all right . . .' I said to Heather.

'I can't think why I shouldn't be all right. I had to do a hell of a lot of being all right while you were up in London all those years.'

She was really in a fighting mood. Only such a mood would make her talk as if the Second World War had been arranged by me as a pretext for leaving her alone at home.

Then she was gone and I turned back to the party but, needless to say, I didn't enjoy it very much. I was just making my way rather dispiritedly over to the drinks table for one last recharging of my glass when the girl who had initially spoken to Heather suddenly appeared at my side. She was wearing very high heels and it struck me that she was not in entirely perfect control of them; she teetered as she came towards me, and when she began to speak I understood why, for she was also slurring her words.

'What have you done with Heather, sweetie?' she asked me, challengingly. 'Where's Heather? You done something with her?'

'She's gone home,' I said.

'Gone home? How do you know that? She tell you?'

'Well, yes, she did tell me,' I said. 'We came together, so she had to make it clear that if I wasn't ready to come home with her I'd be finding my own way home.'

'Go home with her? You live with her or something?'

'She's my wife,' I said.

'Your *wife*? Well, good for Heather . . . so she got there in the end.'

This seemed a reasonable enough statement to cause me to stop and take a good look at the speaker. She was blonde, rather faded, her hair scraped up and piled up on the top of her head; quite a nice blue dress on; the unsteady heels were gold in colour. She had quite a lot of style and it was clear that, normally, she looked after herself well. She peered at my face as if it were something on a different horizon and then narrowed her eyes.

'Let me look at you, sweetie,' she said. 'Let me look at Heather's husband.'

'I didn't catch your name,' I said. 'Mine's Peter Leonard.'

'Hazel. Everybody in Brum knew Heather and Hazel. The terrible twins.' She giggled. 'Not that we were much alike. Inwardly or outwardly. Heather was always much more single-minded. She knew, you know.'

'She knew what?'

For answer Hazel closed one eye in a heavy wink, and tapped the side of her nose with her forefinger in that conspiratorial gesture that's rather gone out in recent years.

'To me, it didn't matter one way or the other,' she said. 'I mean, there we were in Brum, not the brightest place for two girls. It was a nice flat we had, but neither of us could have afforded it on our own. Pricey. Edgbaston way. D'you know Birmingham? Well, don't bother. But the bit we were in, it was quite posh. At first I thought to myself, it'll be enough if we stay out of each other's hair. You know some people, they want to take you over. Heather didn't seem that type. Keeping herself to herself. But turned out better than that. Got along fine, just fine. After the first month or two, we wanted to tell each other things. Any problem came up, couldn't wait to talk it over with Heather. All our problems. Talked half the night, very often. Not that we saw things from the same angle. I was just passing the time. If it was a matter of blokes, well, blokes were just blokes as far as I was concerned. Heather, now . . . knew what she wanted. I just let them come and go. But Heather . . . really was serious about the bloke.'

'Oh, yes,' I said, nodding carelessly to show that I knew all about it. Actually I knew nothing damn-all about it. It had happened during what I thought of as the Long Hiatus, when Heather had disappeared from my life, abruptly, during my second year as an undergraduate – just when she had made that life happy and sane. The reason for her going was that I had dragged my feet about agreeing to her demand for an engagement, or at least a declaration to her parents that I intended to marry her. I didn't see how I could possibly do that, at such an early stage in my life, and by demurring I had lost her. Or so I thought. When, many months later, she had blown into my life again, just as suddenly, she gave me no explanation except a brief sentence or two about having been on a catering course in Birmingham and not having liked it and come away again. Some crazy scheme of her mother's. The whole episode was simply a pool of deep shadow. Here, it seemed, was a chance to shine a beam of light into that pool. Was it wise? On the other hand, could I resist the pull of curiosity, now that I was so close? This Hazel obviously knew something.

'Oh, yes,' I said, playing it cool. 'Yes, that bloke back in the Birmingham days.'

'Yes, Richard was pretty nice.' *Richard!* 'In 's own way. Wouldn't quite have suited me. A bit landed gentry for little Hazel. A bit broad acres. Ancestral towers. I'm from the suburbs. I shall live and die in the suburbs. You can tell that, can't you, when you look at me? Go on, confess. There's something about me says "suburban" right across a room.'

'Well, there's a blend of — '

'Not citified. Not countrified. Suburban, thass our Hazel. I thought I might find some more suburban types here. Don't know Oxford. Nicholas asked me. You know Nicholas?'

'No.'

She jerked her head towards a knot of people who were laughing their heads off over by the fireplace. 'Nicholas said come to the party and stay week-end. Don't really know what's motives are. Don't care much. Just passing the time.' She staggered slightly, steadied herself, and looked at me attentively. 'What do you do, Leonard?'

'I'm a don.'

'Goo' God. So Heather did make it.'

'What can you possibly mean?'

'Got away from the farm. You any idea how much she hated that farm?'

'Well . . .'

'Listen, Leonard, when you meet someone who really hates their background, I mean really *hates* it, 's quite frightening. Heather was really slogging at it with Richard. You could hear them right down the hallway, if you want to know.'

'Slogging . . . ?'

'Trying to get preggers. Had her eye on Richard's ancestral acres. Doing her all-fired damnedest to get pregnant. She had him working on it three, four times a week, and you could hear them right down the — '

'I thought you went everywhere with her. I thought you were the Terrible Twins.'

'We were good friends. Went out a lot. Richard had to be at his dad's place a lot. When Heather wasn't with Richard she was with me.'

'Were you on the catering course with her?'

'What catering course?'

'Why, the one she went to Birmingham to be on. The whole reason why she was . . .' I fell silent.

'Listen, Leonard . . . Whass your surname, by the way? I'd like to know Heather's married name.'

'Carshalton,' I said.

'Leonard Carshalton, what distinguished name. Well, listen, Leonard, sweetie. You obviously know about Richard, but all this stuff about a *catering* course . . . Heather never had any thought of catering or anything else. It was just Richard she was after.'

'But why Birmingham?' I asked weakly.

'Well, that was when his father made him spend six months there, wasn't it? You surely knew all that? How the family money came from some agri-whatsit, tractors and all like that . . .'

309

'Agricultural machinery,' I said.

'Yes, the money came from that and Richard was going to inherit it and take it over one day, and his father made him spend six months in Brum, learning about the factory. He used to turn up at our flat filthy dirty and tired out. First thing he wanted was a bath.'

I looked at Hazel. Her eyes had gone unfocused again. I thought, I shall never see this woman again. Why not just ask her a straight question?

'Hazel,' I said, 'why was it so important to Heather to get pregnant by Richard?'

She went through her nose-tapping routine again.

'Richard,' she said, 'was the kind to do the Decent Thing.'

'Mm.'

'Remember those days, sweetie? The days when men did the Decent Thing?'

'Did he . . . know she was trying to get pregnant?'

Hazel put back her head and laughed. 'Now I *know* you're joking, sweetie,' she said.

Nicholas, whoever he was, now came up to claim Hazel, perhaps remembering that he had invited her to stay the week-end in Oxford and not wanting to find himself upstaged. (He need not have worried.) Hazel beat off the hand he laid on her arm and said to me, 'Heather doesn't like me any more.'

'Doesn't she?'

'No. She didn't want to know me when I said hello to her tonight. She wants to forget that time when we shared a flat. Didn't work, I suppose.'

'Let me drive you home, Hazel,' Nicholas said, leading her away with a firm lock on her forearm.

'Your home or my home?' I heard her ask.

'Mine, of course. Yours is a long way off.'

'Where is my home?' I heard her ask uncertainly.

I hoped she would be all right, but I couldn't spare any attention for worrying about her. I knew I didn't want to stay at the party any more. On the other hand, Heather's suggestion that I should walk round to Episcopus and sleep there was dismally uninviting. I didn't want to face the next few hours alone in my College rooms. I decided to try, even at that hour, to get a taxi to Chinnor. It was a long way, but it might just be possible. I counted the money in my wallet: it should just about stretch that far.

It took me hell's own time to get a taxi firm that would consider a trip like that at this hour, but that was nothing compared with my real troubles. I dialled and dialled, using my host's telephone. By the time I succeeded, only the most hardened core of the guests were still there, finishing up what drink they could find. Our host was sitting on the sofa muttering inaudibly to himself, though whether from impatience to have the place to himself, or because he was drafting in his mind a letter to *The Times*, I could not tell.

When at last I got home and let myself in, Heather was asleep in her half of the bed and showed no sign of waking as I climbed in beside her. That suited me all right. I wouldn't have known, if we had got into talk, what to say to her. There was nothing I felt immediately moved to say. I lay on my back and passively allowed the chaos in my consciousness to settle down until something describable as a 'state of mind' should emerge.

The first thing I felt conscious of was an enormous sense of loss. I felt robbed, stripped, bereft. When I tried to analyse what it was that I felt robbed *of*, it seemed to me that I could put it in one word: motivation.

Here I was, fighting a desperate battle to save our marriage. True, viewed from

310

the outside, nothing was actually threatening our marriage. My wife had not announced her intention of leaving me, nor had I formed any intention to leave her. But my infatuation – to give it no better name – with Mairead had, undeniably, drained our marriage of such life-blood as it had had – which, in fact, had not been all that much. I wanted, however, or at any rate had many reasons for wanting, to put the relationship with Mairead behind me. Lying there in the dark, I saw in my mind Michael's fresh, alert little face and quicksilver body in his blue dressing-gown, as I would see it in a few hours when he woke and came into our room. I had been so determined, after being away from him for much of the time, not to leave him to finish his growing up without me. No, not had been: was. It *must not* happen.

But the motivation? Wasn't it an absolute necessity to love the woman as well as the child?

Well, why shouldn't I love her? She had used me: all right. She had played on my obsessive physical need for her – or for someone like her – and proceeded, first, to receive me handsomely and then manipulate me. Well, I reasoned, why not? Might not happiness have been the end result of it?

It wasn't as if I were too good for such treatment. I wasn't a high spiritual type. I was a pretty selfish sod who had always, on the whole, behaved as a selfish sod behaves. Looking after Number One. It was true that I had no ambition to get rich, nor was I tempted by the ordinary vulgar kinds of power, dominating organizations and ordering people about. That might be held to set me apart from the commonplace worshippers of success. But I knew, in my heart, that I wasn't better than they were, just different.

So why shouldn't Heather, for her own purposes, have used me? If her motive for engineering our marriage had nothing (or very little) to do with loving me, and everything to do with getting away from a background she found unbearable, why should I feel injured?

And then came a second wave, this time of intense pity for Heather. Because, as she must be realizing, expedients like that don't work. Living with another human being, jammed up close to them in the kind of day-and-night physical intimacy that marriage involves, isn't an attractive prospect unless you love that person. If you don't, it is at best wearisome and at worse altogether intolerable.

Heather, with me, was in the wearisome stage. She was bored with me. Perhaps she had never been anything else. But on that basis, I was still supposed to keep out the utterly beautiful, utterly radiant, imperious ... I tried to keep my mind from forming the name of Mairead because the name would bring with it her image. But I failed, of course. The name, and the image, went together, and in that instant my whole being was flooded with longing and regret. *That* was what I had sacrificed, what I had let go, what I had allowed to walk away out of my life.

We had said goodbye and it was now final. I didn't even know where she was: not for certain. I had a few reasonable clues but I didn't actually *know*. I had lost her. It was too late.

Too late! The pain that hit me with that thought was so intense that I actually reared up in bed. Heather still made no movement. Looking back, I'm certain she must have been awake, but with a wise instinct she avoided contact because it would have moved quickly into conflict. Doubtless she sensed the immense distance which, at that moment, separated me from her. Perhaps, for that matter, she was aware of an immense distance on her side, holding her away from me.

I lay down slowly on my back again and stared up at the dark ceiling. I did not, as things stood, know how to go on living. I could see that I *ought* to; what I couldn't see was *how* to.

In spite of all these shocks and traumas, life somehow had to go on. Mostly this was a matter of pushing things down out of sight. The fact of having a routine job to do, requiring one's presence at definite times in a certain place, must have saved many a mind from going to pieces. I think it is from this period of my life that I date my settled conviction that one of the worst misfortunes that can befall a man (women may be different, meshing in with life in different ways) is to have a private income sufficient to release him from the need to earn a wage. There was my work at Episcopus to attend to, and there were the usual preoccupations of family life; whatever I might feel about myself as a husband, I was indisputably a father, a brother, and a son with both parents living. The working week was crammed with teaching, meetings, and one sacred day when I tried to push my own research along: week-ends were filled by family visits and excursions.

The most memorable of these, at this period, was a day spent at Towcester with Brian. Ever since Michael had caught that fascinated glimpse of the K.3. racing car on its trailer, drawn up outside the house in Marston, he had pestered for a closer acquaintance with it – as if his interest in motor-racing had been kindled instantaneously, leaping fully-formed from his forehead like Athene from the forehead of Zeus. On that day at Towcester, therefore, Brian had taken him to see Silverstone racing circuit under construction and told him about the programme of events that were planned for 1947 and – supreme joy! – he had allowed Michael to sit actually in the racing car and grip the steering wheel. They had started the racer's engine, and its throaty crackle had intoxicated the boy – for life, I feared.

On the work front, there were the usual College preoccupations, recruitment to posts in particular. It didn't altogether surprise me, though it came as a disappointment, that Garrity was in the end not elected a Fellow of Episcopus, though he was strongly backed by Ransom with the support of Bax and myself and offstage murmurs of approval from very high in the world of English literature studies. But it was the candidate fielded by Watson who carried the day. For some weeks, Watson had been very busy preparing the ground for a man named Noel Arcady, who he declared would be a very bright ornament of our Common Room. 'Arcady's exactly the kind of man we need,' Watson kept saying. 'He'll bring some sparkle into the place.'

Thinking about this, I looked round the bulk of my colleagues when they were assembled one afternoon after lunch. Given that we were not recruited as professional entertainers, I couldn't see anything particularly dreary or boring about the men I saw around me; but then, as far as I could gather, Watson seemed to think Noel Arcady would take Episcopus College at one bound up to the dizzy heights of worldliness and fashion, rather as if we were to be swept up and suddenly dropped down in the Royal Enclosure at Ascot. At any rate, Arcady was interviewed – not by a meeting of the Fellows but by a small hand-picked committee which Watson managed to keep me out of – and I didn't actually set eyes on this prodigy until, that same evening, he came in to dinner. Impressive, I had to admit, the man was, on what I thought of as a Watsonian level. Tall, good-looking, with a languidly aristocratic manner, he was also, as his conversation soon revealed, clever and quick-witted. Watson had met him on a visit to Cambridge, and, hearing that this young cynosure would soon be looking for employment, had set himself to bring him to Episcopus. He carried with him, as some Cambridge men do, an air of rarefied achievement that could never have grown in the rough and ready atmosphere of Oxford.

Conscious that the only possible chance for Garrity was to present him as the more serious scholar, I tried to engage Arcady in conversation about classical English literature, but didn't know enough about it to make the effort worth while. Mustering the information I had recently acquired in that talk with Bax, I asked him some question about the Parnassus plays, but of course he knew about them, and gracefully guided the talk into an anecdotal channel by recounting some highly amusing story about a production of the three of them at Cambridge that had gone wrong in expected ways, his story studded with names that one was expected to recognize, all the brilliant Cambridge stars. Fed with the admiring questions of Watson, Arcady emerged more and more as the young don who moved easily between the worlds of academic study and the most elevated of literary circles, whose household names he dropped gracefully into his conversation till I found myself beginning to feel that it was probably a mistake to run a candidate like Garrity – so quaint and awkward with his comical bicycle and his fondness for hedgerows and obscure poets – against this dazzling patrician. I knew, fundamentally, that Garrity was the more valuable of the two, but I also recognized the impossibility of getting his nose out in front.

Immersed in these thoughts, I was recalled by Noel Arcady's musical voice: 'Of course one has to be just a little bit careful in handling Morgan,' he said. 'He's the soul of kindness, quite obviously, but even he can have his tender spots that you mustn't tread on.' I was slightly mystified, and it was only when Arcady went on to tell some story about what Morgan had said to Virginia, and what she had said in reply, that I realized 'Morgan' must be E. M. Forster. Peasant that I was, I had not even known that the 'M' in Forster's name stood for 'Morgan'. Clearly I was nowhere. My opinions would not count. Watson, quietly orchestrating the conversation, would make sure that Episcopus did not lose the chance of a man who could drop names like these.

Garrity, by contrast, made a predictable mess of things when he came to the dinner at which he was to be looked over. He had no small talk, which went against him from the beginning; and when someone asked him if he was working on anything in particular at the moment, he answered the question with perfect seriousness, discoursing on the evidence for believing that William Langland was the author of all three versions of *Piers Plowman*, and must therefore have worked on the poem over a period of twenty years. I understand that this view is now generally accepted, but at that time it was disputed, and Garrity was no doubt one of the people who made it generally accepted. But not everyone present shared his passionate interest in the subject, and when, towards the conclusion of the evening, he became involved in a senseless wrangle with someone about Goethe's decision to revive the obsolete metrical form known as *Knittelverse*, not used in German poetry between the sixteenth and eighteenth centuries, the company began to thin and I knew that Arcady would be our next Fellow in English.

I didn't spend a vast amount of time mulling over the revelations I had had from that conversation with the alcoholic Hazel. Yes, they had solved a puzzle that had lain in my mind for years, but somehow it was an old puzzle and the interest had gone out of it. Why Heather had acted as she had during the very early stages of our relationship, what were the precise reasons why we had found ourselves getting married – it was interesting to clear that up, but only as one might solve a yellowed crossword puzzle that had been lying around for ages and suddenly surfaces in a drawer. I could see that Heather, all those years ago, had simply manipulated me; that she had missed her prime target, which was to capture Richard plus ancestral acres, and had settled for me as second best. But I didn't really see how it made any difference, not now, thirteen years later.

It was not the knowledge itself that caused me grief and turmoil, but what followed on from the knowledge: the re-awakening, in a new and terrible intensity, of my longing for Mairead and my regret at having let her go. Mairead! I longed for her, I knew that nothing else, no one else, would save me. Lacking her, my life was a penance. Who cared whether I existed or not? Certainly *I* didn't.

But it was done now, it was over. We had said our final farewells and she had gone back across the sea.

Presumably she was in Dublin. But what use was that to me? Even if I had had an address for her, it would be no use writing to her. She would ignore my letter, thinking it a contemptible sign of weakness.

Well, but – the nagging thought kept on returning – Dublin was not far away. It might happen that I was in Dublin on some perfectly legitimate business. Research, for instance. Any historian of eighteenth-century England ought to have some grip on Irish affairs. How could I understand Irish history if I never went to Ireland? And if to Ireland, then obviously to Dublin... And then supposing I happened to bump into Mairead at a street corner in Dublin, well, it wouldn't actually do us any harm, would it, to exchange a few words in the street? Not that it was at all likely that we would meet. She might not be in Dublin at all. She might easily have been posted to some far-off country. The Diplomatic Service always called on people to travel, and I was not in touch with Mairead.

No, no, I had seen the last of her. All I had left of her was this hole in the centre of my being. Night after night, lying in the darkness, feeling utterly alone although Heather was in the same bed, my thoughts gathered around Mairead. I had no power to prevent them. I re-lived every moment of every meeting she and I had had. I recalled every scrap of our conversation. I have a naturally good memory, and I savoured, pondered, evaluated, every remark we had made and everything that had happened to us, from that first train ride when the man in the duffel coat had been so angry with her about the Treaty Ports to, for example, our day out in Richmond Park when she had tended to be dismissive of Yeats.

Well, I thought, she could knock Yeats as much as she liked, but it was Yeats who had found the only words I could think of that came anywhere near expressing the pain and helplessness that gripped me now:

> I am in love
> And that is my shame
> My language beaten
> Into one name
> What hurts my soul
> My soul adores
> No better than a beast
> Upon all fours.

And surely that was what poets were for, to step forward with the words that managed to encapsulate our deepest experiences, leaving us with the consoling

314

sense that if they could be described in language they might, ultimately, be manageable?

I never knew the moment when I would hear Mairead's voice, as clearly as if she were in the room, ringing in my head. One dusky, rainy winter morning I was in the bathroom, squeezing shaving-cream on to the brush, when I heard her voice demanding, 'What do you tell your students about the Rising of 1641?' And I remembered with shame how I had given her some fobbing-off answer instead of admitting honestly that history, as taught in England, tended to be very reticent about the injustices perpetrated by England against Ireland.

The next time I had leisure, therefore, I investigated that rising and its aftermath, and it soon became clear that if I wanted to know the full consequences for the people of Ireland I would have to read a number of manuscripts that were at Trinity College, Dublin. Thus there was nothing for it but to go to Dublin. Enormous difficulties reared in the way. No currency was available. Every kind of travel restriction was in force. I could not be spared from home; we were coming up to the house-move to Chinnor. I bulldozed on. I was going to spend a week in Dublin during the Easter vacation of 1946, even if the massed bureaucrats of the world should try to stop me.

Why? To look for Mairead? Of course not. I knew I had no hope of starting everything up again with Mairead. She had gone and I had to live with that knowledge. Still, Dublin was the city that might possibly contain her, and that made it sacred in my eyes, the city in all the world that I most wanted to see. And finding out about the Rising of 1641 was a way of communicating with her; it meant that I could reach back into the past, to the moment when she had thrown out that challenge – 'What do you tell your students about the Rising of 1641?' – and, belatedly, rise to it. I could prepare a series of lectures on 'The Seventeenth-Century Foundations of Eighteenth-Century Foreign Policy', and give Irish affairs a prominent place in my narrative. I would dwell in particular detail on the Rising of 1641. And perhaps Mairead, somehow, somewhere, would be aware that I was doing so.

That's how mad I was.

15

Heather and I hadn't gone to Phil's funeral. This was largely because we would have had to take Mike with us, and we didn't want to distress him. He was sad enough about losing Phil as it was. We didn't visit the Burrells for the next couple of weeks either – the dark, chill January weather was against it. The police investigation into Phil's murder seemed to be getting nowhere, and local interest died down.

Then, early one weekday evening, I was at Episcopus, drinking a glass of sherry in the Common Room before dinner, when the porter rang through to say that someone wanted me on the telephone. I was a little jumpy about this; it had bad associations. My mother's call to me to go out and see Brian had come through in exactly these circumstances. What crisis had arisen now, I wondered, as I asked the porter to put whoever it was straight through to me.

It was my father. I could have spoken his words for him, they were so predictable. 'Are you very tied up, Peter? Could you get down here? We could do with a bit of help.'

He never rang for any other reason. 'What kind of help?'

'Well, it's Jim Burrell as a matter of fact. He's round here and we're having a bit of a problem with him.'

'Look,' I said, 'I've finished my day's work and I'm just going to have a meal. As soon as I've eaten it I'll come down. Will that do?'

'Yes, that'll do. But you'll see when you get here that there really is something up. I'm not just fussing.'

'I'm sure you're not, Dad. Don't worry about it. I'll be down as soon as I can.'

When I got down to the Bargeman's, my father waved me straight from the bar into the kitchen. 'Go on through, Peter,' he said. 'You'll see for yourself.'

I went through. My mother met me at the doorway of the kitchen. 'I'm going upstairs, Peter,' she said. 'It'll leave you a free hand. If you talk to him a bit, you can get some idea of what's going on. It started when he came into the bar, about seven o'clock, and said he wanted to see Tom.'

'*Tom?*'

'Yes, Tom, his son. Well, we said Tom wasn't here – if he weren't remembering his lad was dead we didn't want to upset him – and he said he knew he must be because he'd looked up from the street and seen him looking out of the window upstairs. The window of Brian's room, he must have meant.'

She spread her hands in a gesture of helplessness and turned away up the stairs. I went on into the kitchen.

Old Burrell was sitting at the table. He didn't move or speak. There was an empty chair by the hearth, but he was sitting at the table as if he was ready for a game of dominoes or something. Or to interview job applicants. He was bareheaded, a fact that made me suddenly realize that I had very rarely seen him without his pork-pie hat or, sometimes, a frayed old cap. It was the pork-pie he had with him now, lying on the table. The bald crown of his head was covered with large brown freckles. Under the wind-beaten redness of his face his complexion was putty-like. I sat down opposite him as if I were the one who had come in for the game, or the job interview.

We both stayed quite still, not speaking for a long time. At last I began to wonder if he was in some kind of trance. I wasn't sure that he had even seen me, but his eyes must have flickered in my direction, because he finally broke the silence and spoke to me.

'I don't have to tell you how it is, Peter. You knows all about it.'

The safest answer seemed to be 'Yes', and I gave it.

'It happened to you in your turn, like,' said old Burrell, 'and before that it happened to me in my turn.'

'Yes,' I said again.

'When a man's in that grip,' he said, still not looking at me, 'he's in it. He can't move away.'

'No.'

'It happened to you in your turn,' he said again, suddenly turning his red-rimmed eyes on me, 'with my Heather.'

'True enough.'

'You couldn't just walk away. And her in foal.'

'No,' I said. 'I couldn't.'

'Same with me, all them years ago. Thirty-seven years ago. Nearer thirty-eight. Like you with my Heather.'

Thirty-eight years ago? What had happened in 1909?

'What time of year?' I asked, probing at random.

'In the spring,' he answered, staring straight ahead of him. 'It was in the spring. That was why his birthday was mid-winter.'

'Whose birthday?' I asked. But I knew already.

'Phil's,' he said, as if mildly surprised by the question. 'Peg and I had just the one. He was her youngest. Jack never knew. Her husband never guessed from first to last. He might a done, of course. As the years went by he might a looked at the boy and thought . . . Well, it don't matter now. Dead in nineteen-fifteen, Jack was. Only lasted three weeks in France. That was when Peg got so bitter.'

'Bitter, was she?' I murmured promptingly.

'Bitter. But what's the use o' talking? Three weeks and he was gone. Got a telegram, then a letter. She cried all night. And with all them kids. Phil the youngest. Then she started saying it was a judgement on her. Said she'd have to pay for it and I'd have to pay for it. Well, if you ask me, poor Phil's paid for it.'

I was silent. What could I possibly say?

'His neck was all broke open. What was he paying for, with that? Who was better off, for that?' He suddenly stood up, pushing back his chair. I saw that he was wearing breeches and thick woollen stockings, as if about to spend a day walking through thick wet grass. He looked like a countryman in a story-book; but his eyes, as he glared across the room at me, were like those of an animal that has been hunted through city streets. 'I hope they catches 'em,' he shouted. 'And when they catches 'em, they should string 'em up.'

My father, perhaps drawn by the noise of the shouting, opened the door soundlessly, looked at old Burrell and shot an enquiring glance at me. I gestured that I was handling the situation, as far as it could be handled, and he withdrew again.

Old Burrell sat down at the table once more and put his big, gnarled hands over his face. I could hear him weeping quietly. After a long time he took his hands away. 'Phil only wanted to be let alone,' he said in a half whisper. 'He never asked for much. He would a' been quite contented if they'd just let him alone.'

'They should have,' I said.

'I looked after him,' old Burrell said. 'I gave Peg half-a-crown a week so he didn't want for food and clothes. And after the war, when things got more expensive, I gave her more. In the end I was giving her ten shillings.'

'That was a lot,' I said.

'It was a lot,' he said. 'It was the same as the old age.'

We both sat silent for a moment. Then he said, 'It was when she made up her mind to move away. To go up to Wolverhampton where she had that uncle. He had a big house and his wife had died. Plenty of room, and he kept chickens and wanted her to help with 'em. And a couple of pigs. That was when she turned nasty with me. Told me she was going to put Phil in the workhouse. Said her uncle wouldn't keep him.'

'Did they still have workhouses?' I asked.

'Course they did. Had one at Witney. She was going to put him in it and leave him. I felt bad. I'd done my best for him but he hadn't been to school 'cause they wouldn't have him. But I don't see what more I could've done without the whole thing coming out. That wouldn't have been fair to Peg. But she was still bitter with me. Nothing would do but to up and go to Wolverhampton. Nineteen . . . ' he wrinkled his brow ' . . . twenty-six, that was. And that talk about the workhouse for Phil. I couldn't bear to hear her say it. I was married myself then, else I couldn't a got the tenancy. College wouldn't let to a single man without a wife to run the farmhouse. Alice and me, we made up our minds straight away. No point messing about when it's as clear as the road in front of you.'

I wanted to ask him if he had loved his wife, but of course I couldn't. He might not even remember, and in any case I had no right to ask such a thing. 'When you took Phil in,' I said, 'did Alicia know who he was?'

'I never told her,' he said slowly. Then, even more slowly, 'That don't mean she don't know.'

'She's never spoken of it? Even now . . . ?'

'She's never spoke of a lot of things,' he said in a voice so quiet I could hardly hear it.

My mother now entered.

'It's getting late, Jim,' she said gently. 'Won't your wife be worried about you?'

Old Burrell did not seem to understand the question. He looked at her blankly.

'Would you like to speak to her?' my mother asked. When he made no reply, she said, 'We could do it for you if you like, tell her you're here.'

Old Burrell suddenly said, 'I ought to a told the other kids. I ought to a told Tom and Heather as Phil was their own blood, or half of their own blood. They might a let him come closer then. Talked to him more. Brought him in.'

But how could you bring Phil in? I wondered. What could you talk to Phil about? And when Heather as a half-grown girl was suddenly confronted by Phil with his trousers unbuttoned, would she have reacted differently if she had known he was her half-brother?

'I should have stuck to seeing he got taught to read,' old Burrell suddenly said. 'That's where I went wrong. They sent for Peg at the school and told her she had to take him away. Said they couldn't get nothing into his head. They said he could be sent away, to a special school, but she didn't want that. She asked me and I didn't want it neither. Special school! He might never a got out. Sounds more like shutting him up somewhere. He'd be with a lot of kids that were daft. Phil wasn't daft.'

My mother said, 'I'll go and ring up.' She disappeared. The telephone was in a narrow passage at the bottom of the stairs.

'After he come to work for me,' old Burrell said, 'I showed him the numbers. He could count all right, and reckon up. You could send him to buy things. And he could go to Oxford on the bus, and pay his own fare and get it right. He wasn't daft. I learned him the numbers in a week or two. Up to ten he was fine. No, twelve. He knew twelve 'cause he knew there were twelve pennies in a shilling.'

'Did he know how many shillings made a pound?'

Old Burrell shook his head. 'Phil never had pounds. He got his living-place free, so he didn't have to pay a landlord, and I went with him if it was to buy clothes or something big he needed. Phil never had to spend a pound.'

'Hardly any need to count at all,' I said.

'It was for helping round the farm. I used to put numbers on the sacks, like. Sacks of grain, sacks of fertilizer. Anything like that. Feed. Kindling wood. He never mixed up the numbers when he'd once got them in his head. He knew which ones to take out in the field and which ones to fetch and shift about. Phil had plenty of sense. He had a lot more sense than anyone ever give him credit for.'

'Except you,' I said.

'I didn't stand up for him enough,' old Burrell said. 'I didn't do nothing to fight his battles for him. There was a lot more I could a done. I could a been a help to Phil.'

'I don't know what you could have done that you didn't,' I said.

'*You* don't know?' Old Burrell turned his attention on me with surprising alertness. 'What does that mean? You wouldn't expect to know, would you?'

'Well, I suppose if you put it like . . .'

'Why would you know about the kind of life Phil had to live? You never lived a day of it. I tell you I didn't do enough for Phil. I ought to a seen he was all right.'

'Well, you couldn't have done more than you did, surely? You gave him a home, a — '

'A home? You never saw his home. He lived like one of the animals,' old Burrell said heavily. 'My Phil lived like an animal in a shed.'

'Well, but — '

'You never saw where he lived. Even Michael never saw where he lived. Only me sometimes.' He paused. 'And then to finish up like that. Phil, Phil!' He wept.

My mother now came in and said calmly and gently, 'Jim, I've made up a bed for you and I'm going to make a pot of tea.' Old Burrell's initials, J. G., stood for 'James George'. I had never heard him called by either of them.

'I must get home,' he said. 'There'll be the milking at half-past five. Phil used to do it.'

'You can't need to milk at half-past five in the dead of winter. The cows can't be that loaded with milk, they can wait a bit.'

'Is it winter?' he asked. And he turned his eyes towards the window. The curtains were drawn. He stared at them. 'I thought it was spring,' he said.

'No.'

'That's the time when you has to look out,' old Burrell said. 'That's the time when it all comes over you.'

My mother brewed the tea, poured out a cup for Jim Burrell, and put it out in front of him.

'Drink it, before it gets cold,' she said.

'Katie,' he said hoarsely.

'Tell me,' she said.

'I think every man,' old Burrell said slowly, considering his words carefully, 'has a patch of madness in him. It's in his being somewhere. Like a patch of weeds in a garden. Only he can never get near to dig it over.'

'No,' she said. She nodded, encouraging him to go on.

'Every time he gets his fork, or his spade, and goes towards that patch to clean it up, something stops him. He never gets to it.'

My father, who had been engaged in some interminable labour, now entered and sat wearily at the fireside. My mother handed him a cup of tea and stood beside him, her hand resting lightly on his shoulder.

'Every man, in his lifetime,' old Burrell said, 'has done something, or it may be he's done a number of things, that you can't explain, only they must come out of this patch of madness he's got inside him.'

'Don't women have it?' my mother asked.

'No. One here and one there, it might be, but mostly they're in control. They got reasons for what they done. Now you take a man, he'll up and do something for no reason.'

'Or for a hidden reason,' I said.

'No reason at all,' said old Burrell, bringing the flat of his thick hand down on the table. 'Now you take my Tom. I've lost him. Before ever I lost Phil I lost Tom. That's the end of it. Can't get no more, now. And he was a fine lad. Everybody knew that. But he rushed into it. He had to get into one of these damned aeroplanes and rush up into the sky and get into it. Tom. That was his patch of madness.'

'The Air Force — ' my father began.

''Tweren't nothing to do with the bloody Air Force. My Tom was mad for flying in the sky long before he ever went near the Air Force. I could never keep him away from anything that would fly up in the sky with him sitting in it. The sky? He was a farmer's son. He could have spent his life with his boots on good soil, good farming land. But no – it wasn't the land he wanted, it was the sky. And if Tom hadn't been mad, if he could have stayed with his feet on the ground that fed him, he could have looked after Phil. He'd have had to. It's in my will. But Tom's gone because he couldn't keep away from them bloody flying machines, and Phil's gone because he had to go night wandering. I tell you, all of us men have it. A patch of madness in our souls, that's what we've got.'

There was a short silence, then my mother asked, 'What about you, Jim? Have you got a patch of madness?'

'Oh, mine,' he said, 'mine was Peg.'

We all sat there, stalemated. I went to the telephone and spoke to Heather, told her her father seemed fairly quiet and my parents were going to keep him overnight.

'You make the place sound like a hospital,' she said.

'That's what it is, a bit.'

'Is he in a bad state? I mean, what's he *doing*?'

'I'd say he was doing just about the most sensible thing in the circumstances – talking to two people he trusts and feels safe with. He was confused at first,

320

looking for Tom, but he seems to have forgotten that. He talked a lot of stuff out and calmed right down.'

'The poor man. I'm very grateful. Well, for God's sake be careful if you're going to drive back.'

'Right,' I said. 'I'll be about half an hour.'

'Don't drive fast. The roads must be sheets of ice.' And we rang off.

I went back into the kitchen. Everyone had finished drinking tea. My parents were looking at old Burrell in a slightly undecided way. I took charge.

'Time to turn in, Jim,' I said, putting a hand on his shoulder. 'I'll just see you comfortable upstairs before I drive off back to Heather.'

He looked up at me as if wondering what I was doing there. 'Upstairs?'

'Yes, we think it's too late for you to drive out to Cogges in this awful weather. Better wait till it's light, get yourself some rest.'

'That's right, Jim,' my mother said with a sweet smile. 'I've seen to your bed.'

'But you got no room upstairs,' he said, fixing her with an unmoving eye.

'Yes, we have. We've got a spare room. We've had one for years and years, ever since Peter moved out to College, and that must be, ooh, that must be . . .'

'A room you may have,' old Burrell said, 'but it can't be empty, can it?'

'What do you mean, Jim?' my father asked.

'If you puts me in there,' said old Burrell, 'what are you going to do with Tom?'

We were stunned for a moment, and then my mother said, 'Tom isn't here, Jim. There's nobody here except just the family, that you see around you, and yourself, and we're very glad to have you with us.'

'That's as may be,' old Burrell said. 'I don't say as you don't give me a welcome. I believe you've always been a good sort of woman, Katie. I know you speak the truth. But if I go up to that room, where's Tom going to go?'

'Tom isn't here,' my father fairly roared. 'You'll have to take a grip on your state of mind, Jim. I know you've had a shock and it's a hard time for you, but you'll have to see things as they are.'

'That's just it. That's what I did see. I looked up at that window above the street and I see him looking down at me as plain as I'm seeing you.'

'Was he wearing his flying clothes?' I asked.

'He don't wear flying clothes,' old Burrell said. 'He's given up all that load of nonsense. He's back on the farm with me.'

I went back to the telephone. 'Your father's delusions have come back,' I told Heather.

'Can you bring him home with you?' she asked. 'He's not violent or anything?'

'No, I'm fairly sure I could bring him home.'

'Good. He can go to bed tonight here then, and we can get him over to Cogges in the morning after Michael's gone to school.'

'I'll drive him to Cogges now if you like.'

'No. He's my father and I want to look after him. My mother'd be too concerned about saving face. If she thinks he's at the Bargeman's, fine, let her go on thinking it till tomorrow.'

'Well, if you're sure.'

'Bring him,' she said in a decided voice. I hung up and went back to tell my parents what had been settled.

The next job was to get old Burrell into his overcoat and into the car. He was surprisingly docile. During the journey to Chinnor he just sat slumped in his seat, staring forward but obviously not taking anything in. He didn't even ask

321

where we were going. When we got there, I helped him out of the car and he stood looking round at the dark landscape while Heather, who had been watching for our arrival, opened the front door and came out.

As she came up to him he asked her, 'How many acres d'you rent here, Heather?'

'None,' she said. 'There's just a garden.'

'Is it a College farm?' he asked. Obviously he hadn't taken in her answer.

'Yes,' she said, 'it's a College farm, in a way, but we won't discuss it now because you're standing outside and you'll get cold. Come in and have a warm drink and get a night's sleep, Daddy.'

'Where's Alice?' he asked, moving towards the house.

'You'll see Alice in the morning.'

I went to open the garage and put the car away, and when I entered the house Heather was upstairs, putting her father to bed in the spare room. I waited downstairs, pouring myself that stiff drink I hadn't had at the Bargeman's because I knew I would have to drive home over icy roads. When she came down I made a half-hearted attempt to discuss the situation, but Heather didn't want a discussion.

'Look, there isn't actually anything to say,' she said. 'It's just going to have to be coped with. The conventional term for it is a nervous breakdown. Mother'll find some way of presenting it to the world, and she'll also find the best way of keeping him out of sight till he gets better. As far as you and I are concerned, what is there to talk about? Nothing.'

'I don't know. It's pretty serious. When an ageing man loses two sons one after the other like that, even though they were very different — '

'Two *sons?*'

I know it is a cliché to say, 'I could have bitten my tongue off', but this time it was literally true. I really could have done. In my fatigue, my preoccupation, my sheer egotistical stupidity, I had forgotten that Heather didn't know about the revelation her father had made in the kitchen of the Bargeman's Arms. I moved towards her and put a hand on her arm.

'Heather, darling, I'm terribly sorry. I didn't mean to come out with it like that.'

Her face had gone very white. 'How long have you known?'

'Just this evening.'

'Did he tell you?'

'Yes. I had no idea of it myself till he came out with it. Come to think of it,' I babbled desperately, 'it might be a delusion he's been harbouring. Part of his mental breakdown. You know how people — '

'No,' Heather said in a flat voice. 'It isn't a delusion. I can see that now.' She sat down on a kitchen chair. 'Funny that I never saw it before.'

'Heather . . .' I began again.

'I must get up in the morning,' she said. 'I'll have to be up and about early, to give Michael his breakfast and get him off to school before Dad wakes up.'

'But I want to — '

'Don't disturb me. I've got equilibrium now. I have to keep going. I don't want to talk about it, or think about it much. I must be normal and ordinary in the morning. And don't feel bad about it, Peter. It's not your fault.'

We went to bed. In the depths of the night I awoke because the bed was shaken by her silent weeping. I held her close to me. But still she would not talk.

*

The term ground heavily to a halt, the Easter vacation came, and it was time for my trip to Dublin. Heather, of course, was quite clear in her own mind as to my reason for spending a few days in Ireland: it was because I was tired of the food shortages and rationing. 'I don't blame you, wanting to chew your way through some good beefsteaks and spread butter on your toast in the morning,' she said casually when I told her I had made the arrangements. 'I only wish I could think up a good reason why it's essential for *me* to get across the water for a week. Just put a couple of pounds of butter in your suitcase for your family back home, will you?'

I bore this, and more of the same, in silence. Her father, back at Jasmine Farm, was recovering slowly, but the entire episode – and particularly the unwelcome revelation it brought – had been a severe shock to her. I was glad she could joke about my trip, even if resentfully. Also I accepted it as part of a scholar's destiny to have his high idealistic labours misunderstood by those about him. And it was a fact, a bedrock fact, that however mixed may have been my motives for going to Dublin, I did, when I finally got there, benefit enormously as an historian. Among those particular Trinity College manuscripts, concerning Irish affairs in the seventeenth century, there were some examinations taken from men who, by order of the Dublin Government, had been stretched on the rack to make sure they spoke the truth, since it is a well-known maxim among people in power that confessions extorted under excruciating torture are the most reliable.

All in all, the manuscripts made uncomfortable reading for a man who would have liked to hold on to the belief that his bluff, blunt-spoken Englishman, though sometimes a little lacking in polish, was basically a kindly fellow, with his heart in the right place.

I read on in quiet horror. In that calm, dignified T.C.D. library, cries, groans and desperate silences reached me from three centuries before, jangling a mind already alarmed by Belsen and Buchenwald and then Hiroshima and Nagasaki. Coming out each evening into the stately Dublin twilight, walking among those eighteenth-century façades, I wondered by what criteria the human being must ultimately be judged. 'All power tends to corrupt; absolute power corrupts absolutely,' a Catholic historian had written. Yes, and fear puts a bitter edge on the knife of cruelty.

I walked in a dream. Everything conspired to make me see the world from a different perspective. Dublin itself displaced my sense of reality: as a large English-speaking city, where so many of the things I encountered – people's clothes, the weather, the commodities on sale in the shops – were so much what I was accustomed to, it also revealed customs, attitudes, sights and sounds, above all an atmosphere, totally new to me. Everything was like, and yet unlike. Dubliners, like Londoners, had been through years of scarcity; their clothes were shabby, their amenities run-down. But Ireland, unlike England, had not been subjected to the relentless discipline of the war years; fantasy, caprice, impulse, had survived better among them. I had the continual feeling that I was seeing the world from an unexpected angle, through a different window. And then Dublin is not really like an English city to look at. The river, not hidden away as London tries to hide the Thames but flowing demonstratively past the quays, gives it a Parisian air. The houses in the more modest parts of the city centre, away from the grand squares, have an oblong, box-like look that one sees in the workaday quarters of American cities, not in English. Nothing is really surprising – it is not Peking or Istanbul – but neither is anything really familiar.

And Mairead? Did being in Dublin affect my feelings about her? Once again it was hard to say. In some respects it acted as a soothing drug. Now that I could walk down streets she must have walked down, now that I could stand and gaze at the National University where she had spent her student years, she seemed less exotic. My new familiarity with her setting had domesticated my image of her. But it also brought her perilously, agonizingly close.

One afternoon about five o'clock I found that I could drive my attention forward no further. The details in the manuscript I was reading, though as vivid as any I had found, suddenly didn't concern me any more. I stood up. Pausing only to return the manuscript to the custodian's desk, I left the library. Trinity College, like any other college, has a lodge. The lodge has a public telephone. I found the directory, I found the address of the Foreign Service of the Irish Government. Making a note of the street name, I asked the porter where it was. He told me. I went there, pushed open the glass-panelled swing doors, entered. I was pursuing my one image, obeying my one obsession. 'My language beaten / Into one name.' To the bonfire with any more evasions.

The girl behind the information desk was able to reveal only one thing about Mairead: she didn't work in that building. Miss Hoey was not a member of the Dublin Embassy staff and they had no list of names on which she appeared. Was she still in the Diplomatic Service at all? The girl couldn't, or wouldn't, say. Had she been posted abroad? The girl couldn't, or wouldn't, say.

She just looked at me, expressionless and ungiving. She had a pale, dough-like face and pale fair hair with a pale blue ribbon in it. Everything about her was pale, including the tone of her voice.

I turned away and headed for the door and the street outside. I had been a fool to come here: to come to this building, to come to Dublin at all. When, finally, was I going to learn that my love for Mairead, the happiness I had enjoyed with her, had been an episode in my life, nothing more, that it was finished, done with, washed away down the stream of time?

As I turned from the desk, a handsome young woman happened to be crossing the floor of the entrance lobby going from one office to another. Her path took her past the desk, and she paused in her rapid, purposeful walk and said, 'Excuse me. Did I hear you mention the name Mairead Hoey?'

I liked the look of this young person immediately. She was about Mairead's age, with rich clustering dark hair, a face that though round was intelligent, with big, alert eyes, and a figure that in a few more years would be described as 'ample'. She radiated energy. She looked happy.

'Yes,' I said. 'I was enquiring about her. I knew her in London during the war and I've lost touch with her since. I wondered if she was working here now.'

'Oh, no,' the girl said. 'She never has worked here. I know Mairead very well – we were at College together. She was in Sweden till after the war started, and then she went to London and she's stayed there ever since.'

'Ever *since*? She told me she was coming back here.'

'Oh, no.' The girl stopped and a hesitant look came into her large eyes. I could tell what she was thinking: if Mairead had known this man in London, and had told him she was coming back to Dublin, perhaps her object had been to throw him off the scent. Perhaps it would be wrong to give him clues. I could see her regretting the impulse of helpfulness that had made her speak to me at all.

'I haven't any particular business with her,' I hastened to say. 'I . . . wasn't expecting to be in touch with her or anything. It's just that . . . well, it's my first time in Dublin, and you know how your mind goes over all the people you've known who might possibly be around. It couldn't matter less, really.' I wondered if I was piling it on a bit thick. 'Anyway, next time you see her you might say I dropped by and asked about her. I'd like her to know I hadn't forgotten her. My name's Peter Leonard.'

She gave me a look that said she still distrusted me. I said good afternoon and turned away. When she saw that I was definitely taking myself off, she relented and called after me, 'I don't see Mairead very often. She's in the Foreign Section and I'm not. It was when we were at College that I knew her best.'

'Ah,' I said, 'happy days,' and I pushed open the glass door and went into the street, where a light rain was now falling. That, I reflected, was that, and I went into the first bar I came to and began steadily drinking.

Dublin Guinness, of the draught variety, in those days was entirely unlike the Guinness you got anywhere else in the world; it was brewed from the water of the Liffey, and it had a creamy feel as it went over your tongue, followed by a dark, tangy, liquoricey after-taste. Later, when keg brewing came in, it was all the one chemically dead fluid, and it didn't matter where you were on the face of the globe, it was just the same. That was called Progress. But my first visit to Dublin, in 1946, was before Progress and though, thank God, I am not a senseless addict of any alcoholic drink, the draught Guinness you could get in Dublin bars in those days was worth a trip across the water. I was watching the ring of rich froth in my glass slowly going down, therefore, and keeping my mind on the harmless subject of good drinks that don't travel, when a thought struck me that had nothing to do with such matters. It was, simply, the realization that I must find Mairead in London. I must go back to Mr John Dulanty's office, or to the office of whoever was now serving his function on behalf of the Irish Government, and I must enquire for Miss Mairead Hoey. I must refuse to go away until they told me how to reach her. And then, I must reach her.

The next morning, I sailed for Liverpool. I took home with me three abstract items of which I was not in possession when I set out: an appreciation of the high quality of Dublin, Liffey-brewed Guinness; an overview of the consequences to the Irish population of the Rising of 1641 and its suppression; and a certain knowledge that I would find Mairead.

After the long sullen winter of 1945–46, balmy summer had at last arrived. The fields, the woods, the river banks, all were festive with May. Episcopus garden had never seemed to me so beautiful, and its beauty was heightened and made more poignant by the fact that I was never in it enough. I was working drearily hard; trying to freshen up my historical reading, but mostly just straining to stay level with the very heavy teaching commitment that peacetime had brought with it. My visit to London was having to wait. Expansion in numbers, it was now clear, had not as yet brought with it any corresponding expansion in the teaching strength of the University. It just meant that we all had more donkey-work to do; and if anyone imagines that teaching the rudiments of an academic discipline to undergraduates *isn't* donkey-work, he or she is welcome to try it for twelve months.

One Friday afternoon, just about the most beautiful day we had seen that year, I went out into the garden after lunch. It was a full teaching day, with four sixty-minute tutorials in the morning, from nine till one, and two more in the evening, from five to seven. The afternoon, by tradition, was for everyone to relax in, get their strength together, and breathe a little fresh air.

Since it was afternoon rather than morning, most of the benches had members of the public sitting on them, and the paths were alive with people. There was also a fair amount of walking to and fro across the lawn, in spite of notices entreating visitors to keep off the grass. Finally, I spotted a bench that was occupied by only one man, and thankfully I moved towards it. As I came right up to it, I saw that the man was my old poet friend Lamont. His head was bent forward, and he was looking at the pages of a battered notebook.

I sat down beside him, not wanting to disturb his train of thought, but it was not long before he looked up, recognized me, and said, 'Leonard!' I was glad to hear him say this in a pleased tone. I had always admired Lamont.

We got the basic orientation over first. Lamont was spending a week-end in Oxford before going back to his house in the rural north of England. He had only just been discharged from his ship.

'Your ship? You were in the Navy, Lamont?'

'No,' he said. 'I've had a strange war.' He laughed in a slightly self-mocking way, as if it were only to be expected that anything he did, or anything that happened to him, would be more or less strange. 'I've spent the war sailing backwards and forwards across the Atlantic, but not in the Navy. In an ordinary merchantman.'

He seemed inclined to shrug off the subject, to let it go at that, but I was interested. I wanted to get the story out of him. Lamont in a merchant ship? It seemed incongruous.

'Well,' he said, resigning himself to explaining when he saw that I really wanted him to, 'I was inconsistent in my attitude to the war. At least, I was consistent at first – consistent but wrong. I was against it. I even had the intention of registering as a Conscientious Objector. I've always hated fighting – just the idea of fighting, of human beings using their energies to try to do each other harm, in the last resort actually to destroy each other, always seemed to me the ultimate sin, whatever religious point of view you had. At the time the war broke out, I knew only one thing – that I wasn't going to put out a hand to kill anybody. I wasn't going to learn to handle any weapon. I'd no particular objection to being killed, if it had to be, but I wasn't going to kill. That was as far as I'd got.'

'And that changed?'

Lamont was silent, thinking. I stole a look at his face. It was still recognizably the face that had impressed me so much when we were eighteen, but harder, more seasoned. The eyes still had that steadiness and depth which had seemed so remarkable in an adolescent face, but now the rest of his face had, so to speak, grown up to match them. His jaw had a stronger outline now that the last of the puppy-fat had gone. It was the face of a man who has looked deeply into life.

'Lidice changed me,' he said. 'I realized then that the war was necessary. It was unthinkable to ask people to go on knuckling under to a power that could do things like that. And there was no way of getting rid of that power except by fighting it. So I realized I had to support the war: no more talk of registering as a Conscientious Objector. On the other hand I couldn't just slough off that deep repugnance I had to the idea of actual fighting, doing one's best to kill other men.'

Lamont fell silent for a moment. Sitting on that bench with the green leaves whispering all round me of fertility and renewal, I suddenly remembered the words of an Episcopus poet of an earlier generation:

Life, to be sure, is nothing much to lose:
But young men think it is, and we were young.

326

'At any rate it was clear, given my odd psychology,' Lamont was continuing, 'what I had to do. I had to go into something where there was a pretty fair risk of being killed, but absolutely zero risk of killing anyone else. I thought of this and I thought of that, but there was some difficulty about almost everything. In the end I hit on the only cast-iron certainty – something that was virtually asking to get killed and yet was entirely non-aggressive and non-military. The Merchant Navy.'

'Had you any sea-going experience?' I asked.

'Not a day's worth. I'd have been more of a nuisance than a help in sailing any vessel. So I did the only thing possible. I signed on as a steward.'

'A steward?'

'Yes, carrying round the food, clearing away the plates, all that. There were two stewards on the ship I signed on, myself and a man who'd been doing that job for years and showed me the ropes. So there it was. I spent the war going between the galley and the tables, keeping the crew fed. I became a skilled man in the end. I can carry four plates of soup down a narrow companionway in a force seven, and not spill a drop. That was my war service.'

'Were you torpedoed?'

'Twice. The first time they managed to get us on to another ship in the convoy before ours actually went down. The second time I did find myself in the water. I was in it for about twelve minutes, I gather. I gave myself up for lost after about ten seconds. It's cold enough for you to lose consciousness pretty quickly. I was just very lucky. I was hoisted out more or less unconscious.'

'My God,' I said. 'Death came that close and yet he didn't take you.'

'Oh, we lived with death. I remember the most extraordinary sight I saw once. You know some of the ships on that North Atlantic convoy were very, very hastily constructed. They were rushed out of the shipyards at a time when the only thing that mattered was speed of production, to get something that would float out on the water and hope for the best. There was really no time to build them to precision standards. I was on deck, it was about seven o'clock in the morning, and a good steady wind was blowing, nothing like a gale but enough to make the ship work pretty hard to butt through it. I happened to be standing in the bows, looking at the ship next in front of us, when suddenly a change had come over the angle she was sailing at. Her stern came up and of course that meant her bow was going down. Not very steeply, but, you might say, inexorably. She just dug her nose into the water, at that shallow angle, and ploughed in. Exactly what happened, in engineering terms, I don't know, but she put her bow into the sea and just followed it down. I stood and watched. There was nothing anybody could do. No time to launch a boat. I thought of the food cooking in the galley and the charts spread out on the bridge, and chaps who'd come off night watch asleep in the bunks. In about a minute and a half that ship was no more. And we sailed on.'

He ended. I sat silent, looking round at the beautiful garden, rich with glowing flowers and fresh-leaved trees. There seemed to be no way of bringing the two into the same focus. Focus? How could one even get them into the same universe?

'Tell me, Lamont,' I said, 'if it . . . well, seems an acceptable question . . .' I hesitated again. I knew I had to be careful here. 'When you had this kind of experience, did it become harder to go back to thinking about poetry?'

'Exactly the opposite,' Lamont said. 'It made thinking about poetry, and trying to be a poet, seem the only natural thing to do.'

'Yes?'

'Yes. Experiences like that make you very impatient of side-issues. You want

327

to go straight to what really matters. A lot of people think poetry's a way of decorating experience, presenting it in a fancy form. What it actually is, is a way of stripping experience right down to its essence, its heartbeat. And to contemplate life until you render it down to *that* is very like a religious experience. It's the only one some people are capable of.'

'You sound very certain of that. How d'you know it?'

'Because I'm like that myself,' Lamont said.

'You mean writing poetry is the only religious experience you can have?'

'Unless I change,' he said gently.

While we talked, people had been coming past us, hardly noticed, along the gravel path. Now, however, a man approached to whose identity I was instantly alerted. It was Garrity, and at the sight of him I felt slightly ill at ease. Possibly the refusal of the Fellows of Episcopus to take him among their number had cast a shadow over my relationship with him; after all, I was one of these same Fellows.

I need not have worried. Garrity greeted both of us with eager friendliness. He was on a short visit to Oxford, and 'I never miss a chance to take a turn round the garden.' Evidently he knew Lamont, and had known him for some years. He sat down on our bench, produced his awful pipe, began to fill it from an oblong tin labelled 'Capstan Full Strength', and became at once involved with Lamont in a discussion that, as usual, went over my head. It concerned Euhemerus, a Greek in the fourth century B.C. who had propounded a theory that all the myths about the gods had originally been historical narratives celebrating regional heroes, and had gradually undergone a sea-change in the human imagination that put them into the religious orbit: that they had, in fact, begun as history and evolved into theogony.

'Blake, of course,' Lamont was saying, 'saw no need for belief in gods as such because he believed that the human race were themselves divine and that it was only evil institutions and stifling traditions which stopped them from realizing their divinity.'

'Obviously that has a bearing on Euhemerus,' Garrity rejoined in the intervals of drawing madly on his pipe: it seemed to be blocked by years of sludge. 'But there's no need to invoke Blake. A more revealing parallel might be Rilke's conception of Angels. Have you really pondered the full symbolic function of the Angels in Rilke's poetry?'

'Not what I suppose you would call fully. But of course it has occurred to me that . . .'

They went at the subject like a pair of basset hounds on a scent, and I sank into my own thoughts, which were pleasantly sentimental. When our forefathers, I reflected, had built this College, and had endowed it with a beautiful garden, they must have hoped that scholars and poets just like this would sit on simple wooden benches just like this and pursue devoted, impassioned conversations just like this. Glancing at Garrity, as he sat back on the bench with his long, lean shanks thrust out, just as he had sat in that hedge when I had first encountered him, I hoped that the students in the ugly industrial town where he earned his living deserved him, that they didn't simply try to treat him as a cramming-machine for examinations, a purpose for which he wouldn't, in fact, have been much good. I had no grudge against Noel Arcady, but I knew as an absolute certainty that the social aura he carried around with him was mere chaff when set beside the solid nourishing grain of Garrity, chaff that would blow away in the wind.

*

328

All this time I was trying to escape, in a cowardly fashion, from the thought of Mairead. I knew that whatever I did would produce calamity and suffering in one way or another. I couldn't face it, and yet I knew that sooner or later I had to face it, and somehow I managed to hypnotize myself into forgetting about her during long stretches of my waking life. But of course she surfaced all the more in dreams.

I remember one particularly harrowing dream. Heather and I were trying to mend a tractor; she explained to me that my help was essential. 'We haven't got any horses now that the war's over,' she said. 'We have to work with tractors now. We've only got this one and it needs mending.' Protesting that I knew nothing about how tractors worked, I went down on my knees and started trying to dismantle the engine. What made it particularly trying was that for some reason we were working on the tractor on the floor of our living room. Heather kept saying, 'It's the camshaft,' but I didn't know, in the mass of machinery before me, where the camshaft was or what it looked like. As I struggled miserably, I became aware that there was someone else in the room. It was Hazel, the girl who had been Heather's flatmate in Birmingham. She said to me, 'Mairead's outside, sweetie.' I said, 'What does she want? Does she want to come in?' But Hazel only smiled that slightly woozy smile, and I realized that she was still a little drunk, as she had been during our one and only meeting, so I said, 'Please go and ask her what she wants.' I spoke quietly because I was hoping Heather wouldn't hear us. Indeed Heather showed no sign of knowing that Hazel was there, and she now pulled out a steel rod – something like a poker but rather longer – from the engine and said to me, 'This is the camshaft. It needs welding.' The expression was meaningless to me.

At this point Hazel came back and said again, in exactly the same tone as before, 'Mairead's outside.' 'Ask her what she wants!' I shouted, beside myself with frustration, and at the same time I seized the camshaft and tried to break it across my knee. I brought it down with vicious force on the upper part of my leg, but it was my leg that broke. Before my horrified eyes the thigh-bone cracked apart in a jagged fracture, and I woke up. I looked at my watch; it was ten minutes to five. I lay awake, trying vainly to go back to sleep. When Heather woke – or revealed the fact that she was awake, I couldn't tell which – she said to me, 'You talked in your sleep.'

'What did I say?' I asked with a sick feeling of dread.

'You said, "It's the bloody camshaft, it's the bloody camshaft," ' she replied composedly.

Well, I suppose, when you come to think of the symbolism of the whole thing, it *was* the bloody camshaft.

That, in fact, was the experience which pushed me into taking the final plunge. When my nightmares got as near to the surface as that, I realized I had to do something to move the situation forward. What I did was to begin to research where Mairead had been moved to. Going at it methodically, I found out in no very long time that she hadn't been moved anywhere. It had all been a false trail – she hadn't left London at all. There was even a work address where I could write her a letter. I kept it short. I pictured her in a mood not to open any communication from me, so I typed the envelope. I even posted it on a day when I happened to be in London, so that it wouldn't have an Oxford postmark. And I kept it very short, to increase the chances of her reading it to the end:

Mairead, I want to see you. That's an understatement. I more than want to, I desperately need to. Please say yes, and please make a little time available to me. It needn't be more than half an hour, say. And it needn't mean that you are making any concessions. It's just that I want to hear your voice, look at you, and speak to you a little. That is absolutely all. Nothing more unless you want more.

Which I hope and trust you will, I added mentally as I sealed the envelope. But that was as far as I could go. I posted it at Paddington Station, then I settled down to wait for her reply. Nothing happened.

The Leonard family did not travel abroad in the summer of 1946. There was no money to spare, and even if there had been, currency regulations were tight. Besides, where was there to go? Switzerland was too expensive, and as for the other European countries, they were all too smashed up, still struggling to feed their own populations.

We were stuck in England, therefore, and in my listless state I was hardly aware of my surroundings. But even so, one August morning in Oxford High Street, I could not fail to see a woman a few yards ahead of me on the pavement emerge from an antique shop carrying a large flat, rectangular package. From the effortful way the woman lowered the package on to the pavement, I could tell that it was heavy: a painting in a frame, perhaps. She straightened up despairingly, and at the exact moment that she did so I drew level with her so that we were looking into each other's faces. It was Hannah Carshalton.

'Why, hullo,' she said. 'It's . . . uh, Peter Lemming, isn't it, a friend of Dom's from Episcopus?'

'Leonard,' I said. 'But the Peter part is right. You have a good memory, Hannah. We last met before the war, I think. Anyway, what's the problem here?'

'Oh, this. I must have been crazy to buy it. The thing is, I thought they'd deliver to our hotel. Only when I'd bought it and paid for it and they'd wrapped it up, I asked them when they'd bring it round to the Randolph and they just said they couldn't. It seems they don't deliver. They don't have the staff or the gasoline or anything.'

'Well, I'm not surprised. They're mostly like that.'

'So here I am, stuck with it on the sidewalk. I thought I'd just bring it out and hop a cab. But I don't see any.' She looked wildly up and down High Street. 'Has something happened to all the taxis?'

'There never were any. Not ones that cruised about. I've never seen a cruising taxi in Oxford.'

'Well, but how'm I gonna lug this thing all the way to the Randolph? It's a paining in a real king-size frame. I just can't handle — '

'Look, don't worry.' I took charge. 'Here, I'll help you to put it back inside the shop for a few minutes while I go over to St Giles — that's the nearest rank — and get a taxi and send it over here. Then you can take the painting to the Randolph.'

'Oh, that's so kind of you. But won't you come back with the taxi so we can go to the Randolph together and I can at least offer you a drink? It seems such good luck running into you like this. Dom's off for the day and he's got the car, that's why I'm in this jam.'

I hesitated. I ought not to waste my time sitting having a drink with Mrs Carshalton, that was undeniable. On the other hand, I remembered that when I had seen her all those years ago, on that one teatime occasion at Episcopus, I

330

had liked her. She was genuine and human. And anyone who was stuck with Carshalton as a husband had a claim, surely, on one's charitable impulses.

'I'll come back,' I said, 'and we'll take it over together.'

That was how I came to be sitting in the lounge of the Randolph Hotel at noon on a hot, airless day, talking to Hannah Carshalton and drinking a champagne cocktail ('I find them cooling,' she said and I decided to try something new for once). The unwieldy package was leaning against the end of the settee. I had suggested leaving it with the hotel porter, but she had had the men carry it into the lounge because she wanted to show it to me. She was now engaged in cutting the string with a small, neat pair of scissors from her handbag.

'There,' she said at last, peeling away the brown paper. 'That's the paining. I knew I had to have it as soon as I saw it. It gave me a signal that it could help me with my work.'

I looked at it: a rather dark, rather smudgy Victorian oil painting of Dorchester Abbey. It showed a clump of trees, a row of cottages, and the Abbey looming behind, with a thundery sky. I had seen many such paintings. It was not offensive, neither did it do anything for me.

'This will help you with your work?' I said. 'You're a painter?' She hadn't, on our one previous meeting, said anything about work.

'A sculptor. I started in California just at the beginning of the forties. Yes, this'll help me. It's very full of suggestions. The *masses*. The weight of the building here, the dark of these trees here, all bunched up and solid,' she indicated them with the flat of her hand, 'and the fluffy lightness up here of this big cloud, poised just right. It's balanced, but not symmetrically – it's not predictable.'

'I see. You see it as a pure design, not a picture *of* anything.'

'I see all painings as pure design.'

'All of them?'

'Why, yes. As a sculptor I work in masses and counter-stresses. That's what this paining does for me. The colour's pretty conventional, but I don't take much notice of colour. Just weight and density.'

Well, I thought, her position had its own logic. I had no authority to criticize it. Perhaps her sculptures were interesting; how could I know, sitting here with a champagne cocktail in my hand? I took a thoughtful swig at it. Cooling it certainly was; and if she was right about champagne cocktails, she might be right about sculpture too.

'But look, Hannah,' I said, turning to the practicalities, 'you're not going to portage this thing all the way to California?'

She laughed in genuine amusement, at the same time leaning forward and laying her hand momentarily on my forearm in that confiding way I remembered from our first meeting. I was glad she had not given up this habit. It seemed natural to her: it had a warm, huddling-together quality that went with her Jewishness. Rich and free she had always been, yet she had inherited qualities from a people who for long centuries had been forcibly crammed together, layer on layer, in narrow streets from which they were forbidden to emerge.

'No, I'm not taking it to California,' she said. 'I'm buying things for here now. That's what this trip's about.'

'For here?'

'Yes. Dom wants us to get a house in the Cotswolds.'

I was considerably surprised. 'He wants to live in England?'

'Yes. He wants a Cotswold manor house. That's what he's doing today, driving

331

round the Cotswolds with a real estate guy, getting them down to a short list. Then he'll take me out with him and we'll make a final choice.'

I was still struggling with this. 'He really wants to come back? But I thought he'd . . . well, I just pictured the two of you settled in America, probably on the West Coast in the sunshine, for ever.'

'Well, he doesn't want to be here all the time. Or there all the time, for that matter. But air travel's improving all the time. Dom wants to keep well abreast of developments in England.'

'And you? What do you think about coming to live here?'

She shrugged lightly. 'As long as I have a good studio . . . my sculpture's developing very fast right now. And the art market is inner-national, it doesn't matter where you are. I like those Cotswold villages – Lower and Upper Slaughter, Bourton-on-the-Water, Dursley, they're all little jewels. Dom's taken me around. If he can find a good house, I'll enjoy settling into it. And they all have barns and stables and that type of thing, just right for studio conversion. I'll be fine.'

'But what will *he* get out of it? I mean, there he is, settled, with American citizenship I suppose, by this time . . .'

'Yes, he has citizenship. But he doesn't really think he'd get anywhere in American polly-ticks.'

'Politics? Is that what he's interested in?'

'Oh, yes, for some years now. Well, two or three, anyway.'

My mind was working furiously, trying to assimilate all this new material.

'So he's turning towards a political career,' I said slowly. Of course Carshalton would never be content simply to take an interest in politics, to comment on them in an objective spirit. For him, it would have to be a Career. 'And he doesn't think there's much future for him in American politics?'

'No, and I think he's right. He comes over as too English.'

I saw what she meant. 'But surely, he can't think of England at the present moment as anything but even more closed to him, politically, than America? I mean, with his Conservative leanings — '

She stared at me and said, 'Conservative? You mean right-wing? Who can you be talking about, Peter?'

'I'm talking about your husband, of course.'

'But Dom's a Socialist.'

It was a good thing I had finished my champagne cocktail. If I had happened to be drinking it at that moment, I would have gone into an uncontrollable fit of choking.

'Yeah. He started reading *Noo Masses* and *Partisan Review* and all like that. It must have been, oh, back in about '40. Not all that long after we'd settled on the Coast.'

'And he got converted to Socialism by reading left-wing magazines?' It didn't sound like Carshalton.

'Well, it kind of went with it.'

I thought back. Nineteen-forty. All I could remember happening in 1940 was the withdrawal of the British Expeditionary Force from Dunkirk. Then it occurred to me that Socialism of the totalitarian variety might quite easily have seemed a horse worth putting one's shirt on in 1940. After all, Stalin's position in the world was a very strong one, with his western frontiers guaranteed (or so it seemed) by an alliance with Hitler and a free hand in Eastern Europe. That was, I recalled, the year in which Estonia, Latvia and Lithuania, all independent states, were deftly scooped up into the Soviet Union and no questions asked. It was also the year in which Stalin reached out from the Kremlin all the way to Coyoacán, Mexico, and put an ice-pick into the brain of Leo Trotsky.

Yes, I could see, even sitting there holding my empty glass, without time as yet to pursue the matter to its ramifications, that the Left, in its Stalinist form, might have seemed in 1940 to be speaking in a language that Carshalton understood very well. He admired people who got what they wanted. In 1940 Stalin had undeniably been getting a lot of what he wanted.

Yes, Socialism – as defined in the Kremlin and not in the simple egalitarian and humanitarian way favoured by the British Labour Party – had obviously a great deal to offer to the Carshaltons of this world. Not in America, though, where to be even a sympathizer with Communism could make life extremely difficult. So what was Carshalton now doing? Driving round the Cotswolds, looking for a graceful manor house from which he could launch his onslaught on the hearts and minds of his compatriots. He was clever; I had to admit it.

Hannah Carshalton now rose to go. 'I'll tell Dom I ran into you,' she said; 'He'll be real pleased.'

I couldn't see why Carshalton should be pleased at any intelligence concerning me, but I understood that she was simply being agreeable, so I said, 'Yes, do.'

'He didn't really wanna stay in Oxford this time round. He'd rather have been in Gloucester or, what was that other place he thought of? Siren something?'

'Cirencester, I expect.'

'Yes, I think so. He figured either one of those places would be nearer to all the properties we needed to look at. But when we were sedding up this trip, I met someone who knew Paul Nash.'

'Yes?'

'Well! Paul *Nash*!'

It was coming back to me now. 'Yes, of course, the painter. But didn't he die just recently?'

'Yes, that's what's so terribly disappointing. This woman gave me a letter of introduction. I have it here, in my purse – I couldn't bear to leave it behind even though I knew he wasn't around any more. I wanned so *much* to meet him.'

'Yes? Of course he was very – '

'I admired him more than any other artist you had over here. Even more than Moore or Hepworth. And when I say *that* . . . but Nash, wow! Ever since I began to see that art was going to be the most important thing in my life, I'd wannéd to meet Paul Nash, to look into his studio even just for five minutes . . . to think to myself that I'd met him . . . I suppose you met him quite often,' she said wistfully.

'Well . . . actually . . .'

'Don't say *you never met* PAUL NASH! And him living here in Oxford all through the war. Right along the street from here. Two-o-one Ban Berry Road.'

God help me, I hadn't even known he was living here. But then (I clutched at the excuse) one can't know *everything*.

'I went and stood outside the house this morning,' Hannah Carshalton was saying, 'but it didn't tell me anything, just the outside. It was just a house like any other. A woman walked past me and went in, but I couldn't know whether she was Mrs Nash or just a visitor.'

I liked her for having let it go at that, for not having marched up to the front door and banged on it and introduced herself as a disciple from California come to pay homage. I was beginning to like her quite a lot. What a pity she was thrown away on Carshalton! Had she, I wondered, turned to art because there was nothing warm and spontaneous in what should have been her central relationship?

'When did Nash die?' I asked her.

'July eleventh,' she answered promptly.

We stood for a moment in an elegiac silence. I knew little enough of Nash's work, but even I could not have avoided knowing that he had had a tremendous following for some years; reproductions of his paintings were on sale everywhere, and he was one of the official War Artists who had most successfully interpreted the experience of the war.

There was a final flurry of activity when Hannah summoned the hotel porter and gave him instructions about transporting the view of Dorchester Abbey up to the suite of rooms she and Carshalton inhabited. After a moment in which I tried to find room in my mind for so many new thoughts – Carshalton as Socialist! Hannah Carshalton as California sculptress turned Cotswold manor châtelaine! Paul Nash on the Banbury Road! – I thanked her for the champagne and began to make my own way out.

In the doorway of the lounge, though, I almost collided with a tall, stooping figure, walking with a stiff leg and leaning on a stick, that was just entering. This man evidently had such poor sight that he must stoop to peer ahead of him through the furniture, searching for somewhere to sit down. He wore tinted glasses, and his face was skull-like, an impression heightened by his baldness, only the back of his head being clad in hair, and that sparingly.

I muttered an apology for seeming to get in this man's way, and as I stepped aside I looked up into that fleshless face, then froze in my tracks. I knew this man. That is, I had once known him. The figure in front of me was . . . it was Knowlton; careless, laughing, loose-limbed Knowlton, Knowlton of Episcopus. Well, he would never be loose-limbed again, that was for sure. Or careless, or laughing most likely. But what had turned the Knowlton I once knew into the Knowlton I was seeing now?

He recognized me, and a smile spread over the ruined face. 'Hello, Leonard,' he said. 'I was wondering if I'd run into you.' His voice had not changed. Or rather, it had become slightly deeper and more resonant, as if his cavernous chest was now a more reverberative sounding-box for his once light, casual tones.

'Knowlton,' I said. And I'm afraid I just stood there, staring at him.

'I'm glad you recognized me, old thing,' he said with a ghost of his old cheerfulness. 'Some people haven't. I know I'm a bit . . . well, altered, let's say.'

'Of course I recognize you,' I said. This was total insincerity. It hadn't been 'of course' at all. I had almost walked past him.

'Let's sit down a moment,' said Knowlton, limping towards a couple of leather armchairs. 'D'you mind coming over to my left side? Can't hear anything on the right. Makes conversation difficult.' We sat down accordingly. 'Ah,' he sighed, arranging his stiff leg carefully. 'Yes, it changes one's appearance, spending a few years as the guest of our Japanese brethren.'

I was silent. Why had no one told me of this? I had got from Episcopus the names of all the men actually killed in the war; their memorial had been duly cut in stone. But no one had got round to compiling a list of those who had merely been wounded, or taken prisoner.

The waiter now approached and Knowlton ordered a drink and one for me. I didn't want a drink, but it seemed graceless to refuse. There were so few ways in which I could help him, or reach out to him, or express my grief and shock at the suffering that must have been inflicted on him.

It seemed that I should say something. Fully aware of the question's banality, I came out with, 'What brings you to Oxford?'

'To see doctors. That's something I go in for a lot these days. In fact you might say I'm making quite a hobby of it.'

'Um.' I had absolutely no idea what more to say.

'The local wallahs seem to have more or less given up on me. I gather there's something dire going on in my kidneys, and then of course there's the eyesight. That could do with a bit of straightening out. I've got an appointment in Walton Street in a couple of hours' time, in fact. Should get some sort of show on the road.'

'I'm . . . sorry,' I said.

'Yes, I seem to be a bit of a mess, old thing. I suppose I simply wasn't tough enough.'

'Well, you could hardly — '

'You see, I was only a prisoner for a couple of years. The kidney business and eye business were both brought on by vitamin deficiency – you know, living on a cupful of rice a day. Well, some chaps had that for three-and-a-half years, from the fall of Singapore right through to August '45, and they're in better shape than I am. I'm too tall, that's my trouble. To survive that kind of thing you need to be short and stocky. Mistake to be a lanky type like me. Your nerve impulses have to travel too far, I imagine.'

'Oh.' I still had no idea what to say. I just felt terribly sad for him.

'Of course, the gammy leg business wasn't really anybody's fault. I mean, it was just normal warfare. I stopped a bullet with my knee just about as soon as I got into the jungle. I was more or less the first casualty in our unit. When we had to retreat, the other chaps tried to take me with them, but of course I was a hell of a nuisance because I couldn't walk much and I mostly had to be carried. And then I picked up some kind of fever and I was delirious when they actually picked us up, and took us off to some camp. In fact I gather that for about five days I didn't even know I'd been taken prisoner: I thought I was still in the jungle. Quite honestly, old thing, it would have been better for me if I had been.'

'But you wouldn't have survived.'

'That's what I mean,' Knowlton said quietly.

I sat without speaking. This situation was altogether too much for me. The waiter came with our drinks, now approaching Knowlton on his deaf side and speaking into his useless ear. Finally we got it sorted out.

'Funny,' Knowlton said reflectively when the waiter had gone. 'I got the deaf ear when I was clouted on the side of the head with a rifle-butt. My stiff leg made me move rather slowly, you know, and one of the guards gave me some order and evidently felt I didn't jump to it fast enough. Brother Jap tends to be a bit hot-tempered.'

I said the only thing I felt able to say. 'Knowlton, if there's anything I can do to help you, anything *at all*, please tell me what it is.'

'Thanks, old mate.'

'And if you can't think of anything now, this minute, let me know when you do think of something. It doesn't matter when. Just regard that offer as open, always, permanently.'

Knowlton nodded and smiled. As the smile crossed his features he looked, for a brief instant, something like the young man I had known. After it had passed, his face stiffened back into the shape moulded by those months and years of barely endurable agony.

'I'm being looked after splendidly, as a matter of fact,' he said. 'I don't drive a car now, but I have a very good friend who drove me over here and is taking charge of the whole trip, fixing all the appointments and everything. A doctor. How about that for good luck?'

'Sounds fine. What's his name?'

'Stella,' said Knowlton. 'It's a she.'

I was deeply glad to learn that there was a woman somewhere at the centre of Knowlton's smashed life. That old, blessed, unquenchable mending and building instinct – may it be at work here, and may it work with a special singleness of purpose for Knowlton: thus I prayed, silently.

We talked a little more, desultorily, on neutral topics. I gave him such news of Episcopus as I could. How remote it must seem! Surely if the Japanese prison camp was true, Episcopus College must be a dream? But in that case what, between the truth and the dream, were Hiroshima and Nagasaki? What was there to hold on to?

I had to go. I saw Knowlton comfortably settled. He said he would be having lunch with Stella, then going to the Eye Hospital. Would I like to wait and meet Stella? I said no, not this time. I was sure I would have other opportunities. He didn't press me. My real reason was simply that I felt overwhelmed: I didn't want to talk to anyone. I needed to get away by myself, if only for a quarter of an hour.

Knowlton! Knowlton, of all people!

After getting no reply from Mairead to the letter I had written to her in the late spring, I wrote to her again in June. Nothing happened again. I wrote yet again, in much the same terms, in the autumn. Nothing happened again. I was getting used to it now. I supposed that I could easily go on writing substantially the same letter for the rest of my life, even after I had forgotten its original purpose; a Mairead-letter that I wrote every month or so to a dimly apprehended, exalted Presence from whom I requested an interview, not having the slightest idea what I would do if the request should actually be granted.

As Christmas 1946 approached, I sent her a Christmas card, for no better reason than that I was sending a batch out and the kind of message I was becoming accustomed to sending her was short enough to fit into the bit of space round the printed stuff about Wassail and Season's Greetings. I sent it off without much hope.

The Christmas vacation came and, thank God, went. The appalling winter of that year, 1947, the worst since records had been kept, began to bite with a ferocity that crunched down to the bone. To a people jaded and slightly malnourished, still short of food and fuel, it seemed like a grim prolongation of the war, but with the enemy now no longer the Germans but Nature itself.

The Leonard family, in fact, were by no means among the worse sufferers in the early weeks of 1947. One member, Michael, actually enjoyed the same season. Being in the country, we were able to get plenty of logs, so that the house was always warm. And when Michael left the house he revelled in the gleaming snow. Snow-ploughs had been round all the country roads and cut into the deep white drifts, turning the lanes into magic pathways between hard white walls. Michael loved running and sliding on the roads and climbing on and off the high walls. Watching him out of the window as he made snowmen and raced down the slopes on a sledge, I knew he would look back on this period as a happy one. For me, though I escaped the worst hardships of that season, it was like life in a Russian winter, but without the years of adaptation that the Russians bring to it.

In the middle of all this, so preoccupied with the daily struggle to get by that for long stretches I even forgot about Mairead, in late February I received a letter from her. Like mine, it was in a typed envelope, and I opened it with a sheaf of other mail, my mind on other things, pulling out a piece of paper that stopped my heart and left me breathless and dazed. I happened to be by myself in the hall, for which I was immensely grateful.

Peter,
    Thank you for your Christmas card. Since you seem to be so set on a talk with me and have asked for it so repeatedly, I'll be in the bar of the Great Western Hotel on Paddington Station at six o'clock on March 18. I rely on you to be quite sincere about all the things you say in your letters, about not wanting anything beyond just to see me, and all that.

Mairead.

March 18 was still some way off. I don't know how I got through the intervening time, but of course I did somehow. Finally there was only a week to go. Then three days, then one, then a few hours. I looked at my watch very often that afternoon. I got a train that was due to arrive at Paddington at just after four o'clock, wanting to leave enough time for it to be late. It was punctual. I wandered about the Paddington neighbourhood for almost two hours. I went as far as Craven Hill in one direction and St Mary's Hospital in the other. I walked up and down London Street. I went about half a mile down Bishop's Bridge Road, then turned back. I didn't want to be too far from the station, in case I slipped off the kerb and sprained an ankle, and had to hobble back.

I got to the bar at six precisely, timing myself by the big clock on Platform One. I had been standing near it since 5.45, watching the hands move, concentrating all my attention on that clock-face so as to save my sanity, blotting out everything else in the universe except the movement of those two hands.

When the little hand pointed vertically downward and the big hand pointed vertically upward it would be six o'clock. And when I judged that they were within thirty seconds of gaining these positions I turned and began walking down the platform. There was, of course, an element of conjecture in this. So when I say that I entered the bar at six o'clock I understand that my statement is true only in approximate terms. It would not satisfy an engineer. It would not do for Brian, for instance, if he were trying to establish a lap time at Brooklands for the K.3. M.G. But it would pass muster in a court of law.

I found myself alone in the bar. I went up to the counter and ordered a double Irish whisky. This I carried over to the corner of the bench seat that ran round the wall. I put it down, very steadily, without spilling a drop. There was no reason why I should spill a drop. It was only a small glass but a double measure of whisky did not fill it, especially since these were the days before bartenders automatically put large pieces of ice into all short drinks. You only got ice if you asked for it; I had not asked for it.

Suddenly I knew that if Mairead did not come through that door, *immediately*, I would start screaming. I took a grip on myself. It was no use. I drew in my breath and opened my mouth to start screaming. Then she came in through the door.

I let out my breath again and sank against the back of the bench seat, thinking

I was going to faint. Then I remembered the whisky, still untouched, on the table in front of me. As Mairead came towards me I picked up the glass and drained it in one gulp. I remember distinctly that it had no effect on me at all, it went down just like a tablespoonful of tap water.

'Heavens, that was quick,' she said and her face broke into a smile. 'You knocked that back as if you needed it.'

'I just wanted to have an empty glass when I went up to the bar,' I said. 'So we can start fair. What shall I get you?'

She asked for a dry vermouth with ice. I got her one, plus another Irish for me. But I got a small one this time, not a double, and I put a little water with it.

'Well,' Mairead said, lifting her glass, 'here's good luck to us.'

'I've had good luck already,' I said. 'You've come.'

'Yes, I'm here and you're here, but what happens next?'

'We're going to talk.'

'About what?'

I didn't say anything. It wasn't that I had nothing to say; I had too many things and they just jammed in the doorway. Nothing came out. So I just sat and looked at her. She was wearing a blue dress that went perfectly with her eyes and, like them, set off the blackness of her hair. But it was very simple, not at all dressy. It might well have been what she wore at the office on an ordinary working day. Round her neck she had a string of round objects of a reddish colour: coral?

'You know why I needed to see you, Mairead,' I said. 'It's in my letter.'

'That stuff about not being able to live without me?'

'Yes. It happens to be literally true.'

'Isn't that just a way of saying that you've decided you want me?'

'No. It's a way of saying that I can't live without you.'

'You mean you'll actually *die* if we're not together?'

'Yes.'

'Don't be silly, Peter. It takes a lot to kill a person.'

'I know we're not allowed nowadays to talk about people dying of a broken heart. That expression's gone out because medical science has other terms for the causes of death. But it still happens. A person can be driven to a point of unhappiness where they lose the will to live. Then their body takes over and comes up with a disease that has a medical name, and that's what goes down on the certificate.'

'Are you telling me that unless we come back together you're going to die of a broken heart?'

'Yes, that's what I'm telling you, but I don't want you to take it as a threat or emotional blackmail or anything. It's just a statement of fact.'

'Fact! Seems more like a conjecture to me.'

'No, it's fact, perfectly sober objective fact. When we were close together during that couple of years, when we built a life together — '

'Correction. We built part of a life together. There were always fenced-off areas.'

'Yes, there were fenced-of areas, and yet the most vital and most memorable and joyful part of our lives we built together, why deny it?'

She looked down at her hands and said quietly, 'I'm not denying it.'

'When we were building a life together I was happy, as I'd never been before. Then we gave up that life because we thought we owed it to other people to give it up.'

'Not other people. Just one other person: your Heather.'

'And Mike.'

'Mike, I suppose, and yet I didn't feel such pressure coming from him, partly no doubt because I couldn't visualize him. I could always visualize Heather. And then I suppose I thought I might always have a relationship with Mike of one kind or another, but never with Heather.'

'Yes, and I thought – at that time – that I ought to go back to her and cut you out of my life.'

She said, still quietly, 'Well, you did, didn't you?'

'No. I found it didn't work like that. I couldn't just walk away from you. You were round me and I was carrying you with me whether I wanted to or not. And I'll die if I go on trying to live without you.'

'That's not true, Peter. You *won't* die. You'll recover, it'll just take time.'

'Is that what you really think? That people recover?'

She hesitated for a second, then said, 'Yes.'

'You're wrong. When somebody's really broken up by something they don't get over it. They can put on a brave show, but they've died inside and nothing will bring them back to life.'

'Peter,' she said, 'if you could have anything you wanted from me, what would you ask me for?'

'To come to me so that we could be together. For the rest of our lives.'

'As man and wife?'

'If that was the way you thought best. To me personally it wouldn't matter whether or not we had a marriage certificate. I would regard our union as indissoluble because to me it would be indissoluble. That's all one can ever hope for – to be completely decided in one's own mind and to hope that the other person feels the same.'

'But you're married to another woman. You must have felt like that about her, or you wouldn't have married her. You must have been completely decided in your own mind once before, and now you've changed.'

'No, I wasn't. I was confused and boxed in. We had a close physical relationship into which we'd been hurried by my intense need. I went ahead with the marriage because I couldn't see what else to do, and after that I made the best of it. It's an old story.'

'I'm sure a lot of marriages start like that but they don't all end in divorce.'

'Mairead,' I said in a low, urgent tone, 'you know we belong together. You know our place is with one another. Why don't we just give thanks that we've found each other and get on with doing what we have to do? Clear away the obstacles that stand between us, and begin our real lives.'

'I'm sure your wife and son wouldn't be pleased to hear themselves described as obstacles.'

'They're not obstacles, they're living human beings with wants and needs and preferences, and they need to be set free to live their lives too.'

'Is that how Heather'll see it, that she's being set free?'

'No, it isn't how she'll see it, she'll think she's being betrayed.'

'What will happen,' Mairead asked, 'if you just walk out on her?'

'What will happen is that Heather will get a lawyer and tell him to go for my throat. He'll put the screws on me for every penny he can extract. And I'll pay up and look pleasant. I'll sign on the dotted line to give her any colossal sum the court awards, and then I'll pick myself up and reorganize my life and I'll work like a maniac, and take evening classes and do extra exam. marking, and write

339

textbooks, and review historical books in the weekly papers. I'll weed people's gardens and muck out stables if I have to and if I can get the work, anything to survive, and I'll do it with a song in my heart because I'll be doing it so as to be near you.'

Mairead gave a soft smile. And then, woman-like, she attacked from a totally unexpected quarter. 'What about my career?'

'You needn't interrupt it if you don't want to.'

'How on earth could I combine going on with it with coming to Oxford and living with you?'

'Who said anything about coming to Oxford? If you're working in an office in London and you don't want to give it up, fine. I'll get a house in Ealing, which is pretty nearly half-way to Oxford and on the main railway line. I'll get up early every morning and get the train to Oxford, and you can set out at a more civilized hour and go into London on the tube. It goes out that far, as I expect you know.'

'Got it all worked out, haven't you?'

'No. As a matter of fact I hadn't considered it at all. I just came out with Ealing on the spur of the moment, but now that I look at it it's a pretty good idea – I don't think I could find a better solution if I had all the time in the world.'

'Well, what if I were posted abroad?'

'I'd give up my Oxford job and come out with you.'

'And do what?'

'I'd try to get the Embassy to take me on to the staff as a lift attendant or security man or something. Failing that, I'd just stay at home and keep the house and do the cooking ready for you when you came home.'

'You can't cook.'

'I'd learn.'

Mairead laughed. 'And you think you'd be happy doing that?'

'Blissfully.'

Her laugh died away and her smile faded. She looked down at her folded hands, up at me, and said nothing.

'Mairead, my darling, I've sought you out and found you because I want to throw my life at your feet. It's yours, everything that I am and could be is yours for the taking. Please, my love, take it.'

'No,' she said.

At first I thought I hadn't heard her. So intense, so total was my whole being's denial of that syllable that I managed, for a moment, to prevent it from entering my consciousness. But of course it did enter, inexorably, like a gimlet thrusting into a board.

'No?' I repeated wonderingly. 'But Mairead . . . Why? Why no? Surely you must mean yes, don't you?'

'No.'

I fell back against the bench seat. 'All right, I've finished, I don't understand any more. I just don't know where we are.'

Mairead spoke in a low, unhurried voice. But behind each word was the full force of her character, its honesty, its directness.

'I fastened my love on you for two years and then I had to pull away from you.'

'That's what we agreed,' I said feebly.

'Yes, it's what we agreed and it's what we did. The pain of doing that was so awful I had to grow a new self. You talk about people dying of grief, well, in a way I did that. The self I had before was something that belonged to you, and when I went I left it with you. To that extent, I *did* die. So I had to grow a new self. Well, I've grown it now. I'm different. I'm not the same person.'

'I had to adjust to pain too.'

'And yet now you come to me and start talking about starting our old relationship again.'

'Not *that* relationship, Mairead. A new one.'

'What's new about it? You're still married. Heather's still your wife and Mike's still your son. And you talk to me about starting up again – d'you think it's that easy?'

'Look, Mairead, I've got to the end of the line with Heather.'

'Show me your divorce certificate and I'll believe you. Invite me to visit you somewhere that's *your* address, and not yours and hers.'

'All right, I will. These things take time, but I'll – '

'And don't count on it to make any difference to me. I told you I'd had to grow a new self and I have. It's my new self you're looking at now. The old one's dead.'

'Life is change, Mairead.'

'And just think twice before you go on killing people. Heather's built her life round your marriage for donkey's years now, how d'you know it won't kill her when you just walk away?'

'I just – '

'And how d'you know it won't kill Mike? He had to do without you so much during the war, now you're talking about being off again.'

'Children aren't as easily killed as that.'

'They may be. They can very easily be twisted.'

She stood up. 'Thanks for the drink, Peter, and I suppose I ought to feel honoured that you took all that trouble to seek me out again. But that's enough.'

'Mairead . . .' My voice came out as a croak. 'Are you telling me to get out of your life?'

'I'm telling Heather's husband to get out of my life. My new self, the one I had to grow when the old one died, doesn't go in for married men.'

I snatched at that straw. 'And if I *wasn't* Heather's husband?'

'I'll believe that when I see it. I'm certainly making no promises.'

'You mean if I were to come to you one day and say that I was free, no longer married, set up in my own place, ready to start life on a basis of freedom, you might still not want to come to me?'

She was standing, I was sitting. She looked down on me as if I were something in a shop window that she was wondering whether to buy, and thinking probably not.

'Here's the furthest I'll go,' she said at last. 'If I, as I am now with my new self, were to meet you as you might be under those circumstances, you'd start fair. You'd have the same chance of interesting me as anyone else.'

She turned to go. I struggled to my feet. 'Mairead – please! Don't leave me without a lifeline! Tell me at least that you'll let me know where you are.'

'If you mean you want my address, no, Peter. You'd bombard me with letters.'

'I swear to God,' I said, 'I will never write you a letter of more than ten lines, devoted entirely to factual information.'

She thought for a moment, then pulled out a tiny notebook, wrote something, tore off the page and gave it to me. It was a London telephone number.

'Remember,' she said, 'that's only for conveying information. If you pester me I'll never have anything to do with you again – I mean it.'

'I won't pester you,' I said. I stood looking down at the scrap of paper with the figures on it as Mairead picked up her coat and handbag and went out, leaving me alone, looking down at two empty glasses and an empty life.

Slowly I lowered myself on to the bench. I sat there for a long time without moving. I wasn't able to move. Something inside me seemed to be broken. Not only could I not move my body, I couldn't move my mind. I couldn't think of anything. It was just as if I were looking into a white circular disc, something like the reflector of a searchlight.

After I don't know how long, people came and sat at the table beside me, chattering in loud, irritating voices. They broke the spell and got me out of the bar, my coat over my arm. Where now? Out on to the station platform, a train to Oxford, then Chinnor and my homestead?

No. No. I knew I couldn't do that. I must be by myself. Besides, I didn't want Heather to see me like this. She would know at once that something terrible had happened, and it would be intolerably painful if she ignored my distress. And there was Mike. I loved him, perhaps more now than ever, but I didn't feel ready for him.

I went along to the hotel desk and booked a room for the night. I told the receptionist, when she gave me the key, that my luggage was checked in on the station and I would bring it in myself. I had no luggage. I went up and let myself into the narrow impersonal room and lay down on the bed. My mind was still a blank. I was still staring into the searchlight.

After a long time a thought began to form: more precisely, a fear. I feared the hours ahead. I thought I might go mad, shut up in this narrow box. I needed company, the company of someone I trusted; but not, above all not, to talk about Mairead. Not about my emotional situation at all.

Not now, not now. Perhaps not ever.

My need for company was now overwhelming. I knew a few people in London, but in all that city whom did I love and trust? The answer came at once: Harry and Geraldine. The Goodenoughs had recently moved into a flat in Deptford, Harry had a theatre job of sorts, and they had sent me their telephone number. I dialled it. Geraldine answered, chirpy and friendly.

'You're in London? – could you get round to see us?'

'Well – if you can put up with me, dropping in without notice.'

'Course we can. Harry'll be in any time now and I don't even need to ask him. I know he'll be delighted to see you, Peter. And we're planning to eat at home, and there's enough to go round for three.'

'Geraldine – you're the kindest person in the world.'

'I'm only kind to people I like. Now listen carefully while I tell you how to get here.'

I got there. Geraldine opened the door. My first thought was how little she had changed. During the war years we had met rarely and always briefly: I knew she had been employed on some kind of welfare work, helping to resettle people who had been bombed out. She must have had heart-breaking experiences, but outwardly she seemed to me still the cheeky, argumentative undergraduate, the rebel of St Hilda's. She dismissed her war service casually when I asked about it. 'Just making myself useful in little ways. Marking time. It's Harry who really had all the excitement. North Africa and then Italy – hundreds of miles inside a noisy stuffy tank. I daren't think about it. By some miracle I've got him back, that's all I care about.'

Where was Harry? 'On his way home from rehearsal. He telephoned. I told him you were here and he's delighted. He's stopped off to get some wine.'

Then Harry was through the door, big and bear-like, and I hugged him, and felt such relief at being with people I loved and trusted. The Mairead-pain was still there, but I knew the best thing was to pay no attention to it. Before settling down to talk and hear all Harry's news and plans, I rang Heather and told her where I was. I said they had asked me to stay and eat and asked if she minded that I would be home late.

'Late? If you're all the way over to Deptford and you're going to get into talk with those two, I can't see you getting a train from Paddington before midnight, and I can't possibly get in from Chinnor at that hour to pick you up.'

'Well, I quite see that.'

'I think I'll just expect you some time tomorrow.' And she rang off. I couldn't tell if she was angry or not: she had her usual off-hand manner, which probably meant that she knew she was married to an impossible husband who took sudden whims into his head and did things without consulting her, and she would just have to make the best of it. I felt bad. I foresaw that in one way or another I would go on feeling bad for just about the rest of my life.

Harry told me that he was running a Shakespearean theatre in a converted warehouse in the East End, putting on shoe-string productions, very straight, very fast and uncluttered. We opened the wine he had bought in honour of my visit, two bottles of a villainous cheap Spanish red, but so welcome and we all three drank a toast to our friendship. Geraldine told us we were to have ravioli for dinner, she had found an Italian shop in Soho that stocked ravioli, and if you got there when they had just had a consignment you could buy any amount you wanted. Since the little pasta envelopes undoubtedly contained meat, though what meat it was and where it had come from were mysteries better not enquired into, it was perhaps the only unrationed meat on sale in the whole of London; she was very proud of having got some. How typical of them to share it with me! She went off to the kitchen to prepare it, leaving me with Harry.

It was wonderful to talk to him again. There was no one else in the world with whom I could talk so freely. It was his generosity, his openness, that did it, and his lack of a *parti pris*. It was not difficult, in fact, to keep off the subject of Mairead. In any case, I felt that I might have a better chance of coping with that if I could be better sorted out in general. I was so dispersed, so fragmented. I needed a fixed point from which I could make judgments and hold opinions. I had to get myself together, to get my life in order, and to channel my own fretful emotions.

Geraldine and Harry were wonderfully happy together; there must be something to be learnt from that. They were obviously lovers, but equally obviously very good friends who inhabited one another's minds in perfect security, totally unafraid of anything they might find there. I could only see one point in their relationship where dissonance might enter. She was built for the political life, he for the artistic. She took evening classes in the East End on history and politics, raising the awareness of Londoners to their economic and social position and how it could be improved; she was interested in wage structures, employment statistics, legislation. He, on the other hand, was content with a life lived in the creation of illusion as a way to the truth. He wanted to give people dreams and visions, to open their minds to the magic of the world, and let everything else flow from that. I made my intervention just there, at that crucial borderline. With my mind full of recent conversations with Lamont and Garrity – yes, and with Hannah Carshalton, less articulate than the others but just as seriously committed to what she was doing – I knew that these people were finding that art, whichever art they responded to, gave them a star to steer by in the blackest night. What was it they knew and I didn't? Could it be learnt?

'Listen, Harry,' I said when we were settled down with our wine and warm by the gas-fire. 'I'm in a serious mood. I'm full of big questions. It's no good trying to duck them, they're coming over. Here's the first – it's about you.'

'About *me*? What have I done to deserve big questions?'

'You give me the impression of having answered, inside yourself, the biggest one of all. What is it that holds you together?'

'What, me and Geraldine?'

Not for the first time I regretted that English does not have the distinction between *tu* and *vous*. 'No, you, Harry, you yourself. Something holds you together. You're in one piece.'

His big, honest face, surmounted by its shock of hair, turned to me enquiringly. 'Aren't you then, Peter? What's actually the matter?'

'What's the matter is that I can't take hold of all the things I see happening in the world. I have to reckon with them as human experience. But what is human experience? How can one mind comprehend it? Think of the last few years. The war was a series of huge explosions that let out all the extremes that don't usually emerge. And they're so contradictory. The hideous cruelty, the endless destructiveness, and yet at the same time the colossal heroism and self-sacrifice. What is it to be a human animal? I know I'm one of them, but what are they? What, in short, are *we*? What am *I*?'

'D'you have to know all that before you can function?'

'Not before I can function mechanically. But as soon as I need to get down beneath the surface, and especially when I need to make life-decisions, *then* I need to have some self-knowledge. I need to know what humanity is, Harry. I believe you have things to tell me.'

'I do? Why on earth me?'

'Because your life is given to an art and I've noticed that people who pursue an art don't seem troubled by the feeling I have of being dispersed, of not having a centre.'

'That may be just because it takes all their energy and leaves them just no time for the kind of speculation you go in for.'

'It isn't. Harry, please be serious. I don't "go in for speculation", as if speculation were stamp-collecting or photography. I'm just a normally thoughtful person who feels very isolated, drifting without an anchor in a sea that's never been charted. Appalling monsters keep breaking the surface.'

'Talking about anchors, have you talked to anybody religious? They usually claim to have an anchor.'

'I don't really know many religious people. A lot of them are personally very fine, but if I try to discuss anything with them their irrationality puts me off.'

'I see what you mean – not that ordinary rationality's much of a help.'

'No, it isn't. And yet one can't throw reason overboard altogether. The Christians, for instance, with their doctrine of the Atonement, seem to me to be offering an account of the universe that nobody could really hold. I can't think they really hold it themselves. Of course if you tackle them on it they take refuge in saying it's a metaphor.'

344

'Which brings us back to art, I suppose. Art's all metaphor.'

'Well, so it is, Harry, but can you keep going on it?'

'Perfectly well, thank you.'

'I mean, here you are spending your life putting on Shakespeare's plays. Nobody's going to deny the greatness of Shakespeare, but *now*? In the age of the atomic bomb and — '

'I thought,' Harry Goodenough said, 'your problem was that you wanted to understand the nature of the human animal. Well, it's all in Shakespeare. He understood the whole range.'

'Harry, that was 300 years ago and things have *changed*.'

'I'm surprised to hear you say that. An historian. I thought the lesson of history was that nothing changes, except the outer wrapping.'

'In general, yes, but this wrapping is so colossal. Science has put such power into people's hands. That's what upsets poor old Weatherby, for example. He thinks he's living out the Faust legend.'

'Well, so he is. But I don't have to tell you that the best treatment of that legend in English is 300 years old, by Marlowe.'

'Point taken.'

'And you talk about scale,' Harry said, following up his advantage. 'I don't think scale matters. You're thinking of things like the German concentration camps, or Stalin's huge crimes involving vast numbers and the most up-to-date scientific methods. But what's at the bottom of them? Fear, cruelty, aggression: they're not new, are they?'

'No – what's new is the power to inflict them on such a huge scale.'

'The Inquisition was on a pretty wide scale, the cruelties in the Roman arena went on for years and years, and there's always the little matter of Genghis Khan. But as I say, scale is nothing. The blinding of Gloster in *King Lear* is an act of ultimate cruelty represented onstage. If what you're trying to do is come to terms with human cruelty, it's there, acted out for you so that you can contemplate it without feeling that you absolutely *must* intervene and rescue the victims, which is what you'd feel in real life. And Shakespeare also shows us happiness – moments like the reunion of Leontes and Hermione. These may lie outside our individual experience, but the human being is capable of them and he puts them up there for us to share in. And it doesn't matter that they're just individual examples. If it's the nature of a human reality you're after, an individual represen-tation is as good as a mass representation. What you can't find out from one example you can't find out from ten thousand.'

'So you recommend art as a means of making sense of life, Harry?'

He stirred uneasily, as well he might. And when he spoke it was, at first, hesitantly.

'Well, I don't pretend to be a wise man, but what else is there? It's the only means we have of slowing the game down. Experience comes pouring over us in such a headlong torrent, it never stops for a moment, and what's more it doesn't come in manageable form. Something colossal happens in the outside world and just when you want to give your mind to it, something equally colossal happens in your personal life.'

I nodded, thinking of Hiroshima.

'And as far as I can see, art's all we have that's capable of getting hold of life as it rushes by, and arresting it.'

I thought some more. 'But Harry, as an historian I've spent all my working life dealing with material that's designed to act as a brake on experience, to slow it down, to make it keep still long enough to be analysed.'

'What kind of material?'

'Every kind of record. Documents, maps, eyewitness accounts, transcripts of trials . . .'

'Yes, but that stuff's just data. There's no vision built into it, it's just raw material. The artist gives you the raw material you find in the records, but permeated by his vision.'

'So he does the whole job for you? You don't have to do anything for yourself?'

'Don't you believe it. Understanding any of the arts isn't child's play. It calls for effort of a kind that most historians don't know about. Look at the mess the average historian makes when he discusses any work of art. He tries to treat it as a document like any other.'

Geraldine now appeared and summoned us to ravioli. We went to the kitchen. We ate ravioli and with it we opened the second bottle of red wine. Because we were hungry we made only small talk as we actually attacked the food, but by the time we had put away most of it and a pot of coffee was on the stove, we were ready for talk again.

So that we would have a broad enough topic, I deliberately moved the conversation towards politics. I asked Geraldine what were her relations, nowadays, with Communism.

'I'm still a Party member,' she said. 'And I'm still trying to get Harry to pay a subscription and join.'

'Which I won't do,' he said. 'I'm perfectly willing to make a contribution to funds, but to sign up and carry a card – it sticks in my craw.'

'It's the only logical position,' Geraldine said.

'Perhaps that's what I don't like about it. Follow the logic of anything to its natural end and you become the enemy of the human race.'

'So, Geraldine,' I said, 'you left the Party at the time of the Nazi-Soviet Pact, went back into it when Germany and Russia went to war, and you're still in it today.'

'Yes.'

'In spite of the decidedly *un*-peaceful activities of the Soviet Government since peace supposedly broke out.'

'*Peace*! What about the atomic bomb?'

'The atomic bombs I agree were horrible, but they did at least bring the fighting to an end.'

'I don't believe for a minute that it was done to bring the fighting to an end. It was done as a signal to Russia, to show that the West had military supremacy.'

'All right, don't let's argue over that ground. We've both got prepared positions and neither of us could bridge the other. Let's take another issue. If you're a card-carrying Communist, does that mean you approve of everything the Kremlin does?'

'No. You can be a devout Catholic without approving of everything the Papacy does.'

'Well, yes, but I suppose a devout Catholic can stand up in public and actually *criticize* the Papacy. Can a card-carrying Communist? Can you protest, for example, when it seems, as it does now, that the Kremlin would much rather have Franco's government in Spain than the British Labour Party?'

'You seem very certain that you know the thought-processes of the Kremlin.'

'Well, I'm generally certain about what's staring me in the face. If the Kremlin

346

isn't hostile to the British Labour Party – i.e. to the current British Government – they're putting up a remarkably good imitation of hostility, and pretty vicious hostility at that. Come now, Geraldine, Communism hates popular democracy, doesn't it?'

'You've put your finger on it, Peter,' said Harry, pouring more red wine. 'That's what my hesitation about Communism comes down to: they don't trust the people.'

'They trust History,' Geraldine said, 'and they know that History will be made manifest through the people.'

'Only if the people are very carefully shepherded in the way the Party says they must go, with no straying allowed. And the shepherding includes things like suppression of a free press, and a secret police, and labour camps and mass deportations. You've only got to ask yourself how many free elections have been permitted in the parts of Europe that the Red Army was in possession of when the war actually came to a standstill. None at all, as you know. Communism *may* be the best the people could hope for, but just to be on the safe side they're not allowed to hope for anything else. The British Labour Party did at least get in on a free vote.'

'Well, since you press me and since we're friends,' Geraldine said, 'it *is* the one big regret I have about Communism. I do believe their view of political justice is right in theory – I just wish they had a bit more faith in people's ability to know what's good for them. I think it's partly a consequence of their having come to power first in Russia, where the population were so far-flung and backward and so absolutely unacquainted with ideas.'

'Well,' I said, 'Marx himself thought the Revolution would begin in England. That's because the English working class in his day were not only the most oppressed by the first phase of capitalist industrialism, but the most solid and thoughtful. They were like your students at Ruskin. But what actually happened when people like your students got to the levers of power? It was Transport House they worked through, not the Kremlin.'

'That's a step on the way. And a good one.'

'A step on the way? That's not how Moscow sees it.'

'My real worry about Communists,' said Harry, who had been pursuing a train of thought of his own, 'is their absolute confidence that they're right and they have the answer to everything. I don't believe that anybody has that. I'd rather be ruled by politicians who admit that they might sometimes make a mistake.'

'That's the Russian origins again,' Geraldine said. 'You can't govern a village of Russian peasants by telling them you might make mistakes. They came straight from serfdom, where they had to accept absolute authority, to a secular state which had dispossessed the landlords and disbanded the Church. You couldn't just leave them wandering. You had to claim infallibility, for the same reason that the Pope claims it. He has the same problem of being in authority over millions of very poor and very backward people, so of course he tells them he can't be wrong.'

'Yes,' I said, 'but Geraldine, none of us at this table are backward peasants and we *are* acquainted with ideas. Does that mean that Communism's not for us? Or does it just mean that we have to take our place among the leaders of a Communist society and deliberately join in the process of hoodwinking the masses?'

'That's what I meant,' she said, 'when I said a moment ago that I wish the Party had a bit more faith in ordinary people. My ideal would be a Communist

347

government that had been freely elected, in straight competition with other parties. But that's a very distant dream, more distant in this country than any other in Europe. In France and Italy, the Communist Party contests elections and they win quite a lot of seats. In this country, there's only one, Willie Gallacher, and he represents the one place you'd expect him to represent – Glasgow. He's elected by people who feel themselves so far from having any say in how things are run that they might just as well be slaves. By electing a Communist they do at least get people to look at them.'

That was something I could agree with, at any rate. But I found I had once more to head the conversation off. Thinking about the Scots and how they felt neglected by Westminster made me think about the Irish and their historic grievances, and that made me think of Mairead. So I burrowed back into the talk, swerving it back towards Harry's professional work, and his passion for Shakespeare. I smiled, now, as I thought of the evening when he had come to read a paper to the History Discussion Club on early inn-yard stages, and how Geraldine, who had never before set eyes on him, had tangled him up in discussions of the cash-nexus and the break-up of the feudal system, the two of them talking at cross-purposes until Bax intervened. Looking back, I understand now what I didn't then – why Bax had been concerned to protect Geraldine from making a fool of herself. Harry had been in danger of appearing foolish too, of course, but Bax was not in love with Harry. He was in love with Geraldine, and one day that love was to cost him terrible suffering, just as my love for Mairead . . . No. I made a mighty effort and swung my mind into yet another direction.

And so the emergency was dealt with, and the next, and the next, as they arose, until finally I sank, on the sofa and with the makeshift bedding, into sleep.

16

I woke very early the next morning. The room was cold and I felt stiff and cramped. But I didn't mind. I lay back and looked at the chill, austere light that came in through the window, round the edges of the inadequate curtains. It seemed to me to have a challenging quality. It told me to brace myself, to confront life, to stop trying to read its riddles, and instead to bring order to its chaotic jumble.

Harry got up, bumped around in his dressing-gown, lit the gas. The day began. We drank tea. Lumpily, in a stop-and-start fashion, we got dressed, taking turns in the draughty little bathroom. I determined to go to a barber's for a shave. Any barber would lather and shave you in those days: a shave and hot towels, the best refresher in the world.

Harry went off first, to see if the workmen had turned up at his theatre to get on with some repairs. Before he went he said he expected to be seeing me soon. With a surge of gratitude I told him he could count on it. That left Geraldine. I was ready to go. She was ready to go. She looked round the flat, checking that everything was in a fit state to be left for the day. Then, as she moved across the room, she came past me and her eyes met mine. Her quick, busy tread stopped for a moment.

'How are you, Peter?' she said. 'How are you *really*?'

'I don't know. I'm functioning, but I don't know how I am really. I think the truth is that I've got a lot of straightening up to do. Facing facts – and as usual that means making a choice of which particular set of facts I'm going to face.'

'Anything we can do? Harry and I?'

'You've done it. Last night and this morning.'

'Really? What did we do?'

'You helped in two ways. First, by being good reliable friends, the kind I can turn to and feel secure with. Second, by being such a wonderful on-the-hoof example of what it can be like when two people really love each other.'

She grinned, her old *gamine* grin. 'It's not all peaches and cream, you know. We have the most colossal rumpuses sometimes. Or should that be rumpi?'

'I can see with my own eyes that you love each other very much, and absolutely unshakeably, and that's the only thing that's important.'

Her grin faded to an expression of contemplative gentleness. I could tell she was thinking of Harry. Then she said, 'I would never argue with that.'

'Well,' I said, taking my overcoat off a hook, 'I'm off.'

'What are you going to do now?'

'Spend the morning in London and then go back to Oxford.'

'What will you do this morning?'

'I'm not sure. Just walk about, perhaps. Go to Hampstead Heath or somewhere. I've got all this thinking to do.'

'I'll give you one piece of advice,' Geraldine said. 'If you've got a morning free in London, do something Londony. Do something you'd have no chance to do

349

in Oxford. It'll shake your mind up. That'll make it easier for you to do all that thinking. And good luck with it, old Peter.'

I kissed her. There seemed nothing to say. I said nothing. I took my coat and went down the stairs to the street door.

While I was having my shave and hot towels, I decided that her advice had been sound. Do something Londony. Shake up your mind. Well, London was supposed to be the great centre and clearing-house of the arts, and Harry had been telling me to give art a more central place in my life. Since the time at my disposal was the morning, I couldn't go to a theatre or a concert. That meant a picture gallery. They were all in the process of re-opening: during the war, with their treasures stowed away in remote places out of the way of enemy raids, they had either been closed or, in the case of the National Gallery, used for music. In the end, more or less spinning a coin to decide, I went to the Tate. I remember one of the things that decided me was that I knew it was beside the river and I thought I would take a look at the water.

I'll admit it: I'm a Philistine. I had never found it natural to haunt art galleries. As a *dix-huitièmiste* I had gone to the great collections mainly to look at the work of specific eighteenth-century painters from whose work I might learn something about the mind of my chosen epoch. Or I would go to the National Portrait Gallery to stand and gaze at the faces of men and women I was reading, and sometimes writing, about. But art simply as art, art for the sake of what it could tell me about the human condition, I had never adequately considered. I considered it this morning. I wandered to where Turner's paintings hung in all their majesty of flame and shadow, of storm and brilliance. I was exalted, and humbled. I felt that my petty grievances were nothing, that no one who had a pair of eyes and could open them on the world had a right to complain about anything.

Time passed uncounted. Looking at my watch, I realized with a start that it would soon be time to leave the gallery. But first I wanted to follow up Hannah Carshalton's words about Paul Nash. Had she and I anything in common? Would Nash's painting make as profound an impression on me as it had on her? Going to the information desk, I found that a number of Nash's paintings, those completed during the war years, had just been bought by the Tate from the War Artists' Advisory Committee. I asked which room I might find them in, and was told that they were just at that very time being hung and it might be better to go away and come back in a few days. I was in no mood to go away; I wanted to see them now, today. I found my way there.

Nash did not disappoint me. There were men up ladders, they were measuring and calling out instructions to one another, but I ignored all distraction and just looked, looked, looked.

The paintings had a strange, hypnotic effect on me. I can't do art talk, so all I can say is that each one seemed to pull me strongly into its own imaginative world and it was only with an effort that I was able to move on to the next. I was particularly held by one called 'Pillar and Moon'. It showed a stone wall of the kind I had been familiar with all my life, where the blocks of stone are laid down on their sides but surmounted by a row of narrower pieces standing upright. A tall pillar of the same stone stood slightly to the left of centre, with a long line of trees, slanting away and diminishing in perspective, behind it and in front, a field strongly marked with the shadows of their trunks. The painting wasn't abstract – one could see perfectly well what everything in it represented; it was, none the less, a very 'pure' painting with everything in it working hard towards its effect as a picture and not simply as a photographic representation. The scene was lit by a pale, intense light that could be either daylight or exceptionally sharp moonlight, and the moon itself, which seemed in some indefinable but very forceful way to control the scene, was on the same level with the stone ball that topped the pillar, balancing and echoing it. All those strong horizontals, plus the powerful vertical of the pillar, made the painting very steady, but it wasn't lifeless; there was a sense of enormous energy, controlled but ready to break loose, flowing through the lines and shadows.

I stood gazing at this painting, wondering why it was holding me so powerfully; the scene it depicted seemed vaguely familiar, and I found out later that it was actually a painting of a pillar on the perimeter wall of Ascott Park, Stadhampton, a village outside Oxford where I had often bicycled in my boyhood. I had, unthinkingly, looked at this pillar and this avenue of trees many times, but now they confronted me, on the wall of this London gallery, bathed in that dreamlike moonlight, and it seemed to be telling me something about the balance of life-giving strength between the sun and the moon, and about the immense final authority of the earth, with its stillness and strength, and it was as if my own life came back to me through another man's hard-won vision.

I turned to go. But as I did so my eye fell on a painting that had not yet been hung. It was on the floor, leaning against the wall. Clearly it was a Nash – it bore all the obvious signs – and if 'Pillar and Moon' had been fascinating to me, this one was electrifying. I stood back to see it more clearly. Like the rest of Nash's work, it had a strong vein of surrealism and was yet perfectly recognizable on a realistic level. I recognized the scene at once. It was the Cowley dump of shot-down German aircraft, the dump whose organization and surveillance had been one of Brian's duties. My memory went back to the visit I had paid there on the sunlit winter day with the Spitfire stunting in the clear azure of the sky. I saw the two of us standing in the roadway looking at these silent, broken invaders. I heard Brian's voice. 'Right in the middle of the Battle of Britain, we spotted a bloke taking photographs. Walking all around it . . . doing shot after shot . . . Turned out he was an Official War Artist . . . Funny what they'll do, isn't it?' My brother and his team had interrogated Paul Nash.

There was a gallery official of some kind giving instructions to the men who were hanging the paintings. I buttonholed him and asked him if he could tell me the title of this one. He consulted a typewritten list and showed me the item: *Totes meer.* 'Thank you,' I said. 'Dead Sea.' I went back to the painting. I had already taken in – because it was one of the most challengingly obvious features of the picture – that Nash had depicted the smashed planes as forming the wave-shapes of an advancing sea. There were the long ridges of the breakers, there were the crested points of incoming billows. But frozen, immobile. At the lower right-hand corner of the painting was a bank of bare earth, its colour a more or less realistic rendering of the yellowy-brown Oxford clay soil; but Nash had exploited to the full the fact that this could also be the colour of sand on a beach. The sea had tried to seep right over the beach and it had failed and died. It had been frozen into death. But death for that sea meant life for the land that lay beyond the beach.

I stood there, staring at the painting. It was a total statement. There on that canvas was pity, awe, a sense of being aghast at so much destruction: and also a profound sigh of relief and gratitude. Among the many elements with which that picture resonated was one which I knew I was not mistaken about: it was the perfect epitaph for Heather's brother, Tom.

The painting showed a world of death: dead objects, and the implied presence in them of dead men, the young men who had been thrown onto this beach. In the pale night sky a moon, about one-third full, stood within its own nimbus. Of course such a scene, to convey all it had to convey, would have to be lit by moonlight, because the moon's light, though beautiful, is dead; it is beamed from a body without life.

> The moon's a thief,
> For her pale fire she fetches from the sun.

That pale fire brooded over these broken wings and fuselages, reflecting from the dulled metal, casting a shadow. Dead Sea! But at the right-hand edge of the frozen sea, an owl glided on open wings. Realism again: owls must certainly have hunted on that tip, with its crevices and small spaces that would have sheltered rats, mice and voles. But, also, symbolism again. The bird, warm, alert, flying and hungry, was life, whereas the immensely more powerful aircraft were inert, cold and crumpled.

I got myself to Paddington, went into the hotel to retrieve my suitcase, and ate some kind of nameless pie while I waited for a train to Oxford. As I waited I listened to the public address system. All the announcements seemed to concern services that were cancelled because of floods. The spring floods of 1947 were to be the worst on record.

The train finally hissed and clanked in, I took my seat, waited, and it began to hiss and clank out again. Off to Oxford, back to my life and my unanswered problems. The train moved slowly; doubtless there was a risk that the water had loosened sleepers here and there, preparing for a disaster. (It never came; caution won the day.) I looked out as we followed the course of the Thames Valley. Going via Slough and Maidenhead, the railway parts company with the river for a stretch, though I could see floods in the distance, but from Reading onward there were floods all the way. The thaw had been too sudden, too heavy. There had been four feet of snow in the Cotswolds, it had all melted in two days, and the whole lot had come down the Windrush and the Evenlode, both emptying into the Thames just above Oxford. The power of the thaw had knocked aside barriers and obstacles. It was like the thaw in my heart.

Since the railway from London had been built with the expectation of flooding every winter, it was raised high, and in the end we made it. The towers and spires of Oxford came into view, enough to make me breathe, for the ten-thousandth time, a silent prayer of gratitude for that beauty inherited from our forefathers.

In those simpler and more directly nourished days, beauty could be uncomplicated and affirming. It could be made with local skill from local wood and stone, and it could rise straight up from the earth in prayer and wonderment. In our day, beauty was like the beauty of *Totes meer*, wrested in a long struggle from death and destruction, distilled by a long and costly process from everything that made up its opposite. But beauty, once achieved, was one and indivisible.

The train halted for a long time outside Oxford Station, by the cemetery. When we at last pulled in and I came out of the station I couldn't face the thought of seeing anyone, having to talk. I wanted solitude.

I walked up to St Ebbe's, past the little slum houses where I had stood with Geraldine on that hot summer day. Along Brewer Street I went, and when I came out in St Aldate's I turned my face away from the town and towards open country. It was all flooded, but the Abingdon Road was passable because it was mounted on a causeway, as it had been since the early Middle Ages. I went over Folly Bridge, and paused to stare down for a moment at the swirling brown water. The banks had been overflowed, but one could tell from the pace of the water where its central current ran.

I looked down at the Thames, and thought of my parents a mile upstream. I walked on along the Botley Road, the open country coming more clearly into view. The ring-road had not been built then and ahead of me were the low hills, still white with snow, and the dark patches of woodland.

I had decided that I would go back to Chinnor that night, to Heather and Michael, for our evening meal, and talk, and bed: the shell at least of a domestic life. And so I would. But not quite yet. The loneliness, the cold waste all about me, seemed preferable for a while still. The harsh cry of rooks, carried on the afternoon air, seemed preferable. I walked. I left behind the last of the Victorian houses that lined the Abingdon Road. I went past the allotments, or rather the sheets of water under which the allotments lay drowned.

At last, amid the sheeted fields, I came to a halt. All about me, the muted light was sinking towards dusk. The sky was iron-grey, with here and there a ragged patch in the layer of cloud where a gleam of stronger light shone through, to be caught and reflected in the flat fields of water that stretched away on either side.

This was the landscape I had known all my life, but it was so altered by the water that I felt I was seeing it for the first time. Everything I looked at was different: nothing was as I had known it. I understood now why my feet had stopped. It was because of the intolerable sense, pressing down on me from above, that my life had stopped. It had come to a standstill. A direction had to be chosen: now, here, before the light drained down to the point where day became night.

I thought of *Totes meer*. All that ripped and twisted metal, all that violence and pain that had had to be faced and endured so that a nation might live, even to live in the privations, and under the threats, that were our life now.

Totes Meer was half the story. It showed the wreckage of the invader. But the other half of the story was plain to read in it as well. Our victory, our deliverance, had been paid for with abundant wreckage of our own. It had cost young blood and bones and nerves. It had demanded a willingness to risk everything and if need be to lose everything. Our sacrifice had risen to meet the enemy's and in the event it was our sacrifice that had been rewarded. Nothing was cheap. Nothing came easily. Even in the river-valley I was looking at, the Anglo-Saxons had had to beat back the Danes, fierce men with long spears and big axes who rejoiced at the sight of blood. Only the risk-takers survived anyway: everything else was lies. The only question was, what risks were the most worth taking?

A cold wind was blowing. I could stand still no longer. I turned my head from trying to locate the banks of the river where I had grown up, the fields and villages and wooded hills where my life had been lived. But I saw nothing that sent me a clear message. The thaw, coming after so long and so hard a grip of that cruel ice, had been too sudden, too impetuously releasing, too impatient of landmarks and boundaries.

Everything I looked at was different. Nothing was as I had known it.